PENGUIN CLASSICS

THE DEBACLE

ÉMILE ZOLA, born in Paris in 1840, was brought up at Aix-en-Provence in an atmosphere of struggling poverty after the death of his father in 1847. He was educated at the Collège Bourbon at Aix and then at the Lycée Saint-Louis in Paris. He was obliged to exist in poorly paid clerical jobs after failing his *baccalauréat* in 1859, but early in 1865 he decided to support himself by literature alone. Despite his scientific pretensions Zola was really an emotional writer with rare gifts for evoking vast crowd scenes and for giving life to such great symbols of modern civilization as factories and mines. When not overloaded with detail, his work has tragic grandeur, but he is also capable of a coarse, 'Cockney' type of humour. From his earliest days Zola had contributed critical articles to various newspapers, but his first important novel, *Thérèse Raquin*, was published in 1867, and *Madeleine Férat* in the following year. That same year he began work on a series of novels intended to follow out scientifically the effects of heredity and environment on one family: *Les Rougon-Macquart*. The work contains twenty novels which appeared between 1871 and 1893, and is the chief monument of the French Naturalist Movement. On completion of this series he began a new cycle of novels, *Les Trois Villes: Lourdes, Rome, Paris* (1894-6-8), a violent attack on the Church of Rome, which led to another cycle, *Les Quatre Évengiles*. He died in 1902 while working on the fourth of these.

LEONARD TANCOCK spent most of his life in or near London, apart from a year as a student in Paris, most of the Second World War in Wales and three periods in American universities as visiting professor. Until his death in 1986, he was a Fellow of University College, London, and was formerly Reader in French at the University. He prepared his first Penguin Classic in 1949 and, from that time, was extremely interested in the problems of translation, about which he wrote, lectured and gave broadcasts. His numerous translations for the Penguin Classics include Zola's *Germinal*, *Thérèse Raquin*, *L'Assommoir* and *La Bête Humaine;* Diderot's *The Nun*, *Rameau's Nephew* and *D'Alembert's Dream*; Maupassant's *Pierre and Jean*; Marivaux's *Up from the Country*; Constant's *Adolphe*; La Rochefoucauld's *Maxims*; Voltaire's *Letters on England*; Prévost's *Manon Lescaut*; and Madame de Sévigné's *Selected Letters*.

ÉMILE ZOLA

THE DEBACLE
[1870–71]

TRANSLATED
WITH AN INTRODUCTION BY
LEONARD TANCOCK

PENGUIN BOOKS

PENGUIN BOOKS

Published by the Penguin Group
Penguin Books Ltd, 80 Strand, London WC2R ORL, England
Penguin Group (USA) Inc., 375 Hudson Street, New York, New York 10014, USA
Penguin Group (Canada), 90 Eglinton Avenue East, Suite 700, Toronto, Ontario, Canada M4P 2Y3
(a division of Pearson Penguin Canada Inc.)
Penguin Ireland, 25 St Stephen's Green, Dublin 2, Ireland (a division of Penguin Books Ltd)
Penguin Group (Australia), 250 Camberwell Road, Camberwell, Victoria 3124, Australia
(a division of Pearson Australia Group Pty Ltd)
Penguin Books India Pvt Ltd, 11 Community Centre, Panchsheel Park, New Delhi – 110 017, India
Penguin Group (NZ), cnr Airborne and Rosedale Roads, Albany, Auckland 1310,
New Zealand (a division of Pearson New Zealand Ltd)
Penguin Books (South Africa) (Pty) Ltd, 24 Sturdee Avenue,
Rosebank, Johannesburg 2196, South Africa

Penguin Books Ltd, Registered Offices: 80 Strand, London WC2R ORL, England

www.penguin.com

This translation first published in Penguin Classics 1972
16

Set in Monotype Fournier
Printed in England by Clays Ltd, St Ives plc

ISBN-13: 978-0-140-44280-9
ISBN-10: 0-140-44280-4

CONTENTS

INTRODUCTION

La Débâcle, the nineteenth and last but one of the Rougon-Macquart series of novels, the first of which was published in 1871, is in some respects the logical end, the *Götterdämmerung*, of the great saga of the natural and social history of a family during the Second Empire, for the final novel, *Le Docteur Pascal*, will be largely a clearing-up and killing-off of outstanding questions and characters, ending with a vision of the brave new world of science and progress about to be born. The subject is the collapse of Napoleon III's Second Empire in the Franco-Prussian war of 1870 and its destruction on the funeral pyre of the Paris Commune of 1871. Its publication in 1892 was an immense sales success, not only because it was a great war novel and documentary reviving memories in the minds of all but the quite young, but because it was an expression of the painful self-examination still going on in France after the most traumatic humiliation any country had so far received in modern times.

The 1870 war and its sequel in 1871 is one of the watersheds of European history. For a century and a half, from Louis XIV to Napoleon I, the armies of France had ravaged Europe, and the various German states had been invaded, traversed and plundered almost continuously during the Revolutionary and Napoleonic wars. But French arrogance overreached itself when Napoleon III deliberately and unnecessarily provoked Prussia and declared war on 15 July 1870. Seven weeks later, on 1 and 2 September, the French suffered a disastrous defeat at Sedan and Napoleon gave himself up to King William. Why such a total calamity? Leaving aside the various political or psychological factors, which are largely a matter of speculation and point of view and tell us more about the judge than the judged, there are the obvious military reasons. France was unprepared; for years the political opposition had bitterly attacked any attempts at modernization of armaments, and of course immediately after defeat was to round on the régime for being unprepared. The Germans had accurate breech-loading guns made by Krupp, with percussion shells. The French muzzle-loaders, of which Zola gives a detailed description, fired shells which more often than not burst harmlessly in the air. The French rifle, the *chassepot*, was good, but the *mitrailleuse*, an ancestor of the machine-gun, was still on the 'secret' list until shortly before mobilization and the army had no experience of how to use it. Technical incompetence and backwardness were made so much more dangerous by the complacency and over-confidence of all in authority, a small example of which was the issue to officers of maps of *Germany* whereas they had no information on the topography of the difficult mountain terrain of the part of their own country where fighting was bound to occur, and were lured into all sorts of ambushes by highly organized mobile detachments of Germans. And of course rivalries and divided counsels among the commanders were not checked by the weak and sick Emperor. The dash, swagger and bravery of individual French soldiers were no match for the scientific skill and accuracy of the Germans. Flamboyant cavalry charges have no chance against modern technology. In this respect as well as in many others, the 1870 war was the clash of the past and the future, and its lessons were learned by the Germans and ignored by the French.

Zola's novel is the story of this seven-week war and its sequel, and its connection with the Rougon-Macquart saga is tenuous to the point of unimportance, for Jean Macquart, the hero, serves simply as a point of view, or rather, as one of the many points of view. *The Debacle* is unique in Zola's work because it is a strictly historical novel. The other Zola novels may have much factual documentation, some of their characters and incidents may be clearly suggested by known people or events, or the setting may be in a known place described with meticulous accuracy, but the plot is pure invention. *The Debacle*, on the other hand, is the narrative of a very complicated moment in French history so recent that all the events were clearly remembered by all Zola's readers over the age of forty, or even younger, and many details could be immediately verified or challenged. When the book appeared in 1892 the events it described were more recent than those of the 1939–45 war are today. Zola could not risk being caught out on a point of fact, date, time or place, and many of the real persons, soldiers or politicians, mentioned in the story were still there, or their representatives were, and could answer back. Now this peculiar necessity for accuracy in reporting events of extreme complexity, many of them simultaneous and apparently confused but cumulatively of inexorable logic, carries with it the danger that the book might become a tedious chronicle of endless to-ings and fro-ings, comings and goings, to say nothing of repetitions and recapitulations, a sort of game of chess with commentary. All the more so because Zola wanted to make all aspects of the national disaster clear – the causes going back into the Second Empire, the mistakes and miscalculations, incompetence and sheer bad luck, with the resulting demoralization of the troops and the effects upon the lives of civilians of all kinds. How does he achieve clearness while avoiding the dullness of the minute-by-minute list of events? Mainly by skill in construction and by frequently changing the point of view, at the risk of seeming specious and contrived. It is as though he felt compelled by the very complexity of his material to present it in an arrangement remarkably regular and symmetrical even by his own standards, for many of his novels have some orderly arrangement of chapters or parts. Here there are three parts, each of eight chapters, and each part is a very distinct act in the drama.

Act I. The trap. From 6 August, near Mulhouse, we follow the movements of the 7th army corps, mostly through the eyes of one squad of its increasingly weary and demoralized soldiers, as it is moved back through Belfort, by train to Paris but immediately forward again to Rheims, its advance as far as Vouziers, the fatal waste of time there and the false advance and return to Vouziers, then on to Remilly in the Meuse valley and thence into Sedan, surrounded by hills and narrow defiles, every one of which was occupied or dominated by German forces or artillery. And at every stage muddles, supplies sent to wrong places, fuel sent where there was nothing to cook, raw meat where there was no fuel, fodder where there were no horses, guns in one place and ammunition in another, marches and counter-marches. The civilian elements are brought in as the march proceeds, and the exhaustion, hunger and exasperation of the troops become increasingly serious. The stages of this terrible progress from Rheims to Sedan can be followed very easily on the Michelin maps of France, sheets 56 and 53. I have adopted Zola's method of distinguishing between French and German forces by using arabic figures or roman respectively, e.g. 7th army corps (French), IXth army corps (German).

Act II. The disaster. The battle of Sedan, fought on the outskirts of the town and in surrounding villages. The whole action takes place in just over twenty-four hours, from very early in the morning of 1 September until 6 a.m. on the 2nd. The problem is to see clearly the different actions going on in different neighbourhoods and at the same time what was going on inside the town itself in all its complicated detail and from different points of view, and to keep the eye on all these things as they move on simultaneously towards the inevitable catastrophe in which a huge French army, with its wounded, guns, material and horses, is rolled back into a small town quite incapable of feeding or housing it. See map 1.

Act III. The aftermath. 3 September 1870 until May 1871. First, the horrors of the battlefield and captivity of the whole French army in a loop of the river Meuse, the Iges peninsula, where for a week, mostly in bad weather, they had no shelter, next to no food, and droves of captured horses, maddened by hunger, stampeded continually up and down. Even the river water, polluted by corpses, caused terrible dysentery, and the stench was unbearable. Jean Macquart and his friend Maurice Levasseur, whose family had always lived in the region, eventually escape and go to earth at the farm of the latter's uncle, where his twin sister Henriette, whose husband has been shot by the Germans, is also living. Maurice goes back to Paris intending to fight on, is caught in the siege of Paris, is fired by the fever of the insurrection, deserts and becomes a Communard. But Jean, whom Maurice had brought to the farm wounded and almost dying, has to stay there in hiding for months while being nursed back to health by Henriette. They grow to love each other, but the full implications of their feelings are unrecognized even by themselves. Ultimately Jean also makes his way to Paris, re-enlists in the regular (Government) army, and fate decrees that Maurice, now a fanatical Communard, is mortally wounded by Jean during the last desperate resistance when the Communards, and various criminal elements posing as such, set fire to the whole of the centre of Paris. The curtain goes down on the holocaust and Jean's departure, all hope of happiness with Henriette gone, to help build a new France.

Such are the barest bones of the story. But it is clothed with countless incidents, both in military and civilian life, countless authentic facts patiently gathered by Zola, who personally followed out the whole of the route taken in Part I, questioned any local people he could find with personal memories, such as a doctor in Sedan who had helped with the wounded, peasants and notables in and around the town, and in particular Charles Philippoteaux, brother of Auguste Philippoteaux, mayor of Sedan in 1870, and himself mayor of Givonne. He personally conducted Zola to all the places in the battle area and told him of his own glimpse of the Emperor at the farm of Baybel. He is the original of Delaherche, though not necessarily of the latter's fussy officiousness.

The result is one of the best examples of Zola's peculiar gift for taking masses of accurate, verifiable facts or documents and breathing into them life and a formal artistic pattern. Each little incident really happened (local tradition has it that everything in the novel is based on fact except the murder of Goliath, which is Zola's invention), but still the characters are live people with motives and emotions. Zola's art consists in the arrangement and the aesthetic and symbolical value, even as thousands of single notes are combined by a musical mind into a symphony.

But this formal aspect does raise a question in the reader's mind: is it not contrived, does not Zola stretch the long arm of coincidence too far for credibility? It may be objected, and with some justification, that everyone happens to run into the appropriate person exactly when the next twist in the story or next pieces in the jigsaw are required, and that therefore many of the 'fortuitous' meetings are foreseeable, however improbable in real life. Some may feel that the works are visible if not creakingly audible. That may well be. But it is nearly a thousand years since this island of ours experienced invasion and occupation by a foreign power. The sceptical reader should try to picture, say, the clash of the defending English army with the invading Welsh in and around a small town in a river valley traversing a region of wooded hills, such as Bewdley on the Severn or Ross-on-Wye. All that is then needed is that one English soldier should hail from those parts, have local knowledge and relations and friends still living there, and the rest of the meetings and coincidences must follow in such a restricted environment, where everyone knows everyone else. If you place the small town near a frontier (and the Sedan area has been one of the cockpits of Europe all down the ages), there will be traitors who fraternize with the enemy, locals who see a chance of money-making, the underground resistance movements and guerrilla bands, the enemy repressions and penalties. Moreover in a frontier region there are bound to be divided loyalties, families with a foot in both camps, population torn by conflicting linguistic, religious, racial and traditional stresses and strains. Such has always been the painful position of Alsace, Germanic in language and many of its customs, intensely French emotionally, yet often treated with the most tactless lack of understanding by Paris, with its mania for domination and impatience of what it dismisses as *la province*. In a word, as in any drama, the symbolism, real meaning and significant confrontations are more important to the artist than plausibility in the narrow sense. The subject, after all, is war and how it poisons and deforms all human relationships.

Hence not only the apparent speciousness but also the choice of characters and points of view. In a historical novel it is unwise to challenge real history by placing well-known figures in the principal roles, but it is equally unwise to omit all known historical figures and try to give a slice of life in another period or setting, for that will produce a boring archaeological reconstruction. Zola avoids these traps by introducing Napoleon III, MacMahon, Bazaine, Thiers, Gambetta and many others episodically or indirectly, as seen through the eyes of lesser mortals. But the front-rank characters in the novel are typical soldiers or civilians representing various kinds of victims or beneficiaries of war.

In a sense the principal part is a dual one, a pair incarnating the two eternal and irreconcilable facets of the French national character: Jean Macquart and Maurice Levasseur. Jean is balanced, reasonable, hard-working, law-abiding and conservative; Maurice is highly intelligent (although his behaviour makes one wonder), but mercurial, brilliant at chicanery and destructive criticism but less so at construction, nervy, dashing, effervescent, but fatally inclined to collapse hysterically under stress. France has ever been thus, one half practising moderation and common sense, the other flying to the most violent extremes. Jean is not young, he is thirty-nine and has been through personal tragedy. He is, though there is little resemblance, brother of the smug, self-centred Lisa Quenu (*Le Ventre de Paris*) and of the pathetic Gervaise (*L'Assommoir*). But the two girls left home early and went to Paris while he stayed in Provence as a carpenter and then served for seven years in the army, after which he became a farm-hand in a horrible village in the Beauce (*La Terre*). So he has lost touch with them and presumably has never seen his nephews the Lantier boys, Claude (*L'Oeuvre*), Jacques (*La Bête humaine*) and Etienne (*Germinal*), nor Gervaise's daughter by Coupeau, the notorious prostitute Nana. On the farm he was bitterly resented as a stranger by the family of the girl he married, and when his wife was brutally murdered by her own sister lest her bit of land should pass to Jean or his children, he left the land, horrified and broken-hearted, and re-enlisted shortly before the outbreak of war. He is perhaps the most healthy and sane member of the whole Rougon-Macquart tribe and certainly by far the best of the Macquarts. Maurice is hardly young either, being twenty-nine, but he was helped and protected by his twin sister, who sacrificed to send him to Paris and train him as a lawyer, and he still behaves as impetuously as a spoilt child. The friendship of these two men is one of the most beautiful human relationships in all Zola's work. Maurice finds himself in a squad of men under Corporal Macquart. At first there is instinctive aversion and mistrust between the simple peasant and the highbrow intellectual. But Maurice is forced to admire the solid qualities of Jean who in his turn helps Maurice when he is in pain and distress and learns to love him like a brother. Later each saves the life of the other. From then onwards their relationship becomes highly symbolical, as Zola himself is at pains to point out. The two apparently contradictory aspects of France are wedded in this wonderful friendship in which Maurice makes the solid peasant more aware, more sensitive, while Jean makes the brittle, frivolous intellectual deeper and more human. And when this union is torn asunder by the national disaster and Maurice, without his sheet-anchor of common sense, hurls himself into the frenzies of the Commune, Jean, the other France, kills him – accidentally of course – but it symbolizes self-amputation, the cutting out and casting away of a rotten, septic limb which, if retained, would ultimately poison and kill the whole organism.

The other soldiers in the squad are well differentiated types, each heavily charged with symbolism and political significance, possibly a little overdrawn in consequence, but none the less recognizable.

Loubet is the smart-aleck Parisian cockney, a jack of all trades, full of bright ideas and gadgets, the artful dodger but also the wit of the party. Lapoulle is the sheer clodhopper, physically magnificent but slow-witted, amiable and a willing beast of burden, but potentially very dangerous, because he can be cruel and bestial, like the peasants in *La Terre*, and his invincible ignorance and superstitiousness make him a tool for the unscrupulous. Pache, also from the country, is the pious one who furtively says his prayers and is the natural butt of the others. Meek and mild and consequently a bad soldier who breaks down under hardship and conceals some food, he is denounced by Chouteau, who significantly leaves the actual murdering, for a crust of bread, to the brutish Lapoulle. Finally Chouteau, who could be described in three words: a bloody-minded skunk. He is the professional agitator and trouble-maker, the political pub-orator, the demonstrator against everything, who never does anything except to feather his own nest. He escapes from a prisoner-of-war column by causing his best friend Loubet to be done to death, predictably turns up in Paris as a fire-raising and looting Communard, but quickly changes his coat when the other side looks like winning. Chouteau is another example of Zola's consistent hatred and contempt for the violent left-wing agitator type, the thoroughly unsatisfactory workman who is a parasite thriving on the hopes and fears of his fellow-men – Lantier in *L'Assommoir*, Pluchart in *Germinal* – who never did an honest day's work in their lives.

Similarly the officers, almost always seen through the eyes of the common soldiers or civilians, fall naturally into the categories of careerists, like Bourgain-Desfeuilles, or brave, old-fashioned diehards still living out the glories of old France or Napoleon's Grande Armée, like Rochas and Colonel de Vineuil. Most of the higher officers are real historical figures, shown to be incompetent, ambitious and jealous of each other. On his lonely peak is the Emperor Napoleon III, a puppet driven by forces beyond his control, hounded on by Paris and his megalomaniac Empress, ignored by his own military commanders, in constant pain from a mortal illness, a painted figurehead seeking an honourable end but rejected even by death, finding some sort of dignity and strength only at the end when he insists on surrender to avoid further bloodshed.

Zola's treatment of the Emperor is a remarkable example of his attempts, all through his career as a novelist, except perhaps in his final, 'evangelical' stage, to be as fair as possible even to those with whom he has no ideological sympathy. Just as the anti-Catholic found room to bring in some good Christians and saintly priests in the name of the law of averages, if nothing else, so, although himself politically to the left of centre, he had refused to take the facile black-or-white way of demagogues and, for instance in *Germinal*, treat all employers as capitalist oppressors and all workers as innocent victims, but had depicted some good and just employers and some lazy and selfish workers. So, once again, in spite of the tendency throughout the Rougon-Macquart novels to attack retrospectively the Second Empire, Zola cannot bring himself, in common fairness, to overlook the personal tragedy of Napoleon III or the criminal hooliganism of many of the Paris Communards, who are out for destruction, loot and personal power and use for their own ends such starry-eyed idealists as Maurice. Not that Zola holds any brief for the Maurice type, for none is more inhumanly bloodthirsty than the blind intellectual fanatic. Lovable though he may be at times, Maurice has in him the stuff of a Robespierre.

It is this all-embracing humanity, perhaps not sufficiently noticed by some critics, Zola's care to bring in the devotion and beauty of human beings as well as their passions, weaknesses and depravity, that at first sight makes one omission surprising. Here is a novel about soldiers in the demoralizing atmosphere of a campaign, a battle and the subsequent social and political disintegration. Yet although these men are a coarse lot, and some of their language is typically rough, Zola keeps out of their lives almost all sexual behaviour. The man who had recently outraged the respectable with pageants of human lust and bestiality like *La Terre* and *La Bête humaine* now, when dealing with soldiers in wartime, a notorious recipe for sexual looseness, reserves such things for civilians, traitors or Germans. The only Frenchman to have a relationship with a woman is carrying on a pre-war affair, and he is killed a few hours after leaving his mistress's bed. The symbolism of all this hardly needs underlining. Men fighting for their lives not only against the enemy but also against exhaustion, starvation and disease have little inclination for dalliance. That is left to the others.

What of the civilians? They are either innocent victims or motivated by self-interest, and to the latter the war seems either a tiresome interruption of their normal lives or a new chance to do well out of the misfortunes of others. Fouchard, uncle of Maurice and Henriette, will even refuse to sell (let alone give) food or drink to the starving French soldiers because he can get more out of the Germans, yet has the effrontery to claim to be patriotic because he swindles the enemy by selling them rotten meat at exorbitant prices. The mill-owner Delaherche was a Bonapartist before the war and had enthusiastically voted for the régime in the notorious plebiscite, but he becomes disaffected, anti-Bonapartist and potentially pro-German because to go on fighting is so bad for trade. His second wife, Gilberte, is frivolous, promiscuous, irresponsible, exercising her charms on friend and foe alike. A good time is her chief concern.

But Silvine is different. She symbolizes the deepest meaning of the book. In the most gruesome chapter in the whole novel we see her German seducer being slowly bled to death like a pig by the local band of guerrillas brought in to do so by Silvine. She watches it all and their child sees it too. A country violated and laid waste by an invader, or even beaten in war, will never forget and never rest until it has had its revenge. From 1871 until 1914 the statue of Strasbourg in the Place de la Concorde was shrouded in mourning, and France was to dream of *La Revanche*. From 1919 until 1939 Hitler's Germany was to do the same thing the other way round. Such is the futility of war.

In spite of the apparent optimism of the last page, when Jean goes forth to build a new France (and to what end, one might ask, if not to grow strong again and smash the Germans?), this is a profoundly disturbing book in its prophetic vision of the grim realities of the twentieth-century world. All these people are swept along by forces beyond their comprehension and control. Mass movements push the mobs hither and thither, and the individual has little or no freedom or power. Some of the figures in the Commune may possibly have been motivated by patriotic indignation at what they felt was the craven surrender of the Provisional Government of Thiers in the face of Germany's demands, but they certainly were not concerned with the fact that every day of their theatrical heroics prolonged the agony of millions of other Frenchmen who did not happen to live in Paris. The millions are exploited by violent extremists out for their own ends. Urban guerrilla warfare is the cruellest and most cowardly form of so-called social action, involving blackmail of the worst kind, death of innocent men, women and children, intimidation and murder of hostages, looting and destruction of property and art treasures and the pursuance of purely personal vendettas. It brings out the beast in human beings. In our own age, when destruction, fire-raising and murder in crowded cities, always under the cloak of some high-sounding ideological, social, racial or even religious ideal, has become a part of the daily scene almost boring in its regularity, it is perhaps of interest to see into the workings of one of the earliest examples.

Of course it is possible to have differing views about the Paris Commune. Some see it as a glorious manifestation of the fight of the workers for freedom. Not unexpectedly Karl Marx, in *The Civil War in France* (1871), proclaims that 'working men's Paris, with its Commune, will be for ever celebrated as the glorious harbinger of a new society. Its exterminators history has already nailed to that eternal pillory from which all the prayers of their priests will not avail to redeem them.' D. W. Brogan, less lyrical but no reactionary, points out that it was essential that the arrogance and tyranny of Paris over all the rest of France be beaten, above all in the interests of universal suffrage and real democracy. Others again see it as a sinister outburst of violent mob hysteria exploited by a few unscrupulous petty politicians for ends known only to themselves. Zola saw it as a degrading exhibition of human bestiality, with unspeakable atrocities committed by both sides, but his protest is against violence, cruelty and destruction in whatever form and from whatever side. But Zola had over these other commentators the advantage that he was there. He saw it all, for he was not only present but a journalist, having returned to Paris a few days before the revolution of 18 March, after a spell of reporting the doings of the Bordeaux government. He even got into trouble twice and in the atmosphere of indiscriminate killing might have lost his life. To that extent *The Debacle* is an eye-witness account.

One question remains. In spite of his efforts to be fair, and his genuine compassion for Napoleon III as a man, there is little doubt that Zola's overriding object in this novel is to demonstrate that the collapse of France in 1870–71 was due, as he put it, to the rottenness of the tree. In his view the Second Empire had been doomed for years by its own corruption and inefficiency. Was he right? Was he even being fair? Was he playing the familiar political propaganda game? Or was he influenced by the climate of the time when he was writing the novel, and catering for the fashionable prejudices of 1892, that is to say for the inevitable witch-hunt for scapegoats which follows any national disaster? Let a modern historian express his view:

The defeat that wrote finis to the rule of Napoleon III was an external event not an internal development. The Second Empire was not ended by the will of the people. The last plebiscite gave the Emperor almost as large a majority as the first. It was not destroyed by a revolution: there was no revolutionary party with the power to overthrow it. The Empire had simply, in the person of a defeated, aged and ailing Emperor, been overthrown in war, and capitulated to the invader. Its disappearance, before no predestined successor, left only a void. France was thrust into a new age, not deliberately by its own action, or in the fullness of time by the presence of new social forces, but accidentally and prematurely by the fact of military defeat. The intense conservatism of French society in 1871 was revealed by the savage reaction to the Commune of Paris, as it had been in 1848 by the repression of the revolt of the June days. The aim of the ruling classes in 1871 remained what it had been when the Empire was set up, to preserve the fabric of society unchanged; not to make a new France but to save the old one. This was the task which the National Assembly at Bordeaux, elected to get France out of the German war as soon as possible, took upon itself.*

The reader must decide for himself why in Zola's novel the 'intense conservatism of French society in 1871' is personified in Jean, the intelligent, thoughtful working man.

The text used for this translation is the most recent scholarly one in volume 6 of the *Oeuvres complètes* of Émile Zola, published under

*(Alfred Cobban, *A History of Modern France*, vol. 3, p. 9. Penguin Books, 1965)

the general editorship of Henri Mitterand, Paris, Cercle du Livre Précieux, Fasquelle, 1967. The text in the paperback Livre de Poche edition, also published by Fasquelle, is very corrupt, with some grotesque misprints and some whole sentences omitted.

Further information about Zola and this intensely interesting period in French and European history can be found in:

F. W. J. Hemmings, *Emile Zola*, revised edition, Oxford, Clarendon Press, 1966.

D. W. Brogan, *The Development of Modern France (1870–1939)*, London, Hamish Hamilton, 1940 and many later editions. A standard work, with information about almost all the personalities mentioned by Zola.

Frank Jellinek, *The Paris Commune of 1871*, London, Gollancz, 1937. A typical statement of the left-wing point of view.

Robert Baldick, *The Siege of Paris*, London, Batsford, 1964. A day-by-day account, with much contemporary matter and pictures, of the period between September 1870 and January 1871, 'the last full-scale siege of a European capital, the first occasion of the indiscriminate bombardment of a civilian population, the source of immense hardship and suffering, and the origin of a division in the French nation which has still not been healed.'

Alistair Horne, *The Fall of Paris*, London, Macmillan, 1965. The fullest recent account. Not only covers the siege and Commune, but has a clear, concise chapter on the six-week Franco-Prussian war of 1870.

Alistair Horne, *The Terrible Year. The Paris Commune 1871*, London, Macmillan, 1971. A 'coffee-table' book to mark the centenary of the Commune. Excellent short text and lavish illustrations, including many contemporary photographs.

It is no mere convention to thank my wife for her tireless help.

October 1971   L. W. T.

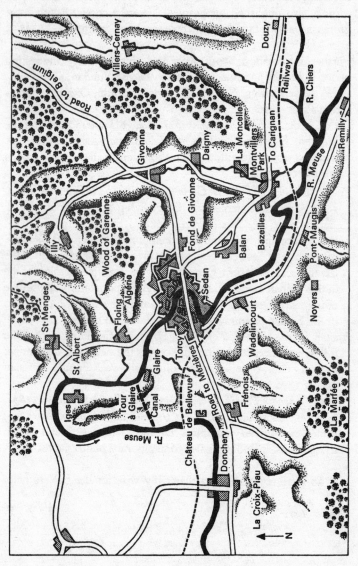

Map 1: *The country around Sedan*

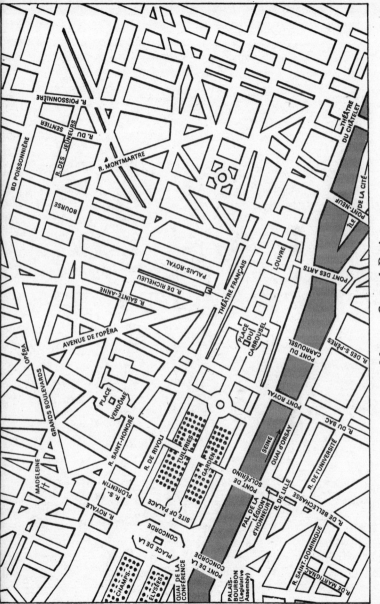

Map 2: *Central Paris*

PART ONE

1

CAMP had been set up two kilometres from Mulhouse, nearer the Rhine, in the middle of the fertile plain. Towards nightfall on this August evening, under an angry sky with heavy clouds, the shelter-tents stretched out and piled arms gleamed, regularly spaced along the battle front, while the sentries with loaded rifles stood watch, motionless, their unseeing eyes staring out at the purple mists of the distant horizon rising from the river.

They had reached there from Belfort at about five. It was now eight and the men had only just got the provisions. But the fire-wood must have been mislaid, for none had been issued. No way of lighting a fire and making some stew. They had had to make do with chewing some biscuit cold, helped down with generous lashings of brandy, which finally put paid to legs already giving way with fatigue. But just behind the piled rifles, near the cook-house, two soldiers were doggedly trying to ignite a heap of green sticks, trunks of young saplings they had slashed down with their bayonets, and which obstinately refused to catch. Dense smoke was rising black and slow into the evening air, infinitely depressing.

There were only twelve thousand men there, all General Fielix Douay had with him out of the 7th army corps. The first division had been summoned the day before and had set off for Froesch-willer; the third was still in Lyons, and he had decided to leave Belfort and advance like this with the second division, the reserve artillery and a division of cavalry not up to full strength. Lights had been reported at Lorrach. A wire from the sub-prefect of Schlestadt said that the Prussians were about to cross the Rhine at Markolsheim. Feeling he was too isolated from the extreme right flank of the other corps and out of communication, the general had been all the more anxious to speed up his advance towards the frontier because news had come the previous day of the disastrous surprise at Wissembourg. At any moment, unless he was himself occupied in repulsing the enemy, he might have reason to fear being called on to support the 1st corps. On that uneasy thundery Saturday, 6 of August, there must have been fighting somewhere over in the Froeschwiller direction: you could see it in the anxious, louring·sky, across which great shudderings and sudden gusts of wind passed, heavy with foreboding. And for the last two days the division had thought it was marching into battle, the soldiers had expected to see the Prussians there in front of them at the end of this long forced march from Belfort to Mulhouse.

The light was fading and retreat was heard in some distant corner of the camp, a drum-roll and sound of bugles, still faint and carried away into the air. And Jean Macquart, who had been busy strengthening the tent by driving the pegs further in, straightened up. At the first rumour of war he had left Rognes, the wound still raw from the drama in which he had lost his wife Françoise and the land she had brought as dowry. He had re-enlisted at the age of thirty-nine, got back his corporal's stripes and been at once drafted to the 106th foot, which was then being brought up to full strength, and he was still amazed sometimes to find himself once again with his cape on his shoulders, for he had been overjoyed to get out of the services after Solferino and not be a sword-waver and killer any more. But what is a chap to do when he hasn't a job, a wife or a bean left under the sun and his heart is turning over inside him with grief and rage? You might just as well have it out on the enemy if they get you down. And now he recalled the exclamation he had made – Oh bugger it, as he hadn't got the guts left to till this old French soil he might as well defend it!

Standing there, Jean looked round the camp in which the retreat was producing a last-minute flurry of activity. A few men were running about, but others, already dropping with sleep, were getting up and stretching, looking tired and irritated. But he was patiently waiting for roll-call with that good-natured, equable reasonableness which made him such an excellent soldier. His mates said that with a bit of education he might have gone a long way. But being just able to read and write, he didn't even covet the rank of sergeant. Once a peasant always a peasant.

But his eye was caught by the greenstick fire which was still smoking, and he hailed the two men still slaving away at it, Loubet and Lapoulle, both in his own squad.

'Oh, turn it up! You're smothering us all.'

Loubet, thin and wiry, who looked a bit of a joker, grinned.

'It's catching, corporal, it really is ... Go on, you, blow!'

He bullied Lapoulle, a great giant of a man who was busting himself, blowing up a hurricane, with his cheeks puffed out like a pair of bellows and purple in the face, his eyes red and streaming.

Two other soldiers of the squad, Chouteau and Pache, the former flat on his back, being a lazy-bones fond of his comfort, the latter squatting and diligently mending a tear in his trousers, burst into laughter, tickled by the fearful face that great clot of a Lapoulle was making.

'Why not turn round and blow from your backside, it'll burn better,' yelled Chouteau.

Jean let them laugh. There might not be many more chances, and for all the serious look of the man, with his full face and regular features, he wasn't in favour of melancholy and deliberately shut his eyes when the men had their bit of fun. But another group caught his attention, yet another soldier in his squad, Maurice Levasseur, who had been talking for the last hour to a civilian, a red-haired gentleman of about thirty-six, with a face like a good-natured dog, with huge blue popping eyes – the short-sighted eyes that had got him exempted from military service. They had been joined by a reserve artilleryman, a sergeant, smart and self-assured with his dark moustache and goatee beard, and all three were chatting away quite oblivious of time as though they were at home.

Out of kindness, to save them from being told off, Jean felt he ought to intervene.

'You had better be going, sir. This is retreat, and if the lieu-tenant should find you ...'

Maurice cut him short.

'You stay, Weiss.'

And to the corporal he snapped:

'This gentleman is my brother-in-law. He had a permit from the colonel, who is a friend of his.'

What business was it of this yokel whose hands still smelt of dung? He himself had passed his law exams the previous autumn, enlisted as a volunteer and thanks to the colonel's influence had been drafted direct to the 106th without going through the square-bashing, though he deigned to wear the knapsack. But from the first minute he had been put off by this illiterate clodhopper in command over him and felt a sullen resentment.

'All right,' Jean quietly answered, 'get yourself run in, it's all the same to me.'

Then he turned away as he saw that Maurice really wasn't lying, for the colonel, Monsieur de Vineuil, happened to come along, with his grand manner, his long sallow face divided in two by his thick white moustache, and he had greeted Weiss and the soldier with a smile. The colonel was hurrying over to a farmhouse that could be seen two or three hundred metres to the left, surrounded by plum orchards, where headquarters had been set up for the night. Nobody knew whether the commanding officer of the 7th corps was there, in the awful grief over the death of his brother, killed at Wissembourg. But Brigadier Bourgain-Desfeuilles, who had the 106th under his command, was certainly there, yapping as usual, quite untroubled by his lack of brains, his skin florid with so much high living, and his heavy body rolling on his stumpy legs. There was increasing activity round the farm; dispatch-riders were coming and going every minute, and yet there was feverish waiting for dispatches, always too slow with news about this great battle which everybody sensed to be decisive and imminent ever since morning. Where had it been fought and what was the outcome at this stage? As night fell it seemed as though mounting anxiety was spreading a lake of darkness over the orchard and the few hayricks around the farm buildings. And it was also being said that a Prussian spy had just been arrested while prowling round the camp and taken to the farm for the general to interrogate. Perhaps Colonel de Vineuil had had some telegram that was making him run so fast.

Meanwhile Maurice had gone on talking to his brother-in-law Weiss and his cousin Honoré Fouchard, the artillery sergeant. Retreat, at first far distant, then gradually getting louder, passed near them, with its brass and drums in the melancholy quiet of dusk, but they did not even appear to notice it. The young man, grandson of a hero of the Grande Armée, was born at Le Chêne-Populeux, where his father, fighting shy of glory, had come down to a humble job of tax-collector. His mother, of peasant stock, had died bringing him and his twin sister Henriette into the world, and Henriette had looked after him from their earliest childhood. He was now here as a volunteer after a long series of misdeeds, the typical dissipations of a weak and excitable temperament, money thrown away on gambling, women and the follies of all-devouring Paris; and all that when he had gone there to finish his law studies and his people had bled themselves white to make a grand gentleman of him. This had hastened his father's death, and his sister, having spent her all, had had the good fortune to find a husband, this reliable fellow Weiss, an Alsatian from Mulhouse, who had been a book-keeper for years at the General Refinery at Le Chêne-Populeux, and was now an overseer for Monsieur Delaherche, one of the biggest clothmakers in Sedan. And Maurice thought he had quite turned over a new leaf, with his nervy nature as quick to hope for the best as to be discouraged by the bad, generous, enthusiastic, but without the slightest stability, blown hither and thither by every passing gust of wind. Fair, small, with a very large head, small neat nose and chin, he had a clever face, with grey, affectionate eyes, a bit wild at times.

Weiss had hurried to Mulhouse the day before the outbreak of hostilities, suddenly anxious to settle a family affair, and the reason why he had taken advantage of Colonel de Vineuil's kindness and come to give his brother-in-law a handshake was that the colonel was uncle of young Madame Delaherche, a pretty widow married last year to the manufacturer. Maurice and Henriette had known her as a young girl through having been neighbours. Also, apart from the colonel, Maurice had found in Captain Beaudoin, the captain of his company, an acquaintance of Gilberte, young Madame Delaherche, and an intimate one, it was said, dating from Mézières when she was Madame Maginot, wife of Monsieur Maginot, Inspector of Forests.

'Give Henriette a kiss for me,' Maurice was saying to Weiss, for he was passionately devoted to his sister. 'Tell her she will be pleased with me and that I mean to make her proud of me at last.'

Tears came into his eyes as he thought of his follies. His brother-in-law, deeply moved himself, changed the subject abruptly and talked to Honoré Fouchard, the artilleryman.

'And as I'm going up Remilly way I'll go and tell Uncle Fouchard I've seen you and you are all right.'

Uncle Fouchard, a peasant with some land and a business as a travelling butcher, was a brother of Henriette and Maurice's mother. He lived at Remilly, up on the hill, six kilometres from Sedan.

'Yes do,' Honoré quietly answered. 'Dad couldn't care less, but go all the same if you would like to.'

At that moment there was a commotion over by the farm and they saw the prowler, the man they had accused of being a spy, coming out quite free, with only one officer. Presumably he had shown his papers and told a tale, for he was simply being turned out of the camp. At such a distance and in the dusk they could not make him out very clearly, but he was huge and square, with reddish hair.

But Maurice uttered a cry.

'Honoré, look ... it's just like that Prussian, you know, Goliath!'

The name made the artilleryman start. He looked with blazing eyes. Goliath Steinberg, the farm-hand, the man who had made trouble between him and his father, who had taken Silvine away from him, the whole nasty story and abominable corruption that still tortured him. He would have liked to rush over and strangle the man, but by now he was beyond the piled arms and disappearing into the night.

'Goliath!' he muttered. 'But it can't be! He's over there with the others ... If ever I run into him!'

He had made a menacing gesture towards the darkening horizon – all that purplish Orient which for him was Prussia. There was a silence and then retreat was heard once more, but far away, fading out towards the end of the camp with a dying softness in keeping with the deepening haze.

'Gosh!' went on Honoré, 'I shall get run in if I'm not there for roll-call. Good night, bye-bye all!'

He gave a final squeeze to both Weiss's hands and strode rapidly towards the hillock on which the reserve artillery was parked, without another word about his father or message for Silvine, whose name burned his throat.

A few more minutes went by and over to the left, where the second brigade would be, a bugle sounded roll-call. Another answered, nearer, and then a third a long way off. Then, one after another they were all blowing together when Gaude, the company bugler, made up his mind in a volley of piercing notes. He was a tall, thin and miserable-looking fellow, clean shaven and with never a word to say, and he blew his calls with the breath of a hurricane.

Then Sergeant Sapin, a skinny little man with big cowlike eyes, began roll-call. He snapped out the names in his high-pitched voice, and the soldiers who had gathered round answered on every note from cello to flute. But then there was a hold-up.

'Lapoulle!' repeated the sergeant, very loud.

Still no answer. And Jean had to dash over to the heap of green sticks which Fusilier Lapoulle, egged on by his mates, was determined to get alight. Now he was flat on his belly and purple in the face, blowing the smoke from the blackening wood straight along the ground.

'For Christ's sake turn it up!' shouted Jean. 'Answer roll-call!'

Lapoulle leaped up in a daze, seemed to understand and bellowed 'Present' in such a savage roar that it made Loubet fall on his backside, it was such a scream. Pache, who had finished his sewing, answered almost inaudibly, like muttering a prayer. Chouteau, full of scorn, didn't even get up, but called out the word and stretched himself out a little more.

Meanwhile Lieutenant Rochas, who was on duty, stood motionless a metre or so away. When the call was over and Sergeant Sapin went up to report that there was nobody missing, he mumbled into his moustache, pointing with a jerk of his chin to Weiss who was still talking to Maurice:

'There's even one too many. What's that character up to over there?'

'Permission from the colonel, sir,' Jean, who had overheard, thought he ought to answer.

Rochas shrugged angrily and without another word continued his tramp along the tents, waiting for lights out, while Jean, whose legs were giving way after the day's march, sat down a few paces from Maurice, whose words reached him at first in a jumble which he didn't listen to, for he himself was weighed down by vague reflections hardly formulated in the depths of his stolid, slow brain.

Maurice was all for war, which he thought was inevitable and vital for the very existence of nations. That had been perfectly plain

29

to him ever since he had gone in for evolutionist ideas, all this theory of evolution which at that time fascinated the younger intellectuals. Is not life a state of war every second? Is not the very condition of nature a continuous struggle, the survival of the fittest, strength maintained and renewed through action, life rising ever young out of death? He recalled the great burst of enthusiasm which had uplifted him when he had had the idea of atoning for his misdeeds by becoming a soldier and going to fight at the front. Perhaps the France of the plebiscite, by handing itself over to the Emperor, did not want war. A week earlier he himself had declared it iniquitous and stupid. People argued about this candidature of a German prince for the throne of Spain, and in the confusion that had gradually developed everybody seemed in the wrong, so that now nobody really knew which side the provocation had come from, and the one inevitable thing had remained unaltered, the inexorable law which at a given moment throws one nation against another. But a great fever of excitement had run through Paris, and he could still see that burning evening, with crowds surging along the boulevards, bands waving torches and shouting: 'To Berlin! To Berlin!' He could still hear the tall, beautiful woman with the regal profile, standing on a coachman's box in front of the Hôtel de Ville, wrapped in the folds of the flag and singing the 'Marseillaise'. Was it all a lie, then? Had the heart of Paris not beaten? And later, as always with him, the nervous elation had been followed by hours of dreadful doubt and revulsion: his arrival in the barracks, the sergeant major who had signed him on, the sergeant who had issued him his uniform, the stinking barrack-room and the revolting filth, the coarse familiarity with his new companions, the routine drill which exhausted his limbs and stupefied his brain. And yet in less than a week he had got used to it and lost his disgust. Then his enthusiasm had taken over again when the regiment had at last set off for Belfort.

From the outset Maurice had been absolutely certain of victory. For him the Emperor's plan was clear: hurl four hundred thousand men at the Rhine, cross the river before the Prussians were ready, separate North Germany from South by a vigorous thrust, and thanks to some striking victory, immediately force Austria and Italy to side with France. Hadn't there been a rumour, at one moment, that the 7th army corps, to which his regiment belonged, was to embark at Brest and land in Denmark to stage a diversion and oblige Prussia to immobilize one of her armies? She would be surprised, overwhelmed on all fronts and crushed in a few weeks. A sheer walk-over, from Strasbourg to Berlin. But since the delay at Belfort he had been tormented by misgivings. The 7th army corps, whose role was to command the Black Forest gap, had reached there in a state of indescribable confusion, incomplete and short of everything. The third division had still not arrived from Italy, the second cavalry brigade was still in Lyons for fear of popular unrest, and three batteries had got lost somewhere or other. Then there was an extraordinary famine, the shops in Belfort which were supposed to supply everything were empty: no tents, no cooking utensils, no body belts, no medical equipment, no smithies, no hobbles for the horses. Not a single medical orderly or clerk. At the last moment they had realized that thirty thousand spare parts, indispensable for rifles, were missing, and an officer had had to be dispatched to Paris and he had brought back five thousand, which he had had a lot of trouble to get out of them. Besides, what upset Maurice was the inaction. They had been there for two weeks and why weren't they advancing? He felt that each day's delay was an irreparable miscalculation, one more chance of victory lost. Confronting the dream-plan there rose up the reality of its execution, that he was to know later but then only felt in an anguished, obscure way: the seven army corps strung out thinly along the frontier from Metz to Bitche and from Bitche to Belfort, everywhere the fighting force below strength, and the four hundred thousand men amounted to two hundred and thirty thousand at the most; generals were jealous of each other, each determined to get the field-marshal's baton for himself and not to help his neighbour; the most appalling lack of foresight, the mobilization and concentration of troops done simultaneously in order to gain time and leading to an inextricable muddle; in fact a slow paralysis, starting at the top from the Emperor, a sick man incapable of any quick decision, which was beginning to creep through the entire army and disorganize it, reduce it to nothing and hurl it into the worst disasters, unable to defend itself. Nevertheless, over and above the vague unease of the waiting, and in the instinctive shrinking from what was to come, the certainty of victory remained.

Suddenly on 3 August the news of the previous day's victory at Saarbrücken had burst upon them. A great victory – well perhaps. But the papers were bursting with enthusiasm – it was the invasion of Germany, the first step on the march to glory, and the Prince Imperial, who had coolly picked up a bullet on the battlefield, began to be a legend. Then two days later, when the surprise and crushing defeat of Wissembourg was known, a howl of rage had burst from people's throats. Five thousand men caught in a trap, men who had stood up to thirty-five thousand Prussians for ten hours, such a cowardly massacre cried out for vengeance! It must be that the leaders were guilty of faulty protective measures and lack of foresight. But it was all going to be put right, MacMahon had called in the first division of the 7th corps, the 1st would be supported by the 5th, and by now the Prussians must have re-crossed the Rhine with our infantrymen's bayonets prodding their backsides. And the thought that there must have been desperate fighting that day, the increasingly feverish wait for news, the general anxiety spread further every minute under the wide, fading sky.

That was what Maurice kept on telling Weiss.

'Oh yes, they've taken a fine old beating today!'

Weiss made no answer, but shook his head with a worried look. He was looking towards the Rhine, too, towards the east where night had already closed down, a black wall, impenetrable, mysterious. After the last notes of roll-call a great silence had fallen over the sleepy camp, hardly broken at all by the footsteps and voices of a few belated soldiers. A light had come on, like a twinkling star, in the living-room of the farmhouse where headquarters staff were sitting up waiting for the dispatches coming in hour by hour, without making things any clearer. The fire of green twigs, at last abandoned, was still smoking with a dense, dismal smoke which a gentle wind was blowing over the restless farmhouse, dirtying the first stars.

'A beating,' Weiss said eventually. 'May God hear your prayer!'

Jean, who was still sitting a few yards away, pricked up his ears, and Lieutenant Rochas, who had overheard this wish with its tremulous doubt, stopped short to listen.

'What!' said Maurice. 'Aren't you completely confident? Do you think a defeat is possible?'

His brother-in-law raised a shaking hand to stop him, and his kindly face suddenly looked tired and pale.

'Defeat, God preserve us from that! You know I belong to this province, and my grandfather and grandmother were murdered by the Cossacks in 1814, and whenever I think of invasion my fists clench of their own accord, and I would fight in my ordinary clothes like a trooper! ... Defeat, no, no! I refuse to consider the possibility.'

His emotion subsided, and he slumped his shoulders in utter weariness.

'But all the same, look here, I'm uneasy ... I know my Alsace well, and I've just come through it again on business, and we Alsatians have seen what was staring the generals in the face but they have refused to see. Oh, we wanted war against Prussia, and had been waiting a long time to settle that old score. But that didn't prevent our having good neighbourly relations with Baden and Bavaria, for we've all got family or friends across the Rhine. We thought they were longing like us to take down the insufferable pride of the Prussians. And calm and resolute though we may be, we've been giving way to impatience and worry for the past fortnight as we've seen how everything is going from bad to worse. From the moment war was declared they have let the enemy cavalry terrify villages, reconnoitre the terrain, cut telegraph wires. Baden and Bavaria are mobilizing and enormous troop movements are going on in the Palatinate, and information from all sides, markets, fairs and suchlike, proves that the frontier is threatened. And when the inhabitants, the mayors of communes, now thoroughly scared, rush to report all that to officers passing through, the latter merely shrug their shoulders: cowardly hallucinations, the enemy is miles away ... When not an hour should have been lost, days and days go by! What can they be waiting for? The whole of Germany to fall on top of us?'

His voice was soft and heartbroken, as though he were repeating these things aloud to himself after having thought them over for a long time.

'Oh, and I know Germany well, too, and the terrible thing is that all you people seem to know as little about it as you do about China ... Maurice, you remember my cousin Gunther, who came last spring and looked me up in Sedan. He is a cousin on my

33

mother's side, his mother was my mother's sister and she married a man in Berlin. And he is typical of them in his hatred of France. Now he is serving as an officer in the Prussian Guard. I can still hear his voice as he said to me that evening when I saw him off at the station: "If France declares war on us she will be beaten." '

This made Lieutenant Rochas, who had contained himself up to then, come forward in a rage. A man of nearly fifty, he was a tall, thin fellow with a long, lantern-jawed face, tanned and leathern. His huge hook nose came down over a wide, strong but good-natured mouth with an untidy bristling grey moustache. Now he went right off the deep end and bellowed in a thundering voice:

'Here, what are you fucking well doing, discouraging the men!'

Without taking part himself in the quarrel Jean thought that really the lieutenant was right, for although he was beginning to be surprised at the long delays and the muddle they were in, he had never had any doubt either about the bloody good hiding they were going to give the Prussians. That was a fact, and that was all they had come here to do.

Weiss was quite taken aback. 'But, lieutenant,' he said, 'I don't want to discourage anybody. On the contrary, I wish everyone knew what I know, because it's best to know so as to be fore-warned and forearmed . . . Now just look at Germany . . .'

He proceeded in his reasonable way to explain his fears: the growth of Prussia after Sadowa, the nationalist movement which put her at the head of the other German states, a great empire in formation, rejuvenated with the enthusiasm and irresistible impetus to achieve its unity; the system of compulsory military service which set up a whole nation in arms, trained, disciplined and with powerful weapons, ready for a long war and still intoxicated with her shattering triumph over Austria; the intelligence and moral strength of this army, under the command of officers almost all young and obeying a commander-in-chief who seemed about to modernize the whole art of war, a man of incomparable prudence and foresight and miraculous clarity of vision. And with that Germany he had the courage to contrast France: the Empire grown old, still acclaimed in a plebiscite but basically rotten because it had weakened the idea of patriotism by destroying liberty, and then turning back to liberalism too late and thereby hastening its own undoing because it was ready to collapse as soon as it stopped satisfying the lust for pleasure it had let loose; the army certainly admirable as a brave lot of men, and still wearing the laurels of the Crimea and Italy, but adulterated by the system of paid substitutes, still in the old routine of the Africa school, too cocksure of victory to face the great effort of modern techniques; and then the generals, most of them nonentities and eaten up with rivalries and some of them quite·stupefyingly ignorant, and at their head the Emperor, a sick man and vacillating, deceived and self-deceiving, and all facing this terrible adventure into which they were blindly hurling themselves, with no serious preparation, like a stampede of scared sheep being led to the slaughter.

Rochas listened to all this, gaping and goggling. His terrible nose was screwed up. Then he suddenly made up his mind to laugh – a huge ear-to-ear laugh.

'What do you think you're waffling about? What does all that cock-and-bull story add up to? It doesn't make sense, it's too silly for me to rack my brains to understand. Go and tell all that to the recruits, but not to me, with my twenty-seven years' service!'

He banged his chest with his fist. The son of a working stone-mason from Limousin, himself born in Paris and hating his father's trade, he had enlisted at eighteen. As a soldier of fortune he had been in the ranks, become a corporal in Africa, sergeant at Sebastopol and lieutenant after Solferino, having put in fifteen years of hard existence and heroic gallantry to achieve this rank, but so lacking in education that he would never make the grade of captain.

'But this is something you don't know about, Mr Knowall ... Yes, at Mazagran I was hardly nineteen and we were a hundred and twenty-three men, not one more, and we held out for four days against twelve thousand Arabs ... Oh yes, for years and years in Africa, at Mascara, Biskra, Dellys and later on the Grande Kabylie and later still Laghouat, if you had been with us, Mister, you would have seen all those bloody wogs bunking off like hares as soon as we came on the scene ... And at Sebastopol, sir, blimey, you couldn't say that was a picnic either. Gales fit to blow your hair off, perishing cold, constant alerts, and then those savages ended by making everything hop! But never mind, we made them hop too, oh yes, with music and in a big frying-pan, what's more! ... And Solferino, you weren't there yourself, sir, so why do you talk about it? Yes, at Solferino, where it was so hot although more rain had come down that day than you have seen in your life, perhaps – at Solferino the thrashing we gave those Austrians – you should have seen them galloping away from our bayonets, going arse over tip to run faster, as if they had fire in their backsides.'

He was bursting with joy, and all the traditional gaiety of the French soldier rang in his triumphant laugh. It was the legendary French trooper going through the world between his girl on one side and a bottle of good wine on the other, conquering the world singing ribald choruses. One corporal and four men, and great armies licked the dust.

Suddenly his voice roared out:

'Beaten! What, France beaten! Those Prussian swine beat us! Us?'

He came up and took Weiss roughly by the lapel of his coat, and his tall, lean body, the body of a knight-errant, expressed utter contempt for the enemy, whoever he was, and he couldn't care less about time and place.

'Just you listen, Mister ... If the Prussians dare to come here we'll send them back home with kicks up the arse. You understand, kicks up the arse all the way to Berlin!'

He made a superb gesture, with the serenity of a child, the candid conviction of the innocent who knows nothing and fears nothing.

'Good God, that's how it is because that's how it is!'

Dazed and almost convinced, Weiss hastened to declare that nothing could suit him better. And Maurice, who was keeping quiet, not daring to rush in with his superior officer present, finally joined in the burst of laughter, for this great oaf of a man, who was a fool in his opinion, warmed his heart. Jean too had been nodding his agreement with the lieutenant's every word. He also had been at Solferino, where it had rained so hard. Now that was what you called talking! If all the officers had talked like that nobody would have cared a damn whether there weren't any stewpans or flannel body-belts!

For a long time now it had been quite dark, and still Rochas was waving his great limbs about in the night. He had only ever managed to read through one book, the victories of Napoleon, which had found its way from a pedlar's box into his knapsack. He was thoroughly wound up now, and all his learning gushed forth in one impetuous cry:

'Austria whacked at Castiglione, Marengo, Austerlitz, Wagram! Prussia whacked at Eylau, Jena, Lützen! Russia whacked at Friedland, Smolensk, Borodino! Spain and England whacked everywhere! The whole world whacked from top to bottom, one side to the other! And are we to be whacked now? Why? How? Has the world been changed?'

He drew himself higher still, raising his arm like a flagstaff.

'Look! There has been fighting over yonder today and we are expecting news. Well, I'll tell you what the news is . . . They have whacked the Prussians, whacked them so as to leave them neither wings nor feet, so that we'll have to sweep up the crumbs!'

Just then a great moan of grief swept across the sombre sky. Was it some night bird's plaint? Was it some mysterious voice from afar, full of woe? The whole camp shuddered in the darkness, and the anxiety which had spread because of the slow arrival of dispatches was thereby heightened to fever pitch. In the distant farmhouse the light by which the headquarters staff were anxiously waiting through the night burned up higher, with the straight, still flame of an altar candle.

It was now ten o'clock, and Gaude rose up from the black ground into which he had disappeared and was the first to blow lights out. Other bugles answered and tailed off one by one in a dying fanfare, as though they were already stupefied with sleep. Weiss, who had not realized it was so late, put his arms tenderly round Maurice: good luck and keep smiling! He would give Henriette a kiss for her brother and go and give his love to Uncle Fouchard. And as he was really going a rumour ran round, a sort of feverish excitement. It was a great victory won by MacMahon: the Crown Prince of Prussia taken prisoner with twenty-five thousand men, the enemy pushed back, destroyed, leaving its guns and baggage in our hands.

'There you are!' was all Rochas exclaimed, in his booming voice.

Then, overjoyed, he ran after Weiss who was hurrying back to Mulhouse:

'With kicks up the arse, sir, kicks up the arse all the way to Berlin!'

A quarter of an hour later another dispatch reported that the army had had to evacuate Woerth and was in full retreat. Oh, what a night! Rochas, knocked out with fatigue, had wrapped his great-coat round him and was asleep on the ground, not bothering about a shelter, as often happened with him. Maurice and Jean had crawled into the tent where Loubet, Chouteau, Pache and Lapoulle were already huddled together with their heads on their knapsacks. There was room for six so long as you kept your knees bent. At first Loubet had made them all laugh away their hunger by giving Lapoulle to believe that there would be chicken at tomorrow's issue of rations, but they were too tired and were soon snoring – let the Prussians come. Jean lay still for a moment close against Maurice; although he was dead tired he couldn't get off to sleep, for what this gent had said was going round and round in his head – the Germans under arms, innumerable and insatiable – and he felt that his companion was not asleep either, but was thinking about the same things. Then Maurice made an impatient movement away from him and Jean realized that he was annoying him. Between the peasant and the intellectual the instinctive hostility, the dislike born of class and education, were like a physical discomfort; yet the former felt a sort of shame at this, an inner unhappiness, and shrank away, trying to escape from the hostile contempt he sensed was there. Although the night was now getting chilly outside, it was so stifling in the tent with all these bodies piled on each other that Maurice, feeling unbearably hot, suddenly jumped up, went out and lay down a few steps away. Jean, feeling wretched, tossed about in a nightmarish half-sleep in which sadness at not being liked mingled with fear of some immense disaster which he thought he could hear galloping out yonder in the unknown.

Hours must have passed, and the whole black, motionless camp seemed crushed beneath the pressure of this limitless, evil darkness laden with something horrible but as yet nameless. Little stirrings could be felt in a lake of blackness, a sudden snore would come from some invisible tent. Or again sounds you didn't recognize – a snorting horse, a sabre rattling, the movement of some late prowler – all quite ordinary noises which took on menacing overtones. Then all of a sudden, near the cookhouse, a great light flared up. It threw the battle front into strong relief in which you caught a glimpse of rows of stacked arms, polished rifle-barrels over which red reflections passed like trickles of fresh blood, and the dark, stiff figures of sentries loomed up in this sudden fire. Was this the enemy whom the officers had been promising for two days and they had been searching for all the way from Belfort to Mulhouse? Then the flame went out in a great fountain of sparks. It was only the heap of green sticks that Lapoulle had worried at for so long, and which after hours of smouldering had flared up like straw.

Frightened by this bright light Jean also rushed out of the tent and nearly tripped over Maurice who was propped on one elbow, watching. The darkness had already returned blacker than ever, and the two men stayed there stretched out on the bare earth, a few metres apart. The only thing visible in the thick darkness was the farmhouse window over yonder in which the light was still burning, the solitary candle that seemed to mark a vigil over the dead. What could the time be? Perhaps two or three. But the headquarters over there was certainly not asleep. The yapping voice of General Bourgain-Desfeuilles could be heard cursing this sleepless night in which he had only been able to keep going with the help of drinks and cigars. New telegrams kept coming in, things must be going wrong, shadowy dispatch-riders could just be discerned galloping madly about. Running feet could be heard, oaths, a sound like a stifled death-cry, then a terrible silence. Was this the end, then? An icy breath blew over the exhausted and anguished camp.

It was then that Jean and Maurice realized that a tall, thin shadow rushing by was Colonel de Vineuil. He must be with Major Bouroche, a big, leonine man. They were exchanging disconnected phrases, unfinished, whispered sentences like you hear in bad dreams.

'It comes from Bâle ... Our first division destroyed ... Twelve hours of fighting, the whole army in retreat ...'

The shadowy figure of the colonel stopped and hailed another shade hurrying along, athletic, slim and dapper.

'That you, Beaudoin?'

'Yes, sir!'

'Oh my dear man, MacMahon beaten at Froeschwiller, Frossard beaten at Spickeren, de Failly immobilized and powerless between

the two . . . At Froeschwiller a single corps against a whole army –
did miracles. But everything swept away, rout, panic, France wide
open . . .'

His voice was choking with tears, the words died away and the
three shades melted and vanished.

Maurice had leapt to his feet, his whole being shuddering.

'Oh my God!' he muttered.

That was all he could find to say, while Jean, with death in his
heart, whispered:

'Oh bloody hell! So that gentleman, your relation, was right
when he said they are stronger than us!'

Maurice could have strangled him, for he was beside himself.
The Prussians stronger than the French! It made his heart bleed.
But the peasant, in his calm and deliberate way, went straight on:

'But it doesn't make any difference, don't you see? You don't
give up just because you've had one knock . . . We've got to bash
'em just the same.'

At that moment a lanky figure rose up in front of them. It was
Rochas, still draped in his greatcoat, who had been awakened out
of his heavy sleep by the vague noises, and possibly by the wind of
defeat. He questioned them, wanted to know.

When after a great struggle he had grasped it, his childlike eyes
showed an immense bewilderment.

More than ten times he repeated:

'Beaten! Beaten how? Why?'

Now the eastern sky was lightening; it was a weird and infinitely
mournful light on the sleeping tents, in one of which you could
begin to pick out the grey faces of Loubet and Lapoulle, Chouteau
and Pache, still snoring open-mouthed. A funereal dawn was
coming up out of the sooty mists rising from the distant river.

2

By about eight the sun dispersed the heavy clouds and a clear,
blazing August Sunday shone out over Mulhouse in the middle of
the great, fertile plain. From the camp, now awake and buzzing
with activity, the bells of all the parishes could be heard hurling

their chimes through the limpid air. That lovely Sunday, day of appalling disaster, had its own gaiety, its brilliant holiday sky.

Suddenly Gaude sounded rations and Loubet was amazed. What was up? Was this the chicken he had promised Lapoulle the day before? Born in the rue de la Cossonnerie, in the central markets, by-blow of a costermonger, he had enlisted 'for a few coppers', as he put it and, after a go at all sorts of trades, he was the cook and his nose was always sniffing out something good to eat. So he went off to find out, while Chouteau the artist – a house-painter from Montmartre, a good-looking chap and a revolutionary, furious at having been called back to the colours after serving his time – was ferociously taking it out of Pache, whom he had come across on his knees behind the tent, saying his prayers. There was a reverend for you! Couldn't he ask that God of his for a hundred thousand a year? But Pache, who came from some outlandish village in Brittany, a puny little specimen with a pear-shaped head, just let himself be teased, with the long-suffering silence of a martyr. He was the butt of the squad, he and Lapoulle, a hulking great brute who had grown up in the marshes of Sologne, who was so ignorant about everything that on the day he had joined the regiment he had asked to see the king. Although the news of the disaster of Froeschwiller had been going round since reveille, the four men were laughing away and going through the usual jobs with their mechanical unconcern.

But then a growl of surprise and jeering went up as Jean, the corporal, accompanied by Maurice, came back from the ration issue with some firewood. At last they were handing out the wood that the troops had waited for in vain last night to warm up the stew. Only twelve hours late.

'Three cheers for the quartermaster!' called Chouteau.

'Never mind, here it is,' said Loubet. 'Now you'll see the lovely stew I'm going to make you!'

He usually took on the eats, and they were all grateful, for he cooked marvellously. But he would pile the most extraordinary jobs on to Lapoulle.

'Go and find the champagne, go and fetch the truffles...'

That morning he hit on a weird idea, typical of a Paris smartie pulling the leg of an innocent.

'Come on, quicker than that! Give me the chicken.'

'Chicken, where?'

'Down there, on the ground ... The chicken I promised you, the one the corporal has just brought!'

He pointed at a big white stone at their feet. Lapoulle was quite nonplussed, but in the end he picked it up and turned it over in his fingers.

'Will you clean that chicken, for God's sake! Go on, wash his feet, wash his neck! With plenty of water, you lazy sod!'

And for no reason, except that it was a lark and the thought of the stew made him feel gay and full of fun, he chucked the stone into the pot of water, together with the meat.

'That's what's going to give it the taste! Oh, didn't you know that? Well, you don't know nothing, you silly sausage. You'll have the arsehole, it's ever so tender, you'll see!'

The squad was tickled pink at the look of Lapoulle, who was now convinced and licking his chops. Oh that cove Loubet, never a dull moment with him! And when the fire began crackling in the sun and the pot began to sing, they all stood round and worshipped with an expression of bliss spreading over their faces as they watched the meat dancing and sniffed the lovely smell beginning to fill the air. Ever since the day before they had been as hungry as wolves and the thought of food was now predominant in their minds. They may have been beaten but that was no reason for not filling themselves. From one end of the camp to the other cookhouse fires were blazing, saucepans were bubbling and there was a voracious, bawling joy amid the chimes still ringing clear from every parish church in Mulhouse.

But just before nine there was a sensation in the air, officers rushed about, and Lieutenant Rochas, who had an order from Captain Beaudoin, came past the tents of his section.

'Come on, everything folded and packed up, we're off!'

'But the stew!'

'Stew another day! We're off at once!'

Gaude blew an imperious call on his bugle. There was consternation and sullen anger. What, leave without food! Not wait even one hour until the stew was eatable! The squad was for drinking the broth anyway, but so far it was nothing but hot water and the uncooked meat was impenetrable, like leather between your teeth. Chouteau muttered terrible oaths. Jean had to intervene and hurry his men on with the preparations. What was all the hurry, then? Clearing off like this, shoving people about with no time to get their strength back! Somebody said in Maurice's hearing that they were marching to meet the Prussians and take their revenge, but he shrugged his shoulders in disbelief. Camp was struck in less than a quarter of an hour, tents folded and strapped on to packs, piles of arms dismantled, and nothing was left on the bare ground but the cooking fires dying down.

General Douay had had serious reasons for deciding on an immediate withdrawal. The dispatch from the sub-prefect of Schlestadt, already three days old, was confirmed, and a telegram said that Prussian camp fires had been sighted again threatening Markolsheim; another telegram said that an enemy corps was crossing the Rhine at Huningue. Details were coming in, full and precise: cavalry and infantry had been sighted, troops on the move from all points and making for their rendezvous. One hour's delay would mean that the line of retreat on Belfort would certainly be cut. Reacting after the defeat, after Wissembourg and Froeschwiller, the general, isolated and with his advance guard useless, could only fall back at once, especially as the morning's news was even graver than that of the night before.

The headquarters staff had set off at a canter, spurring on their horses for fear of being by-passed and finding the Prussians already at Altkirch. General Bourgain-Desfeuilles, foreseeing a tough stretch ahead, had taken the precaution of going through Mulhouse in order to have a copious meal, grumbling at the rush. Mulhouse was in despair as the officers passed through – when news of the retreat spread the inhabitants ran out into the streets protesting at the sudden departure of the troops they had so desperately implored to come. Were they being abandoned, then? Was all the fabulous loot piled up in the station going to be left for the enemy? Was their city itself to be nothing but a conquered city by nightfall? All along the country roads the inhabitants of villages and isolated houses had also taken up positions on their doorsteps in astonishment and alarm. What! Were those same regiments they had seen only yesterday marching to battle, now falling back and running away without fighting? The officers were sullen and spurred on their horses, refusing to answer questions, as though ill-luck were galloping at their heels. Was it true, then, that the

Prussians had crushed the army and were pouring into France from all sides like a river in spate that had burst its banks? Already the population was giving way to mounting panic, and in the still air thought it could hear the distant thunder of invasion, rumbling louder and louder every minute, and already carts were being loaded with chattels, houses were emptying, families were threading their way along the lanes where terror was running riot.

In the confusion of the retreat, along the Rhône–Rhine canal, the 106th had to halt after only one kilometre. Marching orders, badly expressed and even more badly carried out, had jammed the whole 2nd division at this point, and the way through was so narrow, scarcely five metres wide, that the procession looked like going on for ever.

Two hours later the 106th was still waiting at a standstill, facing the endless stream going on ahead of them. Standing in the blazing sun, pack on back and rifle held at ease, the men finally demonstrated their impatience.

'We're the rearguard, I suppose,' said Loubet in his sarcastic voice.

Chouteau blew his top:

'They're roasting us here just to show they don't care a fuck about us. We were here first, we should have gone through.'

On the other side of the canal, over the great fertile plain with its flat roads between hopfields and ripe corn, they could now see the movement of the retreating troops carrying out yesterday's march in the opposite direction, and scornful laughs ran along, a universal burst of furious sneering:

'Here we go galloping along!' Chouteau went on. 'Well, it's a rum idea, this march against the foe they've been stuffing into our ears since the other morning ... No really, it's too funny by half, we get here and then fuck off again with no time even to swallow our stew!'

The exasperated laughter got louder, and Maurice, who was near Chouteau, agreed with him. As they had been stuck there like posts for two hours why hadn't they been allowed to cook their stew and swallow it in peace? Hunger was catching up on them, and they were in a sullen rage about their saucepan emptied out too soon, for they didn't see the necessity for this haste that seemed silly and cowardly to them. Like a lot of hares they were, really!

At that moment Lieutenant Rochas swore at Sergeant Sapin, blaming him for the bad behaviour of his men. The noise brought up Captain Beaudoin.

Silence in the ranks!

Jean said nothing. A veteran of the Italian wars and broken in to discipline, he studied Maurice who appeared to be enjoying Chouteau's bursts of bloody-minded sneering, and was astonished that a real gent like him, a fellow who had had such good schooling, could agree with things that ought not to be said, even if they might be true. If every soldier took it into his head to criticize the officers and give his opinion they wouldn't get very far, and that was a fact.

At last, after yet another hour's wait, the 106th received the order to proceed. But the bridge was still so jammed with the tail end of the division that there was hell's own muddle. Several regiments got mixed up, some companies got carried along willy-nilly, but others were pushed to the side of the road and had to mark time. And to complete the confusion, a squadron of cavalry insisted on riding through and pushed back into the fields some of the stragglers already dropping out of the infantry. After one hour of marching it was an out-and-out rabble, dragging its feet, stringing out in a line and dallying about as though nothing mattered.

So it was that Jean found himself in the rear, lost in a sunken lane with his squad, that he was determined not to let out of his sight. The 106th had vanished and there was not a single man or even officer of the company left. There were only isolated soldiers, a mob of unknown men, worn out at the very start of the day's march, each going at his own pace wherever the paths took him. The sun was killing, it was terribly hot, and their packs, made heavier by the tents and complicated gear which distended them, weighed cruelly on their shoulders. Many of them were unaccustomed to carrying a pack, and in any case they were hampered by their thick service capes that felt as though they were made of lead. All of a sudden a pallid young soldier, whose eyes were filled with tears, stopped and threw his kit into a ditch with a heavy sigh of relief, like the deep breathing of a dying man coming back to life.

'There's somebody with some sense,' murmured Chouteau.

But he went on marching, with his back bent beneath the load. However, when two others had unburdened themselves also, he could hold out no longer.

'Oh, to hell with it,' he said.

And with a jerk of his shoulder he pitched his pack against a bank. No thank you! Twenty-five kilos on his spine, he'd had enough! They weren't beasts of burden, to have to carry all that.

Almost at once Loubet imitated him and forced Lapoulle to do the same. Pache, who made the sign of the cross at every Calvary he came to, loosened the straps and carefully placed all his kit at the foot of a low wall, as though he would be coming back for it. Maurice was the only one still loaded when Jean turned round and saw the men with their shoulders free.

'Pick up your packs; I'm the one who'll cop it!'

But although the men were not yet in open revolt they walked on, grim-faced and silent, pushing the corporal ahead of them along the narrow lane.

'Will you pick up your packs, or I'll report you!'

It was like a whiplash across Maurice's face. Report them! This clodhopper was going to report them because some poor devils were seeking relief for their aching muscles! In a fit of blind rage he loosened his straps too, and dropped his pack by the roadside, staring at Jean in defiance.

'All right,' said Jean in his sensible voice, for he couldn't risk starting a fight, 'we'll settle this tonight.'

Maurice was having terrible trouble with his feet. The big, hard boots that he was quite unused to had turned his flesh into a bloody mess. He was not very robust, and although he had thrown off his knapsack he still felt a sort of open sore all down his spine from the intolerable rubbing of the kit, he didn't know which arm to carry his rifle with, and the weight of it was enough to wind him. But he was even more tormented by the moral agony of one of the fits of depression to which he was subject. These would suddenly come over him quite irresistibly, and then he would witness the collapse of his own will-power and give way to evil instincts, abdicate from his real self, and later cry with shame. His misdeeds in Paris had never been anything but mad fits of 'the other one,' as he called him, the weakling he turned into in his cowardly moments, and who was capable of the meanest actions. And since he had been dragging along in the scorching sun, in this retreat that was more like a rout, he was nothing but an animal in this lost, wandering herd strung out along the roads. It was the after-effect of defeat, of the distant thunder leagues away, whose dying echo was now hounding these panic-stricken men in full flight without having set eyes on an enemy. What was there to hope for now? Surely it was all over? They were beaten, and there was nothing left but to lie down and go to sleep.

'Well, what the hell,' Loubet shouted at the top of his voice with his Cockney laugh, 'but all the same we aren't marching to Berlin!'

To Berlin! To Berlin! Maurice could still hear that cry yelled by the milling crowds on the boulevards during that night of wild excitement which had made him decide to enlist. The wind had changed in a violent storm and here was a terrible about-turn: the whole temperament of the race showed itself in this sublime confidence suddenly crashing down at the very first reverse into the despair which galloped away with these lost soldiers, defeated and scattered before ever striking a blow.

'Oh this rifle's sawing off my paws!' Loubet went on, once again changing shoulders, 'and there's a bleeding tin whistle that can go for a walk!'

Then, referring to the sum he had been paid as a replacement:

'All the same, fifteen hundred francs for this job is daylight robbery! That rich bloke I'm going to get killed for must be enjoying some lovely pipes at his fireside!'

'What about me,' Chouteau groused. 'I had served my time and was just getting out. Well, 'struth, no luck at all to fall into the shit like this!'

He swung his rifle impatiently, then he too flung it violently over the hedge.

'There, off you go, you fucking tool!'

The rifle turned two somersaults and landed in a furrow where it lay at full length, still as a corpse. Others were already flying to join it. Soon the field was full of weapons lying there stiff and for-lorn beneath the sweltering sun. An infectious madness spread, hunger was twisting their guts, boots were hurting their feet, this march was a torture, with unforeseen defeat growling threaten-ingly in their rear. Nothing good left to expect, their leaders losing their grip, the commissariat not even feeding them, anger, frustra-tion, desire to have done with it at once, before even beginning. So what! Let their guns join their packs. In a silly burst of temper and amid the gigglings of a lot of grinning idiots, the guns flew away all down the long, long tail of stragglers stretching back over the countryside.

Before getting rid of his, Loubet made it twirl round beautifully, like a drum-major's stick. Lapoulle, seeing all his mates chucking theirs away, must have thought it was part of the drill, so he imitated their movements. But Pache, in a confused sense of duty to his religious upbringing, refused to do the same and had insults heaped on him by Chouteau, who called him a priest's baby.

'Look at that creep! All because his old cow of a mother made him swallow Our Father every Sunday! Why don't you go and serve Mass, you're too scared to be with your mates!'

Maurice marched on in sullen silence, head down under the scorching sky. All that was left was to go on in a nightmare of atrocious weariness, haunted by phantoms, as though he were going on into an abyss straight in front of him. His whole upbringing as an educated man was collapsing and he was sinking to the low level of these creatures round him.

'Yes,' he suddenly said to Chouteau, 'you're right!'

He had already put his rifle down on a heap of stones when Jean, who was vainly trying to check this disgraceful abandoning of arms, saw him. He went straight for him:

'Pick up that gun of yours at once, at once, do you hear?'

A flood of terrible rage surged up into Jean's face. Usually so placid, always for conciliation, he now had eyes blazing and spoke with the voice of thunderous authority. His men had never seen him like this, and they stood still in amazement.

'Pick up that gun at once or you'll have me to deal with!'

Shaken, Maurice uttered only one word, which he meant to sound insulting:

'Clodhopper!'

'Clodhopper! Yes, a clodhopper is what I am, and you are a grand gent! And that's why you're a swine, yes, a filthy swine! I'm telling you straight!'

Shouts of protest went up, but the corporal went on with extraordinary vehemence:

'When a man's been educated he shows it. If we are yokels and clods you should be setting us all an example because you know

48

more about everything than we do ... Now pick up your gun again, fuck you, or I'll have you shot at the end of the march.'

Maurice picked up the gun, thoroughly cowed. There were tears of rage in his eyes. He marched on, staggering like a drunken man, surrounded by his mates who were now jeering because he had knuckled under. Oh, how he hated that Jean with an undying hate, wounded to the quick by such a hard lesson which he felt he deserved. And when Chouteau muttered at his side that with a corporal like that you waited for a battle and then put a bullet through his head, he saw red and had a clear vision of himself bashing Jean's head in behind some wall.

But then there was a diversion. Loubet noticed that during the row Pache, too, had quietly got rid of his rifle, putting it down at the foot of a bank. Why? He didn't attempt to find an explanation, laughing sheepishly, half pleased with himself and half ashamed like a good little boy being scolded for his first naughtiness. He walked along with arms hanging free, very jolly and cock-a-hoop. Along the interminable sun-baked roads, between the fields of ripe corn or hops, one after another and all looking the same, the stampede went on, and the stragglers, with neither packs nor rifles, were nothing but a wandering rabble tramping along, a hotchpotch of rascals and beggars at whose approach village doors shut in panic.

Just then they met something which put the finishing touch to Maurice's exasperation. A distant heavy rumbling could be heard coming nearer; it was the reserve artillery which had set off last, and suddenly its head appeared round a bend in the road. The demoralized stragglers just had time to throw themselves into the nearby fields. The artillery was moving in column, coming along at a proud canter in fine correct order, a whole regiment of six batteries, the colonel on the outside and near the middle, and the officers in their places. The guns clanked by, keeping strict spacing, each with its ammunition waggon, horses and men. In the fifth battery Maurice recognized his cousin Honoré's cannon. There was the sergeant, proudly mounted on his horse, to the left of the leader, a handsome, fair chap called Adolphe on a sturdy chestnut beautifully matched with the off-horse trotting alongside. In his correct position among the six gunners, sitting in pairs on the cases of the gun itself and its ammunition waggon, was Louis, the gun-layer, a dark little man and Adolphe's mate, his other half, as they said, following the established custom of marrying a mounted man and a foot-slogger. They seemed much taller to Maurice, who had met them in camp, and the gun, with its four horses, followed by the waggon drawn by six more, looked as dazzling as a sun, polished and cherished by all its little world, men and beasts, closely surrounding it with the discipline and tenderness of a well-ordered family. And what hurt him most was the haughty glance his cousin Honoré cast on the stragglers and his sudden amazement when he caught sight of him in the midst of this rabble of unarmed men. The procession was nearly past, with the material for the batteries – waggons, forage-carts, smithies. Then in a final cloud of dust went the reserves, the spare men and horses, who trotted out of sight round another bend in the road with a gradually diminishing din of hoofs and wheels.

'Blimey!' declared Loubet. 'Easy enough to be cocky when you're going by coach!'

The headquarters staff had found Altkirch unoccupied. No Prussians yet. Nevertheless, afraid of being dogged and of seeing them appear at any moment General Douay had decided that the march should go on as far as Dannemarie, which the leading detachments had not reached until five in the afternoon. It was eight and getting dark, and yet the regiments, in a terrible state of confusion and reduced to half strength, had hardly finished bivouacking. The men were worn out and collapsing with hunger and fatigue. Until ten o'clock they could still be seen coming in – hunting for their companies and not finding them – isolated soldiers, little groups, the whole miserable, interminable line of footsore and resentful men strung out along the roads.

As soon as he did manage to rejoin his regiment Jean set about finding Lieutenant Rochas to make his report. He found him and Captain Beaudoin confering with the colonel. All three were in front of a little inn and very concerned about the roll-call and anxious to know the whereabouts of their men. The first words of the corporal to the lieutenant were overheard by Colonel de Vineuil, and he called him over and forced him to tell him the whole story. His long sallow face, in which the eyes looked very black against his snow-white hair and drooping moustache, expressed silent misery.

'Sir,' said Captain Beaudoin, without waiting for his commanding officer's opinion, 'we must shoot half a dozen of these thugs.'

Lieutenant Rochas nodded his agreement, but the colonel made a gesture of helplessness.

'Too many of them . . . what can you do? Nearly seven hundred of them! Who can you pick on out of that lot? . . . And besides, if you please, the general won't hear of it. He goes all fatherly and says he never punished a single man in Africa . . . No, no, there's nothing I can do. It's terrible.'

The captain made so bold as to repeat after him:

'Yes it is terrible . . . It's the end of everything.'

Jean was taking himself off when he heard Major Bouroche, whom he had not noticed standing on the steps of the inn, mutter softly: no more discipline, no more punishment, army done for! Before a week was out the officers would get a few kicks up the backside, whereas if they had coshed one or two of those blighters straight away the rest might have had second thoughts.

Nobody was punished. Officers bringing up the rear, escorting the vehicles of the baggage-train, had had the happy foresight to get the packs and rifles picked up from the roadside. There were only a few missing, and the men were rearmed at dawn on the quiet to hush the matter up. Orders were to strike camp at five, but by four the soldiers were awakened and the retreat on Belfort was pushed forward on the assumption that the Prussians were only a league or two away. Once again the troops had had to put up with biscuits, and they were still dead beat after the short and restless night, with nothing warm in their bellies. That morning, once again, the orderly conduct of the march was jeopardized by this sudden departure.

That day was worse still, utterly miserable. The character of the country had changed, and they had entered a mountainous region with roads up hill and down dale through fir plantations and narrow valleys all tangled with gorse and a mass of golden blossom. But through this gaily-coloured countryside beneath a brilliant August sun, a wind of panic had blown ever more fiercely since the day before. A dispatch advising mayors to warn the inhabitants that they would do well to put away their valuables had just increased the terror to fever-pitch. So the enemy was here? Would there even be time to escape? Everybody thought he could hear the mounting roar of invasion, like the dull thunder of a river in spate, gathering strength at every village from some fresh scare, amid general clamour and lamentation.

Maurice moved on like a sleepwalker, his feet bleeding and his shoulders weighed down with his pack and rifle. His mind had ceased to function and he trudged on through the nightmare that he could see around him. He had lost all consciousness of the tramping of his mates and only felt Jean on his left, worn out by the same fatigue and grief. It was heartbreaking, these villages they went through, the pity of it gripped your heart with anguish. As soon as they saw the troops in retreat, this rabble of exhausted soldiers dragging their feet, the inhabitants got busy and hastened their own flight. And they were so quietly confident a fortnight ago, the whole of Alsace awaiting war with a smile, convinced that the fighting would be in Germany! And now France was invaded and the storm was breaking here, round their homes, in their fields, like one of those terrible hurricanes of hail and thunder that lay waste a whole province in a couple of hours! In front of doors, amid furious confusion, men were loading carts, piling on furniture at the risk of breaking the lot. From upstairs windows women were throwing a last mattress or passing down the cradle they had nearly forgotten. The baby was tied into it and was secured on top amongst legs of upturned chairs and tables. Round at the back they were roping poor old sick grand-dad to a cupboard and carting him off like a piece of furniture. Then there were those who did not possess a cart, but piled their belongings on a wheelbarrow, and yet others were moving off with a load of clothing in their arms, others had only thought of saving the clock, which they clasped to their bosom like a child. They could not take everything, and abandoned furniture or bundles of clothing that had proved to be too heavy were left in the gutters. Some people shut everything up before leaving and the houses looked dead, with doors and windows fastened, but the majority, in their haste and certainty that everything was bound to be destroyed, left their old homes wide open, with doors and windows gaping showing rooms stripped bare, and these were the saddest ones, with the dreadful sadness of a sacked town depopulated by fear – miserable homes open to the four winds, from which the very cats had fled in terror of what was coming. With every village the harrowing sight was more depressing, the numbers of fugitives and people moving out got larger in a growing confusion accompanied by clenched fists, curses and tears.

But it was above all along the main road in the open country that Maurice was choked with grief, for as they approached Belfort the straggle of refugees grew thicker and became an uninterrupted procession. Poor devils who thought they could find safety behind the walls of the fortress! The man belaboured his horse, the wife followed behind, dragging the children. Families pushed ahead, weighed down under their burdens, losing each other, tiny tots unable to keep up with the rest, and all in the blinding whiteness of the road on which the sun poured down like molten lead. Many had taken off their boots and were going barefoot so as to get along faster, and without slackening their pace half dressed mothers were giving the breast to whimpering babies. Scared faces glanced behind and hands gestured wildly as if to shut out the horizon as the wind of panic tousled heads and whipped up hastily put-on clothes. Others, farmers with all their labourers, marched straight across the fields, driving their flocks ahead – sheep, cows, oxen, horses that they had driven out of sheds and stables with their sticks. These were making for the deep valleys, the high plateaux and lonely forests, throwing up the dust-clouds of the great migrations of ancient times, when peoples abandoned their lands to the advancing, all-conquering barbarians. They were all going to live under canvas in some deserted rock fastness, so far from any road that not a single enemy soldier would dare risk his life there. The moving clouds enveloping them disappeared behind clumps of fir trees with the diminishing noise of lowing and trampling herds, whilst the stream of carts and people on foot still flowed along the road, upsetting the march of the troops, and on the outskirts of Belfort it became so concentrated, with its current as irresistible as a river in spate, that several times a halt had to be called.

It was during one of these short halts that Maurice witnessed a scene which stayed in his memory like a slap in the face.

By the roadside there was an isolated house, the dwelling of some poor peasant, the whole of whose little property lay stretched out behind it. He had refused to leave his field, where his roots were too deeply sunk in the soil, and there he was, unable to go unless he left some of his very flesh there. He could be seen in a low-ceilinged room, slumped on a seat, staring with unseeing eyes at these passing soldiers, whose retreat would hand his ripe corn over to the enemy. Standing by him his wife, still quite young, was holding a child while another was clinging to her skirt, and all three were wailing. Then suddenly the front door was flung open and the grandmother appeared, a very old woman, tall and skinny, with bare arms like knotted ropes, furiously waving. Wisps of grey hair came out from under her bonnet and blew round her wizened face, and she was in such a rage that the words she was yelling stuck in her throat and could hardly be heard.

At first the soldiers began to laugh. What a face, silly old geezer! But then the words came through as the old woman shouted:

'Swine! Blackguards! Cowards! Cowards!'

Her voice screamed higher and higher as she spat the insult of cowardice right in their faces. And the laughter died, and a chill ran through the ranks. The men lowered their heads and looked away.

'Cowards! Cowards! Cowards!'

Suddenly she seemed to grow taller still. She drew herself up, gaunt and tragic in her shabby old dress, moving her skinny arm from west to east with such an immense gesture that it seemed to fill the heavens.

'Cowards, the Rhine isn't that way ... The Rhine is over there, cowards, cowards!'

At last the march was resumed, and at that moment Maurice caught sight of Jean's face and saw that his eyes were filled with tears. A shudder came over him and his own suffering became still more acute when he realized that even those oafs had felt the insult which they didn't deserve but had to swallow. Everything was falling to pieces in his poor aching head, and he never knew how he got to the end of that day's march.

The 7th corps had taken the whole day to cover the twenty-three kilometres between Dannemarie and Belfort, and once again night was falling and it was very late when the troops finally bivouacked under the walls of the fortress at the very place from which they had set off to march against the foe four days before. In spite of the late hour and their extreme fatigue the soldiers insisted on lighting their cookhouse fires and making some stew. At last, for the first time since their departure, they were having something hot to eat. Round the fires, in the cool of the evening, noses were buried in messtins and grunts of satisfaction were beginning to be heard when a rumour ran round that astounded the camp. Two new dispatches had come in one after the other: the Prussians had not crossed the Rhine at Markolsheim and there wasn't a single Prussian left in Huningue. The crossing of the Rhine at Markolsheim, the bridge of boats thrown across by the light of huge electric lamps, in fact all these alarming tales were nothing but a nightmare, an unexplained hallucination on the part of the sub-prefect of Schlestadt. And as for the army corps threatening Huningue, the famous army corps of the Black Forest before which Alsace trembled, it was merely composed of a tiny detachment from Württemberg – two battalions and one squadron – which by means of skilful tactics, repeated marches and counter-marches, sudden unexpected appearances, had given the impression that thirty or forty thousand men were involved. To think that that very evening they had almost blown up the Dannemarie viaduct! Twenty leagues of rich country had been laid waste for no reason whatever, in the most idiotic of panics, and at the thought of what they had seen during that deplorable day – populations fleeing in terror, driving their flocks up into the mountains, the stream of carts loaded with chattels flowing towards the town and mingled with multitudes of women and children – the soldiers lost their tempers and exclaimed with ugly sneers.

'No, really, it's beyond a joke!' spluttered Loubet with his mouth full, waving his spoon. 'What! Is that the enemy we were marched against? Nobody there! . . . Twelve leagues forwards, twelve leagues backwards, and not even a cat to be seen! All that for nothing, just for the fun of getting the wind up!'

Chouteau, noisily scraping his messtin, held forth against the generals without mentioning them by name.

'What, those swine? What a lot of bloody fools! Proper runaways they've given us! If they hopped it like that when there was nobody there, wouldn't they half have skedaddled if they had found themselves faced by a real enemy!'

They had flung a fresh armful of wood on the fire so as to enjoy the brightness of the leaping flames, and Lapoulle, luxuriously warming his legs, was exploding with silly, mindless laughter, when Jean, who had at first turned a deaf ear, chipped in in a fatherly way:

'That'll do! If somebody heard you there might be trouble.'

His own simple common sense was just as disgusted by the stupidity of their leaders. But still, you had to see that they were respected, and as Chouteau was still carrying on he cut him short:

'Shut up! Here's the lieutenant, you'd better complain to him if you've any remarks to make.'

Maurice was sitting away on his own, staring at the ground. This was really the end! Hardly had they started before it was all over. This lack of discipline and revolt of the men at the first setback was already turning the army into a rabble with no bond of union, demoralized and ripe for any disaster. Here under the walls of Belfort, these men had not set eyes on a single Prussian and they were defeated.

The following days were full of trepidation and anxiety in their very monotony. So as to find the troops something to do General Douay set them to work on the defences of the fortress, still far from complete. They turned over the ground in a rage and cut into the rock. And no news! Where was MacMahon's army? What was going on in front of Metz? The most extravagant rumours were in circulation and a few Paris newspapers hardly made the enveloping mists of anxiety all that much worse by their contra-dictions. Twice the general had written and asked for orders, and had not even had an answer. But by 12 August the 7th corps was at last brought up to full strength by the arrival of the third division direct from Italy, yet in spite of that there were only two divisions, because the first, beaten at Froeschwiller, had been carried away in the rout and nobody now knew where the current had cast it up. After they had been left for a week, cut off from the rest of France, the order to depart came by wire. There was great rejoicing, for anything was better than this prison life. During the preparations the guessing began again, nobody knew where they were making for: some said to defend Strasbourg and others even talked of a bold thrust into the Black Forest to cut the Prussians' line of retreat.

The next morning the 106th was among the first to leave, piled up in cattle trucks. It was particularly crowded in the truck where Jean's unit was, so much so that Loubet made out he hadn't room to sneeze. As once again the issue of rations had been a complete muddle, and the soldiers had received in spirits what they should have had in food, they were nearly all drunk with a violent and bawling drunkenness that worked itself off in obscene singing. The train went on and on and you couldn't see the others in the truck, so thick was the haze of pipe smoke; the heat was unbearable, with the stink of all these bodies in a heap, and as the truck sped along there issued out of the blackness shoutings that drowned the noise of the wheels and died away across the dreary countryside. It was only at Langres that the troops realized they were being taken back to Paris.

'Oh Christ,' exclaimed Chouteau, already reigning in his corner as undisputed king because of his all-powerful gift of the gab, 'they're going for certain to park us at Charentonneau to prevent Bismarck from going to doss in the Tuileries.'

The others were rolling with mirth, thinking that was a scream, they didn't know why. Anyhow the most trivial incidents on the journey gave rise to deafening booings, yellings and laughter – peasants standing by the line, groups of worried-looking people waiting at little stations for trains to come through in the hope of getting some news – all France scared and jumpy in the face of invasion. And as the engine and train rushed by in a fleeting impression of steam and noise, all the crowds got was the bawling of this cannon-fodder being whisked away. But in a station where they stopped three fashionably dressed ladies, well-to-do towns-people, passed cups of broth round and had a great success. Men wept and kissed their hands in gratitude.

Yet a little further on the filthy songs and savage yellings began again. A little beyond Chaumont the train happened to pass another one full of artillerymen being taken to Metz. Speed had been reduced, and the soldiers in the two trains fraternized in an infernal din. And possibly because they were more drunk, it was the artillerymen who won as they stood waving their fists out of the trucks and shouting everything else down with the violence of desperation:

'To the slaughterhouse! To the slaughterhouse! To the slaughterhouse!'

A great chill, the icy wind of a charnel-house, seemed to be blowing through. A sudden silence fell, in which Loubet's sneering voice could be heard:

'Our chums aren't all that lively!'

'But they're right.' Chouteau took up the point in his pub-orator's voice. 'It's wicked to send off a lot of ordinary chaps to get killed for a lot of balls they don't know the first thing about.'

And so on and so on. He was the typical agitator, the bad work-man from Montmartre, the house-painter who took time off and went on the binge, who half digested bits of speeches heard at public meetings and mixed up a lot of asinine rubbish with the great principles of equality and liberty. He was the know-all and he indoctrinated his comrades, especially Lapoulle, whom he had promised to turn into quite a bloke.

'Can't you see, old cock, it's quite simple. If old Badinguet and Bismarck have a row then let them have it out between them with fists without upsetting hundreds of thousands of men who don't even know each other and don't want to fight.'

The whole truckload laughed and was won over, and Lapoulle, with no idea who Badinguet was and unable to say even whether he was fighting for an emperor or a king, took up the strain like a baby colossus:

'Sure! With fists, and have a drink afterwards.'

But Chouteau had turned towards Pache and was giving him his turn:

'Like you and that God of yours . . . He said you mustn't fight, that God of yours did. So what are you doing here, you silly sod?'

'Well, er . . .' said Pache, quite taken aback, 'I'm not here for my enjoyment . . . Only there's the police . . .'

'The police! Coo, listen to him! Fuck the police! Don't you know, all you chaps, what we should do if we had any sense? When they unload us later on we should piss off – yes, just quietly slope off! And leave that great swine Badinguet and all his crew of tuppenny-ha'penny generals to work it out as they like with their bloody Prussians!'

There was a burst of applause, the brainwashing was working, and Chouteau triumphantly trotted out his theories, a muddied stream in which floated the Republic, the Rights of Man, the corruption of the Empire that had to be thrown down, the treasons of all these men in command of them, each one bribed with a million, as had been proved. He proclaimed himself a revolution-ary – the others didn't even know whether they were republicans, nor, for that matter, how you set about becoming one, except

Loubet the guzzler, who also knew what he believed, never having been for anything but food. However, they were all carried away and shouted against the Emperor none the less, and against the officers and the whole bloody show that they would walk out of, straight they would, at the first sign of trouble. Working on their mounting drunkenness, Chouteau kept his eye on Maurice, the gent, for he was making him laugh and was proud to have him on his side. And so as to work him up as well, he hit on the idea of baiting Jean, who so far was standing still and half asleep, with eyes half closed amid the din. Considering the hard lesson given by the corporal to this volunteer by forcing him to pick up his rifle, if he bore his superior any malice now was the time to set the two men at each other.

'I have heard tell of them as talked about shooting us,' Chouteau went on menacingly. 'Swine who treat us worse than animals, and don't realize that when you've had enough of your pack and rifle it's good-bye, you chuck the whole fucking lot into the field to see if some more'll grow! Well, chums, what would those people say if now we've got them in a corner we chucked them out as well on to the railway line? What about it? Must have an example so that they stop tormenting us with this bleeding war! Death to old Badinguet's lice! Death to the sods who want us to fight!'

Jean had gone very red, with the blood rushing up to his face as it sometimes did in his rare fits of temper. Although he was pinned by his neighbours in a living vice, he got up and went forward with clenched fists and blazing eyes, and he looked so terrible that the other man cringed.

'Christ Almighty! Will you shut your trap, you swine! I haven't said anything for hours because there's nobody left in command and I can't even put you in clink. Yes, one thing is certain, I would have done a good turn to the regiment if I had rid it of a filthy shit like you. But just you listen, if punishments are only talk now you'll have me to deal with. It isn't a matter of corporal any more – just an ordinary bloke who's sick to death of you and is going to shut your jaw. You miserable coward, you don't want to fight! Just say that again and I'll sock you one!'

At once the whole waggon-load turned round, and, caught up by Jean's fine burst of confidence, they left Chouteau high and dry, spluttering and backing away from Jean's big fists.

'I don't give a damn for Badinguet, nor for you either, d'you see? Me, I've never cared two hoots about politics, Republic or Empire, and today, just the same same as when I was working in my field, I never wanted but one thing – happiness for all, law and order and prosperity ... Of course it gets everybody down to have to fight, but that's not to say we shouldn't deal with these slobs coming up discouraging us when it's hard enough to carry on properly as it is. Good God, mates, don't you get worked up when you're told the Prussians are in your own country and that they must fucking well be kicked out?'

With the fickleness of mobs who swing from one passion to another the soldiers applauded the corporal as he repeated his promise to bash the face in of the first man in the squad to talk of refusing to fight. Bravo corporal! We'll soon cook that Bismarck's goose!

And in the middle of this wild oration Jean calmed down and politely said to Maurice, as though he weren't talking to one of the men:

'Now you, sir, you can't be one of these skunks. Come on, we're not beaten yet, and we'll end up by giving these Prussians what for.'

At that moment Maurice felt a warm ray of sunshine pierce him to the heart, and he felt troubled and humbled. So this chap wasn't just a clod, then? He recalled the burning hatred he had felt when he picked up the rifle he had thrown away in an unthinking moment. But he also remembered the revelation when he had seen the two big tears forming in the corporal's eyes when the old grandma with grey hair flying in the wind had insulted them and pointed to the Rhine over there, beyond the horizon. Was it a sense of brotherhood from having gone through the same fatigues and the same sorrows together, which was now carrying away his resentment? Belonging to a Bonapartist family, he had never considered a republic except in a theoretical way; and he felt a certain affection for the person of the Emperor, and he was for war, the essential of nations. Suddenly hope came back to him in one of those leaps of the imagination he knew so well, and the enthusiasm that had made him enlist one evening surged through him once again, filling his heart with the certainty of victory.

'Yes, that's a fact, corporal,' he said perkily. 'We'll give them what for!'

The truck rushed on and on, bearing its load of men in the thick pipe smoke and stifling fug of crowded bodies, hurling the drunken bawling of obscene songs at the anxious crowds on the stations they passed through and the scared peasants standing along the hedges. On 20 August they were in Paris at the Pantin station, and the same evening off they went again, detraining the next day at Rheims, en route for camp at Châlons.

3

VERY much to his surprise Maurice found that the 106th was detraining at Rheims and had orders to camp there. So they weren't going to join up with the army at Châlons? And two hours later, when his regiment had piled arms a league out of the town on the Courcelles side in the broad plain along the Aisne-Marne canal, his surprise was still greater as he learned that the whole army of Châlons had been falling back since that morning and was coming to camp at the same place. And indeed, as far as the eye could see, as far as Saint-Thierry and La Neuvillette and even beyond the Laon road, tents were going up and the fires of four army corps were blazing by evening. Obviously the plan that had prevailed was to take up a position before Paris and wait for the Prussians. He was very pleased about it. Wasn't it wiser?

That afternoon of the 21st Maurice spent wandering round the camp hunting for news. They were quite free, and discipline seemed still more relaxed, and men just came and went as they liked. Eventually he calmly went back to Rheims where he wanted to cash a draft for a hundred francs he had had from his sister Henriette. In a café he heard a sergeant talking about the mutinous spirit of the eighteen battalions of the Garde Mobile de la Seine, which had been sent back to Paris – the sixth in particular had almost killed their officers. Over in the camp generals were being insulted every day, and since Froeschwiller soldiers weren't even saluting Marshal MacMahon. Voices filled the café and a violent argument broke out between two peaceful-looking gentlemen about the number of men the marshal would have under his command. One talked of 300,000, that was silly. The other more reasonably named the four army corps: the 12th brought up to strength with difficulty in the camp with the help of infantry regiments and a division of marines; the 1st, remnants of which had been coming in since 14 August, and which they were re-forming as best they could; and finally the 5th, defeated without a fight and scattered in a rout, and the 7th, which had just arrived, also demoralized and minus its first division which it had just re-discovered in odd units at Rheims – a hundred and twenty thousand men at the most, counting reserve cavalry and the Bonnemain and Margueritte divisions. But the sergeant who had joined in the argument treated this army with withering scorn as a rag-bag of men with no cohesion, a flock of innocents led to the slaughter by fools, and the two gentlemen, afraid of being compromised, made themselves scarce.

Out in the street Maurice tried to find some newspapers, and stuffed his pockets with all the ones he could buy, reading them as he walked along under the big trees in the magnificent boulevards which surround the town. Where were the German armies, then? They seemed to have got lost. There were probably two on the Metz front: the first under the command of General Steinmetz covering the fortress, the second under Prince Friedrich Karl trying to follow the right bank of the Moselle so as to cut Bazaine's route to Paris. But the third army, that of the Crown Prince of Prussia, and the victorious army of Wissembourg and Froeschwiller which was pursuing the 1st and 5th corps, where was it really, in the muddle of contradictory reports? Still in camp at Nancy? Had it been threatening Châlons, which would explain their leaving the camp in such haste, burning stores, equipment, forage and all kinds of provisions? And then again more confusion and the most contra-dictory theories about plans the generals might have. As though he had been cut off from the world, Maurice only learned then what had happened in Paris: the stupefying shock of defeat on a whole people certain of victory, the terrible outburst of emotion in the streets, the recall of both Chambers, the fall of the liberal adminis-tration that had organized the plebiscite, the Emperor deprived of the title of Commander-in-Chief and forced to hand over the supreme command to Marshal Bazaine. Since the 16th the Emperor had been in the Châlons camp, and all the papers mentioned a grand council held on the 17th at which Prince Napoleon and several generals had been present. But there was no agreement between them about the real decisions made, as distinct from facts which had resulted: General Trochu appointed governor of Paris, Marshal MacMahon put at the head of the army of Châlons, which implied complete elimination of the Emperor. One could sense infinite dismay and indecision, contrary plans fighting each other and replacing each other hour by hour. And always the question, where were the German armies? Who were right, those who made out that Bazaine was a free agent, carrying out his withdrawal towards the northern fortresses, or those who said he was already beleaguered in Metz? A persistent rumour told of gigantic battles and heroic struggles going on between the 14th and 20th, a whole week, but nothing was clear except a tremendous clash of arms somewhere far away and out of ken.

Maurice sat on a seat to rest his legs which were worn out with fatigue. Round him the town seemed to be living its normal daily life – nurserymaids under the lovely trees, looking after children, and retired people taking their usual stroll with stately tread. He went back to his papers and came upon an article he had missed before in a violently republican sheet. Suddenly all was clear. The paper affirmed that at the council held on the 17th at the Châlons camp the retreat of the Paris army had been decided upon and the nomination of General Trochu was solely to prepare people for the Emperor's return. But it added that these resolutions had come to grief when confronted with the attitude of the Empress-Regent and the new government. In the Empress's opinion a revolution was inevitable if the Emperor reappeared, and she was credited with the words: 'He would never reach the Tuileries alive.' And so with all her obstinate determination she was set on an advance and a join-up with the army of Metz, whatever happened, and in this she was supported by General Palikao, the new Minister for War, who had a plan for a spectacular and victorious march to link up with Bazaine. Maurice let the paper slip on to his lap and gazing into space thought he could see it all: the two plans struggling against each other, the hesitations of Marshal MacMahon to undertake such a dangerous flanking movement with such unreliable troops, and impatient and increasingly peremptory orders from Paris urging him on to the foolish temerity of this adventure. Then in the midst of this tragic struggle he suddenly had a clear vision of the Emperor deprived of his imperial authority which he had entrusted to the Empress-Regent, stripped of his position as commander-in-chief with which he had just invested Marshal Bazaine, no longer anything at all, a shadow emperor, vague and indefinite, a nondescript, useless object and a nuisance that nobody knew what to do with, spurned by Paris and with no function left in the army, since he had undertaken not even to give an order.

But the following morning, after a thundery night when he had slept outside the tent rolled in his blanket, it was a relief to Maurice to learn that the withdrawal on Paris had prevailed. There was talk of another council held the day before at which the former Vice-Emperor, Monsieur Rouher, had been present as an envoy from the Empress to expedite the march on Verdun, and it was said that the marshal had convinced him of the danger of such a move. Had they had bad news from Bazaine? Nobody dared state this. But the absence of news was in itself significant, and all the more sensible officers were for waiting outside Paris and therefore being the city's army of defence. Convinced that they would retire the next day, since it was said that the orders had been issued, Maurice was in a happy mood and felt like satisfying a childish wish that was bothering him – to escape for once from the messtin and eat somewhere off a tablecloth, have a bottle in front of him, a glass, a plate and all the things he seemed to have been deprived of for months past. He had money and so off he went in search of an inn, as though on an escapade.

It was past the canal, as you enter the village of Courcelles, that he found the meal of his dreams. He had been told the day before that the Emperor was putting up in one of the grander houses of the village, and he had gone that way for a walk out of curiosity. He remembered noticing this inn on a corner, its arbour hanging with fine bunches of grapes already golden and ripe. Beneath this climbing vine there were some tables painted green, and through the open door could be seen the huge kitchen with its ticking clock, Epinal prints gummed to the walls amidst the crockery, and the massive hostess turning the spit. Behind the inn there was a bowling alley. It was friendly, gay and pretty, the typical old-fashioned French eating-house.

A nice buxom girl came up, showing her fine teeth.

'Are you having lunch, sir?'

'Yes, rather! Give me some eggs, a cutlet and cheese ... Oh, and some white wine!'

He called her back.

'Tell me, isn't it in one of these houses that the Emperor is staying?'

'Yes, look, sir, the one straight in front of you. You can't see the house itself, it's behind that high wall with the trees hiding it.'

He went into the arbour, loosening his belt for comfort, choosing a table on which the sun, filtering through the creepers, cast flecks of gold. But his mind kept coming back to the high yellow wall guarding the Emperor. It was indeed a hidden, mysterious house, not even the roof of which could be seen from outside. The entrance was on the other side, on the village street, a narrow street without a shop or even a window, winding its way between dreary walls. Behind them its grounds made a sort of island of dense greenery among the few neighbouring buildings. And then he noticed at the far end of the road a large courtyard surrounded by sheds and stables all cluttered up with a great many carriages and vans, and in all this there was a continual coming and going of men and horses.

'Is all that because of the Emperor?' he asked the waitress by way of a joke as she was spreading a spotlessly white cloth on the table.

'Yes, just that, for the Emperor all by himself,' she answered in her jolly way, glad to be showing her white teeth.

And no doubt informed by the stable-boys who had been coming in for drinks since the day before, she went through the inventory: a general staff of twenty-five officers, the sixty household cavalry and detachment of guides for escort duty, six military police, then the household, comprising seventy-three persons, chamberlains, menservants and waiters, cooks, kitchen hands; in addition, four saddle-horses and two carriages for the Emperor, ten horses for the equerries, eight for the outriders and grooms, to say nothing of forty-seven post horses, an open waggon for personnel, twelve baggage vans, two of which, reserved for the cooks, had won her admiration for the quantity of utensils, plates and bottles inside, all in perfect order.

'Oh, sir, those saucepans, you've no idea! They shine like suns. And all sorts of dishes, receptacles and gadgets for I don't know what all! And a cellar, yes, bordeaux, burgundy, champagne, enough to give a fine old beano!'

In his joy at seeing a white cloth and delight with the white wine twinkling in his glass, Maurice ate two boiled eggs with a gusto he didn't recognize in himself. When he turned his head to the left he could get a view through one of the entrances of the arbour of the great plain dotted with tents – a whole town buzzing with life that had sprung up in the fields of stubble between the canal and Rheims. Only an occasional clump of trees brought a touch of green into the expanse of grey. Three windmills stood there stretching out their skinny arms. But above the jumble of roofs of Rheims, largely hidden in the tops of chestnut trees, the colossal hull of the cathedral stood out against the blue sky, gigantic beside the low houses, in spite of the distance. Back into his mind came schoolboy memories, lessons learned by heart and repeated in a sing-song voice, the coronation of our kings, the phial of holy oil, Clovis, Joan of Arc, all the ancient glories of France.

Then, as the thought of the Emperor in this unpretentious house, so discreetly shut away, made Maurice look back again at the high yellow wall, he had a shock as he read in enormous black letters: Long Live Napoleon! mixed up with obscene scribblings in huge letters. The rain had blurred these letters, but the inscription was obviously old. What a strange thing to see on this wall – the old enthusiastic war-cry which no doubt acclaimed the conqueror, the uncle, and not the nephew! Already he felt all his childhood coming back and singing in his memories, the days when, back in Le Chêne-Populeux, from earliest childhood he listened to tales told by his grandfather, a soldier of the Grande Armée. His mother was dead and his father had had to accept a job as a tax-collector in that twilight of glory which had overtaken the sons of heroes after the fall of the Empire, and the grandfather lived with them on a tiny pension, having come down to the mediocrity of this humble office-worker's home, and his one consolation was to recount his campaigns to his grandchildren, fair-haired twins, a boy and a girl, to whom he was a kind of mother. He would sit Henriette on his left knee and Maurice on his right, and for hours there were Homeric narratives of battle.

Periods ran into each other, and it all seemed to be independent of history in a terrible collision of all the nations. English, Austrians, Prussians, Russians passed by in turn and together, and it was not always possible to know why some were beaten rather than others. But in the end they were all beaten, beaten inevitably in advance, in a surge of heroism and genius that swept armies away like straw. Marengo, the battle of the plain, with its great lines skilfully deployed, its faultless retreat, like a game of chess, by battalions, silent and unruffled under fire; the legendary battle lost at three o'clock, won by six, in which the eight hundred grenadiers of the Consular Guard broke the momentum of the whole Austrian cavalry, in which Desaix came, as he thought, to die but changed an incipient rout into an immortal victory. Austerlitz, with its wonderful sun of victory in the winter mists, Austerlitz, beginning with the capture of the plateau of Pratzen and ending in the terrifying disaster of the frozen lakes, with a whole Russian army corps falling through the ice, men and animals in an appalling crack of doom, while the godlike Napoleon, who of course had foreseen it all, hastened the disaster with a rain of cannon-balls. Jena, the grave of Prussian power, first the sharpshooters firing through the October mists, the impatience of Ney who nearly upset the whole plan, then Augereau coming into line and relieving him, the great collision, with an impact that carried away the enemy's centre, and finally the panic and headlong flight of their vaunted cavalry which our hussars mowed down like ripe oats, filling the picturesque valley with a harvest of men and horses. Eylau, abominable Eylau, the bloodiest of all, a slaughter piling up heaps of hideously mutilated corpses, Eylau red with blood in a blizzard of snow, with its dismal, heroic graveyard, Eylau, still re-echoing with the thunderous charge of Murat's eighty squadrons, cutting the Russian army through and through and strewing the ground with such a thick carpet of bodies that even Napoleon wept. And Friedland, the huge, hideous trap into which once again the Russians fell like a flock of silly sparrows, the strategic masterpiece of the Emperor who knew everything and could do it all, our left wing immovable, imperturbable, while Ney, having taken the town street by street, was destroying the bridges; then our left charging the enemy's right and hurling it into the river, crushing it into this dead-end with such slaughter that the killing was still going on at ten o'clock at night. Wagram, the Austrians out to cut us off from the Danube and constantly reinforcing their right wing to beat Masséna who, though wounded, went on commanding from an open carriage, while Napoleon, crafty Titan, let them get on with it and then suddenly opened a terrible bombardment with a hundred pieces of artillery on their depleted centre, throwing it back over a league whilst the right, appalled at its isolation, gave way before Masséna, the now victorious Masséna, and carried the rest of their army away in the devastation of a broken dam. And finally Borodino, when the bright sun of Austerlitz shone for the last time, a terrifying confusion of men, a turmoil of numbers and obstinate courage, hillocks taken under incessant fire, redoubts carried by storm with naked swords, ceaseless counter-offensives disputing every inch of ground, such fanatical bravery by the Russian guards that victory was only achieved by the furious charges of Murat, the thunder of three hundred cannon firing together and the valour of Ney, whose triumph made him prince of the day. Whatever the battle, the flags floated with the same swirl of glory on the evening air and the same cries of *Vive Napoléon* re-echoed as the camp fires were lit on conquered positions, everywhere France was at home as a conqueror and carried her invincible eagles from end to end of Europe. She had only to plant her foot on a foreign realm and the defeated peoples were swallowed up in the earth.

Maurice was finishing his cutlet, more intoxicated by so much glory rising up and singing in his memory than by the white wine twinkling in his glass, when his eye fell on two soldiers in tatters and covered with mud, like bandits sick of roaming the roads, and he heard them asking the waitress for information about the exact whereabouts of the regiments camping along the canal.

He called them over.

'Come over here, mates ... But you belong to the 7th corps!'

'Yes of course, first division! Oh I can tell you I fucking well do! And if you want to know, I was at Froeschwiller, where it wasn't cold, you can take it from me! ... And my mate here is in the 1st corps and he was at Wissembourg, another hell of a place.'

They told him their stories, how they were swept on in panic and rout, stayed in the bottom of a trench half dead with fatigue and actually both slightly wounded, and after that they had dragged along in the wake of the army and were obliged to stop in towns with exhausting attacks of fever, and were now so far behind the rest that they had only just arrived, feeling a bit recovered and now looking for their squads.

Deeply touched, Maurice, on the point of attacking a piece of Gruyère, noticed their eyes staring voraciously at his plate.

'Mademoiselle, some more cheese, please, and bread and wine ... You'll join me, won't you, mates? I'm having a blow-out. Here's to your very good health.'

They sat down, thrilled. But he felt a chill come over him as he looked at these disarmed soldiers in their pitiful state, with their red trousers and capes so tied up with string and patched with so many odds and ends that they looked like rag-pickers or gypsies wearing out the clothes picked up on some battlefield.

'Oh fuck it, yes,' the taller one began again, with his mouth full, 'it wasn't at all funny there ... You have to have seen it – you tell him, Coutard.'

The smaller one told him, waving his bread about by way of illustration.

'I was just washing my shirt while they were doing the stew .. Just think of it, a filthy hole, a real crater with woods all round that had let those Prussian bastards creep up on all fours without anybody even suspecting ... Then at seven, lo and behold, shells falling into our saucepans. Christ! We didn't give them long, but jumped to our rifles and until eleven at night we really thought we were giving them a prize pasting ... But you must know that there were less than five thousand of us and those sods just went on coming and coming and then some. I was on a little rise lying behind a bush and I saw them coming out straight ahead of me and to right and left, real anthills and streams of black ants, so that when there weren't any more left there were still some more to come. Though I says it as shouldn't, we did all think the officers were a lot of bloody fools to have landed us in a hornet's nest like that, miles from our friends, and let us be flattened out without coming to our help. Well then, our general, that poor bugger General Douay, and he wasn't a fool or a coward either, he went and caught a bullet and was laid out, all four legs in the air. Cleaned out, nobody left! All the same, we held our ground. But there were too many of them and we had to push off. We fought in a field, we defended the station in a racket enough to make you deaf for life. And after that, I don't know, the town must have been taken because we found ourselves on a mountain, the Geissberg, they call it, I think, and there we withdrew into a sort of castle, and didn't we half mow them down, the sods! They jumped up into the air and it was a real pleasure to see them come down again on their noses ... and then, well, they still came on and on, ten to one and guns ad lib. When it's like that all bravery does for you is to leave you dead on the field. Anyway, it was such a mess that we just had to fuck off ... All the same, for a lot of chumps our officers took the biscuit, didn't they, Picot?'

There was a pause. Picot, the tall one, swallowed a glass of white wine and wiped his mouth with the back of his hand.

'That's a fact. Like at Froeschwiller – you must be as barmy as a donkey to fight in such conditions. My captain, who was a smart little bloke, said as much ... The truth is they couldn't have known. A whole army of those buggers fell on us when we were scarcely forty thousand, and our lot weren't expecting to fight that day, and the battle began just afterwards without the officers wanting it, apparently ... Well, I didn't see everything, of course, but what I do know is that the dance started up all over again from one end of the day to the other, and when we thought it was over, not a bit of it, the violins were just tuning up for something better still! First at Woerth, a nice little village with a funny church tower that looks like a stove because they've covered it all with porcelain tiles. I don't know why the hell they ever made us leave it in the morning, because we fought tooth and nail to reoccupy it and didn't manage to. Oh, I'm telling you, mates, we didn't half fight there, and the number of bellies split open, and the brains scattered about, you wouldn't credit it! Then they fought round some other village, Elsasshausen, a name as long as your arm! We were being potted at by lots of guns firing at their ease from the top of a bloody hill we had given up that morning too. And that's when I saw, yes, with my very own eyes, the charge of the cavalry. How they faced death, those buggers! It was a real shame to send horses and men over ground like that, a slope covered with bushes and full of potholes. Especially, for Christ's sake, when it couldn't do any good. Never mind, it was plucky and it warmed your heart ... Then it seemed that the best thing was to go off and get our breath back further away. The village was flaming like a match, and the Badeners, the Württembergers and the Prussians, in fact all the gang, over a hundred and twenty thousand of the bleeders they reckoned it was later, had surrounded us. But was it over, not at all, the band started playing louder still around Froeschwiller! For this is the gospel truth, MacMahon may be a fathead, but he is brave. You should have seen him on his big horse with shells all round him! Anybody else would have sloped off at the outset, deciding there was no disgrace in refusing to fight when you haven't got the wherewithal. But not him. As he had begun he wanted to slog on to the end. And he did, too! You see at Froeschwiller they weren't men, they were wild beasts devouring each other. For nearly two hours the gutters ran with blood ... And then, and then, good God, we had to decamp all the same. And to think they came and told us we had thrown back the Bavarians on our left! God Almighty, if we had been a hundred thousand as well, if we had had enough guns and some chiefs who weren't such bloody clots!'

Coutard and Picot were still violently resentful in their ragged uniforms, grey with dust, as they cut slices of bread and great hunks of cheese, trying to get out of their minds their nightmare memories, there under the pretty trellis with its ripe clusters of grapes pierced by golden shafts of sunlight. Now they came to the fearful rout that had followed: regiments in disorder, demoralized, famished, streaming across the fields, and main roads jammed with a dreadful confusion of men, horses, waggons, cannons, all the wreckage of a shattered army lashed along by the frantic wind of panic. Since they had not had the sense to fall back properly and defend the passes through the Vosges, where ten thousand men could have halted a hundred thousand, they should at least have blown up the bridges and blocked the tunnels. But no, the generals galloped on like mad, and everybody was in such a dazed state, losers and winners alike, that for a time the two armies had lost touch in a blind-man's-buff pursuit in broad daylight, MacMahon scurrying for Lunéville while the Crown Prince of Prussia was hunting for him in the Vosges. On the 7th the remnants of the 1st corps were passing through Saverne like a muddy river in spate bearing away bits of wreckage. On the 8th, at Sarrebourg, the 5th corps tumbled into the 1st like one raging torrent into another; it was in flight too, without having fought, bearing along with it its

71

commander, the pitiful General de Failly, quite unhinged because people were tracing the responsibility for the defeat back to his inaction. On the 9th and 10th the stampede went on, a mad rush that never even glanced behind. On the 11th, in driving rain, they came down towards Bayon in order to avoid Nancy because of a false rumour that that city was in enemy hands. On the 12th they camped at Haroué, the 13th at Vicherey and on the 14th they reached Neufchâteau, where at last the railway gathered up this moving mass of men and shovelled them for three whole days into trains to transport them to Châlons. Twenty-four hours after the departure of the last train the Prussians arrived.

'Oh, what a bloody balls-up!' was Picot's conclusion. 'How we had to use our legs! . . . And us left behind in hospital!'

Coutard was emptying the rest of the bottle into his own glass and his mate's.

'Yes, we had to do a bunk and we're running still . . . Oh well, we feel a bit better all the same because we can drink to the health of those who haven't been done in.'

Then Maurice understood. After the idiotic surprise of Wissembourg the crushing defeat of Froeschwiller was the flash of lightning whose sinister light had suddenly shown up the terrible truth. We were unprepared, with second-rate artillery, less manpower than we had been given to believe, incompetent generals, and the much despised enemy emerged strong, solid and numberless, with perfect discipline and tactics. The thin screen of our seven army corps, stretched out all the way from Metz to Strasbourg, had been dented in by the three German armies as though by three powerful wedges. Hence we were alone, and neither Austria nor Italy would come in, and the Emperor's plan had foundered because of the slowness of the operations and the incompetence of the officers. Even fate worked against us, accumulating tiresome accidents and awkward coincidences, facilitating the Prussians' plan which was to cut our armies in two and roll one part back on Metz to keep it isolated from France while they would march on Paris after destroying the remainder. Now it could be seen to be mathematically worked out: we were bound to be beaten on account of causes the inevitable results of which were plain for all to see, the collision of unintelligent bravery with superior numbers and cool method. Whatever argument there might be about it in the future, the defeat was inevitable, like the physical laws governing the world.

Then Maurice's eyes, lost in a reverie, suddenly focused again on the slogan Long Live Napoleon chalked on the yellow wall in front of him. It gave him a sensation of unbearable distress, a twinge of pain that stabbed him to the heart. So it was true that this France, with her legendary victories, who had marched across Europe with drums rolling, had now been knocked over at the first push by a contemptible little country? Fifty years had sufficed to do it, the world had changed and ghastly defeat was swooping down on the eternal conquerors. He recalled all the things his brother-in-law Weiss had said on the dreadful night outside Mulhouse. Yes, he had been the only one to see clearly and guess at the long-standing hidden causes of our weakness, to sense the new wind of youth and strength blowing from Germany. Was it not the end of one military age and the beginning of another? Woe to whoever stands still in the ceaseless thrust of nations, victory is to those who march in the forefront, the most scientific, the healthiest, the strongest!

But just then there was a noise of laughing and screaming, of a girl struggling with a man and enjoying the fun. It was Lieutenant Rochas in the old dark kitchen with its gay Epinal prints, and he was holding the pretty waitress in his arms, like a conquering hero. He came out into the arbour, where he had a coffee brought to him, and as he had overheard the last words of Coutard and Picot he gaily chipped in:

'Nonsense, my boys, that's nothing! It's just the opening of the ball, and now you are going to see our bloody revenge . . . Well, I ask you, up to now they've been five to one! But that's going to change, you can take it from me. We are three hundred thousand here. All these movements we are carrying out and you don't understand are meant to draw the Prussians after us while Bazaine, who's got his eye on them, will catch them in the rear, and then we'll squash 'em – crack, like this fly!'

He crushed a fly with a loud clap of his hands, and his mirth grew louder and louder for, innocent that he was, be believed in this simple plan, and he was now quite happy again with his faith in unconquerable courage. He kindly pointed out to the two soldiers exactly where their regiments were, then, with a cigar in his mouth, sat down to his coffee in perfect bliss.

'The pleasure was mine, chums,' Maurice said to Coutard and Picot, who thanked him for his cheese and bottle of wine and went off.

He had ordered a cup of coffee too, and looked at the lieutenant, catching a bit of his good humour, though somewhat surprised about the three hundred thousand men when they were hardly one hundred thousand, and at the singular ease with which he crushed the Prussians between the army of Châlons and that of Metz. But he, too, needed illusion so much! Why not still go on hoping, when the glorious past was still singing so loud in his memory? The old inn was so gay with its trellis from which hung the pale grapes of France, golden with sun! Once again he had an hour of confidence that lifted him out of the great, heavy sadness that had been building up in him.

Maurice's eye had momentarily followed an officer of the Chasseurs d'Afrique and an orderly who had cantered out of sight round the corner of the silent house occupied by the Emperor. Then, as the orderly came back alone and stopped with the two horses outside the inn, he called out in surprise:

'Prosper! . . . And I thought you were at Metz!'

He was a man from Remilly, a simple farm-hand he had known when he was a child and used to spend his holidays at Uncle Fouchard's. He had drawn a call-up and had served in Africa for three years when the war broke out, and he looked well in his sky-blue tunic, wide red trousers with blue stripes and red worsted belt, with his long sallow face and his supple, strong yet wonderfully graceful limbs.

'Well, fancy meeting you, Monsieur Maurice!'

But he was in no hurry and led the steaming horses round to the stable, giving a fatherly look, especially at his own. Love of horses, acquired no doubt in childhood when he led the animals to the plough, had made him choose the cavalry.

'We've just come from Monthois, over ten leagues at one go,' he went on when he came back, 'and Zephir will be glad to have something.'

Zephir was his horse. But he himself refused to have anything to eat and just accepted a coffee. He was waiting for his officer, who was waiting for the Emperor. It might be five minutes or two hours. So his officer had told him to put the horses in the shade.

74

And when Maurice's curiosity was aroused and he tried to find out more, he shrugged it off:

'I dunno ... some errand of course ... papers to deliver.'

Rochas looked with a kindly eye at the cavalryman, whose uniform brought back his memories of Africa.

'Where were you over there, my boy?'

'Medeah, sir.'

Medeah! That made them fall to chattering as friends, in spite of rank. Prosper had taken to this life of continual alarms, always on horseback, off to battle as some people go off to the shoot, for some big battue of Arabs. They had one messtin for a gang of ten men, and each gang was a family: one did the cooking, another did the washing, the others set up the tent, looked after the animals, kept the weapons polished. They rode morning and afternoon, loaded with enormous kit, with suns shining down like lead. In the evening they lit big fires to keep off the mosquitoes, and round them they sang the songs of France. Often in the middle of the star-lit night they had to get up and pacify the horses who, irritated by the hot wind, would suddenly bite each other and pull out their tethering posts with furious whinnyings. And then there was the coffee, lovely coffee, which was quite a business to make – they crushed it in a messtin and strained it through a red uniform belt. But there were dark days too, far from any inhabited place and facing the enemy. And then no more singing, no more fun. Sometimes they suffered terribly from lack of sleep, from thirst and hunger. Never mind, they loved this existence of improvisation and adventure, this war of skirmishes, just the kind to bring out the glory of personal bravery, and as much fun as taking over a desert island, enlivened by forays, wholesale theft and looting and the petty pilfering of scroungers, whose legendary feats made everybody laugh, even the generals.

'Ah,' said Prosper, coming over quite serious, 'it isn't like it was there. Here they fight quite differently.'

Answering a fresh question from Maurice, he told of their dis-embarking at Toulon and long and difficult journey to Lunéville, where they had heard about Wissembourg and Froeschwiller. After that he wasn't sure, he got the towns all mixed up: from Nancy to Saint-Mihiel, from Saint-Mihiel to Metz. On the 14th there must have been a big battle, the horizon was on fire, but all he had seen was four Uhlans behind a hedge. On the 16th more fighting and heavy gunfire from six in the morning, and he had been told that on the 18th the dance had started up again, more terrible still. But the Chasseurs weren't there then because on the 16th, while they were waiting by the roadside at Gravelotte to go up to the line, the Emperor, tearing off in his carriage, had picked them up to escort him to Verdun. A nice ride that was, forty-two kilometres at the gallop for fear of being cut off by the Prussians at every moment.

'And what about Bazaine?' asked Rochas.

'Bazaine? They say he was jolly glad the Emperor had left him alone.'

But the lieutenant meant was Bazaine coming? Prosper made a vague gesture: how could anyone say? Since the 16th they had been spending the days in marches and counter-marches in the rain, reconnaissances, outposts that had never seen an enemy. Now he was attached to the army of Châlons. His regiment, two others of the Chasseurs de France and one of the Hussars, made up one of the reserve cavalry divisions, the first, commanded by General Margueritte, whom he spoke of with enthusiasm and affection.

'The old bugger! He's one of the best! But what's the good? All they could think about was making us paddle about in the mud.'

There was a silence. Then Maurice talked for a minute or two about Remilly and Uncle Fouchard, and Prosper was sorry he couldn't go and have a look at Honoré, the sergeant, whose battery must be in camp more than a league away, on the further side of the Laon road. But then the snorting of a horse made him prick up his ears and he got up and went off to make sure Zephir was all right. Gradually soldiers of all arms and ranks were filling the inn, this being the time for coffee and drinks. There wasn't a single table left free and the uniforms made gay splashes of colour against the greenery of creepers flecked with sunshine. Major Bouroche had just sat down next to Rochas when Jean appeared with an order.

'Sir, the captain will expect you at three about duty rosters.'

Rochas nodded to indicate that he would be punctual, and Jean did not go off at once, but grinned at Maurice, who was lighting a cigarette. Since the scene in the train there had been a tacit truce between the two men, as though they were studying each other, but in an increasingly friendly way.

Prosper had come back and was impatient.

'I'm going to have something to eat if my officer won't come out of that dump ... It's no use, the Emperor is just as likely not to come back tonight at all.'

'I say,' asked Maurice, whose curiosity was aroused, 'perhaps it's news of Bazaine you've brought?'

'Could be, they were talking about it at Monthois.'

But at that moment there was a sudden commotion and Jean, who had stopped at one of the entrances to the arbour, turned round and said:

'The Emperor!'

In a moment they were all on their feet. Between the rows of poplars on the white road, a detachment of bodyguards appeared in their uniforms still wonderfully smart and resplendent, with the blazing gold of their cuirasses. Then suddenly came the Emperor followed by another detachment of bodyguard.

Heads were uncovered and a few cheers rang out. As he went by the Emperor looked up; he was very pale and his face was already drawn, his eyes blinking, vague and watery. He seemed to wake up out of a dream, smiled wanly when he saw this sunlit inn and saluted.

At that moment Jean and Maurice distinctly heard Bouroche behind them, muttering after thoroughly examining the Emperor with his practised eye:

'He's a goner!'

Jean, with his limited common sense, had shaken his head: damn bad luck for an army to have a chief like that! Ten minutes later when Maurice, after saying good-bye to Prosper, went off for a stroll and another cigarette or two, feeling contented after his good lunch, he carried with him this picture of the Emperor, so pallid and ineffectual, trotting past on his horse. This was the conspirator, the dreamer lacking the energy when the moment comes for action. He was said to be a very good man, quite capable of a great and generous thought and very tenacious in his silent determination; he was very brave too, a fatalist scorning danger, always prepared to face his destiny. But at times of crisis he seemed all in a daze, as though paralysed when faced with having to do anything and powerless to react against fortune if she turned against him. It made Maurice wonder whether there was not some special

77

physiological condition underlying this, aggravated by pain, whether the illness from which the Emperor was obviously suffering was not the cause of the increasing indecision and impotence he had been showing since the outset of the campaign. It might have been the explanation of it all. A stone in a man's flesh, and empires collapse.

That evening after roll-call there was a sudden activity in the camp, with officers running to and fro giving orders, fixing the departure for the following morning at five. It was for Maurice a shock of surprise and disquiet to realize that everything was altered once again. They were not now going to fall back on Paris but march to Verdun to link up with Bazaine. There was a rumour that a dispatch had come from him during the day indicating that he was putting into effect his movement of retreat; and then Maurice remembered Prosper and the officer who had come from Monthois, it might well have been to bring a copy of that dispatch. So, thanks to the continual vacillation of Marshal MacMahon, it was the Empress-Regent and the council of ministers who were having their way, in their fear of seeing the Emperor return to Paris and their obstinate determination to drive the army forward at all costs in order to make a supreme attempt to salvage the dynasty. And the wretched Emperor, this poor man who no longer had a job in his own empire, was to be carried round like some useless clutter in the baggage of his troops, condemned to drag after him the irony of his imperial establishment, his lifeguards, coaches, horses, cooks, vanloads of silver utensils and champagne, all the pomp of his robe of state, embroidered with imperial bees, trailing the roads of defeat in the blood and mire.

Midnight came and Maurice was still not asleep. A feverish dozing with nightmare dreams kept him tossing and turning in his tent. In the end he got up and went out, and was relieved to be on his feet and breathing the cool air, feeling the wind lash his face. The sky was now overcast with thick clouds and the night was very dark, an endless waste of shadows lit only occasionally by the dying fires of the colour-lines, like stars. Yet in this black peace, heavy with silence, you could sense the steady breathing of the hundred thousand men lying there. Then Maurice's distress melted away and there came upon him a feeling of brotherhood, full of indulgent affection for all these living, sleeping men, thousands of whom would soon sleep the sleep of death. They were a decent lot of chaps really. Not very well disciplined, and they stole and drank. But how much they were already going through, and what an excuse they had in the general break-up of their country! The glorious veterans of Sebastopol and Solferino were already only a small minority mixed in with troops who were too young and incapable of a long resistance. These four army corps, hastily bodged together, with no firm links between them, were the army of desperation, the scapegoats sent to the sacrifice in an effort to avert the wrath of destiny. That army was about to climb its Calvary to the very end and redeem the sins of all with the red stream of its blood and find its greatness in the very horror of disaster.

It was then, in that expectant darkness, that Maurice became aware of a great duty. He ceased entertaining vainglorious hopes of winning fabulous victories. This march to Verdun was a march to death, and he accepted it with a cheerful, firm resignation, since one has to die anyway.

4

On 23 August, a Tuesday, at six in the morning, camp was struck and a hundred thousand men of the army of Châlons were on the move and soon flowing in an immense stream, a river of men momentarily spreading out into a lake and then resuming its course. In spite of yesterday's rumours it came as a great surprise to many of them that instead of continuing the retreat they were turning their backs on Paris and going somewhere eastwards into the unknown.

By five in the morning the 7th corps still had no ammunition. For the past two days the artillerymen had half killed themselves unloading the horses and supplies in the goods yard cluttered with material coming in from Metz. And it was only at the last minute that some trucks loaded with cartridges were discovered in the inextricable confusion of trains, and a fatigue party, including Jean, managed to shift two hundred and forty thousand of them in hastily requisitioned carts. Jean issued the regulation hundred rounds to each man in his squàd at the very moment when the bugler Gaude sounded the order to march.

The 106th was not to go through Rheims itself, the order being to go round the city and rejoin the main Châlons road. But once again they had not thought of staggering the times, so that the four army corps set out at the same time and a terrible muddle ensued where they had to get on to the same sections of road. At every moment artillery and cavalry cut across lines of infantry and brought them to a halt. Whole brigades had to stand by for an hour. Worst of all, a terrible storm broke scarcely ten minutes after departure, with deluges of rain that soaked the men to the skin and added to the weight of their packs and capes. However, the 106th had been able to set off again as the rain eased off, while in a field nearby some Zouaves, obliged to wait longer still, had thought out a game to keep themselves in a good humour; they bombarded each other with clods of earth, great lumps of mud which spattered all over their uniforms, giving rise to gales of mirth.

The sun came out again almost at once, a glorious sun on this hot August morning. And cheerfulness returned; the men were like a line of washing hanging out in the open air, and very soon they were dry, like muddy dogs fished out of a pond, joking about the festoons of caked mud they were carrying on their red trousers. There was a fresh halt at every road junction. At the last outlying houses of Rheims there was a final halt in front of a pub which was doing a roaring trade.

Maurice thought he would treat the squad, by way of wishing them all good luck.

'Do you mind, corporal?'

Jean hesitated a moment and then accepted a glass. Loubet and Chouteau were there too, the latter now all obsequious since the corporal had made himself felt, and also Pache and Lapoulle, both good types so long as you didn't get across them.

'Here's to your very good health, corporal,' said Chouteau in smarmy tones.

'And to you, and we must all try to bring back our heads and our feet,' answered Jean politely, and everyone laughed in agreement.

But they were off again and Captain Beaudoin came by with a shocked air, while Rochas looked the other way, for he was indulgent towards his men's thirsts. Already they were out on the Châlons road, an endless, tree-lined ribbon running straight ahead across the vast plain – interminable cornfields, broken here and there by big hayricks and wooden windmills turning their sails. Further northwards lines of telegraph poles marked other roads where they could make out the dark columns of other regiments on the march. There were even quite a few cutting straight across the fields in dense masses. Ahead to the left a brigade of cavalry was trotting along in the dazzling sun. The whole great featureless horizon, empty, depressing and limitless, was coming to life and peopling itself with streams of men pouring from all sides, like continuous runs from some gigantic anthill.

By about nine the 106th left the Châlons road and took the one to Suippes, on the left, another straight ribbon going on for ever. They marched in two files with a space between, leaving the middle of the road clear. Only officers used that, as they wished, and Maurice noticed their worried look, which contrasted with the good humour and contented jollity of the soldiers, who were as happy as children to be on the move at last. As the squad was almost at the head he even had a distant glimpse of the colonel, Monsieur de Vineuil, and was struck by his despondent look as his tall and stiff figure swayed gently with his horse's step. The band had been left in the rear, together with the regimental kitchens. Then with the division came the ambulances and equipment, followed by the supply column of the whole corps – an immense convoy, forage waggons, covered vans for provisions, carts for baggage – a procession of vehicles of all kinds more than five kilometres long, the endless tail of which could be seen at the rare bends of the road. And finally at the very end of the column the livestock brought up the rear, a ragged herd of huge oxen tramping along the road in a cloud of dust, the meat, still alive and whipped along, for a migrating tribe of warriors.

Meanwhile Lapoulle every now and then was humping up his pack with a jerk of the shoulders. On the pretext that he was the strongest he had been loaded with the implements common to the whole squad, the big stewpan and the can with the water. This time they had even entrusted him with the company shovel, making out it was an honour. Not that he minded, but laughed away at a song with which Loubet, the tenor of the squad, was enlivening the

81

tedious march. As for Loubet, his pack was celebrated, and you could find a bit of everything in it: underclothes, spare shoes, needle and thread, brushes, chocolate, a knife, fork and spoon, a mug, to say nothing of the regulation rations of biscuits and coffee; and although the rounds of ammunition were there too, and on top of the lot the rolled blanket, tent and pegs, it all looked as though it weighed nothing, so skilled was he at packing his trunk, as he called it.

'Fucking awful country, though!' Chouteau repeated at intervals, casting a contemptuous eye on the dreary plains of this barren Champagne.

The vast stretches of chalky earth went on and on without end. Never a farm, never a soul, nothing but flights of rooks like specks of black on the grey immensity. Far away to the left some pine woods, almost black, crowned the gentle undulations where the sky began, while to the right the course of the Vesle could be made out by an unbroken line of trees. And in that direction, behind the hills, they had seen for the last league a huge amount of smoke going up in billows that finally united to blot out the horizon with a terrifying cloud of fire.

'What's burning over there?' everybody was asking.

The explanation ran from end to end of the column. It was the Châlons camp which had been blazing for two days, set on fire by the Emperor's order to prevent hoards of supplies falling into Prussian hands. The rearguard cavalry, it was said, had been ordered to set fire to a great warehouse called the yellow store, full of tents, tent-pegs, matting beds, and to the new store, a huge enclosed shed in which were piles of messtins, boots, blankets, enough to equip another hundred thousand men. Stacks of forage, also fired, were burning like giant torches. At this sight, witnessing these livid, swirling clouds rolling over the distant hills and filling the sky with mourning for the irreplaceable, the army marching across the dreary plain fell into a sullen silence. Under the sun no sound could be heard except the beat of their steps, but heads were turned willy-nilly towards the ever spreading smoke which, like a doom-laden cloud, seemed to be following the column for yet another league.

Cheerfulness came back at the main halt in a field of stubble where the soldiers could sit on their packs and have a bite to eat.

The big square biscuits were meant for dunking in soup, but the little round ones, crisp and light, were a real treat that had only the one drawback that they made you terribly thirsty. When his turn came, Pache, by request, sang a hymn that the whole squad took up as a chorus. Jean smiled good-naturedly and let them get on with it, and Maurice's confidence began to return as he saw everybody's enthusiasm and the orderliness and good humour of this first day's march. The rest of the stage was covered in the same perky way, but the last eight kilometres seemed tough. They had left the village of Prosnes to their right and had abandoned the main road and cut across fallow land and some sandy heathland dotted with little plantations of pine, and the whole division, followed by its endless supply column, wound its way in and out of these woods, ankle-deep in the sand. The waste land stretched ever further, and there was nothing to be seen in it but a straggling flock of sheep guarded by a big black dog.

At last, at about four, the 106th halted at Dontrien, a village on the banks of the Suippe. The little stream runs between clumps of trees and the ancient church in its churchyard is completely shaded by a huge horse-chestnut. The regiment pitched its tents on the left bank in a sloping field. The officers said that the four army corps were camping for that night along the Suippe from Aubérive to Heutrégiville, passing through Dontrien, Bétheniville and Pont-faverger in a front nearly five leagues long.

Gaude sounded rations straight away and Jean had to run, for the corporal was the chief supplier and had to be always ready. He took Lapoulle with him and they returned after half an hour loaded with a rib of fresh-killed beef and a bundle of wood. Three animals out of the herd in the rear had already been slaughtered and cut up. Lapoulle had to go back for the bread which had been baking since noon at Dontrien itself, in the village ovens. On this first day everything was really in abundance except wine and tobacco, and as a matter of fact there never would be any issue of these.

When he got back Jean found Chouteau putting up the tent, assisted by Pache. He watched them for a minute like an experienced old soldier who wouldn't give tuppence for the job they were doing.

'All right if it keeps fine tonight.' he said. 'Otherwise, if there were any wind we should all go down into the river ... Here, let me show you.'

He wanted to send Maurice for water in the big can, but he was sitting on the grass with his boot off, examining his right foot.

'Hallo, what's up with you?'

'It's the stiffening that's taken the skin off my heel ... My other boots were done in and I was silly enough to buy these at Rheims because they were a good fit. I ought to have chosen a pair of boats.'

Jean knelt down, took up the foot and turned it over very gently, like a child's foot, shaking his head.

'You know, this isn't funny at all ... Mind what you do. A soldier who's lost his feet is no use for anything but the scrap-heap. My captain in Italy always used to say that you win battles with your legs.'

So he ordered Pache to go and fetch the water. Anyhow the river was only fifty metres away. And while he was doing so Loubet kindled the wood in the hole he had dug in the ground so that he could at once put the stew over it – the big dixie of water into which he placed the meat, neatly tied up with string. Then it was sheer bliss just to watch the stew bubbling. The whole squad, now free of fatigues, lay stretched out on the grass round the fire like a family, full of tender care for the cooking meat, while Loubet solemnly skimmed the pot with his spoon. Like children and savages, their only instinct was to eat and sleep in this rush towards the unknown with no tomorrow.

But Maurice had found in his pack a paper he had bought in Rheims, and Chouteau asked:

'Any news about the Prussians? Read it to us.'

Under the growing authority of Jean they were sharing the jobs well. Maurice obligingly read out the interesting bits of news while Pache, the housewife of the outfit, mended his cape for him and Lapoulle cleaned his rifle. First it was a great victory for Bazaine, who had knocked out a whole Prussian army corps in the Jaumont quarries, and this work of imagination was served up with dramatic details – men and horses crushed to death among the rocks, total annihilation, not even any corpses left intact to bury. Then there were plentiful details on the pitiful state of the German troops since they had been in France: soldiers ill fed, badly equipped, reduced to absolute destitution, dying in hordes along the roads, struck down by fell diseases. Another article reported that the King of Prussia had diarrhoea and that Bismarck had broken his leg as he leaped out of the window of an inn in which the Zouaves had nearly caught him. That's grand! Lapoulle grinned from ear to ear, and Chouteau and the others, without showing the slightest sign of doubt, were cock-a-hoop at the idea of soon picking up Prussians like sparrows in a field after a hailstorm. They were especially tickled about Bismarck's going arse over tip. Oh those Zouaves and Turcos weren't half a lot, they were! All sorts of fairy tales went round – Germany was terrified and angry, saying it was unworthy of a civilized nation to get savages like that to defend her. Although they had already been decimated at Froeschwiller they were apparently still intact and invincible.

The little clock-tower at Dontrien struck six and Loubet shouted:

'Supper-time!'

The squad solemnly sat round in a ring. At the last moment Loubet had discovered some vegetables at a near-by peasant's. Complete banquet: a stew smelling of carrots and leeks, as soft on the stomach as velvet! Spoons banged hard in the little messtins. Then Jean, who was serving, had to share out the beef that day with the strictest impartiality, for eyes were sharp and there would have been grumblings if one portion had looked bigger than another. They mopped up everything and were up to their eyes in it.

'Oh Christ,' declared Chouteau, lying back when he had finished, 'well, anyhow that's better than a kick up the backside!'

Maurice, too, was very full and very happy, having stopped thinking about his foot where the pain had gone off a bit. He was now quite reconciled to this brutish comradeship that brought him down to the common level of mateyness which comes from sharing the physical needs of life. And that night, too, he slept the same deep sleep as his five tentmates, all in a heap together and glad to be warm in these heavy dews. It should be added that Lapoulle, egged on by Loubet, had gone and pinched great armfuls of straw from a near-by rick, and in this the six chaps snored away as in a feather bed. Under the clear night sky, from Aubérive to Heutrégiville, all along the pleasant banks of the Suippe which meanders between the willows, the camp fires of the hundred thousand men lit up the five leagues of plain like a trail of stars.

At sunrise coffee was made by crushing the beans in a messtin with a rifle-butt and throwing them into boiling water, then the grouts were precipitated to the bottom by adding a drop of cold water. That morning the sun rose with regal magnificence amid great clouds of purple and gold, but even Maurice no longer paid any attention to these spectacles of horizon and sky, and only Jean, the discerning countryman, looked anxiously at the red dawn which warned of rain. And, as just before leaving there had been an issue of the bread baked the day before and the squad had received three long loaves, he went for Loubet and Pache who had tied them outside their packs. But tents were folded and bags tied up and they took no notice. It was striking six by all the village churches when the whole army moved off, gaily resuming its advance in the early morning confidence of a new day.

In order to rejoin the Rheims–Vouziers road the 106th cut through almost at once on cross-country roads and climbed through fields for over an hour. Below them and to the north they could see Bétheniville, where it was said the Emperor had spent the night. When they were on the Vouziers road the plains of the previous day began again, the poor fields of barren Champagne rolled on and on with heartbreaking monotony. Now the Arne, a miserable little stream, ran along to their left, while to the right the bare fields stretched on for ever, prolonging the horizon with their flat lines. They went through villages, Saint-Clément with a single line of houses winding on each side of the roadway, Saint-Pierre, a bigger place with prosperous folk who had barricaded their doors and windows. At about ten came the main halt near another village, Saint-Etienne, where the soldiers were over-joyed to find some tobacco still left. The 7th corps had been divided into several columns and the 106th was marching alone with nothing behind it but a battalion of Chasseurs and the reserve artillery, and Maurice looked back in vain at each bend of the road for the immense column which had interested him the day before: the herds had gone and there was nothing but guns rolling along, magnified by these bare plains and looking like black, long-legged grasshoppers.

Past Saint-Etienne the road became atrocious, climbing by gentle humps amid the vast barren fields in which the only growth was the eternal pinewoods with their black foliage, so depressing against the chalky earth. They hadn't crossed such a desolate area before. Badly surfaced, soaked by the recent rains, the road was a real sea of mud, diluted grey clay in which your feet stuck as if it were pitch. Everybody was extremely tired, and the exhausted men seemed to make no headway. And then to cap it all, it suddenly began to pour with terrible violence. The artillery almost stuck there in the quagmire.

Chouteau was carrying the squad's rice ration, and out of breath and furious with the load weighing him down he threw it away, thinking nobody was looking. But Loubet had seen.

'You're making a mistake, mate, shouldn't do things like that because later on your pals 'll have to tighten their belts.'

'Don't you believe it,' answered Chouteau. 'As they've got everything, they'll give us some more at the next stop.'

So Loubet, who was carrying the bacon, convinced by this argument, got rid of that too.

Maurice was having more and more trouble with his foot, and obviously the heel was inflamed again. He was limping so painfully that Jean became more and more concerned.

'Not so good? Starting up again?'

Then, as they called a short halt to let the men get their breath back, he gave him a bit of good advice.

'Take your boots off and walk barefoot, the cold mud will take away the smarting.'

And Maurice was indeed able in this way to keep up without too much difficulty and he felt a deep sense of gratitude coming over him. It was a real stroke of luck to have a corporal like this, an old soldier knowing all the tricks of the trade, a yokel and not very polished, obviously, but a good type all the same.

It was late when they reached Contreuve where they were to bivouac after crossing the Châlons–Vouziers road and going down a steep hill into the Semide gorge. The country was changing, and it was already the Ardennes. From the big bare hills above the village where the 7th corps was to camp, the valley of the Aisne could be made out in the distance veiled in the pale mist of the rainstorms.

By six Gaude had still not sounded rations, so Jean, for the sake of something to do, and also because he was worried about the rising wind, wanted to put up the tent himself. He showed his men how you should choose a site on a gentle slope, drive in the pegs at an angle and dig a gulley round the canvas for drainage. Maurice was exempt from all fatigues because of his foot, so he looked on and was surprised at the shrewd skill of this big, raw-boned fellow. He himself was dead beat but was kept going by the hope which was being reborn in every heart. They really had marched hard from Rheims, sixty kilometres in two stages. If they went on at this rate and straight ahead they would without doubt knock out the IInd German army and join up with Bazaine before the IIIrd, that of the Crown Prince of Prussia, said to be at Vitry-le-François, had had time to move up to Verdun.

'Look here, are they going to let us peg out with hunger?' asked Chouteau, realizing that it was seven o'clock and no issue had been made.

Jean had prudently ordered Loubet to light a fire all the same and put on a pan of water, and as there was no wood he had to shut his eyes when Loubet got some by simply ripping off the palings from a near-by garden. But when Jean mentioned doing some rice and bacon they had to own up that the rice and the bacon had been dumped in the mud along the Saint-Etienne road. Chouteau told a barefaced lie and swore that the package must have come untied and dropped from his pack without his noticing.

'You're a lot of swine!' Jean shouted furiously. 'Throwing food away when there are so many poor buggers with empty stomachs!'

And it was just the same over the three loaves that had been tied outside the packs: nobody had listened to him and the rains had soaked them and turned them into a soggy mess you couldn't bite on at all.

'We're in a nice old mess!' he said. 'We had plenty of everything, and now look at us without a crust to eat ... You're a lot of fucking swine!'

Then the sergeants' call was sounded for orders to be given, and Sergeant Sapin, with his doleful air, came to warn the men in his section that as any issue of supplies was impossible they would have to manage with their marching rations. Apparently the supply convoy was stuck on the road because of the bad weather. As for the herd of cattle, they must have got lost owing to contradictory orders. It came out later that as the 5th and 12th corps had gone up to Rethel that day, where the general headquarters was to be billeted, all the provisions had drained towards that town, together with the population, all agog to see the Emperor, with the result that the country had emptied itself before the eyes of the 7th: no meat left, no bread, no people even. And as the last straw, by some misunderstanding, supplies for the commissariat had been sent to Le Chêne-Populeux. Throughout the campaign this was the continual despair of the poor quartermasters, about whom all the soldiers complained, and for the most part their only offence was that they reached agreed places dead on time, but the troops never went there.

'You bloody swine!' repeated Jean, beside himself with rage. 'It's just what you deserve and you aren't worth all the trouble I'm going to have to root something out for you, for after all it's my job not to let you starve to death on the road.'

He went off to explore as any good corporal should, taking with him Pache, whom he liked for his gentleness, although he did find him a bit too given to priests.

But a minute or so earlier Loubet had spotted a little farm two or three hundred metres away, one of the last habitations of Contreuve, where he thought he could make out quite a bit of trade going on. He got hold of Lapoulle and said:

'Let's bugger off on our own. I've an idea there's something to scrounge over there.'

Maurice was left to give an eye to the pan of boiling water, with orders to keep up the fire.

He sat on his blanket with his boot and sock off so that his bad place could dry. He was interested in watching the camp, with all the squads running about now that they were not expecting any issue of food. The truth was dawning on him that some were continually going without everything while others lived in perpetual abundance, according to the foresight and adroitness of the corporal and his men. In the enormous amount of activity going on round him, in and out between stacked arms and tents, he saw some who had not even been able to light themselves a fire, others, already resigned, who had bedded down for the night, but in contrast others busy eating with great relish something or other, but certainly something good. What also struck him was the good order of the reserve artillery camped higher up on the bluff. The setting sun appeared between two clouds and lit up the guns from which the artillerymen had already cleaned off all the mud from the roads.

Meanwhile General Bourgain-Desfeuilles, the brigade commander, had installed himself comfortably in the little farmhouse that Loubet and his mates had their eye on. He had found a quite acceptable bed and was at table in front of a large omelette and roast chicken, which put him in a charming good humour, and as Colonel de Vineuil happened to be there about some service detail he had invited him to dinner. So they were both eating, waited on by a big fair-haired yokel who had only been working for the farmer for three days, having said he was an Alsatian, a refugee displaced by the disaster of Froeschwiller. The general talked freely in front of this man, discussed the army's march and then asked him about the route and distances, forgetting that he was not a native of the Ardennes. The total ignorance displayed by the general's questions finally upset the colonel, for he had lived in Mézières. He gave a few exact pieces of information which drew the cry from the general:

'Well, isn't it silly? How can you expect us to fight in a terrain we don't know!'

The colonel made a vague gesture of despair. He knew that immediately war was declared they had issued to every officer maps of Germany, but certainly not one possessed a map of France. What he had seen and heard during the past month had finished him, and all he had left was his courage, which made him loved rather than feared by his regiment as a somewhat weak and limited commander.

'You can't eat in peace!' the general shouted. 'What are they yapping like that for? Go and find out, you.'

But the farmer appeared, exasperated and gesticulating, in tears. He was being robbed – Chasseurs and Zouaves were looting his home. To begin with he had been unwise enough to open his shop, being the only one in the village who had any eggs, potatoes and rabbits. He sold without being too extortionate, pocketed the money, delivered the goods, and that resulted in more and more buyers who swamped the place, muddled him and finally rough-handled him and took the lot without paying. The reason why so many countryfolk during the campaign hid everything, refused even a glass of water, was this terror of the steady, irresistible advance of the tide of men that swept them out of their homes and carried away home and all.

'Oh, leave us alone, my good man,' said the general, irritated. 'I should have to shoot a dozen of these characters everyday. How can I?'

He had the door shut so as not to have to go and deal with it himself, while the colonel explained that there had been no issue of rations and the men were hungry.

Outside, Loubet had spied a field of potatoes, and he and Lapoulle had thrown themselves upon it, digging with both hands, tearing them out and filling their pockets. But then Chouteau, looking over a low wall, gave them a whistle call and they ran over and shouted for joy: it was a flock of geese, ten magnificent geese parading majestically in a narrow yard. At once a council was held and Lapoulle was pushed forward and made to climb over the wall. The combat was fierce, the goose he seized nearly cut his nose off with the snapping scissors of its beak. Then he grasped it by the neck and tried to strangle it, but all the time it beat on his arms and stomach with its powerful legs. He had to smash its head with his fist and yet it was still struggling as he hurried away, pursued by the rest of the gaggle tearing at his legs.

When the three got back, hiding the beast in a sack with the potatoes, they found Jean and Pache just coming back and equally pleased with their expedition, carrying four loaves and a cheese they had bought from some nice old girl.

'The water's boiling, we'll make some coffee,' said the corporal. 'We've got bread and cheese, it'll be a real party!'

Suddenly he caught sight of the goose lying outspread at his feet, and couldn't help laughing. He felt it with an experienced hand and was full of admiration.

'Good God, what a lovely bird! It must weigh over twenty pounds.'

'It's a bird we happened to meet,' explained Loubet in his professional funny-man's voice, 'and she wanted to make our acquaintance.'

Jean made a sign meaning that he didn't want to know any more. You had to live after all! And besides, why the hell shouldn't they have this banquet – a lot of poor sods who had forgotten what poultry tasted like?

Loubet was already blowing up the fire. Pache and Lapoulle were plucking the goose for all they were worth. Chouteau, who had run off to get some string from the artillerymen, came back and hung it between two bayonets in front of the roaring fire, and Maurice was detailed to turn it every now and again with a touch of his finger. The fat dripped down into the communal messtin. It was a triumph of string roasting. The whole regiment, attracted by the lovely smell, came and stood round, and what a feast! Roast goose, boiled potatoes, bread and cheese! When Jean had carved the goose the squad tucked into it up to their eyes. There was no question of portions, each man stuffed as much into him as he could take. They even took a piece over to the artillery who had provided the string.

That evening, as it happened, the officers of the regiment were going hungry. Owing to a mistake in instructions the canteen van had gone astray; probably it had followed the main column. When the men went short because food had not been issued they usually managed to scrounge something to eat, they helped each other and the squads pooled their resources. But the officer, left to himself and isolated, had no alternative but starvation as soon as the canteen went wrong.

So Chouteau, who had heard Captain Beaudoin carrying on about the disappearance of the provision van, had a good sneer when, from the depths of the carcass of the goose, he saw him go by with his stiff, unbending air. He indicated him with a look out of the corner of his eye.

'Just look at him, his nose is twitching . . . he'd give five francs for the parson's nose.'

They all roared at the captain's hunger, for he had never managed to be popular with his men, being too young and too strict, a real slave-driver they called him. For a moment it looked as though he was going to tell the squad off for the scandal they were creating with their goose. But probably the fear of giving away his own hunger made him move on, head in the air as though he had seen nothing.

But as for Lieutenant Rochas, his guts were just as tormented with terrible hunger, and he was prowling round the blissful squad openly laughing. He was worshipped by the men, first because he loathed the captain for being a puppy from Saint-Cyr, and also because he himself had shouldered the knapsack the same as the rest of them. Not that he was always as easy-going as that, being so rude sometimes that you could punch his head.

Jean first glanced for confirmation from his mates and then stood up and made Rochas follow him to the back of the tent.

'I say, sir, no offence meant, but if you would like . . .'

And he slipped him half a loaf of bread and a messtin in which he put a thigh of the goose sitting on six large potatoes.

They didn't need rocking to sleep that night either. All six were digesting the bird for all they were worth. And they had the corporal to thank for the solid way he had pitched the tent, for they didn't even notice a violent squall at about two in the morning, with a deluge of rain; tents were blown away, men woke up in a panic, soaked to the skin and forced to run for it in the dark, but theirs stood up to it and they were perfectly sheltered, without a single drop of wet, thanks to the gulleys that took away the storm water.

Maurice woke up at dawn, and as they were not to start off again until eight he thought he would go up to the top of the hill to where the reserve artillery were camped and have a word with his cousin Honoré. After a good night's rest his foot was not so painful. It was still a matter of wonderment to him how well the parking was done, the six guns of each battery correctly in line, and behind them the ammunition waggons, gun-carriages, forage waggons and smithies. Further off the tethered horses were neighing with their nostrils turned towards the rising sun. He found Honoré's tent at once, thanks to the perfect order allocating a line of tents to all the men on the same gun, so that the first glance at a camp tells you the number of guns.

When Maurice arrived the artillerymen were up already and having their coffee, and a row was going on between Adolphe, the leading driver and the gun-layer Louis, his mate. They had been together for three years, according to the custom that coupled a driver and a gunner, and all the time theirs had been a perfect marriage except when they were eating. Louis, who was better educated and more intelligent, accepted the dependent position in which any horseman keeps a foot-slogger, and he it was who put up the tent, did fatigues, looked after the cooking, while Adolphe saw to his two horses with an air of absolute superiority. But Louis, a swarthy, thin type cursed with a ravenous appetite, rebelled when the other, a very tall man with a big fair moustache, was by way of helping himself as though he was the master. That particular morning the squabble was because Louis, who had made the coffee, accused Adolphe of drinking the lot. Someone had to see that they made it up.

Every morning as soon as he woke up Honoré went to inspect his gun and saw to it that the night's dew was wiped off, just as he might have rubbed down a beloved horse for fear it might catch a chill. There he was with a fatherly eye, watching it gleaming in the cool morning air, when he caught sight of Maurice.

'Oh hallo, I knew the 106th was somewhere about, I had a letter from Remilly yesterday and was coming down ... Let's go and have a white wine.'

So that they could be alone together he took him off to the little farmhouse that the soldiers had plundered the day before, and in which the farmer, incorrigibly out for the main chance, had fitted up a sort of bar by broaching a cask of white wine. He was serving it on a plank outside the door at four sous a glass, helped by the farm-hand he had taken on three days earlier, the fair giant, the Alsatian.

Honoré was clinking glasses with Maurice when his eyes fell on this man. For a moment he stared at him, thunderstruck. Then he gave vent to a terrible oath:

'Fucking hell! It's Goliath!'

He leaped up and made as if to fly at his throat. But the farmer, thinking his house was going to be sacked once again, jumped back and locked the door. There was a moment of scrimmage and all the soldiers rushed up as the furious sergeant shouted himself hoarse:

'Open the door, open it, you fucking sod! He's a spy, I tell you he's a spy!'

Maurice was quite sure now, too. He had had no trouble in recognizing the man they had let go at the camp at Mulhouse for want of proof, and this man was Goliath, once the farm-hand at his Uncle Fouchard's at Remilly. When at last the farmer consented to open his door they searched everywhere in vain, the Alsatian had vanished, this blond giant with the honest face whom General

Bourgain-Desfeuilles had questioned unavailingly the day before, and in front of whom, over the meal, he had so carelessly revealed his own secrets. The fellow had probably jumped out of a back window they found open, but they hunted all round in vain – this great big man had vanished like a wisp of smoke.

Maurice had to take Honoré away, for in his despair he was going to say too much in front of his mates, who had no need to share in all these miserable family affairs.

'Christ, I would have loved to throttle him! In any case that letter I had just had had made me furious about him!'

They sat down by a haystack a few yards away from the farmhouse and Honoré gave his cousin the letter.

It was the old, old story, this unhappy love affair of Honoré Fouchard and Silvine Morange. She was a dark girl with meek eyes who had lost her mother when she was quite a child, the mother being a factory worker in Raucourt who had been seduced. Dr Dalichamp, who had obligingly stood godfather (he was a kindly soul always prepared to adopt the babies of the poor girls he delivered), had placed her as a maid at old Fouchard's. It was true that this old peasant, who had become a butcher for love of gain, hawking his meat round twenty neighbouring parishes, was as miserly as hell and as hard as nails, but he looked after the girl and she would do well if she worked. Anyhow, she would be saved from the lusts of the factory. And of course it happened that in old Fouchard's establishment the son of the house and the young maid fell in love. Honoré was sixteen then and she was twelve, and when she was sixteen and he twenty he had drawn lots for the call-up and to his delight drawn a lucky number and so resolved to marry her. Nothing had passed between them beyond a good deal of kissing and embracing in the barn – an unusual purity which was part and parcel of the thoughtful and level-headed character of the young man. But when he mentioned marriage to his father, the outraged and obstinate old man declared that it would only be over his dead body, and he calmly kept the girl on, hoping that they would have their fun together and get it over with. For nearly another eighteen months the young pair were madly in love and full of desire but never touched each other. Then after a terrible scene between the two men, the son, who could not stand any more of it, enlisted and was sent to Africa while the old man insisted on keeping the maid, who pleased him. Then the awful thing happened: one evening two weeks later Silvine, who had sworn to wait for him, found herself in the arms of a farm-hand who had been taken on a few months before, Goliath Steinberg, the Prussian as they called him, a big, good-natured fellow with close cropped fair hair and round pink face always smiling, who had been the friend and boon companion of Honoré. Had old Fouchard slyly encouraged this to happen? Had Silvine given herself in a moment of thoughtlessness, or had she been half raped when she was sick with misery and still worn out with weeping over the separation? She did not know herself and was aghast, pregnant and now accepting the necessity of marriage to Goliath. Not that he refused on his side, ever smiling, but he put off the formality until the baby's arrival. Then suddenly, on the very eve of the birth, he vanished. It was said later that he went and worked at another farm near Beaumont. Three years had gone by since then, and nobody now doubted that this Goliath, such a nice chap, who so enjoyed giving babies to the girls, was one of those spies with whom Germany filled our eastern provinces. When Honoré had heard this story in Africa he spent three months in hospital, as though the fierce sun of those parts had felled him with a hot iron on the back of the neck, and he had never used a leave to go back home, for fear of seeing Silvine and the child.

While Maurice was reading the letter Honoré's hands were trembling. The letter was from Silvine and it was the first and only one she had ever sent him. What emotion had stirred this submissive, silent girl, whose beautiful dark eyes would sometimes take on an expression of extraordinarily fixed determination in her life of continual service? She simply wrote that she knew he was at the war and that should she never see him again it hurt her too much to think he might die believing she didn't love him. She still loved him, she had never loved anybody else, and she repeated this for four pages in the same sentences that came back again and again, with no attempt to find excuses or even to explain what had happened. And not a word about the child, nothing but an infinitely sad good-bye.

The letter touched Maurice deeply, for his cousin had told him the whole story long ago. He looked up and saw that he was in tears, and he put a brotherly arm round him.

'Poor Honoré!'

But already the sergeant was fighting down his emotion. He carefully put the letter away in his breast pocket and buttoned up his coat.

'Yes, things like that upset you ... Oh, the swine! If only I could have strangled him! Oh well, we shall see.'

The bugles sounded for striking camp, and they had to run to get back to their own tents. As a matter of fact the preparations for departure were held up, and the troops waited about with full kit on until nearly nine. The commanders seemed to be in some uncertainty, and already the fine determination of the first two days had gone, when the 7th corps had covered sixty kilometres in two stages. And a fresh piece of news, rather strange and alarming, had been going the rounds since first thing: the march northwards of the three other army corps, the 1st to Juniville, the 5th and 12th to Rethel, was quite illogical, and it was being explained by lack of supplies. Weren't they making for Verdun, then? Why a day lost? The worst thing was that the Prussians couldn't be far away now, for the officers came and warned the men not to lag behind because any laggard was liable to be picked up by reconnoitring enemy cavalry.

It was the 25th of August, and later, remembering Goliath's disappearance, Maurice was convinced that he was one of those who gave information to the German High Command on the exact route of the march of the army of Châlons and who influenced the change of tactics of the third army. The very next day the Crown Prince of Prussia left Ruvigny and the manoeuvre was under way, the flanking attack, the gigantic encircling movement carried out by forced marches and with admirable efficiency across Champagne and the Ardennes. Whereas the French would hesitate and wander round and round in the same place as though they were suddenly struck with paralysis, the Prussians covered as much as forty kilometres a day like a huge circle of beaters herding the human game they were pursuing towards the forest on the frontier.

Anyhow, they set off at last, and that day as it happened the army pivoted on its left, the 7th corps only covered the two short leagues between Contreuve and Vouziers, whilst the 5th and 12th stood still at Rethel and the 1st stopped at Attigny. From Contreuve to the Aisne valley the plains began again and were even barer; as it neared Vouziers the road wound through the grey earth between desolate hillocks with never a tree or a house, as depressing as a desert, so that the very short march was fatiguing and boring and seemed to be terribly long. By noon a halt was called on the left bank of the Aisne and they bivouacked on the barren ground of the last escarpments overlooking the valley and commanding the Monthois road which ran along the river and by which the enemy was expected to come.

Maurice was completely thunderstruck when he saw coming along the Monthois road the Margueritte division – all the reserve cavalry whose job was to support the 7th corps and scout for the left flank of the army. It was rumoured that it was making for Le Chêne-Populeux. Why leave unprotected the one wing that was threatened? Why take these two thousand horsemen, who should have been deployed as scouts many leagues away, and move them to the centre where they must be absolutely useless? The worst of it was that as they blundered right into the manoeuvres of the 7th they nearly cut up its columns into an inextricable muddle of men, guns and horses. Some of the Chasseurs d'Afrique had to wait nearly two hours outside Vouziers.

By sheer chance Maurice caught sight of Prosper, who had taken his horse to a pond, and they could talk for a moment. He seemed quite lost and dazed, knowing nothing and having seen nothing since Rheims. Oh, but yes, he had seen two Uhlans, chaps who appeared and disappeared and nobody knew where they came from or where they went. Stories were already going round about four Uhlans galloping into a town with revolvers in their hands, dashing through it, conquering it, and twenty kilometres away from their own army corps at that. They were everywhere, they preceded the enemy columns like a swarm of buzzing bees, a moving curtain behind which the infantry could disguise its movements, marching with complete security as in peace time. Maurice felt sick at heart as he saw the road jammed with cavalry and hussars being so badly employed.

'Oh well, so long,' he said, shaking Prosper's hand. 'Perhaps they'll still need you up there.'

But the cavalryman seemed to be exasperated at the job they were making him do. He patted Zephir sorrowfully and said:

'Don't you believe it! They work the horses to death and do nothing with the men. It's disgusting.'

That evening when Maurice went to take off his boot to look at his heel which was throbbing and burning hot, he tore away the skin. The blood came and he uttered a cry of pain. Jean was close by and seemed full of anxious sympathy.

'Look here, this is getting bad, you'll find yourself laid up . . . must look after it. Let me have a go.'

He knelt down, washed the place himself and dressed it with some clean material from his knapsack. And his movements were like a mother's, he had the gentleness of a man of long experience whose big hands can be delicate when need arises.

Maurice could not help being overcome by a great tenderness, his eyes went misty, and the language of friendship rose from his heart to his lips in an immense longing for affection, as though in this clodhopper he had loathed some time ago and despised only yesterday he had found a lost brother.

'You're a bloody good chap, you are . . . thank you, mate.'

Jean, beaming with pleasure, answered with his serene smile:

'And now look here, boy, I've still got some tobacco left. What about a cigarette?'

5

ON the next day, the 26th, Maurice woke up all aches and pains, with his shoulders hurting after a night in the tent. He still had not got used to the hard ground, and as the previous night the men had been ordered not to take off their boots, and sergeants had come round in the dark, feeling to make sure that everybody was booted and gaitered, his foot was not much better and was painful and burning, to say nothing of the fact that he must have got a thorough chill in his legs from being unwise enough to stick them out of the tent to stretch them.

Jean said at once:

'Look, my boy, if we've got to march today you'd do well to see the M.O. and get yourself bunged in a van.'

But nobody knew anything and the most contradictory tales were going round. At one time they thought they were going on, camp was struck and the whole army corps began moving and went through Vouziers, leaving only one brigade of the second division on the left bank of the Aisne to keep an eye on the Monthois road. Then suddenly, at the other side of the town, on the right bank, they halted and piled arms in the fields and meadows stretching along on both sides of the Grand-Pré road. At that moment the departure of the 4th hussars, cantering away along that road, gave rise to all sorts of conjectures.

'If we're stopping here I shall stay with you,' declared Maurice, who hated the thought of the M.O. and the ambulance.

It was soon known that they were to camp there until General Douay had had definite information about the movements of the enemy. Since the moment on the previous day when he had seen the Margueritte division going back towards Le Chêne, he had felt increasingly anxious, knowing that he was no longer covered and that there was not a single man guarding the defiles through the Argonne, so that he could be attacked at any moment. He had therefore dispatched the 4th hussars to reconnoitre as far as the defiles of Grand-Pré and La Croix-aux-Bois, with orders to bring back news at all costs.

On the previous day, thanks to the energy of the mayor of Vouziers, there had been an issue of bread, meat and forage, and that morning at about ten the men had just been authorized to make some stew for fear they might never have time later, when a second departure of troops, the Bordas brigade, which set off down the road taken by the hussars, once again set everyone speculating. What now? Were they off again? Weren't they going to be left to eat in peace now that the pot was on the fire? But the officers explained that the Bordas brigade was detailed to occupy Buzancy, a few kilometres away. But others, to be sure, said that the hussars had run into a large number of enemy detachments and that the brigade was being sent to relieve them.

These were a few delightful hours of rest for Maurice. He stretched himself out on the grass half way up the hill on which his regiment was camping, and in his listless, exhausted state he looked at the green valley of the Aisne, with the fields and clumps of trees through which the river meanders lazily. In front of him and at the head of the valley Vouziers rose up in an amphitheatre, its terraces of roofs dominated by the church with its narrow spire and domed tower. Down by the river the high chimneys of the tanneries were smoking and at the other end could be seen the buildings of a big flourmill white amid the greenery at the water's edge. This view of a little town nestling in the green grass seemed full of a gentle charm to him, as though he had recovered his former vision as a sensitive dreamer. His boyhood came back, and the excursions he used to make to Vouziers in the old days when he lived at Le Chêne, his birthplace. For an hour he was lost to the world.

The stew had been eaten a long time ago and still they were waiting about when, at nearly half past two, the whole camp was permeated by a vague but increasing restlessness. Orders flew hither and thither, the fields were evacuated and all the troops climbed up and took positions on the ridges between two villages, Chestres and Falaise, about four or five kilometres apart. Already the sappers were digging trenches and throwing up ramparts while to the left the reserve artillery was on top of a mound. The tale went round that General Bordas had sent a dispatch rider to report that having met superior forces at Grand-Pré he was obliged to fall back on Buzancy, and that gave rise to fears that his line of retreat to Vouziers might soon be cut. That was why the commander of the 7th corps, thinking an attack was imminent, had moved his men into combat positions to sustain the first shock until the rest of the army could come to his support, and one of his aides-de-camp had gone off with a letter to the marshal, warning him about the situation and asking for help. So as he was frightened of being obstructed by the interminable supply column which had rejoined the corps during the night and which was now dragging after him again, he had made that set off at once, sending it any old where in the Chagny direction. It was battle order.

'So this is really it this time, sir?' Maurice ventured to ask Rochas.

'Yes, it bloody well is!' he answered, waving his long arms. 'You'll see whether it's hot enough in a minute.'

All the men were thrilled. Since the battle line had been drawn from Chestres to Falaise the excitement of the camp had heightened still more and the men were becoming feverishly impatient. So they were going to see them at last, these Prussians the papers said were so exhausted with marches, so undermined by diseases, famished and in rags! And the hope of bowling them over at the first go revived everyone's spirits.

'It's a good job we've found each other!' declared Jean. 'We've been playing hide and seek long enough since losing each other over there on the frontier after their battle ... But are these the ones who beat MacMahon?'

Maurice could not answer him, for he wasn't sure. From what he had read at Rheims it seemed very unlikely that the IIIrd army, commanded by the Prussian Crown Prince, could be at Vouziers when only two days before it could scarcely have camped nearer than Vitry-le-François. There had of course been talk of a IVth army put under the command of the Crown Prince of Saxony which was to operate on the Meuse; it must be that one, although such an early occupation of Grand-Pré astonished him because of the distances. But what finally muddled him was his amazement when he heard General Bourgain-Desfeuilles interrogating a peasant from Falaise to find out whether or not the Meuse flowed through Buzancy and if there were some strong bridges there. Moreover in his fool's paradise the general declared that they would be attacked by a force of a hundred thousand men from Grand-Pré whilst another sixty thousand were coming via Sainte-Ménehould.

'How's the foot?' asked Jean.

'Can't even feel it now,' Maurice laughed. 'If there's a fight it'll be all right.'

It was true. He was upheld by such nervous excitement that he felt as if he were not touching the ground. To think that all through the campaign he hadn't yet fired a single round. He had been to the frontier, he had spent the awful night of suspense outside Mulhouse, without setting eyes on a single Prussian or firing a shot, and he had had to retreat to Belfort, to Rheims, and once again he had been marching towards the enemy for five days with his rifle still virgin and useless. He was possessed by a growing need, a dull rage urging him to take aim and fire anyway, to steady his nerves. It was nearly six weeks since he had joined up in a burst of enthusiasm, dreaming of battle the next day, and all he had done was wear out his poor, delicate, civilian feet running away or marking time, miles from any battlefield. That was why, in this universal mood of expectation, he was one of the most impatient watchers of that main road to Grand-Pré stretching away dead straight between its fine trees. Beneath him the valley wound along, the Aisne making a kind of silver ribbon amid the willows and poplars, but his eyes could not help coming back to that road down there.

There was an alert at about four. The 4th hussars returned after a long detour, and tales of fights with Uhlans went the rounds, getting magnified as they went, and this endorsed everybody's conviction that an attack was imminent. Two hours later another dispatch rider came in, explaining in scared tones that General Bordas daren't leave Grand-Pré now because he was sure that the Vouziers road was cut. This was not yet the case, since the rider himself had come through freely, but at any minute it could be a fact, and General Dumont, in command of the division, left at once with the one brigade he had remaining, to relieve his other brigade in peril. The sun was going down behind Vouziers, whose line of roofs stood out black against a great cloud of red. For a long time the brigade could be seen moving between the double row of trees until in the end it was lost in the deepening shadows.

Colonel de Vineuil came to make sure that his regiment was in a good position for the night. He was astonished not to find Captain Beaudoin at his post; and as he came back at that very moment from Vouziers, giving the excuse that he had been to lunch with the Baroness de Ladicourt, he received a severe reprimand, which he heard in silence, looking the essence of the good officer.

'My boys,' the colonel kept saying as he moved about among the men, 'we may be attacked tonight and certainly shall be tomorrow at dawn ... Hold yourselves ready and remember that the 106th has never run away.'

They all applauded him, for in the mood of fatigue and discouragement that had been growing on them since their departure they all preferred a showdown to put an end to it. Rifles were checked and pins changed. As they had had a hot meal in the morning they made do with coffee and biscuit. The order had been not to go to bed. Outposts were placed at fifteen hundred metres, and sentries posted as far as the banks of the Aisne. All the officers sat up round camp fires. And every now and then the flickering light of one of these fires picked out against a low wall glimpses of the gaudy uniforms of the Commander-in-Chief and his staff – shadowy figures darting to and fro, running towards the road, listening out for the sound of horses' hoofs in this intense anxiety about the fate of the third division.

At about one in the morning Maurice was posted as an advance sentinel on the edge of a plum orchard between the road and the river. The night was as black as ink. As soon as he was alone in the crushing silence of the sleeping countryside he was conscious of a feeling of fear creeping over him, an awful fear he had never known before and could not overcome, and it made him shake with anger and humiliation. He turned round to reassure himself with the sight of the camp fires, but they must have been hidden by a little wood, and all he had behind him was a wall of blackness; the only lights were a few very distant ones still burning in Vouziers, where the inhabitants, who had no doubt been alerted, were terrified at the thought of a battle and were staying up. What really froze him with fear was to find out when he brought his rifle to his shoulder that he could not even see the sights. Then the most cruel period of waiting set in, with all the strength of his being concentrated on the sense of hearing alone, his ears straining for imperceptible sounds and ending by roaring in his head like thunder. Some distant running water, a light rustling of leaves, the flight of an insect, all became huge, reverberating noises. Was it a galloping of horses, an endless rumbling of artillery coming straight at him from over there? To his left had he heard a cautious whisper, voices being kept down, some advance column crawling through the darkness, preparing a surprise attack? Three times he was on the point of firing to raise the alarm. His uneasiness was increased by the fear of being mistaken and looking ridiculous. He had knelt down with his left shoulder propped against a tree, and it seemed to him that he had been there for hours and been forgotten. The army must have gone off without him. Then suddenly his fear vanished, he heard quite clearly the rhythmical step of soldiers marching along the road he knew was only a couple of hundred metres away. At once he felt sure that they were troops in distress, the ones who had been so impatiently waited for – General Dumont bringing back the Bordas brigade. Just then someone came and relieved him, his turn of duty had hardly lasted the regulation one hour.

It was indeed the third division returning to camp, and that was an immense relief. But precautions were redoubled because information received confirmed everything they thought they knew about the enemy's approach. The few prisoners they brought back, sombre Uhlans in their long cloaks, refused to talk. Daybreak, the grey dawn of a rainy day, came up in the continuing expectancy which frayed everybody's nerves. The men had not dared to sleep for fourteen hours. At about seven Lieutenant Rochas said that MacMahon was on the way with a whole army. The truth was that General Douay had had, by way of a reply to his dispatch sent the day before predicting the inevitable fight before Vouziers, a letter from the marshal telling him to hold on until he could send him some support: the advance had been stopped, the 1st corps was making for Terron, the 5th for Buzancy, while the 12th would stay at Le Chêne in reserve. So the wait took on an even greater significance, it was no longer a simple fight to come, but a great battle involving the whole of the army that had been headed away from the Meuse and was now on the march further south in the Aisne valley. So once again they dared not cook their hot stew but had to make do with coffee and biscuit, for the final reckoning was fixed for noon, everybody said without knowing why. An aide-de-camp had been sent off to the marshal to hasten the arrival of reinforcements, the approach of the two enemy armies being more and more certain. Three hours later a second officer galloped off for Le Chêne, where General Headquarters was, from which he was to bring back immediate orders, so much had anxiety increased following news from the mayor of some little country place who claimed to have seen a hundred thousand men at Grand-Pré while a hundred thousand more were coming up via Buzancy.

By noon still not a single Prussian. By one, by two, still nothing. Everybody was getting sick of it, and sceptical as well. Jeering voices began to poke fun at the generals. Perhaps they had seen their own shadows on the wall. They voted to get them some glasses. A fine lot of jokers to have upset everybody like this if nothing was coming! Some wag called out:

'So it's going to be Mulhouse all over again?'

This wrung Maurice's heart with bitter memories. He recalled that idiotic flight and panic that had swept the 7th corps along without a single German being seen for ten leagues around. And now it was all starting again, he felt it quite clearly, with no mistake about it. Now that the enemy had not attacked twenty-four hours after the skirmish at Grand-Pré it must have been that the 4th hussars simply ran into some mounted reconnaissance. The main forces must still be a long way off, possibly even two days' march. All at once this thought horrified him as he considered how much time had been lost. In three days they had not covered two leagues, from Contreuve to Vouziers. On the 25th and 26th the other army corps had gone northwards on the pretext that they had to restock with foodstuffs, whereas now, on the 27th, lo and behold they were going southwards to accept a challenge nobody was offering. Following the 4th hussars towards the abandoned passes in the Argonne, the Bordas brigade had thought it was lost and dragged in the whole division to help, then the 7th corps and then the whole army, all to no purpose. Maurice thought of the inestimable value of each hour in this wild scheme of joining up with Bazaine, a plan which none but a general of genius could have carried out, and with seasoned troops, on condition that he took everything by storm, straight ahead through every obstacle.

'We're finished,' he said to Jean, seized with despair in a sudden brief moment of lucidity.

Then as the other opened his eyes wide, not following, he lowered his voice and went on for him alone, referring to the commanders:

'More stupid than wicked, that's certain, and always out of luck! They don't know anything, never foresee anything, they've got no plan, no ideas, no lucky breaks ... Can't you see, everything is against us, we're done for!'

This discouragement that Maurice reasoned out, being an intelligent and educated fellow, gradually grew and weighed on all the troops who were immobilized for no reason and worn out with waiting. In an obscure way doubt and suspicion about the true situation were doing their work in their thick heads, and there was not a man left, however dim-witted, who didn't feel uneasy about being badly led, held up for no reason, shoved somehow or other into the most disastrous adventure. What the hell were they buggering about there for, with no Prussians coming? Either let them fight at once or go somewhere and get a good night's sleep. They'd had enough. Since the last aide-de-camp had gone off to bring back orders anxiety was growing every minute, groups had formed and were arguing at the tops of their voices. The officers, who were in sympathy with this agitation, did not know what answers to give to soldiers who ventured to ask questions. So at three, when word went round that the aide-de-camp was back and that they were going to fall back, there was relief in every heart and a sigh of real joy.

So wise counsels were to prevail at last! The Emperor and the marshal, who had never been in favour of this march on Verdun and were now alarmed to know that once again they had been out-manoeuvred and were going to be confronted by the army of the Crown Prince of Saxony as well as that of the Crown Prince of Prussia, were giving up the improbable link-up with Bazaine in order to retreat via the northern strongholds and swing round on Paris. The 7th corps received orders to make for Chagny via Le Chêne, while the 5th was to march on Poix and the 1st and 12th on Vendresse. Very well, then, as they were falling back, why had they advanced to the Aisne, why so many days lost and so much fatigue when it was so easy and logical to go straight from Rheims and take up strong positions in the valley of the Marne? Was there no master plan, no military skill, nor even plain common sense, then? But now the wondering stopped and all was overlooked in delight at this most reasonable decision, the only right one to get them out of the hornets' nest they had run into. From the generals down to the ranks they all had the feeling that they would recover their strength and be invincible before Paris, and that it was there of necessity that they would defeat the Prussians. But they had to evacuate Vouziers before dawn so as to be on the march towards Le Chêne before an attack came, and at once the camp was filled with extraordinary animation, with bugles sounding, orders being given in all directions, and already baggage trains and administration were going on ahead so as not to impede the rearguard.

Maurice was overjoyed. Then, while he was trying to explain to Jean the manoeuvre of withdrawal they were going to execute, he let out a cry of pain. His state of elation had gone, and he became conscious of his foot again, like a lump of lead on the end of his leg.

'What, is that starting up again?' The corporal was very concerned, but with his practical mind he had an idea.

'Listen, kid, you told me yesterday that you knew people in that town. You ought to get the major's permission to get a lift to Le Chêne, where you could get a good night's sleep in a good bed.

Tomorrow, if you are walking all right, we can pick you up as we go through. How does that strike you?'

In Falaise itself, the village near which they were camping, Maurice had run into an old friend of his father's, a small farmer who in any case was going to take his daughter to an aunt's in Le Chêne, and his horse was already harnessed to a trap.

But with Major Bouroche things nearly went wrong from the very first words.

'It's my foot, doctor, it's got the skin off . . .'

'Don't call me doctor . . . who sent me a bloody soldier like this?'

As Maurice was nervously trying to apologize he went on:

'I'm the major, don't you understand, you clot?'

Then, realizing the sort of person he was dealing with, he must have felt a bit ashamed, for he stormed louder than ever:

'Your foot, that's a nice tale! All right, all right, you can have permission. Go in a carriage, go in a balloon. We've got enough Tired Tims and Weary Willies here!'

When Jean helped Maurice up into the trap the latter turned round to thank him and the two men hugged each other as though they were never to see each other again. How could you tell, in all the confusion of retreat, with these Prussians about? Maurice was still surprised at the deep affection that already tied him to this fellow. Twice more he turned round and waved him good-bye, and so he left the camp, where they were preparing to light big fires to deceive the enemy while they slipped off quite noiselessly before dawn.

On the road the farmer moaned continuously about the times being out of joint. He had not had the courage to stay at Falaise, and now he was already sorry he wasn't still there, repeating that he was ruined if the enemy set fire to his house. His daughter, a lanky, colourless creature, was snivelling. But Maurice, who was drunk with fatigue, did not hear, for he was asleep on his seat, lulled by the smart trot of the little horse, which covered the four leagues from Vouziers to Le Chêne in under an hour and a half. It was not yet seven, and dusk was hardly setting in when the young man, startled out of sleep and shivering, got down at the canal bridge on to the open space in front of the narrow yellow house where he was born and where he had lived twenty years of his existence. He made for it automatically although the house had been sold eighteen months before to a veterinary surgeon. When the farmer asked him if he could help he answered that he knew quite well where he was going and thanked him very much for his kindness.

But in the middle of the little three-sided space, by the well, he stood still, puzzled, his mind a blank. Where was he aiming for? Then he remembered he was making for the notary's, whose house adjoined the one in which he had grown up, and whose mother, the very old and kind Madame Desroches, as a neighbour used to spoil him when he was a child. But he hardly recognized Le Chêne, for this normally dead-and-alive little town was in a state of uproar caused by the presence of an army corps camped just outside, filling the streets with officers, dispatch riders, camp-followers, prowlers and hangers-on of all kinds. Of course he knew the canal cutting through the town from end to end and dividing the central square, and the narrow stone bridge connecting the two triangles; and on the further side the market hall was still there with its moss-covered roof, the rue Berond going off to the left and the Sedan road to the right. But from where he was he had to look up and see the clock tower with its slate roof above the notary's house to be sure this really was the quiet corner where he had played hopscotch long ago, for the rue de Vouziers in front of him, as far as the Hôtel de Ville, was buzzing with a solid mass of people. On the open space itself he thought an area was being kept clear and men were heading off sightseers. And there, to his surprise, he saw a large space taken up behind the well by a large park of carriages, vans, carts, a whole encampment of baggage he had certainly seen before.

The sun had gone down into the straight and blood-red water of the canal and Maurice was making up his mind when a woman who had been looking at him for a minute or two exclaimed:

'Good Lord, can it be possible? Surely you are the Levasseur boy?'

Then he recognized Madame Combette, the chemist's wife on the square. As he was telling her that he was going to beg for a bed for the night from that nice Madame Desroches, she pulled him away, obviously disturbed.

'No, no, come over to us, I'll explain . . .'

When she had carefully closed the shop door behind her:

'So you don't know, my dear boy, that the Emperor is lodging at the Desroches's. The house has been commandeered for him and they are not all that pleased with the great honour, I can tell you. When you think that the poor old mother, a woman well past seventy has been forced to give up her own room and go and sleep up in the garret in a maid's bed! . . . Look, all you can see out there on the square is to do with the Emperor – his luggage in fact, if you see what I mean!'

Maurice then recalled those carriages and vans, all the grand paraphernalia of the imperial household he had seen at Rheims.

'Oh my dear boy, if only you knew the things they unpacked from there – silver plate and bottles of wine, hampers of provisions, fine linen and everything! It went on for two whole hours. I wonder where they have managed to stow so many things, for it isn't a big house . . . Just look at the fire they've lit in the kitchen.'

He glanced over at the little white two-storey house on the corner of the square and the Vouziers road, a serene, respectable-looking house, and the inside, the central passage-hall on the ground floor, the four rooms on each floor, all came back to his mind as though he had been there only yesterday. There was already a light in the first-floor window nearest the corner that looked on to the square, and the chemist's wife explained that that was the Emperor's room. But as she had said, the place which blazed most brightly was the kitchen, the windows of which, on the ground floor, looked on to the Vouziers road. Never had the inhabitants of Le Chêne seen such a show. An ever-rolling stream of sightseers blocked the street, gaping at this furnace on which an Emperor's dinner was roasting and boiling. So as to get some air, the cooks had thrown the windows wide open. There were three chefs in spotless white jackets busy in front of chickens spiked along an immense spit, stirring sauces in enormous saucepans of copper gleaming like gold. Old men couldn't remember having seen so much fire and so much food cooking at once at the Lion d'Argent, even for the grandest weddings.

Combette the chemist, a bustling little man, came in very excited by all he had seen and heard. He seemed to be in the know, being deputy mayor. It appeared that at about half past three MacMahon had wired Bazaine that the arrival of the Crown Prince of Prussia at Châlons forced him to fall back on the northern fortresses, and another telegram was going off to the Minister of War warning him also about the retreat, explaining the terrible danger the army was in of being cut off and annihilated. The wire to Bazaine could run there if it had good legs, for all communication with Metz seemed to have been cut off for some days. But the other wire was more disturbing, and lowering his voice the chemist said he had heard a high officer say: 'If anybody tells them in Paris, we're up the spout!' Everybody was aware of the pertinacity with which the Empress-Regent and the cabinet were urging an advance. Anyhow the confusion was getting worse every hour, and the most extraordinary tales came in about the approaching German armies. The Crown Prince of Prussia at Châlons – was it possible? Then, what troops had the 7th corps run into in the gorges of the Argonne?

'At General Headquarters they know nothing,' the chemist went on with a despairing wave of the arms. 'Oh, what a mess! But still, it's all right so long as the army is in retreat by tomorrow.'

Then his real kindness came out:

'Look here, my young friend, I'm going to put a dressing on that foot of yours, you'll have a meal with us and sleep up there in my apprentice's little room. He's sloped off.'

But being still obsessed with the need to see and know, Maurice wanted above all to carry out his first idea and go and see old Madame Desroches opposite. He was surprised not to be stopped at the door which in spite of the tumult of the square outside was left open and not even guarded. People were continually going in and out, officers and orderlies, and it seemed as if the commotion in the blazing kitchen was affecting the whole house. Yet there was no light on the stairs and he had to feel his way up. On the first floor he paused a few seconds with thumping heart in front of the door of the room where he knew the Emperor was, but in that room there was not a sound, it was as still as death. And up at the top, on the threshold of the maid's room where she had had to retreat, old Madame Desroches was at first afraid of him. Then, when she saw who it was:

'Oh my child, what a dreadful time to meet again! I would gladly have given up my house to the Emperor, but some of the people with him really are too uncouth! If you knew how they have taken everything, and they'll burn everything too, with the huge fire they're making ... He, poor man, looks like death, and so sad ...'

When the young man took his leave, trying to cheer her up, she came with him and leaned over the banister.

'Look,' she whispered, 'you can see him from here ... Oh, it's all up with us, that's certain. Good-bye, my boy.'

Maurice stayed rooted to a step on the dark staircase. By craning his neck he could see through a fanlight a sight that remained stamped on his mind for ever.

The Emperor was there in this simply furnished, cold room, sitting at a little table on which his dinner was served and which was lit by a candle at each end. Behind, two aides-de-camp were standing in silence. A major-domo was standing by the table, in attendance. And the glass had not been used, the bread had not been touched, a chicken breast was going cold in the middle of the plate. The Emperor, motionless, was gazing at the cloth with the same vacillating, lack-lustre, watery eyes he already had at Rheims. But he looked more tired, and when he had made up his mind, as though it were an immense effort, and taken two mouthfuls, he pushed all the rest away with his hand. He had dined. An expression of secretly borne pain made his pale face look even more ashen.

Downstairs, as Maurice was passing the dining-room, the door was suddenly thrown open and he saw in the flickering candle-light and in the steam rising from dishes, a whole table of equerries, aides-de-camp, court officials busy emptying the bottles unloaded from the vans, swallowing down chickens and mopping up sauces, all with loud conversation. Now that the telegram to the marshal had gone off all these people were delighted at the certainty of retreat. In a week's time they would have clean beds at last, in Paris.

This made Maurice suddenly conscious of the terrible fatigue weighing him down: now it was certain that the army was falling back all he had to do was sleep until the 7th corps came through. He crossed the open space again, found himself back in Combette's shop, where he ate as in a dream. Then it seemed that somebody was dressing his foot and taking him up to a room, and after that, black night and nothingness. He slept, knocked right out, scarcely breathing. After an indeterminate time, hours or centuries, his sleep was interrupted by a shudder of panic, and he sat up in the darkness. Where was he? What was this continuous rumbling of thunder that had woken him up? He sudddenly remembered and ran to the window to look. Down in the dark square where the nights were usually so quiet the artillery was on the move in a cease-less trot of men, horses and cannon, shaking the little dead houses. This sudden departure filled him with unreasoning anxiety. What-ever was the time? It struck four at the Hôtel de Ville. He was endeavouring to be sensible, telling himself that it was simply the beginning of the execution of the order for retreat given the day before, when what he saw as he turned his head upset him more than ever. There was still a light in the corner window of the notary's house, and at regular intervals the shadow of the Emperor could clearly be seen in dark silhouette.

Maurice quickly pulled on his trousers to go downstairs, but Combette appeared, holding a candlestick and gesticulating.

'I saw you from down there, on my way back from the Hôtel de Ville, so I came up to say . . . Just think of it, they haven't let me go to bed, and for the past two hours the mayor and I have been dealing with fresh requisitions . . . Yes, once again the whole thing has been changed . . . Oh, that officer who didn t want the wire to be sent to Paris was bloody well right!'

He went on for a long time in short, disconnected sentences, and in the end the young man understood, and he was silent and sick at heart. At about midnight a telegram from the War Office had reached the Emperor in reply to that of the marshal. The exact text was not known, but an aide-de-camp had said out loud at the Hôtel de Ville that the Empress and cabinet were afraid of a revolution in Paris if the Emperor returned there and left Bazaine in the lurch. The telegram was misinformed about the true position of the Germans and, appearing to believe that the army of Châlons had advanced further than it really had, it insisted in extraordinarily passionate terms on a march straight ahead come what may.

'The Emperor sent for the marshal,' went on the chemist, 'and they were shut up together for nearly an hour. Of course, I don't know what they can have said, but what all the officers have repeated is that the retreat is off and the march to the Meuse is on again . . . We have requisitioned all the bakehouses in the town for the 1st corps which will replace the 12th here in the morning. The

12th's artillery, as you see, is now leaving for La Besace ... This really is the end, and you are off to battle!'

He stopped, for he, too, was looking at the lighted window at the notary's. Then he went on in an undertone, as though tortured by curiosity:

'What can they have said to each other, I wonder? ... Funny all the same, to fall back at six in the evening before the threat of danger, and at midnight to rush headlong into the same danger, although the situation remains identical!'

Maurice was still listening to the rumbling of the guns down there through the dark little town, this uninterrupted trotting past, this stream of men flowing towards the Meuse, to the terrible unknown of tomorrow. On the ordinary, thin curtains over the window he could still see the shadow of the Emperor regularly passing to and fro. This sick man, kept up by insomnia, was pacing up and down, feeling the need to keep moving in spite of his pain, his ears filled with the noise of those horses and men he was allowing to be sent to their death. So only a few hours had been enough and it was now disaster, deliberately chosen, accepted. What indeed could the Emperor and the marshal have said to each other, both perfectly aware of the doom towards which they were moving, convinced in the evening of defeat in the appalling circumstances in which the army would find itself and surely not able to change their minds by morning, when the peril was increasing hour by hour? General Palikao's plan, an all-out march on Montmédy, which already by the 23rd was on the rash side, still perhaps just possible on the 25th, became by the 27th an act of pure lunacy, given the continual vacillating of the command and the growing demoralization of the troops. If they were both aware of all this why were they giving in to the pitiless voices hounding them on in their indecision. Perhaps the marshal was merely a blinkered and obedient soldier showing his greatness by his abnegation. And the Emperor, no longer in command, was just waiting for fate to decide. Their lives, and the lives of the army, were being asked for and they were giving them. This was the night of the crime, the abominable night of the murder of a nation, for from that moment onwards the army was in peril, a hundred thousand men were being sent to the slaughter.

Thinking over these things, shivering in despair, Maurice still

114

followed that shadow on Madame Desroches's thin muslin – that feverish, pacing shadow driven on by the relentless voice from Paris. Had not the Empress, that very night, wished for the Emperor's death so that her son might reign? March on! March on! Never look back, in rain, through mud, to extermination, so that this crucial game of the dying Empire be played out to the last card. March on! March on! Die like a hero on the heaped corpses of your people, fill the whole world with wonder and awe if you want it to forgive your successors! And without doubt the Emperor was marching on to death. Downstairs the kitchen was no longer ablaze, the equerries, aides-de-camp and officials were fast asleep and the whole building was in blackness; but alone the shadow paced ceaselessly up and down, resigned to the inevitability of the sacrifice amidst the deafening din of the 12th corps still going by in the dark.

It suddenly occurred to Maurice that if the advance were to be resumed the 7th would not come up through Le Chêne at all, and he saw himself left behind, cut off from his regiment, a deserter. The pain in his foot had gone; skilful dressing and some hours of absolute rest had brought down the inflammation. When Combette had given him a pair of his own boots, wide ones in which he felt comfortable, he wanted to be on his way, and at once, hoping he might still find the 106th on the road from Le Chêne to Vouziers. The chemist tried in vain to keep him, and was on the point of deciding to take him back himself in his own trap and just drive about in the hope of finding them, when the apprentice Fernand reappeared, explaining that he had been to see his girl cousin. He was a tall, weedy youth, looked a bit of a ninny, and he harnessed the horse and took Maurice. It was not quite four, a deluge of rain was falling from an inky sky, and the lanterns of the vehicle shone palely, hardly lighting the road in the great, sodden countryside, full of gigantic noises which brought them to a halt at every kilometre, thinking an army must be on the move.

And just outside Vouziers Jean had not slept either. Since Maurice had explained how the retreat was going to save the whole situation, he had kept awake, preventing his men from straying too far away, waiting for the order to leave which the officers might give at any moment. At about two, in the pitch darkness starred with red fires, a great noise of horses went through the camp: it was the cavalry setting off as advance guard for Ballay and Quatre-Champs so as to keep an eye on the roads from Boult-aux-Bois and La Croix-aux-Bois. One hour later the infantry and artillery began to move in their turn, finally giving up their positions at Falaise and Chestres, which they had obstinately defended for two whole days against an enemy who never appeared. The sky was overcast and it was still dark night as each regiment went off with the utmost silence, a procession of men disappearing into the blackness. But all hearts were beating with joy, as though they had escaped from an ambush. They already saw themselves at the walls of Paris and on the eve of taking their revenge.

Jean peered into the thick darkness. The road was lined with trees and it looked to him as though it went across open meadows. Then there were some ups and downs. They were entering a village which must be Ballay when the heavy clouds which darkened the sky burst into a deluge of rain. The men had already had so much wet that they had even given up grousing about it and just hunched their shoulders. But after Ballay, as they were approaching Quatre-Champs, the wind began to blow in furious squalls. Beyond there, when they had climbed up on to the great plateau stretching with its bare fields all the way to Noirval, the hurricane raged and they were lashed by a frightful cloudburst. And there, in the middle of this endless plain, came an order to halt which stopped all the regiments one by one. The whole 7th corps, thirty-odd thousand men, was standing there in a mass when day dawned – a muddy day in streams of grey water. What was up now? Why this halt? Already the ranks were getting restive, and some were suggesting that the order to march had been reversed. They had been made to stand easy but forbidden to break ranks and sit down. Sometimes the gale swept over the high plain with such force that they had to move close to each other so as not to be blown along. The rain blinded them and stung their skin, a freezing rain which got under their clothes. Two hours went by, an interminable wait, nobody knew why, and once again anxiety gripped every heart.

As it grew lighter Jean tried to get his bearings. He had been shown the Le Chêne road going off north-west up a hill the other side of Quatre-Champs. Well, why had they turned right instead of left? What interested him was the headquarters set up in La

Converserie, a farmhouse perched on the edge of the plateau. They seemed to be very perturbed there, with officers running about and arguing and gesticulating. But nothing was coming, what could they be waiting for? The plateau formed a sort of circus — bare stubble stretching on and on, dominated on the north and east by wooded uplands; southwards there were extensive thick woods while to the west could be seen a glimpse of the Aisne valley with the little white houses of Vouziers. Below La Converserie the slate steeple of Quatre-Champs stood out, drowned in sheets of rain which seemed to be melting away the few miserable mossy roofs of the village. As Jean ran his eye up the hilly road he saw quite clearly a trap bowling quite fast along the stony track which was now a torrent.

It was Maurice, who from the hill opposite as he came round a bend had spotted the 7th. He had been casting round for two hours, misled by peasants' instructions, taken the wrong way by the artful bloody-mindedness of his driver, who was scared to death of the Prussians. As soon as he reached the farmhouse Maurice leaped down and at once found his regiment.

Jean gaped in amazement.

'What, you! Why? We were going to pick you up!'

Maurice put all his anger and distress into one gesture.

'Oh yes? Well, we're not going up that way now, we're going over there, to be killed, the whole lot of us!'

After a pause Jean, grim-faced, said: 'All right, anyhow you and I will be knocked out together.'

And as they had parted so the two met again, with an embrace. In the still driving rain the private soldier rejoined the ranks while the corporal set the example, streaming wet but making no complaint.

By now the news was going round, and it was official. The retreat to Paris was off, and once again they were marching towards the Meuse. An aide-de-camp from the marshal had just brought orders for the 7th corps to go and camp at Nouart, whilst the 5th, heading for Beauclair, would take the right flank and the 1st would replace at Le Chêne the 12th, which was marching on La Besace, on the left wing. The reason why thirty-odd thousand men had been standing about there waiting in the furious gales for three hours was that General Douay, in all the deplorable muddle of this fresh change of plan, was terribly worried about the whereabouts of the baggage train sent on ahead the day before towards Chagny. They had to wait until it had rejoined the main body. It was being said that this convoy had been cut in half by that of the 12th at Le Chêne. On top of that, part of the equipment – all the smithies for the artillery – having taken the wrong road was now on its way back from Terron via the Vouziers road, where it was certain to fall into German hands. Never had there been a greater muddle, nor more anxiety.

Then a mood of out and out despair came over the soldiers. Many of them were for sitting down on their packs in the mud on that soaking plain and just waiting for death in the rain. They sneered at their commanding officers and insulted them: a nice lot they were, hadn't the brains of a louse, undid in the evening what they had done in the morning, did damn all when the enemy wasn't there and did a bunk as soon as he showed himself! Utter demoralization finished off the job of turning this army into a rabble with no faith in anything, no discipline, being led to the slaughter by sheer chance. Over towards Vouziers some rifle fire had broken out – shots between the rearguard of the 7th corps and the advance guard of the German troops – and all eyes had been turned towards the valley of the Aisne in which swirling clouds of thick black smoke were rising into a clear patch of sky. They realized it was the village of Falaise, set on fire by the Uhlans. The men were filled with rage. What! The Prussians were there now! They had waited for them for two days, to give them time to get there, and then decamped! In a dim sort of way, even in the dullest heads, there developed a fury at the irreparable error that had been committed, this idiotic delay, this trap into which they had fallen: the scouts of the IVth German army keeping the Bordas brigade busy and so halting and paralysing one by one all the corps of the army of Châlons in order to give the Crown Prince of Prussia time to hurry along with the IIIrd army. And now, thanks to the marshal's ignorance, for he still didn't know what troops he had confronting him, the junction was being effected, and the 7th and 5th corps were going to be harried with a continual threat of disaster.

Maurice watched Falaise blazing on the horizon. But there was one bit of comfort: the baggage train they thought was lost made its appearance from the Le Chêne road. At once, while the first division remained at Quatre-Champs to wait for the interminable baggage train and protect it, the second set off again and made for Boult-aux-Bois through the forest, while the third took up a position to the left, on the heights of Belleville, to safeguard communications. As the 106th at last left the plain just when the rain redoubled its fury and continued the iniquitous march to the Meuse and the unknown, Maurice had another vision of the shadow of the Emperor pacing up and down wearily behind old Madame Desroches's little curtains. Oh, this army of hopelessness, this doomed army being sent to certain annihilation to save a dynasty! March on! March on, never looking behind, in rain, through mud, to extermination!

6

'GOD's truth!' said Chouteau, waking up next morning aching and frozen in the tent, 'I could do with some broth with lots of meat all round!'

At Boult-aux-Bois, where they had camped, all they had had issued to them the night before had been a meagre ration of potatoes, for the commissariat was more and more crazy and disorganized by continual marches and counter-marches, and never met the troops at the prearranged times and places. With the roads all out of action they never knew where to take the travelling herds of cattle, which meant that there would soon be famine.

'Yes, bugger it, roast geese are all over and done with,' groaned Loubet as he stretched himself.

The squad was sulky and sullen. When you didn't eat it wasn't so good. And besides, there was this incessant rain and this mud they had been sleeping in.

Having spotted Pache making the sign of the cross after silently saying his morning prayer, Chouteau exploded again:

'Why don't you ask that God of yours to send us each a couple of bangers and half a pint?'

'Oh, if only I had a loaf and as much bread as I wanted,' sighed

Lapoulle, who suffered more from hunger than the others, and was tortured by his enormous appetite.

But Lieutenant Rochas made them shut up. They should be ashamed of themselves, always thinking about their bellies! He quite simply tightened his trouser-belt. Since things had gone decidedly to the bad and they could now hear distant gunfire he had regained all his obstinate confidence. Since those Prussians were now here, well, it was simple, they were going to fight them! He shrugged his shoulders behind Captain Beaudoin, this youngster as he called him, who was terribly put out by the definite loss of his baggage, tight-lipped, pale-faced, always in a temper. Going without food, well, that could be managed, but what outraged him was not being able to change his shirt.

Maurice had woken up feeling depressed and nervous, though his foot was no longer inflamed thanks to the wide fitting boots. But after yesterday's deluge his cape was still heavy with wet, and that had left him aching in every limb. On water fatigue for the coffee, he glanced over the plain on one edge of which Boult-aux-Bois is situated: forests rise up west and north and a ridge climbs up to the village of Belleville, whilst eastwards towards Buzancy are wide flat stretches of land with slight undulations in which hamlets nestle. Was that the direction from which the enemy was expected? On his way back from the stream with his canful of water he was hailed by a distressed family of peasants at their cottage door who asked him whether the soldiers were really going to stay this time and defend them. Three times already, acting on contradictory orders, the 5th corps had crossed and re-crossed their district. The day before they had heard gunfire in the direction of Bar. Certainly the Prussians were not more than two leagues away. When Maurice told these poor folk that the 7th corps was probably setting off too, they took it very badly. So they were being let down, so the soldiers didn't come to fight, then, for they saw them appearing and disappearing, but always running away.

'Anybody what wants sugar,' said Loubet as he served the coffee, 'has only got to stick his thumb in and wait till it melts.'

But nobody was amused. Coffee without sugar was pretty awful anyway, but if only they had some biscuit! On the plain at Quatre-Champs the day before, almost everybody, for the sake of something to do while hanging about, had finished off the provisions in his pack and swallowed the last crumbs. But fortunately the squad discovered a dozen potatoes, which were shared out.

Maurice, whose stomach was in a bad way, moaned:

'If I had known at Le Chêne I'd have bought some bread!'

Jean listened but said nothing. He had had a row first thing with Chouteau, whom he wanted to send on wood fatigue and who had insolently refused, saying it wasn't his turn. Since everything had been going from bad to worse, indiscipline was on the increase, and the officers were reaching the stage of not daring to reprimand anyone. Jean with his sweet reasonableness had realized that he must play down his authority as a corporal for fear of provoking overt rebellion. So he had turned into a good fellow, appearing to be just a comrade to his men, to whom his experience was still of great value. If his squad wasn't as well fed as it had been, anyway it was not dying of hunger as so many others were. But Maurice's distress upset him in particular, for he felt that he was weakening, and he watched him with an anxious eye, wondering how this delicate young man would ever manage to go through with it.

When Jean heard Maurice complain about having no bread he got up and disappeared for a moment and then came back after rummaging in his pack. Slipping a biscuit into Maurice's hand, he said:

'Here you are, hide it, I haven't enough for everybody!'

'But what about you?' asked the young man, very touched.

'Me? Oh, never you fear ... I've still got two left.'

It was true, he had treasured three biscuits in case there was any fighting, knowing you can get terribly hungry on a battlefield. Anyhow he had just had a potato. That'd do for him. See later on.

At about ten the 7th moved off again. The marshal's original intention must have been to sent it via Buzancy to Stenay, where it would have crossed the Meuse. But the Prussians, outstripping the army of Châlons, must be at Stenay already, and were even said to be at Buzancy. So, turned back northwards, the 7th had had orders to make for La Besace, twenty-odd kilometres from Boult-aux-Bois, in order to go on from there the day after and cross the Meuse at Mouzon. It was a surly departure, the men were grumbling, with their stomachs unsatisfied and their limbs unrested, worn out by the fatigues and delays of the previous days, and the officers, sullen and yielding to the general apprehension about the catastrophe they were heading for, complained about the inaction and were annoyed because they had not gone to Buzancy to reinforce the 5th corps, whose gunfire had been heard there. That corps must also be in retreat and going up towards Nouart, while the 12th was leaving La Besace for Mouzon and the 1st heading for Raucourt. It was like the stampede of a herd hurried and harried by the dogs, all jostling each other on the way to the longed-for Meuse, after endless delays and dodderings.

When the 106th followed its cavalry and artillery from Boult-aux-Bois in the great stream of three divisions streaking the plain with marching men, the sky clouded over again with slow-moving, angry clouds that put the finishing touch to the men's gloom. The 106th itself kept to the main Buzancy road, with its magnificent lines of poplars. At Germont, a village with dunghills steaming outside the doors in a row on each side of the road, women were sobbing and picking up their children in their arms and holding them out to the passing troops as if they wanted them to be taken away. There was nothing left in the village – not a mouthful of bread or even a potato. Then instead of going on towards Buzancy the 106th turned to the left, going up in the direction of Authe, and the men, seeing Belleville once again on the rise at the other side of the plain, which they had been through the day before, knew for a certainty that they were retracing their steps.

'Christ!' muttered Chouteau, 'do they take us for teetotums?'

Loubet added:

'There's a lot of tuppeny-ha'penny generals for you, all going this way and that! You can see our legs don't cost them nothing.'

They were all losing their tempers. You don't wear men out like this just for the fun of walking them about. Over the bare plain between the gentle ups and downs, they moved on in column in two lines, one on each side of the road, between which the officers move up and down. But gone was the time, as in Champagne the day after Rheims, when the march was cheered with jokes and songs, when their packs were carried gaily and the load on their shoulders was lightened by the hope of racing the Prussians and beating them. Now they dragged their feet in angry silence, hating their rifles which bruised their shoulders and the packs that weighed them down, having lost all faith in their commanders and giving way to such hopelessness that they were only marching ahead like a herd of cattle lashed by the whip of fate. The wretched army was beginning to climb its hill of Calvary.

Meanwhile Maurice had been very interested for the last few minutes because over to the left, where there rose some low hills, he had seen a horseman emerge from a clump of trees in the distance. Almost at once another appeared, and then another. All three stood there motionless, no bigger than your fist, looking as small and as clear-cut as toy soldiers. The thought was passing through his mind that it must be an isolated detachment of hussars, some reconnaissance on its way back, when he was astonished to see shining points on their shoulders, probably the light catching gold epaulettes.

'Look over there!' he said, nudging Jean who was next to him. 'Uhlans!'

The corporal opened his eyes wide.

'Well I'll be damned!'

And Uhlans they were – the first Prussians the 106th had seen. Jean had been campaigning for nearly six weeks now, and not only had he not fired a single round, but so far he hadn't seen an enemy either. Word ran round, all heads were turned and curiosity grew. They looked very nice, those Uhlans.

'One of them looks jolly fat,' remarked Loubet.

But to the left of the little wood, on a piece of level ground, a whole squadron appeared. In view of this threatening appearance a halt was called in the column. Orders came along and the 106th took up a position behind the trees by a stream. Already the artillery was dashing back and establishing itself on a hillock. Then for nearly two hours they stayed there in battle formation and killed time, but nothing else happened. On the horizon the mass of enemy cavalry stood motionless. Realizing at last that precious time was being lost, the army resumed its march.

'Ah well,' Jean murmured regretfully, 'it won't be this time!'

Maurice too felt his hands itching with the desire to fire at least one shot. Once again he went over the mistake that had been made the day before by not going to support the 5th corps. If the Prussians were not attacking it must be because they still had not enough infantry at their disposal, which meant that their displays of cavalry in the distance could have no other object than to delay the movement of the French army corps. Once again they had fallen into the trap. And as a matter of fact from that moment onwards the 106th constantly spotted Uhlans to the left on every bit of high ground, following them, keeping an eye on them, disappearing behind a farmhouse only to reappear round the tip of a wood.

Gradually the soldiers' nerves got frayed as they saw themselves ensnared at a distance as though in the meshes of some invisible net. Even Pache and Lapoulle were saying: 'They're beginning to get us down and it would do us good to slosh 'em one or two!'

But still they went on marching and marching, painfully, with dragging steps that quickly got tired. During this uncomfortable day's march they felt the enemy drawing nearer on all sides, as you are conscious of a thunderstorm on the way before it appears over the horizon. Strict orders had been issued about the proper conduct of the rearguard, and there were no more laggards because it was certain that the Prussians behind would snap up everything and everybody. Their infantry was coming up at a terrific speed while the French regiments, harassed and paralysed, were marking time.

At Authe the sky cleared, and Maurice, taking his bearings by the sun, realized that instead of going on towards Le Chêne, a good three leagues further on, they were turning to march due east. It was two o'clock and now they were suffering from unbearable heat after shivering in the rain for two days. The very circuitous road climbed across barren plains. Not a house or a living soul, nothing but a few widely scattered dismal little woods to break the dreariness of the wilderness, and the depressing silence of these solitary places made itself felt on the soldiers who were trudging along, heads down and sweating. At length Saint-Pierremont came into sight, a few deserted houses on a little hill. They did not go through the village, and Maurice noted that they were immediately turning left and reverting to the northerly course towards La Besace. Now he understood that the route had been chosen in an attempt to reach Mouzon before the Prussians. But could they pull it off with such weary and demoralized troops? At Saint-Pierrement the three Uhlans had reappeared far away at a bend in the road from Buzancy, and as the rearguard was leaving the village a battery was disclosed and a few shells came over but did no harm. They did not reply, but went on marching more and more wearily.

From Saint-Pierremont to La Besace is a good three leagues, and when Maurice said so to Jean he made a gesture of despair: the men would never do twelve kilometres, he could tell by infallible signs, they were out of breath and their faces looked desperate. The road was still climbing between two slopes which were gradually closing in. They had to call a halt. But this rest made their limbs ache still more, and when they had to set off again it was worse than ever: the regiments were not making any progress and men were falling by the wayside. Seeing Maurice looking paler and paler and rolling his eyes with exhaustion, Jean uncharacteristically chattered away, trying to take his mind off it all with a torrent of words and keep him awake in the automatic marching movement which had become just instinctive.

'So your sister lives in Sedan, does she? We may go that way.'

'Sedan, never! That's not our way, that would be crazy.'

'Is she young, your sister?'

'But she is the same age as I am. I told you we were twins.'

'Is she like you?'

'Oh well, she's fair just the same. Oh, such soft, curly hair! ... Very small, thin face, and not at all the boisterous kind, oh dear no! Dear Henriette!'

'You are very close to each other?'

'Yes, yes.'

There was a pause, and glancing at Maurice Jean saw that his eyes were closing and that he was on the point of falling down.

'Now, now lad ... Hold yourself up, for God's sake ... Give me your gun a minute, that'll give you a rest ... We're going to leave half the blokes on the road, and it isn't possible to go much further today, God knows!'

Straight ahead he had just caught sight of Oches, with its few miserable hovels terraced on a hillside. It is dominated by the church, all yellow and perched up high among the trees.

'That's where we're going to sleep tonight, for certain.'

He had guessed right. General Douay, seeing the exhaustion of his troops, gave up hope of ever making La Besace that day. But what settled it for him was the arrival of the supply train, this damned convoy he had been dragging after him ever since Rheims, the three leagues of which – vehicles and animals – so terribly hampered his march. From Quatre-Champs he had ordered it to be sent straight on to Saint-Pierremont, and it was only at Oches that the vehicles rejoined the main body, and in such a state of exhaustion that the horses were refusing to move. It was five o'clock already and fearing to get involved in the gorge of Stonne, the general thought he should give up the idea of finishing the day's march laid down by the marshal. So they stopped and camped, the baggage down below in the meadows, guarded by one division, while the artillery took up a position behind on the higher ground, and the brigade that was to act as rearguard the next day stayed on a bluff opposite Saint-Pierremont. Another division, of which the Bourgain-Desfeuilles brigade was a part, bivouacked behind the church on a broad plateau flanked by an oak wood.

Night was already falling when at last the 106th could settle down on the edge of this wood, for there had been so much confusion about the choice and allocation of sites.

'To hell with it!' Chouteau said furiously, 'I'm not going to eat anything, I'm going to sleep!'

That was the universal chorus. Many of them hadn't the strength to put up their tents, and went off to sleep where they fell, like inert lumps. And besides, before you could eat you would have to have an issue from the commissariat, and the commissariat, which was waiting for the 7th at La Besace, was not at Oches. In the general break-up and loss of control there was not even the bugle call for orderly corporals. Food was just catch as catch can. From that time on there were no more regular issues, and soldiers had to live on the rations they were supposed to have in their packs, and their packs were empty, very few could find a crust or even the crumbs of the abundance they had contrived to live on at Vouziers. There was some coffee left and so the less tired still had some sugarless coffee.

When Jean wanted to share by eating one of his biscuits and giving Maurice the other, he saw that he was fast asleep. It crossed his mind to wake him up, but then he stoically put the biscuits back in his pack, with infinite care as though he were hiding some gold, and he himself made do with coffee like the others. He had insisted on the tent being put up and in it they were all lying flat out when Loubet came back from an expedition bringing some carrots from a nearby field. There was no possibility of cooking them, so they munched them raw, but that only aggravated their hunger. They made Pache quite ill.

'No, no, let him sleep on,' Jean said to Chouteau who was shaking Maurice to give him his share.

'Ah,' said Lapoulle, 'tomorrow, when we are in Angoulême, we shall get some bread ... I once had a cousin who was a soldier in Angoulême. Good garrison there.'

There was general stupefaction. Chouteau shouted:

'Angoulême, what do you mean? ... That silly sod thinks he's in Angoulême!'

It was impossible to get any explanation out of Lapoulle. No, he thought they were going to Angoulême. He was the one who, when they had sighted Uhlans that morning, had maintained that they were Bazaine's men.

The camp fell into inky blackness and a deathly silence. Although the night was chilly fires had been forbidden. The Prussians were known to be only a few kilometres away, and even noise was kept down for fear of alerting them. The officers had already warned the men that they were setting off at about four in the morning to make up for lost time, and everybody was greedily snatching some sleep and dead to the world. The heavy breathing of these multitudes rose up in the darkness above the far-flung encampments, like the breathing of the earth itself.

A sudden shot woke up the squad. It was still pitch dark, it might be about three. They all leaped to their feet, the alert ran along the lines and it was believed to be an enemy attack. But it was only Loubet, who couldn't sleep any more and so had thought of going into the oak wood where there might be rabbits. What a binge they would have if he brought back a pair of rabbits for his mates at dawn! But as he was looking for a good place to shoot from he heard some men coming towards him, snapping twigs and talking, and he panicked and fired his shot, thinking he had got some Prussians to deal with.

Maurice, Jean and others were already running up when a hoarse voice croaked:

'Don't fire, for God's sake!'

On the edge of the wood was a tall, gaunt man whose thick, bushy beard could just be made out. He had on a grey smock pulled in at the waist with a red belt, and carried a rifle slung over his shoulder. He at once explained that he was French, a sergeant in the guerrillas, and that he had come with two of his men from the Dieulet woods to bring some information to the general.

'Here, Cabasse, Ducat!' he shouted behind him. 'Come on, you lazy buggers!'

The two men had probably been scared, but now they came up. Ducat was short and stocky, pasty-looking with thinning hair, Cabasse tall and wiry, swarthy faced with a long, thin nose.

By now Maurice had had a close look at the sergeant, which gave him a shock, and now he asked:

'Tell me, aren't you Guillaume Sambuc, from Remilly?'

When after some hesitation the man nervously admitted that he was, Maurice recoiled slightly, because this Sambuc was said to be a terrible scoundrel, a worthy son of a family of woodcutters who had gone to the bad – the father, a drunkard, had been found one night in a wood with his throat cut, the mother and daughter had taken to begging and thieving and ended up in some brothel. This one, Guillaume, was a poacher and did a bit of smuggling. Only one whelp out of this litter of wolves had grown up to be respectable, Prosper, of the African Cavalry, who before he was lucky enough to get into the army had become a farm-hand because he hated the forest.

'I saw your brother in Rheims and at Vouziers,' Maurice went on. 'He is quite well.'

Sambuc did not answer, but to cut things short:

'Take me to the general. Tell him it's the guerrillas from the Dieulet woods who have an important message to deliver.'

On their way back to camp Maurice thought about these freelance companies on whom so many hopes had been built, and who already were giving rise to complaints on all sides. They were supposed to carry on guerrilla warfare, lie in wait for the enemy behind hedges, harass him, pick off his sentries and keep an eye on the woods from which no Prussian would ever get out alive. But the truth of the matter was that they were becoming the terror of the peasants, whom they were not defending at all and whose fields they were plundering. Out of hatred for regular military service all the drop-outs were rushing to join these gangs and enjoy freedom from discipline, roam at large like a lot of bandits out on the spree, sleeping and guzzling any old where. The recruits in some of these companies were deplorable types.

'Cabasse! Ducat!' Sambuc went on shouting, looking behind at every step. 'Come on, you lazy devils!'

Maurice felt that these two were just as terrible. Cabasse, the tall, wiry one, a native of Toulon, had once been a waiter in a Marseilles café and ended up in Sedan as an agent for produce from the south, and had almost been run in over some story of theft which remained obscure. Ducat, the short, fat one, had been a process-server at Blainville, but had been forced to sell out after some unsavoury adventures with little girls, and only recently had again narrowly escaped the assizes for the same disgusting behaviour at Raucourt, where he worked as a book-keeper in a factory. He could bandy Latin quotations, whereas the other one could hardly read, but they made a nice pair, a disturbing pair of shady customers.

The camp was already awake. Jean and Maurice took the men to Captain Beaudoin, who took them to Colonel de Vineuil. The latter interrogated them, but Sambuc, conscious of his own importance, was determined to see the general, and as General Bourgain-Desfeuilles, who had slept at the house of the parish priest of Oches, had just appeared at the presbytery door, very put out at being woken up in the middle of the night to face another day of famine and fatigue, he gave these men a furious reception.

'Where have they come from? What do they want? Oh, it's you, the guerrillas! Another lot of Weary Willies, eh?'

'Sir,' explained Sambuc, quite unruffled, 'we and the others hold the Dieulet woods.'

'Dieulet woods, where's that?'

'Between Stenay and Mouzon, sir.'

'Stenay, Mouzon, never heard of them! How do you expect me to know where I am with all these new names?'

Colonel de Vineuil, feeling embarrassed, intervened discreetly to remind him that Stenay and Mouzon were on the Meuse, and that as the Germans had cut off the first of these towns they were going to attempt to cross the river by the bridge at the second, further north.

'Anyway, sir,' Sambuc went on, 'we've come to warn you that the Dieulet woods are now full of Prussians ... Yesterday, as the 5th corps was leaving Bois-les-Dames, it was engaged near Nouart. ...'

'What, was there fighting yesterday?'

'There certainly was, sir. The 5th corps was in a battle and with-drew, and it must be at Beaumont tonight . . . So while some of our comrades have gone to tell them about the enemy movements, we thought we would come and tell you what the situation is so that you can go to their aid, for they are certainly going to be up against sixty thousand men tomorrow morning.'

This figure made General Bourgain-Desfeuilles shrug his shoulders.

'Sixty thousand men! Hang it all, why not a hundred thousand? . . . You're dreaming, my dear fellow. Fear has made you see double. There can't be sixty thousand men so near us. We should know if there were!'

He would not be persuaded. In vain Sambuc called on Ducat and Cabasse for corroboration.

'We have seen the cannons,' the southerner affirmed, 'and those buggers must be crazy to risk them on those forest tracks where you sink in up to your shins on account of the rain there's been these last few days.'

'Somebody is guiding them, for sure,' declared Ducat.

But since Vouziers the general had given up believing in this concentration of the two German armies which everybody, he said, had been dinning into his ears. He did not even think it worth while having the men taken to the commander of the 7th corps – to whom, actually, they thought they had been talking. If one had paid attention to all the yokels and tramps who brought so-called information, one wouldn't have advanced a single step without being shunted right and left into absurd adventures. However, he did order the three men to stay and travel with the column because of their local knowledge.

'All the same,' Jean said to Maurice as they went back to fold the tent, 'those three are decent blokes to have done four leagues cross-country to warn us.'

Maurice agreed, and he knew the men were right, for he too knew the district, and he was just as much a prey to deadly anxiety at the thought that the Prussians were in the Dieulet woods and on the move towards Sommauthe and Beaumont. He was sitting down now, already feeling wretched before the march had even begun, his stomach empty and his heart sick with anguish at the dawn of a day he felt was bound to be terrible.

Upset at seeing him looking so pale, Jean asked in a fatherly way:
'Not too good? Is it still that foot of yours?'

Maurice shook his head. His foot was now quite all right with these wide boots.

'Hungry then?'

Seeing he did not answer, Jean took one of the two biscuits out of his pack without being seen, and then, telling a simple lie:

'Look here, I have saved you your share . . . I ate the other one just now.'

Day was breaking as the 7th left Oches, making for Mouzon via La Besace, where it should have slept that night. The accursed supply column had left first with the first division, and if the proper army waggons which had first-rate horses made good speed, the others, the requisitioned ones, mostly empty and useless, dawdled astonishingly on the gradients of the gorge of Stonne. The road climbs, particularly after the hamlet of La Berlière, between wooded hills which overlook it. At about eight, when the two remaining divisions were at last beginning to move, Marshal MacMahon appeared and was furious to find still there troops which he thought had left La Besace that morning with only a few kilometres to do to be right on time at Mouzon. And so he had a violent altercation with General Douay. It was decided that the first division and the supply train should be left to continue their march to Mouzon, but that the two other divisions, so as not to be slowed down any more by the cumbersome advance guard, would take the road to Raucourt and Autrecourt so as to cross the Meuse at Villers. This once again meant turning northwards, in the haste the marshal was making to put the river between his army and the enemy. Cost what it may, they had to be on the right bank that evening. And the rearguard was still at Oches when a Prussian battery opened fire from a distant height near Saint-Pierremont, renewing the tactics of the day before. At first they made the mistake of answering their fire, but then the last troops pulled out.

Until about eleven the 106th made its way slowly along the winding road in the gorge of Stonne, between the high hills. On the left the crests rose bare and precipitous, but on the right woods grew down the gentle slopes. The sun had come out again and it was very hot in the narrow valley, frighteningly lonely. After you leave La Berlière, dominated by its tall, dreary Calvary, there is not a single farm, not a living soul or animal grazing in the meadows. The men, so weary and famished the day before, were already dragging their feet, disheartened and full of smouldering anger.

Then suddenly, as they were halted by the roadside, gunfire thundered to the right. The firing was so clear and loud that the battle could not be more than two leagues away. The effect on these men, so weary of retreating and sick of waiting about, was extraordinary. They all leaped to their feet, full of excitement, forgetting their fatigue: why weren't they marching? They wanted to fight, to be killed rather than go on running away helter-skelter like this, and without knowing where or why.

General Bourgain-Desfeuilles had just gone up a hill to the right, with Colonel de Vineuil, to reconnoitre the country. They could be seen on the top, between two clumps of trees, field-glasses raised, and at once they sent down an aide-de-camp who was with them to ask for the guerrillas to be sent up if they were still there. A few men, Jean, Maurice and some others, went up with them in case any help should be needed.

As soon as the general saw Sambuc he bawled:

'What a damn silly place this is with these hills and woods going on for ever ... here, you, where is it, where's the fighting?'

Sambuc, with Ducat and Cabasse always at his heels, listened and scanned the wide horizon without answering. Maurice, who was standing by him, looked too and was impressed by the immense stretch of valleys and hills, like an endless sea with huge, slow waves. Forests made patches of dark green on the yellow earth, and in the blazing sun the distant hilltops faded into a russet haze. Although nothing could be seen, not even a single puff of smoke in the pale sky, the guns were still booming like the sound of a distant but approaching storm.

'That's Sommauthe to the right,' Sambuc finally said, pointing to a lofty crest covered with green. 'Yoncq is over there to the left ... It's at Beaumont where the fighting is, sir.'

'Yes, Warniforêt or Beaumont,' Ducat confirmed.

The general mumbled some half audible words.

'Beaumont, Beaumont, you never know in this bloody part of the world.'

Then aloud:

'How far is Beaumont from here?'

'About ten kilometres, by the road from Le Chêne to Stenay which is down there.'

The gunfire never stopped and seemed to be moving from west to east in a continuous rolling of thunder. Sambuc went on:

'Golly, it's warming up! I expected it, and I warned you this morning, sir, it is certainly the batteries we saw in the Dieulet woods. By now the 5th corps must be having to deal with the whole of that army coming from Buzancy and Beauclair.'

There was a silence while the distant battle thundered louder. Maurice almost bit his tongue off, for he had a mad desire to scream. Why weren't they marching to battle, now, without all this talk? He had never felt so worked up. Each round made his heart leap, lifted his spirit and gave him a desperate urge to be there, to be in it, to get it over. Were they once again going to skirt along the edge of this battle, rub elbows with it without firing a shot? It was against all reason to drag them round like this ever since the declaration of war, and always running away! At Vouziers all they had heard was shots from the rearguard. At Oches the enemy had just bombarded them for one minute – in the back. And still they were running away, this time they weren't even going to race to the help of their comrades! He glanced at Jean who was very pale, like himself, with a feverish light in his eye. Every heart was leaping at this clarion call of the guns.

But then there was a fresh delay because a staff officer was climbing the narrow path up the hill. It was General Douay hurrying with an anxious look on his face. When he had personally questioned the guerrillas he gave vent to a cry of despair. Even if he had been warned that morning, what could he have done? The marshal's order was categorical, they must cross the Meuse by nightfall at all costs. And besides, how could one possibly at this stage reassemble troops strung out on the road to Raucourt so as to redirect them at full speed towards Beaumont? Wouldn't they get there too late in any case? The 5th must already be retreating towards Mouzon, and the gunfire showed this clearly as it moved further and further eastwards like a disastrous hailstorm moving away. General Douay raised both arms above the vast horizon of valleys and hills in a gesture of helpless fury, and the order was given to continue the march to Raucourt.

And what a march! Deep in the gorge of Stonne between the

high peaks, while to the right behind the woods the cannon went on roaring. At the head of the 106th Colonel de Vineuil rode bolt upright on his horse, with his ashen face raised and his eyelids blinking as though he were holding back his tears. Captain Beaudoin silently chewed his moustache, while Lieutenant Rochas was softly muttering obscenities and curses against everybody including himself. And even among those soldiers who did not want to fight, among the least brave, there was developing an urge to bawl and bang in anger at the continual defeat and rage at sloping off yet again with weary, uncertain steps while these bloody Prussians were slaughtering their comrades over yonder.

At the foot of the Stonne gorge, down which the route zigzags between hillocks, the roadway widens out and the troops were passing through broad meadows broken by clumps of trees. The 106th, which was now in the rearguard, had expected to be attacked at any moment since leaving Oches, for the enemy was dogging the column step by step, keeping his eye on it, obviously waiting for the favourable moment to take it in the rear. His cavalry was utilizing all the ups and downs of the terrain to try to catch it on the flanks. Several squadrons of the Prussian Guard were seen to debouch from behind a wood, but they stopped in the face of a demonstration by a regiment of hussars which came along and kept the road clear. Thanks to this respite the retreat went on in fairly good order, and they were nearing Raucourt when something they saw redoubled everyone's uneasiness and put the finishing touch to the men's demoralization. They suddenly saw a mob rushing down a side road – wounded officers, soldiers out of control and without weapons, supply waggons galloping, men and animals all in flight, panic-striken before the wind of disaster. It was all that was left of a brigade of the first division which had been escorting the supply train that had set out that morning for Mouzon via La Besace. A terrible piece of ill-luck, a mistake in the route had thrown them and part of the train right into the rout of the 5th corps at Varni-forêt, near Beaumont. Surprised by a flank attack and outnumbered, they had fled, and panic was driving them on, bleeding, haggard, half-crazed, knocking over their own comrades in their terror. Their tales spread alarm; it was as though they had been flung there by the rumbling thunder of the cannon that had gone on since noon without a break.

By the time they were going through Raucourt, anxious haste was turning into a stampede. Should they turn right towards Autrecourt so as to cross the Meuse at Villers as had been decided? Worried and hesitating, General Douay feared he might find the bridge jammed, or perhaps even in Prussian hands. So he preferred to go straight ahead along the valley of Haraucourt in order to reach Remilly before nightfall. After Mouzon, Villers, and after Villers, Remilly. They were still going northwards with the galloping Uhlans behind them. There were only six more kilometres to do, but it was already five o'clock, and what overwhelming fatigue! They had been on their feet since dawn, had taken twelve hours to cover barely three leagues, standing about and getting tired in endless delays, and subjected to the strongest emotional strains and fears. For two nights the men had hardly slept at all and they had never satisfied their hunger since Vouziers. They were collapsing for want of food. In Raucourt things were pitiful.

This little town is prosperous, with its numerous factories, main street with fine buildings on each side, its charming church and town hall. But the night spent there by the Emperor and Marshal MacMahon, with all the paraphernalia of General Headquarters and the imperial household, followed by the passage through the town of the whole of the 1st army corps which had flowed along the street all the morning like a river, had exhausted all the town's resources, emptying bakeries and grocers' and making a clean sweep even of the crumbs in the townspeople's homes. There was no more bread, wine or sugar to be found – nothing drinkable or eatable. There had been ladies standing at their front doors giving away glasses of wine and cups of broth until the last drops had gone from casks and saucepans. And now it was all gone, and by the time the first regiments of the 7th corps began to come through at about three the people were in despair. What, was it starting all over again? And still going on and on? Once again the main street was thronged with men, dead beat, covered with dust, dying of hunger, and they hadn't a mouthful of anything to offer them. Many of the men stopped and knocked at doors, held out their hands in front of windows, begging for a crust of bread to be thrown to them. There were women in tears as they made signs that they couldn't, that they had nothing left.

At the corner of the rue des Dix-Potiers, Maurice came over faint and reeled. When Jean rushed up to him:

'No, leave me here, this is the end . . . I'd rather peg out here.'

He flopped by the roadside. The corporal put on purposely the brutality of an angry N.C.O.

'Christ! What's the good of a fucking soldier like that! Do you want to be picked up by the Prussians? Come on, up you get!'

Then seeing that the young man made no answer, but looked white as a sheet, his eyes half closed and half swooning, he went on swearing, but in a tone of infinite pity.

'Christ Almighty! Christ Almighty!'

He ran to a near-by fountain, filled his messtin with water and came back and bathed the other's face. Then, with no concealment this time, he took the last biscuit out of his pack, the one he had saved so jealously, broke it up into small pieces which he poked into Maurice's mouth. The famished man opened his eyes and devoured the food.

'But what about you?' he suddenly remembered, 'Haven't you had anything, Jean?'

'Oh, I'm all right, I've got a tougher hide than you and I can wait. A good drink of frog juice and I shall be right as rain.'

He had filled the messtin again and he drank it off in one gulp, clicking his tongue. But his face, too, looked as pale as death, and he was so tortured with hunger that his hands were shaking.

'Off we go! Come on boy, got to rejoin the others.'

Maurice let himself be carried away like a child. No woman's arms had ever held him as close and warm as this. In the collapse of everything, amidst this utter misery, with death staring him in the face, it was an ineffable comfort to feel another person loving him and looking after him; and possibly the thought that this heart that was all his belonged to a simple man, a peasant who had never left the land and whom at first he had looked on with distaste, now added a wonderful tenderness to his gratitude. Was this not the brotherhood of the earliest days of the world, friendship before there was any culture or class, the friendship of two men united and become as one in their common need of help in the face of the threat of hostile nature? He heard his own humanity beating in Jean's breast, and so he was proud on his own account to feel him there, stronger, helping, devoting himself. And Jean, who did not analyse what he felt, found a great joy in protecting in his friend the refinement and intelligence that were still so rudimentary in himself. Since the violent death of his wife in a dreadful tragedy, he thought he had no heart, he had sworn never again to look at those creatures on whose account a man suffers so much, even when they are not being evil. And so friendship became a sort of broadening out for both of them: they might not kiss, but they touched each other's very souls, the one was part of the other, however different they might be, on this terrible road to Remilly, one upholding the other and the two of them making a single being in pity and suffering.

As the rearguard was leaving Raucourt the Germans were entering it at the other end, and two of their batteries were set up at once on the heights to the left and started firing. At that moment the 106th on the road going down beside the Emmane was in the line of fire. A shell brought down a poplar on the river bank and another buried itself in a field near Captain Beaudoin, but did not explode. But all the way to Haraucourt the gorge went on narrowing, and they wormed their way into a narrow corridor dominated on both sides by wooded crests, and if even a handful of Prussians were in ambush up there disaster was certain. Bombarded from the rear and with the threat of a possible attack from right and left, the troops could not help advancing with ever increasing anxiety, and were in a great hurry to get out of this dangerous pass. This inspired a final burst of energy even in the most exhausted. The same soldiers who just before had dragged their feet from door to door in Raucourt were now stepping out quite perky and revived under the stinging lash of peril. Even the horses seemed to realize that a minute lost might have to be paid for very dearly. The head of the column must have reached Remilly when there was a sudden halt to the march.

'Fuck it all!' said Chouteau. 'Are they going to leave us standing here?'

The 106th had not yet reached Haraucourt, and the shells were still raining down.

As the regiment was marking time, waiting to set off again, one exploded to their right which fortunately did not wound anyone. Five interminable, terrifying minutes went by and still they made no move, there was some obstacle blocking the road further on, some wall had apparently sprung up. The colonel stood up in his stirrups and shuddered as he looked, for he was conscious of the mounting panic of his men behind.

'We've been sold down the river, everybody knows that,' Chouteau went on in a dangerous voice.

There broke out murmurings and then a swelling growl of exasperation under the lash of fear. Yes, yes, they had been brought here to be sold, to be handed over to the Prussians. The relentless piling-up of mishaps and the countless mistakes made had planted in these limited minds the idea of betrayal as the only possible explanation of such a series of disasters.

'We've been sold,' repeated panic-stricken voices.

Then Loubet thought up something.

'It's that sod of an Emperor further on, stuck across the road with all his luggage, just to hold us up.'

The news at once flew round. It was affirmed that the jam was due to the movement of the imperial household cutting across the column. There was an outbust of execration, with abominable words, all the hatred prompted by the insolence of the Emperor's servants, taking over whole towns to sleep in, unpacking their provisions, their hampers of wine, their silver plate in front of soldiers stripped of everything, lighting roaring fires in kitchens while other poor buggers tightened their belts. Oh, that bloody Emperor with neither throne nor power, like a lost child in his Empire, being carried round now like a useless parcel in the baggage of his troops, condemned to drag about with him the irony of his gala household, his bodyguard, carriages, horses, vans, all the pomp of his state robe embroidered with bees, used to sweep up the blood and mud on the highways of defeat!

One after another two more shells came down. Lieutenant Rochas had his cap knocked off by a bit of shrapnel. The ranks closed and there was a thrust, a sudden surging wave which communicated itself further and further. Voices were spluttering with rage, Lapoulle was furiously bawling for them to get a move on. In another minute, perhaps, there was going to be an appalling catastrophe, a stampede that would crush men to death in a struggling mass.

The colonel turned round, looking very grim.

'Now now, my boys, my boys, be a bit patient. I have sent somebody to find out . . . we are just going . . .'

But they were not just going, and the seconds were like centuries. Jean had already taken hold of Maurice's hand, and with perfect self-control was softly explaining to him that if the chaps were to start shoving the two of them would jump to the left and climb up through the woods on the other side of the river. He cast his eye round to find the guerrillas, thinking that they must know the by-ways, but somebody said they had sloped off on the way through Raucourt. And then the march suddenly started again, they rounded a bend in the road and from there onwards were screened from the German batteries. Later on it was known that in the confusion of that unfortunate day it was the Bonnemain division, four regiments of cuirassiers, who had cut across the 7th corps and stopped it in this way.

Night was falling by the time the 106th went through Ange-court. The hilltops went on to the right, but the gorge widened out on the left and a bluish valley appeared in the distance. At last, from the heights of Remilly, there could be seen through the evening mists a ribbon of pale silver in the immense panorama of meadows and cultivated land. It was the Meuse, the longed-for Meuse, where there would be victory, it seemed.

And Maurice, pointing to little distant lights twinkling merrily through the trees in this rich valley, making à charming picture in the tints of twilight, said to Jean, with the joyful relief of a man finding himself back in his beloved homeland:

'Oh, look down there . . . that's Sedan!'

7

In Remilly there was a dreadful mix-up of men, horses, and vehicles jamming the street which zigzags down the hill to the Meuse. Half way down, in front of the church, some guns had got their wheels locked together and could not be moved in spite of much swearing and banging. At the bottom of the hill, where the Emmane roars down a fall, there was a huge queue of broken-down vans blocking the road, while an ever-growing wave of soldiers was struggling at the Croix de Malte inn, but not getting so much as a glass of wine.

This desperate pressure came up against a stoppage further on, at the southern end of the village, separated by a clump of trees from the river, over which the engineers had thrown a pontoon bridge that morning. To the right there was a ferry, and the ferry-man's house stood white and isolated amid tall weeds. Big fires had been lit on both banks, and the flames leaped up now and again and filled the night with a glare that made the water and banks as light as day. Then it was possible to see the huge pile-up of waiting troops, for the footbridge allowed only two men to cross at once, while on the bridge proper, three metres wide at the most, the cavalry, artillery and baggage-train moved at a mortally slow walking-pace. It was said that a brigade of the 1st corps was coming up, thirty-odd thousand men who, believing the enemy was at their heels, were in feverish haste to reach safety on the opposite bank.

There was a moment of despair. What! They'd been marching since first thing with no food, they had just got themselves out of the terrible gorge of Haraucourt by putting a sprint on, and all that so as to bang their heads, in this alarm and confusion, against an impassable wall! It might be hours and hours before the turn of the last comers, and everyone was fully aware that even if the Prussians dared not continue pursuing them through the night they would be there by daybreak. But the order to pile arms was given, and they camped on the great bare hills along the sides of which the Mouzon road runs, and the lower slopes of which run down to the meadows by the Meuse. Behind them, on the top of a plateau, the reserve artillery took up battle positions and trained their guns on the gorge so as to bombard the exit should need arise. And once again the waiting set in, full of resentment and anxiety.

The 106th was halted in a field of stubble above the road and looking over the great plain. The men had been loath to put down their rifles, and kept glancing behind them in their nagging fear of an attack. They all looked hard-faced and grim, and said nothing beyond occasional sullen mutterings of anger. It was nearly nine and they had been there for two hours, but although they were desperately tired they could not sleep but lay stretched out on the ground, their nerves on edge and ears cocked for the smallest distant sound. They could not struggle any more against their gnawing hunger – they would eat something over on the other side of the river, and they would eat grass if they couldn't find anything else. But the congestion only seemed to be getting worse, the officers General Douay had posted by the bridge came back every twenty minutes with the same maddening story that hours and hours would still be needed. Eventually the general made up his mind to fight a way through to the bridge for himself. He could be seen struggling about in the mob, hurrying people on.

Sitting against a bank with Jean, Maurice made the same gesture towards the north that he had made before.

'Sedan is in the background . . . Oh, and that is Bazeilles over there . . . And then Douzy and Carignan to the right . . . I expect it'll be at Carignan that we shall be concentrated . . . Oh, if it were light you would see there's plenty of room!'

His gesture took in the immense valley, full of darkness. The sky was not so black that you could not make out the pale course of the river across the panorama of black fields. Clumps of trees made darker patches, especially a row of poplars to the left, which cut off the horizon like a fantastic dike. Then in the background behind Sedan, with its sprinkling of bright little lights, was a heap of blackness as if all the forests of the Ardennes had drawn across their curtain of age-old oaks.

Jean looked back at the pontoon bridge below.

'Just look at that! The whole thing's buggered up and we shall never get across.'

The fires on both sides of the river were blazing higher and their light was so intense that the frightening scene stood out with nightmarish clarity. Under the weight of the cavalry and artillery passing over since morning the pontoons supporting the baulks of timber had sunk lower, so that the flooring was a few centimetres under water. At that moment the cuirassiers were crossing two by two in an uninterrupted line, emerging from the shadows on one bank and disappearing into the shadows on the other, and as the bridge itself could no longer be seen they appeared to be walking in the water, or on top of water luridly ablaze with dancing fires. The horses were whinnying as, manes standing on end and legs stiff, they moved forward in terror of the shifting ground they felt giving way beneath them. Standing in the stirrups and tugging the reins, the cuirassiers went on and on, draped in their long white cloaks and showing only their helmets flaming with red reflected fire. They might have been taken for phantom horsemen riding to a ghostly war with hair flaming.

A deep lament rose from Jean's parched throat:

'Oh, I am famished!'

But most of the men round them had gone to sleep in spite of the clawing at their stomachs. Excess of fatigue had taken away their fear and knocked them out on their backs, with their mouths gaping, dead to the world under the moonless sky. From end to end of the bare hills the time of waiting had sunk into a deathly silence.

'Oh, I am hungry, so hungry I could eat earth!'

This was the cry that Jean, usually so tough and so silent, could not hold in any longer, but let out in spite of himself in the delirium of hunger, having had nothing to eat for nearly thirty-six hours. And then Maurice made up his mind, seeing that their regiment would probably not cross the Meuse for two or three hours.

'Look here, I've got an uncle not far from here, Uncle Fouchard, you know, I told you about him. It's up there, only five or six hundred yards, and I was wondering, but as you are hungry . . . My uncle will give us some bread, so what the hell!'

He took his friend away, and Jean let himself be led. Old Fouchard's little farmhouse was at the end of the Haraucourt defile, near the plateau on which the reserve artillery had taken up its position. It was a low house with a fair number of outbuildings, a barn, cowshed and stable, and on the opposite side of the road, in a sort of coach-house, he had set up his business as a travelling butcher, his own abattoir where he slaughtered the animals himself, which he then hawked round the villages in his cart.

As they drew near Maurice was surprised to see no light.

'Oh, the old skinflint will have barricaded everything up, and he won't open the door.'

What he saw then made him stop still in the middle of the road. In front of the farmhouse there were a dozen or so soldiers on the prowl, marauders no doubt looking for what they could pick up. They had begun by calling out, then they had knocked, and now, seeing that the house was black and silent, they were banging on the door with rifle-butts trying to break the lock. Voices were bawling:

'Go on, for God's sake, knock the fucking thing in, there's nobody at home!'

Suddenly the shutter of an attic window flew open and a lanky old man in a smock, bareheaded, appeared with a candle in one hand and a gun in the other. His face jutted out under his tousled white mane, a deeply wrinkled face with a strong nose, big pale eyes and a firm chin.

'Are you a lot of thieves breaking everything down?' he shouted in a harsh voice. 'What do you want?'

The soldiers fell back, a bit abashed.

'We're dying of hunger, we want something to eat.'

'I've got nothing, not even a crust . . . Do you think we can feed hundreds of thousands of men, just like that? . . . This morning it was another lot, yes, General Ducrot's lot, and they came through and took everything.'

One by one the soldiers came nearer.

'Open the door just the same. We'll have a rest and you'll dig something out.'

They were already banging again when the old man put his candle down on the bar and took aim with his gun.

'As sure as that's a candle, I'll blow out the brains of the first one to touch my door!'

Then there was nearly a pitched battle. They shouted curses up at him and one voice yelled that they'd better settle this bloody yokel's hash – just like all the others he'd rather chuck his bread into the river than give a mouthful to a soldier. Rifles were already being raised and they were on the point of shooting him at almost point-blank range, but he did not even recoil, but stayed there, furious and immovable, in full view in the candlelight.

'Nothing at all! Not a crust! They've taken the lot!'

Maurice was horrified and leaped forward, with Jean after him.

'Comrades . . .'

He struck down the soldiers' rifles and looked up, pleading:

'Look, do be sensible. Don't you recognize me? It's me!'

'Me! Who's me?'

'Maurice Levasseur, your nephew.'

Old Fouchard picked up his candle again. Obviously he recognized him. But he persisted in his determination not to give away even a glass of water.

143

'Nephew or not, how do I know in this cut-throat darkness? Go on, bugger off, the whole lot of you, or I'll shoot!'

And all through the vociferations and threats to shoot him down and set fire to the whole show he went on with the one cry which he repeated twenty times over:

'Bugger off, the whole lot of you, or I'll shoot!'

'Even me, Dad?' suddenly asked a loud voice above all the din.

The others drew back and a sergeant appeared in the flickering light from the candle. It was Honoré, whose battery was less than two hundred metres away and who for two hours had been fighting an irresistible urge to come and knock at this door. He had sworn he would never cross the threshold again and in all his four years of service he had never exchanged a single letter with the father he was now addressing so curtly. Already the marauding soldiers were in a huddle, conferring busily. The old boy's son, and an N.C.O. as well! Nothing doing, it wasn't so good, they'd better look somewhere else. And off they went, and vanished into the inky darkness.

When old Fouchard realized that he had been saved from looting he simply said, with no emotion whatever, as though he had seen his boy the day before:

'Oh it's you . . . all right, I'm coming down.'

It took a long time. Doors could be heard being unlocked and locked again – quite a performance by the sort of man who makes sure nothing is left lying about. Then at last the door opened, but barely ajar, and held by a strong hand.

'Come in, you and nobody else!'

Yet he could not refuse asylum to his nephew, though it went visibly against the grain.

'All right, you too.'

And he was by way of shutting the door pitilessly on Jean, and Maurice had to entreat him. But he was immovable : no, no, he didn't want any strangers and thieves in his house and breaking up his furniture. Finally Honoré butted with his shoulder and let their mate in, and the old man had to give way, muttering vague threats. He had hung on to his gun. When he had taken them into the living-room and stood his rifle against the sideboard and put the candle on the table, he fell into a sullen silence.

'Look here, Dad, we're starving. Surely you can give us some bread and cheese!'

He made no answer and did not appear to hear, but kept going over to the window to listen in case some other lot should come and besiege his house.

'Look, Uncle, Jean is like a brother to me. He went without everything for me. And we've been through so much together.'

He was still going round to make sure nothing was missing, and did not even look at them. At last he made up his mind, but still never said a word. He suddenly picked up his candle and left them in the dark, taking care to lock the door behind him so that nobody could follow. They heard him going down the cellar stairs. Once again it took a very long time. When he came back, after renewed barricading, he placed in the middle of the table a large loaf and a cheese, still in the silence which, now that his anger had died down, was simply strategic, for you never know where talking might lead you. In any case the three men threw themselves at the food revenously, and the only sound now was the frenzied noise of their jaws.

Honoré got up and went to fetch a jug of water from the sideboard.

'Father, you might have given us some wine!'

Having now regained his composure and being sure of himself, Fouchard found his tongue again.

'Wine! I haven't got any, not a drop left! The other lot, the Ducrot lot, have drunk, eaten and pinched everything.'

He was lying, and try as he would it showed in the blinking of his pale bulging eyes. Two days before he had spirited away all his livestock, the few domestic animals he kept and the ones destined for his butchery, taking them by night and hiding them nobody knew where, in the depths of which wood or which abandoned quarry. And he had just been spending hours concealing everything in the house – wine, bread and the most unimportant provisions, even flour and salt, so that in fact all the cupboards could have been ransacked in vain. The house was swept clean. He had even refused to sell anything to the first soldiers who had appeared. You never knew, there might be better opportunities later, and vague ideas about trading were taking shape in the head of this patient and cunning miser.

Maurice, having eaten almost his fill, was the first to talk.

'And my sister Henriette, how long is it since you saw her?'

The old man was still walking up and down, casting glances at Jean, who was putting away enormous hunks of bread; and then, without hurrying, as though after long reflection:

'Henriette, yes, last month in Sedan ... But I saw Weiss, her husband, this morning. He was with his boss, Monsieur Delaherche, who had taken him out with him in his carriage to see the army go through at Mouzon, just for the jaunt.'

An expression of heavy irony passed across the peasant's inscrutable face.

'But still, they may well have seen too much of the army and not have enjoyed themselves very much, because by three you couldn't move on the roads, they were so cluttered up with soldiers on the run.'

In the same level and almost indifferent voice he gave a few details about the defeat of the 5th corps, taken by surprise at Beaumont just as they were preparing a meal, forced to withdraw and kicked back to Mouzon by the Bavarians. A lot of fleeing soldiers, rushing panic-stricken through Remilly, had called out to him that de Failly had once again sold them to Bismarck. Maurice recalled the frantic marches of the last two days, the orders from MacMahon stepping up the retreat so as to cross the Meuse at all costs, when they had lost so many precious days in incomprehensible hesitations. Now it was too late. Perhaps the marshal, who had been furious at finding the 7th corps in Oches when he thought it was at La Besace, had been convinced that the 5th was already encamped at Mouzon, whereas it was dallying at Beaumont and letting itself be annihilated. But what can you expect from troops badly commanded, demoralized by delay and flight, dying of hunger and fatigue?

Fouchard had finally come to a halt behind Jean, astounded to see the chunks disappearing, and coldly sarcastic:

'You feel better, don't you?'

The corporal looked up and answered with the same peasant aplomb:

'Just beginning, thank you.'

Ever since he had been there Honoré had stopped now and again, in spite of his great hunger, and looked round thinking he heard a noise. The reason why after a great struggle he had broken his oath never to set foot in this house again was that he was urged on by an irresistible desire to see Silvine once more. He had kept under his shirt, in fact next to his body, the letter he had had at Rheims, that affectionate letter in which she told him she still loved him, and that she would never love anyone but him in spite of Goliath and the baby, little Charlot, she had had by this man. And now he could think of nothing but her and was worried because he had not seen her yet, while at the same time holding himself in check so as not to betray his anxiety to his father. But passion won, and he asked in a voice he tried to make sound natural:

'And what about Silvine, isn't she here now?'

Fouchard looked quizzically at his son, and his eyes twinkled with hidden amusement.

'Oh yes, oh yes.'

Then silence, and he spat very deliberately. After a pause Honoré had to go on:

'Well, has she gone to bed?'

'No, no.'

Finally the old man condescended to explain that he had gone as usual that morning to market in Raucourt, taking her with him in the cart. Because soldiers were going through the town that was no reason for people to give up eating meat and for business to stop. So, as always on Tuesdays, he had taken a sheep and a quarter of beef and he was finishing selling them when the arrival of the 7th corps had landed him in the middle of a terrible shindy, everybody running about and knocking each other over. So he had been afraid of somebody taking his horse and cart and had gone, not waiting for Silvine, who was doing some errands in the town.

'Oh, she'll get back all right,' he concluded in his calm voice. 'She will have taken refuge in Dr Dalichamp's house, he's her godfather ... She's a brave girl, for all her look of only being able to do what she's told ... Certainly she's got lots of good points.'

Was he teasing? Or was he trying to explain why he was keeping on this girl who had come between him and his son, and that in spite of the Prussian's child from whom she refused to be parted? Once again he cast his sly glance and laughed to himself.

'Charlot is asleep in there, in her room, and she won't be long, I'm sure.'

Honoré's lips were trembling, and he looked so hard at his father that the latter resumed his walking up and down. Silence fell again, an endless silence while he automatically cut himself some more bread, still chewing. Jean went on too, without feeling any need to say a word. But Maurice had had enough to eat, and with his elbows on the table he looked round at the old sideboard and the old clock and daydreamed about the holidays he had spent at Remilly long ago with his sister. The minutes ticked by, the clock struck eleven.

'Hell,' he murmured, 'we mustn't let the others go without us.' He went over and opened the window, and Fouchard did not object. The whole black valley was scooped out below like a rolling sea of shadows. Nevertheless, when your eyes became accustomed to it you could make out quite clearly the bridge lit by the fires on either bank. There were still cuirassiers crossing, looking in their big white cloaks like phantom riders whose horses, whipped on by a wind of terror, were walking on the water. And that went on and on endlessly, and always at the same speed like a slow-moving vision. To the right the bare hills, where the army was sleeping, were still wrapped in a death-like stillness and silence.

'Oh well,' went on Maurice with a gesture of despair, 'it'll be tomorrow morning now!'

He had left the window wide open, and old Fouchard seized his gun, cocked his leg over the rail and jumped out with the agility of a young man. For a minute or two he could be heard walking away with the regular step of a sentinel, then nothing could be heard but the distant roar of the crowded bridge. No doubt he had sat down on the roadside, feeling more secure there where he could see danger coming and be ready to leap back and defend his home.

Now Honoré was watching the clock every minute, and his nervousness was growing. It was only six kilometres from Raucourt to Remilly, hardly more than one hour's walking for a strapping young woman like Silvine. Why wasn't she back, for it was hours since the old man had lost her in the confusion of a whole army corps all over the place, blocking all the roads? He felt certain that some catastrophe had happened, and he visualized her caught in some horrible adventure, running panic-stricken across the fields, trampled on by horses.

Suddenly all three jumped to their feet. A sound of running feet was coming down the road, and they heard the old man loading his gun.

'Who's that?' he shouted arrogantly. 'Is it you, Silvine?'

No answer. He threatened to fire and repeated his question. Then a breathless, scared voice managed to say:

'Yes, yes, it's me, Monsieur Fouchard.'

Then she asked at once:

'What about Charlot?'

'In bed and asleep.'

'Oh good, thank you.'

Then she gave up hurrying and fetched a deep sigh, breathing out all her anxiety and fatigue.

'Go in through the window,' Fouchard went on. 'I've got company.'

She jumped in through the window, but stood dumbfounded when she saw the three men. In the flickering light of the candle she could be seen: very dark with thick black hair, fine large eyes which in themselves made her beautiful, set in an oval face denoting calm and steady resignation. But then the sudden sight of Honoré brought all the blood up from her heart to her cheeks; and yet she was not surprised to find him there, indeed she had been thinking of him while she was running all the way from Raucourt.

His voice failed him and he almost reeled, but put on an appearance of the utmost calm:

'Good evening, Silvine.'

'Good evening, Honoré.'

But then she turned away so as not to burst into tears. She smiled at Maurice, whom she recognized. Jean embarrassed her. As she felt stifled she took off the scarf she had round her neck.

Honoré went on, avoiding the affectionate terms of long ago:

'We were worried about you, Silvine, because of all the Prussians coming.'

She suddenly went pale and her face fell, and glancing involuntarily towards the room where Charlot was asleep she gestured with her hand as though she were fending off some abominable vision, and murmured:

'The Prussians, oh yes, yes, I saw them!'

She sank on to a chair, exhausted and then told them her story;

that when the 7th corps had overrun Raucourt she had fled to the house of her godfather, Dr Dalichamp, hoping that old Fouchard would think of going there for her before he went home. The main street was jammed with such a crush of people that even a dog would not have ventured along it. She had waited patiently until about four, not too worried, making bandages with some ladies for the doctor who, thinking that they might perhaps send some wounded from Metz and Verdun if there was any fighting round there, had been busy for a fortnight fixing up a casualty station in the big room at the town hall. Some people had come and said that the station might be needed at once, and in fact by noon they had heard gunfire in the direction of Beaumont. But that was still a long way off and nobody was worried; and then all of a sudden, just as the last French soldiers were leaving Raucourt, a shell came down with a terrific noise and smashed in the roof of a house quite near. Two more followed; it was a German battery shelling the rearguard of the 7th. There were already some wounded from Beaumont at the town hall and it was feared that a shell might finish them off as they lay on straw mattresses waiting for the doctor to deal with them. Mad with terror, the wounded men got up and tried to go down into the cellars in spite of their smashed limbs which were making them scream with pain.

'And then,' she went on, 'I don't know how it happened, but there was a sudden silence ... I had gone upstairs to a window looking on to the road and the open country. I couldn't see a soul, not one red-trouser, and then I heard loud, heavy steps, and a voice shouted something and all the rifle-butts hit the ground together. There, at the end of the street, were a lot of little, dark, dirty-looking men with big ugly heads surmounted by helmets like the ones our firemen wear ... I was told they were Bavarians. Then as I looked up I saw, oh, thousands and thousands of them coming along all the roads, over the fields, through the woods, in close-packed ranks, endlessly. A black invasion, like black grasshoppers, on and on, so that in no time you couldn't see the ground for them.'

She shuddered and again made the gesture of driving the horrible memory away.

'And then you've no idea what went on ... It seems these men had been on the march for three days and had just been fighting like maniacs at Beaumont. So they were starving and half crazy, with their eyes popping out of their heads. The officers didn't even attempt to hold them in check and they all broke into houses and shops, smashing in doors and windows, breaking furniture, looking for something to eat and drink, swallowing anything that came to hand ... I saw one of them in Simmonot's, the grocer's, ladling treacle out of a tub with his helmet. Others were gnawing at pieces of raw bacon. Others chewed flour. It had already been said that there was nothing left as our soldiers had been passing through for forty-eight hours, and yet they could still find things – hidden stores no doubt – and so went on deliberately destroying everything, thinking they were being refused food. In less than an hour grocers, bakers, butchers and even private houses had their windows smashed, cupboards rifled, cellars broken into and emptied. At the doctor's – you just can't imagine it – I found one great lout eating all the soap. But it was in the cellar that the real pillage went on. From upstairs you could hear them down there howling like wild beasts, breaking bottles, opening the taps of casks, and the wine gushed out with a noise like a fountain. They came up with their hands red after paddling about in all that spilt wine ... And this is the sort of thing that happens when men go back to savagery: Monsieur Dalichamp tried in vain to prevent a soldier from drinking off a litre of laudanum he had discovered. That poor devil must be dead by now, he was in such agonies when I left.'

She began shaking violently, and covered her eyes with both hands so as not see any more.

'No, no, I've seen too much, I can't say another word!'

Old Fouchard, who had stayed out in the road, had come and stood by the window to listen, and this tale gave him food for thought; he had been told that the Prussians paid for everything, were they going to start thieving now? Maurice and Jean were also listening intently to all these details about the enemy that this girl had just seen, and whom they had never succeeded in setting eyes on in a whole month of war. But Honoré, lost in thought and betraying his emotions by the expression of his mouth, was only interested in her, and thinking of nothing but the old trouble that had separated them.

Just then the door of the next room opened and the child Charlot appeared. He must have heard his mother's voice, and he ran over in his nightshirt to kiss her. Pink, fair and very chubby, he had a mop of light curly hair and big blue eyes.

Silvine was startled at seeing him so suddenly, as if taken off her guard by the picture he conjured up. Was it that she did not recognize him, this beloved child of hers, that she should now look at him in terror as though he were a nightmare come to life? She burst into tears.

'My poor darling!'

She crushed him wildly in her arms and held him to her, while Honoré, deathly pale, saw the extraordinary likeness between Charlot and Goliath, the same square, blond head, the whole Germanic race in a lovely, healthy child, fresh and smiling. The son of the Prussian, or 'that Prussian', as all the jokers in Remilly called him! And here was this French mother holding him to her heart while she was still overwhelmed and haunted by the sight of the invaders!

'Now, my poor lamb, be a good boy and come back to bed ... Come along to bye-byes, sweetie.'

She carried him off. When she came back from the next room she had stopped crying and recovered her calm face, with its expression of placidity and courage.

It was Honoré who started the conversation again, in a hesitant voice:

'And what about the Prussians?'

'Oh yes, the Prussians ... Well, they had broken up every-thing, and pillaged, eaten and drunk everything. They stole the linen too, towels, sheets and even curtains, which they tore into long strips to bandage their feet with. I saw some whose feet were just one raw mass, they had marched so far. In front of the doctor's house I saw a lot of them sitting down in the gutter with their boots off and winding round their feet women's chemises trimmed with lace, no doubt stolen from Madame Lefèvre, the wife of the manufacturer ... The looting went on until the evening. Houses had no doors left, and through all the openings on the ground floor gaping on to the road you could see the remains of the furniture inside, an absolute shambles that infuriated ordinary sensible people. I was so beside myself that I couldn't stay there any longer. They tried to keep me, saying the roads were blocked, that I would get killed for certain, but it was no use, and I left, and took to the fields on the right as soon as I got out of Raucourt. Cartloads of French and Prussians were coming in from Beaumont. Two of them passed quite close to me in the darkness and there were shouts and moans, and oh, I ran and ran over fields and through woods, I don't remember where, but I did a big detour round Villers ... Three times I hid when I thought I could hear soldiers. But I only met one woman who was running too. She was getting away from Beaumont, and she told me things that would make your hair stand on end ... Anyway, here I am and feeling miserable, just miserable!'

Once again she was choked with sobs. Some obsession kept bringing her back to these things, and she repeated what the woman from Beaumont had told her. This woman, who lived in the main street of the village, had seen the German artillery going through since nightfall. Along both sides was a hedge of soldiers holding resin torches, lighting the roadway fiery red. And in the middle the stream of horses, cannon and ammunition waggons tore through at a furious gallop. It was a hell-for-leather ride to victory, a devilish hunt for French troops to finish off and do to death in some black hole. Nothing was respected, they smashed everything and simply went on. Horses that stumbled had their harness cut off at once and were rolled over, trampled on and thrown out as bits of bleeding wreckage. Some men trying to cross the road were similarly knocked down and cut to pieces by the wheels. In this hurricane the drivers, who were dying of hunger, did not stop but caught loaves of bread thrown to them while the torch-bearers held out joints of meat for them on the points of their bayonets. Then with the same points they gave the horses a dig so they reared up in terror and galloped faster still. The night went on and on and still the artillery passed through with the increasing violence of a tempest, amid frantic cheering.

In spite of listening attentively to this story Maurice, overcome with fatigue after the voracious eating, had dropped his head between his arms on the table. Jean struggled on a little longer and then he too gave in and went off to sleep at the other end. Old Fouchard had gone down the road again, and so Honoré found himself alone with Silvine who was sitting quite still now, facing the wide open window.

Then he stood up and went over to the window. The night was still immense and black, swollen as it were with the laboured

breathing of the troops. But louder noises, knockings and crackings, were coming up now because the artillery was crossing down
there over the half-submerged bridge. Horses were rearing, scared
by the running water. Ammunition waggons slipped over to one
side and had to be pushed completely into the river. As he saw this
painful, slow retreat to the opposite bank which had been going on
since the day before and would certainly not be completed by dawn,
the young man thought of the other artillery tearing through
Beaumont like a rushing torrent, overwhelming everything, pounding man and beast so as to go faster.

Honoré went up to Silvine and said softly, in the frightening
darkness:

'Are you unhappy?'

'Oh yes, I am unhappy.'

She sensed that he was going to refer to the thing, the abominable thing, and lowered her eyes.

'Tell me, how did it happen? I'd like to know.'

She could not answer.

'Did he force you? . . . Did you consent?'

She stammered out almost inaudibly:

'Oh God, I don't know, I swear I don't even know myself . . .
But you see, it would be wrong to tell a lie, and I can't find excuses!
No, I can't say he used force . . . You had gone, I was out of my
mind, and the thing happened, I don't know, I don't know how!'

She could not go on for crying, and he, deathly pale and on the
point of tears too, waited a minute. And yet the thought that she
could not lie to him gave him some comfort. Then he went on
questioning her, for his mind was tormented by all sorts of things
he could not yet understand.

'So Father has kept you on here?'

She did not even look up, but became quieter and resumed her
air of brave resignation.

'I do my job. I have never cost much for my keep, and as there is
an extra mouth besides me he has taken advantage of it to cut my
wages . . . Now it is clear that whatever he orders I've got to do.'

'But what about yourself? Why have you stayed?'

That surprised her so much that she looked him in the eyes.

'But where do you expect me to go? At any rate my little boy
and I can eat here and we are left alone.'

They fell silent again but now each was looking into the other's eyes, while in the distance down in the dark valley the noises of the crowd swelled up as the rumbling of the guns over the pontoon bridge went on and on. The darkness was rent by a loud cry, some cry of a man or beast, and infinitely sad.

'Listen, Silvine,' he went on slowly, 'you sent me a letter which gave me great joy ... I wouldn't ever have come back here. But that letter, I've read it again this evening, and it says things that couldn't be said better.'

At first she went white when she heard him refer to that. Perhaps he was vexed that she had dared to write, like some brazen hussy. But then as he went on explaining she blushed very red.

'I know that you don't believe in lying, and that's why I believe what is on the paper. . . . Yes, now I quite believe it ... You were right to think that if I had died in the war without seeing you again it would have been a great sorrow to me to pass away like that thinking you didn't love me ... And so, as you do still love me, as you have never loved anyone else ...'

He got tongue-tied and could not find the right words, trembling with overwhelming emotion.

'Listen, Silvine my dearest, if those Prussian swine don't kill me, I still want you – yes, we'll get married as soon as I'm back home.'

She jumped up, and with a cry fell into the young man's arms. She could not speak, and all the blood in her veins seemed to be in her face. He sat down on the chair and took her on his knee.

'I've thought it over a lot, and that was what I had to come here and tell you ... If Father won't consent, well, we'll go away, the world is a big place ... And your child, well, we can't do him in, can we? There'll be lots more as well, and I shall end up by not being able to pick him out of the crowd.'

It was forgiveness. She still fought against this immense happiness and murmured at long last:

'No, it isn't possible, it's too much. You might live to regret it some day ... But how good you are, Honoré! And how I love you!'

He silenced her with a kiss. Already she had given up trying, unable to reject the happiness coming to her, the whole blissful life she thought had gone for ever. With an instinctive, irresistible urge she threw both her arms round him and clasped him to her, kissing him in her turn with all the strength a woman can find, like a lost treasure regained and hers alone, that nobody would take away from her any more. He was hers again, this man she had lost, and she would die rather than let him be taken from her yet again.

But at that moment there rose from below a noise like a great reveille, peopling the thick darkness. Orders were shouted, bugles sounded and a host of shadows were rising out of the bare ground, an indistinct, moving sea already flooding down towards the road. Below, the fires on each bank were nearly out, and all that could be seen was vague, trampling masses, neither was it clear whether they were still crossing the river. Never before had such anguish, dismay and terror stalked through the shadows.

Old Fouchard had come back to the window shouting that they were off. Jean and Maurice woke up, shivering and aching, and jumped to their feet. Honoré quickly squeezed Silvine's hand in his.

'We've sworn . . . wait for me.'

She could find nothing to say, but put her whole soul into a last long look as he leaped out of the window, racing off to rejoin his battery.

'Good-bye, Father.'

'Good-bye, my lad.'

That was all, peasant and soldier parted again as they had met, with no embrace, a father and son who could get along quite well without having to see each other.

When they too had left the farmhouse, Maurice and Jean galloped down the steep slopes. At the bottom they found no sign of the 106th; all the regiments were already on the move, and they had to keep running and were redirected right and left. But in the end, when they were frantic in the dreadful confusion, they fell in with their company, led by Lieutenant Rochas. As for Captain Beaudoin and the regiment itself, they were somewhere or other, no doubt. And then Maurice was astounded to see that this multitude of men, horses and guns was leaving Remilly and making for Sedan along the road on the left bank. What on earth was going on? So they had given up crossing the Meuse and were retreating northwards!

A cavalry officer standing there, heaven knows why, said quite audibly:

'Good God, we should have cleared out on the 28th, when we were at Le Chêne!'

Other voices were explaining the manoeuvre, and news began coming in. At about two in the morning an aide-de-camp from Marshal MacMahon had come and informed General Douay that the whole army had orders to fall back on Sedan without losing a minute. Routed at Beaumont, the 5th corps was sweeping away the three others in its own disaster. At that moment the general, who was keeping watch by the pontoon bridge, was horrified to see that his third division had crossed the river alone. It would soon be light and they might be attacked at any minute. So he sent word to all officers under his command to make for Sedan each one as best he could by the most direct route. And he himself, abandoning the pontoon bridge which he ordered to be destroyed, hurried off along the left bank with his second division and reserve artillery, while the third followed the right bank, and the first, thrown into disarray at Beaumont, was fleeing in disorder nobody knew where. Of the 7th corps, which had still not seen any fighting, there were only odd sections left, lost on the roads, galloping in the darkness.

It was not yet three, and the night was still dark. Although he knew the district, Maurice had no idea where he was going, and could not recover his wits in the rushing torrent of this crazy mob filling the road. Quite a few men who had escaped from the disaster at Beaumont, soldiers of all arms, in rags, covered with dust and blood, were mingling with the regiments and spreading despondency. The same murmuring sound arose from the whole valley, beyond the river as well, other trampling herds, other fugitives, the 1st corps which had just left Carignan and Douzy, the 12th corps from Mouzon with the remnants of the 5th, all unnerved, carried away by the same logical, invincible force which ever since the 28th had been thrusting the army northwards and ramming it into the impasse where it was to perish.

However, a grey dawn came as the Beaudoin company was going through Pont-Maugis, and Maurice saw where he was, with the hills of Liry on the left and the Meuse along the right of the road. This grey dawn revealed Bazeilles and Balan looking utterly dreary in the mists over the fields, while a livid, nightmarish, tragic Sedan could be made out on the horizon against the immense dark curtain of forest. And after Wadelincourt, when they at last reached the

Torcy gate, there had to be a parley, with begging and threats, almost a regular siege, to make the governor lower the drawbridge. It was five o'clock. The 7th corps entered Sedan, knocked out with fatigue, hunger and cold.

8

In the crush in the Place de Torcy at the end of the Wadelincourt road, Jean became separated from Maurice, and he ran madly about in the milling throng but could not find him. This was a real blow because he had accepted the young man's offer to take him to his sister's, where they could have a rest and even sleep in a proper bed. There was such confusion, with all the regiments mixed up and no route orders or officers left, that the men were more or less free to do what they liked. There would still be time to sort yourself out and find your own lot again when you had had a few hours' sleep.

Really alarmed, Jean found himself on the Torcy viaduct above the broad meadows that the governor had had flooded with water from the river. Then, having gone through another gate, he crossed the Meuse bridge and it seemed to him, in spite of the growing daylight, that it was getting dark again in this constricted town, hemmed in between its ramparts, with dank streets between tall buildings. He couldn't even remember the name of Maurice's brother-in-law. Where should he go? Whom could he ask? His feet were only carrying him on now because of the automatic movement of walking, and he felt he would fall down if he stopped. Like a drowning man, all he could hear was a dull roaring in his ears, and all he could see was the continual flow of the tide of men and animals carrying him forward. As he had had something to eat at Remilly his main trouble was lack of sleep, and all round him fatigue was more powerful than hunger, and the herd of shadows was staggering along the unknown streets. At every step a man collapsed on the pavement, fell into a doorway and stayed there as if dead, fast asleep.

Looking up, Jean read a name-plate: Avenue de la Sous-Préfecture. At the far end there was a monument in a garden. And at the corner of the avenue he saw a cavalryman, a Chasseur d'Afrique, whom he thought he knew. Wasn't it Prosper, the chap from Remilly he had seen at Vouziers with Maurice? The man had dismounted, and the horse, sick-looking and unsteady on his legs, was suffering so much from hunger as to be on the point of stretching his neck to eat the planks of the baggage-wagon drawn up at the kerb. The horses had had no rations for two days and were dying of exhaustion. His big teeth were grating like a file on the wood and the man was in tears.

Jean went on, but turned back thinking this man might know the address of Maurice's relatives, but he had gone. Then he was in despair, and wandered from street to street, found himself at the Sub-Prefecture, pushed on as far as the Place Turenne. There he thought for one moment he was saved when he saw Lieutenant Rochas and a few men of the company in front of the Hôtel de Ville at the foot of the statue of Turenne. If he couldn't rejoin his friend he would link up with the regiment again and at any rate sleep in a tent. Captain Beaudoin not having reappeared – he had been carried along and landed somewhere else – the lieutenant was trying to collect his men together, asking for information and trying in vain to find out where their camp was. But as they advanced into the town the company, far from growing, was fading away. One soldier gesturing wildly, went into a pub and never reappeared. Three others stopped at the door of a grocer's, their interest held by some Zouaves who had banged a hole in a little cask of spirits. Quite a few were already stretched out across the gutter, others set off to go somewhere, but fell down again, overcome with fatigue and quite dazed. Chouteau and Loubet, nudging each other, disappeared down a dark alley behind a fat woman carrying a loaf of bread. By then only Pache and Lapoulle, with a handful of others, were left with the lieutenant.

At the foot of the bronze statue of Turenne Rochas was making a great effort to stay on his feet with his eyes open. When he saw Jean he muttered:

'Oh, it's you, corporal. What about your men?'

Jean waved a vague arm to indicate that he didn't know. But Pache, pointing at Lapoulle, answered, melting into tears:

'Here we are, only two of us left . . . Oh God have mercy on us, it's too awful!'

The other one, the big eater, looked voraciously at Jean's hands, outraged to see them empty at this juncture. Perhaps in his sleep-walking state he had dreamed that the corporal had gone for the issue of rations.

'Bloody hell!' he growled. 'Got to squeeze me belly in again!'

Gaude the bugler, leaning against the railings while waiting for the order to blow fall-in, had slipped straight down and gone to sleep flat on his back. One by one they all gave in to sleep and were snoring away dead to the world. Only Sergeant Sapin was still standing, with his eyes wide open and his nose screwed up in his little pale face as though he were reading his own doom on the horizon of this unknown town.

By now Lieutenant Rochas had given in to the irresistible urge to sit down on the ground. He tried to give an order.

'Corporal, we must ... we must ...'

He couldn't find his words, for his mouth was clogged by fatigue, and suddenly he went over as well, knocked out by sleep.

Afraid of falling on the pavement too, Jean moved off. He was determined to find a bed. From the other side of the square, through a window of the Hôtel de la Croix d'Or, he had perceived General Bourgain-Desfeuilles already in his shirtsleeves and preparing to slip between some fine white sheets. What was the point of being conscientious and putting up with any more? He had a sudden burst of joy when a name sprang up in his memory, the name of the cloth manufacturer who was the employer of Maurice's brother-in-law: Monsieur Delaherche. Yes, that was it! He stopped an old man who was passing.

'Monsieur Delaherche's?'

'Rue Maqua, almost at the corner of the rue au Beurre, a nice big house with carvings on it.'

Then the old man ran after him.

'I say, you belong to the 106th, don't you? If you are looking for your regiment, it went off again down by the castle. I've just run into the colonel, Monsieur de Vineuil, whom I knew when he was at Mézières.'

But Jean was off with a gesture of wild impatience. Oh no, now he was sure of finding Maurice he wasn't going to sleep on the hard ground. But there was a slight feeling of guilt nagging inside him as he conjured up a vision of the colonel with his tall figure, a man so resistant to fatigue in spite of his age, sleeping like his men under canvas. But then he entered the Grande-Rue and finally asked a little boy who took him to the rue Maqua.

It was there that a great-uncle of the present Delaherche had built in the last century the huge factory which had not gone out of the family for a hundred and sixty years. There are textile mills like this in Sedan dating from the early years of Louis XV, mills as big as the Louvre, with regal, majestic façades. The one in the rue Maqua had three floors with lofty windows framed with classical carvings, and inside there was a palatial courtyard still planted with the original elms dating from the founding of the business, gigantic trees. Three generations of Delaherches had made sizeable fortunes there. The father of Jules, the present proprietor, had inherited the mill from a cousin who had died childless, and so it was a younger branch of the family that was now in charge. Jules's father had increased the prosperity of the firm, but he was a gay fellow and had made his wife unhappy. So she, when she was widowed, trembling lest her boy should start on the same fun and games, had tried to keep him completely dependent, like a grown-up good boy, until he was past fifty, having married him off to a simple and pious woman. The terrible thing is that life takes its revenges. His wife died, and Delaherche, never having been allowed any youth, fell head over heels in love with a young widow of Charleville, the pretty Madame Maginot, about whom various tales were whispered, and in spite of his mother's remonstrances he had married her the previous autumn. Sedan, a very puritanical town, has always been severe on Charleville, a city of gaiety and fun. Not that the marriage would ever have been concluded had not one of Gilberte's uncles been Colonel de Vineuil, who was by way of being promoted to general. This connexion and the thought that he had become a member of a military family, were very gratifying to the cloth manufacturer.

The day before, in the morning, Delaherche, learning that the army was to pass through Mouzon, had been out with Weiss, his book-keeper, for the drive that old Fouchard had mentioned to Maurice. Tall and heavily built, with a high colour, strong nose and thick lips, he was an outgoing kind of man with the middle-class Frenchman's enjoyment and interest in watching fine parades of troops. Having been told by the chemist at Mouzon that the Emperor was at Baybel farmhouse, he had gone up as far as there, had seen him, and even almost spoken to him – quite a thrilling adventure that he had never stopped narrating since his return. But what a terrible return it was, through the panic at Beaumont and on the roads blocked with fugitives! A score of times the carriage had nearly capsized in ditches, and it was dark before the two men had made their way back through ever recurring obstacles. This pleasure jaunt, the army that Delaherche had travelled two leagues to see go by and which carried him brutally back in the stampede of its retreat, this whole unforeseen and tragic tale had made him say ten times over on the way back:

'And to think that I thought it was marching to Verdun and didn't want to miss the chance of seeing it! Well, I've seen it now, and I think we're going to see it at Sedan, and more of it than we want!'

That morning he was awakened at five by the 7th corps going through the town with the loud noise of open sluice-gates. He had dressed with all speed, and the first person he saw in the Place Turenne proved to be Captain Beaudoin. The year before, in Charleville, the captain had been one of pretty Madame Maginot's group of intimates, and Gilberte had introduced him before their marriage. A story had formerly gone the whispered rounds that the captain, having no favour left to desire, had withdrawn with tactful delicacy in favour of the cloth manufacturer, not wanting to stand between his mistress and the very great fortune which was coming her way.

'What, you!' exclaimed Delaherche. 'Good Lord, what a state you're in!'

Beaudoin, normally so correct and well groomed, was in fact in a lamentable condition, with dirty uniform and black hands and face. He was exasperated at having fallen in with some Turcos and couldn't understand how he had lost his own company. Like everybody else, he was dropping with hunger and fatigue, but that was not what caused his most acute misery; what put him out most of all was not having changed his shirt since Rheims.

'Just think of it!' he at once began moaning. 'They lost my luggage at Vouziers. Fools and rogues, I'd break their necks if I got hold of them! ... Nothing left, not even a handkerchief or a pair of socks! It's enough to drive you mad, it really is!'

Delaherche at once insisted on taking him to his own home, but he demurred: oh no, he didn't even look human, he didn't want to give everybody a fright. Delaherche had to swear that neither his wife nor his mother would be up yet. And besides, he would give him soap and water, clean underclothes, in fact anything he needed.

It was striking seven when Captain Beaudoin, all washed and brushed up, wearing one of the husband's shirts under his uniform, appeared in the grey-panelled dining-room with its lofty ceiling. Madame Delaherche senior was there already, for she always rose at dawn in spite of her seventy-eight years. She was quite white, and her nose had got even more pointed and her mouth never laughed now in her long, thin face. She rose to her feet and was exceedingly polite, inviting the captain to sit down in front of one of the cups of coffee and milk already poured out.

'But perhaps, sir, you would rather have some meat and wine after such a tiring time?'

He protested.

'No, thank you very much indeed, Madame, just some milk and bread and butter, that would suit me best.'

At that moment a door was gaily thrown open and Gilberte came in with outstretched hand. Delaherche must have warned her, for as a rule she never got up before ten. She was tall, looked lithe but well built, with beautiful black hair and lovely dark eyes, and yet a very fair skin, a laughing face, a bit harum-scarum and without a trace of malice. Her beige dressing-gown with red silk embroidery had come from Paris.

'Oh, captain,' she gushed, as she shook the young man's hand, 'how kind of you to have come to see us in our dead-and-alive part of the world!'

But she was the first to laugh at her own scatterbrained talk.

'Oh aren't I silly? You could certainly do without being in Sedan in these circumstances. But I'm so glad to see you again!'

Her fine eyes shone with delight. Madame Delaherche, who must have been aware of the tittle-tattle of the Charleville gossips, sat bolt upright, watching them both closely. The captain, on his side, was being very discreet, behaving like a man who had simply kept happy memories of a hospitable home where he had been made welcome.

They had breakfast, and at once Delaherche came back to his

excursion of the day before, unable to resist the itch to tell the story once again.

'Do you know, I saw the Emperor at Baybel.'

He was off, and nothing could stop him after that. First there was a description of the farmhouse, a large, square building with an inner courtyard, shut off by railings, and standing on a little hill overlooking Mouzon to the left of the Carignan road. Then he came back to the 12th corps that he had gone right through as they were camping among the vines on the slopes – superb troops, gleaming in the sunshine, the sight of whom had filled him with great patriotic joy.

'And there I was, sir, when the Emperor suddenly came out of the farmhouse where he had gone for a break to rest and eat. He was wearing a cloak thrown over his general's uniform, although the sun was very hot. Behind him a manservant was carrying a folding seat. I didn't think he looked at all well, oh no! stooping and walking with difficulty, his face yellow, in fact a sick man ... And that didn't surprise me because the chemist at Mouzon who had advised me to go on as far as Baybel had just told me that an aide-de-camp had been to him for medicine ... yes, you know, remedies for ...'

The presence of his mother and his wife prevented him from describing more clearly the diarrhoea from which the Emperor had been suffering since Le Chêne, and which had compelled him to stop like this at farmhouses along the route.

'So, in a word, the servant set up the folding seat on the edge of a cornfield, at the point of a wood, and the Emperor sat down ... He stayed there motionless, all huddled up, looking like some old pensioner warming his aches and pains in the sun. He scanned with his dull eyes the vast horizon, the Meuse below him flowing along the valley and opposite him the wooded slopes with summits going away into the distance, the peaks of the Dieulet woods on the left, the green hilltops of Sommauthe on the right ... He was surrounded by aides-de-camp and high ranking officers, and a colonel of dragoons who had already asked me for directions had just signed to me not to go away, when suddenly ...'

Delaherche rose to his feet for he was approaching the gripping climax of the narrative, and he wanted to add action to the words.

'Suddenly there are shattering explosions, and lo and behold, right opposite, this side of Dieulet woods, shells describe parabolas in the sky ... Upon my soul, it looked to me like a firework display let off in broad daylight ... Naturally in the Emperor's entourage there are exclamations, expressions of anxiety. My colonel of dragoons rushes back and asks me if I can say exactly where the fighting is. Without any hesitation I say: 'At Beaumont, no doubt whatever.' He returns to the Emperor, across whose knees an aide-de-camp was unfolding a map. The Emperor refused to believe they could be fighting at Beaumont. Well, I couldn't insist, could I? Especially as the shells were careering through the sky and falling nearer, following the Mouzon road ... It was then, just as I am looking at you now, sir, that I saw the Emperor turn his ashen face in my direction. Yes, he looked at me for a moment with his lacklustre eyes, full of mistrust and sadness. Then his head was bowed again over the map and he did not move again.'

Delaherche had been an ardent Bonapartist at the time of the plebiscite, but since the first reverses he admitted that the Empire had made some mistakes. However, he still defended the dynasty and pitied Napoleon III, who was being deceived by everybody. So according to him the people really responsible for our disasters were none other than the republican deputies in the opposition who had prevented the voting of the necessary numbers of men and financial credits.

'And did the Emperor go back to the farmhouse?' asked Captain Beaudoin.

'Well, sir, I really don't know, I left him on his campstool. It was midday, the battle was getting closer and I was beginning to be concerned about getting home ... All I can add is that a general, to whom I pointed out Carignan in the distance on the plain behind us, seemed amazed to learn that the Belgian frontier was there, a few kilometres away. Oh poor Emperor, he has some wonderful servants!'

Gilberte, smiling and quite at her ease, as of old in her widowhood when she entertained in her drawing-room, concerned herself with the captain, passing him toast and butter. She tried to insist on his accepting a room or a bed, but he declined, and it was settled that he would only lie down for a couple of hours on a settee in Delaherche's study before rejoining his regiment. As he was taking the sugar-basin from the young woman, old Madame Delaherche, who kept her eyes glued on them, clearly saw them link fingers; so now she knew.

A maid had just come in.

'Sir, there's a soldier downstairs asking for Monsieur Weiss's address.'

Delaherche was not proud, as they say, and enjoyed talking to the lowly of this world, out of a love of chattering and popularity.

'Weiss's address, well, that's funny! . . . Bring the soldier in.'

Jean came in, so exhausted that he was reeling. Seeing his captain sitting at table with some ladies, he started slightly in surprise and drew back the hand he was automatically putting out to support himself against a chair. Then he briefly answered the questions of the manufacturer, who was playing up the common touch, the soldier's friend. In a few words he explained his friendship with Maurice and why he was looking for him.

'He is a corporal in my company,' the captain said at last, to cut things short.

He interrogated Jean in his turn, for he was anxious to know what had happened to the regiment. And as Jean said that the colonel had recently been seen going through the town at the head of his remaining men, on the way to camp to the north, Gilberte once again spoke too quickly with the usual impulsiveness of a pretty young woman not given to much thought.

'Oh why didn't my uncle come and have breakfast here? . . . We could have had a room ready for him . . . Suppose we send somebody to look for him?'

But old Madame Delaherche made a gesture of sovereign authority. In her veins flowed the ancient bourgeois blood of the frontier towns, with all the manly virtues of unbending patriotism. She only broke her severe silence to say:

'Never mind Monsieur de Vineuil, he is doing his duty.'

That caused some embarrassment. Delaherche took the captain off to his study and wanted to see for himself that he rested on the settee, and Gilberte, in spite of the reprimand, fluttered off like a bird flapping its wings, blithe and gay just the same in the storm, while the maid who had been put in charge of Jean took him through the yards of the factory and into a maze of passages and stairs.

The Weisses lived in the rue des Voyards, but the house, which belonged to Delaherche, communicated with the huge main building in the rue Maqua. This rue des Voyards was at that time one of the strangest in Sedan, a narrow lane, damp and darkened by the rampart with which it ran parallel. The roofs of the lofty house-fronts almost touched each other and the dark entries were like mouths of caves, especially at the end where the high wall of the school towered. But Weiss, who occupied the whole of the third floor rent free, including heating, was well off, living right by his office to which he could go down in his slippers all under cover. He was a contented man since he had married Henriette, whom he had waited for so long, ever since he had first known her at Le Chêne in the house of her father the tax-collector. She had been a housewife from the age of six, taking her dead mother's place, while he, having got a job in the General Refinery as a practically unskilled labourer, had educated himself and worked his way up to the position of ledger clerk by hard study. And even then, before he made his dream come true, he had had to wait for the death of the father, and then there had been the terrible follies of the brother in Paris, this Maurice, whose twin sister was a sort of servant to him, and had sacrificed her whole life to make him a gentleman. Brought up as a Cinderella at home, having learned little more than how to read and write, she had sold the house and furniture and still not filled the hole made by the young man's extravagances when the kindly Weiss had hastened to offer all he possessed, with his strong arms and his heart. Touched to tears by his affection, and being very sensible, after careful thought she had agreed to marry him, for she was full of tender esteem if not of passionate love. Now fortune was smiling on them, Delaherche had talked of making Weiss a partner in the business. It would be perfect happiness when children came.

'Mind how you go!' said the maid, 'the stairs are very steep.'

And indeed he was stumbling about in pitch darkness when a door was quickly opened and the stairs were flooded with light. He heard a gentle voice saying:

'Here he is.'

'Madame Weiss,' said the maid, 'here's a soldier who is asking for you.'

There was a happy little laugh and the gentle voice answered:

'Good, good, I know who he is.'

As the corporal, tongue-tied and awkward, was hesitating at the door:

'Come in, Monsieur Jean ... Maurice has been here for two hours and we've been expecting you so impatiently!'

Then in the subdued light of the room he saw her, strikingly like Maurice, with that extraordinary likeness of twins which is a sort of duplication of faces. But she was shorter and even slighter, more frail-looking, with a largish mouth, small features and a lovely head of fair hair, the light gold of ripe oats. The main thing that made her different from him was her grey eyes, calm, brave eyes in which there lived on all the heroic soul of their grandfather, the hero of the Grande Armée. She was not a great talker and moved noiselessly, and her movements were so neat, and her gentleness so radiant that as she passed by you felt her like a caress in the air.

'Come this way, Monsieur Jean,' she said again. 'Everything will be ready in a moment.'

He made vague sounds and could not even find words to thank her in his emotion at being welcomed just like a brother. In any case his eyes were closing of their own accord and he could only see her through the invincible sleepiness which was overtaking him like a sort of mist through which she floated like a wraith not touching the ground. Was she only a beguiling vision, this woman who was offering help and smiling at him with such simplicity? He thought she was taking his hand and that he felt hers, small, strong and as reliable as an old friend's.

From that moment onwards Jean lost any clear consciousness of events. They were in the dining-room, there was bread and meat on the table, but he couldn't even have found the strength to carry the pieces to his mouth. There was a man sitting on a chair. Then he realized it was Weiss, whom he had seen at Mulhouse. But he could not take in what the man was saying in such a worried voice and with slow, weary gestures. On a camp-bed set up in front of the stove Maurice was already fast asleep, his face motionless, looking like a corpse. Henriette was busying herself round a divan, on which she had put a mattress, and was now bringing a bolster, pillow and blankets, and then with quick skilful hands white sheets, lovely white sheets, white as snow.

Oh, those white sheets, sheets so desperately longed for! They were all Jean could see. He had not taken off his clothes properly or slept in a bed for six weeks. It felt like the impatient greed of a child, an irresistible passion to slip into this cool whiteness and lose himself. As soon as they left him alone he stripped down to his shirt and had his feet bare, and went to bed and satisfied this hunger with the grunt of a contented animal. The pale morning light came in through the high window, and as he was sinking into sleep he half opened his eyes and had one more vision of Henriette, an even more vague and disembodied Henriette tiptoeing back to put on a table at his side a carafe and glass she had forgotten. She seemed to pause there a few seconds looking at them both, her brother and him, with her gentle smile, infinitely kind. Then she faded away. And he slept between the white sheets dead to everything.

Hours, years went by. Jean and Maurice no longer existed, dreamless, not even conscious of the faint pulse in their veins. Ten years or ten minutes, time no longer counted; it was like the revenge of their overwrought bodies, satisfying themselves in the death of their whole being. Suddenly, jerked back by the same shock, they both woke up. What was the matter? What was going on? How long had they been asleep? The same pale light was falling from the high window. They felt knocked out, with stiff joints, and their limbs felt more tired and their mouths more dry than when they had gone to bed. Fortunately they couldn't have slept for more than an hour. So they were not surprised to see Weiss on the same chair, apparently waiting for them to wake up, and still in the same attitude of dejection.

'Oh Lord,' muttered Jean, 'we must get up and get back to the regiment by noon.'

He jumped to the floor with a little exclamation of pain and pulled on his clothes.

'By noon!' Weiss repeated. 'Do you realize it's seven in the evening, and you've been sleeping for about twelve hours?'

Seven o'clock, good God! This was terrifying. Jean, already fully dressed, was for running. But Maurice, still in bed, was moaning that he had lost the use of his legs. How were they to get back to their mates? Hadn't the army moved on? They both began to get angry, they shouldn't have been allowed to sleep on so long. But Weiss made a gesture of despair.

'Good Lord, considering all they've done you've been wise to stay in bed.'

He had been wandering round Sedan and its outskirts all day. He had only just come in, disgusted at the inaction of the troops this whole day, the 31st, so valuable and lost in some inexplicable delay. There was only one possible excuse, the extreme fatigue of the men, and even then he didn't see why the retreat had not continued after the few essential hours of rest.

'Of course,' he went on, 'I don't presume to understand, but I have the feeling, yes, I feel that the army is very badly placed in Sedan ... The 12th corps is at Bazeilles, where there was a little fighting this morning; the 1st is strung out all along the Givonne from the village of La Moncelle to the Garenne woods; while the 7th is camping on the plateau of Floing and the 5th, already half destroyed, is huddled right under the ramparts of the castle ... And that's what frightens me, knowing that they are all standing round the town like that, just waiting for the Prussians. If it had been me, I'd have got away at once towards Mézières. I know the country, and there's no other line of retreat, or else we shall be pitched back into Belgium ... And then besides, come and see something ...'

He took Jean's hand and led him to the window.

'Look over there, on the crest of those hills.'

The window looked out over the ramparts and the near-by buildings to the valley of the Meuse south of Sedan. The river was winding across the broad meadows, with Remilly on the left, Pont-Maugis and Wadelincourt opposite, Frénois on the right; and the hills spread out their green slopes – first Le Liry, then La Marfée and La Croix-Piau, with their extensive woods. In the evening light the immense horizon looked profoundly peaceful, limpid as crystal.

'Don't you see over there along the tops those black lines moving like a procession of black ants?'

Jean opened his eyes wide and Maurice, kneeling on his bed, craned his neck.

'Oh yes,' they exclaimed together. 'There's one line, and there's another, and another and another! It's crawling with them.'

'Well,' said Weiss, 'those are the Prussians ... I've been watching them ever since this morning, and they keep going on and on! Oh, I can tell you, if our soldiers are waiting for them they are in a hurry to get here! And all the inhabitants of this town have seen them, same as me, and really the generals are the only ones with their eyes blindfolded. I was talking just now to a general and he shrugged his shoulders and told me that Marshal MacMahon was absolutely convinced he had scarcely seventy thousand men opposing him. God grant he is well informed ... But just look at them, the ground is covered with them, and still they come and come, like black ants!'

At that moment Maurice threw himself back on the bed and burst into violent sobbing. Henriette was coming in with the smiling face she had had that morning, but she ran over in alarm.

'What is it?'

But he pushed her away.

'No, no, leave me alone, I've never given you anything but trouble. When I think that you went without clothes and I was at college! Oh yes, an education I've made fine use of! And then I pretty nearly dishonoured our name, and I don't know where I'd be now if you hadn't bled yourself white to pay the price of my idiocy.'

She began to smile again.

'Really, my poor darling, you're not waking up in a very happy mood ... But you know all that is over and forgotten. Aren't you doing your duty as a Frenchman now? Since you enlisted I've been very proud of you, I really have.'

She turned to Jean as though to call in his help. He looked at her and was a little taken aback to find her not so pretty as before, but thinner and paler now he was no longer seeing her through the near-hallucination of his fatigue. What was still striking was the likeness to her brother, and yet all the profound difference between their natures showed clearly at that moment. He was as highly-strung as a woman, shattered by the disease of the age they were living in, going through the historical and social crisis of his race, capable of passing from one minute to the next from the most noble enthusiasms to the most craven discouragements, but she, so weak-looking, a self-effacing Cinderella with the resigned look of a little housewife, had the firm brow and brave eyes of the blessed stock that martyrs are made of.

'Proud of me!' exclaimed Maurice. 'There's no reason at all for that, really there isn't. For a whole month now we've been running away like the cowards we are.'

'Well, after all,' said Jean with his usual good sense, 'we aren't the only ones, we do what we are told to do.'

But at that the young man's attack burst out more violently than ever.

'That's just what I mean, and I've had enough! ... Doesn't it make you weep tears of blood, these continual defeats, these fools of commanders, these soldiers just being led by stupid people to the slaughterhouse like a lot of cattle? ... Now look at us here in a blind alley. It is perfectly clear that the Prussians are closing in from every direction and we are going to be crushed, the army is doomed ... No, no, I'm staying here, I prefer to be shot as a deserter. Jean, you can go without me. No, I'm staying here.'

He fell back on to the pillow in another flood of tears. It was an irresistible nervous reaction, an all-destroying collapse, one of those sudden plunges into despair and contempt for the world and for himself to which he was so often subject. Knowing him well, his sister remained calm.

'It would be very wrong, Maurice dear, to desert your post at the moment of danger.'

He sat up with a jerk.

'All right, give me my gun and I'll blow my brains out, it will be quicker.'

He pointed to Weiss, standing still and silent.

'You see, he's the only sensible one, yes, he's the only one who has seen clearly ... Do you remember, Jean, what he was saying to me outside Mulhouse a month ago?'

'That's quite true, he said we should be beaten.'

They recalled the scene, that night of anxiety, that nerve-racking wait during which all the disaster of Froeschwiller could already be sensed in the dismal sky, while Weiss was voicing his misgivings – Germany well prepared, better led, aroused in a great burst of patriotism, France in disarray, a prey to disruption, unprepared and distraught, with neither the commanders, nor the men nor the weapons needed. Now the dreadful prophecy was coming true.

Weiss's hands trembled as he raised them. His amiable face expressed the deepest grief.

'Oh, I don't feel at all triumphant about being right! I'm not very bright, but it was so obvious when you knew how things were ... But all the same, if we are beaten we can kill some of those accursed Prussians. That is the one consolation, I still don't think we shall get out of this, and I want some Prussians not to get out of it either, heaps of Prussians, enough to cover all that land over there!'

He stood up and waved his arm over the whole valley of the Meuse. There was a flame in those bulging, short-sighted eyes that had disqualified him for military service.

'God, yes, I'd fight if I was free! I don't know whether it's because they are now masters in my own part of the country, in Alsace where already the Cossacks had done so much harm before, but I can't think of them and visualize them here without at once being seized with a furious desire to make a dozen of them bleed to death . . . Oh, if I hadn't been turned down on medical grounds, if I were a soldier!'

Then, after a pause:

'But then, who knows?'

It was the rebirth of hope, the need to believe victory was always possible, held even by the most disillusioned. Maurice, already ashamed of his tears, listened and clung anew to this dream. And indeed, only yesterday hadn't a rumour run round that Bazaine was at Verdun? Fortune owed a miracle to this France she had made glorious for so long. Henriette had slipped away in silence and when she returned she was not surprised to see her brother up and dressed and ready to go. She insisted on seeing them both eat something. They had to sit down at the table, but each mouthful stuck in their throats and made them feel sick, heavy as they still were with sleep. Being a man of foresight, Jean cut a loaf in two, and put half in Maurice's pack and half in his own. It was getting dark, they must go. Henriette, standing by the window looking out at the Prussian troops in the distance on La Marfée, the black ants ceaselessly on the move and now gradually disappearing in the growing darkness, let an involuntary moan escape her:

'Oh war, how atrocious war is!'

Thereupon Maurice teased her, taking his revenge:

'What, little sister, you urge us to fight and then curse war?'

She turned round and flung at him, valiant as ever:

'It's true, I loathe it and think it's unjust and horrible . . . Perhaps it's simply because I am a woman. These killings make me sick. Why can't they talk it out and come to an understanding?'

Jean, good fellow that he was, nodded in agreement. Nothing seemed easier to him, as a plain, uneducated man, than for everybody to come to terms so long as they produced good reasons. But Maurice, back in his scientific world, was thinking of war as a necessity, war like life itself, the law of the universe. Wasn't it man, a soft-hearted creature, who introduced the conception of justice and peace, whereas impassive nature is nothing but a continual fight to the death?

'Come to an understanding!' he exclaimed. 'Yes, centuries from now! If all the peoples formed only one nation you might just conceive the coming of that golden age, but even then wouldn't the end of war mean the end of humanity? . . . I was silly just now, we must fight since it is the universal law.'

But then he too smiled and took up Weiss's phrase.

'But then, who knows?'

Once again the morbid exaggeration of his highly strung nature made him give in to unquenchable illusion and a need for deliberate blindness.

'By the way,' he went on gaily, 'what about cousin Gunther?'

'Cousin Gunther?' said Henriette. 'But he belongs to the Prussian Guard . . . Are they in these parts?'

Weiss made a gesture of ignorance, and so did the two soldiers, who couldn't say, since even the generals themselves had no idea what enemy forces they had opposite them.

'Let's be off, I'll show you the way,' he said. 'I found out just now where the 106th is camping.'

Then he told his wife that he would not come back, but go and sleep at Bazeilles. He had recently bought a cottage there that he had just made ready for them to use until the cold weather began. It was next door to a dyeworks belonging to Monsieur Delaherche. He was worried about the provisions he had already stored in the cellar, a cask of wine, two sacks of potatoes, and was sure, he said, that marauders would loot the place if it stayed empty, but he would probably keep it safe if he slept in it that night. While he was talking his wife looked him straight in the eyes.

'Don't you worry,' he went on with a smile, 'all I want to do is to keep an eye on our few sticks of furniture. I promise you that if the village is attacked or there is the slightest danger I shall come back at once.'

'You go,' she said. 'But come back or else I shall come and fetch you!'

As they were leaving Henriette kissed Maurice tenderly. Then she put out her hand to Jean and held his in her own for a few seconds, in a friendly grip.

'I am putting my brother in your charge again. Yes, he has told me how good you have been to him and I love you for it!'

He was so embarrassed that all he could do was squeeze her strong little hand in return. Once again he felt the impression he had had when they first came, of Henriette with hair like ripe corn and so blithe and gay in her unobtrusive way that she filled the air round her with a kind of caress.

Down below they were back in the dark Sedan of the morning. Already the narrow streets were melting into the dusk, and the roadways were cluttered up with mysterious activity. Most of the shops were shut, and houses seemed dead, whereas out in the open there was an appalling crush. But still they had managed without too much difficulty to get to the Place de l'Hôtel de Ville when they ran into Delaherche, who was wandering about to see what he could see. He at once exclaimed how delighted he was to see Maurice, told them how he had just taken Captain Beaudoin back to Floing where his regiment was, and his usual self-satisfaction increased when he heard that Weiss was going to sleep out at Bazeilles, for as he had just told the captain, he had made up his mind to spend the night there at his dyeworks, just to keep an eye on things.

'Weiss, we'll go there together, but first let us go down to the Sub-Prefecture where we might catch a glimpse of the Emperor.'

Ever since he had nearly spoken to him at the Baybel farmhouse, he could think of nothing but Napoleon III, and eventually he roped in the two soldiers as well. Only a few groups of people were standing about on the Place de la Sous-Préfecture and talking softly to each other, but scared-looking officers dashed through every few minutes. The colour of the trees was already fading into a dreary shadow, and to the right the sound of the Meuse could be heard as it flowed noisily past the buildings. In the crowd it was being said that the Emperor, who had decided to leave Carignan much against his will at eleven o'clock on the night before, had absolutely refused to push on as far as Mézières, because he wanted to stay in the danger zone and not demoralize the troops. Others said that he was no longer there but had fled, leaving by way of a substitute one of his lieutenants wearing his uniform, whose

175

striking personal resemblance took the army in. Others swore on their word of honour that they had seen vehicles loaded with the imperial treasure going into the garden of the Sub-Prefecture – a hundred million in gold, in brand-new twenty-franc pieces. The truth was that it was merely the paraphernalia of the Emperor's household, the passenger coach, the two carriages, the dozen vans which had caused such a stir as they went through the villages of Courcelles, Le Chêne, Raucourt, and had grown in popular imagination until they had become an immense train of vehicles which had brought the army to a standstill and had at last landed up here, accursed and ashamed, concealed from all eyes behind the lilac bushes of the Sub-Prefecture.

Near Delaherche, who was on tiptoe watching the ground-floor rooms, an old woman, some poor charwoman from near-by, with bent body and knotted, work-stained hands, was mumbling between her teeth:

'An Emperor . . . I'd like to see one . . . yes, just for the sake of seeing . . .'

Suddenly Delaherche seized Maurice's arm, exclaiming:

'Look, there he is! . . . See, there in the left-hand window . . . Oh no, I'm making no mistake, I saw him yesterday quite near . . . He lifted the curtain, yes, that pale face pressed against the window-pane.'

The old woman had overheard and stood open-mouthed. It was indeed, pressed against the window-pane, a wraith with a cadaverous face, lack-lustre eyes, drawn features and a colourless moustache, in this final torture. And the old girl, quite taken aback, turned away at once and walked off with a gesture of sovereign contempt.

'That an Emperor? Well, of all the sillies!'

A Zouave was there too, one of the soldiers on the loose and in no hurry to get back to the corps. He waved his rifle, swearing and spitting out threats, and said to a mate:

'Just wait a minute while I put a bullet through his fucking head!'

Delaherche intervened in great indignation. But the Emperor had already disappeared. The loud swash of the Meuse went on and an unspeakably doleful moan seemed to have passed by in the deepening shadows. Other vague sounds could be heard far away. Was it the terrible order: March on! March on! shouted from Paris, which had hounded this man on from stage to stage, dragging the irony of his imperial escort along the roads of defeat until he was now cornered in the frightful disaster he had foreseen and come deliberately to meet? How many decent, ordinary people were about to die through his fault, and what an utter breakdown of this sick man's whole being, this sentimental dreamer, silent while dully awaiting his doom!

Weiss and Delaherche took the two soldiers as far as the plateau of Floing.

'Good-bye,' said Maurice, embracing his brother-in-law.

'No, no! Au revoir, good gracious me!' cried Delaherche in his jolliest manner.

Jean, with his instinctive sense of direction, at once found the 106th, whose tents were aligned up the slope to the plateau behind the cemetery. It was now almost dark, but you could still make out the roofs of the town in great dark masses, and beyond them Balan and Bazeilles in the fields opening out as far as the line of hills from Remilly to Frénois; to the left stretched the black patch of the Garenne woods and down on the right gleamed the pale ribbon of the Meuse. For a moment Maurice watched the huge panorama vanish into the darkness.

'Ah, here comes the corporal!' said Chouteau. 'Has he come back with the rations?'

A buzz of conversation arose. All through the day the men had been coming back singly or in dribs and drabs and in such confusion that the officers had given up even asking for explanations. They kept their eyes shut and were glad to welcome those who consented to return.

As a matter of fact Captain Beaudoin had only just got back, and Lieutenant Rochas had only returned at about two o'clock with the straggling company reduced by two thirds. Now it was more or less up to strength. Some of the soldiers were drunk, others were still famished, not having been able to scrounge a bit of bread. And once again rations had not turned up. Loubet, however, had contrived to cook some cabbages pinched from a garden somewhere, but he had neither salt nor fat and their stomachs were still crying out for something to eat.

'Come on, corporal, you're a sly one, you are!' Chouteau repeated with a leer. 'Oh, it's not for myself, I've had a very good meal with Loubet at a lady's house.'

Anxious faces looked towards Jean, the squad had been waiting, especially Lapoulle and Pache, the unlucky ones, who hadn't picked anything up, counting on him, for he could have got flour out of a stone, as they put it. So Jean, moved with pity and conscience-stricken at having abandoned his men, divided between them the half loaf he had in his pack.

'Oh Christ, oh Christ!' Lapoulle kept on saying as he chewed, finding no other word in his growl of satisfaction, while Pache said under his breath a Paternoster and an Ave to make sure that God would send him his daily bread again tomorrow.

The bugler Gaude had blown roll-call at full blast, but not retreat, and the camp fell at once into deep silence. And it was then, when he had checked that his half-section was complete, that Sergeant Sapin, with his sickly-looking face and screwed-up nose, said quietly:

'There will be a lot missing this time tomorrow.'

As Jean looked at him he added with quiet certainty, gazing far away into the darkness:

'Oh, as for me, I shall be killed tomorrow.'

By now it was nine, and the night looked like being bitterly cold, for the mists had risen off the Meuse, hiding the stars. Maurice, lying beside Jean under a hedge, shivered and said they would do well to go and lie down in the tent. But neither of them could get to sleep, for since the rest they had had they were more tired and aching than ever. They envied Lieutenant Rochas near them who, scorning any cover, and simply wrapped in a blanket, was snoring like an old campaigner on the wet ground. Then for a long time they watched with interest the little candle flame burning in a large tent where the colonel and some officers were sitting up late. All the evening Monsieur de Vineuil had looked very worried because he had had no orders for the following morning. He felt his regiment was exposed too far forward, although he had already drawn back and abandoned the forward outpost occupied that morning. General Bourgain-Desfeuilles had not been seen – he was said to be ill in bed at the Hôtel de la Croix d'Or, and the colonel had to decide to send an officer to warn him that the new position looked dangerous, the 7th corps being so spread out because it was obliged to defend too long a line from the loop of the Meuse to the Garenne woods. It was certain that the battle would begin with the daylight, so there were not more than seven or eight hours of this great black calm left. Maurice was very surprised to see, as the little glimmer of light in the colonel's tent went out, Captain Beaudoin pass quite close to him, skirting the hedge with furtive steps, and disappear in the direction of Sedan.

The night steadily thickened as the vapours rising from the river obscured everything in a dismal fog.

'Are you asleep, Jean?'

He was, and so Maurice was alone. The thought of joining Lapoulle and the others in the tent made him feel sick and tired. He listened to their snores answering those of Rochas, and felt envious. It may well be that if great captains sleep soundly on the eve of a battle it is simply because they are tired out. Nothing could now be heard coming from the great camp, lost in the darkness, but the heavy breath of sleep, a gigantic but gentle breathing. Nothing really existed clearly, he only knew that the 5th corps must be camping down there beneath the ramparts, that the 1st stretched from the Garenne woods to the village of La Moncelle, while the 12th, over on the other side of the town, was occupying Bazeilles; and everything was asleep, and the slow pulse of sleep was coming from the first tents to the last from the intangible depths of shadow over more than a league. Then beyond all that there was another unknown, and its sound also sometimes reached his ears, so distant, so soft that he might have thought it was just a noise in his own ears – a far away galloping of cavalry, a muffled roar of cannon, but above all a heavy tramp of marching men, the procession up there of the black human ant-hill, the invasion, the enveloping that even night itself could not halt. Were there not somewhere over there fires going out, occasional voices calling, a great and ever growing anguish pervading this last night as they all waited in terror for the day?

Maurice's groping hand had found Jean's, and only then did he fall asleep, reassured. Nothing was left but one distant bell in Sedan, tolling the hours one by one.

PART TWO

—

1

At Bazeilles, in the dark little room, a sudden shock made Weiss leap out of bed. He listened. It was gunfire. He felt for the candle, which he had to light so as to see the time by his watch: four o'clock and only just beginning to get light. He seized his spectacles and looked up and down the main street, the Douzy road which runs through the village, but it was filled with a kind of thick dust and he could not make anything out. So he went into the other room, the window of which looked over on to the fields towards the Meuse, and he realized that the morning mists were coming off the river and obscuring the horizon. The gunfire was louder from over the river, beyond this veil. Suddenly a French battery replied, so near and with such a din that the walls of the little house shook.

The Weisses' house was about in the centre of Bazeilles, on the right before you reach the Place de l'Eglise. The front, standing a little back, faced the road and had only one storey above the ground floor with three windows, and a loft above, but there was quite a large garden behind which sloped down to the meadows and from which could be seen the immense panorama of the hills from Remilly to Frénois. Weiss, in the excitement of new owner-ship, had not gone to bed until nearly two after he had buried all the provisions in his cellar and worked out how to protect the furniture as well as possible from bullets by draping the windows with mattresses. He felt anger rising within him when he reflected that the Prussians might come and sack this house he had longed for so much, acquired with so much difficulty and so far enjoyed so little.

But he was hailed by a voice from the road:

'I say, Weiss, can you hear that?'

Downstairs he found Delaherche, who also had wanted to sleep at his dyeworks, a large brick building adjoining. In any case all the employees had fled through the woods and reached Belgium, and the only person left guarding the premises was the caretaker, a stonemason's widow named Françoise Quittard. And she was all of a tremble and very upset, and would have gone with the others if she had not had her boy, young Auguste, a lad of ten, so ill with typhoid that he could not be moved.

'I say,' Delaherche said again, 'can you hear that, it's really starting . . . It would be wise to get straight back to Sedan.'

Weiss had solemnly promised his wife to leave Bazeilles at the first real sign of danger, and at that time he was quite determined to keep his promise. But so far there was only an artillery duel going on at long range and a bit haphazard in the mists of dawn.

'For goodness sake let's wait a bit longer,' he said, 'there's no hurry.'

It should be said that Delaherche's curiosity was so lively and so busy that it gave him courage. He had not had a wink of sleep because he was so interested in the preparations for the defence. General Lebrun, in command of the 12th corps, had been warned that he would be attacked at dawn and had spent the night taking up position in Bazeilles, for he had orders to prevent at all costs its being occupied. Barricades blocked the main street and all side streets, and every house had its garrison of two or three men, every alleyway and garden was turned into a fortress. By three o'clock, in the inky darkness, the troops had been silently awakened and were manning their combat posts, with rifles freshly greased and pouches filled with the regulation ninety rounds of ammunition. Therefore the first round of enemy gunfire had taken nobody by surprise, and the French batteries, in the rear between Balan and Bazeilles, had immediately begun to reply just to show they were there, for in the mist they were only firing by guesswork.

'You know,' Delaherche went on, 'the dyeworks will be strongly defended . . . I have a whole section. Come and look.'

And indeed forty or more marines had been posted there, under the command of a lieutenant, a tall, fair man, very young, who looked energetic and determined. His men had already taken over the building, some were making loopholes through the first-floor shutters facing the road, and others constructing battlements in the low wall of the yard overlooking the fields at the back.

It was in the middle of this yard that Delaherche and Weiss

found the lieutenant on the look-out, trying to see into the distance through the morning mist.

'This damn fog!' he muttered. 'We aren't going to be able to fight by feel.'

Then, after a pause and with no apparent transition:

'What day is it today?'

'Thursday,' said Weiss.

'Thursday, quite right, so it is. Well I'm damned! We don't know quite what we *are* doing, as though the world didn't exist.'

But just then there leaped out from the ceaseless background of gunfire a rapid fusillade at the end of the fields themselves, five or six hundred metres away. It was like a stage effect: the sun was rising, the mists of the Meuse dispersed in shreds of fine muslin, the blue sky appeared, cleared itself and was cloudless. It was the flawless morning of a lovely summer day.

'Oh,' exclaimed Delaherche, 'they're crossing the railway bridge. Can you see them going along the line, trying to reach ... But how idiotic not to have blown up the bridge!'

The lieutenant made a gesture of silent rage. The blast holes were charged, he explained; only, after fighting the day before for four hours to recapture the bridge, somebody had forgotten to light the fuse!

'Just our luck,' he snapped.

Weiss looked on, trying to take it all in. The French occupied a very strong position in Bazeilles. Built along both sides of the Douzy road, the village dominated the plain, and the only way to get to it was by this route, turning to the left in front of the castle, while another road to the right leading to the railway turned off at the Place de l'Eglise. So the Germans had to cross the meadows and ploughed fields, wide open spaces alongside the Meuse and the railway line. Their habitual prudence being well known, it seemed unlikely that the main attack would come from this direction. And yet dense masses of them were still coming over the bridge, in spite of the massacre from *mitrailleuses* set up at the entrance to Bazeilles, and those who did get through at once took shelter among the few willows, and columns re-formed and advanced. That was where the ever-growing fusillade was coming from.

'Well fancy!' said Weiss. 'They are Bavarians, I can see the tufts on their helmets quite clearly!'

But he thought he could make out other columns, half hidden behind the railway line, that were making for their right, trying to reach the trees some way off so as to swing back on Bazeilles in an oblique movement. If they succeeded by this means in gaining cover in the park of Montvillers the village could be taken. That was a quick and vague impression, but as the frontal attack grew in intensity it faded from his mind.

He suddenly looked round at the heights of Floing which could be seen to the north rising above the town of Sedan. A battery up there had opened fire and puffs of smoke rose in the bright sunshine, then the detonations followed very clear. It might be about five o'clock.

'Here we go,' he murmured, 'this will open the ball.'

The lieutenant was watching too, and he made a gesture of absolute certainty as he said:

'Oh, Bazeilles is the key point. It's here that the outcome of the battle will be decided.'

'Do you think so?' asked Weiss.

'No doubt about it. It's obvious that that was in the marshal's mind when he came last night to tell us to let ourselves be killed to the last man rather than allow the village to be occupied.'

Weiss nodded, cast his eye round the horizon, then ventured hesitantly, as though talking to himself:

'Oh no, oh no, that isn't it . . . I'm afraid of something else, yes, and I daren't put it into words.'

He fell silent. All he did was open his arms very wide, like the jaws of a vice, and turning to the north he brought his hands together as if the two jaws were suddenly closed.

That was what he had been afraid of since the day before, with his local knowledge and in view of the movements of the two armies. Even now, when the great valley lay spread out in the radiant sunshine, his eyes went over to the hills on the left bank where, all through a day and a night, such a black swarm of German troops had been marching by. A battery was firing from above Remilly. Shells were beginning to come over from another that had taken up its position at Pont-Maugis on the river bank. He folded his eyeglasses, putting one lens over the other so as to examine the wooded slopes more carefully, but all he could see was the little puffs of smoke from the guns surmounting more of the heights every minute: then, that river of men that had been flowing over there – where was it massing at the present time? Above Noyers and Frénois, on La Marfée, he did eventually make out, at the corner of a clump of pines, a group of uniforms and horses, probably officers, some headquarters staff. And the loop of the Meuse was further away, barring the west, and in that direction there was no way of retreat towards Mézières except one narrow road through the Saint-Albert gap between the river and the forest of the Ardennes. That was why the day before he had ventured to mention this sole line of retreat to a general he had chanced to meet in a cutting in the valley of the Givonne and who, he found out later, was General Ducrot, commander of the 1st corps. If the army did not withdraw at once by that route, but waited to be cut off by the Prussians as they crossed the Meuse at Donchery, it would certainly be immobilized with its back to the frontier. It was already too late by that evening, for it was reported that the bridge was occupied by Uhlans – yet another bridge that had not been blown up, this time because nobody had thought to bring any gunpowder. In despair Weiss told himself that the flood of men, the black swarm, must be in the plain of Donchery and making for the Saint-Albert gap, throwing its advance guard to Saint-Menges and Floing, where he had taken Jean and Maurice the evening before. In the brilliant sunshine the church tower of Floing could be seen a long way off, like a fine white needle.

Then eastwards there was the other jaw of the vice. Although he could see to the north, from the plateau of Illy to that of Floing, the whole battle-line of the 7th corps, supported in a feeble way by the 5th, which had been stationed in reserve beneath the ramparts, he could not know what was going on further east along the valley of the Givonne, where the 1st corps was stretched from the Garenne woods to the village of Daigny. But guns were roaring in that direction as well, and the battle must be joined in the Chevalier wood at this end of the village. His disquiet came from the fact that some country folk had said the day before that the Prussians had reached Francheval, so that the movement going on in the west via Donchery was also happening in the east via Francheval, and the jaws of the vice would succeed in meeting over in the north at the Calvary of Illy if the double pincer movement was not halted. He knew nothing about military science, had nothing but his own common sense, and he shuddered as he contemplated this immense triangle, one side of which was the Meuse and the two others were made up by the 7th corps on the north and the 1st on the east, while the 12th occupied the extreme point on the south, and all three had their backs to the others, waiting, God knew how or why, for an enemy coming from all directions. In the middle, at the bottom of a pit, was the town of Sedan, armed with obsolete cannon, with neither munitions nor provisions.

'Now look,' he said, repeating his gesture with arms out wide and hands coming together, 'that's what it's going to be like if your generals don't watch it ... They're just keeping you amused at Bazeilles.'

But he put it badly and in a muddled way, and the lieutenant, who did not know the district, could not follow. So he shrugged his shoulders impatiently, full of scorn for this bourgeois with his overcoat and glasses who thought he knew more about it than the marshal. Annoyed at hearing him say again that the attack on Bazeilles was probably only intended as a diversion to conceal the real plan, he cut it short by saying:

'Oh shut up! ... We'll chuck those Bavarians of yours into the Meuse and then they'll see whether we're being kept amused!'

In the last few minutes the enemy snipers seemed to have got nearer, for bullets were hitting the brick wall of the dyeworks with a thud, and now the soldiers protected by the low wall of the yard were replying. Every second was marked by the sharp crack of rifle fire.

'Chuck them into the Meuse, yes, no doubt,' murmured Weiss, 'and walk over their bodies to get back on to the Carignan road, very nice too!'

Then, to Delaherche who had ducked behind the pump to avoid the bullets:

'I don't care what they say, the real plan should have been to get away last night to Mézières, and if I were them I'd rather be there than here ... Anyway, they'll have to fight because now any retreat is impossible.'

'Are you coming?' asked Delaherche, who for all his burning curiosity was beginning to wilt. 'If we hang about any longer we shan't be able to get back to Sedan.'

'Yes, just a minute and I'll follow you.'

In spite of the danger he stood on tiptoe, determined to see for himself. On the right, the meadows had been flooded by order of the governor, and the vast lake stretching from Torcy to Balan protected the town, a sheet of water, pale blue in the morning sun. But the water stopped at the beginning of Bazeilles, and the Bavarians had in fact advanced through the grass, taking advantage of every hollow or tree. They might be about five hundred metres away, and what struck him was the deliberateness of their movements, the patience with which they gained ground, exposing themselves as little as possible. Moreover they were supported by powerful artillery, and the fresh, pure air was full of the screaming of shells. He looked up and saw that the battery at Pont-Maugis was not the only one firing at Bazeilles: two others, half way up Le Liry, had opened fire, shelling the village and even raking with fire the open ground of La Moncelle where the reserves of the 12th corps were, as far as the wooded slopes of Daigny, occupied by a division of the 1st corps. Moreover all the hilltops along the left bank seemed to be bursting into fire. Guns seemed to be springing up out of the ground, it was like a ring steadily extending: a battery at Noyers firing on Balan, a battery at Wadelincourt firing on Sedan, a battery at Frénois, under La Marfée, a formidable battery whose shells passed over the town to burst among the troops of the 7th corps on the plateau of Floing. These beloved hills, this line of crests he had always thought of as there for the beauty of the view, enclosing the valley with such lovely greenery, Weiss was now looking at with anguish and terror, for they had suddenly turned into a frightful, gigantic fortress busily smashing the useless fortifications of Sedan.

A little fall of plaster made him look up. It was a bullet that had chipped a bit off his house, one side of which he could see over the party wall. This annoyed him very much, and he fumed:

'Are those bastards going to demolish it for me?'

Then he was startled by another little thud behind him. He looked round and saw a soldier, who had been shot through the heart, falling on his back. The legs made a few convulsive movements, the face stayed young and calm, suddenly still. This was the first man killed, and Weiss was particularly upset by the crash of his rifle as it fell on the cobbles of the yard.

'Oh no, I'm off!' stammered Delaherche. 'If you're not coming, I'm going on my own.'

The lieutenant who was sick to death of them, chimed in:

'Certainly, gentlemen, you would be well advised to go ... We may be attacked at any minute.'

Then, after another glance at the meadows where the Bavarians were gaining ground, Weiss made up his mind to follow Delaherche. But first he wanted to double-lock his house on the other side, the road side. He was finally joining his friend when a new sight rooted them both to the spot.

At the end of the street, about three hundred metres away, the Place de l'Eglise was being attacked by a strong force of Bavarians coming from the Douzy road. The regiment of marines responsible for defending the square appeared to slacken fire for a moment as if to let them advance. Then suddenly, when they were massed right in front of them, there was an extraordinary and unforeseen manoeuvre: the French soldiers threw themselves to one side or the other of the road and many lay flat on the ground, and, through the space thus suddenly opened, the machine guns, concentrated in a battery at the other end, suddenly belched forth a hail of bullets, sweeping the enemy force away. The soldiers leaped up again with one bound and charged with bayonets on the scattered Bavarians, which pushed and toppled them right back. Twice the process was repeated with the same success. At the corner of a narrow lane three women were still in a little house and there, in one of the windows, they were calmly laughing and applauding, apparently delighted to see the show.

'Oh damn,' Weiss suddenly said, 'I forgot to shut the cellar door and take the key ... Wait for me, I shan't be a minute.'

The first attack seemed to have been repulsed, and Delaherche, giving in to his curiosity again, was in less of a hurry. He was standing in front of the dyeworks talking to the caretaker, who had come for a moment out of the door of the room she occupied on the ground floor.

'Poor Françoise, you should come with us. It's terrible, a woman on her own in the middle of all these horrors.'

She raised her trembling arms.

'Oh sir, of course I should have gone but for my little Auguste's illness ... Come in, sir, and you'll see.'

He did not go in, but craned his neck and shook his head on seeing the lad in a spotlessly clean bed, his face flushed with fever, staring at his mother with burning eyes.

'Well, yes, but why don't you carry him away? I will fix you up in Sedan ... Wrap him up in a warm blanket and come with us.'

'Oh no, sir, it isn't possible. The doctor said I would kill him ... If only his poor father were still alive! But there are only the two of us now and we must save ourselves for each other ... And besides, those Prussians surely won't do any harm to a woman on her own and a sick child!'

Weiss reappeared at that moment, satisfied that he had barricaded everything in his house.

'There! If they want to get in they'll have to smash up the whole show ... Now let's be off, and it's not going to be all that easy either. Let's slip along near the houses so as not to be hit by something.'

And indeed the enemy must have been working up for a fresh attack, for the fusillade redoubled its intensity and the screaming of shells never let up. Two had already come down on the road a hundred metres away and another had buried itself in the soft earth of the garden without exploding.

'Oh Françoise, I want to give your little Auguste a kiss,' Weiss went on. 'But he's not as bad as all that, another couple of days and he'll be out of danger ... Cheer up, and now hurry indoors and don't show your nose outside.'

At last the two men were setting off.

'Be seeing you, Françoise.'

'Be seeing you, gentlemen.'

At that very second there was an appalling crash. A shell had demolished a chimney of Weiss's house and fallen on to the pavement, where it went off with such an explosion that all the windows nearby were broken. A thick dust and heavy smoke at first hid everything from sight. Then the front of the dyeworks could be seen gaping wide, and Françoise had been flung across the door-step, dead, with her back broken, her head smashed in, a lump of human flesh, red and horrible.

Weiss rushed back. Almost incoherent, he could only stammer out swear words:

'Bloody hell! Bloody hell!'

No doubt about her being dead. He stooped and felt her hands. and as he straightened up he saw the flushed face of the child Auguste who had raised his head to look at his mother. He did not speak, he did not cry, but only stared at this horrible, unrecognizable body with his eyes monstrously magnified by fever.

'Oh God,' Weiss at last managed to say, 'they're killing women now!'

He was now standing up again and shaking his fist at the Bavarians whose helmets were beginning to reappear by the church. The sight of the roof of his house half stove-in by the falling chimney put the finishing touch to his mad fury.

'Filthy sods! You kill women and destroy my home! No, no, it's not possible, I can't go away like this. I'm staying here!'

He dashed off and came back in a single bound with the rifle and cartridges of the dead soldier. For special occasions, when he wanted to see clearly, he always had on him a pair of spectacles which he did not usually wear, out of a touching sense of embarrassment and vanity in front of his young wife. Now he quickly took off his folding glasses and replaced them with the spectacles, and this heavily-built bourgeois in his overcoat, with his round, jolly face transfigured by rage, looking almost comically and sublimely heroic, began firing into the mass of Bavarians at the end of the street. It was in his blood, as he always used to say, this urge to pick a few of them off, ever since the tales of 1814 he had been told in his childhood away in Alsace.

'Oh, the filthy sods! The filthy sods!'

He fired non-stop and so fast that the barrel of his gun began to burn his fingers.

Clearly the attack was going to be terrible. The fusillade from the meadows had died down. The Bavarians were masters of the little stream fringed with poplars and willows, and were now preparing for an assault on the houses defending the church square, and so their snipers had prudently drawn back. The sun shone in golden splendour on the great stretch of grassland, dotted with a few black patches, the bodies of killed soldiers. So the lieutenant had moved out of the yard of the dyeworks, leaving a sentry there, realizing that the danger was now going to be on the street side. He quickly disposed his men along the pavement, with orders that in the event of the enemy's capturing the square they should barricade themselves in the first floor of the building and resist there to the last bullet. Lying on the ground, sheltering behind stones or taking advantage of the slightest projections, the men were firing all out, and along this wide, sunlit and empty street there was a hurricane of lead with streaks of smoke, like a hailstorm blown by a high wind. A young girl was seen running across the road in terror, but she was not hit. But then an old man, a yokel in a smock, was insisting on getting his horse into a stable, and he was struck in the forehead by a bullet with such force that it knocked him into the middle of the road. The roof of the church was blown in by a shell. Two other shells had set fire to houses, which blazed up in the bright light with cracklings of timber. And poor Françoise's body, smashed beside her sick child, the old peasant with a bullet through his skull, the destruction and the fires goaded to exasperation inhabitants who had preferred to die there rather than run away into Belgium. Bourgeois, workmen, people in overcoats or overalls, all of them were firing frenziedly through the windows.

'Oh, the swine!' shouted Weiss. 'They've gone right round ... I saw them quite clearly going along the railway line ... Listen, can't you hear them over there to the left?'

And indeed rifle fire had broken out behind the park of Montvillers, the trees of which bordered the road. If the enemy occupied that park Bazeilles was lost. But the very violence of the firing proved that the commander of the 12th corps had foreseen this manoeuvre and that the park was being defended.

'Mind what you're doing, clumsy!' shouted the lieutenant, forcing Weiss to flatten himself out against the wall. 'You'll get cut in half!'

This stout man in his spectacles, so courageous, had ended by rousing his interest, though he had to smile; and as he heard a shell coming he had pushed him aside in a brotherly way. The projectile fell some ten metres away and burst, covering them both with shrapnel. The civilian was still standing, but the lieutenant had both legs broken.

'This is it,' he murmured. 'I've got my packet.'

Knocked down on the pavement, he had himself put in a sitting posture against the doorway, near the dead woman lying across the step. And his young face kept its keen, steadfast expression.

'Never mind that, boys, just listen to me . . . Fire away and take your time. I'll tell you when to go for them with bayonets!'

He continued in command, head up, keeping an eye on the distant enemy. Another house opposite was on fire. The crackling of bullets and explosions of shells rent the air which was filled with dust and smoke. Soldiers fell at every street corner and the dead, isolated or in heaps, made dark, bloodstained patches. Over the village, swelling in an immense clamour, was the threat of thousands of men bearing down upon a few hundred brave men resolved to die.

Delaherche, who had never stopped calling to Weiss, asked for the last time:

'Aren't you coming? Oh well, don't then! I'll leave you, goodbye!'

It was now about seven, and he had hung about too long. As long as the houses lasted he took advantage of doorways and bits of wall, squeezing into the tiniest corners at each burst of firing. He would never have believed he was so young and agile as he glided along as lithe as a snake. But at the end of Bazeilles, when he had to negotiate nearly three hundred metres of empty, open road, raked by the batteries at Le Liry, he felt himself shivering although he was soaked in sweat. For one moment he was able to get along bent double in a ditch, but then he had to run for it, madly, straight ahead, his ears full of explosions like peals of thunder. His eyes smarted as though he were walking through fire. It seemed to go on for an eternity. Suddenly he saw a little house on the left, and he leaped for it and shelter, and a huge weight was lifted from him. There were people all round him, men and horses. At first he had not recognized anyone. Then what he saw amazed him.

Surely it was the Emperor with all his staff? For all the personal knowledge he had boasting about since he nearly spoke to him at Baybel, he hesitated, and then stood gaping. It was indeed Napoleon III, who looked taller now that he was on horseback, and his moustache was so waxed and his cheeks were so rouged that he at once thought he looked much younger, and made up like an actor. Surely he must have had himself made up so as not to go round displaying to the army the horror of his colourless face all twisted with pain, his fleshless nose and muddy eyes. Having been warned at five in the morning that there was fighting at Bazeilles, he had come like a silent, gloomy ghost with its flesh all brightened up with vermilion.

There was a brickworks there, affording some protection. On the other side the walls were being pitted with bullets, and every second a shell came down on the road. The whole escort had stopped.

'Your Majesty,' a voice ventured, 'it really is dangerous . . .'

But the Emperor turned and made a sign to his staff to go and stand in the narrow lane that ran along the side of the brickworks. There men and horses would be completely hidden.

'Really, sir, it's madness . . . Sir, we beg of you . . .'

But all he did was repeat his gesture, as though to indicate that the sudden appearance of a group of uniforms on the open road would certainly attract the attention of the batteries on the other side of the river. And he advanced all alone amid the bullets and shells, unhurriedly, with his usual gloomy, indifferent bearing, going to meet his destiny. Perhaps he could hear behind him that implacable voice hounding him on, the voice screaming from Paris: 'March on! March on! Die like a hero on the piled-up corpses of your people, fill the whole world with admiration and awe so that your son may reign!' So he went on, urging his horse at a gentle trot. For a hundred metres he went on. Then he stopped and waited for the end he had come to find. Bullets whistled by like a hurricane, and a bursting shell had bespattered him with earth. Still he waited. His horse's mane stood on end and its skin was twitching as it recoiled instinctively in the face of death which passed by at every moment but had no use for either man or beast. Then after this seemingly endless wait the Emperor, with his fatalistic resignation, understood that his hour was not yet, and slowly returned as though all he had wanted to do was reconnoitre the exact position of the German batteries.

'Sir, what courage! . . . For pity's sake don't expose yourself any more . . .'

But with another gesture he invited his staff to follow him, without sparing them this time any more than he spared himself, and he rode up towards La Moncelle over the fields and the open ground of La Rapaille. One captain was killed and two horses were brought down. He passed in front of the regiments of the 12th corps, who watched him come and go like a ghost, with no salute, no acclaim.

Delaherche had witnessed all this. It made him shudder, especially when he reflected that as soon as he left the brickworks he also would be right in the path of the firing. He waited about and listened to some dismounted officers who had stayed there.

'But I tell you he was killed instantly, a shell cut him in two!'

'No he wasn't. I saw him carried off . . . Just a straightforward wound, a splinter in the buttock . . .'

'What time?'

'About six-thirty, an hour ago . . . Up there near La Moncelle, in a sunken road . . .'

'So he's gone back to Sedan?'

'Yes, of course, he's in Sedan.'

Who were they talking about? Delaherche suddenly realized that it was Marshal MacMahon, wounded while inspecting the outposts. The marshal wounded! Just our luck, as the lieutenant of the marines had put it. He was thinking about the consequences of the accident when a dispatch-rider tore past, shouting to a friend he recognized:

'General Ducrot is commander-in-chief! The whole army is to be concentrated at Illy to withdraw towards Mézières.'

He was already galloping away into Bazeilles under renewed fire, and Delaherche, appalled by all these extraordinary bits of news, one after another, and in danger of finding himself caught in the retreating army, made up his mind and ran all the way to Balan, whence he regained Sedan at last without too much trouble.

In Bazeilles the dispatch-rider went on galloping, looking for officers to give orders to. And the news galloped too – Marshal MacMahon wounded, General Ducrot appointed commander-in-Chief, the whole army falling back on Illy.

'What? What are they saying?' asked Weiss, his face blackened with powder. 'Retreat to Mézières now! But it's madness, they'll never get through!'

He was full of despair and remorse at having advised this course the day before, and to General Ducrot of all people, who was now in supreme command. Of course it was all right the day before, and there was then no other line to take: retreat, immediate retreat through the Saint-Albert gap. But by now that route must be cut, the whole black swarm of Prussians had gone that way into the plain of Donchery. And, to weigh one act of folly against another, there was now only one left, and that was a desperate and courageous one, to throw the Bavarians back into the Meuse and pass over them and go back along the Carignan road.

Weiss, pushing up his glasses every second, explained the position to the lieutenant who was still propped against the door, with both legs gone, white and bleeding to death.

'Sir, I assure you I am right ... Tell your men to hold on ... You can see we're winning. One more effort and we'll chuck them into the Meuse!'

And indeed the second Bavarian attack had been repulsed. Once again the machine guns had raked the church square, and piles of corpses blocked the roadway in the bright sunlight, and from all the little alleys the enemy was being thrust back with the bayonet into the fields in headlong flight riverwards, which would certainly have become a rout if fresh troops had reinforced the exhausted and thinned ranks of the marines. Moreover, in the Montvillers park the fusillade was not making very much progress, which showed that on that side also a few reinforcements would have cleared the wood of the enemy.

'Tell your men that, sir ... with bayonets, with bayonets!'

White as wax, and in an expiring voice the lieutenant still found the strength to murmur:

'You hear, boys, with the bayonet!'

That was his last breath, and he expired, head up and steadfast, eyes open, still watching the battle. Already the flies were hovering and settling on the smashed face of Françoise, and the child Auguste from his bed in a feverish delirium, kept calling and asking for a drink in a low, imploring voice.

'Mummy, wake up, get up ... I'm thirsty, I'm ever so thirsty.'

But the command was clear, officers had to order a retreat, however upset they were at not being able to take advantage of the success they had had. Obviously General Ducrot, haunted by fear of being encircled by the enemy, was sacrificing everything to the crazy attempt to get out of their clutches. The church square was evacuated, the troops fell back from alley to alley and soon the street was empty. Women were heard crying and wailing, men were swearing and brandishing their fists in anger at seeing themselves abandoned in this way. Many shut themselves in their houses, resolved to defend themselves and die.

'Well I'm not clearing out!' shouted Weiss, beside himself with rage. 'No, I'd rather leave my dead body here. Just let them come and break up my furniture and drink my wine!'

Nothing else now existed but his rage, the inextinguishable fury of the conflict when he thought that the foreigner might enter his home, sit on his chair, drink out of his glass. It made his whole being turn over, took away his ordinary existence, his wife, his business and his reasonable, middle-class prudence. He shut and barricaded himself in his house, and there he roamed round and round like a caged beast, going from room to room making sure that all openings were blocked. He counted his ammunition, he had about forty rounds left. Then, as he was going to have a last look towards the Meuse to make sure that there was no attack to fear from the meadows, his eye was caught once again by the range of hills on the left bank. Puffs of smoke clearly indicated the positions of the Prussian batteries. Once again he saw, dominating the formidable batteries of Frénois, at the angle of the little wood on La Marfée, the group of uniforms, this time more of them and looking so brilliant in the bright sunshine that by putting his folding glasses over his spectacles he could see the gold of epaulettes and helmets.

'Filthy buggers! Filthy buggers!' he repeated, shaking his fist.

Up there on La Marfée it was King William and his general staff. He had come there at seven from La Vendresse, where he had slept the night, and he was up there, away from all danger, with the valley of the Meuse, the battlefield, stretching out before him on all sides. The immense relief map went from one end of the sky to the other, and he, standing on the hill, looked on as though from a throne reserved for him in this gigantic box at a gala performance.

In the middle, against the dark background of the forest of the Ardennes, draped across the horizon like a curtain of antique verdure, Sedan stood out with the geometrical lines of its fortifications, lapped by the flooded meadows and river on the south and west. In Bazeilles houses were already on fire and the village was half obscured with the dust of battle. Then eastwards, from La Moncelle to Givonne, all that could be seen was a few regiments of the 12th corps and the 1st, crawling like lines of insects across the stubble and sometimes disappearing in the narrow valley where the hamlets were hidden; and on the opposite side the other rising ground could be seen, light-coloured fields with the green patch of the Chevalier wood. But what could be most clearly seen was the 7th corps, to the north, filling with its moving black dots the plateau of Floing, a broad band of reddish earth stretching from the little Garenne wood down to the grassland by the river. Beyond that there was still Floing, Saint-Menges, Fleigneux, Illy, villages huddled away in the ups and downs of the land in a rugged piece of country broken up by escarpments. To the left also was the loop of the Meuse, with its slow waters, pale silver in the bright sun, enclosing the peninsula of Iges in its vast meandering detour, cutting off all routes to Mézières and only leaving between its further bank and the impassable forests the one outlet of the Saint-Albert gap.

The hundred thousand men and five hundred cannon of the French army were there packed together and hounded into this triangle. And when the King of Prussia turned westwards he saw another plain, that of Donchery, empty fields extending to Briancourt, Marancourt and Vrigne-aux-Bois, a waste of grey earth, powdery-looking under the blue sky, and when he turned to the east there was yet again, opposite the huddled French lines, an immense vista, a crowd of villages, Douzy and Carignan first, then as you go up, Rubécourt, Pouru-aux-Bois, Francheval, Villers-Cernay, right on to La Chapelle, near the frontier. In all directions the land belonged to him, he could move at will the two hundred and fifty thousand men and the eight hundred guns of his armies, he could take in with one sweeping look their invading march. Already on one side the XIth corps was advancing on Saint-Menges, while the Vth corps was at Vrigne-aux-Bois and the Wurttemberg division was waiting near Donchery; on the other side, even though trees and hills were in the way, he could guess what moves were being made, for he had just seen the XIIth corps penetrating the Chevalier wood and knew that the Guards must have reached Villers-Cernay. These were the jaws of the vice, the Crown Prince of Prussia's army on the left and that of the Crown Prince of Saxony on the right, and they were opening and irresistibly closing round while the two Bavarian corps were hammering away at Bazeilles.

At King William's feet, from Remilly to Frénois, the almost continuous line of batteries were ceaselessly thundering, pounding La Moncelle and Daigny with shells and firing right over the town of Sedan to rake the plateaux to the north. It was not much after eight in the morning, and he was awaiting the inevitable outcome of the battle, his eyes on the giant chessboard, busily manoeuvring this dust-storm of men, the furious attack of these few black dots in the midst of eternal, smiling nature.

2

AT first light on the plateau of Floing, in a thick fog, Gaude's bugle sounded reveille for all it was worth. But the air was so saturated with moisture that the merry tune was muffled. Nevertheless the men of the company, who had not even had the heart to put up the tents but had rolled themselves up in the canvas and lain in the mud, did not even wake up but were like a lot of corpses already with pallid faces, stiff with fatigue and sleep, and had to be shaken one by one and pulled out of their torpor. They rose up as if from the dead, ghastly looking, with eyes full of the terror of being alive.

Jean had roused Maurice.

'What's up? Where are we?'

He looked about him, scared, but only saw the grey sea of fog in which the shades of his comrades were floating. You couldn't make out anything twenty metres in front of you. You lost all sense of direction, and he could never have said which way Sedan was. Just then his ear caught the far off sound of gunfire somewhere.

'Oh yes, the fighting is to be today ... Good, we shall get it over!'

Voices round him were saying the same thing, and there was a feeling of grim satisfaction, the need to get out of this nightmare at last by seeing those Prussians, whom they had come to find and from whom they had been running away for so many mortal hours. So they were going to give them a bit of rifle-fire and unload themselves of these cartridges they had carted so far without firing a single one! This time, they all felt, it was the inevitable battle.

'Where's that firing?'

'As far as I can tell,' Maurice answered, 'it seems to me to be over towards the Meuse, but the devil take me if I have the faintest idea where I am!'

'Look here chum,' the corporal said, 'you and I aren't going to get separated because, you see, you've got to have the know-how if you don't want to land in trouble. I've already been through all this, and I'll keep my eyes open for you as well as myself.'

By now the squad were beginning to grouse and get angry at having nothing hot to put in their stomachs. Can't light a fire with no dry wood in bloody awful weather like this! At the very moment when the battle was opening the question of the belly came back imperiously, decisively. Heroes perhaps, but bellies first and foremost. To eat, that was the sole concern, and with what rapture they skimmed the pot on good stew days, and what childish, savage tempers when bread was short!

'When you don't eat you don't fight,' declared Chouteau. 'I'll be buggered if I risk my skin today!'

The revolutionary was raising his head again in this great oaf of a house-painter, the Montmartre orator, the public-bar theorist who spoiled the few good ideas he picked up here and there in the most appalling mess-up of rubbish and lies.

'Besides,' he went on, 'what did they fucking well take us for, telling us the Prussians were dying of starvation and diseases, that they hadn't even got no shirts left and that you could meet them on the roads all dirty and ragged like a lot of tramps?'

Loubet began to laugh. He was a real Parisian smart aleck, who had dabbled in all the dubious jobs at the Markets.

'Don't you believe it, we're the ones pegging out in poverty, the ones people'd give a penny to when we go by with our cracked boots and scarecrow's clothes. And what about those famous victories? And that was a nice joke too, when they told us how Bismarck had been taken prisoner and that they had kicked a whole army of them into a quarry ... Balls! They were fucking well having us on!'

Pache and Lapoulle listened and clenched their fists, nodding furiously. And others were getting worked up too, for the final effect of these continuous lies in the papers was disastrous. The men had lost all confidence and no longer believed anything. The imaginings of these overgrown children, at first so fertile in wild hopes, were now collapsing into wild nightmares.

'Of course it's easy enough to see,' went on Chouteau, 'it's got a simple explanation, we've been sold down the river ... You all know that.'

Lapoulle's simple peasant mind was outraged each time this phrase cropped up.

'Sold down the river! Oh aren't they shits!'

'Sold, like Judas sold his Master,' murmured Pache, always haunted by biblical memories.

Chouteau was triumphant.

'It's quite simple, good Lord, we know the figures ... MacMahon has had three million and the other generals a million each for bringing us to this place ... It was all fixed up in Paris in the spring, and last night they fired a rocket just to tell them it was all ready and they could come and get us!'

Maurice was disgusted by the stupidity of this invention. Formerly Chouteau had amused him and almost won him over with his back-street smartness. But at the moment he could not stand this trouble-maker, the bad workman who spat on all the jobs so as to put off the others.

'Why do you say such absurdities?' he shouted. 'You know it isn't true!'

'What do you mean it isn't true? ... So it isn't true that we've been sold? ... Oh I say, your lordship, are you one of them too, one of that lot of fucking bastards?'

He advanced menacingly.

'Look here, it's about time it was said, Mister La-di-da, because we might not wait for your friend Bismarck but cook your goose straight away.'

The others were beginning to mutter, and so Jean thought he had better intervene.

'Now you shut up! I'll report the first one to move.'

But Chouteau sneered and booed at him. He didn't give a hoot for his report! He would fight or he wouldn't, just as he felt inclined, and they'd better not get across him any more, because he hadn't got bullets for Prussians only! Now that the battle was under way what little discipline had been maintained by fear was collapsing: what could anyone do to him? He'd just piss off when he had had enough. He began a slanging match, working the others up against the corporal who let them die of hunger. Yes, it was his fault that the squad hadn't had anything to eat for three days while the other blokes had had soup and meat. But of course the gentleman went out guzzling with his lordship and the tarts. Oh yes, they'd been seen in Sedan all right!

'You've blued the squad's money, and don't you dare to deny it, you bleeding swindler!'

Then things turned nasty. Lapoulle began clenching his fists, and Pache, for all his meekness, was crazed with hunger and demanding an explanation. The most sensible was Loubet once again, who began laughing his knowing laugh, saying it was daft for Frenchmen to be going for each other when the Prussians were just over there. He didn't hold with quarrels, whether with fists or guns, and referring to the few hundred francs he had received as a conscript's replacement, he added:

''Struth, if they think my carcass isn't worth more than that I'll give them something for their money.'

Maurice and Jean, annoyed by this mindless aggressiveness, were shouting back in self-defence when a loud voice came out of the fog:

'What's up? What's all this about? Which bloody fools are having a row now?'

Lieutenant Rochas appeared, in his rain-soiled képi and cape with buttons off, his whole lean and gawky person in a pitiful state of neglect and shabbiness. But that didn't affect his victorious cockiness, and his eyes were shining and his moustache bristling.

'Sir,' Jean said, beside himself with rage, 'what's up is these men shouting about the place that we have been betrayed ... Yes, they say our generals have sold us ...'

In Rochas's limited mind this idea of treason was not far from seeming the obvious thing, for it explained defeats he could not admit to.

'Well, what the fuck does it matter to them if we are sold? What business is it of theirs? It doesn't alter the fact that the Prussians are here and that we've got to give them one of those thrashings you don't forget in a hurry.'

Away behind the thick curtain of fog the gunfire at Bazeilles was continuous. He waved his arms with a sweeping gesture.

'Well, this time here it is! We're going to chase them back home with the butts of our rifles!'

For him, since he had heard the gunfire, everything else was wiped out: the delays, lack of direction on the march, demoralization of the troops, the disaster at Beaumont, the final agony of the forced retreat on Sedan. But since they were actually fighting, wasn't victory certain? He had learned nothing and forgotten nothing, and he kept his swaggering contempt for the enemy, his total ignorance of modern conditions of warfare, his obstinate certainty that a veteran of Africa, the Crimea and Italy was unbeatable. It really would be too silly to start again at his age!

A sudden laugh opened his jaws wide. He had one of those bursts of maty affection that made the soldiers worship him in spite of the ticking-off he sometimes handed out.

'Listen, boys, instead of squabbling it would be better to have a drink. Yes, I'm going to stand you all a drink and you can drink my health!'

And from a pocket deep in his cape he produced a bottle of brandy, adding with his triumphant air that it was a present from a lady. And indeed he had been seen the evening before at a table in a pub at Floing getting very fresh with the barmaid whom he had on his knee. By now the soldiers were laughing like mad, holding out their messtins into which he was gaily pouring.

'My lads, drink to your girlfriends if you've got any, and drink to the glory of France ... That's all I know about, so here's to fun!'

'Quite true, sir, here's to your health and everybody else's.'

They all drank, warmed up and friends again. This drink was a real treat in the chilly morning just before marching against the enemy. Maurice felt it running down into his veins, giving him the warmth and semi-tipsiness of illusion. Why shouldn't they beat the Prussians? Didn't battles have their surprises in store, the sudden changes of fortune that history looked at in wonderment? This devil of a man went on to say that Bazaine was on the march and was expected before the evening, and although it was actually Belgium he pointed to, when indicating the route Bazaine was taking, Maurice indulged in one of those upsurges of hope without which he could not live. Perhaps this was the moment of revenge after all.

'What are we waiting for, sir?' he ventured to ask. 'Aren't we going to start?'

Rochas made a sign meaning that he had no orders. Then after a pause:

'Has anyone seen the captain?'

There was no answer. Jean recollected having seen him stealing away after dark towards Sedan, but a prudent soldier should never see an officer when off duty. So he was keeping his mouth shut, when turning round he saw a shadowy form coming along the hedge.

'Here he is,' he said.

It was indeed Captain Beaudoin. He amazed them all by the smartness of his dress – his spotless uniform and polished boots contrasted violently with the bedraggled state of the lieutenant. Moreover there was about him a certain elegance, something of the lady-killer in his white hands and curled moustache, a vague perfume of Persian lilac such as pervades the well-stocked dressing-room of a pretty woman.

'Just look at that!' sneered Loubet. 'So the captain's found his luggage again!'

But nobody smiled because he was known to be difficult. He was detested and kept his men in their places. A real bastard, according to Rochas. Ever since the first reverses he had looked positively outraged, and the disaster that everybody had foreseen seemed to him bad form rather than anything else. A convinced Bonapartist and heading for the highest promotion, backed up by several salons, he felt his fortune sinking into all this mud. It was said that he had a very fine tenor voice to which he already owed a great deal. Not without intelligence, though knowing nothing about his profession, he was solely concerned with being acceptable, and he was also very brave, if necessary, but no fanatic.

'What a fog!' was all he said, thankful to find his own company again which he had spent the last half-hour looking for as he was afraid of being lost.

Immediately after that an order at last came through and the battalion moved forward. New billows of fog must have been coming up from the Meuse, for they almost groped their way along in a sort of whitish dew coming down in a fine drizzle. At that moment Maurice was struck by a vision – Colonel de Vineuil suddenly looming ahead, motionless on his horse at the junction of two roads, very tall and pale, like a marble statue of despair, his mount shivering in the morning cold with his nostrils open and turned away towards the guns. But most striking of all, ten paces to the rear the regimental flag, already out of its cover and held by the lieutenant on duty and flapping in the soft moving whiteness of the vapour, seemed to be up in a sky of dreams, an apparition of glory, trembling and on the point of vanishing away. The golden eagle was soaking wet and the silk tricolor, on which the names of victories were embroidered, looked faded and dirty, riddled with old wounds, and the only thing to stand out from all this dimness was the gleaming enamel of the arms of the cross of honour attached to the tassels.

Flag and colonel disappeared, swallowed up in a new cloud, and the battalion still advanced without knowing where it was going, as though in damp cotton wool. They had come downhill and were now climbing again up a narrow lane. The command to halt rang out. And there they stood easy, their packs weighing down on their shoulders, forbidden to move. They must be on some high land, but it was still impossible to see twenty paces and nothing could be made out. It was now seven, and the gunfire seemed to have come nearer, fresh batteries were firing on the other side of Sedan, nearer and nearer.

'Oh well,' Sergeant Sapin said in his matter-of-fact way to Jean and Maurice, 'I shall be killed today.'

He hadn't opened his mouth since reveille, but was lost in a dream, with his delicate face, large beautiful eyes and prim little nose.

'Well, that's a nice idea!' protested Jean. 'Can anyone say what he'll get? You know there's none for nobody and some for everybody.'

'Oh, as far as I'm concerned it's as though it was done already ... I shall be killed today!'

Heads turned round and asked if he had seen that in a dream. No, he hadn't dreamed anything, just felt it, and there it was.

'Still, it's annoying, because I was going to get married when I got home.'

His eyes wandered off again and he saw his own life. Son of a small grocer in Lyons, spoilt by his mother who had died, and unable to get on with his father, he had stayed with the regiment, fed up with everything and refusing to be bought out. Then on one of his leaves he had come to an understanding with a girl cousin, come to terms with life, and together they had worked out an attractive project for opening a business, thanks to the small sum she would bring with her. He had had some schooling – reading, writing and arithmetic. For the past year he had lived only for the joy of this future life.

He shivered and shook himself free of this dream, then calmly repreated:

'Yes, it's annoying, I shall be killed today.'

The talking stopped and the wait went on. There was no knowing even whether they had their backs or their fronts to the enemy. Vague sounds came now and again out of the foggy unknown: rumbling of wheels, tramping of feet, distant trotting of horses. These were troop movements hidden by the mist, all the manoeuvres of the 7th corps taking up its battle positions. But in the last few minutes the mist seemed to be thinning out. Shreds blew up like wisps of gauze and odd corners of the horizon came into sight, still indistinct, like the murky blue of deep water. It was in one of these breaks that the regiments of Chasseurs d'Afrique that formed part of the Margueritte division could be seen moving along like a procession of phantom riders. Bolt upright in their saddles, in their full regimentals with broad red belts, they were spurring on their mounts, slender creatures half hidden by their complicated kit. Squadron after squadron, they all emerged from the murk and went back into it as though they were melting in the fine drizzle. No doubt they were a nuisance and were being moved further off because nobody knew what to do with them, as had been the case since the outset of the campaign. They had been used just occasionally as scouts, and as soon as battle was joined they were moved from valley to valley as an expensive luxury.

Maurice watched them and thought of Prosper.

'Look,' he murmured, 'perhaps that's him over there.'

'Who?' asked Jean.

'That chap from Remilly, you remember, whose brother we met at Oches.'

But by now they had gone, and there was a sound of rapid galloping and a staff officer appeared down the hill. This time it was Jean who recognized General Bourgain-Desfeuilles, waving his arms wildly. So he had at last deigned to leave the Hôtel de la Croix d'Or, and from his bad temper it was clear enough that he was annoyed at having been up so early, to say nothing of deplorable conditions of lodging and food.

His stentorian voice carried as far as them.

'Oh, for God's sake, as though I knew! Moselle or Meuse, there's some water down there anyway!'

However the fog was really lifting. It was quite sudden, as at Bazeilles, like a stage set discovered behind the floating curtain as it slowly goes up into the flies. The bright sun poured down from a blue sky. At once Maurice realized where they were standing waiting.

'Oh,' he said to Jean, 'we're on the Algérie plateau . . . See over there, across the valley opposite us, that's Floing. And over there is Saint-Menges, and beyond that Fleigneux. And then right behind in the Ardennes forest, where you see those scraggy trees on the horizon, that's the frontier.'

He went on pointing things out. The plateau of Algérie was a belt of red earth about three kilometres long that sloped gently from the Garenne wood to the Meuse, from which it was separated by the meadows. It was there that General Douay had stationed the 7th corps, in despair at not having enough men to defend such a long drawn-out line and link up firmly with the 1st corps which was at right angles to him, occupying the valley of the Givonne, from the Garenne wood to Daigny.

'It's huge, isn't it, huge!'

Maurice turned and with a wave of the hand went round the horizon. From the plateau of Algérie the whole battlefield lay stretched out to the south and west: first Sedan, with its citadel dominating the rooftops, then Balan and Bazeilles with a pall of smoke that never went away. Then, beyond, the heights of the left bank, Le Liry, La Marfée, La Croix-Piau. But it was westwards, more especially, towards Donchery that the view was extensive. The loop of the Meuse surrounded the Iges peninsula with a pale ribbon, and there could be seen very clearly the narrow Saint-Albert road, running between the river bank and a steep cliff on top of which, far away, was the little Seugnon wood, a tail-end of the woods of La Falizette. The road from Vrigne-aux-Bois and Donchery came out at the top of the rise at the Maison-Rouge crossroads.

'You see, that's the way we could fall back on Mézières.'

But at that very minute the first round of artillery fire came from Saint-Menges. In the distance a few wisps of mist were still hanging about and nothing could be seen clearly except a vague shape moving through the Saint-Albert gap.

'Ah, here they come,' said Maurice, instinctively lowering his voice and not mentioning the Prussians by name. 'We're cut off, it's all up!'

It was not yet eight. The gunfire getting stronger in the Bazeilles direction could now be heard eastwards too, out of sight up the Givonne valley – it was just at the moment when the army of the Crown Prince of Saxony, emerging from the Chevalier wood, came up against the 1st corps before Daigny. And now that the XIth Prussian corps, marching on Floing, was opening fire on General Douay's troops, the battle was joined in all directions, from north to south round this immense perimeter of many leagues.

That was when Maurice fully realized the irreparable mistake that had been made in not falling back on Mézières during the night. But the consequences were not yet quite clear to him. It simply was that some deep instinct of danger made him glance anxiously at the neighbouring heights overlooking the plateau of Algérie. If they hadn't had time to effect a retreat, then why hadn't they decided to occupy those heights backing on to the frontier so that they could go into Belgium if they were thrown back? Two points looked especially menacing, the round hilltop of Le Hattoy, above Floing to the left, and the Calvary of Illy, a stone cross between two lime trees on the right. On the previous day General Douay had put a regiment in occupation on Le Hattoy, but being too exposed it was withdrawn at dusk. As for the Calvary of Illy, it was to be defended by the left wing of the 1st corps. The land extending between Sedan and the Ardennes was a vast expanse of bare earth, deeply indented with valleys, and the key to the position was obviously there, at the foot of that cross and those two lime trees, from which the whole of the surrounding country could be raked by gunfire.

Three more rounds of gunfire were heard, then a whole salvo. This time they saw smoke rise from a little hill to the left of Saint-Menges.

'Here we come,' said Jean. 'This is our turn.'

And yet nothing happened, the men were still just standing easy, and had nothing else to do except look at the fine arrangement of the second division drawn up in front of Floing with its left wing running at right-angles towards the Meuse to hold off an attack from that side. Eastwards the third division stretched as far as the Garenne woods below Illy, while the first, which had been very depleted at Beaumont, was a second line of defence. During the night the engineers had run up some defence works. Even now, under the opening fire of the Prussians, they were still making dug-outs and throwing up breastworks.

A fusillade burst out at the lower end of Floing, but was over almost at once, and Captain Beaudoin's company was ordered to fall back three hundred metres. They were entering a huge square cabbage-field when the captain snapped out:

'Everybody down!'

They had to lie flat. The cabbages were wet with heavy dew, and their thick greeny-yellow leaves retained drops as pure and bright as big jewels.

'Set your sights at four hundred,' the captain called out next.

Maurice supported the barrel of his rifle on a cabbage in front of him. But you couldn't see anything down at ground level like this, for the earth stretched on and was quite featureless, cut up by greenery. He nudged Jean, who was stretched out on his right, and asked him what the hell they were supposed to be doing. Jean, as an experienced soldier, showed him a battery they were installing on a near-by hillock. Clearly they had been positioned here to support this battery. Out of curiosity he stood up to see whether Honoré and his cannon were involved, but the reserve artillery was in the rear, protected by a clump of trees.

'For Christ's sake,' bawled Rochas, 'lie down, will you!'

Maurice had hardly got down again before a shell whistled overhead. From then on they never stopped. The range was only gradually adjusted, the first came well beyond the battery, which began to fire also. As a matter of fact many shells did not explode because they were deadened in soft earth, and at first there were plenty of jokes about the clumsiness of these bloody sauerkraut-eaters.

'Oh well,' said Loubet, 'their fireworks are duds.'

'I expect they've pissed on them!' added Chouteau with a grin.

Even Lieutenant Rochas joined in.

'I told you those silly sods can't even aim straight with a cannon!'

But then a shell burst ten metres away, spattering the company with earth. Although Loubet said something funny about the chaps getting out their clothes-brushes, Chouteau went pale and stopped talking. He had never been under fire, nor for that matter had Pache or Lapoulle, in fact nobody in the squad except Jean. Eyelids fluttered over worried eyes, and voices went thin as though they could not get out properly. Maurice had sufficient self-control to make an attempt at self-examination: he was not afraid yet, for he didn't think he was in any danger, and all he felt was a slight discomfort under the diaphragm, while his mind went blank and he couldn't put two ideas together in his head. Yet if anything his hopes were rising in a sort of elation since he had been struck with admiration at the discipline of the troops. He reached the state of no longer doubting victory if they could get close to the enemy with the bayonet.

'Funny,' he remarked, 'it's full of flies.'

Three times already he had heard what he took for a swarm of bees.

'Oh no,' laughed Jean, 'they're bullets.'

Other faint buzzings passed over. The whole squad looked round and began to take interest. It was irresistible, the men screwed their necks round and couldn't keep still.

'Look here,' Loubet advised Lapoulle, delighting in his simplicity, 'when you see a bullet coming all you've got to do is put one finger up in front of your nose like this, and that cuts the air and the bullet passes to the right or the left.'

'But I can't see them,' said Lapoulle.

At explosion of laughter burst around him.

'Oh the artful old devil, he can't see them! Open your optics, you fool! Look, there's one, there's another! ... Didn't you spot that one? It was green.'

Lapoulle opened his eyes wide, put one finger in front of his nose, while Pache was fingering the scapular he always had on him and would have liked to spread it out to make a breast-plate to cover all his chest.

Rochas, who had remained standing, called out in his chaffing way:

'No harm in saying hallo to shells, my boys, but it's no use for bullets – too many of 'em!'

Just then a piece of shell smashed in the head of a soldier in the front rank. Not even a cry – a jet of blood and brains, that was all.

'Poor bugger,' Sergeant Sapin said simply. He was very calm and very pale. 'Whose turn next?'

But after that nobody could hear anybody else speak. The frightful din was what upset Maurice most. The battery near-by was firing incessantly, with a continual roar that shook the very ground, and the *mitrailleuses* were worse still, rending the air, intolerable. Were they going to stay like this a long time, lying in the middle of the cabbages? They still could see nothing and knew nothing. It was impossible to have the slightest conception of the battle as a whole – was it even a real big battle? Above the bare line of the fields the only thing Maurice recognized was the round wooded top of Le Hattoy, a long way away and still unoccupied. Not that a single Prussian could be seen anywhere on the horizon, just puffs of smoke going up and floating for a moment in the sunshine. As he looked round he was very surprised to see down in a lonely valley, isolated by steep slopes, a peasant unhurriedly ploughing, guiding his plough behind a big white horse. Why lose a day's work? The corn wouldn't stop growing or people living just because there was fighting going on.

Overcome with impatience Maurice stood up. Casting his eyes round he again saw the batteries at Saint-Menges which were bombarding them, surmounted by lurid smoke, and in particular he saw once again the road from Saint-Albert black with Prussians, a milling horde of invaders. Already Jean was pulling at his legs and bringing him roughly down to the ground again.

'Are you crazy? You'll leave your body here!'

Rochas swore at him too:

'Will you lie down! Who landed me with a lot of bloody fools getting themselves killed without orders?'

'But sir,' Maurice said, 'you're not lying down, are you?'

'Oh, it's different for me, I have to know!'

Captain Beaudoin was also courageously standing, but he never opened his mouth, for he was out of touch with his men, and seemed unable to stand still, but kept on walking from end to end of the field.

Still waiting, nothing happening. Maurice felt suffocated beneath the weight of his pack which was pressing on his back and chest in this prone posture, so painful for any length of time. The men had been urged not to jettison their packs except in the very last resort.

'Look here, are we going to stay like this all day?' he finally asked Jean.

'May well be! At Solferino it was in a field of carrots, and we stayed there for five hours with our noses to the ground.'

Then, being a practical fellow, he went on:

'What are you complaining about? We aren't too bad here, and we shall have plenty of time to expose ourselves a bit more. We all get our turn, I can tell you. If you all got killed at the beginning, well, there wouldn't be anyone left for the end!'

'Oh,' Maurice suddenly cut in, 'look at that smoke on Le Hattoy ... They've taken Le Hattoy, now we're for it.'

For a short time his anxious curiosity, in which there was an element of his original fear, had some real reason. He kept his eyes fixed on the round top of the hill, the only mound he could see above the flat stretch of great fields on his eye level. Le Hattoy was much too far away for him to make out the crews of the batteries the Prussians had just installed there, and all he could really see was the puffs of smoke at each discharge over a copse in which the guns must be concealed. As he had felt earlier, it was a really serious thing that the enemy had taken this position that General Douay had had to give up defending. It commanded all the surrounding plateaux. All at once the batteries opened fire on the second division of the 7th corps and decimated it. Now they were getting the range, and the French battery near which the Beaudoin company was lying had two of its crew killed in quick succession. A splinter even came and wounded one man in their own company, a quartermaster whose left heel was blown off and who began shrieking with pain as though he had suddenly gone mad.

'Shut up, you fool!' cried Rochas. 'What's the sense in bawling like that for a silly little trouble in your foot!'

The man was suddenly calmed, he stopped and relapsed into a motionless lethargy, nursing his foot.

The formidable artillery duel went on, getting steadily fiercer over the heads of the prostrate regiments in the baking and depressing country where there was not a soul to be seen in the blazing sun. Nothing but this thunder and hurricane of destruction rolling through the solitude. The hours were to pass one after another and it would never stop. Yet already the superiority of the German artillery was becoming clear, their percussion shells almost all went off at enormous distances, whereas the French ones with fuses had a much shorter range and most often exploded in the air before reaching the target. And no other resource was left but to make oneself as small as possible in the furrow where one was cowering! Not even the relief, the thrill of going off the deep-end and firing a rifle, for who was there to fire at since you still couldn't see anybody on the empty horizon!

'Are we ever going to fire?' Maurice kept on saying in a flaming temper. 'I'd give five francs to see one of them. It's maddening to be machine-gunned like this and never be able to answer back!'

'Just wait, it'll come, I expect,' said Jean mildly.

A galloping on their left made them look up. They recognized General Douay, followed by his staff, who had hurried over to gauge the morale of his troops under the murderous fire from Le Hattoy. He seemed satisfied, and was giving some orders when General Bourgain-Desfeuilles also appeared, emerging from a sunken road. The latter, although a court soldier, was trotting quite unruffled amid the shells, hidebound in his African colonial routine and having learned nothing. He was shouting and gesticulating like Rochas.

'I'm expecting them. I'm expecting them now for a showdown at close quarters.'

Seeing General Douay he came over.

'General, is it true about the marshal's wound?'

'Yes, unfortunately . . . I've just had a note from General Ducrot in which he said that the marshal had named him commander-in-chief of the army.'

'Oh, so it's General Ducrot! Well, what are the orders?'

The general made a gesture of despair. Since the previous day he had felt that the army was doomed, and had insisted in vain that the positions at Saint-Menges and Illy must be occupied in order to cover a retreat on Mézières.

'Ducrot is going back to our plan, all troops are to concentrate on the plateau of Illy.'

He made the same gesture again, as though to say it was too late.

The noise of gunfire drowned his words, but the meaning had reached Maurice's ears and he was appalled. What! Marshal MacMahon wounded and General Ducrot in command instead, the whole army in retreat north of Sedan? And these terrible facts unknown to the soldiers, the poor devils getting killed, and this dreadful gamble dependent on a mere accident, the whim of a new command! He felt the confusion and final chaos into which the army was falling, with no chief, no plan and pushed about in all directions, while the Germans were making straight for their goal with their clear judgement and machine-like precision.

General Bourgain-Desfeuilles was already moving off when General Douay, who had just received a new message delivered by a dust-stained hussar, recalled him in stentorian tones.

'General! General!'

His voice was so loud and so thunderous with surprise and emotion that it could be heard above the noise of the artillery.

'General! It's no longer Ducrot in command, it's Wimpffen! ... Yes, he turned up yesterday in the middle of the Beaumont rout, to take over the command of the 5th corps from de Failly. And he writes that he has an official letter from the Minister of War putting him at the head of the army in the event of the command becoming vacant. And we don't fall back any more, orders are now to regain and defend our original positions.'

General Bourgain-Desfeuilles listened goggle-eyed.

'Good God!' he said. 'So long as we know ... For my part I don't give a damn anyway!'

He galloped away, not really interested at bottom, having only looked upon the war as a quick means of gaining promotion to general of division, and only too anxious that this stupid campaign should come to an end as soon as possible, as it was proving so unsatisfactory to everybody.

Then there came a burst of mirth from the soldiers of the Beaudoin company. Maurice said nothing, but he was of the same opinion as Chouteau and Loubet, who went off into scornful laughter. Gee up! Whoa back! Any old way you like! Look at that fine lot of officers who were all hand in glove and never looked after number one – I don't think! When you had officers like that wasn't the best thing you could do to go off and have a kip? Three commanders-in-chief in three hours, three clots who didn't even quite know what there was to do and gave different orders! No, straight, it was enough to make God Almighty in person lose his temper and throw his hand in! And then the inevitable accusations of treason began again – Ducrot and Wimpffen were out for Bismarck's three million, same as MacMahon.

General Douay had stayed alone at the head of his staff, looking into the distance at the Prussian positions, lost in an utterly depressing dream. For a long while he examined Le Hattoy, shells from which were falling at his feet. Then, having turned towards the plateau of Illy, he summoned an officer to take an order over to the brigade of the 5th corps he had borrowed from Wimpffen the day before and which linked him up with General Ducrot's left. Once more he was clearly heard saying:

'If the Prussians captured the Calvary we couldn't hold on here for an hour, but would be thrown back into Sedan.'

He left, disappearing with his escort round a bend in the sunken road, and the gunfire redoubled its intensity. Perhaps they had spotted him. The shells, which so far had only been coming from straight in front, now began to rain down obliquely from the left. They were the batteries on Frénois and another battery on the Iges peninsula, and they were directing a cross-fire with those on Le Hattoy. The whole plateau of Algérie was being swept by them. From then on the situation of the company became terrible. Men concerned with watching what was happening in front of them had this new worry in their rear and did not know which threat to dodge. Three men were killed in quick succession, and two wounded men were screaming.

So it was that Sergeant Sapin met the death he was expecting. He had turned round and he saw the shell coming when it could no longer be avoided.

'Ah, here it is!' was all he said.

His little face, with its big, beautiful eyes, was merely deeply sad, with no terror. His belly was split open. He moaned:

'Oh, don't leave me here, take me away to the ambulance, please ... Take me away!'

Rochas wanted to shut him up, and was on the point of telling him brutally that with a wound like that there was no point in upsetting all his comrades. But then he was touched:

'Poor old chap, just wait a bit for the stretcher-bearers to come for you.'

But the wretched man went on, crying now, maddened by the dream of happiness departing with his life-blood.

'Take me away, take me away ...'

Captain Beaudoin, whose jangled nerves were no doubt exasperated by this moaning, asked for two willing men who would carry him into a little spinney close by, where there must be a mobile ambulance. With one bound Chouteau and Loubet leaped up, forestalling the others, and seized the sergeant, one by the shoulders and the other by the feet, and started carrying him off at the double. But on the way they felt him stiffen and expire in a final convulsion.

'Look here, he's dead,' declared Loubet. 'Let's drop him!'

Chouteau stuck to it furiously.

'Get a move on, you lazy sod! I'm not bloody well dumping him here and getting called back!'

They held to their course with the body as far as the spinney, threw it down under a tree and cleared off. They were not seen again until evening.

The fire intensified, the battery close by had been reinforced with two guns and in the mounting din Maurice was seized by fear, insane fear. At first he had not had this cold sweat and painful sensation of collapse in the pit of the stomach, the irresistible urge to get up and run, screaming. Perhaps even now it was only due to thinking too much, as happens in sensitive and nervous natures. But Jean, who was keeping an eye on him, gripped him with his strong hand and made him stay near him, reading this fit of cowardice in the worried darting of his eyes. He swore at him softly and paternally, trying to shame him out of it with harsh words because he knew that you put courage back into men by giving them a kick up the backside. Others had got the shivers too. Pache had tears in his eyes and was whimpering with a soft, involuntary wail, like a little child's, which he could not stop. And then Lapoulle had an accident – such an upset of the bowels that he pulled his trousers down there and then, with no time to get to the hedge. He was cheered and they threw clods of earth at his bare arse displayed to bullets and shells. Many of them were taken short in this way, and relieved themselves amid obscene mirth which restored everyone's courage.

'You cowardly bugger,' Jean was saying to Maurice, 'you're not going to shit yourself like them . . . I'll sock you one on the jaw if you don't behave yourself!'

He was putting new heart into him with these rough words when all of a sudden, four hundred metres in front of them, they saw ten or so men in dark-coloured uniforms coming out of a little wood. They could tell by their pointed helmets that they were Prussians at last, the first Prussians they had seen within range of their rifles since the beginning of the campaign. Other squads of them followed the first, and in front of them they could make out the little clouds of dust sent up from the ground by shells. It was all clearly defined, the Prussians were sharply outlined like little tin soldiers set out in perfect order. Then, as the shells rained thicker they went back and disappeared into the trees.

But the Beaudoin company had spotted them and could still see them there. Rifles had gone off of their own accord. Maurice was the first to fire his, and Jean, Pache, Lapoulle and all the others followed. No order had been given, and the captain wanted to stop the firing and only gave in when Rochas waved his arm indicating that the men needed this relief. So at last they were firing, they were using this ammunition they had been carting round for over a month without ever letting any off! Maurice above all was heartened, with something to do for his fear, intoxicating himself with detonations. The edge of the wood looked dreary and not a leaf stirred, nor had a single Prussian reappeared. They were firing all the time at motionless trees.

Having glanced up, Maurice was surprised to see Colonel de Vineuil a few paces away, on his big horse, man and beast quite undisturbed as though made of stone. With his face to the enemy the colonel waited in the hail of bullets. The whole 106th must have closed in there, other companies were lying in the adjoining fields and the rifle-fire was spreading from one to another. A little to the rear Maurice also saw the flag and the strong arm of the subaltern who was bearing it. But now it was not that ghostly flag half lost in the morning mist. In the blazing sun the golden eagle shone forth and the silk tricolor gleamed in brilliant tones in spite of all the wear and tear of battles. Against the blue sky, in the hurricane of gunfire, it floated like a flag of victory.

Why shouldn't they win now that they were fighting? Maurice and all the others went mad and fired as though to kill the distant wood, in which a slow silent rain of twigs came down.

3

HENRIETTE could not get to sleep all night, tortured by the thought that her husband was at Bazeilles, so near to the German lines. In vain she kept reminding herself of his promise to come home at the first sign of danger, and every minute she was straining her ears, thinking she could hear him. At about ten, before going to bed, she opened the window, leaned out and forgot all about time.

It was a very dark night and she could hardly make out beneath her the cobbles of the rue des Voyards, a dark, narrow passage between the old houses. Further off, towards the school there was only the smoky star of a street lamp. From down there somewhere there came up a musty smell of cellars, the miaowing of a fighting cat, the heavy tread of some stray soldier. Then behind her, from all over Sedan, there came unusual sounds, rapid gallopings, and rumbling noises like premonitions of death. As she listened her heart thudded faster, but still she did not recognize her husband's step round the corner.

Hours went by, and now she was worried by distant lights out in the country beyond the ramparts. It was so dark that she had to make an effort to place things. That great pale sheet down there must be the flooded meadows. So what was that light she had seen come on and then go out up there, perhaps on La Marfée? Others flared up in all directions, at Pont-Maugis, Noyers, Frénois, mysterious lights twinkling as if over a countless multitude teeming in the night. And then another thing, extraordinary noises startled her, like the tramp of a people on the move, snorting of animals, clashing of arms, a whole cavalcade in this infernal darkness.

Suddenly a single cannon shot rang out, terrifying in the absolute silence that followed. It froze her blood. What could it be? No doubt some signal, some manoeuvre successfully carried out, an announcement that they were now ready over there and that the sun could come out.

At about two Henriette threw herself on the bed, fully clothed, not even bothering to shut the window. She was overcome with fatigue and anxiety. What was the matter with her, shivering like this as though she had a temperature, for she was usually so placid, so light on her feet that you hardly heard her busying herself about. She fell into a troubled doze, numbed with a persistent sensation of impending doom in the black sky. Suddenly she was dragged from the depths of her uneasy sleep by the gunfire starting again with dull, distant boomings, but this time it went on, regular and persistent. She sat up, shuddering. Where was she? She did not recognize or even see the room, which seemed to be filled with dense smoke. Then she understood – the fog rising from the river near by must have got into the room. Out there the gunfire was getting heavier. She jumped up and ran to the window to listen.

Some church clock in Sedan was striking four. Day was just breaking, evil-looking and murky in the brownish fog. Impossible to see anything, she could not make out the school buildings a few metres away. Oh God, where were they firing? Her first thought was for her brother Maurice, for the reports were so muffled that they seemed to be coming from the north and over the town. Then, and there was no doubt about it, they were firing there, in front of her, and she trembled for her husband. It was at Bazeilles for certain. And yet she felt reassured again for a few minutes because the detonations seemed occasionally to be coming from her right. Perhaps the fighting was at Donchery where she knew they had not been able to blow up the bridge. And then she was seized by cruel uncertainty – was it Donchery, was it Bazeilles? With the noises in her head it was impossible to tell. Soon the torture was such that she felt she could not stay there waiting any longer. Quivering with an imperative need to know, she threw a shawl over her shoulders and went out to find news.

Down in the rue des Voyards Henriette had a moment of hesitation because the town seemed so dark still in the impenetrable fog which enveloped it. The light of dawn had not reached down to the damp cobbles between the black walls of the old houses. In the rue au Beurre all she saw was two drunken Algerians with a girl in a sleazy bar lit by one flickering candle. She had to turn into the rue Maqua before she found any sign of life – shapes of soldiers furtively making their way along the pavements, probably deserters looking for somewhere to hide; a tall cuirassier wandering about, sent to find his captain and knocking violently on doors; a stream of bourgeois sweating with fear because they had dallied so long in deciding to pile into a cart and try to see whether there was still time to reach Bouillon in Belgium, where half Sedan had been emigrating over the past two days. She instinctively made for the Sub-Prefecture, feeling sure she would get some information there, and as she wanted to avoid meeting anybody she thought she would cut through side streets. But at the rue du Four and rue des Laboureurs she could not get through, for there was an unbroken line of guns, gun-carriages and ammunition waggons that must have been parked in this back street the day before and apparently forgotten. There was not even a single man guarding them. It struck cold into her heart to see all this useless artillery dismally sleeping abandoned in these deserted alleys. So she had to retrace her steps through the Place du Collège towards the Grand-Rue where, in front of the Hôtel de l'Europe, orderlies were holding horses in readiness for high officers whose loud voices could be heard coming from the dining-room, which was brilliantly lit. On the Place du Rivage and Place Turenne there were still more people, groups of worried townsfolk, women and children mingling with some of the soldiers who had deserted and were running wild, and there she saw a general come swearing out of the Hôtel de la Croix d'Or and gallop off madly without bothering about knocking everyone down. For a moment it looked as if she might go into the Hôtel de Ville, but in the end she took the rue du Pont de Meuse and went on to the Sub-Prefecture.

Never before had Sedan given her this impression of being a tragic, doomed town as it did now, seen in the murky, misty early morning. The very houses seemed dead, and many had been abandoned and empty for two days, others remained hermetically sealed and one sensed inside them a frightened insomnia. It was a really shivery morning, with streets still half deserted and only peopled by anxious shadows or enlivened by some hurried departure, with doubtful characters still hanging about since the day before. It was beginning to get lighter and soon the town would become crowded and overwhelmed by the disaster. It was half-past five and the noise of the gunfire, deadened between these lofty, dark buildings, could hardly be heard.

At the Sub-Prefecture Henriette saw the concierge's daughter Rose, a fair, delicate-looking pretty little thing, who worked at the Delaherche mill. She went straight to the lodge. The mother was not there, but Rose greeted her in her charming way.

'Oh, dear lady, we're simply dropping! Mother has just gone for a little rest. Just think, all night long and we have had to be on our feet with these continual comings and goings!'

And without waiting to be asked, she talked on and on, thoroughly worked up about the extraordinary things she had seen since the day before.

'Oh, the marshal slept all right, he did. But the poor Emperor! No, you can't imagine what he is going through. Just fancy, yesterday evening I went upstairs to help put out some linen. Well, going into the room next to the bathroom I heard groans, yes, groans, as though somebody was dying. And there I stood trembling, and my blood ran cold when I realized that it was the Emperor ... It seems he has some awful illness that makes him cry out like that. When there are people about he holds it in, but as soon as he is alone it gets the better of his self-control, and he shouts and moans fit to make your hair stand on end.'

'Where has the fighting been this morning, do you know?' asked Henriette, trying to cut her short.

Rose waved the question aside and went on:

'So you see, I wanted to find out, so I went up again four or five times during the night and glued my ear to the wall ... He was still moaning and hasn't ever stopped, and hasn't slept a minute, I'm quite sure ... Isn't it awful to be in such pain, with all the worries he must have on his mind, for it's a real mess, a madhouse. Upon my word, they all look mad! And always somebody else arriving, and doors banging, and people in a temper and others crying, and the whole building is being pillaged, everything upside down, what with the officers drinking out of bottles and lying in beds with their boots on! When you come to think of it, it is really the Emperor who is the nicest and takes up least room in the corner where he goes off and hides so as he can moan!'

Then as Henriette repeated her question:

'Where the fighting is? At Bazeilles, they've been fighting there since first thing. A soldier on horseback came to report it to the marshal who went straight to the Emperor to warn him ... It's already ten minutes since the marshal went off, and I think the Emperor must be joining him because up there they're dressing him ... I saw just now they were combing his hair and dolling him up with all sorts of stuff on his face.'

But knowing now what she wanted to know, Henriette fled.

'Thanks, Rose, I'm in a hurry.'

The girl obligingly escorted her to the street and threw in by way of a farewell:

'You're very welcome, Madame Weiss. I know I can say anything to you.'

Henriette hurried back home to the rue des Voyards. She was certain she would find her husband back, and she even thought that if he didn't find her at home he would be very worried, and that made her quicken her step still more. As she approached the house she looked up, thinking she could see him up there leaning out of the window, watching for her return. But the window was still wide open and empty. When she got up there and had glanced round the three rooms she was sick at heart on finding nothing but the icy fog and the continual rumbling of cannon. The firing out there never stopped. She went back to the window for a moment. Now that she knew what was happening, even though the wall of morning mist was still impenetrable, she could follow out the battle going on at Bazeilles, with the crackling of machine-guns and shattering volleys of the French batteries replying to the distant volleys of the German ones. One had the impression that the detonations were getting closer together and that the battle was getting fiercer every minute.

Why wasn't Weiss back? He had so solemnly promised to come home at the first attack! Henriette's anxiety steadily grew as in her imagination she saw obstacles, the road cut, shells already making retreat too perilous. Perhaps something dreadful had happened to him. She thrust the thought aside, finding in hope a strong incentive for action. She thought for a moment of setting off in that direction to meet her husband, but second thoughts held her back – they might cross, and then what would happen to her if she missed him? And what agonies he would go through if he came back and didn't find her. But the courage needed for a visit to Bazeilles at that moment seemed perfectly natural to her and not a case of foolhardy heroism, just part of her function as an active wife quietly carrying out whatever the proper running of her home demanded. Where her husband was she would be, that was all.

But then she made a sudden gesture and said aloud, as she left the window:

'And Monsieur Delaherche . . . I'll go and see.'

It had just occured to her that the mill-owner had slept at Bazeilles too, and that if he was back she would get news from him. She went downstairs again at once, but instead of going out by the rue des Voyards she crossed the narrow courtyard and took the passage leading to the huge factory buildings, the monumental frontage of which looked on to the rue Maqua. As she emerged into what was once the inner garden, now paved over except for a lawn surrounded by some superb trees, giant elms dating from the last century, she was at first surprised to see a sentry posted in front of the locked door of a coach-house, until she remembered that she had heard the day before that the cash of the 7th corps was deposited there, and it struck her as odd that all this gold, millions it was said, was hidden in this coach-house while they were already killing each other all round. But just as she was going up the service stairs to get to Gilberte's room another surprise brought her to a standstill, such an unexpected encounter that she came down the three steps she had already climbed, wondering whether she dared to go up and knock. A soldier, a captain had crossed her path, swift as a vision, and vanished. Nevertheless she had had time to recognize him, having seen him in Charleville at Gilberte's when she was still Madame Maginot. She walked about in the courtyard for a few moments, looked up at the two lofty windows of the bedroom, the shutters of which were still closed. Then she made up her mind and went up all the same.

On the first floor she thought she would knock on the door of the dressing-room as an intimate childhood friend who sometimes came for a morning chat. But this door had not been shut properly in a hurried departure, and was ajar. She only had to give it a push and she was in the dressing-room and then in the bedroom. It was a room with a very lofty ceiling from which hung voluminous red velvet curtains which surrounded the whole bed. Not a sound, the sultry silence of a happy night, nothing except a regular, almost inaudible breathing in an atmosphere vaguely scented with essence of lilac.

'Gilberte!' she whispered.

The young woman had gone to sleep again at once, and in the dim light coming through the red window curtains she had her pretty round face, set in the pillow, resting on one of her bare arms and surrounded by her lovely rumpled black hair.

'Gilberte!'

She stirred, stretched, but did not open her eyes.

'Yes, good-bye ... Oh, never mind ...'

Then, looking up, she recognized Henriette.

'Oh, it's you! ... What's the time, then?'

When she learned that it was just six she was somewhat embarrassed and joked to cover it up, saying it was no time for waking people out of their sleep. Then in answer to the first question about her husband:

'But he hasn't come back yet, he won't before nine, I think. What makes you think he will come home so early?'

Henriette, seeing her smiling away in drowsy contentment, had to insist.

'I'm telling you, they've been fighting in Bazeilles since dawn, and as I'm worried about my husband ...'

'Oh my dear, you've no need to be,' exclaimed Gilberte. 'Mine is so cautious that he would have been here hours ago if there had been the slightest danger ... Get along with you, so long as he doesn't come back there's no need to worry.'

This thought made a strong impression on Henriette, for it was quite true that Delaherche was not the sort of man to take pointless risks. She was quite reassured, went over and pulled back the curtains and pushed open the shutters, and the room was lit up by the bright pinkish light from the sky in which the sun was beginning to pierce the fog with gold. One of the windows was half open and you could now hear the gunfire in this big warm room, so close and shut in until a moment ago.

Gilberte, half sitting up, with one elbow on the pillow, looked at the sky with her lovely light eyes.

'So there's some fighting,' she said.

Her nightdress had slipped down and one of her shoulders was bare, showing her soft pink skin through the strands of her dark hair, and a strong aroma of love came from her awakening body.

'They're fighting so early, oh dear! It's so silly to fight!'

But Henriette's eye had been caught by a pair of army gloves, a man's gloves, forgotten on a table, and she had not managed to restrain a start. Then Gilberte went very red and drew her over to the bed with a confused and affectionate movement and buried her face in her shoulder.

'Yes, I felt sure you knew, that you had seen ... My dear, you mustn't judge me too harshly. He's an old friend, I told you about him and me at Charleville in the old days, don't you remember?'

She spoke more softly still and went on sentimentally but with a little giggle:

'He begged so hard yesterday when I met him again ... Just think, he's fighting this morning and he might get killed ... I couldn't refuse, could I?'

It was heroic and charming in its tender gaiety, this last present of pleasure, this night of happiness freely bestowed on the battle eve. That was what was making her smile, with her bird-brained frivolity, despite her embarrassment. She would never have had the heart to shut her door, since everything worked together to facilitate the meeting.

'Do you blame me?'

Henriette had looked very serious while she was listening. Such things took her aback because she did not understand them. Perhaps she was different. Since first thing that morning her heart had been with her husband and her brother out there under fire. How could anyone sleep so peacefully and go in for such carefree dallying when loved ones were in peril?

'But my dear, doesn't it make your heart ache not to be with your husband, or even that young man? Don't you think all the time that at any minute they may be brought back to you broken and disfigured?'

With a quick movement of her adorable bare arm Gilberte thrust away the awful vision.

'Oh my God, what *are* you saying? You really are horrid, spoiling my morning like this! No, no, I refuse to think about it, it's too depressing!'

Even Henriette could not help smiling. She recalled their childhood, when Gilberte's father, Major de Vineuil, was appointed customs officer for Charleville after being invalided out and had sent his daughter to a farm near Le Chêne-Populeux because he was worried about her cough. He was haunted by the death of his wife who had been carried off very young by tuberculosis. The little girl was only nine, and already she was restless and coquettish, went in for play-acting, dressing herself up as a queen in any old things she could find, keeping silver paper from chocolate to make bracelets and crowns. She remained like that later, and at twenty had married Maginot, a forestry inspector. She disliked Mézières, all shut in by its ramparts, and continued to live in Charleville, where she preferred the freer life brightened up with parties. Her father had died and she enjoyed absolute freedom with an easy-going husband who was such a nonentity that she had no scruples. Provincial gossip had given her many lovers, but she had only really let herself go with Captain Beaudoin out of the vast numbers of uniforms she had lived among thanks to the former connexions of her father and her relationship with Colonel de Vineuil. There was no vice in her, she simply loved pleasure, and it seemed quite clear that in taking lovers she had been indulging her irresistible need to be beautiful and gay.

'It's very wrong to have started up with him again,' Henriette finally said in her serious tone.

But Gilberte at once shut her mouth with one of her pretty, affectionate gestures.

'Oh my dear, but how could I do anything else, and it was only for once ... You know I would rather die than deceive my new husband.'

They both stopped talking and stayed in an affectionate embrace, though so profoundly unlike each other. At that moment they could hear the beating of their hearts and might have understood the different languages of those hearts – the one living for her own happiness, giving herself, sharing herself, the other filled with a single devotion with the great silent heroism of noble souls.

'Yes, they're fighting, it's true,' cried Gilberte at long last. 'I must hurry up and get dressed.'

Since they had been silent the sound of gunfire had indeed seemed louder. She jumped out of bed, got Henriette to help her, not wanting to call her maid, putting on shoes, getting quickly into a dress so as to be ready to receive anybody or go downstairs if necessary. As she was quickly finishing her hair there was a knock, and recognizing old Madame Delaherche's voice she ran to open the door.

'Of course, Mother dear, do come in.'

With her usual thoughtlessness she let her in without noticing that the army gloves were still there on the table. Henriette rushed to seize them and throw them behind an armchair, but in vain. Madame Delaherche must have noticed them, for she remained speechless for several seconds, as though she could not get her breath. She instinctively ran her eyes round the room, let them pause on the red curtained bed, still all unmade and in disorder.

'So it was Madame Weiss who came up and woke you . . . You managed to sleep, my dear.'

Obviously she had not come to say that. Oh dear, this marriage that her son had insisted on going into against her will, at the dangerous age of fifty, after twenty years of a frigid married existence with a disagreeable, scraggy woman! He had been so reasonable until then, and was now carried away by a youthful passion for this pretty widow who was so flighty and frivolous! She had made up her mind to keep an eye on the present, and now here was the past coming back! But should she say anything? As it was she only existed as a silent reproach in the home, always stayed shut up in her room, and was unbending in her religious life. But this time the disloyalty was so flagrant that she resolved to tell her son.

Gilberte blushed and answered:

'Yes, I did manage to get a few hours of good sleep . . . You know Jules still hasn't come back.'

Madame Delaherche cut her short with a gesture. She had been worrying ever since the gunfire began, and watching out for her son's return. But she was a heroic mother. And then she remembered what she had come to do.

'Your uncle the colonel has sent Major Bouroche with a pencilled note to ask whether we could fit up a casualty station here. He knows we've got room in the mill, and I've already put the yard and drying-shed at their disposal ... Only you ought to go down ...'

'Oh yes, straight away! Straight away!' said Henriette, joining in. 'We'll help.'

Gilberte herself seemed very concerned and enthusiastic about this new role as a nurse. She just took the time to tie a lace scarf over her hair and the three women went down. As they reached the archway down below, through the open gate they saw some people gathered in the street. A low vehicle was slowly coming along, a sort of trap with one horse being led by a lieutenant in the Zouaves. They thought it was the first wounded being brought in.

'Yes, yes, here it is, come in!'

But they were quickly undeceived. The wounded man lying on the floor of the trap was Marshal MacMahon, part of whose left buttock had been shot away, and he was being brought to the Sub-Prefecture after an emergency dressing in a gardener's cottage. He was bareheaded and half undressed, and the gold braid on his uniform was soiled with dirt and blood. Without speaking he lifted his head and looked about him vaguely. Then seeing the three women standing horrified and wringing their hands as this great disaster went by – the whole army stricken in its commander-in-chief as the very first shots were fired – he nodded slightly with a wan paternal smile. A few onlookers standing by had doffed their hats. Others were already busily explaining that General Ducrot had been appointed commander-in-chief. It was half past seven.

'And what about the Emperor?' Henriette asked a bookseller standing at his door.

'He went by nearly an hour ago,' answered the neighbour. 'I went along with him and saw him go out by the Balan gate. There's a rumour that his head has been shot off.'

The grocer opposite was angry.

'Come off it, that can't be true! Only the brave give their lives.'

Towards the Place du Collège the trap carrying the marshal disappeared into the swelling crowds, among whom the most far-fetched reports from the battlefield were already going round. The mist was thinning and the streets filling with sunshine.

But then there came a harsh voice from the courtyard:

'Ladies, it isn't there you are wanted, but in here!'

All three went in and found themselves confronted by Major Bouroche, the medical officer, who had already thrown his uniform jacket into a corner and put on a big white apron. His huge head with coarse bristling hair and leonine face seemed flaming with urgency and energy above all this still unstained whiteness. He struck them as so terrible that they were instantly subjugated, obeying his every sign and rushing to satisfy him.

'We've got nothing . . . Give me some linen, try and find some more mattresses, show my chaps where the pump is . . .'

They rushed about busily and became simply his servants.

The mill was a very good choice for an ambulance station. There was in particular the drying-shed, an enormous room with glass at the end where there was ample room for a hundred beds, and at one side there was a shed which would be ideal for operating: a long table had been brought in, the pump was quite near, and those with minor injuries could wait on the lawn just near, which happened to be very pleasant, for the lovely old elms were delightfully shady.

Bouroche had preferred to establish himself straight away in Sedan, foreseeing the massacre and the appalling pressure that would force the troops back into the town. He had merely left, close to the 7th corps, behind Floing, two mobile ambulance units for first aid, from which the wounded could be sent on to him after emergency dressings. All the stretcher-bearing squads were out there with the job of picking up under fire any men who fell, and they had the carts and vans. And apart from two of his assistants left on the battlefield Bouroche had brought his staff, two assistant medical officers and three juniors, which might be enough to cope with the operations. In addition there were three dispensers and a dozen medical orderlies.

But he was still fuming, being a man unable to do anything without passion.

'What are you up to now? Put those mattresses closer together . . . We'll put some straw in that corner if necessary.'

The guns were roaring, and he knew that the work would be coming in at any moment now, vehicles full of bleeding flesh, and he was frantically fitting up the big and still empty room. Then there were other preparations going on in the shed: boxes of dressings and medicaments all open and set out on a plank, packets of lint, bandages, compresses, linen, splints for fractures; while on another shelf beside a large pot of ointment and a bottle of chloroform the sets of instruments were laid out, all of shining steel, probes, pincers, knives, scissors, saws, an arsenal of every kind of point and blade for probing, making incisions, slicing, cutting off. But there were no bowls.

'You must have some basins, buckets, saucepans, any old thing ... We can't muck ourselves up with blood up to our eyes, can we? And sponges, try and get me some sponges!'

Madame Delaherche rushed off and came back followed by three maids loaded with all the bowls they could find. Standing by the instruments Gilberte had beckoned Henriette over and shown them to her with a little shudder. They held each other's hands and stood there in silence, expressing with the pressure of their hands the vague terror, pity and anxiety overwhelming them.

'Oh my dear, to think of having a limb cut off!'

'Poor creatures!'

On the big table Bouroche had had a mattress put and was covering it with oilcloth when a clatter of horses' hoofs was heard under the archway. It was the first ambulance coming into the courtyard, but it only contained ten slightly wounded men sitting facing each other, most of them with an arm in a sling, a few with head wounds and bandaged foreheads. They got out themselves with just a little help and the examination began.

As Henriette was gently helping a very young soldier with a bullet wound in his shoulder to get his cape off, which made him cry out in pain, she noticed the number of his regiment.

'But you belong to the 106th! Are you in the Beaudoin company?'

No, he was in Ravaud's. But he did know Corporal Jean Macquart, and thought he was right in saying that his squad had not yet been in action. This very vague piece of information was enough to cheer her up, though; her brother was alive so far, and she would be quite all right when she had embraced her husband, whom she was still expecting at any minute.

Just then Henriette looked up and was amazed to see, standing in a group of people a few steps away, Delaherche, holding forth about the terrible dangers he had just come through between Bazeilles and Sedan. How had he got here? She hadn't seen him come in.

'Isn't my husband with you?'

But Delaherche, whose mother and wife were enjoying questioning him, was in no hurry.

'Just a minute.'

He took up his story again:

'Between Bazeilles and Balan I was nearly killed twenty times. A hail of bullets and shells – no, a hurricane! ... And I ran into the Emperor, oh, very brave! Then from Balan here I dashed ...'

Henriette pulled his arm.

'My husband?'

'Weiss? Oh, he stayed there, Weiss did!'

'There? What do you mean?'

'Yes, he picked up a dead soldier's rifle, he's fighting.'

'Fighting – but why?'

'Oh, he's quite off his head. He simply wouldn't come with me, so I left him, naturally.'

Henriette looked at him with staring eyes. There was a silence. Then she calmly made up her mind.

'All right, I'm going there.'

She was going there, but how? But it was impossible, crazy. Delaherche began again about the bullets and shells sweeping the road. Gilberte had seized her hand again to stop her, and Madame Delaherche also tried in vain to point out the absurd rashness of her idea. She said again in her quiet, calm way:

'No, there's nothing you can say, I'm going.'

She insisted, and all she would agree to take was Gilberte's black lace head-scarf. Still hoping to convince her, Delaherche finally declared he would go with her, at any rate as far as the Balan gate. But at that moment he caught sight of the sentry who throughout the commotion of the installation of the casualty station had gone on pacing up and down in front of the coach-house in which the cash of the 7th corps was being kept under lock and key. He remembered and was afraid, and went to see if the millions were still there. Meanwhile Henriette was already on her way under the archway.

'Wait for me! My word, you're as crazy as your husband!'

But as another ambulance vehicle was coming in they had to let it pass. This was smaller, with only two wheels, containing two badly wounded lying on stretchers. The first one they brought out, with infinite care, was nothing but a mass of bleeding flesh with one hand smashed and the whole of one side torn through by a shell splinter. The second one had his right leg crushed. At once Bouroche had this one placed on the mattress and began the first operation, with orderlies and his assistants ceaselessly running to and fro. Madame Delaherche and Gilberte were sitting near the lawn, rolling bandages.

Outside, Delaherche caught up with Henriette.

'Look here, my dear Madame Weiss, you're not going to do such a silly thing . . . How do you think you can get to Weiss out there? He can't even still be there by now, and must have taken to the fields to get back . . . I assure you that Bazeilles is unreachable.'

But she was not listening, and walked on faster, entering the rue du Ménil to get to the Balan gate. It was nearly nine, and Sedan had emerged from the dark, shivery morning and desolate, blind awakening in the thick fog. A sultry sun cast hard shadows of the houses, the roadway was filled with an anxious crowd, through which dispatch-riders were continually galloping. Groups formed round the few unarmed soldiers who had already come back into the town, some slightly wounded, others in a state of extraordinary emotional tension, gesticulating and shouting. And yet the town would still have had its everyday look were it not for the shops with shutters closed and dead-looking façades in which not a single blind was open. Moreover there was this continual gunfire making everything tremble, stones, ground, walls and even the slates on the roofs.

Delaherche was a prey to the most unpleasant inner struggle, torn between his duty as a brave man which bade him not to desert Henriette and his terror of going back along the Bazeilles road under shell-fire. Suddenly, just as they reached the Balan gate they were separated by a number of officers coming in on horseback. People were packed tight near the gate, waiting for news. He ran along looking for the young woman, but in vain, she must be beyond the walls and hurrying along the road. He did not push his zeal any further, but was surprised to catch himself saying aloud:

'Oh, what the hell! It's too ridiculous!'

So he wandered about in Sedan, a citizen full of curiosity and not wanting to miss any of the sights, but also full of growing anxiety. What was it all going to lead to? If the army was beaten wouldn't the town be in for a very bad time? The answers to these questions remained obscure and depended too much on the turn of events. But that did not prevent him from trembling for his mill, his buildings in the rue Maqua, even though he had moved away all his valuables and hidden them in a safe place. He went to the Hôtel de Ville and found the council in permanent session. He hung about there for a long time but learned nothing new unless it was that the battle was going very badly. The army did not know whom to obey, moved backwards by General Ducrot during the two hours of his command and forwards again by General de Wimpffen who had succeeded him, and these incomprehensible comings and goings, positions they had to reconquer after abandoning them, the whole absence of any plan or energetic leadership were precipitating the disaster.

Next Delaherche moved on to the Sub-Prefecture to find out whether the Emperor had reappeared or not. The only news anyone could give him was about Marshal MacMahon whose wound, not at all dangerous, had been dressed by a surgeon and who was now peacefully in bed. But towards eleven, while he was still tramping the streets, he was held up for a moment in the Grande-Rue in front of the Hôtel de l'Europe by a slow procession of horsemen covered with dust whose weary mounts were going at a walking pace. At their head he recognized the Emperor, returning after spending four hours on the field of battle. Death hadn't any use for him, obviously. In the anguished sweat of this ride through defeat the make-up had gone from his cheeks and his waxed moustache had got soft and drooping, the ashen face had taken on the agonized stupor of a dying man. An officer who dismounted in front of the hotel began explaining to a group of people the route they had followed, from La Moncelle to Givonne all along the little valley, among the soldiers of the 1st corps whom the Saxons had thrown back on to the right bank of the stream; and they had come along the road in the cutting of Fond de Givonne, in such a jam already that even if the Emperor had wanted to go back to his front line troops he could only have done so with the greatest difficulty. Besides, what was the good?

As Delaherche was listening to these details a loud report shook the neighbourhood. It was a shell that had demolished a chimney in the rue Sainte-Barbe, near the Keep. There was a panic, and women screamed. He had flattened himself against a wall when another explosion shattered the windows of a house near-by. This was getting terrible if they were bombarding Sedan, and he raced home to the rue Maqua, so possessed with anxiety to know the worst that without stopping he rushed up to the roof where there was a flat terrace with a view over the town and its surroundings.

He was at once reassured, for they were firing right over the town and the German batteries on La Marfée and Frénois were aiming beyond the built-up area so as to rake the plateau of Algérie. He even found the flight of the shells interesting – the immense curve of light smoke they left above Sedan, like invisible birds leaving trails of grey feathers. To begin with it seemed clear that the few shells that had smashed roofs round him had been strays. They were not yet bombarding the town. But on a more careful examination he felt that they must be in reply to the odd shots fired from the fort. So he turned round and studied the citadel to the north, a complicated and formidable system of fortifications, blackened walls, green panels of glacis, innumerable geometrical bastions and topping all the three gigantic hornworks, that of the Ecossais and the Grand Jardin and La Rochette, with menacing angles; and further west, like a Cyclopean projection, the Nassau fort, followed by the Palatinate fort, towering above the Ménil district. The impression they made on him was a melancholy one of enormity and childishness. What was the point of it now, with these guns whose projectiles flew so easily from one end of the sky to the other? In any case the fortress was unarmed, with neither the necessary pieces of artillery nor the ammunition nor the men. For the past three weeks, or barely as long as that, the governor had been organizing a National Guard of citizens willing to man the few guns in working order. That was why three cannon were firing from the Palatinate while a good half dozen were at the Paris gate. But there were only seven or eight rounds available per gun, and so they spaced out the shots, letting one off every half hour and only for honour's sake at that, for the shells went no distance, but fell in the fields opposite. So the enemy batteries contemptuously sent an occasional answer back, out of charity.

What interested Delaherche was these batteries. He was casting a keen eye on the slopes of La Marfée when he thought of the field glasses with which he used to amuse himself looking at the surrounding country from up there. He went down to find them, came back and took up his position, and as he was getting his bearings by moving them along in little jerks, making fields, trees and houses go by, he spotted, above the big Frénois battery, the group of uniforms that Weiss had thought he could make out from Bazeilles at the corner of a pinewood. But thanks to the magnification he could easily have counted these staff officers, so clearly could he see them. Some of them were half lying in the grass, others were standing in groups, and in front there was one man standing alone, a shrivelled, thin-looking man in a plain uniform, but he felt that this man was the master. It was indeed the King of Prussia, scarcely half a finger high, like one of those tiny tin soldiers children play with. Of course he did not know this for certain until later, but he kept his eye on him, always coming back to this tiny figure, whose face, no bigger than a dot, was just a pale speck beneath the wide blue sky.

It was not yet noon, and the King had been following the mathematical, inexorable march of his armies since nine. They went on and on according to their prearranged routes, completing the circle, closing step by step the wall of men and guns round Sedan. The army from the left, coming from the flat plain of Donchery, was still debouching from the Saint-Albert gap, it was past Saint-Menges and was beginning to reach Fleigneux. And he could distinctly see, behind the XIth corps which was violently engaged with the troops of General Douay, the Vth corps filtering along under cover of the woods and making for the Calvary of Illy, while batteries joined with batteries in an ever longer line of thundering guns until the whole horizon was on fire. The army on the right was now occupying the whole of the Givonne valley, the XIIth corps had taken La Moncelle, the Prussian Guards had gone through Daigny and were already following the little stream up its valley, also making for the Calvary, having forced General Ducrot to fall back behind the Garenne wood. Just one more thrust and the Crown Prince of Prussia would link up with the Crown Prince of Saxony in the open fields on the very verge of the Ardennes forest. South of the town Bazeilles could no longer be seen, for it was hidden in the smoke of fires and in the wild dust of a fight to the death.

The King had been calmly looking on and waiting since first

thing. One or two hours more, perhaps three, it was only a matter of time, one cog moved the next and the crushing machine was in action and would finish its job. Under the wide, sunny sky the battlefield was shrinking, and this furious mêlée of black dots was piling itself thicker and thicker round Sedan. A few windows were gleaming in the town, one house seemed to be on fire to the left towards La Cassine. But further off, in the now deserted fields towards Donchery and Carignan, all was peaceful and bathed in light, the silvery waters of the Meuse, the trees looking happy to be alive, the great fertile plains, the broad green meadows beneath the blazing noonday sun.

The King had asked briefly for some bit of information. On the colossal chessboard he wanted to know everything and keep a hand on this multitude of men under his command. To his right a flight of swallows, scared by the gunfire, wheeled upwards very high and was lost to sight in the south.

4

At first Henriette could make good speed along the Balan road. It was not much after nine, and the wide street between houses and gardens was still passable, though as she approached the village it became increasingly blocked by fugitives and troops on the move. As each fresh wave of people came along she hugged the wall and managed to slip past all the same. Being very small and inconspicuous in her dark dress, with her lovely fair hair and little pale face half hidden by the black lace scarf, she passed unnoticed and nothing slowed her lithe, quiet step.

But in Balan itself there was a regiment of marines blocking the road, a solid mass of men waiting for orders in the shade of the big trees which concealed them. She stood on tiptoe but could not see the end of them. Yet she tried to make herself smaller still and wriggle through. Elbows shoved her away and she felt rifle-butts sticking into her. She had done some twenty steps when there were shouts and protests. A captain turned round and let fly at her:

'Here, woman, are you mad? Where are you off to?'

'I'm going to Bazeilles.'

'Bazeilles? What are you talking about?'

There was a general burst of laughter, and they pointed her out to each other and joked. The captain joined in the mirth and went on:

'Bazeilles, my dear, I wish you could take us with you! ... We were there just now and I hope we're going back, but I warn you that you won't feel cold there.'

'I'm going to Bazeilles to join my husband,' Henriette declared in her gentle voice, and her light blue eyes kept their quiet determination.

The laughter stopped, and an old sergeant got her away from them and forced her to turn back.

'Poor child, you can see it's impossible for you to get through ... It's no woman's job to go to Bazeilles just now ... You'll find that husband of yours later. Now come along, do be sensible!'

She had to give in and stood still, jumping up every minute to see as far as she could, obstinately determined to go on her way. She gathered a little information from what she heard round her. Officers were bitterly complaining about the order to retreat which had made them abandon Bazeilles at quarter past eight when General Ducrot, taking over from the marshal, had got it into his head to try to concentrate all the troops on the plateau of Illy. The worst of it was that the 1st corps having fallen back too soon and thus handed over the Givonne valley to the Germans, the 12th, already under strong attack from the front, had been outflanked on its left. And now General de Wimpffen had succeeded General Ducrot and the original plan was in favour again, so that orders were coming in to reoccupy Bazeilles at all costs and throw the Bavarians into the Meuse. Wasn't it crazy to have made them give up a position that they had now got to retake? They were prepared to face death, but really – not for fun!

There was a great surge of men and horses and General de Wimpffen appeared, standing in his stirrups, his face radiant and his voice inspired, shouting:

'My friends, we can't fall back, it would be the end of everything ... If we have to beat a retreat it will be on Carignan and not on Mézières ... But we shall win, you beat them this morning, and you will beat them again!'

Off he galloped and disappeared along a road going up to La

Moncelle. It was rumoured that he had had a violent altercation with General Ducrot, each of them defending his own plan and attacking the opposite one, one declaring that their retreat via Mézières had not been feasible since first thing in the morning, the other prophesying that before nightfall the army would be surrounded unless they withdrew on to the plateau of Illy. Each accused the other of not knowing the terrain nor the true situation of the troops. The worst of it was that they were both right.

But for a moment Henriette had had her mind taken off her hurry to get on. She had recognized a Bazeilles family stranded there at the roadside, a family of poor weavers, the man and wife and three girls, the eldest of whom was only nine. They were so shattered and dazed with exhaustion and despair that they could go no further and had collapsed by a wall.

'Oh, dear lady,' the woman said to Henriette, 'we've got nothing left ... You know our home was on the Place de l'Eglise. Well, a shell set fire to it. I don't know how the children and ourselves got out alive.'

The three little girls began crying and screaming again at the thought of it, while the mother went into details about their disaster, with wild gestures.

'I saw the loom burning like dry firewood. The bed and the furniture blazed up quicker than handfuls of straw ... And even the clock, I didn't have time to bring that away.'

'God Almighty!' swore the man, with big tears in his eyes. 'What's going to become of us?'

In order to calm them Henriette just said, in a slightly unsteady voice:

'You are together, both safe and sound, you have your little girls, what are you complaining about?'

Then she questioned them about what was happening in Bazeilles, whether they had seen her husband, what her house looked like when they left. But in their trembling, frightened state their answers were contradictory. No, they hadn't seen Weiss. Yet one of the little girls said she had seen him on the pavement, with a big hole in the middle of his head, and her father boxed her ears to make her shut up because, he said, she was lying for certain. As for the house, it must have been all right when they left, and they even remembered noticing that the door and windows were carefully shut as though there wasn't a soul there. At that time, in any case, the Bavarians were still only occupying the Place de l'Eglise, and had to take the village street by street, house by house. But of course they had had quite a way to come and perhaps by now the whole of Bazeilles was on fire. And the poor wretches went on talking about these things with vague, panic-stricken gestures as they called to mind the awful sight of the blazing roofs, blood flowing and the dead covering the ground.

'And what about my husband, then?' she asked.

They made no further answer, but sobbed into their clasped hands. She stood there in atrocious anguish, firm, but her lips were quivering slightly. What was she to believe? However much she told herself that the child was mistaken, she could see her husband lying there in the street with a bullet-hole in his head. And then she was worried about this hermetically sealed house. Why? Wasn't he still there, then? Suddenly the certainty that he had been killed struck a cold fear into her heart. But perhaps he was only wounded; and her need to go there and be there returned so inexorably that she would have tried once again to force a way through, there and then, if the bugles had not sounded the advance.

Many of these young soldiers had just come from Toulon, Rochefort or Brest, they were almost completely untrained and had never been under fire, yet since first thing they had been fighting as bravely and reliably as veterans. These men who had marched so badly from Rheims to Mouzon, worn out by the unaccustomed strain, were now revealing themselves in the face of the enemy to be the best disciplined and the most fraternally united by a bond of duty and self-sacrifice. The bugles had only to sound and back they went into the firing-line, and they resumed the attack even if their hearts were full of resentment. Three times they had been promised the support of a division which never came. They felt let down, written off as expendable. By sending them back against Bazeilles after making them evacuate it somebody was asking all of them to give up their lives. They were perfectly aware of this, and yet they would give their lives without question, closing their ranks, leaving the protection of the trees, and go back into the shells and bullets.

Henriette heaved an immense sigh of relief. At last they were marching! She followed on in the hope of getting there with them, and was prepared to run if they ran. But already once again they came to a halt. By now projectiles were raining down, and to occupy Bazeilles would mean reconquering every metre of the way and seizing alleyways, houses, gardens to right and left. The front ranks had opened fire and now they were only advancing in fits and starts, and the smallest obstacles caused many minutes' delay. She would never get there if she stayed like this at their tail waiting for victory. So she made up her mind and threw herself to the right along a path between two hedges that went down towards the meadows.

Henriette's plan was to reach Bazeilles through these stretches of meadow that bordered the Meuse. Not that she was very clear about it herself. Suddenly she stopped, stuck on the edge of a little pool that prevented her from going on in that direction. It was the flooding, this low-lying ground turned into a defensive lake, and she had not thought of that. For a moment she thought of going back, but then, at the risk of leaving her shoes in it, she went on, working along the edge, sinking ankle-deep in the muddy grass. For a hundred metres it was possible, but then she ran up against a garden wall and the land sloped downwards, so that the waters lapped the wall and were two metres deep. Impossible to get through. She clenched her small fists and had to take the firmest grip on herself so as not to burst into tears. When the first shock was over she skirted the wall the other way and found a narrow lane between a few houses. This time she thought she was saved, for she knew this maze of odd, twisting alleys, a tangle that did in the end lead to the village.

But there the shells were falling. Henriette stood rooted to the spot, very pale in the deafening noise of a frightful explosion, and hit by the blast. A shell had exploded only a few metres away from her. She looked back at the heights on the opposite side of the river, from which puffs of smoke from the German batteries were rising, and she understood, but went on again, with eyes fixed on the horizon, looking for shells so that she could dodge them. The rash temerity of her journey was not devoid of cool-headedness, indeed it had all the brave calm that a good little housewife can muster. She simply wanted not to be killed, to find her husband and take him home so that they could live happily again. The bombardment was incessant, and she glided along by the walls, taking cover behind stone bollards or any sort of shelter. But then came an open space, a piece of street that had been demolished and was already covered with rubble, and she was pausing at the corner of a barn when, down at ground level sticking out of a sort of hole, she caught sight of a child's inquisitive face, watching intently. It was a little boy of ten, barefoot and with torn shirt and trousers, some kid on the prowl who was thoroughly enjoying the battle. His little black eyes were sparkling and he uttered exclamations of delight at each explosion.

'Oh aren't they fun! Stay there, here comes another. Bang! That one didn't half go! Don't move, don't move!'

With each shell, he did a dive into the hole, and reappeared, popping up his head like a bird whistling, then dived down again.

Henriette noticed that the shells were coming from Le Liry, whilst the batteries of Pont-Maugis and Noyers were now only firing at Balan. She could clearly see the smoke at each discharge, and almost at once she heard the whining, followed later by the explosion. There must have been a short break, for the clouds of thin vapour slowly cleared away.

'Bet you they're having a drink,' shouted the kid. 'Quick, quick, let me take your hand and we'll run for it.'

He took her hand and pulled her along and, bent double, they both ran side by side across the open space. At the end, as they threw themselves behind a haystack, they saw another shell coming, and it fell right on the barn where they had been just before. The din was appalling, the barn collapsed.

The kid danced about with glee, finding it all a scream.

'Hooray – there's a nice smash-up! It was about time, too, wasn't it?'

But once again Henriette came up against an impassable obstacle, garden walls and no way through. Her little companion went on laughing and said you could always get by if you wanted to. He clambered up on to the coping of a wall and helped her over. They jumped down into a vegetable garden between rows of beans and peas. Walls everywhere. So to get out of it they had to go through a gardener's cottage. The boy went first, whistling and swinging his arms, ready for anything. He pushed open a door, found himself in a room, went through to another in which there was an old woman, probably the only living soul still there. She looked dazed, and was standing by a table. She watched these two unknown people walking like this through her home, but didn't say a word to them, nor they to her. They were out at the other side in a narrow lane that they were able to follow for a short distance. Then fresh difficulties arose, and so it went on for nearly a kilometre, walls had to be scaled or hedges got through, they took the shortest cuts they could, through coach-house doors, windows of houses, just as it chanced on the route they managed to follow. Dogs barked, and they were nearly knocked down by a madly galloping cow. But they must be getting near now, for there was a smell of burning, and at every moment big, ruddy clouds like floating, gauzy material veiled the sun.

Suddenly the boy stopped and planted himself in front of Henriette.

'I say, Missis, where are you off to like this?'

'But you can see, I'm going to Bazeilles.'

He whistled and gave vent to a high-pitched laugh like a truant from school who is having a grand time.

'Bazeilles . . . Oh no, I don't want that, I'm off somewhere else. Ta-ta!'

He turned on his heel and went off as he had come, without her knowing where he came from or where he was going. She had found him in a hole in the ground, she lost sight of him at the corner of a wall, and would never see him again.

Left alone, Henriette felt strangely frightened. That puny child with her was hardly a protection, but his chatter had been a distraction. Now, though normally so courageous, she was trembling. The shells were no longer coming over, the Germans had stopped firing on Bazeilles, no doubt for fear of killing their own men, now masters of the village. But for some minutes she had heard bullets whistling, that buzzing of big flies she had heard about and which she recognized. In the background so many hellish noises were mingled together that she could not even pick out the sound of the rifle fire from the violence of the din. As she rounded the corner of a house, right by her ear there was a dull thud and plaster falling which pulled her up; a bullet had chipped a lump off the façade, and she went very pale. Then before she had time to wonder whether she dared go any further she felt a kind of hammer-blow on the forehead and fell to her knees, dazed. A second bullet had ricocheted and caught her just above her left eyebrow, but it had only made a nasty graze. When she put both hands to her forehead and took them away they were red with blood. But she had felt her skull solid and unharmed under her fingers, and said aloud, to give herself courage:

'It isn't anything, it isn't anything . . . come on, I'm not afraid, no, I'm not afraid!'

And it was true. She got to her feet again and walked on among the bullets with the detachment of a person outside herself, beyond reasoning, prepared to give her life. She even gave up protecting herself, walking straight in front of her, head held high, only quickening her step in the hope of getting there sooner. Bullets spattered round her, and a score of times she might have been killed, but she appeared not to notice. Her lithe step, with her quiet, unfussed efficiency, seemed to help her to slip, slender and supple, through the danger that she escaped. She was in Bazeilles at last, and cut across a field of lucerne to rejoin the main road, the village high street. As she emerged on to it she saw, two hundred metres to her right, her house on fire. In the bright sun the flames could not be seen, but half the roof had already fallen in and the windows were belching clouds of black smoke. She rushed forward, running for all she was worth.

Weiss had been marooned there since eight in the morning, cut off from the withdrawing troops. Suddenly his return to Sedan had become impossible, for the Bavarians, who had come out through the park of Montvillers, had cut the line of retreat. He was alone with his gun and the remaining rounds of ammunition, when he saw ten soldiers in front of his door who like him had been left behind, isolated from their comrades, and they were looking round for some shelter where they could at least sell their lives as dearly as possible. He at once ran downstairs and opened the door to them, and from then on the house had a garrison, a captain, a corporal and eight men, all in a fury of desperation and determined never to surrender.

'What, you one of them, Laurent!' exclaimed Weiss, amazed to find among them a lanky fellow with a rifle picked up beside some dead body.

Laurent, in his blue shirt and trousers, was a gardener in the village, about thirty, who had recently lost his mother and his wife in the same influenza epidemic.

'Why shouldn't I be in it?' he answered. 'I've got nothing left but my own carcass, and that's mine to give if I want to ... And besides, you know, I enjoy it because I'm not a bad shot and it's going to be fun to finish off one of those buggers with each go!'

The captain and corporal were already looking over the house. Nothing doing on the ground floor, and they just pushed the furniture against the door and windows to barricade them as securely as they could. So it was in the three little rooms on the first floor and in the loft that they organized the defence, and they approved of the preparations already made by Weiss, the mattresses reinforcing the venetian blinds and the loopholes he had made here and there between the slats. As the captain ventured to lean out to take stock of the surroundings he heard a child crying.

'What's that?' he asked.

There came back into Weiss's mind the sight of the sick child Auguste, with his face flushed with fever against the white sheets, calling his mother who could never answer again, lying on the pavement with her head smashed. With a gesture of grief at this vision he replied:

'A poor little kid whose mother has been killed by a shell, and he's crying there next door.'

'Oh Christ,' muttered Laurent, 'we've got to make them pay for all this!'

So far only a few stray bullets were hitting the front of the house. Weiss and the captain, together with the gardener and two of the men, had gone up into the attic from which it was easier to keep an eye on the road. They could see at an angle as far as the Place de l'Eglise, which was now in the hands of the Bavarians, who were still advancing only with great difficulty and with extreme caution. At the corner of a lane a few infantrymen still held them at bay for nearly a quarter of an hour with such murderous fire that the dead were piling up. And then it was a single house, even an angle between two walls that they had to take before being able to move on. Sometimes through the smoke a woman could be seen with a rifle shooting from one of the windows. It was a baker's shop in which there were some stranded soldiers together with the inhabitants, and when the house was taken, there were screams and a fearful vision of people being hustled across to the opposite wall: a flood in which could be glimpsed a woman's skirt, a man's jacket, a mane of white hair, and then the rattle of a firing squad and blood splashing up to the coping of the wall. The Germans were inflexible: any person not belonging to the armed forces who was found with weapons was shot at once, having wilfully deprived himself of all legal rights. In the face of the furious resistance of the village their anger was rising, and the terrible losses they had been suffering for nearly five hours provoked them to take atrocious reprisals. The gutters were running red and the dead were blocking the roadway, some crossroads were mere charnel-houses from which came the gasps of the dying. So then they could be seen throwing lighted straw into every house they captured after a fight, and others ran along with torches or sprinkled walls with paraffin. Soon whole streets were on fire and Bazeilles went up in flames.

Hence now in the centre of the village there only remained Weiss's house, with its shutters closed, like a menacing fortress, determined never to give in.

'Look out, here they come!' cried the captain.

A volley from the attic and the first floor laid low three Bavarians who were creeping along by the walls. The others fell back and took cover in all the corners along the road; the siege of the house began, such a rain of bullets lashed the front that it was like a hailstorm. For nearly ten minutes this fusillade went on, making holes in the plaster but not doing much harm. But one of the men the captain had taken up with him into the attic was imprudent enough to show himself at a dormer window, and he was killed instantly with a bullet through the forehead.

'Dammit, that's one less!' grunted the captain. 'Do be careful, there aren't so many of us that we can get killed for fun!'

He had taken a rifle himself and was firing from behind a shutter. But it was Laurent the gardener whom he admired the most. Kneeling with the barrel of his rifle supported in the narrow slit of a loophole, as though he were stalking game, he never let off a shot unless he was quite sure, and he even announced the result in advance.

'Now for the little blue officer over there, I'll get him in the heart . . . The other one further off, the tall skinny one, between the eyes . . . The fat one with the ginger beard – he's getting me down, one in the belly for him . . .'

And each time the man fell, killed instantly, hit in the place he had indicated, and he went on calmly, with no rush, having plenty to do, as he put it, for it would take some time for him to kill them all off one by one like this.

'Oh, if only my eyes were any good!' Weiss kept saying furiously.

He had just broken his glasses and was very annoyed. He still had the folding ones, but he could not keep them firmly on his nose because of the sweat running down his face, and consequently he often fired at random, over excited and with shaky hands. A mounting passion was triumphing over his normal coolness.

'Don't be in a hurry, it's no good at all,' said Laurent. 'Look, take aim carefully at that one over there without his cap, on the corner of the grocer's . . . But that's fine, you've smashed his foot, look at him jigging about in his own blood.'

Weiss looked at him and went a bit pale. He murmured:

'You finish him off.'

'What, and waste a bullet! Oh no. More use to do in another of them.'

The assailants must have noticed this formidable fire from the windows in the attic. Not a single man could step forward but he stayed there for good. So they brought up some fresh troops with orders to riddle the roof with bullets. That made the attic untenable, for the slates could be pierced as easily as sheets of thin paper, and the bullets came in on all sides, buzzing like bees. Each second meant risk of death.

'Let's go down,' said the captain. 'We can still hold out on the first floor.'

But as he was making for the ladder a bullet got him in the groin and knocked him backwards.

'Too late, dammit!'

Weiss and Laurent, helped by the one remaining soldier, insisted on getting him down although he shouted that they were not to waste their time over him: he had got his ticket and he could peg out up there just as well as downstairs. Yet when they had laid him on a bed in a first-floor room he was still determined to direct the defence.

'Fire into the middle of them and don't bother about anything else. So long as your fire doesn't slacken they're much too prudent to take any risks.'

The siege of the little house indeed looked like going on and on for ever. A score of times it had seemed on the point of being taken in the storm of iron beating upon it, and in the midst of these squalls and through the smoke it still was standing, holed and gashed, torn to bits and yet spitting forth bullets from every crack. The attackers were exasperated at being held up for so long and losing so many men over a shanty like this, and they yelled and fired from a distance without daring to charge forward and smash in the ground-floor door and windows.

'Look out!' shouted the corporal, 'that shutter's coming down!'

The impact of the bullets had forced a shutter off its hinges. But Weiss rushed and pushed a cupboard against the window, and Laurent could go on firing, shielded by that. One of the soldiers lay at his feet, his jaw smashed and losing a lot of blood. Another was hit in the throat by a bullet and reeled over to the wall where he made a continual snoring noise, with his whole body jerking in convulsions. They were now down to eight, not counting the captain, who was too weak to speak but propped up on the bed was still giving orders by signs. The three first-floor rooms were beginning to be as untenable as the loft, for the tattered mattresses were no longer stopping the bullets: bits of plaster jumped from the walls and ceiling, furniture was being broken and sides of cupboards splitting as though under the axe. Worst of all, ammunition was running short.

'What a pity!' grumbled Laurent. 'It's going so well.'

Weiss had a sudden idea.

'Wait a moment.'

He had thought of the dead soldier up there in the loft. He went up and searched him for the ammunition he must have. A whole section of roofing had fallen in and he could see the blue sky, a patch of gay light which astonished him. To avoid being killed he crawled along on his knees. Then, when he had the ammunition, another thirty or so rounds, he hurried down at full speed.

Down below, as he was sharing this new supply with the gardener, a soldier uttered a scream and fell on his face. They were now only seven, and immediately after only six, the corporal getting a bullet through his left eye which blew out his brains.

From then on Weiss lost all consciousness of what was happening. He and the five others went on shooting like mad things, finishing off the ammunition and not even thinking they could surrender. The floors of the three little rooms were strewn with bits of furniture. The dead blocked the doorways and one wounded man in a corner went on and on with his pitiful moaning. Everywhere blood stuck to their feet. A red trickle had gone down the stairs. The air was scarcely breathable, thick and with a burning taste of gunpowder, an acrid, sickening smoke, almost total darkness streaked by the flames of the rifle-fire.

'Good God!' exclaimed Weiss. 'They're bringing up cannon!'

It was true. Feeling they would never be able to liquidate this handful of fanatics who were holding them up like this, the Bavarians were bringing up a cannon into position at the corner of the Place de l'Eglise. Perhaps they would get through once they had demolished the house with gunfire. The honour they were being done by having artillery trained on them put the finishing touch to the wild glee of the besieged men, who sneered in utter scorn. The cowardly lot of sods with their cannon! Still on his knees, Laurent took careful aim at the gunners, picking off his man each time and preventing the gun from being served, so that it took five or six minutes before the first shot was fired. It went too high and only took off a bit of the roof.

But the end was in sight. They searched the dead in vain, there was not a single round of ammunition left. Exhausted and haggard, the six men felt about for something to hurl out of the windows and crush the enemy. One of them showed himself, vociferating and brandishing his fists; he was immediately riddled with lead, and they were only five. What could they do next? Go downstairs and try to escape through the garden and over the fields? But just then there was a tumult down below and a furious mob surged up the stairs: it was the Bavarians who had at last surrounded the house, smashed the back door and come in. There was a free fight in the little room among the corpses and bits of broken furniture. One of the soldiers had a bayonet through his chest and the two others were taken prisoner, while the captain, who had just breathed his last, remained there with his mouth open and arm raised as if giving an order.

Meanwhile an officer, a heavy, fair man with a revolver and bloodshot eyes popping out of their sockets, had caught sight of

Weiss and Laurent, one in his overcoat and the other in his blue cotton shirt, and he addressed them furiously in French:

'Who are you? What are you two doing here?'

Then seeing them blackened with powder he understood and heaped curses on them in German, his voice choking with rage. He was by way of raising his pistol to blow their brains out when the soldiers under his command rushed and seized Weiss and Laurent and bundled them down the stairs. The two men were carried along on this human tide, out into the road and across to the wall opposite with such vociferations that the officers' voices could no longer be heard. So that for another two or three minutes, while the big fair officer was trying to detach them in order to proceed with their execution, they could stand up and see everything.

Other houses were on fire and Bazeilles would soon be nothing but a furnace. Tongues of flame were beginning to come from the lofty windows of the church. Soldiers chasing an old lady out of her house had forced her to give them some matches so as to set fire to her bed and curtains. By degrees the fires were spreading as straw firebrands were thrown and quantities of oil poured about. It was now nothing but a war of savages frenzied by the length of the struggle, avenging their dead, the heaps of their dead on which they had to tread. Bands of men were bawling amid the smoke and sparks, in a frightful din made up of all kinds of noises, the moans of the dying, shots, crashed buildings. People could scarcely see each other for great livid clouds of swirling dust, which stank intolerably of soot and blood as though filled with the abominations of massacre, and which hid the light of the sun. The killing was still going on, with destruction in every corner: the wild beast let loose, the raving madness of men in the act of destroying their fellow men.

And then Weiss saw his own house burning there in front of him. Soldiers had run up with torches, others were feeding the flames by throwing in bits of furniture. In no time the ground floor was ablaze and the smoke was issuing from all the holes in the walls and roof. Already the dyeworks next door was catching fire as well and, most horrible thing, you could still hear the voice of the child Auguste lying in bed calling for his mother in his feverish delirium, while the poor creature's skirt, as she lay there across the doorstep with her head bashed in, was beginning to burn.

'Mummy, I'm thirsty ... Mummy, give me a drink of water ...'

The flames roared up, the voice stopped, and all that could be heard was the deafening cheering of the victors.

Above the noises and shouting rose a terrible shriek. Henriette appeared at that moment and saw her husband against the wall facing a firing squad that was getting ready.

She rushed to embrace him.

'Oh God, what is it? They aren't going to kill you?'

Weiss looked at her, dazed. What, his wife, this woman he had yearned for so long and whom he worshipped with such loving devotion! He woke up with a shudder. What had he been doing? What had he stayed there for, firing a rifle instead of going back to her as he had sworn he would? In a flash he saw his happiness lost in a brutal separation, for ever. Then he caught sight of the blood on her forehead and said in a faltering, almost off-hand way:

'Are you wounded, dear? ... You were mad to come.'

She roughly cut him short:

'Oh there's nothing the matter with me, just a scratch. But you, you, why are they holding you? I won't let them kill you!'

The officer was busying himself in the middle of the cluttered road to give his squad a little more distance, when he saw this woman hanging on to the neck of one of the prisoners and he said angrily, in French again:

'Oh no, none of that nonsense! Where have you come from? What do you want?'

'I want my husband!'

'Your husband, what, that man there? He has been sentenced, and justice has got to be done.'

'I want my husband.'

'Look here, be sensible ... Get out of the way, we don't want to do any harm to you.'

'I want my husband.'

So, abandoning the effort to convince her, the officer was going to give orders for her to be torn away from the prisoner's arms, when Laurent, who so far had said nothing, but had been standing there quite unmoved, ventured to intervene:

'I say, captain, I was the one who bumped off so many of your lot, so let me be shot, that's all right. And what's more I've got

249

nobody, neither mother, wife nor child ... But this gentleman is married ... So let him go and then you can settle my account.'

Beside himself now, the captain bellowed:

'That's enough talk! Are you trying to pull my leg? Come on, I want a volunteer to take this woman away.'

He had to repeat the order in German. A soldier stepped forward, a thickset Bavarian with a huge head bristling with red beard and hair, in the midst of which all that could be seen was a wide potato nose and big blue eyes. He had blood on him and looked horrible, like one of those cave-dwelling bears, hairy wild beasts red with the prey whose bones they have been cracking.

In heart-rending tones Henriette went on crying:

'I want my husband, kill me with my husband.'

The officer energetically beat his breast, declaring that he was not a murderer, and if there were some who killed innocent people, it wasn't him. She had not been sentenced and he would cut his own hand off rather than touch a hair of her head.

Then as the Bavarian was coming she clung to her husband's body with all the strength of her limbs, frantically.

'Oh my darling, please keep me, let me die with you!'

Weiss was weeping bitterly, but without answering her he struggled to wrench the desperate woman's convulsive fingers from his shoulders and waist.

'So you don't love me any more, and want to die without me! Hold on to me and they'll get tired of it and kill us both together!'

He had pulled away one of her little hands and he pressed it to his mouth and kissed it while working at the other to make it let go.

'No, no, keep me, I want to die.'

At last, with a great effort, he held both her hands. So far he had avoided speaking and remained mute. Now all he said was:

'Good-bye, dearest wife.'

And immediately he deliberately threw her into the arms of the Bavarian, who carried her away, struggling and screaming, while, perhaps to calm her, keeping up a stream of guttural talk. With a violent effort she got her head free and saw everything.

It lasted less than three seconds. Weiss's folding glasses had slipped down during the parting, and he quickly replaced them on his nose as though he wanted to look death squarely in the face. He backed against the wall and folded his arms, and the face of this big, good-natured fellow in his tattered jacket shone with radiance, admirable in beauty and courage. Next to him Laurent had simply thrust his hands into his pockets. He looked outraged at this cruel scene, the abomination of these savages killing men before the eyes of their wives. He drew himself up, looked at them insolently and spat out in contempt:

'Filthy swine!'

But the officer had raised his sword, and the two men fell like logs, the gardener face to the ground and the other, the accounts clerk, on his side along the wall. Before expiring he had a final convulsion, his eyelids flickered and his mouth twitched. The officer came up and turned him over with his foot to make sure he was not still alive.

Henriette had seen it all, the dying eyes looking for her, the dreadful spasm of his end, the heavy boot kicking his corpse. She even stopped screaming, but silently, furiously, bit whatever she could, a hand her teeth came up against. The Bavarian uttered a cry of intense pain, flung her down and nearly knocked her out. Their faces touched, and she was never to forget that red beard and hair flecked with blood, those blue eyes staring and mad with rage.

Later Henriette could not clearly remember what had happened next. She had had only one desire, to go back to her husband's body, take it away and watch over it. But as in a nightmare one obstacle after another sprang up and stopped her every move. A fresh and violent fusillade had broken out and a great deal of manoeuvring took place among the German troops occupying Bazeilles: it was the arrival at long last of the Marines, and the fight began again so fiercely that she was thrown back down an alley to the left with a mob of panic-stricken inhabitants. In any case the outcome of the struggle could not be in doubt, for it was too late to recapture the abandoned positions. For nearly another half-hour the Marines fought doggedly on and gave their lives with superb dash, but the enemy was continually being reinforced from every side, the meadows, the roads, the park of Montvillers. Nothing could now dislodge them from the village they had bought at such a price, where thousands of their men lay in blood and flames. Destruction was now completing its work, and nothing was left but a charnel-house of scattered limbs and smoking ruins. Bazeilles, murdered, demolished, was disappearing into ashes.

Henriette caught one last glimpse of her little home where the floors were falling into a whirlpool of fire. Opposite, she could still see her husband's body lying by the wall. Then a fresh wave caught her again, the bugles were sounding the retreat and she was carried along somehow in the midst of the fleeing troops. She just became an object, a piece of flotsam washed along in a swirling stream of people flowing along the road. She lost any idea of what was happening until she found herself in Balan, in somebody's kitchen, where she was sobbing with her head on a table.

5

AT ten o'clock up on the plateau of Algérie Beaudoin's company was still lying among the cabbages, not having moved from that field since first thing. The cross-fire from the batteries of Le Hattoy and the Iges peninsula was increasing in intensity and had just killed two more of their men, and still no order to advance. Were they going to spend all day there, to be shot down without a fight?

And now the men had not even the relief of letting off their own rifles. Captain Beaudoin had managed to stop the firing, a furious and pointless fusillade against the little wood opposite, in which not a single Prussian seemed to have stayed. The sun was scorching and they were baked alive, lying like this on the ground under a blazing sky.

Jean turned round and saw with alarm that Maurice had let his head fall on the ground, his cheek was against the earth and his eyes shut. His face was white and still.

'Hallo, what's up?'

It simply was that Maurice had gone to sleep. The waiting and his exhaustion had knocked him out even though death was hovering all round. He woke up with a start, opened wide, serene eyes which at once took on again the frightened, haunted expression of battle. He never knew how long he had been asleep. He felt he was emerging from a timeless, delicious nothingness.

'Fancy, isn't that funny, I've been asleep! Oh, it's done me good.'

It was true that he was less conscious of the painful tightness in his head and ribs, the strait-jacket of fear that makes your bones crack. He teased Lapoulle, who was worrying about the disappearance of Chouteau and Loubet and talking of going to look for them – lovely idea that was, to go and take cover behind a tree and smoke a pipe! Pache would have it that they had been kept by the ambulance people who were short of stretcher-bearers. That's not a pleasant occupation either, going round picking up the wounded under fire. Then, tormented as ever by his rustic superstitions, he added that it was bad luck to touch the dead, you might die yourself.

'Oh shut up, for God's sake!' shouted Lieutenant Rochas. 'As though you would!'

Colonel de Vineuil, riding by on his tall horse, turned his head, and he smiled for the only time since the early morning. Then he relapsed into his immobility, always unmoved under fire, waiting for orders.

Maurice's interest was being caught by the stretcher-bearers, and he watched them as they searched among the ups and downs of the terrain. There must be a first-aid post behind the hedge at the end of the sunken lane and it was the men from there who had set about exploring the plateau. A tent was being quickly set up while the essential material was unloaded from a van, the few instruments and pieces of apparatus, bandages, the wherewithal for quick dressings before the wounded were dispatched for Sedan as and when transport could be made available; and soon it would not be. There were only orderlies at that point. But it was the stretcher-bearers whose heroism was steadfast and inconspicuous. They could be seen in their grey uniforms with the red cross on their caps and armbands, slowly, quietly risking their lives under fire to get to places where men had fallen. They crawled on all fours, trying to utilize ditches and hedges and any mound or dip without showing off by needlessly exposing themselves. Then as soon as they found men lying on the ground their hard task began, for many of these men had lost consciousness, and they had to distinguish the wounded from the dead. Some had stayed lying on their faces with their mouths in a pool of blood and were choking to death, others had their gullets full of mud as though they had bitten off lumps of earth, others lay in heaps higgledy-piggledy, arms and legs contorted and ribs nearly crushed. With great care the bearers freed and lifted the ones still breathing, straightened out their limbs,

253

raised their heads and cleaned them as best they could. Each man had a can of fresh water, but was exceedingly sparing with it. Often they could be seen kneeling for minutes at a time trying to revive a wounded man and waiting for him to open his eyes.

Some fifty metres away to the left Maurice watched one trying to locate the wound of a young soldier from whose sleeve blood was trickling drop by drop. There was a haemorrhage that the red-cross man found eventually and stopped by compressing an artery. In urgent cases they simply took immediate precautions, avoiding harmful movements in fracture cases, binding up limbs and immobilizing them so as to make it safe to move the men. And transport then became the main problem: they supported the walking cases, carried others in their arms like children or pickaback, or again they worked in pairs of three or four together according to the degree of difficulty, making a chair with joined hands, or supporting their legs and shoulders. Beside the regulation stretchers there were also all kinds of ingenious devices, stretchers improvised from rifles tied together with straps from packs. And from all directions all over the plain being raked by gunfire, they could be seen singly or in groups, moving along with their burdens, keeping their heads down, testing the ground with their feet with cautious, admirable heroism.

As Maurice was watching one of them on his right, a puny, delicate-looking young man who was carrying a heavily-built sergeant on his back and struggling along on his tired legs like a worker ant transporting a grain of wheat too heavy for it, he saw them pitch over and vanish in a shell-burst. When the smoke had blown away the sergeant reappeared, lying on his back but with no fresh wound, while the bearer lay with his belly ripped open. And another busy ant ran up, and after turning over and examining his dead comrade he picked up the wounded man again and carried him away on his back.

So Maurice chipped Lapoulle:

'I say, chum, if you prefer that job go and give them a hand!'

For some little time the batteries on Saint-Menges had been at it like fury, and the hail of shells had got thicker. Captain Beaudoin, still nervously going up and down in front of his company, decided to approach the colonel. It was a pity to wear down the men's morale for hours and hours without giving them anything to do.

'I have no orders,' was the colonel's stoical answer.

Once again General Douay was seen galloping past, followed by his staff. He had just had a meeting with General de Wimpffen, who had hurried there to beg him to hold on, which he thought he could promise to do, but on the strict understanding that the Calvary of Illy, on his right, would be defended. If the Illy position was lost he could answer for nothing and retreat would be inevitable. General de Wimpffen declared that troops from the 1st corps were going to occupy the Calvary, and indeed almost at once a regiment of Zouaves could be seen taking it over. Hence General Douay, now reassured, agreed to send the Dumont division to support the 12th corps which was very hard pressed. But a quarter of an hour later, as he was on his way back from seeing that his left was in good shape, he uttered an oath on looking up and seeing that the Calvary was deserted, the Zouaves had gone, the plateau had been abandoned and the hellish fire from the Fleigneux batteries was in any case making it untenable. In desperation, foreseeing disaster, he was hastening towards the right when he ran into a stampede of the Dumont division falling back in disorder and panic, mixed up with the remains of the 1st corps. The latter, after its withdrawal, had not succeeded in regaining its morning positions, abandoning Daigny to the XIIth Saxon corps and Givonne to the Prussian Guard, forced northwards through the Garenne woods and bombarded by batteries the enemy was placing on every hilltop from one end of the valley to the other. The terrible ring of iron and fire was tightening, a part of the Guard was continuing its advance on Illy from east to west, rounding the hills, while from west to east, behind the XIth corps, now in possession of Saint-Menges, the Vth was steadily moving on past Fleigneux, bringing its guns further forward with insolent unconcern, so convinced of the ignorance and impotence of the French troops that it did not even wait for the infantry to support it. It was midday, and the whole skyline was ablaze, thundering and cross-firing at the 7th and 1st corps.

Then, as the enemy artillery was thus preparing for the final attack on the Calvary, General Douay made up his mind to make a last effort to recapture it. He dispatched orders, threw himself in person into the midst of the fugitives from the Dumont division, succeeded in forming a column which he hurled on to the plateau.

It held good for several minutes, but the bullets were whistling by so thick and fast, and such a storm of shells was sweeping over the bare fields that panic broke out at once, throwing the men back down the slopes, bowling them along like wisps of straw blown by a sudden squall. The general obstinately sent in more regiments.

A dispatch rider, as he galloped by, shouted an order to Colonel de Vineuil through the frightful din. The colonel was already standing in his stirrups and his face was radiant. With a great wave of his sword towards the Calvary he shouted:

'Our turn at last, boys! Up there and at 'em!'

Deeply stirred, the 106th began to move. The Beaudoin company was one of the first to get to its feet, amid jokes among the chaps who said they were rusty and had earth in their joints. But after a few steps they had to throw themselves into a trench that they came across because the fire got so fierce. Then they ran on bent double.

'Mind how you go, young fellow-me-lad!' Jean said more than once to Maurice. 'This is the crunch . . . Don't show the tip of your nose or it'll get blown off! Keep your bones well inside unless you want to leave a few on the road. The ones who get back after this lot will be pretty good.'

Maurice could hardly hear for the tumult and racket of the crowd filling his ears. He no longer knew whether he was afraid or not, carried along at a run by all the others, with no will-power of his own except to get it over at once. To such an extent had he become just one single wave of this rushing torrent that when there was a sudden ebb at the far end of the trench, caused by the prospect of the open ground still to be climbed, he at once felt panic come over him and was ready to run away. Instinct took over, his muscles ran amok, obeying every wind that blew.

Men were already turning back when the colonel rushed up.

'Now look here, boys, you're not going to let me down and act like a lot of babies . . . Remember, the 106th has never retreated, and you would be the first to disgrace our flag . . .'

He urged on his horse and blocked the way against those who were turning tail, finding some word for each one, talking of France in a voice breaking with emotion.

Lieutenant Rochas was so moved that he fell into a furious rage and began belabouring the men with his sword as though it were a stick.

'You bleeding lot of sods, I'll get you up there with kicks up the arse! Will you do as you're told, if not, the first man to turn on his heels – I'll sock him one on the jaw!'

But violence of this kind, soldiers driven into the firing line by kicks, did not appeal to the colonel.

'No, no, lieutenant, they're all going to follow me ... Aren't you, boys? ... You're not going to let your old colonel have it out with the Prussians on his own! Come on, up and at 'em!'

Off he dashed, and they all went after him, for he had said that in such a fatherly way that you couldn't let him down unless you were a lot of shits. But he was the only one to cross the bare fields quite calmly, on his tall horse, while the men scattered and ducked like snipers, taking advantage of every bit of shelter. The land went uphill and there were a good five hundred metres of stubble and beet patches before the Calvary was reached. Instead of the classical assault as in manoeuvres, in straight lines, all that could soon be seen was humped backs creeping along on the ground, soldiers alone or in little groups crawling or suddenly jumping up like insects and reaching the top by dint of agility and subterfuge. The enemy batteries must have spotted them, for shells were raking the ground so often that the explosions never stopped. Five men were killed; a lieutenant had his body cut in two.

Maurice and Jean had had the good luck to find a hedge behind which they could run along unseen. But a bullet ploughed through the side of the head of one of their companions, who fell at their feet. They had to kick him to one side. However, the dead no longer counted, there were too many of them. The horror of the battlefield, a wounded man they saw shrieking and holding his entrails in with both hands, a horse still dragging itself along on its broken legs, all this frightful agony had ceased to touch them. All they suffered from now was the overpowering heat of the noonday sun gnawing at their shoulders.

'Oh, how thirsty I am!' muttered Maurice. 'I feel as if I had some soot down my throat. Can't you smell scorching, like burning wool?'

Jean nodded.

'It was the same smell at Solferino. I suppose it's the smell of war . . . Oh, I've still got some brandy left, and we can have a nip.'

They coolly stopped there for a moment, behind the hedge. But far from quenching their thirst the brandy burned their insides. It was the limit, this taste of scorching in their mouths. And they were dying of hunger too. They would have liked to take a bite at the half loaf Maurice had in his pack, only how could it be done? All along the hedge behind them other men were constantly coming up and pushing into them. At last they dashed with one bound across the last slope and were on the plateau at the foot of the Calvary, the old cross weatherbeaten by wind and rain between two scraggy lime trees.

'Oh thank God, here we are!' said Jean. 'But the thing is to stay here!'

He was right, it wasn't exactly the most pleasant of spots, as Lapoulle pointed out in a doleful voice which tickled the company. Once again they all lay stretched out in the stubble, but that didn't save three men from being killed. Up there it was hell's own hurricane let loose, shells coming over so thickly from Saint-Menges, Fleigneux and Givonne that the earth seemed to be throwing up a fine mist as it does in heavy thunder rain. Clearly the position could not be held for long unless some artillery came as soon as possible to back up the troops so rashly engaged. General Douay, it was said, had ordered two reserve batteries to be brought up, and every second the men anxiously glanced over their shoulders expecting the guns which never came.

'It's ridiculous, ridiculous!' Captain Beaudoin kept on saying as he went on with his jerky walking up and down. 'You don't send a regiment up into the air like this without supporting it immediately.'

He noticed a dip in the land to his left and called to Rochas:

'I say, lieutenant, the company should take cover over there.'

Rochas stood there without moving, but shrugged his shoulders.

'Oh, captain, here or there, what's it matter, the dance is just the same . . . Better not to move.'

At that Captain Beaudoin, who never swore, burst out in a rage:

'But fucking hell, we shall stay here for good, the whole lot of us. We can't just let ourselves be done in like this!'

He insisted on looking personally into the better position he had pointed out. But before he had gone ten steps he vanished in an explosion, and his right leg was smashed by a piece of shell. He was thrown on to his back and uttered a scream like a startled woman.

'It was bound to happen,' muttered Rochas. 'It's no good fidgeting about so much. What you've got coming to you, comes.'

The men of his company, seeing their captain fall, leaped up, and as he was crying for help and begging to be taken away, Jean also ran over to him and Maurice after him.

'Friends, in God's name don't leave me here, take me to the ambulance!'

'Lord, captain, that's not so easy to do ... But we can always try.'

They were thinking out how best to take hold of him when they saw, behind the hedge they had been following, two red-cross men apparently looking for a job. They waved at them frantically and persuaded them to come over. They would be saved if they could reach the ambulance station without mishap. But it was a long way, and the hail of bullets was getting still thicker.

The ambulance men had bound the leg up tight to hold it in place, and then were carrying the captain on a bandy-chair with his arms round their necks, when Colonel de Vineuil, who had been informed, came up as fast as he could urge his horse. He had known the young man since he graduated from Saint-Cyr and was fond of him, and he was visibly very upset.

'Poor old chap, be brave ... It won't be anything much, and they'll soon put you right.'

The captain made a sign of relief as though he had been greatly heartened.

'No, no, it's all over, and I prefer it like that. What is so exasperating is waiting for what you can't avoid.'

He was carried off, and the bearers were lucky enough to reach the hedge without trouble, and they hurried along it with their burden. When the colonel saw them vanish behind the trees where the ambulance was, he sighed with relief.

'But, sir,' Maurice exclaimed, 'you are wounded too!'

He had only just noticed the officer's left boot which was covered with blood. The heel must have been torn off and a piece of the upper had even penetrated the flesh.

M. de Vineuil nonchalantly leaned over in the saddle and

glanced at his foot which must have been very painful and weighing down his leg.

'Yes, yes,' he muttered. 'I picked that up just now ... It's nothing, it doesn't prevent me from sitting on my horse.'

And as he went back to take his place at the head of his regiment, he added:

'When you're on horseback and can stay there you can always manage.'

At last the two reserve batteries were coming up, which was an immense relief to the anxious men, for whom these guns were the rampart, the salvation, the thunder from heaven which would silence the enemy cannon over yonder. Moreover it was a superb sight, the parade-ground arrival of the batteries in battle order, each piece followed by its ammunition waggon, the drivers mounted on the near-horses and holding the off-horses by the bridle, the gunners on the boxes, with the corporals and sergeants galloping in their regulation positions. They might have been on parade, carefully keeping their distances as they advanced at a furious pace across the fields with the dull roar of thunder.

Maurice, who had lain down again in a furrow, got up all excited and said to Jean:

'Look over there, the one taking the left position is Honoré's battery. I recognize the men.'

With a quick back-hander Jean knocked him down again.

'Just you get down and lie doggo!'

But even with their cheeks to the ground they both kept the battery in sight, very interested in the manoeuvre, and their hearts beat wildly as they watched the calm, active bravery of these men, from whom they still expected victory.

The battery suddenly came to a halt on a bare hilltop to the left, and in a matter of a minute the gunners jumped down from their boxes and uncoupled the limbers, the drivers left the guns in position, wheeled their horses to move fifteen metres to the rear and remain motionless, facing the enemy. The six guns were already trained, spaced well apart in three pairs commanded by lieutenants, all six being under the orders of a captain, a very tall thin man who paced fussily up and down the plateau.

'Range sixteen hundred metres!' the captain could be heard shouting after he had done his rapid calculations.

The target was to be the Prussian battery to the left of Fleigneux which was behind some brushwood and making the Illy Calvary untenable.

'You see,' Maurice went on with his explanations, for he couldn't stop talking, 'Honoré's gun is in the centre section. There he is, leaning over with his gun-layer. The layer is young Louis, we had a drink together at Vouziers, don't you remember? And over there the offside driver, the one sitting up so stiffly on his mount, a lovely arab, that's Adolphe . . .'

The gun with its crew of six and sergeant, and beyond it the limber and its four horses mounted by two drivers, beyond that the ammunition waggon with its six horses and three drivers, still further off the supply and forage waggons and the smithy, the whole string of men, animals and equipment stretched out in a straight line for a good hundred metres to the rear, to say nothing of the spare horses, spare ammunition waggon, animals and men to fill the gaps, who were standing over to the right so as not to remain uselessly exposed in the line of fire.

Meanwhile Honoré was busy with the loading of his gun. The two centre gunners were already on their way back with the charge and shell from the ammunition waggon where the corporal and artificer were in charge and at once the two men at the muzzle put in the charge of powder wrapped in serge, which they pushed carefully down with the ramrod, then slid in the shell, the studs of which squeaked along the rifled barrel. The assistant layer quickly exposed the powder with his wire and pushed the fuse into the touch-hole. Honoré wanted to train the first round himself, and half lying on the mounting, he turned the adjusting screw to find the range, indicating the direction with a continuous movement of his hand to the gunner behind, who with a lever moved the gun very gradually further right or left.

'That's about it,' he said, straightening up.

The captain came and checked the range, bending his tall form almost double. At each gun the assistant layer, string in hand, stood ready to pull the striker, the saw-edged blade that ignited the cap. Orders were called slowly by numbers:

'Number one, fire! . . . Number two, fire!'

The six rounds went off, the guns recoiled and were brought back, while the sergeants saw that their range was much too short.

They adjusted it and the operation began again, always the same, and it was this slow precision, the mechanical job coolly done which kept up the men's morale. Their gun, like a favourite animal, gathered a little family round it, drawn close together by their common occupation. It was the tie that bound them, their one care, for which everything existed – waggon, vans, horses and men. Hence the great cohesion of the whole battery, calm and serene like a well-run household.

The first salvo had been greeted with cheers by the 106th. At last they were going to shut those Prussian guns up. But there was immediate disappointment when they saw that the shells stopped half way and mostly went off in the air before reaching the thickets over there in which the enemy artillery was concealed.

'Honoré,' Maurice went on, 'Honoré says that the others are all old crocks compared with his ... Oh, his gun, he'd sleep with it, you'll never find another like it! Look at his doting eyes, and how he has it wiped in case it should be too hot!'

He was joking with Jean, for they both felt cheered by the fine calm bravery of the gunners. But after three rounds the Prussians had readjusted their fire: too long at first, it had become so accurate that the shells were falling straight on the French guns, while the latter, for all their efforts to lengthen the range, were still not getting there. One of Honoré's gunners, the one to the left of the muzzle, was killed. His body was pushed aside and the loading went on with the same careful, unhurried regularity. Projectiles were coming down from all directions and exploding, but round each gun the same methodical operations went on – charge and shell put in, range checked, shell fired, gun wheeled back into position – as though the men found their job so absorbing that it prevented their seeing or hearing anything else.

But what struck Maurice most was the attitude of the drivers fifteen metres to the rear, sitting bolt upright on their horses, facing the enemy. Adolphe was there, broad-chested, with his heavy fair moustache in the middle of his red face, and you really had to be jolly brave to watch the shells coming straight at you, without batting an eyelid or even being able to bite your thumbs to take your mind off it. The gun crews who were working had something else to think about, but the drivers, motionless, could see nothing but death and had plenty of leisure to think about it and wait for it to come. They were forced to stand facing the enemy because if they had turned their backs men and beasts might have been seized by an irrestible urge to run away. Seeing the danger you face up to it. There is no heroism less in evidence or greater.

Yet another man had had his head blown off, two of the horses on one van were agonizing with their bellies ripped open, and the enemy was keeping up such a murderous fire that the whole battery was going to be put out of action if they hung on to the same position. This terrible bombardment must be foiled in spite of the difficulties of a change of position. Without further hesitation the captain called out the order:

'Limber up!'

The dangerous movement was carried out with marvellous speed: the drivers about-turned again and brought up the limbers, which the gun crews coupled to the guns. But in carrying out this movement they had strung themselves out into a long front which the enemy took advantage of to redouble his fire. Three more men were lost. The battery cantered on, described an arc over the fields and took up its position some fifty metres further to the right, beyond the 106th on a little eminence. The guns were uncoupled, the drivers once again found themselves facing the enemy, and the bombardment started up again without a break and with such violence that the ground shook without pause.

This time Maurice uttered a cry. Once again, in three rounds, the Prussian batteries had readjusted their fire, and the third shell had fallen right on Honoré's gun. He was seen leaping forward and feeling the fresh damage with a trembling hand – a big piece chipped off the bronze muzzle. But the gun could still be loaded, and the routine went on after they had cleared the wheels of the body of another of the crew, whose blood had splashed on to the gun-carriage.

'No, it isn't young Louis,' Maurice went on, thinking aloud. 'There he still is, laying his gun, though he must be wounded, for he's only using his left arm . . . Poor little Louis, his marriage with Adolphe was doing so well as long as he, the foot-slogger, for all his superior education, remained the humble servant of the driver, the mounted man . . .'

Jean, who had kept quiet, broke in with a cry of anguish:

'They'll never hold out, we're done for!'

It was true, and in less than five minutes this second position had become as untenable as the first. Projectiles rained down upon it with the same precision. One shell demolished one gun and killed a lieutenant and two men. Not one of the rounds went astray, so that if they stuck there any longer there would not be a single cannon or gunner left. It was a crushing, overwhelming defeat.

Then the captain's voice rang out a second time:

'Limber up!'

The movement started again, the drivers galloped, did their about-wheel so that the crews could hitch up the guns. But this time in the middle of the manoeuvre a splinter of shell went through Louis's throat and tore away his jaw, and he fell across the trail he was in the act of picking up. And as Adolphe was coming up, just when the line of teams was sideways on, there was a furious volley: he fell with his chest split open and arms flung out. In a final convulsion he put his arms round the other man, and they remained twisted together in a fierce embrace, wedded even in death.

Already, in spite of slain horses and the disorder the murderous volley had spread in the ranks, the whole battery was climbing a slope and establishing itself further forward, a few metres from where Maurice and Jean were lying. For the third time the guns were uncoupled, the drivers found themselves facing the enemy while the crews opened fire again at once with obstinate, invincible heroism.

'It's the end of everything!' said Maurice in a broken voice.

It really seemed as though earth and sky were intermingled. Rocks split and dense smoke sometimes darkened the sun. In the midst of the frightful din the horses looked dazed and stupefied, with their heads down. The captain stood out wherever he was, for he was too tall. He was cut in two and fell like a broken flagstaff.

It was above all round Honoré's gun that the activity went on, unhurried and steadfast. Stripes or no stripes, he had to get down to the job, for only three of his crew were left. He did the laying and pulled the striker while the three others went to the ammunition waggon, loaded, worked with the cleaning brush and ramrod. They had asked for men and horses from the reserve to fill the gaps made by death, but these were a long time coming and meanwhile they had to make do. The maddening thing was that they were still not reaching target and their shells almost all exploded in the air without doing much harm to those terrible batteries on the other side whose fire was so deadly accurate. But Honoré suddenly let out an oath that could be heard above all the noise of firing – of all the bad luck, the right wheel of his gun had been smashed! Fuck it all, with one leg gone the poor old girl was pitched on her side, nose in the earth, all lopsided and no good for anything! He wept bitter tears and put his groping hands round her neck as though he could set her on her feet again by the sheer warmth of his affection. A gun that was the best of them, the only one to have landed a few shells over there! Then he was seized by a crazy resolve to replace the wheel there and then under fire. When he had gone himself with one of the crew and found a spare wheel in the waggon, the tricky operation began, the most dangerous there could be on the battlefield. Fortunately the relief men and horses had at last come, and two fresh gunners gave a hand.

So once again the battery was in confusion. Foolhardy heroism could not be taken any further. The order to fall back definitely could not long be delayed.

'Get a move on, chums!' Honoré kept urging them. 'We'll take her away with us anyway, and they won't get her!'

That was his idea – his gun must be saved, just as you save the flag. And he was still talking when he was struck down, his right arm torn off and his left side split open. He fell over his gun and there he stayed as though lying on a bed of state, his head straight on his shoulders and his face intact and beautiful in its anger as it turned towards the foe. A letter had slipped out of his torn uniform, clenched in his fingers, and his blood was staining it drop by drop.

The only lieutenant still alive called the order:

'Limber up!'

One waggon had blown up with a noise like fireworks fizzing and exploding. They had to decide to take the horses from another ammunition waggon to save a gun whose team was laid out. And this last time, when the drivers had wheeled round and coupled the four remaining guns, they galloped off and never stopped for a thousand metres until they were behind the first trees of the Garenne wood.

Maurice had seen it all. With a little shiver of horror he went on repeating in a mechanical voice:

'Oh, poor devil! Poor devil!'

This sorrow seemed to make his gut-twisting pain worse than ever. The animal within him was in revolt, he was at the end of his tether and he was dying of hunger. His eyes were worrying him, and he did not even realize the danger the regiment was now in since the battery had had to retire. At any minute the plateau could be attacked by heavy forces.

'Look here,' he said to Jean, 'I've got to have something to eat. I'd rather eat and let them kill me afterwards!'

He opened his pack and took out the loaf with both hands shaking, and began to bite into it voraciously. Bullets whistled by and two shells went off only a few metres away. But nothing existed for him any more, there was only his hunger to be appeased.

'Want some, Jean?'

Jean was watching him dully, with goggling eyes, for his own stomach was tortured by the same desire.

'Yes, damn it, I do. It hurts too much.'

They shared it out and finished the loaf off greedily, not bothering about anything else as long as a mouthful was left. It was only afterwards that they caught sight of the colonel again, on his tall horse with his bleeding boot. The 106th was broken on all sides. Some companies had already had to take to flight. So, forced to yield to the torrent, he raised his sword and said with tears in his eyes:

'Boys, you are in God's hands, though He hasn't found much use for us!'

He was surrounded by groups of fugitives, and disappeared into a dip in the ground.

Then, without knowing how they got there, Jean and Maurice found themselves behind the hedge with the remnants of their company. There were only forty men left at the most, commanded by Lieutenant Rochas, and the flag was with them: the second lieutenant carrying it had rolled the silk round the staff to try to save it. They ran along to the end of the hedge and threw themselves down among some little trees on a slope, where Rochas made them reopen fire. The men were now scattered like snipers and were under cover and could hold out, especially as a big cavalry manoeuvre was going on to their right, and regiments were being brought back into line to support it.

Then Maurice understood the slow, inexorable encircling movement that had just reached its completion. In the morning he had seen the Prussians pouring out through the Saint-Albert gap, reaching Saint-Menges, then Fleigneux, and now behind the Garenne wood he could hear the thundering cannon of the Guards and was beginning to see other German uniforms coming over the slopes of Givonne. In a few minutes' time the ring would close and the Guards would join up with the Vth corps and envelop the French army in a living wall, a deadly girdle of artillery. It must have been some desperate idea of making one last effort, an attempt to break this moving wall, that was behind the massing of a division of reserve cavalry, that of General Margueritte, behind a fold in the hills, in readiness for a charge. They were going to charge against death, with no possible outcome, for the honour of France. Thinking of Prosper, Maurice witnessed the terrible spectacle.

Ever since first thing that morning Prosper had done nothing but urge his horse on in continual marches and counter-marches from end to end of the plateau of Illy. They had been awakened at dawn man by man, without any bugle calls, and to brew some coffee they had managed to put a coat round each fire so as not to give their presence away to the Prussians. Since then they had known nothing of what was going on, they had heard gunfire and seen smoke and distant movements of infantry but, in the complete inactivity in which the generals left them, they knew nothing of the progress of the battle. Prosper was falling about with sleep. This was their great trouble: after bad nights and accumulated fatigue an overpowering drowsiness overcame them as they were gently rocked by the movement of their horses. Prosper had hallucinations, saw himself on the ground and snoring on a mattress of pebbles, dreamed that he was in a nice bed with white sheets. For minutes on end he really dozed off in the saddle and was merely a parcel on the move, borne along wherever his trotting mount liked to take him. Sometimes mates of his had fallen off their horses like that. They were all so dead beat that bugles no longer roused them and they had to be kicked out of oblivion and on to their feet.

'But what the hell are they up to with us, what are they up to?' Prosper went on repeating to keep this irresistible torpor at bay.

The guns had been roaring for six hours. As they went up a hill he had had two comrades killed at his side by a shell, and a bit further on three others were left on the ground riddled with bullets coming from nobody knew where. It was exasperating to be out on this useless and dangerous military parade across the battlefield. Finally at about one he realized that they had at any rate made up their minds to have them killed decently. The whole Margueritte division, three regiments of Chasseurs d'Afrique, one of French and one of hussars, had been asembled in a dip of the land slightly below the Calvary, to the left of the road. The trumpets had sounded dismount. And the officers' command rang out:

'Tighten girths, secure packs.'

Prosper dismounted, stretched himself and stroked Zephir. Poor Zephir! He was as woebegone as his master, worn out with the silly job he was being made to do. Added to that, he was being made to carry a whole world of stuff: clothing in the saddlebags and rolled coat on top, shirt, trousers, knapsack with medical supplies behind the saddle, and slung across him the bag with provisions, to say nothing of the water-bottle, can and messtin. The rider's heart was filled with pity and affection as he tightened the straps and made sure everything was secure.

It was a nasty moment. Prosper was no more a coward than the next man, but he lit a cigarette because his mouth was so dry. When you are about to charge, every man can really tell himself: 'This time I shall stay there!' This lasted a good five or six minutes, and it was being said that General Margueritte had gone ahead to reconnoitre. They waited. The five regiments were drawn up in three columns, each column seven squadrons deep – plenty of cannon-fodder.

Suddenly the trumpets sounded 'To horse!' and almost immediately another call: 'Draw swords!'

The colonel of each regiment had already galloped forward to his battle position twenty-five metres ahead of the main body. The captains were in their positions at the head of their men. And the waiting began again, in deathly silence. Not a sound, not a breath in the blazing sun. Only their hearts beat fast. One more order, the last, and this inert mass would begin to move and hurtle with the speed of a hurricane.

Just then an officer appeared over the brow of the hill, on his horse, wounded and supported by two men. At first they did not recognize him. Then a muttering began, which spread into a deafening clamour. It was General Margueritte, shot through the jaw by a bullet and near to death. He could not speak. He waved his arm towards the enemy.

The clamour grew louder still.

'Our general! Revenge, revenge!'

Then the colonel of the first regiment raised his sword in the air and shouted in a voice like thunder:

'Charge!'

The trumpets sounded and the mass began to move, at first at a trot. Prosper was in the front rank, but almost at the end of the right wing. The greatest danger was in the centre, where the enemy instinctively concentrates his fire. When they had scaled the top of the Calvary hill and were beginning to go down the further side towards the broad plain he had a clear view, some thousand metres ahead, of the Prussian squares against which they were being hurled. For all that, he was riding in a dream, feeling as light and disembodied as a man in his sleep, with an extraordinary vacuum in his brain which left him without a single idea – in fact a machine functioning with irresistible impetus. They kept repeating 'Close up! Close up!' so as to close the ranks as tightly as possible and give them a granite-like solidity. Then as the pace quickened and changed into a mad gallop, the Chasseurs d'Afrique, as in the Arab fashion, uttered wild yells that maddened their mounts. This furious gallop soon turned into a diabolical race, hell's own stampede, with its savage catcalls accompanied by the patter of bullets like hailstones on metal things, messtins, water-bottles, the brass on uniforms and harness. In this hail blew a hurricane of wind and din that made the earth tremble, and into the sunshine rose a smell of scorching wool and the sweat of savage beasts.

After five hundred metres Prosper took a fall when a dreadful swerving movement sent everything flying. He seized Zephir by the mane and managed to get back into the saddle. The centre raked by the enemy fire and forced back, had faltered, while the two wings whirled round and fell back in order to recover their impetus. It was the inevitable, foreseeable annihilation of the first squadron. The ground was littered with dead horses, some killed outright, others still writhing in violent death-throes, and un-horsed men could be seen running as fast as their little legs would carry them, looking for another horse. The plain was already strewn with dead, many riderless horses were still careering about and making of their own accord for their place in the line and dashing on into the enemy fire at a mad pace as if drawn on by the smell of powder. The charge was resumed and the second wave was now advancing with increasing fury, men bent low along their horses' necks, holding their sabres at the knee, ready to slash. Two hundred metres more were covered amid the deafening clamour. But once again the centre gave way, men and animals fell and stopped the charge with the inextricable clutter of their corpses. So the second squadron was mown down in its turn, annihilated, yielding its place to those who followed.

Then, in the heroic determination of the third charge, Prosper found himself involved with hussars and French chasseurs. Regiments no longer meant anything, and now there was simply an enormous wave continually breaking and re-forming to carry away all it met. He no longer had any notion of what was happening, but abandoned himself to his horse, that good old Zephir he loved so much and who seemed to have been driven crazy by a wounded ear. He was in the centre now, other horses were rearing and falling round him, some men were thrown to the ground as though they were blown down, while others, killed instantly, were still in the saddle, still charging with unseeing eyes. And this time, behind the two hundred fresh metres gained, the fields came back into view covered with dead and dying. There were some with their heads rammed into the ground. Others had fallen on their backs and were staring at the sun with terrified eyes starting from their sockets. There was a big black horse, with its belly open and vainly trying to get back on to its feet because its legs were caught in its entrails. Under the increasing fire the wings turned about yet again and gathered themselves together for another furious return.

So it was at last only the fourth squadron, the fourth wave, that came into contact with the Prussian lines. Prosper, with raised sabre, slashed on helmets and dark uniforms which he saw through a haze. Blood was flowing, and he noticed that Zephir's mouth was bleeding, and thought it was from biting into the enemy ranks. The clamour all round was such that he could not hear himself shout, though his throat felt lacerated by the yelling that must be coming out of it. But behind the first Prussian line there was another, and another and yet another. Heroism was unavailing, for these deep masses of men were like tall vegetation into which horses and men disappeared. However many you mowed down there were still plenty there. Fire continued with such intensity at point-blank range that some uniforms were set alight. Everything collapsed and was swallowed up amid the bayonets, chests cut open and skulls split. Regiments were going to leave two thirds of their strength there, and all that remained of this famous charge was the glorious folly of having attempted it. All of a sudden Zephir was hit by a bullet full in the chest and down he went, crushing beneath him Prosper's right haunch, and the pain was so intense that he lost consciousness.

Maurice and Jean had looked on at the heroic gallop of the squadrons, and they exclaimed in anger:

'Good God, what's the use of being brave?'

They went on firing their rifles as they crouched behind the brushwood on the little hillock where they found themselves sniping. Rochas himself had picked up a rifle and was shooting. But this time the Illy plateau was well and truly lost, and the Prussian troops were swarming on to it from all sides. It must have been about two o'clock, the junction was now completed, and the Vth corps and the Prussian Guard had met and closed the trap.

Jean was suddenly knocked over.

'I've got my ticket,' he muttered.

It had been like a violent hammer-blow on the top of his head, and his képi was knocked off and lay in shreds on the ground behind him. For a moment he thought his skull was open and his brains exposed, and for a second or two he dared not feel with his hand for he was certain there would be a hole. When he did venture his fingers came away red from a copious bleeding. The pain was so terrible that he fainted.

Just then Rochas was ordering them to fall back. There was a Prussian company not more than two or three hundred metres away. They would be caught.

'Don't rush, turn round and fire as you go. We'll find each other down there by that low wall.'

But Maurice was in desperation.

'Sir, we aren't going to leave our corporal here, are we?'

'If his number's up what do you propose to do about it?'

'No, no, he's breathing all right ... Let's carry him!'

With a shrug of the shoulders Rochas suggested that they couldn't clutter themselves up with everybody who fell. On the battlefield the wounded cease to count. So Maurice implored Pache and Lapoulle:

'Come on, give me a hand. I'm not strong enough on my own.'

They took no notice, couldn't hear, were only concerned with themselves, with the sharpened instinct of self-preservation. Already they were moving along on their knees as fast as they could go, out of sight behind the wall. The Prussians were now only a hundred metres away.

Weeping with rage, Maurice, now alone with the unconscious Jean, took him in his arms and tried to carry him. But he was indeed too weak, fragile in build as well as overcome with fatigue and suffering. If only he could still see an ambulance man! He searched with desperate eyes, thinking he could make out some of them among the fugitives, and waved wildly. Nobody came back. He summoned all his remaining strength, took hold of Jean again and managed to move some thirty paces, and when a shell burst near them he thought it was all over and that he too was going to die on the body of his friend.

But he slowly got up again, felt himself all over, nothing wrong, not a scratch. Why not run away? There was still time, he could reach that low wall in a few bounds and would be safe. His fear came back and was turning into panic. He took one leap and was rushing away when he was checked by a bond stronger than death. No, it was impossible, he couldn't abandon Jean. His whole body would have bled, the brotherly love that had grown up between this peasant and himself went down into the depths of his being, the very root of life itself. Perhaps it went back to the earliest days of the world, and it was as if there were only two men left in existence, and the one could not abandon the other without abandoning himself.

If Maurice had not eaten that crust of bread under fire an hour before he would never have found the strength to do what he now did. Not that he could remember anything about it later. He must have got Jean up on to his shoulders and then dragged himself along, with a score of failures and fresh starts, through stubble and briars, tripping over every boulder but somehow getting up again. Only invincible will-power kept him going and gave him strength that would have carried a mountain. Behind the low wall he found Rochas and the few men of the squad, still firing, defending the flag which the subaltern was holding under his arm.

No line of retreat had been indicated to the various army corps in the event of failure. This muddle and lack of foresight left each general free to act as he thought fit, and now they all found themselves being thrown back into Sedan in the formidable clutches of the victorious German armies. The second division of the 7th corps was withdrawing in reasonably good order, but the remnants of the other divisions, intermingled with those of the 1st corps, were already rushing towards the town in a frightful rabble, a torrent of anger and terror sweeping along men and beasts alike.

And then Maurice saw with joy that Jean's eyes were opening, and as he ran over to a little stream for water to wash his face, he was very surprised to see once again on his right, down in a quiet valley, sheltered by the steep hills, the same peasant he had seen in the morning, who was still slowly ploughing, guiding his plough behind a big white horse. Why lose a day? They might be fighting, but that was no reason why the corn should stop growing and the world stop living.

6

Up on the flat roof where he had gone to take in the situation, Delaherche once again became impatient to know. Of course he could see that the shells were passing over the town and that the three or four which had damaged the roofs of neighbouring houses must be just casual replies to such slow and inefficient fire from the Palatinate fort. But he could not make out anything about the battle itself, and there was inside him an urgent need for information, sharpened by fear of losing his fortune and his life in the catastrophe. So he went down, leaving his telescope trained in the direction where the German batteries were.

But when he got downstairs he was held for a moment by the state of the central garden of the factory. It was nearly one, and the casualty station was crammed with wounded. The line of vehicles coming through the gateway was endless. Already the regulation two-wheel or four-wheel carts were insufficient, and now artillery ammunition waggons were appearing, forage or supply vans, any-thing that could be commandeered on the battlefield, and now indeed there were even traps and farm carts taken from farms and hitched to stray horses. Into them had been piled wounded picked up by the first-aid men and given emergency dressings. It was a horrible unloading of poor wretches, some with the greenish pallor of death on them, others purple with congestion, many unconscious, others screaming, some so stupefied that they gave themselves to the orderlies with terrified eyes while others died of shock as soon as they were touched. The crowd was so dense that all the mattresses in the huge low shed were on the point of being used up, and Major Bouroche ordered the straw to be used, a large supply of which he had had put at one end. But so far he and his assistants could cope with the operations. All he had asked for was another table, with a mattress and American cloth over it, in the operating shed. An orderly quickly thrust a towel soaked in chloroform under the patient's nose. Little steel scissors gleamed, saws made a tiny file-like sound, blood squirted out in sudden jets, to be stopped at once. Patients for operation were brought up and carried away in a rapid shuttle-service, with just time for the American cloth to be wiped with a sponge. At the further end of the lawn, behind a clump of laburnums, into the charnel-house they had had to make there to get the dead out of the way, they also threw amputated legs and arms and all the bits of flesh and bone left on the tables.

Madame Delaherche and Gilberte were sitting under one of the big trees and could not manage to roll enough bandages. Bouroche, rushing by red-faced and with his apron already red, threw a bundle of linen to Delaherche and shouted:

'Look here, why don't you do something and make yourself useful!'

But the mill-owner protested:

'Excuse me, I must go again and find out what the news is. We don't know whether we're alive or dead.'

He touched his wife's hair with his lips.

'Poor Gilberte, to think that one shell can set fire to all this! It's terrifying.'

She was very pale, she looked up and glanced round with a shudder. Then her involuntary, irresistible smile came to her lips.

'Oh yes, terrible, all these men being cut up . . . It's funny that I can stick it without fainting.'

Madame Delaherche had watched her son kiss the young woman's hair. She made a little movement as though to thrust the thing out of sight, thinking of the other one, the man who must also have kissed that hair last night. Her old hands shook and she murmured:

'Oh God, what suffering! It makes you forget your own.'

Delaherche went off, saying he would be back in a moment with definite news. Even in the rue Maqua he was surprised by the number of soldiers coming back with no weapons, their uniforms in tatters and filthy with dust. But he could not get any exact details out of those he took the trouble to question: some answered in a daze that they didn't know, others talked so much and with such a frenzy of gesture and extravagance of words that they might have been mad. So he instinctively made for the Sub-Prefecture again, with the idea that all the news went there. As he was crossing the Place du Collège two cannons, probably the only two left out of a battery, dashed up and were stopped by a kerbstone. In the Grande-Rue he had to admit that the town was beginning to get overcrowded with the first fugitives. Three hussars who had lost their horses were sitting in a doorway and sharing a loaf, two others were slowly leading their horses along by the bridle with no idea where to stable them, officers were frantically running hither and thither, apparently not knowing where they were making for. On the Place Turenne a second lieutenant advised him not to hang about because quite a few shells were coming down, and a fragment had even broken the railing surrounding the statue of the Great Captain, conqueror of the Palatinate. And indeed, as he slipped quickly along the rue de la Sous-Préfecture, he saw two projectiles burst with a terrific noise on the Meuse bridge.

He was standing in front of the concierge's lodge trying to think up an excuse to ask for one of the aides-de-camp and question him, when a young voice hailed him:

'Monsieur Delaherche! . . . Come in quick, this is no time to be outside.'

It was Rose, his employee, whom he had forgotten. Thanks to her all doors would open for him. He went into the lodge and accepted a seat.

'Just fancy, it's made Mother ill and she's gone to bed. As you see, there's only me because Dad is a National Guard at the citadel. Just now the Emperor wanted to show that he was still brave, and he went out again and managed to get to the end of the street, as far as the bridge. One shell even fell in front of him and the horse of one of his equerries was killed. And then he came back again ... Well, what can you expect him to do?'

'So you know how things are ... What are these gentlemen saying?'

She looked at him in amazement. She was still young and fresh and gay, with her pretty hair and childlike eyes, busying herself about the place amid these abominations that she didn't really understand.

'No, I don't know anything ... At about twelve I took a letter up for Marshal MacMahon. The Emperor was with him ... They were shut up together for an hour, the marshal in bed and the Emperor sitting on a chair close to the bed. That I do know because I saw them when somebody opened the door.'

'Well, what were they talking about?'

She stared at him again and could not help laughing.

'I don't know, how do you expect me to know? Nobody in the world knows what they said to each other.'

Of course it was true, and with a gesture he apologized for his silly question. Yet he was haunted by the thought of this fateful conversation: how important it must have been and what decision had they reached?

'Now,' Rose went on, 'the Emperor has gone back to his private room where he is in conference with two generals who have just come from the battlefield.'

She stopped short and glanced at the steps.

'Look, that's one of them ... And there's the other.'

He quickly went out and recognized General Douay and General Ducrot, whose horses were waiting. He watched them mount and gallop away. After the evacuation of the plateau of Illy they had hurried separately to warn the Emperor that the battle was lost. They gave him details of the situation; the army and Sedan were from now on hemmed in on all sides, and the disaster would be appalling.

In his room the Emperor paced up and down in silence for some time, with the faltering step of a sick man. There was only one aide-de-camp there with him, standing silent by a door. He went on walking to and fro between the fireplace and the window, and his haggard face was now drawn up by a nervous tic. His back seemed even more bowed, as though a whole world was collapsing upon it, and his lifeless eyes beneath the heavy lids betokened the resignation of the fatalist who has played his last card against destiny and lost. Yet each time he came back to the open window he paused there and winced.

At one of these momentary pauses he raised a shaky hand and murmured:

'Oh, those guns, those guns, ever since first thing!'

Indeed the thunder of the batteries at La Marfée and Frénois was extraordinarily loud at that particular place. The rumbling of the thunder shook windowpanes and the very walls themselves with an obstinate, ceaseless, exasperating din. And he must be thinking that from then onwards the struggle was hopeless and any further resistance criminal. What was the point of any more bloodshed, limbs mangled, heads blown off, still more dead added to the other dead throughout the campaign? Since they were beaten and it was finished, why go on with the massacre? Enough abomination and grief was already crying to high heaven.

The Emperor came back to the window and again raised his trembling hands:

'Oh those guns, those guns, on and on!'

Perhaps the terrible vision of his responsibilities rose before him, of the bleeding corpses his misdeeds had strewn over the fields in thousands; perhaps it was just the sentimental pity of a dreamer's heart, of a good man haunted by humanitarian ideas. In this dreadful blow of fate that broke off and carried away his own fortune like a wisp of straw he could find tears for others, and was horrified at the continuing useless butchery, too weak to bear it any longer. Now this murderous cannonade seemed to hit him in the chest and redouble his pain.

'Oh those guns, those guns, stop them at once, at once!'

This Emperor without a throne since he had handed over his powers to the Empress-Regent, this commander-in-chief who no longer commanded since he had invested Marshal Bazaine with the supreme command, now had a reawakening of power, an irresistible

277

desire to be master one last time. Ever since Châlons he had effaced himself, had not given a single order, but resigned himself to being a nondescript, useless thing, an embarrassing package transported in the army baggage. The Emperor in him was aroused, but only for defeat, and the first and only order he was still to give, out of a heart filled with terror and pity, was to hoist the white flag over the citadel and ask for an armistice.

'Oh those guns, those guns . . . Get anything, a sheet, a table-cloth! Hurry and say they must be stopped!'

The aide-de-camp rushed out and the Emperor went on with his stumbling walk from the fireplace to the window while the batteries thundered on, shaking the whole building.

Down below Delaherche was still talking to Rose when a duty sergeant rushed in.

'Mademoiselle, we can't find anything and I can't run a maid to earth . . . You don't happen to have any white material, a piece of white cloth?'

'Would you like a towel?'

'No, no, that's not big enough . . . Half a sheet, for example.'

Rose was already obligingly running to a cupboard.

'But I haven't got a sheet cut in half! . . . A big piece of white material? No, I can't see anything that would do . . . Oh, but would you like a tablecloth?'

'Yes, that's fine. That'll do perfectly.'

As he went off he added:

'We're going to make it into a white flag that will be put up over the citadel to ask for peace . . . Thanks very much, Mademoiselle.'

Delaherche almost jumped for joy in spite of himself. At last they were going to be quiet! Then, this joy seemed unpatriotic and he checked it. But all the same his heart throbbed with relief, and he saw a colonel, a captain and the sergeant run out of the Sub-Prefecture. The colonel was carrying the rolled cloth under his arm. Delaherche thought he would follow them, and left Rose, who was very proud of having supplied this piece of linen. At that moment it was striking two.

In front of the Hôtel de Ville Delaherche was pushed about by a stream of scruffy soldiers coming down from the Cassine district. He lost sight of the colonel and set aside his curiosity to see the white flag run up. He would certainly not be allowed to enter the Keep, and besides, as he heard that shells were coming down on the school a new fear came over him – suppose his mill had caught fire since he left it. He hurried along, giving in again to his feverish need to keep on the move and finding relief in the mere fact of rushing about like this. But the streets were blocked by groups of people and there were fresh obstacles at every corner. It was only back in the rue Maqua again that he sighed with pleasure on seeing the monumental front of his house intact, with no smoke or sparks. He went in, shouting from a distance to his mother and his wife:

'Everything's all right, they're running up the white flag and there's going to be a cease fire!'

Then he stopped dead, for the sight of the ambulance station was truly horrifying.

In the huge drying-shed, the big door of which was left open, not only were all the mattresses occupied, but there was no room even on the straw scattered at the one end. They were beginning to put down straw between the beds, packing the wounded tight against one another. Already there were more than two hundred of them and they were still coming in. A white light from the big windows lit up all this heap of human suffering. Sometimes, if somebody was moved too roughly, there would be an involuntary scream. The hot, damp air was filled with the gasps of the dying. At the far end a soft, almost sing-song whimpering went on and on. Then the silence was deeper still, it was a kind of resigned stupor, the miserable exhaustion of the death-chamber, only relieved by the footsteps or whispers of the orderlies. Wounds hastily dressed on the battlefield, and some even still uncovered, could be seen in all their distress amid tattered coats and torn trousers. Feet were sticking out with boots still on, but crushed and bleeding. Limbs were dangling loose from knees and elbows that looked as if they had been broken with a hammer. There were crushed hands, fingers almost torn off and only held on by a thread of skin. Fractured legs and arms were the most common things, stiff with pain and heavy as lead. But the most upsetting wounds were gaping stomachs, chests or heads. Some men's trunks were bleeding through dreadful gashes, and knots of twisted entrails pushed up the skin, vital organs that had been pierced or hacked, twisted men into grotesque attitudes and paroxysms. Lungs had been shot right through, some with a hole so tiny that there was no bleeding, but others with an open gash through which the life-blood ebbed away in a red stream, and unseen internal haemorrhages struck men down all of a sudden in raving delirium and turned them black. Heads had suffered even worse things, smashed jaws with tongue and teeth a bleeding mess, eye-sockets driven in and eyes half out, skulls split open with brains visible. All those whose spinal cord or brain had been reached by bullets were like corpses, in a deathlike coma, while the others, those with fractures or feverish temperatures, were softly begging for something to drink.

Then in the operating shed next door there was a fresh horror. In this first rush only urgent operations were being done, the ones that had to be done because of the desperate condition of the patients. Any danger of haemorrhage made Bouroche decide on immediate amputation. Neither could he stop to look for bullets buried in wounds and remove them if they had lodged in some dangerous place, such as the bottom of the neck, the region of the armpit or groin, or in the elbow or back of the knee. Other wounds that he preferred to leave for observation were just dressed by orderlies under his supervision. Already he had done four amputations, spacing them out by taking 'rest' periods, during which he extracted a few bullets, between the major operations, and now he was beginning to tire. There were only two tables, his and one where one of his assistants was working. They had hung up a sheet between the two so that men being operated on could not see each other. However well they were sponged down the tables remained red, and the buckets they emptied a few steps away over a bed of daisies – buckets in which a single glassful of blood was enough to turn the clear water red – looked like pailfuls of pure blood, great sploshes of which covered the flowerbeds in the lawn. Although the fresh air came in freely a revolting stench rose from the tables, bandages and instruments in the sickly smell of chloroform.

A kindly man at bottom, Delaherche was shuddering with pity when his attention was caught by a landau coming through the gateway. Presumably this grand carriage was all they had managed to find, and it was piled with wounded, eight of them one on top of the other. Delaherche uttered a cry of astonishment and horror when he saw that the last one to be carried out was Captain Beaudoin.

'Oh, poor fellow! . . . Just a minute, I'll call my mother and my wife.'

They rushed up, leaving the bandage-rolling to two maids. The orderlies who had seized the captain were carrying him into the shed and were about to lay him on a heap of straw when Delaherche noticed on a mattress a soldier motionless, with ashen face and staring eyes.

'But look, that one's dead!'

'Oh yes, so he is,' murmured an orderly. 'No use having him cluttering up the place.'

And he and a comrade took the corpse and carried it off to the charnel-house they had made behind the laburnums. There were already a dozen or so dead put out there just as they had stiffened at the end, some with feet thrust out as though they had been on the rack with pain, others all deformed and twisted in horrible postures. Some were grinning, with white eyes and teeth showing between turned-back lips, and many of them, with drawn and terribly sad faces, were still weeping bitterly. One very young fellow, short and thin with half his head gone, was still convulsively clasping on his heart with both hands a woman's photo, one of those dim photos from a suburban shop, and it was splashed with blood. And at the feet of the dead were the heaps of arms and legs, and in fact anything cut out or hacked off on the operating tables, the sweepings of a butcher's shop when he had swept the refuse of flesh and bones into a corner.

When she saw Captain Beaudoin Gilberte had shuddered. Oh God, how pale he looked as he lay on that mattress, with his face quite white under the dirt that soiled it! The thought that only a few hours ago he had held her in his arms and was so full of life and smelt so sweet, froze her with horror. She knelt down.

'How dreadful, my dear! But it isn't anything, is it?'

She automatically took out her handkerchief and dabbed his face, finding him unbearable in that state, filthy with sweat, earth and powder. She felt she was relieving his pain by cleaning him up a little.

'It isn't anything, is it? It's only your leg!'

The captain, who was in a sort of drowsy sleep, opened his eyes with difficulty. He recognized his friends and was trying to smile at them.

'Yes, only my leg . . . I didn't even feel it happen, I thought I had stumbled and was falling . . .'

But he was finding it difficult to speak.

'Oh I'm thirsty, I'm thirsty.'

Then Madame Delaherche, who had been leaning over the other side of the mattress, got busy. She ran off for a glass and a flask of water with a few drops of brandy in it. When the captain had greedily drunk off a glass she had to share out the rest between the other wounded near-by – every hand was stretched out and urgent voices were imploring. A Zouave, for whom there was none left, burst into tears.

Meanwhile Delaherche was trying to speak to the major so as to get some favourable treatment for the captain. Bouroche had just come into the shed with his bloodstained apron and heavy face sweating, looking as if it was on fire under his leonine mane, and as he went by men raised themselves up and tried to stop him, all anxious to be seen to at once, to be helped and to know: 'Come to me, doctor, me!' He was pursued by incoherent prayers and clutching fingers touched his clothes. But he was entirely wrapped up in his job, puffing wearily as he went on organizing the work without listening to anybody. He talked aloud to himself, counted the cases on his fingers, giving them numbers and classifications: this one, that one, then the other, one, two, three, a jaw, an arm, a leg, while the assistant with him listened hard so as to try to remember.

'Major,' said Delaherche, 'there's a captain here, Captain Beaudoin . . .'

Bouroche cut him short.

'What! Beaudoin here? Oh, poor bugger!'

He went and stood in front of the wounded man. But he must have seen at a glance how serious the case was, for he went straight on, without even stooping to examine the injured leg.

'All right, they'll bring him to me straight away, as soon as I have done the operation now being got ready.'

He went back to the operating shed, followed by Delaherche, determined not to let him go for fear he might forget his promise.

This time it was the disarticulation of a shoulder by the Lisfranc method, what surgeons call a nice operation, a neat and quick job, scarcely forty seconds in all. They were already chloroforming the patient, and an assistant seized his shoulder with both hands, four fingers of each under the armpit and the thumb on top. Then Bouroche, armed with his long knife, shouted: 'Sit him up,' grasped the deltoid, cut into the arm and through the muscle; then stepping back he detached the joint in one go and the arm was off, amputated in three movements. The assistant had moved his thumbs along to stop the blood from the humeral artery. 'Lay him down again!' Bouroche couldn't help chuckling as he went on to the ligature, for he had done the job in thirty-five seconds. All that had to be done now was to pull the bit of loose flesh down over the wound, like a flat epaulette. It was a nice, tricky business because of the danger, as a man could empty out all his blood in three minutes through the humeral artery, to say nothing of the risk of death every time you sit a patient up when he is under chloroform.

Delaherche was frozen with horror and would have liked to run away. But there was no time, the arm being already on the table. The soldier who had had his arm amputated, a recruit, a hefty peasant, was regaining consciousness and caught sight of the arm being taken by an orderly to the place behind the laburnums. He glanced at his shoulder and saw it cut and bleeding. He flew into a furious rage.

'Oh Christ, what a bloody silly trick you've done!'

Bouroche was too tired to answer at once. Then with man-to-man heartiness:

'I did it for the best, I didn't want you to peg out, my boy ... Anyhow, I did consult you, and you said yes!'

'I said yes! I said yes! How could I know what I was saying?'

His anger vanished and he began to cry bitterly.

'What's the fucking good of me now?'

He was carried back to the straw, the American cloth and table were vigorously swabbed, and once again the pails of red water were thrown over the lawn and bloodied the whole bed of daisies.

Delaherche was amazed that he could still hear the guns. Why hadn't they stopped? Surely Rose's tablecloth must now be hoisted above the citadel. It seemed, on the contrary, that the Prussians' fire was growing in intensity. The ear-splitting din shook even the least nervous from head to foot in growing distress. It could hardly be good for operators or patients, for these explosions pulled your insides out. The whole ambulance station was upset by them and being strained to breaking-point.

'It was over, what are they going on for?' cried Delaherche, straining his ears all the time, thinking that each shot he heard was the last.

Then as he was making for Bouroche to remind him about the captain, he was astonished to find him on a bale of straw on the ground, lying on his front with both arms bare to the shoulders and thrust into two buckets of ice-cold water. At the end of his moral and physical resources, the major was trying to relax like this, for he was stunned and knocked out by immense sadness and despair – at one of those moments when a practitioner is in agony over his own apparent powerlessness. Yet he was a strong man, thick-skinned and stout-hearted. But he had been struck by the 'what's the use?' and the feeling that he would never do it all, could never do it all, had suddenly paralysed him. What was the use? Death would always come out the strongest!

Two orderlies brought Captain Beaudoin up on a stretcher.

'Major,' Delaherche ventured to say, 'here's the captain.'

Bouroche opened his eyes, took his arms out of the pails, gave them a shake and wiped them on the straw. Then getting up on to his knees:

'Oh yes, fuck it, another of them! ... Oh well, come on, the day's not over yet!'

Already he was on his feet and refreshed, shaking his leonine head with its tawny mane, having got himself back to normal by professional habit and ruthless self-discipline.

Gilberte and Madame Delaherche had followed the stretcher and they remained standing at a little distance when the captain had been laid on the mattress with the American cloth over it.

'Right, it's above the right ankle,' Bouroche was saying, for he always talked a lot to take the patient's mind off it. 'Not too bad in that place, you get over it quite well ... Let's have a look at it.'

But it was clear that he was worried about the torpor of Beaudoin's condition. He looked at the emergency dressing, which was just a simple band, tightened and held over the trouser-leg by a bayonet sheath. He muttered between his teeth, wondering what sort of silly clot had done that. But then he suddenly went quiet for he understood – it must have happened on the journey, in the landau full of wounded, that the bandage had come loose and slipped down, no longer pressing on the wound, and that had caused a severe haemorrhage.

Bouroche took it out violently on an orderly who was helping him.

'You clumsy sod, cut it away, quick!'

The orderly cut away the trouser leg and pants underneath, also the sock and boot. The leg and the foot could now be seen, colourless bare flesh flecked with blood. Above the ankle there was a terrible hole into which the fragment of shell had driven a piece of red cloth. A lump of jagged flesh and muscle was sticking out of the wound in a mass of pulp.

Gilberte had to support herself against one of the posts of the shed. Oh that flesh, such white flesh, and now bloody and mangled! For all her horror she could not take her eyes off it.

'Gosh!' declared Bouroche. 'They've made a fine old job of you!'

He touched the foot, which was cold, and he could feel no pulse. His face became very grave, with a puckering of the lip that he always had over desperate cases.

'Gosh!' he said again. 'That's a bad foot!'

The captain, whose anxiety woke him out of his daze, watched him and waited, and at length he said:

'You think so, major?'

Bouroche's tactics were never to ask a wounded man directly for the usual permission when an amputation was clearly necessary. He preferred the patient to come round to it himself.

'Bad foot!' he murmured as though thinking aloud. 'We shan't be able to save it.'

Nervously Beaudoin went on:

'Look here, it's got to be faced, major. What do you think?'

'I think you are a brave man, captain, and that you're going to let me do what's necessary.'

Beaudoin's eyes lost their lustre and seemed to cloud over with a sort of reddish mist. He had understood. But in spite of the unbearable fear choking him, he answered simply and with courage:

'Carry on, major.'

The preparations did not take long. Already the assistant had in readiness the cloth soaked in chloroform and it was at once held under the patient's nose. Then, at the exact moment when the brief spasm preceding unconsciousness occurred, two orderlies moved the captain along on the mattress so as to have his legs accessible, and one held the left leg and supported it, while an assistant seized the right and squeezed it tight with both hands up near the groin to compress the arteries.

When she saw Bouroche drawing near with his narrow knife Gilberte could bear it no longer.

'No, no! It's horrible!'

She was swooning and holding on to Madame Delaherche, who had to put her arm out to save her from falling.

'Why stay, then?'

Yet both women did stay. They turned their heads away, trying not to see, and stood there rooted to the spot and trembling, clinging to each other although there was so little love lost between them.

It was certainly at this hour of the day that the thunder of the guns was at its worst. It was now three, and Delaherche, feeling let down and exasperated, declared that it was beyond his comprehension. For now there was no doubt about it that, far from stopping, the Prussian batteries were redoubling their fire. Why? What was going on? It was a hellish bombardment, the ground shook and the very air was on fire. All round Sedan the eight hundred pieces of German equipment, a girdle of bronze, were firing at once, blasting the fields with a continuous thunder, and this converging fire, all these surrounding heights aiming at the centre, would burn and pulverize the town within two hours. The worst of it was that shells were beginning to come down on houses again. More and more crashes could be heard. One shell went off in the rue des Voyards. Another knocked a bit off one of the tall chimneys of the mill and rubble came down outside the shed.

Bouroche glanced up and growled:

'Do they want to finish our wounded off? This row is unbearable.'

However, the orderly was holding the captain's leg out straight, and, with a rapid incision all round, the major cut the skin below the knee, five centimetres below the point where he intended to cut through the bones. Then at once, using the same thin knife which he did not change so as not to waste time, he took off the skin and raised it all round like peeling an orange. But as he was about to cut through the muscles an orderly came up and whispered into his ear:

'Number two's gone.'

In the appalling din the major could not hear.

'Speak up, for God's sake! Those bloody guns are splitting my ears.'

'Number two's gone.'

'Which is number two?'

'The arm.'

'Oh, all right ... Well, bring along number three, that's the jaw.'

With wonderful skill, and without any hesitation, he cut the muscles with a single stroke right down to the bones, laying bare the tibia and fibula between which he put a three-tailed compress to keep them in position. Then he cut them through with one stroke of the saw. The foot remained in the hands of the orderly who was holding it.

There was little loss of blood thanks to the pressure being applied higher up round the thigh by the assistant. The ligature of the three arteries was rapidly done. But the major was shaking his head, and when his assistant had taken away his fingers he examined the wound, and feeling sure that the patient could not yet hear he murmured:

'It's the devil, there's no blood coming through the arterioles.'

And he finished his diagnosis with a gesture: one more poor bugger done for! Fatigue and an immense sadness had come back to his sweating face, the despairing 'what's the use?', since they weren't saving four out of ten. He mopped his brow and began to put back the skin to do the three stitchings.

Gilberte had just turned round again, as Delaherche had told her it was all over and she could look. But she did see the captain's foot that the orderly was taking away behind the laburnums. The charnel-house was still piling up, two more dead were laid out there, one with his mouth unnaturally open and black, looking as though he were still shrieking, and the other screwed up in an awful death-struggle that had reduced him to the size of a sickly and deformed child. Worst of all, the pile of human remains was now overflowing on to the path. Not knowing where he could decently put the capain's foot, the orderly hesitated and then made up his mind to throw it on to the pile.

'Well, that's that!' said the major to Beaudoin as they revived him. 'You'll be all right now.'

But the captain had nothing like that happy awakening that follows successful operations. He sat up a little and then fell back, gasping in a lifeless voice:

'Thank you, major. I'm glad it's over.'

But then he felt the sting of the spirit dressing. And as the stretcher was being brought up to take him away a terrible explosion shook the whole factory. It was a shell that had exploded behind the shed, in the little yard where the pump was. Windows were shattered and a thick smoke came into the ambulance station. In the other hall the wounded had risen in panic from their straw beds and were all screaming with fear and trying to run away.

Delaherche rushed off in a frenzy to assess the damage. Were they going to burn down and destroy his house now? What on earth was going on, then? If the Emperor wanted it to stop why had they started again?

'For God's sake, stir your stumps!' Bouroche bawled to the orderlies. 'Come on, wash down the table and bring me number three!'

They swabbed the table and once more threw the pails of water over the lawn. The bed of daisies was now nothing but a blood-stained mess, greenery and flowers all mangled up in blood. The major, to whom number three had been brought, began by way of a restful change to look for a bullet which after breaking the lower jawbone must have buried itself under the tongue. There was a great deal of blood which made his fingers all sticky.

In the main hall Captain Beaudoin was back on his mattress, and Gilberte and Madame Delaherche had followed the stretcher. Even Delaherche, upset though he was, came and chatted for a moment.

'Just relax, captain, we'll get a room ready and have you with us.'

But the stricken man roused out of his stupor and had a moment of lucidity.

'No, I'm sure I'm going to die.'

He looked at all three of them with staring eyes full of the fear of death.

'Oh, captain, what are you saying?' murmured Gilberte, trying

288

to smile through her terror. 'You'll be up and about in a month.'

He shook his head, now looking only at her, and his eyes betrayed an immense longing for life and dismay at going off like this before his time and without exhausting the joys of life.

'I'm going to die, I'm going to die ... Oh it's awful!'

Then he caught sight of his dirty, torn uniform and black hands and seemed to be embarrassed about being in such a state in front of women. He felt ashamed of letting himself go like this, and the thought that he was lacking in good manners finally gave him back quite a jaunty air. He managed to go on in a joking tone:

'Only, if I die I should like to die with clean hands ... Madame, it would be so kind of you if you could moisten a towel and give it to me.'

Gilberte ran off and came back with the towel and insisted on wiping his hands herself. From then on he displayed very great courage, anxious to end like a man of good breeding. Delaherche said comforting things and helped his wife to make him presentable. As she watched this dying man, and both husband and wife busying themselves for him in this way, old Madame Delaherche felt her resentment melt away. Once again she would hold her peace, though she knew and had sworn to tell her son everything. What was to be gained by casting a blight on the home since death was washing away the sin?

It was soon over. Captain Beaudoin was losing strength and he relapsed into his exhaustion. His forehead and neck were bathed in icy sweat. He opened his eyes again for a moment and groped as though he were feeling for an imaginary blanket that he began to pull up to his chin with a weak but determined movement of his twisted hands.

'Oh I'm cold, I'm so cold.'

And he departed, snuffed out with not even a gasp, and his face, calm but drawn, had kept its expression of infinite sadness.

Delaherche saw to it that the body was placed in a near-by coach-house instead of being thrown on to the heap. He tried to force Gilberte, who was weeping uncontrollably, to go indoors. But she said she would be too frightened now to be alone, and preferred to stay with her mother-in-law amid the activity of the ambulance station, which took her mind off things. In a moment she was off to give a drink to a Chasseur d'Afrique who was wandering in delirium, and then she helped an orderly to bandage the hand of a young soldier, a twenty-year-old recruit, who had walked all the way from the battlefield with a thumb off, and as he was nice and funny, joking about his wound with the detached air of a Parisian wag, she even managed to laugh with him.

During the death agony of the captain the bombardment seemed to have got still worse, and a second shell had come down in the garden and had snapped one of the century-old trees. Terrified people were screaming that the whole of Sedan was on fire, and indeed a major fire had broken out in the Cassine district. It was the end of everything if this bombardment went on with such violence for long.

'It just isn't possible, I'm going back!' said Delaherche, beside himself.

'Where to?' asked Bouroche.

'The Sub-Prefecture, of course, to find out whether the Emperor is having us on when he talks about running up the white flag.'

For a few seconds the major remained stunned by this idea of the white flag, defeat, capitulation, coming in the midst of his powerlessness to save all these poor bloodstained devils being brought to him. He made a gesture of furious despair.

'Oh go to the devil! We're all done for anyway!'

Outside Delaherche found it more difficult to push his way through the troops who had swelled in numbers. Every minute the streets were getting more crowded with the stream of straggling soldiers. He questioned some of the officers he met and none had seen the white flag over the citadel. Finally a colonel said he had caught a momentary glimpse of it – just being run up and lowered again. That would explain everything, for either the Germans had not had time to see it or, seeing it appear and disappear, they had redoubled their fire realizing that the end was near. There was even a rumour already about the crazy anger of a general who had dashed forward when the white flag appeared, snatched it down with his own hands, breaking the staff and trampling the cloth underfoot. So the Prussian batteries were still firing, shells were raining down on roofs and in the streets, houses were burning and a woman had her head smashed at the corner of the Place Turenne.

Delaherche did not find Rose in the porter's lodge at the Sub-

Prefecture. Every door was open and the rout was setting in. So he went up the stairs, every person he ran into was in a panic and nobody asked him any questions. As he was hesitating on the first floor he saw the girl.

'Oh, Monsieur Delaherche, it's all going to pieces ... Look sharp if you want to see the Emperor.'

And indeed to his left a door was ajar, and through the opening the Emperor could be seen once again taking his faltering walk between the fireplace and the window. He kept on walking, never stopping in spite of his intolerable pain.

An aide-de-camp had gone in, and he it was who had neglected to shut the door after him, so the Emperor could be heard asking in a voice exhausted with grief:

'But why, sir, are they still firing, since I had the white flag run up?'

This torture had become unbearable, the gunfire never stopping, but increasing in violence every minute. He could not go near the window without being cut to the heart. More blood, more human lives cut off and through his fault! Every minute added more dead to the pile, pointlessly. Tender-hearted dreamer that he was, he could not stand it, and ten times already he had asked his desperate question of people coming in:

'But why are they still firing, since I had the white flag run up?'

The aide-de-camp muttered some answer Delaherche could not catch. Not that the Emperor had stopped, for he was continually giving in to his compulsive need to go back to that window where the ceaseless thunder of gunfire made him feel faint. His pallor was more marked than ever, and his long, tragic, drawn face, with the morning's make-up not properly wiped off, betrayed his agony.

Just then a bustling little man in a dusty uniform, whom Delaherche recognized as General Lebrun, crossed the landing and pushed open the door without having himself announced. At once, yet again, the anguished voice of the Emperor could be heard:

'But, general, why are they still firing, since I had the white flag run up?'

The aide-de-camp came out and the door was shut, and Delaherche could not hear the general's reply. The scene had vanished.

'Oh,' Rose said again, 'it's all going to pieces, I can tell from those gentlemen's faces. Now there's that cloth of mine, that I shan't see again! Some of them say it's been torn up . . . In all this it's the Emperor who makes me feel so sorry, for he's more of a sick man than the marshal, and would be better off in bed than in that room where he's wearing himself out with always walking up and down.'

She was deeply moved, and her pretty fair face was full of sincere pity. So Delaherche, whose Bonapartist fervour had been cooling off remarkably for two days, thought she was a bit silly. But downstairs he stayed with her a minute or two longer watching out for General Lebrun's departure. When he came down again Delaherche followed him.

General Lebrun had explained to the Emperor that if he wanted to ask for an armistice a letter signed by the commander-in-chief of the French army would have to be delivered to the commander-in-chief of the German forces. Then he had undertaken to write this letter and go in search of General de Wimpffen who would sign it. He was now bearing the letter, but was only too afraid of not finding the general, not knowing whereabouts on the battle-field he might be. Moreover the pack in Sedan was so thick that he had to ride his horse at a walking pace, which enabled Delaherche to keep up with him as far as the Ménil gate.

Once out on the main road General Lebrun went at a gallop, and he was fortunate enough to see General de Wimpffen as soon as he reached Balan. The latter had written only a few minutes before to the Emperor: 'Sir, come and put yourself at the head of your troops, and they will think it an honour to open up a way for you through the enemy lines.' And so the very mention of the word armistice threw him into a furious rage. No, no, he wouldn't sign anything, he was determined to fight! It was then half past three, and it was soon afterwards that the heroic and desperate attempt was made, the last thrust to open up a gap through the Bavarians by marching once again on Bazeilles. So as to put some heart back into the troops they spread a lie by shouting 'Bazaine is coming, Bazaine is coming!' Since first thing in the morning this had been the dream of so many who thought they could hear the guns of the army of Metz every time a new battery of the Germans was un-covered. About twelve hundred men were scraped together, stray soldiers from every corps and every arm, and the little column dashed gloriously at full speed along the bullet-swept road. At first it was sublime, falling men did not check the impetus of the rest, and they covered nearly five hundred metres with truly reckless courage. But soon the ranks began thinning, and even the bravest fell back. What could they do against overwhelming odds? It was simply the crazy folly of an army chief who did not want to be beaten. In the end General de Wimpffen found himself alone with General Lebrun on the Balan–Bazeilles road, which they had to abandon for good. There was nothing to be done but retreat into Sedan.

As soon as he had lost sight of the general, Delaherche hurried back to his mill with but one idea in his head, which was to go up again to his observation post and follow events from a distance. But on reaching home he was held up for a moment by running into Colonel de Vineuil, who was being brought in with his blood-soaked boot, half unconscious on some hay in the bottom of a farm cart. The colonel had insisted on trying to rally the remnants of his regiment until he had fallen off his horse. He was taken straight up to a first-floor room, and Bouroche hurried up but found it was only a cracked ankle-bone and so merely bandaged the wound after extracting bits of boot-leather. He was overwhelmed and at the end of his tether, and rushed down again shouting that he would rather cut off one of his own legs than go on doing his job in such a messy way, without proper materials or the essential assistance. And indeed down below they had reached the stage of not knowing where to put the wounded, and had decided to put them on the lawn, in the grass. There were already two rows of them waiting and loudly complaining in the open air, with shells still coming down. The number of men brought in to the station since noon was over four hundred, and the major had asked for more surgeons, but all they had sent was one young doctor from the town. He simply could not cope with it, and he examined, cut through flesh, sawed through bones and sewed up again almost beside himself and in despair at seeing more work being brought than he was getting through. Gilberte was sick with horror and overcome with nausea at so much blood and tears, and she had stayed with her uncle the colonel, leaving Madame Delaherche down below to give drinks to the fevered and wipe the sweating faces of the dying.

Up on his flat roof Delaherche tried to get a quick impression of the situation. The town had been less damaged than had been feared and only one fire was sending up thick black smoke in the Cassine district. The Palatinate fort had stopped firing, having probably run out of ammunition. Only the guns at the Paris gate were still firing an odd round now and again. What interested him immediately was that they had once again run up the white flag over the Keep, but they couldn't be seeing it from the battlefield, for the firing was still as heavy as ever. Some roofs in the foreground concealed the Balan road and he could not follow the movements of troops there. Moreover, having put his eye to the telescope which was still trained in that direction, he once again had picked out the German Headquarters which he had already seen there at noon. The master, that diminutive tin soldier, as big as half your little finger, in whom he thought he had recognized the King of Prussia, was still standing there in his dark uniform, in front of the other officers, most of whom were lying on the grass and all shining with gold braid. There were foreign officers there, aides-de-camp, generals, court officials, princes, all provided with field glasses, and since early morning they had been following the death-struggles of the French army like a play. And now the terrible drama was drawing to its close.

From these wooded heights of La Marfée King William had just witnessed the conjunction of his troops. It was all over, the third army, under the command of his son the Crown Prince of Prussia, which had come via Saint-Menges and Fleigneux, was taking possession of the plateau of Illy, whilst the fourth, commanded by the Crown Prince of Saxony, was reaching the rendezvous through Daigny and Givonne, by means of a detour round the Garenne woods. The XIth corps and the Vth thus joined hands with the XIIth corps and the Prussian Guard. The supreme effort to break out of this circle as it was closing, the useless and glorious charge of the Margueritte division, had torn from the King a cry of admiration: 'Oh, what brave fellows!' Now the inexorable, mathematical enveloping movement was nearly complete, the jaws of the vice had come together and he could take in at a glance the immense wall of men and guns hemming in the defeated army. To the north the embrace was tightening and driving fugitives back into Sedan before the ceaseless fire from batteries in an unbroken line all along the horizon. To the south, Bazeilles, conquered, deserted and tragic, was burning itself out, sending up clouds of smoke and sparks, while the Bavarians, now occupying Balan, were levelling their guns three hundred metres from the town gates. And the other batteries along the left bank at Pont-Maugis, Noyers, Frénois, Wadelincourt, which had been firing non-stop for nearly twelve hours, were thundering louder than ever and completing the impassable girdle of fire right to below where the King was standing.

King William, who was getting tired, gave up using his field glasses for a minute and went on watching with the naked eye. The slanting sun was descending towards the woods and was about to set in a pure cloudless sky. It gilded the whole vast panorama, and shed on it such a clear light that the smallest details stood out with striking clarity. He could pick out the houses of Sedan, with their little black bars across the windows, the ramparts, the fortress, the complicated defensive system with its ridges in high relief. And scattered all round in the countryside, the fresh, gaily-painted villages looked like toy farms, Donchery to his left, on the edge of its flat plain, Douzy and Carignan to his right in the meadows. You could almost have counted the trees of the forest of the Ardennes, and its ocean of green stretched out of sight to the frontier. In this horizontal light the Meuse, with its meanderings, had become a river of pure gold. The atrocious, bloody battle itself, seen from such a height in the setting sun, was like a delicate painting: dead horsemen and disembowelled horses flecked the plateau of Floing with gay splashes of colour; further to the right, towards Givonne, the final scramble of the retreat made an interesting picture with the whirling of black dots running about and falling over themselves; and again in the Iges peninsula to the left a Bavarian battery with its guns the size of matches looked like a piece of nicely adjusted mechanism, for the eye could follow its regular, clockwork movements. It was unhoped-for, overwhelming victory, and the King had no remorse, faced as he was by these tiny corpses, these thousands of men less than the dust on the roads, the great vale in which the fires of Bazeilles, the slaughter of Illy, the anguish of Sedan, could not prevent unfeeling nature from being beautiful at this serene end of a perfect day.

Then suddenly Delaherche saw, climbing the slopes of La Marfée, a French general in a blue tunic on a black horse, preceded by a hussar with a white flag. It was General Reille, detailed by the Emperor to bear this letter to the King of Prussia:

Sir, my Brother,

Not having been able to die among my troops, it only remains for me to put my sword in Your Majesty's hands.

Truly Your Majesty's brother, Napoleon.'

In his anxiety to stop the killing, since he was no longer master, the Emperor was giving himself up, hoping to touch the conqueror's heart. Delaherche saw General Reille halt ten paces from the King, dismount and go forward to hand over the letter, unarmed and with only a riding-whip. The sun was going down in a great pink radiance, the King sat down on a chair, leaned against the back of another chair which was held by a secretary, and answered that he accepted the sword and would be waiting for an officer to be sent to negotiate the terms of the capitulation.

7

Now all round Sedan, from all the lost positions – Floing, the plateau of Illy, the Garenne woods and the valley of the Givonne, the Bazeilles road – a panic-stricken flood of men, horses and cannon was pouring towards the town. This fortress, on which they had had the disastrous idea of depending, was proving to be a terrible snare, a shelter for fugitives, a sanctuary into which even the bravest men let themselves be lured in the general demoralization and panic. Behind those ramparts they imagined they would at last escape from the terrible artillery which had been thundering for nearly twelve hours; all conscience and reason had fled, the animal had run away with the human and there was nothing left but the mad rush of instinct stampeding for the hole in which to go to earth and sleep.

At the foot of the little wall, when Maurice bathed Jean's face with the cold water and saw him open his eyes, he cried out with joy:

'Oh, dear old sod, I thought you were done for ... And no offence meant, but you weigh a ton!'

Still dazed, Jean seemed to be waking out of a dream. Then he must have realized and remembered, for two big tears ran down his cheeks. So this Maurice, this puny boy he loved and looked after like a child, had in this surge of affection found enough strength in his arms to carry him as far as here!

'Half a mo, let me have a look at that cranium of yours.'

The wound was nothing much, just a grazing of the scalp, which had bled a lot. The hair, now matted with blood, had acted as a pad. So he took care not to wet it, so as not to reopen the place.

'There, now you've been cleaned up you've got a human face again. Just a second and I'll fix you up with a hat.'

So he picked up the képi of a dead soldier and carefully put it on Jean's head.

'Just the right size ... Now if you can walk we're both smart boys.'

Jean stood up and shook his head to see if it felt all right. All he felt now was a bit of a headache. He'd be fine. He was overcome with a simple man's emotion and threw his arms round Maurice and clasped him tight to his heart. The only words he could find were:

'Oh my dear boy, my dear boy!'

But the Prussians were coming, and the vital thing was not to dally behind that wall. Lieutenant Rochas was already retreating with his small band of men protecting the flag, still being carried under the second lieutenant's arm, rolled round its staff. Lapoulle, being very tall, could raise himself and still fire a few more rounds over the coping, but Pache had slung his rifle over his shoulder, presumably deeming that enough was enough and that now some food and sleep would be desirable. Jean and Maurice, bent double, hurried after them. There was no lack of ammunition or rifles, you only had to stoop down. They rearmed themselves, having left everything over there, kit and all, when one had had to carry the other on his shoulders. The wall ran right along to the Garenne wood, and the little band, thinking it was in safety, darted behind a farm building and from there reached the trees.

'Ah,' said Rochas, still keeping his fine, unshakable confidence, 'we'll get our breath back here for a minute before going back to the offensive.'

But with the very first steps they all felt they were entering an inferno; they could not go back again, but had to go on through the wood, their only line of retreat. It was now a terrifying wood, a wood of despair and death. Realizing that troops were falling back

297

through it, the Prussians were riddling it with bullets and raking it with gunfire. It was being lashed by a hurricane, all movement and howling and shattering of branches. Shells cut trees in two, bullets brought leaves down like rain, groans seemed to come out of the split trunks and sobs come down with branches wet with sap. It was like the distress of a fettered mob of men, the terror and cries of thousands of people nailed to the ground and unable to flee from the hail of bullets. No anguish ever moaned so loud as in a bombarded forest.

At once Maurice and Jean, who had rejoined their mates, lost their nerve. At that moment they were going through a glade of tall trees and could run. But the bullets were whistling in a crossfire, from which directions it was impossible to tell and so dart safely from tree to tree. Two men were killed, hit in the back, hit in the front. Right in front of Maurice an age-old oak had its trunk pulverized by a shell and crashed down with the majesty of a tragic hero, smashing everything around it. And as he jumped back a colossal beech on his left had its head knocked off by another shell, broke and collapsed like a pillar in a cathedral. Where could they run? Which was the best direction to go? On all sides nothing but falling branches, it was like being in a huge building threatened with collapse as in room after room the ceilings were falling in. Then, when they had leaped into a thicket to escape from this crashing of big trees, it was Jean's turn to be almost cut in two by a projectile which mercifully did not explode. This time they could not make any headway through the inextricable tangle of bushes. Twigs caught their shoulders and tall grasses clung round their feet, sudden walls of brushwood brought them to a standstill, while foliage flew round them as the giant scythe swept through the wood. By their side another man was killed instantly by a bullet through the forehead, but he remained standing, jammed between two birches. A score of times as they were held prisoners by this thicket they felt death pass by.

'Christ!' said Maurice. 'We'll never get out of here!'

He was ashen and his trembling had come back, and Jean, so brave as a rule, who had comforted him that morning, was going pale, too, and feeling as cold as ice. It was fear, horrible fear, catching and irresistible. Once again they were parched with thirst, an intolerable dryness in the mouth, a contracting of the throat with an acute, strangling pain. And with it other discomforts, a feeling of sickness in the pit of the stomach, pins and needles pricking their legs. In this wholly physical sensation of fear that crushed their heads as in a vice, they could see thousands of black dots rushing past as if they could pick out the bullets in the flying cloud.

'Oh what bloody awful luck!' muttered Jean. 'I mean, it makes you wild being here and getting killed for other people when those other people are somewhere quietly smoking their pipes.'

Maurice, his face drawn and wild-looking, went on:

'Yes, why me and not somebody else?'

It was the revolt of the self, the self-centred rage of the individual unwilling to sacrifice himself for mankind and cease to be.

'And besides,' added Jean, 'if only we knew the reason, if there was any point in it!'

Then, looking up at the sky:

'And then this bleeding sun won't make up its mind to fuck off! When it's set and it's dark they'll stop fighting, maybe.'

For ages now, with no means of knowing the time and not even being conscious of the flight of time, he had been looking out for the slow decline of the sun, which seemed to have stopped altogether above those woods on the further side of the river. It was not even cowardice now, but an imperious and growing need not to hear shells and bullets any more, but to go away, anywhere, and bury oneself in the depths of the earth and find oblivion. If it were not for what other people thought, or the glory of doing one's duty in front of one's fellows, he would go beserk and run away instinctively, at full speed.

And yet once again Maurice and Jean got used to it, and out of the very excess of their panic there grew a sort of don't-care intoxication which had something brave about it, and they ended by not even hurrying any more through that accursed wood. The horror had intensified still more among this population of bombarded trees killed at their posts and falling on all sides like steadfast, gigantic soldiers. Under the greenwood tree, in the lovely half-light, down in mysterious bowers carpeted with moss, brutal death passed by. The solitary waterbrooks were violated, dying men gasped their lives away in the most secret nooks where hitherto none but lovers had ventured. One man with a bullet through his chest had time to shout 'Got me!' as he fell on his face, dead. Another, both of whose legs had been smashed by a shell, went on laughing, not realizing he was wounded, but thinking he had merely stumbled over a tree-root. Others, with limbs shot through and mortally wounded, went on talking and running for a few steps before collapsing in a sudden spasm. At the first moment even the deepest wounds could hardly be felt, and it was only later that the appalling sufferings began and poured themselves forth in screams and tears.

Oh, that treacherous, massacred forest, that amid the sobs of dying trees was gradually filling with the agonized shrieks of the wounded! At the foot of an oak Maurice and Jean saw a Zouave with his entrails exposed, who was howling endlessly like an animal being slaughtered. And further on a man was on fire, his blue belt was burning and the flame reached up to his beard and singed it; but his back must have been broken for he was unable to move and was crying bitterly. And then a captain, with his left forearm gone and his right side slit down to the thigh, was flat on his belly and dragging himself along on his elbows, imploring somebody, in a dreadful high-pitched voice, to finish him off. More and still more were in abominable suffering, scattered along the grassy walks in such numbers that you had to watch out so as not to tread on them as you moved. But wounded and dead had ceased to count. Any comrade who fell was left there and forgotten, with never a glance behind. It was just fate. Now the next – me perhaps!

Suddenly, as they were coming to the edge of the wood, a cry was heard.

'Help!'

It was the second-lieutenant who was carrying the flag, and he had just had a bullet in the left lung. He had fallen and blood was gushing from his mouth. Seeing somebody coming, he found enough strength to pull himself together and shout:

'The flag!'

Rochas leaped back in one bound, took the flag, the staff of which had been broken, while the second lieutenant murmured in a voice choking with bloody foam:

'I've got my ticket, I don't care a damn. Save the flag.'

There he stayed alone, writhing on the moss in this lovely woodland dell, clawing at grass with his clenched hands, his chest heaving in a death-struggle that went on for hours.

At last they were out of this fearful wood. Apart from Maurice and Jean there only remained out of the little group Lieutenant Rochas, Pache and Lapoulle. Gaude, whom they had lost, emerged in his turn from a thicket and ran to rejoin his mates, with his bugle slung over his shoulder. It was a real relief to find themselves in open country and breathing freely. The whistling of bullets had stopped, and shells were not coming down on this side of the valley.

Then they suddenly heard somebody cursing and swearing in front of the gateway to a farmyard, and they saw a furious general on a steaming horse. It was General Bourgain-Desfeuilles, the commander of their brigade, also covered in dust and looking dog-tired. His big red face, the face of a man who does himself well, expressed the state of exasperation he was thrown into by the disaster, which he took as a personal misfortune. The soldiers had not set eyes on him since early that morning. Presumably he had got himself lost on the battlefield, running about after the scattered remains of his brigade, and quite capable of letting himself be killed in his anger with the Prussian batteries for sweeping away the Empire and his prospects as an officer well thought of at the Tuileries.

'Blast it all!' he bawled. 'Isn't there anybody left here? Can't you get any information in this buggering country?'

The farm people must have fled into the woods. Finally a very old woman appeared at the door, some old servant left behind and kept there by her bad legs.

'Here, Ma, come here! . . . Which way's Belgium?'

She stared at him stupidly, apparently not understanding. Then he went right off the deep-end, forgetting he was speaking to a woman and bellowing that he didn't mean to be caught in a trap like a mug by going back to Sedan – he was going to fuck off abroad, he was, and bloody quick too! Some of the soldiers had come up and were listening.

'But sir,' said a sergeant, 'you can't get through now, there are Prussians everywhere. It was all right this morning, you could have done a bunk then.'

There were stories going the rounds already about companies cut off from their regiments who had unintentionally crossed the frontier, and others who had even managed courageously to get

through the enemy lines before they had completed the encircle-
ment.

Beside himself, the general raised his arms.

'Come on, with some good chaps like you couldn't we get anywhere we wanted? I can surely find fifty stalwart fellows ready to
fight it out.'

Then, turning back to the old woman:

'Oh damn it all, Ma, why can't you answer? Where's Belgium?'

This time she did understand. She waved her skinny hand
towards the great woods:

'That way, that way.'

'What's that you're saying? ... Those houses you can see
beyond the fields?'

'Oh, further than that, much further! Right over there!'

The general spluttered with rage.

'Oh it makes you sick, a bloody hole like this. You don't know
what to make of it. Belgium was over there and you were afraid
of stumbling into it without knowing, and now you want to get
there it's gone ... No, no, this is the end, let 'em take me and do
what they like with me, I'm going to sleep.'

He spurred his horse, bouncing in the saddle like a bladder blown
up with the wind of anger, and galloped off towards Sedan.

There was a bend in the road and they went down into Fond-de-
Givonne, a district shut in between steep slopes, where the road
climbing towards the woods was flanked by little houses and
gardens. It was so clogged by a stream of refugees that Lieutenant
Rochas found himself pushed back with Pache, Lapoulle and
Gaude, against a pub on a corner of the crossroads. Jean and
Maurice had a job to get to them. And they were all amazed to hear
a thick, drunken voice addressing them:

'Well, fancy meeting you! ... Hallo chums! ... Well, it's a
small world, isn't it?'

Behold, it was Chouteau in the pub, leaning out of one of the
ground-floor windows. He was very drunk and went on between
hiccups:

'Look here, don't worry if you're thirsty ... Plenty left for my
pals.'

He waved shakily backwards, summoning somebody still at the
back of the room.

'Come here, you lazy sod ... Give these gents something to drink.'

It was Loubet's turn to appear, holding a full bottle in each hand and waving them about for fun. He wasn't as drunk as the other one, and he shouted in his Parisian smart-aleck voice, putting on the nasal voice of a soft-drink vendor on a public holiday:

'Nice and cool! Nice and cool! Who wants a drink?'

They had not been seen since they had gone off ostensibly to carry Sergeant Sapin to the ambulance post. They had no doubt been wandering about ever since and dodging spots where shells were falling. They had landed up here in this pub which was then being looted.

Lieutenant Rochas was outraged.

'Just you wait, you swine. I'll give you booze! And while all the rest of us are pegging out in the thick of it all!'

But Chouteau refused to accept the reprimand.

'Look here, you silly old sod, there's no more lieutenant about it, there's only free men ... Haven't the Prussians given you enough, then? Do you want a bit more?'

They had to hold back Rochas, who was threatening to do him in. Loubet, of all people, bottle in hand, was trying to keep the peace.

'Now, now, give over, no point in scrapping, we're all brothers together!'

Catching sight of Lapoulle and Pache, two of their mates in the squad:

'Don't you be soft, come in here, you two. Let's give your throats a rinse for you.'

Lapoulle had a moment's hesitation, feeling vaguely that it was wrong to have a good time while other poor buggers were at their last gasp. But he was so all in and knocked up with hunger and thirst! He suddenly made up his mind, and with one bound and without a word he nipped into the pub, shoving Pache in front of him, who was just as silent and tempted, and gave in. They never reappeared.

'Lot of swine!' repeated Rochas. 'They should all be shot!'

Now he only had Jean, Maurice and Gaude left with him, and all four were more or less swept along in spite of themselves by the torrent of fugitives filling the whole width of the road. The pub was already far behind. It was a rabble pouring down into the ditches of Sedan in a muddy stream, like the earth and stones washed down into the valleys when a storm strikes the hills. From all the neighbouring uplands, down all the slopes and coombs, along the Floing road, through Pierremont, past the cemetery and the parade ground, as well as through Fond-de-Givonne, the same mob rushed on and on in an ever quickening gallop of panic. How could you blame these wretched men who had been waiting motionless for twelve hours, exposed to the shattering artillery of an invisible enemy against whom they could do nothing? Now the batteries were catching them in front, on either side and in the rear, and their fire converged more and more as the army retreated into the town, until whole heaps of men were being flattened out into a human mush in the foul hole into which they had been swept. A few regiments of the 7th corps, especially on the Floing side, did fall back in reasonable order. But in Fond-de-Givonne there were neither ranks nor officers, the troops shoved each other along in a desperate herd made up of all sorts: Zouaves, Turcos, light cavalry and infantry, mostly unarmed, in dirty and ragged uniforms, with black hands and faces, staring bloodshot eyes and thick lips swollen through having bawled so many oaths. Now and again a riderless horse would come rearing along, knocking soldiers over and leaving behind it a wake of terror where it had cut through the crowd. Cannons would tear through like mad things, batteries in confusion whose drivers behaved as though they were mad drunk and ran over everything without warning. On and on went the herd in a solid procession shoulder to shoulder, a mass flight in which gaps were immediately filled with the instinctive haste to get to shelter, behind a wall.

Jean looked up westwards again. Through the thick cloud of dust kicked up by feet the sun's rays still shone on sweating faces. The weather was lovely, the sky wonderfully blue.

'But it doesn't half get you down,' he kept saying, 'this fucking sun that won't make up its mind to go.'

Then Maurice, seeing a young woman being pushed back against a house and almost crushed to death by the crowd, was suddenly horrified to realize that it was his sister Henriette. For nearly a minute he just saw her and remained gaping. She it was who spoke first, without seeming to be surprised.

'They shot him at Bazeilles . . . Yes, I was there . . . So as I want to get his body back I thought . . .'

She never named the Prussians or Weiss. Everybody must understand, and Maurice certainly did. He was devoted to his sister and he burst into tears.

'Oh my poor darling!'

When she had pulled herself together at about two o'clock Henriette had found herself at Balan, in the kitchen of some people she did not know, with her head on the table, crying. But her tears dried up. In this quiet and delicately made woman a heroine was already being born. She was without fear and her soul was steadfast, invincible. In her grief all she thought of was recovering her husband's body and burying him. Her first idea was to go back to Bazeilles there and then, but everybody dissuaded her and pointed out that it was absolutely out of the question. So she set about looking for somebody, some man to go with her and take the the necessary steps. She thought of a cousin, formerly assistant manager of the General Refinery at Le Chêne when Weiss worked there. He had been very fond of her husband and surely he would not refuse to help. For the last two years, after his wife had received a legacy, he had retired to a nice house and garden, L'Ermitage, the terraces of which were near Sedan, on the other side of the Fond-de-Givonne valley. This was where she was making for in spite of obstacles, held up at every step, and in continual danger of being trampled on and killed.

She rapidly explained the idea to Maurice, who approved.

'Cousin Dubreuil has always been so good to us . . . He'll be useful to you.'

Then he, too, had an idea. Lieutenant Rochas wanted to save the flag. It had already been suggested that it should be cut up and that each man should carry a piece under his shirt, or again that it should be buried at the foot of a tree and that bearings be taken so that it could be dug up later. But it was too depressing to think of this flag being cut to pieces or buried like a dead thing, and they wished they could think of something else.

So when Maurice proposed giving the flag to somebody quite reliable who would hide it and if necessary defend it until the day it could be returned intact, they all agreed.

'Very well,' he said to his sister, 'we'll go with you to see whether Dubreuil is at L'Ermitage . . . In any case I don't want to leave you.'

It was not easy to get out of the crush, but they managed to and hurried up a sunken lane to the left. Then they found themselves in a real labyrinth of paths and lanes, quite a little township of market gardens, pleasure grounds and country homes, small properties all mixed up with each other, and these little lanes and alleys ran along between walls, made sharp turns and came to dead ends – a marvellous system of fortifications for guerrilla warfare, with corners that ten men could defend for hours against a regiment. And already shots were going off in there, for this district over-looked Sedan and the Prussian Guard was coming in on the opposite side of the valley.

When Maurice and Henriette, followed by the others, had hurried left, then right, between two endless walls, they suddenly emerged in front of the wide open gate of L'Ermitage. The estate, with its little park, was on three broad terraces, on one of which stood the building, a large square house reached by an avenue of ancient elms. Opposite, across the narrow, deep valley, there were other properties on the edge of a wood.

The door left brutally open worried Henriette.

'They aren't here. They must have gone.'

And indeed, foreseeing certain disaster, Dubreuil had decided to take his wife and children to Bouillon the day before. But the house was not empty, and even from a distance and through the trees you could tell that something was going on inside. As she was venturing into the avenue the corpse of a Prussian soldier made her jump back.

'Blimey!' exclaimed Rochas. 'There's already been some spar-ring here!'

Anxious to find out, they all pushed on towards the house, and what they saw made it plain: the ground-floor doors and windows must have been smashed in with rifle-butts, the gaping holes opened into looted rooms, and furniture thrown outside was lying on the gravel terrace at the bottom of a flight of steps. In particular there was a drawing-room suite in sky-blue, a settee and twelve easy chairs standing higgledy-piggledy round a big side-table, the white marble top of which was split across. And Zouaves, chasseurs and infantrymen were running about behind the buildings and in the avenue firing over the valley into the little wood opposite.

'Sir,' a Zouave told Rochas, 'we found those Prussian sods in the middle of sacking everything. You can see we've put paid to their account . . . Only the buggers always come back ten to one, and it's not going to be a picnic.'

Three other bodies of Prussian soldiers were laid out on the terrace. As Henriette was staring at them, doubtless thinking of her husband, also lying over there and disfigured with blood and dirt, a bullet hit a tree just behind her. Jean darted forward.

'Don't stay there! Quick, quick, hide in the house!'

Now that he had seen her again, looking so changed and overcome with distress, his heart was bursting with pity as he remembered how she had struck him only the day before, a smiling housewife. At first he had not found anything to say to her, not knowing even whether she recognized him. He would have liked to devote himself to her and bring back into her life some peace and joy.

'Wait for us inside . . . as soon as there is any danger we'll find a way of getting you out up that way.'

She made a gesture of indifference.

'What's the use?'

But her brother was urging her too, and she had to go up the steps and stay a minute inside the hall, whence she could see right down the avenue. From then on she watched all the fighting.

Maurice and Jean were standing behind one of the nearest elms. The century-old trunks were gigantic and could easily provide cover for two men. Further off bugler Gaude had joined Lieutenant Rochas, who was obstinately hanging on to the flag as there was nobody to entrust it to, and he had set it down next to him against the tree while he fired his rifle. Each tree-trunk had its man, and all along the avenue Zouaves, chasseurs and marines kept behind cover except when they poked out their heads to fire.

In the little wood opposite the number of Prussians must have been steadily building up, for their fire was getting heavier. There was nothing to be seen except an occasional glimpse of a man dashing from one tree to another. A country house with green shutters was also occupied by snipers who were firing out of the open ground-floor windows. It was now about four o'clock, and the sound of gunfire was slackening and gradually stopping, and yet here men were still killing each other as though in some personal feud down in this remote dingle, from which the white flag hoisted on the Keep could not be seen. Right on until it was dark, and despite the armistice, there were pockets of fighting going obstinately on like this, and rifle fire went on in the Fond-de-Givonne district and the gardens of Petit-Pont.

For a long time they went on riddling each other with bullets from one side of the valley to the other. Now and again any man who was unwise enough to emerge from cover went down with a bullet through his body. Three more were killed in the avenue. One wounded man had fallen on his face and was gasping horribly, but nobody dreamed of turning him over to relieve his agony.

Looking up suddenly Jean saw Henriette who had calmly come back and was slipping a sack under the poor devil's head by way of a pillow after she had turned him over on to his back. He rushed and pulled her roughly back behind the tree where he was sheltering with Maurice.

'Are you trying to get yourself killed?'

She did not seem to realize how rash she was.

'No, of course not . . . But it makes me frightened, being alone in that hall . . . I'd rather be outside.'

And so she stayed with them. They made her sit down at their feet against the tree while they went on firing their last rounds right and left with such fury that all fear and fatigue had gone. They had reached a state of complete unawareness and were acting automatically, with nothing in their minds, having even lost the instinct of self-preservation.

'Look, Maurice,' Henriette suddenly said, 'isn't that dead man just over there a soldier in the Prussian Guard?'

For a few minutes she had been looking at one of the bodies left behind by the enemy, a stocky fellow with a bushy moustache, lying on his side on the gravel of the terrace. His spiked helmet had rolled down near them, its chinstrap broken. The corpse was indeed wearing the Guard's uniform – dark-grey trousers, blue tunic, white braid, and rolled coat slung round like a bandolier.

'I tell you, he's a guardsman . . . I've got a picture at home . . . And then what about the photo cousin Gunther sent us?'

She stopped talking and walked calmly over to the dead man before they could stop her, and leaned over him.

'Red shoulder-straps,' she called out, 'oh, I could have taken a bet on it!'

She came back with a hail of bullets whistling about her ears.

'Yes, red shoulder-straps, it just had to be . . . Cousin Gunther's regiment!'

After that neither Maurice nor Jean could get her to keep still under cover. She was constantly on the move, sticking out her head, determined, come what may, to watch the little wood, with one fixed idea. They went on firing and jerked her back with their knees if she ventured too far out. Presumably the Prussians were beginning to think they were now sufficiently numerous and ready to attack, for they were now showing themselves in a flood spilling out between the trees, and they were sustaining terrible losses as each French bullet was accurate and picked off its man.

'Look,' said Jean, 'perhaps that's your cousin. That officer coming out of the house with the green shutters opposite.'

It was certainly a captain, recognizable by the gold collar of his tunic and the golden eagle shining on his helmet in the light of the afternoon sun. He had no epaulettes, had a sabre in his hand and was shouting an order in staccato tones, and the distance was so short, a bare two hundred metres, that he could be seen quite clearly, with his slim build, pink, hard face and little fair moustache.

Henriette scrutinized him with her piercing eyes.

'Yes, it's him all right,' she said without any surprise. 'I recognize him perfectly.'

With a furious movement Maurice was already taking aim.

'Our cousin! . . . Oh Christ, he's going to pay for Weiss!'

But she leaped up in terror and pushed the rifle to one side, and the shot spent itself in the sky.

'No, no, not between relations, not between people who know each other . . . It's an abomination!'

She became a woman again, and collapsed behind the tree, weeping hysterically. She was overcome with horror, full of nothing but terror and grief.

Meanwhile Rochas was having his moment of triumph. Round him the firing of a handful of soldiers, inspired by his stentorian voice, had so intensified at the sight of the Prussians that the latter fell back into the little wood.

'Stick to it, boys! Don't slack off! ... Look at those fat pigs doing a bunk! We'll settle their hash!'

He was cheerful and now apparently full of immense confidence again. There hadn't been any defeats. That handful of men opposite was the German army, and he was going to kick them arse over tip, nothing easier. His tall lean body, his long bony face with its beak of a nose coming down over his big mouth, was all laughing with a bragging joy, the joy of the trooper who has conquered the world between having his girl and a bottle of good wine.

'It goes without saying, boys, that's what we're all here for, to give them a bloody licking. Can't finish any other way, it would be too much of a change to be beaten, now wouldn't it? Beaten! Is that possible? One more effort, lads, and they'll piss off like hares!'

He bawled and waved his arms, such a fine chap with his ignorant illusions that the soldiers laughed with him. Suddenly he shouted:

'With kicks up the arse! With kicks up the arse all the way to the frontier! Victory! Victory!'

But then, just when the enemy opposite really looked as though he was falling back, a terrible fusillade burst out on the left. It was the inevitable turning movement – a whole detachment of the Guards that had come round by way of Fond-de-Givonne. From that moment defence of L'Ermitage was out of the question, for the dozen or so soldiers still defending the terraces were caught between two fires and in danger of being cut off from Sedan. Some of them fell, and there was a moment of great confusion. Already the Prussians were coming over the wall of the estate and running along the paths in such numbers that fighting began with the bayonet. One Zouave in particular, bareheaded and with his coat off, a fine man with a black beard, was doing a terrific job, smashing through breastbones and sinking into soft stomachs, wiping his bayonet, red with the blood of one, on the body of another, and when the bayonet snapped he went on smashing in skulls with his rifle-butt, until at length, when a false move finally disarmed him, he leaped at a big Prussian's throat with such a flying leap that they rolled together on the gravel as far as the broken-in kitchen door, in a mortal embrace. Between the trees and in every corner of the lawns similar slaughter piled up the dead. The fight was at its most deadly in front of the flight of steps, round the sky-blue settee and chairs, a furious hand-to-hand set-to with men firing point-blank into each other's faces, tearing each other with tooth and claw for want of a knife to slit open each other's breasts.

Then Gaude, with that doleful face of his, suggesting the man who has had his troubles but never refers to them, was seized with heroic bravado. In this final defeat, well knowing that the company was wiped out and not a single man could answer his call, he seized his bugle, put it to his lips and blew Fall In with such a blast that he seemed to want to make the dead rise to their feet. The Prussians were nearly there, but he never budged, blowing louder still, a complete fanfare. A shower of bullets struck him down, and his last breath flew away in a brassy note and filled the sky with shuddering.

Rochas stood there uncomprehending, having made no attempt to run away. He waited, stammering:

'Well, what's up? What's up?'

It never entered his head that it could be defeat. Everything was being changed nowadays, even the way you fought. Oughtn't those chaps to have waited across the valley for them to go and beat them? It was no use killing them, they still went on coming. What was the matter with this buggering war in which they got ten men to crush one and the enemy only showed himself in the evening after throwing you into confusion all day long with precautionary gunfire? Flabbergasted and wild-eyed, having understood nothing so far about the campaign, he felt himself being enveloped and carried away by some superior force he could not resist any more, even though he went on with his obstinate cry:

'Courage, lads, victory is just round the corner!'

All the same, he had quickly taken up the flag again. This was his last thought, he must hide it so that the Prussians wouldn't get it. But although the staff was broken it caught in his legs and he nearly fell. Bullets hissed around, and feeling death coming he ripped off the silk flag and tore it up, trying to do away with it. It was then that he was struck in the neck, chest and legs, and he collapsed among the bits of tricolor as though he were dressed in them. He lived for a minute more with staring eyes, seeing perhaps a true picture of war as it is, a ghastly struggle for life that can only be accepted with serious resignation, as one does a law. Then, with a little cough, he departed with the wonderment of a child, like some poor limited creature, a carefree insect squashed by nature's vast, impassive machine. With him perished a legend.

As soon as the Prussians arrived Jean and Maurice had withdrawn from tree to tree, protecting Henriette as much as they could behind them. They never stopped shooting, firing one round and then gaining shelter. Maurice knew there was a little gate at the top of the park, and luckily they found it open. All three quickly got away. They had emerged into a narrow by-way which wound between two high walls. But when they came to the end of it some firing made them run up another lane to the left which unfortunately proved to be a dead end. They had to rush back and turn right under a hail of shot. They never knew afterwards what roads they had taken. There was still rifle fire going on at every turn of the wall in this inextricable labyrinth. Fighting was lingering on in gateways, and the smallest obstacles were being defended and attacked by storm with fearful tenacity. All of a sudden they came out on to the Fond-de-Givonne road quite near Sedan.

For the last time, Jean looked up westwards where the sky was filling with a great pink light, and at last he sighed with immense relief:

'Oh, that bloody sun, at last it's going down!'

They were now all three running and running without stopping for breath. Round them the tail end of the fugitives was still filling the roadway with a constantly mounting pressure like a torrent in spate. When they reached the Balan gate they had to wait in an appalling mêlée. The chains of the drawbridge were broken and the only way open was a pedestrian footway, so that guns and horses could not get through. At the castle postern and the Cassine gate they said the crush was even more frightening. It was the headlong rush of all the remnants of the army pelting down the slopes and throwing themselves into the town with a noise like an open sluicegate or water going down a drain. The fatal attraction of these city walls corrupted even the bravest.

Maurice seized Henriette in his arms, and trembling with impatience:

'Surely they aren't going to shut the gate before everyone's got in.'

This was what the crowd was afraid of. But to right and left

312

soldiers were already camping on the grass slopes, while the batteries of artillery had tumbled into the ditches in a jumble of pieces of equipment, ammunition waggons and horses.

Repeated bugle-calls resounded, soon to be followed by the clear notes of the retreat. Straggling soldiers were being called in. Some were still running up at full speed, and isolated shots went off in some outlying neighbourhoods, but fewer and fewer. Detachments were left on the benches inside the parapet to defend the approaches, and eventually the gate was closed. The Prussians were not more than a hundred metres away. They could be seen coming and going on the Balan road, calmly setting about occupying houses and gardens.

Maurice and Jean, pushing Henriette in front of them to protect her from being jostled, were among the last to enter Sedan. It was striking six and already nearly an hour since the bombardment had stopped. Gradually even the isolated rifle shots gave over. Then nothing was left of the deafening noise and hateful thunder that had been roaring ever since sunrise – nothing but the peace of death. Night was coming, falling into a mournful, frightening silence.

8

At about half past five, before the closing of the gates, Delaherche had gone back yet again to the Sub-Prefecture in his anxiety about what was going to happen now that he knew the battle was lost. He stayed there nearly three hours, tramping up and down the paved courtyard on the watch and questioning any passing officer, and in this way he learned about the rapid sequence of events: General de Wimpffen's resignation tendered and then withdrawn, the plenary powers he had received from the Emperor to go to the Prussian General Headquarters and obtain for the beaten army the least harsh conditions, then the meeting of the war council to decide whether they should attempt to carry on the war by defending the fortress. During this meeting, attended by a score of high-ranking officers, which seemed to him to last a century, he went up the flight of steps twenty times. At eight-fifteen General de Wimpffen suddenly emerged looking very flushed and with swollen eyes, followed by a colonel and two other generals. They leaped into the saddle and rode off over the Meuse bridge. It was capitulation, accepted as inevitable.

Delaherche, feeling reassured, realized that he was dying of hunger and decided to go home. But as soon as he was outside he was pulled up short by the terrible confusion that had developed. The streets and open spaces were jammed and bursting, so full of men, horses and equipment that the compact mass looked as though it must have been forced in by some gigantic ram. While the regiments that had retired in good order were camping on the ramparts, the scattered remnants of every corps, the fugitives from all arms, a milling throng, had submerged the town and piled up like a tidal wave that had congealed and frozen solid, in which you could not move arms or legs. The wheels of guns, waggons and countless vehicles had fouled each other. Horses, whipped and shoved in all directions, had no room to go forwards or backwards. And the men, taking no notice of threats, were breaking into houses, devouring whatever they found and lying down wherever they could, in rooms or in cellars. Many had fallen asleep in doorways and were blocking entries. Some, too weak to go any further, were lying on the pavement dead asleep, not even stirring under feet that bruised their limbs, preferring to be trodden on rather than to have to make the effort to go somewhere else.

This made Delaherche realize the urgent necessity of surrender. At certain road junctions ammunition waggons were touching each other, and just one Prussian shell, if it landed on one of them, would blow up the others, and the whole of Sedan would flare up like a torch. Besides, what could be done about such a collection of desperate men, overcome with exhaustion and hunger and with no ammunition and no supplies? It would have needed a whole day simply to clear the streets. The fortress itself had no armament and the town had no provisions. At the meeting these had been the reasons given by the wiser men who kept a clear view of the situation in spite of their deep patriotic grief, and even the most hot-headed officers, the ones who shouted emotionally that no army could give in like this, had had to hang their heads, being unable to think of any practical measures to start the fight again next day.

Delaherche managed with difficulty to fight his way through the pack and cross the Place Turenne and the Place du Rivage. As he passed the Hôtel de la Croix d'Or he caught a depressing glimpse of the dining-room, in which some generals were sitting in silence at an empty table. There was nothing left, not even any bread. But General Bourgain-Desfeuilles, who was storming about in the kitchen, must have found something, for he stopped talking and then ran up the stairs awkwardly holding in both hands something in greasy paper. There was such a crowd staring in from the pavement through the window at this glum board, swept clean by famine, that Delaherche had to shove with his elbows, feeling caught in a web, and sometimes being pushed back and losing what headway he had gained. But when he got to the Grande-Rue, the wall of people was impassable, and for a moment he gave up hope. Here all the guns in a battery seemed to have been piled on top of each other. So he made up his mind and climbed up on to the gun-carriages, stepped over the guns themselves, leaping from wheel to wheel at the risk of breaking his legs. Then there were horses in the way, and he stooped down and was reduced to making his way between the legs and under the bellies of these poor, half-starved creatures. After struggling for a quarter of an hour he reached the top of rue Saint-Michel, but there the growing number of obstacles frightened him, and he thought he would go along that street and get round via rue des Laboureurs, hoping that these back streets would be less crowded. But as ill-luck would have it there was a brothel down there, besieged by a lot of drunken soldiers, and fearing he might fare badly in some shindy he retraced his steps. So then he fought on and got to the end of the Grand-rue, sometimes balancing on cart-shafts, sometimes climbing over vans. In the Place du Collège he was actually carried along on people's shoulders for some thirty metres. He fell off and nearly had his ribs broken, only getting away by climbing some railings. When at last he reached rue Maqua, in a sweat and torn to shreds, he had been wearing himself out for an hour since leaving the Sub-Prefecture to do a journey that usually took him under five minutes.

To prevent the garden and ambulance station from being over-run, Major Bouroche had taken the precaution of posting two pickets at the entrance. This was a relief to Delaherche, to whom it had just occurred that his home might be given up to looting. In the garden the sight of the temporary hospital, ill-lit by a few lanterns and giving off a foul smell of sickness, once again struck a chill into his heart. He tripped over a soldier asleep on the paving-stones and recollected the existence of the cash of the 7th corps, which this man had been guarding since that morning, and, no doubt forgotten by his officers, he was so dead beat that he had lain down. The house itself looked empty and the ground floor was quite dark, with the doors wide open. The servants must have stayed in the ambulance station, for there was nobody in the kitchen, where only one miserable little lamp was smoking. He lit a candle and went softly up the main staircase so as not to wake up his mother and his wife, whom he had begged to go to bed after such a heavy day and such terrible emotions.

But as he went into his study he had a shock. A soldier was stretched out on the sofa on which Captain Beaudoin had slept for some hours the day before, and he only understood when he recognized Maurice, Henriette's brother; particularly as when he turned round he saw another soldier on the carpet, wrapped in a blanket, the Jean whom he had seen the day before. They were both knocked out, dead to the world. He did not stay there, but went on into his wife's room next door. There was a lamp burning on the corner of a table, and an eerie silence. Gilberte had thrown herself across the bed fully dressed, for fear of some disaster, presumably. She was sleeping very peacefully, and by her bedside Henriette was asleep too, sitting on a chair with just her head resting on the bed, but her sleep was disturbed by nightmares, and there were big tears under her lids. He stood there looking at them both for a moment and was tempted to wake Henriette up and find out. Had she been to Bazeilles? Perhaps if he asked her she could give him some news about his dyeworks. But pity came over him, and he was withdrawing when his mother appeared noiselessly at the door and beckoned him to follow.

As they went through the dining-room he expressed his astonishment:

'What, not in bed yet?'

She first shook her head and then whispered:

'I can't sleep, I'm in an armchair beside the colonel . . . He's now got a very high temperature and keeps on waking up and asking questions. I don't know how to answer. You come and have a look at him.'

Monsieur de Vineuil had already dropped off to sleep again. His long, red face with its bushy, snow-white moustache could just be made out on the pillow, for Madame Delaherche had shielded the lamp with a newspaper and all that part of the room was in semi-darkness, while the bright light shone on her as she sat stiffly in the armchair with her hands hanging loose and eyes far away in a tragic dream.

'Just a minute,' she murmured, 'I think he's heard you, he's waking up again.'

The colonel was indeed opening his eyes again, and he gazed at Delaherche without moving his head. Then he recognized him and at once asked in a voice weak with fever:

'It's all over, isn't it? They're capitulating.'

Delaherche caught his mother's eye and was on the point of telling him a lie. But what was the point? He said with a gesture of weariness:

'What do you expect them to do? If you could see the state of the streets in the town! . . . General de Wimpffen has just gone to the Prussian headquarters to discuss terms.'

Monsieur de Vineuil shut his eyes again and he gave a long shudder and moaned softly:

'Oh God! Oh God!'

Keeping his eyes shut he went on in gasps:

'Oh, what I wanted . . . they should have done it yesterday . . . Yes, I knew the terrain and I told the general what I was afraid of . . . but nobody would listen to him either . . . Up there, above Saint-Menges, as far as Fleigneux, all the heights occupied, the army dominating Sedan, commanding the Saint-Albert gap . . . There we were waiting in quite impregnable positions, the Mézières road still open . . .'

His words were getting mixed up, he mumbled a few more unintelligible words as his vision of the battle, born of a high fever, gradually faded out and vanished into sleep. In his sleep perhaps he was still dreaming of victory.

'Does the major think he'll pull through?' Delaherche whispered.

Madame Delaherche nodded.

'All the same, it's terrible, those wounds in the foot,' he went on. 'He'll be a long time in bed, won't he?'

This time she made no reply, herself lost in the great grief of the defeat. She belonged to an already bygone age, that of the old, sturdy frontier bourgeoisie, so fierce in former days in defence of its towns. In the strong lamplight her severe face with its thin nose and tight lips expressed her anger and suffering, the feeling of revolt which made sleep impossible for her.

So Delaherche felt isolated and filled with dreadful distress. His unbearable hunger was coming on again, and he thought it must just be weakness that was draining him in this way of all his courage. He tiptoed out of the room and went down to the kitchen again, candlestick in hand. But he found it drearier than ever, with the stove out, the cupboard bare and cloths thrown all over the place as if the wind of disaster had blown through there and taken with it all the life and joy of anything that can be eaten or drunk. At first he thought he would not discover even a crust, for the odd bits of bread had gone down to the ambulance station in the soup. But then in the back of a cupboard he came upon some of yesterday's beans that had been overlooked. He devoured them with neither butter nor bread, standing there and not daring to go upstairs for such a meal, which he hurried through in this dismal kitchen which the guttering little lamp made stink of paraffin.

It was not much after ten, and Delaherche had nothing he could do while waiting to know whether the capitulation was really going to be signed. He had a nagging worry that the struggle might be resumed, and a terror of what would happen then which he kept to himself and which weighed heavily on him. Having gone up to his study again, where Maurice and Jean had not moved, he tried in vain to stretch out in an armchair, but sleep would not come, and noises of exploding shells made him jump up again just as he was dropping off. The dreadful bombardment of the day had stayed in his ears, and he listened in terror for a minute and was left trembling at the heavy silence surrounding him. Not being able to sleep, he preferred to get up, and wandered through the dark rooms, avoiding the one in which his mother was watching over the colonel, for her fixed stare following him round got on his nerves. Twice he went back to see whether Henriette had awakened, and paused and watched how peaceful his wife's face was. Until two in the morning, not knowing what to do, he went up and down from one place to another.

It could not go on for ever. Delaherche decided to go back yet again to the Sub-Prefecture, knowing that there would be no rest for him so long as he did not know. But down below, when he saw the jammed street, his heart failed him. He would never have the strength to get there and back with all these obstacles, the very memory of which made him feel exhausted. He was still hesitating when Major Bouroche came in, puffing and blowing and swearing.

'Christ! It's enough to kill you!'

He had had to go the the Hôtel de Ville to beg the mayor to requisition some chloroform and send him some by dawn because his supply had run out, operations were imperative and he was afraid, as he put it, that he would be obliged to mince up the poor buggers without putting them to sleep.

'Well?' asked Delaherche.

'Well, they don't even know whether the chemists have still got any!'

But the textile manufacturer was not interested in chloroform and he went on:

'Never mind that ... Is it over? Have they signed with the Prussians?'

The major waved his arms violently.

'Nothing settled yet. Wimpffen has just come back ... It seems that those sods are making demands they should get a thick ear for ... Oh well, let's all start again and all peg out, it'd be better that way!'

This made Delaherche go very pale.

'But is what you are saying quite certain?'

'I had it from those gentry in the town council who are having a permanent session ... An officer had come in from the Sub-Prefecture and told them all about it.'

He went into details. The interview between General de Wimpffen and General von Moltke and Bismarck had taken place at the Château de Bellevue, near Donchery. He was a terror, that von Moltke, cold and hard, with the pasty face of a mathematical chemist who won battles in his study by algebra! He at once made it clear that he knew all about the desperate plight of the French army: no food, no ammunition, demoralization and disorder, the absolute impossibility of breaking the iron ring tightly closed round it, while the German armies occupied the strongest possible positions and could burn the town down in two hours. He coldly dictated his wishes: the whole French army to be taken prisoner with its arms and baggage. Bismarck merely backed him up, looking like an amiable bloodhound. Thereupon General de Wimpffen had worn himself out trying to resist these conditions, the harshest ever imposed upon a defeated army. He talked of its ill-luck, the heroism of the soldiers, the danger of pushing a proud people too far, and for three hours he had threatened, begged, talked with desperate and superb eloquence, asking them to intern the vanquished army in Central France or even in Algeria, and the sole concession obtained in the end was that officers who would bind themselves in writing and on their honour not to fight again would be allowed to go home. Anyhow, the armistice was to be extended until the following morning at ten. If by then the conditions were not accepted, the Prussian batteries would open fire again and the town would be destroyed.

'It's ridiculous!' exclaimed Delaherche. 'You don't burn down a town that's done nothing to deserve it!'

The major put the finishing touch to his panic when he added that some officers he had seen at the Hôtel de l'Europe were talking of a mass break-out before daybreak. Since the German demands had become known emotion had risen to fever-pitch, and the most extravagant projects were being put forward. Even the idea that it would not be honest to take advantage of the darkness and violate the truce stopped nobody, and the most crazy plans were bandied about – resumption of the march on Carignan right through the Bavarians, under cover of darkness, the plateau of Illy recaptured by surprise, the Mézières road cleared, or again an irresistible dash to leap with one bound into Belgium. Others, it was true, said nothing, for they were conscious of the inevitability of the disaster and, with a happy cry of relief, would have accepted anything, signed anything so as to be done with it.

'Good night,' concluded Bouroche. 'I'm going to try and get a couple of hours' sleep. I need it badly.'

Left on his own, Delaherche was outraged. What, were they really going to start fighting again and burn Sedan down? It was becoming inevitable, and this appalling thing would certainly come about as soon as the sun was sufficiently high above the hills to give enough light for the horrible massacre. Once again he automatically climbed the steep stairs to the attics and found himself among the chimneys on the narrow ledge overlooking the town. But at that hour up there he was in total darkness, in an endless rolling sea of black waves and at first he could not make out anything whatever. The factory buildings below him were the first things to emerge in vague masses he could recognize: the engine-house, the loom-shops, drying-sheds, stores; and the sight of the huge block of buildings, his pride and wealth, broke him down with self-pity as he reflected that in a few hours nothing would be left of it but ashes. His eyes went up to the horizon and travelled along this black immensity in which tomorrow's threat lay dormant. Southwards in the Bazeilles direction sparks were blowing over houses which were collapsing in ashes, while northwards the farm in the Garenne woods which had been set on fire that evening was still burning and throwing a bloody glare on to the trees. No other fires, only those two blazes, and between them a bottomless chasm with nothing but scattered, frightening noises. Over there, maybe a long way off, maybe on the ramparts, somebody was crying. He tried in vain to pierce the veil and see Le Liry, La Marfée, the batteries at Frénois and Wadelincourt, the circle of bronze beasts of prey that he sensed were there, straining forward with open jaws. As he brought his eyes back to the town round him, he could hear its anguished breathing. It was not merely the uneasy sleep of the soldiers lying in the streets, the faint creakings of the mass of men and animals and cannons. What he seemed to be hearing was the anxious insomnia of townspeople and neighbours who couldn't sleep any more than he could, but were feverishly waiting for daylight. They must all be aware that the capitulation was not signed, and were all counting the hours and shudderingly thinking that if it were not signed there would be nothing for them to do but go down into their cellars and die there, crushed and buried beneath the ruins. He thought a wild voice came up from the rue des Voyards crying Murder! amid a sudden clicking of rifles. He stayed there leaning over into the thick night, lost in a misty starless sky, and taken with such a shivering that all the hairs on his body seemed to be standing on end.

Down below Maurice woke up on the sofa at daybreak. Aching all over, he lay still and stared at the window gradually lightening in a grey dawn. Horrible memories came back, the lost battle, flight, disaster, all with the sharp clarity of the morning after. He could see it all again in the minutest detail, and the defeat pained him terribly, penetrating to the depths of his being as if he felt personally guilty. He considered his own pain, analysed himself and recovered his old faculty of tearing himself to pieces, but more successfully than ever. Was he not just the ordinary man, the man in the street of the period, highly educated no doubt, but crassly ignorant of all the things that ought to be known, and moreover conceited to the point of blindness, perverted by the lust for pleasure and the deceptive prosperity of the régime? Then his mind moved on to another vision – his grandfather, born in 1780, one of the heroes of the Grande Armée, the victors of Austerlitz, Wagram and Friedland; his father, born in 1811, who had come down to bureaucracy, a humdrum salaried official, tax-collector at Le Chêne-Populeux, where he had burnt himself out; and finally himself, born in 1841, brought up to be a gentleman, a qualified lawyer and capable of the worst sillinesses and greatest enthusiasms, beaten at Sedan in a catastrophe that he knew must be immense and mark the end of a world. The degeneration of his race, which explained how France, victorious with the grandfathers, could be beaten in the time of their grandsons, weighed down on his heart like a hereditary disease getting steadily worse and leading to inevitable destruction when the appointed hour came. If it had been victory he would have felt so brave, so triumphant! In defeat he was as weak and nervous as a woman and giving in to one of those fits of despair in which the whole world collapsed. There was nothing left. France was dead. He began sobbing and cried, putting his hands together and going back to the faltering prayers of his childhood:

'Oh God, take me away ... Oh God, take away all these poor, suffering people!'

Jean, wrapped in his blanket on the floor, began to move. Then he sat up in astonishment.

'What's up, lad? Are you ill?'

Then, realizing that it was another lot of what he called 'those ideas' you should put out to roost, he turned fatherly.

'Now, now, what's the matter, boy? Mustn't get yourself into a state like this over nothing!'

'Oh,' exclaimed Maurice, 'it's all up – we might as well get ready to be Prussians.'

As his friend, being a hard-headed, uneducated man, showed surprise, he tried to make him understand the impoverishment of the race, its extinction in a necessary stream of fresh blood. But the countryman obstinately shook his head and turned down the explanation.

'What! My field no longer my field? Am I supposed to let the Prussians take it away from me before I'm quite dead and while I've still got my two arms? ... Come off it!'

Then it was his turn to express what he thought, awkwardly and as the words came. All right, they had had a bloody licking, for sure! But they weren't all dead, were they, and there were still some of them left and they would manage to build the house again if they were sensible blokes, worked hard and didn't drink what they earned. In a family, if you take the trouble to put something aside you always manage to get by even in the worst trouble. In fact, sometimes it isn't a bad thing if you do get a good clip on the ear, it makes you think. Of course it was true that there was something rotten somewhere or some limb was septic, well, it was better to see it on the ground, chopped off, than to die because of it as if you had the plague.

'Done for, oh no, no,' he said several times. 'I'm not done for, I don't feel a bit like that!'

And, although he was wounded, his hair still matted with blood from the graze, he struggled up in an unquenchable urge to live, to handle a tool or a plough and rebuild his house, as he put it. He came from the old, unchanging, careful soil, from the land of reason, hard work and savings.

'All the same,' he went on, 'I feel sorry for the Emperor ... Things looked as if they were going well and corn was selling. But he has been too stupid, that's certain, and people shouldn't get themselves into such a mess.'

Maurice was still cast down, and he made a gesture of despair once again.

'Oh I quite liked the Emperor really, for all my ideas about liberty and republicanism ... Yes, I had it in my blood from my grandfather, I suppose. And now that's all gone rotten as well, what are we going to come down to?'

His eyes looked wild and he uttered such a moan of grief that Jean, now really worried, was on the point of jumping up when he saw Henriette come in. She had just woken up, hearing voices in the next room. A dismal grey light now filled the room.

'You've come at the right time to give him a talking to,' he said, pretending to be joking. 'He's not being a good boy.'

But the sight of his sister looking so pale and tragic had shaken Maurice into a salutary fit of compassion. He opened his arms and invited her to come to him, and when she flung herself into his arms he was filled with a great tenderness. She was weeping too, and their tears mingled.

'Oh my poor, poor dearest, I could kick myself for not being braver so as to console you! ... Good, kind Weiss, the husband who loved you so much! What are you going to do? You've always been the victim, and never complained. Haven't I given you enough sorrow as it is, and who can tell how much more I may give you!'

She stopped him by putting her hand on his mouth, and at that moment Delaherche came in, almost out of his mind with exhaustion. He had finally come down from the roof, ravenous again with one of those nervous hungers made worse still by fatigue, and as he had gone back to the kitchen to get something warm to drink he had come upon the cook with a relation of hers, a carpenter from Bazeilles, whom she was giving some mulled wine. And this man, one of the last to stay behind in the midst of the fires, had told him that his dyeworks was completely destroyed, a heap of rubble.

'What vandals they are!' he spluttered to Maurice and Jean. 'All is really lost now, and they'll set fire to Sedan this morning as they did to Bazeilles yesterday. I'm ruined, ruined!'

Then he noticed the bruise on Henriette's forehead, and remembered that he had not yet been able to speak to her.

'Oh yes, of course, you went there, and that's where you got that ... Oh, poor Weiss!'

Then, seeing from her red eyes that she knew her husband was dead, he let out an appalling detail that the carpenter had just told him.

'Poor Weiss! It seems they burned him ... Yes, they collected the bodies of the civilians they had shot, poured paraffin on them and threw them into the middle of a burning house.'

Henriette listened to this, frozen with horror. Oh God, not even the consolation of claiming and burying her beloved dead, the wind would scatter his ashes! Maurice once again tightened his arms round her, calling her his poor Cinderella in a caressing voice and begging her not to give in to her grief too much – she was so brave!

After a pause Delaherche, who had been at the window watching it getting lighter, turned round quickly to say to the two soldiers:

'Oh, I forgot . . . I came up to tell you that down there in the coach-house where they deposited the cash, there's an officer distributing the money to the men so that the Prussians don't get it . . . You should go down, some money might be useful if we aren't all dead by tonight.'

It was sound advice. Maurice and Jean went down after Henriette had consented to take her brother's place on the sofa. As for Delaherche, he went through the adjoining room in which Gilberte, with her calm face, was still sleeping like a child, and the sounds of talking and crying had not even made her turn over. And from there he peeped into the room in which his mother was watching over Monsieur de Vineuil, but she had dozed off in her armchair and the colonel, his eyes shut, had not moved, for he was exhausted by fever.

He opened his eyes wide and asked:

'Well, it's all over, isn't it?'

Vexed by this question which caught him just when he was hoping to escape, Delaherche answered angrily, keeping his voice down:

'Oh yes, all over until it starts again! Nothing's been signed.'

The colonel went on very softly, beginning to wander again:

'Oh God, let me die before the end! . . . I can't hear the guns. Why have they stopped firing? . . . Up there at Saint-Menges and Fleigneux we're commanding all the routes, and we'll throw the Prussians into the Meuse if they try to come round Sedan and attack us. The town is at our feet like an obstacle strengthening our positions . . . Come on the 7th! We'll take the lead, the 12th will cover the retreat . . .'

His hands went up and down on the sheet as though he were riding his horse in his dream. Gradually they slackened and his words thickened and he fell asleep again. The hands stopped, and he remained motionless, knocked out.

'Have a rest,' Delaherche whispered. 'I'll come back when I get some news.'

After making sure that he had not awakened his mother he made his escape and disappeared.

Down in the coach-house Jean and Maurice did find a paymaster, sitting on a kitchen chair with only a little whitewood table in front of him, and no pen, no receipts, no papers of any kind, doling out fortunes. All he did was thrust his hands into money-bags bursting with gold coins, and without even bothering to count he quickly put handfuls into the képis of all the sergeants of the 7th corps who were passing him in line. It was understood that the sergeants would share out the sums among the soldiers in their half-sections. Each one received it awkwardly, like a ration of coffee or meat, and went off in embarrassment, emptying the képi into his pockets so as not to be out in the street in broad daylight with all that gold. Not a word was being said, and there was no sound except the clear tinkle of the coins, to the amazement of these poor devils seeing themselves loaded with riches when there wasn't a loaf of bread or litre of wine left to be bought.

When Jean and Maurice came up the officer at first held back the handful of gold louis he was holding.

'You're not sergeants, either of you . . . Only sergeants have the right to handle . . .'

But, tired already and anxious to get it done with:

'Oh well, you, the corporal, have some all the same . . . Hurry up there, next!'

He had dropped the coins into the képi Jean was holding out. Jean, staggered by the amount – nearly six hundred francs – wanted Maurice to have half at once. You never knew, they might get separated.

They shared it out in the garden, near the ambulance station, and then they went in there as they recognized their company drummer Bastian lying on the straw almost by the door. He was a fat, jolly chap and he had had the ill-luck to get a stray bullet in the groin at five o'clock, after the battle was over. He had been at death's door since yesterday.

In the dim morning light, time for waking up in the hospital, the sight of the place chilled them with horror. Three more wounded had died during the night without anybody noticing, and the orderlies were busy carrying off the bodies and making room for others. Yesterday's operation cases, still half asleep, opened staring eyes and gazed bewildered at this vast dormitory of suffering, where a herd of half-slaughtered creatures were lying on the straw. For all the sweeping and mopping up of the night before, after the bleeding butchery of the operations, the floor had not been properly wiped and there were trails of blood here and there, and a big sponge stained red and looking like brains was floating in a pail, and an odd hand with broken fingers had been dropped near the shed door. These were the bits fallen from the butchery, the awful refuse of the day after a massacre, lit up by the gruesome light of dawn. The normal bustling and noisy life of the earlier hours had given way to a sort of apathy under the pressure of fever. Only now and again was the reeking silence broken by some incoherent moan, muffled by sleep. Glazed eyes looked frightened of the daylight, coated mouths breathed foul breath, the whole ward was relapsing into that endless succession of livid, disgusting, agonizing days through which these wretched wounded were to exist, and from which after two or three months they might emerge with a limb missing.

Bouroche, coming on again after a few hours' rest, paused in front of the drummer Bastian, then went on with an imperceptible shrug of the shoulders. Nothing to be done. But the drummer had opened his eyes again and seemed to come back to life as his keen glance followed a sergeant who had had the bright idea of coming in holding his képi full of gold in his hand to see if any of his men might be here among these poor devils. Other sergeants came in and gold began to rain down on the straw. Bastian, who had managed to sit up, held out the shaking hands of a dying man:

'Me! Me!'

The sergeant was for going on as Bouroche had. What was the point? But then an instinct of kindness prevailed, and without counting he threw some coins into the already cold hands.

'Me! Me!'

Bastian had fallen back. He tried to catch the gold that eluded his grasp, clutching for some time with stiff fingers. Then he died.

'Night-night, the gent has blown out his candle!' said a neighbour, a dark wizened little Zouave. 'Too bad just when you've got something to stand yourself a drink!'

This man had his left foot in an appliance, but he managed to lift himself and crawl on his elbows and knees as far as the dead man and pick up the lot, looking into his hands and ransacking the folds of his coat. When he got back to his own place he realized he was being looked at, but all he said was:

'No need for it to get lost, is there?'

Maurice felt sick at heart in this atmosphere of human misery and got Jean away quickly. As they re-crossed the operating shed they saw Bouroche, exasperated at not having got any chloroform, deciding to amputate all the same the leg of a poor young fellow of twenty. They hurried away so as not to hear.

At that moment Delaherche was coming in from the street. He beckoned them over and said:

'Come upstairs quick. We're going to have breakfast, cook has managed to get some milk. Can't really say I'm sorry, we can do with something hot!'

Try as he would, he could not repress all his exultant joy. He lowered his voice and added, beaming:

'This time it really is it! General de Wimpffen has gone off again to sign the capitulation.'

Oh, what a tremendous relief, his factory saved, the dreadful nightmare lifted, life going to start up again, painful no doubt, but life, life! It was nine o'clock and young Rose, who had come to this part of the town to get some bread from an aunt who had a baker's shop – the streets were now somewhat clearer – had told him all that had happened that morning at the Sub-Prefecture. At eight o'clock General de Wimpffen had called a new council of war, more than thirty generals, and told them the outcome of his move, his useless efforts and the harsh demands of the victorious enemy. His hands were shaking and deep emotion filled his eyes with tears. He was still speaking when a colonel from the Prussian head-quarters had appeared as an emissary on behalf of General von Moltke to remind them that if a decision was not reached by ten firing would begin again on Sedan. So the council, in the face of dire necessity, could only authorize the general to go again to the Château de Bellevue and accept everything. He must be there by now and the whole French army must be prisoners, together with arms and baggage.

Rose had then gone into details about the extraordinary sensation the news was creating in the town. At the Sub-Prefecture she had seen officers tearing off their epaulettes and weeping like children. On the bridge cuirassiers were throwing their sabres into the Meuse, and a whole regiment had passed across, each man throwing his own, watching the water splash and close over it. In the streets soldiers were taking hold of their rifles by the barrel and breaking off the butts against the wall, and gunners who had taken the moving parts out of *mitrailleuses* were getting rid of them down the sewers. Some were burying or burning flags. In the Place Turenne an old sergeant had climbed up on a bollard and was insulting the commanders, calling them cowards as though he had suddenly gone off his head. Others looked stunned and wept silently. But also it had to be admitted that others, and the majority, had expressions of joy in their eyes and happy relief permeating their whole being. At last this was the end of their misery, they were prisoners, they wouldn't be fighting any more! For so long they had been suffering from too much marching and not enough eating! Besides, what's the point of fighting if you aren't the ones who are winning? If their officers had handed them over so as to put an end to it straight away, well, a good job too! It was so nice to think they were going to get some white bread again and sleep in beds!

Upstairs, as Delaherche went into the dining-room with Maurice and Jean, his mother called him.

'Come here, I'm worried about the colonel.'

Monsieur de Vineuil, with his eyes open, was going on aloud with the delirious visions of his fever.

'What does it matter if the Prussians do cut us off from Mézières . . . look, now they're getting round the Falizette wood, and others are following up the Givonne stream . . . We've got the frontier behind us and we'll jump across it in one bound when we've killed as many of them as possible . . . That's what I wanted to do yesterday . . .'

But his blazing eyes had seen Delaherche. He recognized him and seemed to sober down and emerge from the hallucination of his dreams into the terrible reality, asking for the third time:

'It's all over, isn't it?'

This time the mill-owner could not repress the explosion of his gratification.

'Yes, thank God, all quite over . . . The capitulation must be signed by now.'

The colonel struggled violently up, despite his bandaged foot, and he seized his sword, which was on a chair, and tried to break it. But his hands were too shaky and the blade slipped.

'Look out, he'll cut himself!' exclaimed Delaherche. 'It's dangerous, take it out of his hands.'

It was Madame Delaherche who took possession of the sword. Then, seeing Monsieur de Vineuil's despair, instead of hiding it as her son told her to, she herself broke it with one smart tap over her knee, with a superhuman strength she would not have thought her old hands capable of. The colonel had sunk down again and he was crying as he looked at his old friend with infinite tenderness.

Meanwhile in the dining-room cook had served bowls of coffee for everybody. Henriette and Gilberte were up, the latter refreshed after a good night's sleep, with bright face and laughing eyes, and she tenderly embraced her friend Henriette, saying she felt for her from the depths of her heart. Maurice sat next to his sister while Jean, feeling a bit awkward, had to accept coffee, too, and sat opposite Delaherche. Madame Delaherche would not hear of sitting down at table, and she was taken a bowl which she agreed to drink. But the breakfast of the five people there, at first silent, soon livened up. They were all the worse for wear and very hungry, and how could they help being glad to be there alive and well when thousands of poor devils were still lying all over the countryside? In the big cool dining-room the snow-white cloth was a joy to look at, and the piping hot coffee and milk seemed delicious.

They started talking. Delaherche had recovered the poise of the rich industrialist, and with the patronizing good fellowship of an employer enjoying popularity, who disapproves only of failure, he came back to Napoleon III, whose face had been haunting him for two days as he gaped in curiosity. He addressed Jean, having only this simple man to talk to.

'Oh yes, sir, I can say that the Emperor has been a bitter disappointment to me ... It's all very well for his flatterers to plead extenuating circumstances, but obviously he is the prime cause, the sole cause of our misfortunes.'

He was already forgetting that as an ardent Bonapartist he had worked for the success of the plebiscite only a few months earlier. He had even given up pitying the man who was to become the Man of Sedan, but laid on him the iniquity of them all.

'An incompetent, as we are bound to agree now, but that in

itself would not matter ... A mere visionary, a crackpot who seemed to pull things off as long as luck was on his side ... No, you see, there's no point in trying to work up our sympathy for him by saying he's been deceived and that the Opposition denied him the necessary men and credit. It is he who has deceived us, and his misdeeds have landed us in the awful mess we are in.'

Maurice did not want to be drawn in, but could not repress a smile, while Jean, embarrassed by this political talk and afraid of saying something silly, merely said:

'But still, they do say he's a nice man.'

But these few words, quietly said, made Delaherche sit up. All the fear he had felt and all the worries he had been through burst out in a cry of exasperation turned to hatred.

'A nice man, oh yes, that's easy to say! ... Do you know, sir, that my mill has been hit by three shells, and that it's no fault of the Emperor's that it hasn't been burnt down! ... Do you know that I, yes I, am going to lose a hundred thousand francs over this ridiculous business? ... Oh no, oh no, France invaded, set on fire, exterminated, industry brought to a standstill, commerce destroyed, it's too much ... A nice man of that kind we've had quite enough of, and God save us from him! ... He's down in the mud and blood, let him stay there.'

With his fist he went through the energetic motions of shoving down some struggling wretch under the water and holding him there. Then he greedily finished off his coffee. Gilberte had involuntarily smiled at Henriette's sorrowful absent-mindedness as she fed her like a child. When the bowls were empty they lingered in the peaceful and happy atmosphere of the big dining-room.

At that very time Napoleon III was in the weaver's humble cottage on the Donchery road. By five in the morning he had insisted on leaving the Sub-Prefecture, feeling ill at ease with Sedan all round him like a reproach and a threat, and moreover he was still tormented by the need to appease his tender heart by obtaining better conditions for his unhappy army. He wanted to see the King of Prussia. He had taken a hired carriage and gone out along the broad main road lined with poplars, on the first stage of exile in the early chill of dawn, conscious of all the lost greatness left behind in his flight. And on that road he had met Bismarck, who had hurried there in an old cap and polished jackboots, with the one object of keeping him occupied and preventing his seeing the King so long as the capitulation was unsigned. The King was still at Vendresse, fourteen kilometres away. Where could they go? Under what roof could they wait? Far away, lost in a storm-cloud, the Tuileries palace had vanished. Sedan already seemed leagues behind and cut off by a river of blood. No more imperial palaces in France, no more official residences, not even a corner in the home of the most humble of his officials where he could dare to sit down. So he elected to end up in the weaver's home, the humble house he saw by the roadside, with its little cabbage-patch sur-rounded by a hedge, its one upstairs room and dark little windows. The room upstairs was simply whitewashed, with a tiled floor, and the only furniture was a whitewood table and two wicker chairs. There he tried for hours to possess his soul in patience, first with Bismarck, who smiled when he heard him talking about generosity, and later alone in his misery, with his ashen face glued to the window-panes, still looking at this French soil, this river Meuse flowing along, so lovely, through the broad fertile meadows.

Then next day and the days after came the other horrible stages: the Château de Bellevue, that desirable upper-class residence with view over the river, in which he spent the night weeping after his interview with King William; the cruel departure, avoiding Sedan for fear of the anger of the defeated and starving, the bridge of boats the Prussians had thrown across the river at Iges, the long detour round the north of the town, the cross-country roads and byways well away from Floing, Fleigneux and Illy, and all this lamentable flight in an open carriage; and then, on the tragic plateau of Illy, strewn with corpses, the legendary meeting of the miserable Emperor, who could not now even bear the motion of the horse, but had cowered in the pain of an attack, perhaps auto-matically smoking his eternal cigarette, with a party of prisoners, haggard and covered with blood and dust, being taken from Fleigneux to Sedan, moving to one side of the road to let the carriage pass, some silent but others beginning to grumble, and again others getting more and more exasperated and bursting into booing, with fists shaking in a gesture of insult and cursing. After that came still more endless crossings of the battlefield, a league of bumpy roads among the wreckage and the dead staring with wide open, accusing eyes, the bare countryside, great silent forests, the frontier at the top of a rise; then the end of everything, going down on the other side, the road lined with conifers in a narrow valley.

And what a first night of exile at Bouillon, in an inn, the Hôtel de la Poste, surrounded by such a mob of French refugees and mere sightseers that the Emperor had thought he ought to make an appearance, amid murmurings and catcalls! The room, with three windows on the square and the river Semoy, was the standard kind of room – chairs covered in red damask, mahogany mirror-fronted wardrobe, mantelpiece with spelter clock flanked by sea-shells and vases of artificial flowers under glass. Small twin beds on either side of the door. The aide-de-camp lay in one and was so tired that he was dead asleep by nine. In the other the Emperor tossed and turned for hours, unable to sleep, and if he got out of bed to relieve the pain by walking about, the only way to take his mind off it was to look at the pictures on the wall each side of the fireplace, one representing Rouget de l'Isle singing the 'Mar-seillaise' and the other the Last Judgement, a furious blast of trumpets by Archangels summoning all the dead from out of the earth, the resurrection of the slaughtered in battle coming up to bear witness before God.

In Sedan the paraphernalia of the imperial household, the cumbersone, accursed baggage, had remained forlorn behind the sub-prefect's lilac bushes. Nobody knew how to spirit it all away out of the sight of the poor people dying of hunger, for the look of aggressive insolence it had acquired and the dreadful irony due to defeat were becoming so intolerable. They had to wait for a very dark night. The horses, the carriages, the vans, with their silver casseroles, spits, hampers of vintage wine, took their leave of Sedan in deepest mystery and went off into Belgium too, through dark byways, almost noiselessly, like thieves in the night.

PART THREE

1

THROUGHOUT the endless day of the battle Silvine had never stopped watching Sedan from the hill on which old Fouchard's farmhouse stood, and in the thunder and smoke of guns she was tortured by the thought of Honoré. And the following day her anxiety increased because of the impossibility of getting accurate news, with Prussians guarding the roads, refusing to answer questions and in any case knowing nothing themselves. Yesterday's bright sun had gone and rain showers cast a melancholy gloom over the valley.

Towards evening old Fouchard, also finding his self-imposed silence a torment and not giving his son much thought, but anxious to know how he might be affected by other people's troubles, was standing at his door hoping to see something happen when he noticed a tall fellow in a smock, who had been prowling along the road for a minute or two looking very ill at ease. When he recognized him he was so surprised that he called out in spite of three passing Prussians:

'What, is that you, Prosper?'

The Chasseur d'Afrique frantically signed to him to be quiet, then he approached and said softly:

'Yes, it's me. I've had enough of fighting for nothing, so I've sloped off ... I say, Pa Fouchard, I suppose you don't want a farm-hand?'

At once the old man recovered all his wariness. As a matter of fact he did want one. But there was no point in saying so.

'A new hand, oh dear no, not just now ... But come in all the same and have a drink. I'm certainly not going to leave you high and dry in the middle of the road.'

Indoors, Silvine was putting the stew on the fire and little

335

Charlot was hanging on to her skirt, playing and laughing. At first she did not recognize Prosper, although he had worked with her once, and it was only when she was bringing two glasses and a bottle of wine that she looked at him. She uttered an exclamation, but she was only thinking about Honoré.

'Oh, you've come from there, haven't you? Is Honoré all right?'

Prosper started to answer, then hesitated. For two days he had been living in a daze, going through a violent sequence of vague things that had left no clear impression on his mind. True, he thought he had seen Honoré's dead body lying over his gun, but he could no longer vouch for it, and why upset people when you're not sure?

'Honoré,' he mused, 'I don't know ... I can't say ...'

She looked hard at him and insisted.

'You haven't seen him, then?'

He slowly spread his hands and shook his head.

'How do you think I can know? Such a lot of things have happened, such a lot! You see, out of all this bloody battle I should have my work cut out to tell you as much as that! No, not even the places I have been through ... It makes you just silly, it really does!'

He drank off a glass of wine and sat there miserably gazing far away, into the mists of his memory.

'All I can remember is that night was already falling when I came to ... When I had my fall while charging, the sun was high in the sky ... I must have been there for hours, with my right leg crushed under poor Zephir, who had had a bullet right in the chest ... I can tell you, it wasn't a bit funny being in that position, with heaps of dead comrades all round and not even a cat about, with the thought that I was going to peg out too unless somebody came and picked me up. I tried very carefully to get my thigh free, but no use, Zephir weighed as much as five hundred thousand devils. He was still warm. I stroked him and talked to him, calling him nice things. And this is what I shall never forget: he opened his eyes again and made an effort to lift up his poor head which was lying on the ground next to mine. So we started talking: "Well, old cock," I said, "no offence meant, but do you want to see me kick the bucket along with you? Is that why you're hanging on to me so hard?" Of course he didn't answer yes, but all the same I could see

336

in his eyes what a terrible thing it was for him to leave me. And I don't know how it happened, whether he did it on purpose or whether it was just a spasm, but he gave a sudden jerk that shifted him to one side. I was able to stand up, but oh what a state I was in, with my leg like a lump of lead! . . . Never mind, I took Zephir's head in my arms and went on saying nice things to him, anything that came from my heart, that he was a good horse, that I was very fond of him, that I would always remember him. He listened and seemed so glad! Then he gave another jerk and died, and his big, blank eyes had never left me. Still, it's a funny thing, and nobody will believe me, and yet it is the solemn truth that he had big tears in his eyes . . . Poor Zephir, he was crying just like a man . . .'

Prosper had to break off, choked with sorrow and crying himself. He drank another glass of wine, then went on with his story in broken and disconnected sentences. It was getting darker and now there was nothing left but a red streak of light along the horizon over the battlefield, lengthening indefinitely the shadows of dead horses. He must have stayed a long while by his, unable to go away, with his leg gone dead. But then a sudden wave of panic had made him walk in spite of it – a desire not to be alone, to be with friends and not be so frightened. In the same way, from all sides, ditches, thickets and all sorts of odd corners, forgotten wounded men were dragging themselves along, trying to find each other, to get together in groups of four or five, little communities in which it was less terrible to share their last agonies and die. So it was that he had come across two soldiers of the 43rd in the Garenne wood, who had never had a scratch but who had gone to earth there like hares, waiting for nightfall. When they realized that he knew the lie of the land they told him their plan: to clear off into Belgium, reaching the frontier through the woods before daylight. At first he refused to take them, for he would have preferred to head for Remilly at once, knowing he could find refuge there, but where could he get a smock and some trousers from? And besides, from the Garenne wood to Remilly, from one side of the valley to the other, there was no hope of getting through the many Prussian lines. So he did agree to act as a guide to the two comrades. His leg had got some life back into it, and they were fortunate enough to get somebody at a farm to let them have some bread. They heard a distant clock strike nine as they set off again. The only place where

337

they got into danger was at La Chapelle, where they ran right into an enemy post which rushed to arms and fired into the darkness, while they for their part tore along on all fours into some bushes amid the whistling of bullets. After that they stayed in the woods, straining their ears and groping their way. As they came round a bend in a path they crept along and then jumped on the shoulders of a lone sentry and slit his throat with a knife. After that the roads were clear and they went on their way laughing and whistling. At about three in the morning they reached a little Belgian village, woke up a kind-hearted farmer who at once let them into his barn where they slept soundly on some bundles of hay.

The sun was already high in the sky when Prosper woke. Opening his eyes while his mates were still snoring, he saw their host harnessing a horse to a big farm cart loaded with loaves of bread, rice, coffee, sugar and all kinds of provisions, concealed under sacks of charcoal. He found out that the good man had two married daughters in France, at Raucourt, and he was going to take these provisions to them, knowing that they had been left quite destitute after the Bavarians had passed through. He had obtained the necessary safe-conduct first thing that morning. At once Prosper was seized with a mad desire to sit on the seat of that cart as well and go back to the place for which he was already dying of homesickness. Nothing simpler, he could get off at Remilly, which the farmer had to go through in any case. It was all fixed up in three minutes, they lent him the trousers and smock he needed so badly, the farmer gave out everywhere that he was his farm-hand, and by about six he got off at the church, after being stopped only two or three times at German posts.

'No, really, I'd had enough,' Prosper went on after a pause. 'I wouldn't have minded so much if they'd put us to some good use as they did in Africa. But to move left just so as to move back right, to feel you're absolutely no use, it isn't any sort of existence at all ... And now my poor Zephir is dead and I'd be quite alone, so the only thing I can do is go back to the land. Better than being a prisoner with the Prussians, isn't it? ... You've got some horses, Monsieur Fouchard, and you'll see whether I can love them and look after them!'

The old man's eyes glittered. He held up his glass once again and concluded the business without undue haste:

'Oh well, as it will help you I don't mind if I do ... I'll take you on ... But as to any wages, can't discuss that until the war is over, because I don't really need anybody and times are too hard!'

Silvine was still sitting there with Charlot on her lap, and she had never taken her eyes off Prosper. When she saw him getting up to go straight off to the stable and get to know the horses, she asked him once again:

'So you haven't seen Honoré?'

The question, suddenly hitting him again, made him jump, as though it had shone a sudden ray of light into a dark corner of his memory. He hesitated again and then made up his mind.

'Look, I didn't want to upset you just now, but I believe Honoré is still out there.'

'Still there? What do you mean?'

'Yes, I think the Prussians have done for him. I saw him lying back over a cannon, with his head held high and a hole under the heart.'

There was a silence. Silvine turned a ghastly white, and old Fouchard looked stunned, then put his glass back on the table, where he had finished off the bottle.

'Are you sure?' she gasped.

'Yes of course I am, as sure as you can be of anything you've seen ... It was on a little mound, near three trees, and I think I could go there with my eyes shut.'

For her it was the end of the world. This man who had forgiven her, bound himself with a promise, whom she was to marry as soon as he came back from the army after the campaign was over! And they had taken him away from her, he was out there with a hole under the heart! Never had she felt she loved him so much, and now an urge to see him again, to have him to herself in spite of all, even though buried in the ground, lifted her out of her usual passivity.

She put Charlot down roughly and exlaimed:

'Right, I shan't believe it until I've seen for myself ... As you know where the place is you're going to take me there. And if it's true and we find him we'll bring him back home.'

Tears choked her words and she collapsed on the table, shaken with bitter sobs, and the child, outraged at having been roughly handled by his mother, burst into tears as well. She took him back and clasped him to her, uttering disjointed words:

'Poor child, poor child!'

Old Fouchard was thunderstruck. He really did love his son in his own fashion. Old memories must have come back from long ago when his wife was still alive and Honoré was still going to school, and two big tears formed in his red eyes too and rolled down his brown leathery cheeks. He had not cried for over ten years. He began to mutter oaths, and worked himself up into a rage because his son belonged to him and yet he wouldn't ever see him again.

'Oh Christ, it makes you wild to have only one boy and then have him taken away!'

But when some sort of calm was restored Fouchard was very put out to hear Silvine still talking about going to find Honoré's body out there. She was quite set now in a desperate, unshakable silence, with no more lamenting, and he hardly recognized her, normally so docile, doing everything with resignation, for her big submissive eyes that alone gave her such beauty had taken on a fierce decision in her pale face under the thick, dark hair. She had snatched off a red scarf from round her shoulders and was all in black like a widow. He pointed out the difficulties of the search, the risks she might run, how little hope there was of finding the body, but all in vain. She gave up even anwering him, and he realized that she would go off on her own and do something silly unless he did something about it, and that worried him still more because of the possible complications he might run into with the Prussian authorities. So in the end he decided to go and see the Mayor of Remilly, who was a distant cousin of his, and between them they made up a tale: Silvine was given out to be the real widow of Honoré and Prosper became her brother, and on the strength of that the Bavarian colonel, billeted at the lower end of the village in the Hôtel de la Croix de Malte, agreed to issue a pass for the brother and sister authorizing them to bring back the husband's body if they could find it. By now it was dark, and the utmost they could get out of Silvine was that she would wait until daylight before setting out.

Next morning Fouchard said he would never consent to having one of his horses harnessed for fear of not seeing it again. Who could say that the Prussians wouldn't confiscate the horse and cart? He did at last consent with a very bad grace to lend the donkey, a little grey donkey, whose small trap was just big enough to take a man's body. He gave lengthy instructions to Prosper, who had slept well but was rather uneasy about the expedition now that, after a good rest, he was trying to get his memory clear. At the last minute Silvine ran and fetched the bedspread from her own bed, which she folded and put on the floor of the trap. As she was going she ran back to kiss Charlot.

'Daddy Fouchard, I am entrusting him to you, mind he doesn't play with the matches.'

'Yes, yes, don't you worry.'

Preparations had taken a long time, and it was nearly seven when Silvine and Prosper, walking behind the little trap drawn by the grey donkey with its head down, descended the steep slopes of Remilly. It had rained heavily during the night, and the roads had turned into rivers of mud, and great angry clouds were racing across the dreary, depressing sky.

Prosper had made up his mind to take the shortest route by going straight through Sedan. But just before Pont-Maugis a Prussian post stopped the trap and held it up for over an hour, and when the pass had been through the hands of several officers the donkey was allowed to go on its way on condition that it went the long way round through Bazeilles by taking a side road to the left. No reason was given – perhaps they were afraid of adding to the traffic in the town. When Silvine crossed the Meuse by the railway bridge, that fatal bridge that had not been blown up, and which incidentally had cost the Bavarians so many lives, she saw the body of an artilleryman floating down as though he were having a nice swim. He was caught by a tuft of grass, stayed still a moment, then turned over and set off again.

In Bazeilles, which the donkey walked slowly through from end to end, it was total destruction, all the abominable ruin that war can inflict when it passes over like a mad, devastating hurricane. The dead had already been collected, so there was not a single corpse left on the road, and the rain was washing the blood away, though there were still some red puddles and remains that couldn't be looked at too closely, fragments of flesh on which you thought you could still see hair. But the really heartbreaking impression came from the ruins themselves of this village of Bazeilles, so pretty only three days earlier, with its gay houses in their gardens, and now smashed to smithereens, reduced to nothing but bits of wall blackened by flames. The church was still burning like a huge funeral pyre of smoking beams in the middle of the square, and from it rose an unceasing column of black smoke, spreading out over the sky like the plumes on a hearse. Whole streets had gone, with nothing left on either side, nothing but heaps of calcined stones beside the gutters, a mess of soot and ash like thick inky mud covering everything. On all four corners of every crossroads the corner houses were flattened out and it looked as though they had been blown away by the tempest of fire. Others were less damaged, and one was standing in isolation whilst the ones on each side of it were riddled by bullets and their carcasses stood there like fleshless skeletons. An unbearable stench arose, the sickening smell of fire, and in particular the pungent smell of paraffin, which had been poured freely all over the floors. Then there was the silent pathos of what people had tried to save, poor little bits of furniture thrown out of windows and smashed on the pavements, rickety tables with broken legs, cupboards with sides off or fronts split, clothes lying about, torn or dirty, all the pitiful odds and ends of pillage disintegrating in the rain. Through a gaping house-front and collapsed floors, a clock could be seen quite intact on a mantel-piece high up a wall.

'Oh the swine!' growled Prosper, whose blood, the blood of a soldier until two days before, was boiling at the sight of such an abomination.

He was clenching his fists, and Silvine, very scared, had to calm him down with a look every time they met a picket along the road. The Bavarians had posted sentries in front of houses still burning, and these men, with rifles loaded and fixed bayonets, seemed to be guarding the fires so as to let the flames finish their work. Sight-seers or interested parties wandering round were headed off with a threatening gesture and a guttural oath if they persisted. Groups of inhabitants, keeping their distance, said nothing but were boiling with rage inside. One quite young woman, with unkempt hair and mud-stained dress, would not be moved from in front of the ruins of a little house, wanting to search among the red-hot cinders in spite of the sentry keeping people away. It was said that her child had been burnt to death in that house. Suddenly, as the Bavarian was savagely pushing her away, she spat her furious despair in his face, curses made up of blood and filth, obscene words in which she at last found some slight relief. He obviously did not understand, but looked at her nervously and moved back. Three of his companions ran up and freed him from the woman, whom they took away screaming. In front of the ruins of another house a man and two little girls had collapsed on the ground with fatigue and misery, and they were crying together, with nowhere to go, having seen everything they possessed disappear into ashes. A patrol came along and cleared off the sightseers, and the street was left empty with only the grim, hard sentries keeping a watch to make sure that their dastardly orders were respected.

'The swine! The swine!' Prosper repeated under his breath. 'It'd be a pleasure to strangle one or two of them!'

Once again Silvine made him keep quiet. She shuddered with horror. In a coach-house untouched by the fire a dog that had been shut in and forgotten for two days was howling with a continuous moan so heartrending that it seemed to fill with terror a louring sky from which a grey drizzle had started to come down. And then it was that they met something just outside the Mont-villers park. There were three big carts loaded with dead, those refuse carts that come along the streets every morning, and into which men shovel the muck of the day before. In a similar way they had been filled with corpses, stopping by each one, which was then chucked in, and setting off again with wheels bumping along until the next stop a bit further on; and they had gone right through Bazeilles until they were heaped up. They were now standing in the road waiting to be taken to the town dump, the nearby charnel-house. Feet were sticking up in the air. A head, half off, was dangling. When the three carts moved off again, bumping over the potholes, a very long bloodless hand hanging down rubbed against a wheel; and it was gradually wearing away, rubbed right down to the bone.

The rain stopped when they were in the village of Balan. Prosper persuaded Silvine to eat a bit of bread that he had had the fore-thought to bring with him. It was eleven already. As they neared Sedan a Prussian post stopped them once again, and this time it was terrible, for the officer shouted at them and even refused to return their pass, which he said was forged – in very good French, moreover. On his orders soldiers had taken the donkey and trap into a shed. What was to be done? How could they go on? Almost at her wit's end, Silvine had an idea; she thought of cousin Dubreuil, a relation of old Fouchard, whom she knew and whose property, L'Ermitage, was only about a hundred paces away up the lanes, overlooking the neighbourhood. Perhaps they would take some notice of him, a local resident. She took Prosper with her, for they were quite free to come and go so long as they left the cart. They hurried up there and found the gate of L'Ermitage wide open. As they began to walk along the avenue of great elms they were amazed at the sight that met their eyes.

'Golly!' exclaimed Prosper. 'Some people are having a good time!'

At the bottom of the steps, on the gravel terrace, quite a jolly party was going on. Round a marble-topped table was a circle of armchairs and a settee, covered with sky-blue satin, making a strange open-air drawing room that must have been rained on since the day before. At each end of the settee two Zouaves were lolling, apparently bursting with laughter. A little infantryman in an armchair was leaning forward, holding his sides. Three others were nonchalantly supporting their elbows on the arms of their chairs and a cavalryman was putting out his hand to take up a glass from the table. They had obviously raided the cellar and were having a party.

'But how can they still be here?' muttered Prosper, still more amazed as he went nearer. ' Don't the buggers care two hoots about the Prussians?'

But Silvine's eyes stared and she screamed with a sudden movement of horror. The soldiers were stock still, they were dead. The two Zouaves were stiff, their hands were twisted and they had no faces left – their noses had been cut off and the eyes were out of their sockets. The grin of the one holding his sides was due to a bullet having split open his lips and broken his teeth. It really was horrifying, these poor creatures chatting there in the angular postures of dummies, with glassy stares and mouths open, all frozen and still for ever. Had they dragged themselves there while still alive so as to die together? Or was it rather that the Prussians had thought it was fun to collect them and sit them in a ring by way of having a laugh at the traditional French sociability?

'Funny idea of a joke!' said Prosper, turning pale.

He looked at the other dead, lying all over the avenue, under trees and on the grass, thirty or so brave fellows amongst whom lay the body of Lieutenant Rochas, riddled with bullets and wrapped in the flag, and he went on in a serious voice and with great respect:

'They've had a fine set-to here! I'd be surprised if we found the gentleman you're looking for.'

Silvine was already entering the house, the battered doors and windows of which were gaping and open to the wet. There was nobody there, of course, the owners must have gone before the battle. But as she insisted on going on as far as the kitchen she uttered another scream. Two bodies had rolled under the sink, a Zouave, a fine man with a black beard, and a huge Prussian with red hair, and the two were locked in a furious embrace. One had his teeth sunk into the other's cheek, their arms had stiffened in death but not let go and were still cracking each other's broken spines. The two bodies were tied together in such a knot of eternal hatred that they would have to be buried together.

Prosper hurried Silvine away, since there was nothing for them to do in this wide open house full of death. When they got back in despair to the post which had detained the donkey and trap, they had the good fortune to find with the churlish officer a general who was touring the battlefield. The latter asked to look at the pass and then returned it to Silvine with a gesture of sympathy, meaning that they were to let this poor woman go with her donkey and look for her husband's body. She and her companion lost no time in going up towards the Fond-de-Givonne with the little cart, in accordance with the new order not to go through Sedan.

Then they turned left to get up to the plateau of Illy by the road through the Garenne wood. But there again they were delayed, and many times thought they would not get through the wood because there were so many obstacles. At every step the way was blocked by trees cut down by shells and felled like giants. This was the forest that had been bombarded, from end to end of which the gunfire had hacked down century-old beings, as though through a square of the old guard, standing firm and immovable like veterans. On all sides tree-trunks lay denuded, cut through, split open like human breasts. This destruction, with its slaughter of branches shedding tears of sap, had the tragic horror of a human battlefield. And there were human bodies too, soldiers who had died with the trees, like brothers. A lieutenant, with blood coming from his mouth, still had both hands digging into the ground, tearing out handfuls of grass. Further on a dead captain was lying on his front with his head up, shrieking with pain. Others seemed to be asleep in the undergrowth, and a Zouave, whose blue belt was burnt, had his beard and hair completely singed off. Several times they had to move a body to one side so that the donkey could get along the narrow woodland track.

When they reached a little coomb the horror suddenly came to an end. The battle must have passed over without touching this lovely corner of nature. Not a single tree had been touched, no wound had bled on the mossy bank. A brook swirled its little eddies along and the path that followed it was shaded by lofty beech trees. The cool running water and soft rustle of greenery had a pervasive charm and was delightfully peaceful.

Prosper stopped the donkey and let it drink from the stream.

'Oh isn't it lovely here!' He could not help expressing his relief.

Silvine looked round and was astonished and slightly shame-faced to feel that she was refreshed and happy too. Why should there be such peaceful happiness in this lovely spot when all around there was nothing but mourning and grief? She made a gesture indicating urgent haste.

'Quick, quick, let's get on ... Where is the place? Are you sure you saw Honoré?'

Fifty paces further on they really came out on to the plateau of Illy, and the bare plain suddenly opened out in front of them. This time it was a real battlefield, with bare ground stretching away to the horizon under the wide and dreary sky from which the heavy rain was still coming down in torrents. Here there were no piles of dead, all the Prussians must have been buried already, for there was not one to be seen among the bodies of the French scattered along roads, in fields and hollows, according to the tide of battle. The first one they saw against a hedge was a sergeant, a fine figure of a man, young and strong, who seemed to have a smile on his parted lips, and his face was peaceful. But a hundred paces further on there was another lying across the road, and he was horribly mutilated, with half his head blown off and his brains had splashed down over his shoulders. And then after the isolated bodies here and there, came little groups. They saw seven men in a row, one knee on the ground and rifle to shoulder, picked off as they were firing, and near them a non-commissioned officer had fallen as he was giving a command. The road wound on through a narrow defile and there the horror came upon them again as they saw a sort of ditch into which a whole company seemed to have rolled, mown down by machine-gun fire: it was filled with an avalanche of bodies which had fallen into a twisted and broken lot of men whose claw-like hands had scraped at the yellow clay but failed to get a hold. A black flight of crows moved off cawing, and already swarms of flies were buzzing above the bodies, returning obstinately in their thousands to drink fresh blood from the wounds.

'But where is it?' Silvine repeated.

Then they skirted a ploughed field covered all over with knapsacks. Some regiment being hard pressed must have got rid of them there in a fit of panic. Odds and ends scattered over the ground bore witness to episodes in the fight. Képis here and there in a field of beet looked like big poppies, and bits of uniform, shoulder-tabs, sword-belts spoke of fierce contact in one of the few hand-to-hand fights in the formidable twelve-hour artillery duel. Most frequently of all they were continually tripping over weapons, swords, bayonets, rifles, and in such quantities that they seemed to be growing out of the ground, a harvest that had sprung up in one abominable day. Messtins and water-bottles were strewn over the roads, all sorts of things that had fallen out of torn knapsacks – rice, brushes, cartridges. Field after field of immense devastation, fences torn down, trees looking as if they had been burnt in a fire, the earth itself pitted with shell-holes, trodden down hard by stampeding mobs and so ravaged that it seemed condemned to eternal sterility. Everything was soaked in the dismal rain, and there rose a pungent smell, the smell of battlefields, made up of rotting staw and burnt cloth, a mixture of decay and gunpowder.

Weary of these fields of death through which she felt she had been walking for leagues, Silvine looked round her with growing anguish.

'Where is it? Where is it, then?'

Prosper made no answer for he was getting worried himself. What upset him even more than the corpses of his mates were the bodies of the horses, poor horses lying on their sides, which they kept meeting in large numbers. There were some really pitiful ones in dreadful attitudes, decapitated or with bellies split open and entrails coming out. Many were on their backs, with bellies swollen and four legs sticking up in the air like snow posts, dotting the plain as far as you could see. Some of them were still not dead after two days of agony, and at the least sound they raised their suffering heads, turned right and left and dropped them again; others did not move but occasionally uttered a loud scream, the plaint of a dying horse, so unmistakable and so terribly grief-stricken that the very air trembled. Prosper's heart ached as he thought of Zephir and that he might possibly see him again.

Suddenly he felt the ground shake under the galloping hoofs of a furious charge. He turned round and just had time to shout to Silvine:

'Mind the horses! The horses! Get down behind that wall!'

Over the top of a near-by slope some hundred horses, riderless, some still carrying a full pack, were bearing down on them at breakneck speed. These were the stray animals left on the field of battle, who had instinctively gathered in a herd. They had had no hay or oats for two days, and had eaten the scanty grass, cropped hedges and even gnawed the bark of trees. Whenever hunger caught them in the belly like a prick of the spurs, they all set off together in a mad stampede, charging straight through the empty, silent country, trampling on the dead and finishing off the wounded.

The storm was approaching and Silvine just had time to pull the donkey and trap into the shelter of the low wall.

'Oh God! They'll smash everything!'

But they leaped over the obstacle and nothing was left but the rumbling of thunder, and already they were galloping off in another direction and diving into a sunken road and on to the corner of a wood behind which they vanished.

When Silvine had brought the donkey back on to the road she insisted on an answer from Prosper:

'Look here, where is it?'

He stood there looking at the four corners of the horizon.

'There were three trees, I must find those three trees ... Bless

348

you, you don't see all that clearly when you're fighting, and it isn't easy to know afterwards which way you went!'

Seeing some people to his left, two men and a woman, he thought he would ask them. But as he went up to them the woman ran off and the men brandished threatening fists. He saw yet more and they all avoided him and ran off into the bushes like cunning, prowling animals, they were dressed in rags, unspeakably dirty, with crafty, evil-looking faces. Then he realized that where these horrible people had passed, the dead, were bootless with bare, grey-looking feet, and he understood that these were the prowling thieves who followed the German armies, the plunderers of corpses, a gypsy crew of vultures who moved in the wake of the invasion. A tall thin fellow rushed away from him with a sack over his shoulder and pockets jingling with watches and silver coins stolen from pockets.

But one boy of thirteen or fourteen let Prosper approach, and when Prosper, realizing the boy was French, told him off roundly, he protested. What, couldn't you earn your own living now? He picked up rifles and was given five sous for each one he found. That morning he had run away from his village, having had nothing to eat since the day before, and he had been taken on by a Luxembourg dealer who had an arrangement with the Prussians about this harvest of guns on the battlefield. The truth of the matter was that the Prussians were afraid that these weapons, if picked up by peasants in this frontier region, might be taken into Belgium and thence get back into France. So there was quite a swarm of poor devils looking for rifles at five sous a time, ratting about in the grass like those women you see bent double picking dandelions in the meadows.

'What a dirty trade!' growled Prosper.

'Well, you must live,' said the boy. 'I'm not robbing anyone.'

As he was a stranger in those parts and could not give any directions he merely pointed out a little farmhouse where he had seen some people.

Prosper thanked him and was moving off to go back to Silvine when he caught sight of a rifle half buried in a furrow. At first he took care not to point it out. But then he suddenly turned back and found himself calling:

'Look, there's one over there. That'll mean another five sous!'

As they were making for the farm Silvine saw other peasants

digging long trenches. But these people were working under the direct orders of Prussian officers who were standing stiff and silent with just a switch in their hands, superintending the work. The inhabitants of the villages had been set to work to bury the dead for fear that the rainy weather might hasten decomposition. There were two cartloads of bodies and a gang was unloading them and quickly laying them side by side very close together, without searching them or even looking at their faces, and three men with large shovels followed on and covered the row with such a thin layer of earth that already the rain was opening up little cracks. So hastily was the job done that before a fortnight was up a pestilence would be rising through all these cracks. Silvine could not help stopping on the edge of the trench and looking at these pitiful bodies as they were brought along. She was shuddering with the horrible fear that in each bloody face she would recognize Honoré. Was he that dreadful one with no left eye? Or the one with the broken jaw? If she didn't hurry up and find him on this featureless, endless plain they would certainly take him away from her and bury him in the dump with the others.

So she rushed back to Prosper, who had gone with the donkey to the farmhouse door.

'Oh God, where is he? Ask them, keep on asking!'

But there were only Prussians in the farmhouse, with a servant and her child who had come back from the woods where they had nearly died of hunger and thirst. It was a little corner of sociable family life, well-earned rest after the labours of the previous days. Soldiers were carefully brushing their uniforms which were hanging over the clothes-lines. One was finishing off a skilful darning job on his trousers, and the cook of the party had a big fire going in the middle of the yard, on which the soup was bubbling in a large saucepan, giving off a nice smell of cabbage and bacon. The conquest was already being organized with perfect, quiet efficiency. You would have taken these men for a lot of business people back home and smoking their long pipes. On a seat by the door a big red-haired man had lifted the servant's child in his arms, a kid of five or six, and was jumping him up and down and saying nice things to him in German, enjoying seeing the child laugh at this funny language with its harsh syllables that he couldn't understand.

Prosper turned away at once, fearing some fresh trouble. But these Prussians really were good fellows. They grinned at the little donkey and didn't even take the trouble to see their pass.

Then began a frantic hunt. The sun appeared for a moment between two clouds, but it was already low down on the horizon. Were they going to be benighted in this endless graveyard? A new downpour obscured the sun again, and there was nothing round them but the dismal waste of rain, like a dust-storm of water effacing everything, roads, fields. trees. He no longer knew where he was, had lost his bearings and said so. The donkey trotted along behind them at the same even pace, head down and pulling his little cart with his resigned, docile gait. They went north, then came back towards Sedan. They lost all sense of direction, twice went back on their tracks when they realized they were passing the same things again. Probably they were going round in a circle, and ultimately they pulled up, tired and desperate, at a point where three roads met, lashed by the rain and too exhausted to go on looking.

But then they heard some moaning, and pushed on as far as a lonely cottage to the left, where they found two wounded men in a room. The doors were wide open and for two days they had been shivering in a fever with their wounds not even dressed, and had not seen a living soul. Above all they were tormented by thirst amid all this pouring rain lashing the windows. They could not move and at once cried 'Water! Water!' – the cry of agonized longing with which the wounded pursue anybody who passes, at the slightest sound of footsteps that drags them out of their torpor.

When Silvine had brought them some water Prosper recognized that the more seriously wounded one was a comrade of his, a Chasseur d'Afrique of his own regiment, and he realized that they could not be far from the place where the Margueritte division had charged. The wounded man managed to wave vaguely: yes, it was over that way when you turn left after a big field of lucerne. Silvine was for setting off again at once with the information. She called in a passing team of men who were collecting the dead and asked them to help the two wounded men. She had already taken the donkey's halter and was pulling him over the slippery ground so as to get quickly down there past the lucerne.

Prosper suddenly stood still.

'It must be somewhere here. Look, there are the three trees on the right. Can't you see the wheel marks? There's an ammunition waggon broken down over there ... Here we are at last!'

Silvine rushed over in a very agitated state and looked into the faces of two dead men, gunners lying at the side of the road.

'But he's not here, he's not here! You can't have seen properly ... Yes, it must have been one of those funny ideas that made you see things!'

She was gradually giving way to a wild hope and uncontrollable joy.

'Suppose you had made a mistake and he's still alive! Yes, he must still be alive as he isn't here!'

Then she uttered a little moan, for turning round she found herself on the actual position of the battery. It was appalling, the very ground was ploughed up as if there had been an earthquake, with wreckage strewn everywhere and dead men blown in all directions in frightful postures, with twisted arms, legs bent back, heads awry, yelling with wide open mouths showing all their white teeth. A corporal had died with his hands over his eyes, clenched in terror, trying not to see. Some gold coins a lieutenant had had in a money-belt had come out with his blood and entrails. The 'married couple', Adolphe the driver and Louis the gun-layer, were lying one on top of the other with their eyes out of their sockets and were locked in a fierce embrace, united in death. And there at last was Honoré, stretched out on his crippled gun as though lying in state, his side and one shoulder mangled but his face intact and beautiful in its anger, still looking out towards the Prussian batteries.

'Oh my darling,' Silvine moaned, 'my darling ...'

She fell on her knees on the wet ground and joined her hands in a spasm of wild grief. This word darling, the only one she could find, expressed the love she had lost, this man who in his goodness had forgiven her and consented to take her for his wife in spite of everything. Now her hope was at an end and she would cease to be really alive. She had never loved another and would love him for ever. The rain was giving over, and a flight of crows cawing above the three trees frightened her like some evil menace. Was her beloved dead, recovered with such difficulty, to be taken from her again? She dragged herself over on her knees and with a trembling hand drove away the greedy flies buzzing above the wide open eyes she still hoped would look at her.

Then she caught sight of a bloodstained piece of paper clutched in Honoré's fingers, and anxiously tried to pull it out in little jerks. The dead man refused to give it up and held on so tight that it could only have been torn away in pieces. It was the letter she had written him, that he had kept between his skin and his shirt, and he had squeezed it in his hand for a farewell in death's final convulsion. Recognizing it, she was filled with a deep joy in the midst of her grief and quite overwhelmed by this proof that he had died thinking of her. Oh yes, yes, she would let him keep the beloved letter, and not take it from him as he was so determined to take it with him into the earth. A fresh outburst of weeping brought her some relief, for her tears were warm and sweet now. She stood up, kissed his hands and his forehead, repeating the one word of infinite love:

'My darling, my darling.'

But the sun was going down, and Prosper had gone and brought the coverlet, and spread it on the ground. Slowly and respectfully they lifted Honoré's body, laid him on this, wrapped it round him and carried him to the cart. The rain was threatening to start again, and they were setting off once more with the donkey, a sad little procession across the malignant plain, when they heard a distant rumbling of thunder. Again Prosper cried:

'The horses! The horses!'

It was another charge of the horses roaming at large and famished. This time they were coming across a huge flat field in a solid mass, manes flying and nostrils flecked with foam, and a slanting ray of the red sun sent the shadow of their frantic race right across the plain. Silvine at once threw herself in front of the trap with her arms in the air as though to stop them with a gesture of fury and fear. Mercifully they swerved to the left, turned aside by the slope of the land. They would have pounded everything to pieces. The earth shook and their hoofs sent up a shower of stones like a hail of shrapnel that hurt the donkey's head. Then they vanished into a deep ravine.

'Hunger is spurring them on,' cried Prosper. 'Poor creatures!'

Silvine bandaged the donkey's ear with a handkerchief and took the bridle again. The little funeral procession re-crossed the plain in the opposite direction to start the two leagues between them and Remilly. At every step Prosper paused to look at dead horses, grief-stricken at going away like this without seeing Zephir again.

A little way below the Garenne wood, as they were bearing left to go back the same way as in the morning, a German post demanded to see their permit. This time, instead of keeping them out of Sedan, the guard ordered them to go through the town, or else they would be arrested. There was no answering back, it was fresh orders. In any case that would shorten their return journey by two kilometres, and as they were dead tired they were glad.

However, in Sedan itself they were very badly held up. As soon as they had passed through the fortifications they were overcome by a foul stench, and a bed of filth came up to their knees. The town was disgusting, an open sewer in which the defecation and urine of a hundred thousand men had been piling up for three days. All sorts of other muck had thickened this human dunghill – straw and hay itself rotting with the droppings of animals. Even worse, the carcasses of horses which had been slaughtered and cut up in the open street poisoned the air. Offal was decaying in the sun, heads and bones were lying in the street, alive with flies. Plague would certainly break out unless this layer of horrible filth was quickly swept down into the drains, for in the rue du Ménil and rue Maqua and even the Place Turenne it was as much as twenty centimetres deep. Moreover white posters had been put up by the Prussian authorities mustering all inhabitants for the next day and ordering all persons, whoever they were, workmen, shopkeepers, professional people, magistrates, to set to work with brooms and shovels under the threat of the severest penalties if the town was not clean by evening. Already the chief magistrate could be seen in front of his home raking over the roadway and shovelling the muck into a wheelbarrow.

Silvine and Prosper, who had taken the Grande-Rue, could only proceed very slowly through the fetid slime. And besides at every moment the way through the town was barred by some uproar, because it was the time when the Prussians were combing through the houses to dig out hidden soldiers determined not to give themselves up. At about two o'clock on the day before, when General de Wimpffen had come back from the Château de Bellevue after signing the capitulation, a rumour had run round at once that the army taken prisoner was to be interned in the Iges peninsula while waiting for arrangements to be made for it to be moved to Germany. A very few officers thought they would take advantage of the clause giving them their freedom on condition that they signed an undertaking not to fight again. Only one general, it was said, had made the undertaking, and that was General Bourgain-Desfeuilles, using his rheumatism as a pretext. That morning he had been booed on his departure, as he climbed into a carriage in front of the Hôtel de la Croix d'Or. Disarmament had been going on since first light; the soldiers were made to file across the Place Turenne and throw their arms – rifles and bayonets – on to a pile in a corner that grew like a tip of scrap-iron. A Prussian detachment was there, commanded by a young officer, a tall, pale fellow in a sky-blue tunic and wearing a round cap with cock's feathers, who superintended the operation with an air of lofty correctness, wearing white gloves. When a Zouave in a moment of revolt had refused to give up his rifle the officer had him taken away, saying without a trace of German accent: 'Shoot that man!' The others went on miserably filing past, throwing their rifles down mechanically, anxious to have done with it. But how many were already disarmed, the ones whose rifles lay scattered all over the countryside! And how many had been in hiding since yesterday, dreaming of disappearing in the indescribable confusion! Houses had been taken over and were full of these stubborn men who refused to answer and buried themselves in corners. The German patrols scouring the town found some of them even crouching under furniture. And as many of them, even when discovered, obstinately refused to come out of the cellars, the patrols simply fired on them through gratings. It was a manhunt, a horrible battue.

On the Meuse bridge the donkey was stopped by a great crush of people. The officer commanding the post guarding the bridge was suspicious, thinking there might be some smuggling of bread or meat, and insisting on checking what was in the cart. He pulled back the cover, took one horrified look at the corpse and waved them through. But still they could not get on because the crowd got denser; it was one of the first convoys of prisoners being taken to the Iges peninsula by a detachment of Prussians. The herd went on and on, men shoving each other and treading on each other's heels, looking ashamed in their tattered uniforms and averting their eyes, and their hunched backs and dangling arms suggested beaten men without even a knife left to cut their own throats. The harsh commands of their guards urged them on like the lashing of a whip in their mute confusion, in which the only other sound was the flop-flop of heavy boots in the thick mud. There had been yet another shower, and nothing could be more distressing than this rabble of humiliated soldiers, looking like tramps or beggars on the road.

Prosper, as a veteran African campaigner, felt his heart thumping with helpless rage. Suddenly he nudged Silvine and pointed at two of the passing soldiers. He had recognized Maurice and Jean being taken off with the rest, walking side by side like two brothers, and when the little cart started up again at the tail of the convoy he was able to follow them with his eye as far as Torcy, on the flat road leading to Iges through gardens and small-holdings.

'Ah', murmured Silvine, glancing towards Honoré's body and distressed at what she saw, 'perhaps the dead are happiest!'

Night caught them at Wadelincourt, and it had been dark for a long time when they got back to Remilly. Seeing the body of his son old Fouchard was overcome with amazement, for he was convinced it would never be found. He had spent the day concluding a nice bit of business. The current price for officer's horses stolen on the battlefield was twenty francs each, and he had got three for forty-five.

2

As THE column of prisoners was leaving Torcy there was such a crush that Maurice was cut off from Jean. He tried to catch up but got even more lost. By the time he reached the bridge over the canal which cuts across the isthmus of the Iges peninsula, he was mixed up with a lot of Chasseurs d'Afrique and could not get back to his own regiment.

The bridge was defended by two guns facing the peninsula. Immediately past the canal the Prussian headquarters had set up a post in a large house under an officer responsible for receiving and guarding the prisoners. The formalities were brief, the incoming men were simply counted like sheep as the crowd came through and not much notice was taken of uniforms or numbers, after which the crowds poured in and camped wherever the roads took them.

Maurice thought he could venture to speak to a Bavarian officer who was calmly smoking as he straddled a chair.

'Which way for the 106th regiment of the line, sir?'

Was this one of the few officers who did not understand French? Or did he find it amusing to misdirect a poor devil of a soldier? He smiled, raised his hand and pointed straight on.

Although he belonged to this part of the world, Maurice had never been into the peninsula, so from then onwards he was on a voyage of discovery, as though he had been cast up on a desert island. At first he skirted along the side of La Tour à Glaire on his left, a fine country house with its charming little park on the river Meuse. The road next followed the river, flowing to the right at the foot of steep banks. Gradually the road climbed in wide bends, going round the little hill in the centre of the peninsula, and there were some disused quarry workings with narrow wandering paths. Still further, at water level, was a mill. Then the road turned away and went downhill again to the village of Iges, built on a slope and connected to the opposite bank by a ferry where the Saint-Albert textile mill was. And finally ploughed fields and meadows stretched out, a great expanse of flat, treeless land enclosed by a bend in the river. Maurice looked carefully among the ups and downs of the hill-slope, but in vain – he could only see cavalry and artillery settling down there. He asked again, this time a corporal in the Chasseurs d'Afrique, but he knew nothing. It was getting dark and he sat down for a moment on a roadside stone because his legs were tired.

In the sudden fit of depression that came over him he saw on the far side of the Meuse the hated fields where he had fought two days before. In the fading light of this day of rain everything took on a ghastly appearance, a horizon of mud stretching on endless and dismal. The Saint-Albert gap, the narrow road along which the Prussians had come, ran parallel with the bend of the river as far as the whitish screes of some quarries. Beyond the slopes of the Seugnon were the feathery treetops of the Falizette wood. But straight ahead of him, a little further to the left, Saint-Menges stood out, with the road coming down to the ferry, and then the summit of Le Hattoy in the middle. Illy was far away in the distance, Fleigneux buried behind a fold in the land, Floing nearer and to the right. He recognized the field in which he had waited for hours lying among the cabbages, the plateau that the reserve artillery had tried to defend, the crest where he had seen Honoré die on his smashed gun. The abomination of the disaster all came back and filled him with pain and disgust until he felt sick.

But for fear of being caught in the dark he had to go on with his quest. Perhaps the 106th was encamped in the low-lying part beyond the village, but all he found there was a few characters on the prowl, so he decided to go right round the peninsula, following the loop of the river. As he crossed a field of potatoes he took the precaution of pulling up a few plants and filling his pockets. The potatoes were unripe, but it was all he had, as most unfortunately Jean had insisted on carrying both the loaves Delaherche had given them when they left. What struck him now was the number of horses he met on the bare slopes that went gently down from the little hill in the middle to the Meuse in the Donchery direction. Why had all these animals been brought here, and how were they going to be fed? It was quite dark by the time he came to a little wood by the river, in which he was surprised to find the Emperor's Household Cavalry already encamped and drying their things round big fires. These gentlemen camping on their own had good tents, bubbling saucepans and a cow tethered to a tree. He at once noticed that they were looking askance at him in his ragged infantry uniform covered with mud. But they did let him bake his potatoes in the ashes, and he withdrew and sat under a tree a hundred metres away to eat them. It had stopped raining, the sky had cleared and the stars were shining very bright in the dark blue vault. He realized that he would be spending the night here and would have to continue his search in the morning. He was collapsing with fatigue, and the tree would at least give him some shelter should the rain start again.

But he could not get to sleep and was haunted by the thought of the huge prison open to the night air in which he felt shut in. The Prussians had had a really bright idea in herding into this place the eighty thousand men left of the army of Châlons. The peninsula might be three kilometres long by one and a half wide, plenty of room to park the huge rabble of disarmed men. He was well aware of the continuous barrier of water surrounding them, with the loop of the Meuse on three sides and at the base the by-pass canal linking the closest points of the river. Just there was the only way through, the bridge defended by two guns. So it was the simplest thing in the world to guard this camp in spite of its great area. He had already noticed the line of German sentries strung along by the water's edge on the opposite bank at fifty-pace intervals with orders to shoot any man trying to escape by swimming. Uhlans were patrolling behind, linking the different posts, and further off, scattered over the open country, you could have counted black lines of Prussian soldiers, a threefold living and moving girdle hemming in the imprisoned army.

Now, with his staring, sleepless eyes, he could see nothing but darkness lit here and there by camp fires. Yet beyond the pale ribbon of the Meuse he could still make out the motionless forms of the sentries. In the starlight they stood there straight and black, and at intervals he could hear their guttural calls – the menacing call of the watch tailing off into the swash of the river. These harsh foreign syllables cutting through a lovely starlit night in France revived in him all the nightmare of two days earlier, in the places he had seen but an hour ago, on the plain of Illy still strewn with dead, and in the horrible outskirts of Sedan where a whole world had collapsed. Lying there with his head on the root of a tree in the dampness of the woodland, he relapsed into the despair that had gripped him the day before on the sofa in Delaherche's home. What hurt his injured pride still more and tortured him now was the question of the morrow. He felt an urge to measure the extent of the fall and know what sort of ruins yesterday's world had left. Now that the Emperor had surrendered his sword to King William, didn't it mean that this hateful war was over? But he recalled what two of the Bavarian soldiers escorting the prisoners to Iges had said to him: 'Us in France! Us all in Paris!' In a half-doze he suddenly realized what was happening: the Empire swept away amid universal execration, a Republic proclaimed in an outburst of patriotic fervour, and the legend of 1792 conjuring up shadowy figures, soldiers in the mass uprising, armies of volunteers purging the homeland of the foreigner. It was all jumbled up in his poor sick head, the extortions of the conquerors, the bitterness of conquest, the determination of the conquered to fight to their last drop of blood, captivity for the eighty thousand men held there, first in this peninsula and later in German fortresses for weeks, months, possibly years. Everything was breaking up and crashing down for ever in endless woe.

The cry of the sentries gradually grew louder and then burst into a shout right opposite him. Now wide awake, he was turning over on the hard earth when a shot tore through the silence, followed by a splashing sound and the short struggle of a body falling straight down into the water. Presumably some poor devil had been shot through the heart while trying to escape by swimming across the Meuse.

Maurice was up by sunrise. The weather was still bright and he was anxious to rejoin Jean and the rest of his company. He thought for a moment of searching once again in the middle of the peninsula, but then decided to finish going right round. And as he reached the bank of the canal he saw what was left of the 106th, about a thousand men camping on the towpath and only sheltered by a thin row of poplars. If on the night before he had turned to the left instead of going straight on he would have caught up with his regiment at once. Almost all the regiments of the line were huddled together there along the canal bank from La Tour à Glaire to the Château de Villette, another country house surrounded by a few hovels away in the direction of Donchery; and they had all planted themselves near the bridge, that is near the only way out, with the same instinct for freedom that makes large flocks of sheep crush each other to death against the gate leading out of the fold.

Jean shouted for joy:

'Oh, it's you at last! I thought you were in the river!'

There he was, with the rest of the squad, Pache and Lapoulle, Loubet and Chouteau. The last two, having slept in a doorway in Sedan, had been brought in again in the big round-up. The whole company had no other leader now but the corporal, death having cut down Sergeant Sapin, Lieutenant Rochas and Captain Beaudoin. Although the conquerors had abolished ranks and decided that prisoners only had to obey German officers, the four of them had still clung to Jean, knowing how sensible and experienced he was and good to follow in difficult circumstances. So that morning harmony and good humour reigned despite the foolishness of some and the bloody-mindedness of others. To begin with, he had found them a fairly dry spot for the night, between two ditches, where they had stretched themselves out, having only one piece of canvas between them. Then he had just got hold of some wood and a pan, in which Loubet had made them some nice hot coffee that cheered them up. It had stopped raining, and the day bade fair to be superb, they still had some biscuit and bacon left, and besides, as Chouteau remarked, it was a pleasure not to have to obey anyone any more but mess about as you liked. They were shut up, no doubt, but there was plenty of room. In any case they would be off in a day or two. So altogether this first day, Sunday the 4th, passed very happily.

Even Maurice, feeling better now he had rejoined his companions, found nothing much to grumble about except the German bands which played all through the afternoon on the opposite side of the canal. And towards evening there was hymn-singing as well. Beyond the cordon of sentries little groups of soldiers could be seen singing slow and loud to celebrate the Sabbath.

'Oh that music!' Maurice almost screamed in exasperation. 'It's getting under my skin!'

Jean, more phlegmatic, just shrugged.

'After all, they've got their reasons for being pleased. And perhaps they think they're entertaining us ... It hasn't been a bad day, we mustn't grumble.'

But towards dusk it began raining again. That was disastrous. Some soldiers had broken into the few empty houses on the peninsula and a few others had managed to put up tents. But the majority had no protection of any kind, not even a blanket, and had to spend the night in the open with rain pouring down on them.

At about one in the morning Maurice, who had dozed off exhausted, woke up in an absolute lake. The ditches, swollen by the rain, had overflowed and submerged the ground on which he was lying. Chouteau and Loubet were swearing with rage and Pache was shaking Lapoulle who was sleeping on like a log, lake or no lake. Then Jean remembered the poplars along the canal and ran to take shelter under them with his men, who spent the rest of that fearful night bent nearly double with their backs against the tree

361

trunks and legs bent up under them to avoid the heaviest of the drips.

The following day and the one after that were really dreadful, with such frequent and heavy showers that their clothes never had time to dry on their bodies. Famine was setting in, with no biscuit, bacon or coffee left. During these two days, the Monday and the Tuesday, they lived on potatoes stolen from fields near-by, and even these were becoming so scarce by the end of the second day that the soldiers with any money were buying them at five sous each. True, bugles still sounded rations, and the corporal had even hurried off to a big shed at La Tour à Glaire, where it was rumoured that rations of bread were being issued. But the first time he went he had waited there for three hours to no purpose, and the second he had had a row with a Bavarian. If the French officers could do nothing, being powerless to act, had the German headquarters parked the beaten army in the rain with the idea of letting them die of hunger? It didn't look as though any precaution had been taken or any effort made to feed the eighty thousand men whose death-agony was beginning in this horrible hell the soldiers were beginning to call the Camp of Hell, a name denoting anguish that would haunt even the bravest for ever.

When he got back from these long fruitless waits in front of the shed, Jean, usually so phlegmatic, lost his temper.

'Are they just pulling our legs, calling when there's nothing there? Bugger me if I put myself out any more!'

Yet at the first suggestion of a call he rushed off again. They were inhuman, these regulation bugle calls, and they had another effect which broke Maurice's heart. Each time the bugles sounded the French horses, abandoned and wandering about on the other side of the canal, tore along and jumped into the water to rejoin their regiments, maddened by these fanfares they recognized and which acted on them like a dig of the spurs. But they were exhausted and so were dragged off by the current, and few of them reached the other side. They struggled pitifully, and so many of them were drowned that their swollen, floating bodies were already blocking the canal. And those that did reach land acted as though they had gone mad and galloped away over the empty fields of the peninsula.

'More meat for the crows!' Maurice said sadly, remembering the disturbing numbers of horses he had seen. 'If we stay here a few more days we shall all be devouring each other ... Oh, the poor creatures!'

The night of Tuesday to Wednesday was particularly horrible. Jean, who was beginning to be seriously worried about Maurice's over-tense state, made him wrap himself up in an old blanket they had bought from a Zouave for ten francs, while he himself, with his cape soaked like a sponge, received the full force of the deluge which went on all night. The position under the poplars was becoming untenable; it was a river of mud, and the saturated earth held the water in deep puddles. The worst of it was that their stomachs were empty, the evening meal having consisted of two beetroots among the six men, and they had not even been able to cook them for want of dry wood, so that the cold sugary taste had soon turned into an intolerable burning sensation; to say nothing of the beginnings of dysentery caused by fatigue, bad food and persistent damp. More than ten times, Jean, propped against the trunk of the same tree, with his legs in the water, had put out his hand to feel whether Maurice had thrown off his covering in his restless sleep. Since his friend had saved him from the Prussians on the plateau of Illy by carrying him in his arms he had been repaying his debt a hundredfold. Without reasoning it out he was giving him his whole being, he was forgetting himself entirely for love of him, and this love was indefinable but imperishable, though he had no words to express what he felt. He had already taken the food out of his own mouth, as the chaps in the squad put it, but now he would have given his own skin to clothe him, protect his shoulders and warm his feet. In the midst of the savage egotism all round him in this corner of suffering humanity maddened by hunger, he probably owed to this total self-abnegation the unlooked-for blessing of keeping his unruffled calm and health of mind, for he was the only one who was still strong and had not lost his head.

And so, after that horrible night, Jean carried out an idea that had been going round in his head.

'Look here, young fellow-me-lad, as they're not giving us anything to eat but forgetting all about us in this bloody hole, we've got to stir our stumps a bit if we don't want to peg out ... Can you still walk all right?'

Mercifully the sun had come out and Maurice was quite warmed up.

'Of course, my legs are all right!'

'O.K., then we're going off to see what we can find ... We've got some money, and I'll be damned if we don't find something to buy. And don't let's bother about the others, they're just not worth it, let them work it out for themselves!'

As a matter of fact he was disgusted by the sly selfishness of Loubet and Chouteau, who stole everything they could and never shared anything with their mates. Neither was there anything to be got out of Lapoulle, who was a clod, or Pache, who was a worm.

So the two of them took the road Maurice had already been along, by the river. The gardens of La Tour à Glaire and the house had already been laid waste and looted, the lawns ploughed up as though by storm-floods, trees felled, buildings broken into. A bedraggled mob of soldiers, covered with mud, hollow-cheeked and with feverish, shining eyes, were camping out like a lot of gypsies, living like wolves in rooms filthy with excrement, for they dared not go out in case they lost their places for the night. And further on, up the slopes, they went through the cavalry and artillery, formerly so well drilled but now demoralized, too, going to pieces in this torturing hunger which maddened the horses and sent men off over the meadows in marauding bands. On the right they saw an endless queue of artillerymen and Chasseurs d'Afrique slowly moving past a mill where the miller was selling flour, two handfuls of it in their handkerchiefs for a franc. But they were afraid of waiting too long and went on, hoping to find something better in the village of Iges. But when they reached there they were filled with consternation to find it bare and grim like an Algerian village after the locusts have passed, not a scrap left of anything to eat, bread, vegetables or meat, and the miserable houses looked as though people had scratched all through them with their nails. It was said that General Lebrun had put up in the mayor's house. He had tried in vain to arrange an issue of vouchers payable after the war so as to facilitate the feeding of the troops. There was nothing left, and money was useless. Even the day before one biscuit had fetched two francs, a bottle of wine seven, a little tot of brandy one franc, a pipeful of tobacco fifty centimes. And now officers had to guard the general's house and the surrounding hovels with drawn swords because continual bands of marauders were breaking down doors and stealing even lamp-oil to drink.

Three Zouaves hailed Maurice and Jean. With five of them they might be able to pull something off.

'Come on . . . There are some horses pegging out, and if only we had some dry wood . . .'

Then they made a rush at a peasant's cottage, broke off cupboard doors and tore the thatch off the roof. Some officers with revolvers dashed up and drove them away.

When they saw that the few inhabitants left in Iges were as miserable and starved as the soldiers, Jean was sorry they had turned their noses up at the flour at the mill.

'Let's go back, there may still be some left.'

But Maurice was beginning to get so tired and weak for want of food that Jean left him in a hole in a quarry, sitting on a rock, staring at the broad horizon of Sedan. Jean, after queueing for threequarters of an hour, came back eventually with some flour in a bit of rag. And all they could do was eat it just like that, out of their hands. It wasn't too bad, it had no smell and an insipid taste like dough, but it did cheer them up a bit. They were even lucky enough to find a natural pool of pure rain-water in a rock and they joyfully quenched their thirst.

Jean suggested staying there for the afternoon, but Maurice impatiently dismissed the idea.

'No, no, not here! It'd make me ill to have all this in front of my eyes for long.'

With a trembling hand he pointed at the immense horizon, Le Hattoy, the plateaux of Floing and Illy, the Garenne woods, all these hateful scenes of massacre and defeat.

'While I was waiting for you just now I had to turn my back on it, for I should have ended up by screaming with rage, yes, howling like a dog being teased beyond endurance . . . You can't imagine how it hurts me, it's driving me mad!'

Jean looked at him, and this wounded and bleeding pride astonished him, and he was perturbed to catch once again the wild look of insanity in his eyes that he had seen already. He tried to make a joke of it.

'All right, that's easy, we'll have a change of scene.'

So they wandered about until evening wherever the paths took them. They explored the low-lying part of the peninsula hoping to find some more potatoes, but the artillerymen had taken the ploughs and turned over the fields, gleaning and picking up everything. They retraced their steps and once again passed through crowds of idle, slowly dying men, starving soldiers walking about in their hunger or lying on the ground listless, having collapsed with exhaustion in their hundreds in the hot sun. They themselves frequently gave in and had to sit down, but then a kind of exasperated bravado set them on their feet again and they resumed their prowl, goaded on by the animal instinct to hunt for food. This seemed to have been going on for months, and yet the minutes sped quickly by. In some of the enclosed fields on the Donchery side they were frightened by the horses and had to take refuge behind a wall, where they stayed a long time, their strength gone, looking with unseeing eyes at these stampedes of crazed animals against the red sky of sunset.

As Maurice had foreseen, the thousands of horses interned with the army and which could not be fed were a menace that increased in seriousness each day. They had begun by eating the bark of trees, then they had attacked trellises and fences, any sort of planks they could find, and now they were devouring each other. They could be seen hurling themselves on each other to tear the hair from their tails, which they chewed madly, foaming at the mouth. But it was above all at night that they became terrible, as though darkness brought them nightmares. They would gather together and charge at the few tents standing, looking for straw. It was useless for the men to light big fires to keep them off; the fires seemed to excite them still more. Their whinnyings were so pitiful and unnerving that they seemed like the roaring of wild beasts. If you drove them away they came back fiercer and more numerous than ever. And every minute during the hours of darkness you could hear a long cry of agony from some stray soldier trampled to death in this mad stampede.

The sun was still on the horizon when Jean and Maurice, on their way back to camp, were surprised to come upon the four other members of the squad lying in a ditch and looking as though they were hatching some evil plot. Loubet called them over and Chouteau said:

'It's about tonight's meal ... We are starving and it's thirty-six hours since we've had anything inside us ... Well, as there are some horses, and as horsemeat's not bad ...'

'You will be in on it, won't you, corporal?' went on Loubet. 'Because the more of us there are the better, with such a big animal ... Look, there's one over there we've been trailing for an hour, that big chestnut that looks sick. It'll be easier to finish him off.'

He pointed to a horse struck down by hunger on the edge of a ravaged beet field. The horse was on his side and now and again he raised his head and looked round dolefully with a great sigh of misery.

'Oh what a long wait!' grumbled Lapoulle, tortured by his huge appetite. 'I'll knock him out, shall I?'

But Loubet stopped him. No thank you! And get into a row with the Prussians, who had forbidden the killing of a single horse on pain of death, for fear that an abandoned carcass might start off plague ... So they had to wait until it was quite dark, which was why all four were now in the ditch keeping watch with glittering eyes, which were never taken off the animal.

'Corporal,' ventured Pache in a slightly quavery voice, 'you know all about these things, could you kill him without hurting him?'

With a gesture of disgust Jean refused to do the cruel job. That poor dying creature, oh no, no! His first impulse had been to run away and take Maurice with him so that neither should take part in this horrible butchery. But seeing how ill his friend looked, he reproached himself for being so squeamish. After all, good heavens, that's what animals are for, to feed men. They couldn't let themselves die of starvation when there was meat there. He was glad to see Maurice cheering up a little in the hope that they would get a meal, so he said in his good-humoured way:

'Well, really, I've no idea, and if we've got to kill him without pain ...'

'Oh balls!' cut in Lapoulle. 'You watch me!'

The two newcomers sat in the ditch and the wait was resumed. Every so often one of them stood up and made sure that the horse was still there stretching his neck towards where the cool air of the Meuse came from, towards the setting sun, to drink in what life was left there. At last, when dusk had slowly come down, the six stood up; in this savage watch they were impatient with the slowness of nightfall, keeping a look-out in all directions, nerves on edge in case anybody should see them.

'Oh blast it all!' cried Chouteau. 'Now's the time!'

The countryside could still be seen in the dim light of dusk. Lapoulle ran first, followed by the five others. He had taken with him from the ditch a big round stone, and he rushed at the horse and began bashing in his skull with both arms straight as though using a club. But at the second blow the horse attempted to stand up. Chouteau and Loubet threw themselves across the horse's legs, trying to hold him down and shouting for the others to help. The horse whinnyed in an almost human voice in his bewildered grief, and began to struggle and would have broken the men like glass if he had not already been half dead with starvation. But his head was moving too much and the blows were going wide. Lapoulle could not finish him off.

'Christ, his bones aren't half hard! Hold on to him and let me do him in!'

Jean and Maurice were frozen with horror and did not hear Chouteau calling, but stood there with arms dangling and unwilling to join in.

All of a sudden Pache, in an instinctive burst of religious compassion, fell on his knees, put his hands together and began to mumble some prayers as people do at the bedside of the dying:

'Lord, have mercy upon him . . .'

Once again Lapoulle missed his aim and only took an ear off the wretched horse, who fell over with a loud cry.

'What a minute,' growled Chouteau, 'we've got to finish this off, he'll get us pinched . . . Don't you let go, Loubet!'

He had taken a knife out of his pocket, a little knife with a blade hardly longer than your finger. And sprawling on top of the animal's body, with one arm round its neck, he buried the blade, digging about in the living flesh, hacking lumps out until he found and severed the artery. He jumped to one side as the blood spurted out like water from a spout, while the feet pawed about and convulsive twitchings ran along the skin. It took nearly five minutes for the horse to die. His great staring eyes, full of grief and terror, were fixed on the grim-faced men waiting for his death. They grew dim and went out.

'Oh God,' muttered Pache, still on his knees, 'succour him, take him into Thy holy keeping . . .'

Then, when the horse had stopped moving, they were very hard

368

put to it as to how to get the best cuts. Loubet, who was a jack of all trades, did show them how to set about getting the fillet. But he was a clumsy butcher and in any case only had the little knife, and he floundered about in this warm flesh, still pulsing with life. Lapoulle, impatient as always, started helping him by opening up the belly quite unnecessarily and the carnage became appalling. They rummaged with furious haste in the blood and entrails like wolves worrying the carcass of the prey with their fangs.

'I don't know what cut this can be,' Loubet finally said, straightening up, his arms burdened with an enormous lump of meat. 'But anyhow here's enough to fill us all up to the eyes.'

Sick with horror, Jean and Maurice had turned away. Nevertheless hunger was driving them, and they followed the rest when they ran away so as not to be caught near a horse that had been cut open. Chouteau had made a discovery, three large beetroots somebody had dropped, and took them. Loubet, to get his arms free, had thrown the meat over Lapoulle's shoulders, and Pache carried the squad's saucepan, which they took about with them in case they had any lucky find. All six ran and ran without stopping to breathe, as though they were being chased.

Loubet suddenly stopped them all.

'This is silly, we've got to think where we can cook it.'

Jean, who was beginning to feel better now, suggested the quarries. They weren't more than three hundred metres away, and there were hidden caves where you could light a fire without being seen. But when they got there all sorts of difficulties cropped up. First there was the question of wood; fortunately they found a quarryman's wheelbarrow, and Lapoulle kicked the planks apart with his heel. Then there was absolutely no drinking water. During the day the hot sun had dried up the little pools of rainwater. There was a pump, but it was too far away, at the manor of La Tour à Glaire, and you queued there until midnight and thought yourself lucky if, in the scrimmage, some comrade didn't knock the lot out of your can with his elbow. The little wells in the neighbourhood had been exhausted for two days and you got nothing out of them but mud. That left only the water of the Meuse, and the banks were just across the road.

'I'll go with the pan,' said Jean.

They all protested.

'Oh no! We don't want to be poisoned, it's full of corpses!'

It was true, the Meuse was carrying along bodies of men and horses. They could be seen floating past every minute, with swollen bellies and already decomposing and going green. Many of them had got caught in the weeds near the banks and were filling the air with stench as they constantly bobbed up and down in the water. Nearly all the soldiers who had drunk this abominable water had had sickness and dysentery after frightful colic.

And yet they had to make up their minds to it. Maurice explained that the water would no longer be dangerous once it had been boiled.

'All right, I'll go,' said Jean again, taking Lapoulle with him.

By the time the pan was on the fire, full of water and with the meat in it, it was really dark. Loubet had peeled the beetroots so as to cook them in the broth – a stew that would be out of this world, as he put it – and they all kept the flames up by pushing pieces of the barrow under the pan. Their long shadows danced weirdly in this rocky cavern. But then they could wait no longer and threw themselves on to this disgusting brew and tore the meat into shares with wild, impatient fingers, without waiting to use a knife. But all the same it made them heave. It was the lack of salt in particular that upset them, for their stomachs refused to keep down this insipid mess of beet-root and bits of half-cooked, gluey meat tasting like earth. Almost at once they began throwing it up. Pache could not go on, Chouteau and Loubet cursed the devil's own nag they had had so much trouble to turn into a stew and which was now giving them the belly-ache. Lapoulle was the only one who dined copiously, but later in the night it nearly did him in when he had gone back with the three others to sleep under the poplars.

On the way Maurice, without a word, had taken Jean's arm and pulled him down a side path. The others filled him with a kind of furious disgust, and he had made a plan which was to go and sleep in the little copse where he had spent the first night. It was a good idea, and Jean strongly approved of it when he had lain down on sloping ground quite dry and sheltered by dense foliage. They stayed there until broad daylight and even slept a deep sleep which somewhat restored their strength.

The following day was a Thursday, but they no longer knew how they were living, and were simply glad that the fine weather seemed to have come back. Jean persuaded Maurice, in spite of his reluctance, to go back to the canal to see whether the regiment was to leave that day. Each day now prisoners were leaving for German fortresses in detachments of a thousand to twelve hundred. Two days earlier they had seen a party of officers and generals setting off for the train at Pont-à-Mousson. Everybody was in a frenzy of desire to get away from this awful Camp of Hell. Oh, if only their turn could come! When they found the 106th still camping on the towpath, in the growing confusion of so much suffering, they really were in despair.

And yet that day Jean and Maurice really thought they were going to get something to eat. Beginning that morning, quite a system of trading had developed between the prisoners and the Bavarians across the canal. Money was thrown to them in a handkerchief and they returned the handkerchief with some black bread or coarse tobacco scarcely dried out. Even the soldiers who had no money had contrived to do business by throwing over regulation white gloves which the Germans seemed to like. For two hours, all along the canal, this primitive bartering caused packages to fly to and fro. But when Maurice sent over a five-franc piece in his tie, the Bavarian who was sending back a loaf threw it, either out of clumsiness or for a nasty joke, so that it fell into the water. Roars of laughter from the Germans. Twice Maurice persisted, and twice the loaf went in. Then some officers ran up to see what the laughter was about, and they forbade the men to sell anything to the prisoners on pain of severe penalties. The trading stopped and Jean had to calm Maurice down, for he was shaking his fists at these robbers and yelling at them to return his five-franc pieces.

In spite of the bright sunshine it was another terrible day. There were alerts, two bugle calls that made Jean run to the shed where rations were supposed to be issued. But both times all he got out of it was jostling in the crush. The Prussians, so remarkably organized themselves, still showed a callous indifference towards the defeated army. As a result of complaints from Generals Douay and Lebrun they had indeed had a few sheep and cartloads of bread brought in, but they took so few precautions that the sheep were stolen and the carts ransacked as soon as they reached the bridge, so that troops camped more than a hundred metres away still got nothing. Only prowling thieves and gangs who attacked convoys got anything to eat. And so Jean, tumbling to it, as he put it, took Maurice with him to the bridge so that they too could lie in wait for food.

It was already four in the afternoon, and they had still had nothing to eat on this lovely sunny Thursday, when to their great joy they suddenly caught sight of Delaherche. A few of the better-off people in Sedan were managing with much trouble to get an authorization to go and see prisoners and take food to them, and more than once already Maurice had expressed his surprise at having no news of his sister. As soon as they recognized Delaherche a long way off, carrying a basket and with a loaf of bread under each arm, they made a rush, but even then they reached him too late, for there had been such an immediate pushing and shoving that the basket and one of the loaves had stayed in the scrum, been wafted away, done the vanishing trick. And Delaherche hadn't even noticed.

'Oh my poor friends,' he stammered, dumbfounded, deflated, having come with a smile on his lips and the jolly man-to-man tone he adopted in his desire for popularity.

Jean had seized the last loaf and was defending it, and while Maurice and he sat at the roadside and devoured it in great mouthfuls Delaherche told them the news. His wife, thank God, was very well. He was a bit worried about the colonel, who had fallen into a state of great exhaustion, although Madame Delaherche sat with him from morning till night.

'What about my sister?' asked Maurice.

'Oh yes, of course, your sister ... She came with me and she carried the two loaves. But she had to stay there on the other side of the canal. The guards would never agree to let her pass ... You know the Prussians have absolutely prohibited women from coming into the peninsula.'

Then he told them about Henriette and her vain efforts to see her brother and help him. By chance she had come face to face with cousin Gunther in Sedan – he was a captain in the Prussian Guard. He was going past with his stiff, hard look, pretending not to see her. And she herself, feeling sick as though he were one of her husband's murderers, had at first quickened her step. But then, in a sudden reversal of mood that she did not understand herself, she had gone back and told him everything about Weiss's death in a harsh, reproachful voice. On hearing about this horrible death of a relation of his he had simply made a gesture: it was the fortune of war and he might just as well have been killed himself. Hardly any change of expression had shown on his soldier's face. Then, when she had mentioned her brother, now a prisoner, and begged him to use his influence so that she could see him, he had refused to take any step. Orders were explicit, and he spoke of the will of Germany as of a religion. On leaving him she had had the distinct impression that he thought he was in France as a righteous judge, with the intolerance and arrogance of the hereditary enemy brought up in hatred of the race he was chastising.

'Anyway,' Delaherche concluded, 'you will have had something to eat tonight, and I am very sorry, but I'm afraid I can't get another permit.'

He asked if they had any errands he could do, and kindly took pencilled letters that other soldiers entrusted to him, for Bavarians had been seen laughing as they lit their pipes with letters they had promised to send off.

As Maurice and Jean were walking with him to the bridge Delaherche exclaimed:

'Look! There she is, Henriette!... You can see her waving her handkerchief.'

Beyond the line of sentries, in the crowd, they did make out a little, slim figure and a white point moving in the sun. They were both deeply moved and had tears in their eyes as they raised their arms and answered her with frantic waving.

The next day, Friday, was the most terrible of all for Maurice. And yet, after another quiet night in the little copse, he had had the good luck to eat some bread again, for Jean had discovered a woman in the Château de Villette who sold some at ten francs a pound. But that day they witnessed a gruesome scene which haunted them long afterwards like a nightmare.

On the previous day Chouteau had noticed that Pache had given up grumbling and looked dreamy and contented like a man who has eaten his fill. This at once suggested to him that the artful dodger must have a secret hoard somewhere, especially as that morning he had noticed that he went off for about an hour and then reappeared with a furtive smile and his mouth full. Surely he had had some stroke of luck and got hold of some food in one of the scrimmages. So Chouteau worked Loubet and Lapoulle up, especially the latter. Well, of all the filthy shits, to have something to eat and not share it out with his mates!

'Tell you what, we'll follow him tonight. We'll see if he dares to stuff his guts all on his own when other poor sods are dying of hunger all round him.'

'Yes, yes, you're right, we'll follow him,' Lapoulle echoed furiously. 'Then we shall see!'

His fists were clenched, and the mere hope of having something to eat at last was turning him into a madman. His huge appetite tormented him more than the others, and it was such a torture that he had tried to chew grass. Since the night before last, when the horsemeat and beetroot had given him such awful dysentery, he had had nothing at all, for his great body was so clumsy although it was so strong that he never got hold of anything in any scrum for food. He would have given his life-blood for a pound of bread.

As night was falling Pache slipped away among the trees of La Tour à Glaire and the three others stealthily followed.

'He mustn't suspect,' whispered Chouteau. 'Be careful in case he turns round.'

But some hundred paces further on Pache obviously thought he was alone, for he began walking fast without even bothering to look back. They had no trouble in following him as far as the quarries and were at his heels as he was moving two large stones and getting half a loaf out from underneath. It was the end of his provisions, still enough for one meal.

'You fucking fraud!' bawled Lapoulle. 'So that's why you hide! Give me that, it's my share.'

Give up his bread, why should he? Little shrimp he might be, but anger stiffened him up, and he hugged the bread to his bosom with all his strength. He was hungry too.

'Piss off, do you hear! It's mine!'

As Lapoulle raised his fist he took to his heels and ran down from the quarry to the open land towards Donchery. The three others gave chase at full speed, breathing hard. But he was leaving them behind, for he was lighter in build and so frightened and so determined to keep what was his own that he seemed to be borne by the wind. He had covered nearly a kilometre and was nearing the little copse by the river when he ran into Jean and Maurice, who were coming back to their place for the night. As he went by he shouted for help, but they were so astonished by this man-hunt galloping past them that they remained rooted at the edge of a field. And so they saw it all.

As ill-luck would have it Pache tripped over a stone and went down. Already the three others had caught up, swearing, yelling and worked up by the chase, like a pack of wolves let loose on their prey.

'Give us that, fuck you,' shouted Lapoulle, 'or I'll do you in.'

He was raising his fist again when Chouteau handed him the knife, ready open, with which he had bled the horse.

'Here you are, here's the knife!'

Jean rushed forward to stop a murder, and he lost his head, too, and talked of turning them all in, which brought on him a nasty sneer from Loubet, who called him a Prussian because there were no higher ranks any more, and the Prussians were the only ones who issued orders.

'For Christ's sake,' roared Lapoulle, 'are you going to give it me?'

In spite of the terror that had drained the colour from his face Pache held the bread to his chest tighter still, with the obstinacy of a hungry peasant who won't give up anything that is his.

'No!'

Then it was all over, the brute thrust the knife into his throat so violently that the poor devil did not even make a sound. His arms slackened, the bit of bread fell to the ground into the blood that had spurted out.

In the face of this stupid, insane murder Maurice, who had not moved until then, seemed to go suddenly out of his mind as well. He threatened the three men with his fists and called them murderers with such vehemence that his whole body was shaking. But Lapoulle did not seem even to hear. He stayed on the ground, crouching by the body, devouring the bread, red splashes of blood and all, with a wild, brutish look as though besotted by the noise of his own jaws, while Chouteau and Loubet, seeing how terrible he was as he appeased his hunger, did not even dare to ask for their shares.

The real night had come, but it was a bright night with a beautiful starlit sky, and Maurice and Jean, who had come back to their copse, could now only see Lapoulle prowling to and fro along the Meuse. The two others had gone, no doubt back to the canal towpath, worried about the body they had left behind. But Lapoulle seemed afraid to go back there and rejoin his mates. Clearly what with the shock of the murder and the heavy discomfort after bolting the big hunk of bread too fast, he was overcome with uneasiness, and that kept him on the move but he did not dare to go back along the path blocked by the corpse, hesitating, unable to make up his mind. Was it remorse awakening in his muddled soul, or merely fear of being discovered? So he roamed up and down like an animal behind the bars of its cage, with a sudden, growing urge to run away, an urge that hurt like a physical pain which he felt would kill him if he did not satisfy it. He must run, run at once and get away from this prison in which he had killed a man. But he threw himself down and for a long time he stayed there cowering in the grass on the river bank.

Maurice too was in a restless state and said to Jean:

'Look, I can't stand it here any longer. I tell you I shall go mad ... I'm surprised how my body has stood up to it. I feel pretty fit, but my mind is going, yes it is, I'm sure. If you keep me one more day in this hell I'm done for ... Please, I beg of you, let's get out, and at once!'

He began to develop extravagant plans for escape. They would swim across the Meuse, throw themselves upon the sentries and strangle them with a bit of string he had in his pocket, or again knock them out with bits of rock, or again buy them over with money, put on their uniforms and go through the Prussian lines.

'Stop it, chum,' said Jean, very worried. 'It frightens me when you talk such rubbish. Is any of that sensible, is it possible? We'll see tomorrow, chuck it.'

Although he too felt sick with anger and disgust, he hung on to his good sense even though weakened by hunger and in the midst of the nightmares of this existence that was reaching the rock-bottom of human suffering. And as his friend got more hysterical and wanted to dive into the Meuse, he had to hold him back and even rough-handle him, though his eyes were full of tears as he pleaded and scolded. But then suddenly:

'Oh, look!'

They had heard a splash, and then they saw Lapoulle, who had made up his mind to drop into the river, having thrown off his cape so as to be freer in his movements, and his shirt was clearly visible as a light patch moving on the dark current. He began to swim and slowly went upstream, no doubt looking for a suitable place to land, but on the opposite bank the slender outlines of the motionless sentries could clearly be seen. A sudden flash tore through the darkness and the sound of a shot echoed as far as the rocks of Montimont. The water merely swirled as though a pair of oars were badly churning it up. That was all, and Lapoulle's body, the white patch, was left to float gently downstream.

The next day, Saturday, at dawn, Jean took Maurice back to the camp of the 106th with the fresh hope that they would leave that day. But there were no orders, and it looked as though their regiment had been forgotten. Many had gone and the peninsula was emptying, and those left behind were falling into black depression. For eight long days minds had been getting more and more unhinged in this hell. The rain had stopped, but the pitiless glaring sun had only changed the kind of torture. The heat wave put the finishing touch to the men's exhaustion and bade fair to turn the cases of dysentery into an alarming epidemic. The dung and urine of all this army of sick men filled the air with the vilest stenches. It was now impossible to walk along the Meuse or the canal, so overpowering was the stink of drowned horses and men rotting among the reeds. In the fields the horses that had died of starvation were now decomposing, and the pestilential smell was so violent that the Prussians, who were beginning to be afraid for themselves as well, had brought some picks and shovels and were forcing the prisoners to bury the bodies.

And yet that Saturday saw the end of the famine. As they were fewer and provisions were coming in from all directions, they went abruptly from extreme deprivation to the most generous abundance. They had as much bread, meat and even wine as they wanted, and ate from morn till night enough to kill themselves. Night came and they were still eating, and went on until the next morning. Many died of it.

All day long Jean had been wholly taken up with watching Maurice who, he felt, was capable of any folly. He had been drinking and was talking of clouting a German officer so as to be taken away. And in the evening, having discovered a free corner in a cellar in the outbuildings of La Tour à Glaire, Jean thought it might be wise to go and sleep there with his friend who might be calmed down by a good night's rest. But it was the most terrible night of their stay, a night of sheer horror during which they never closed their eyes. The cellar was full of other soldiers, and two of them were lying in the same corner as them, dying of dysentery which had drained their bodies. As soon as it was quite dark they kept up a continuous inarticulate moaning, with disjointed cries that became a death-struggle of increasing intensity. In the pitch darkness this death-rattle was so horrible that the other men lying near-by who wanted to get to sleep lost their tempers and shouted to the dying men to shut up. They did not hear, and the death-rattle went on, swelled up and drowned everything else, while from the outside came the drunken bawlings of comrades who were still gorging, still not getting enough.

Then a time of distress set in for Maurice. He had tried to get away from this dreadful painful moaning which brought him out into a cold sweat of anguish, but as he was feeling his way on to his feet he had trodden on somebody's limbs and fallen down again, hemmed in with these dying men. After that he did not even try to escape. The whole awful disaster came back to him from the time of leaving Rheims to the crushing blow at Sedan. It seemed to him that the agony of the army of Châlons was only now coming to its end in the inky blackness of that cellar where two soldiers were gasping out their lives and preventing their mates from sleeping. The army of despair, the herd of sacrificial victims sent as a burnt offering, had paid for the sins of all with the red streams of its blood at each of the stations of its *Via Crucis*. And now, slain without glory, spat upon, it was going down to martyrdom under this chastisement whose harshness it had not deserved. It was too much, and it filled him with wrath and made him hunger for justice, with a burning passion to be revenged on destiny.

When dawn came one of the soldiers was dead and the other still gasping.

'Come on, boy, let's clear out of here,' said Jean gently. 'We'll get some fresh air, it'll be better.'

But when they got outside, on this beautiful and already warm morning, and had gone along the river until they were near the village of Iges, Maurice became even more worked up, and shook his fist at the great sunny horizon of the battlefield, the Illy plateau straight opposite, Saint-Menges to the left and the Garenne wood to the right.

'No, no, I can't, I simply can't look at that any more. It's having that in front of me that turns me over inside and splits my head open. Take me away! Take me away, now!'

It was another Sunday, and peals of bells came from Sedan, and already a German band could be heard in the distance. But still there were no orders for the 106th and Jean, alarmed at Maurice's increasingly hysterical condition, made up his mind to try a trick he had been meditating since the day before. In the road, in front of the Prussian post, a party was being assembled for leaving, that of another regiment, the 5th infantry. There was considerable confusion in the ranks, and an officer whose French was not much good was having trouble with checking. So both of them, having first pulled the collar band and buttons off their tunics so as not to be given away by the number, slipped into the middle of the crowd, crossed the bridge and found themselves outside. Evidently the same idea had occurred to Chouteau and Loubet, for they saw them behind, with their furtive, murderers' eyes.

Oh what a relief that first happy minute was! In the outer world it seemed like a resurrection, with dancing light, unlimited air, all their hopes flowering anew. Whatever troubles they might have to face now, their fears had gone and they even laughed at them as they made their way out of the nightmare of the Camp of Hell.

3

THAT morning Jean and Maurice heard the gay sound of French bugles for the last time, and now they were marching along the road to Germany in the herd of prisoners, preceded and followed by detachments of Prussian soldiers while others guarded them on either side with fixed bayonets. Now all they heard at each post was German trumpets with their brassy, dreary sound.

Maurice was glad to see that the column was turning left and going through Sedan. Perhaps he would be lucky enough to catch one more glimpse of his sister Henriette. But the five kilometres between the Iges peninsula and the town were enough to take the edge off his joy at feeling himself out of the sink of filth in which he had suffered nine days of torment. But this pathetic convoy of prisoners was a new kind of torture, with these weaponless men dangling their useless hands, being driven like sheep with hurried and frightened steps. Dressed in rags, filthy from having been left in their own excrement, emaciated after fasting for over a week, they looked like nothing but a lot of vagrants and suspicious characters that the police had roped in from the streets. From Torcy onwards, as men stood still and women came to the doors to stare at them with sullen sympathy, Maurice was overcome with shame and looked down at the ground, a bitter taste in his mouth.

Jean, more down-to-earth and more thick-skinned, was only concerned with their silliness in not having brought away a loaf each. In the sudden scurry of their departure they had even left without eating anything, and now once again hunger was tiring them out. Other prisoners must have been in the same state, for many were holding out money and begging to be sold something. One very tall man in particular, who looked terribly ill, was waving a gold coin with his long arm over the heads of the escorting soldiers, and despairing of finding anything to buy. Then it was that Jean, who was certainly on the look-out, spotted in the distance a pile of a dozen loaves in front of a baker's shop. Quickly, before the others, he threw down five francs and tried to pick up two of the loaves. Then as the Prussian near him brutally shoved him back, he insisted on trying at any rate to recover his money. But already the captain in charge of the column was running up. He was a bald-headed little man with an arrogant face, and he threatened Jean with the butt of his revolver and swore he would crack open the skull of the first man who dared to move. They all lowered their heads and looked down, and the march continued with the thud of feet and the resentful submissiveness of a herd of animals.

'Oh to give that one a clout!' Maurice muttered furiously. 'A good back-hander and ram his teeth in!'

After that he couldn't bear the sight of this captain, with his supercilious face that cried out to be hit. Now that they were entering Sedan proper over the Meuse bridge, the scenes of brutality recurred, and there were more of them. A woman, probably a mother, wanted to kiss a young sergeant and was pushed away so violently with a rifle-butt that she fell on the ground. On the Place Turenne the townspeople were rough-handled because they threw food to the prisoners. In the Grande-Rue one of the prisoners slipped down as he was taking a bottle a lady gave him, and was kicked to his feet again. For a whole week now Sedan had been witnessing this human livestock from the defeat being driven along with sticks, but could not get used to it, and with each new lot was moved by a sullen fever of pity and revolt.

Jean was thinking of Henriette too, and then he suddenly thought of Delaherche. He nudged his friend.

'I say, keep your eyes open in a minute if we go along that street!'

And indeed, as soon as they entered rue Maqua, they caught sight of several heads hanging out of one of the enormous windows of the mill. Then they recognized Delaherche and his wife Gilberte leaning out, with the tall, austere figure of Madame Delaherche standing behind them. They had some loaves of bread and he was throwing them down to the hungry men holding out shaky, imploring hands.

Maurice at once saw that his sister was not there, but Jean was worried at the speed with which the loaves were flying, and afraid there would be none left for them. He waved his arms and yelled:

'Save some for us! Save some for us!'

It was almost a happy surprise for the Delaherches. Their sombre, compassionate faces lit up and they could not restrain gestures of joy at the meeting. Gilberte insisted on throwing the last loaf into Jean's arms, which she did with such charming clumsiness that she burst into a peal of pretty laughter.

Not being able to stop, Maurice turned round backwards and as he went along shouted an anxious question:

'What about Henriette? Henriette?'

Delaherche answered with a long sentence, but his voice was lost in the tramp of feet. He must have realized that the young man had not caught what he said, for he made many signs, and repeated one especially, southwards. But already the column was entering rue du Ménil, and the façade of the factory, with the three heads leaning out, disappeared, but a hand still waved a handkerchief.

'What did he say?' asked Jean.

Maurice was very upset and still vainly looking back.

'I don't know, I didn't understand . . . Now I shall be worried so long as I don't get any news.'

The tramp went on, with the Prussians hurrying them up with the arrogance of conquerors, and the herd left Sedan by the Ménil gate, in a thin line, scampering along as though it was being worried by the hounds.

When they went through Bazeilles Jean and Maurice thought of Weiss and looked for the ashes of the little house that had been so valiantly defended. At the Camp of Hell they had been told about the devastation of the village, the fires and the massacres, but what they saw was worse than their most horrible dreams. After twelve days the heaps of ruins were still smoking. Tottering walls had fallen and not ten houses were left intact. They did find some consolation in the numbers of barrows and carts they saw full of Bavarian helmets and rifles picked up after the battle. This proof that they had killed a lot of these murderers and fire-raisers was some comfort.

The halt for lunch was to be at Douzy. They did not reach there without considerable suffering because the prisoners tired very quickly in their half-starved condition. Even the ones who had blown themselves out with food the day before were giddy, liverish and tired; for, far from restoring their lost strength, this gluttony had weakened them still more. And so when they stopped in a meadow to the left of the village the poor devils dropped on the grass, too dispirited to eat. There was no wine, and kind women who had tried to come with bottles were chased away by the guards. One of them fell and twisted her ankle, and there were cries and tears and a harrowing scene while the Prussians, who had confiscated the bottles, drank them. This pity and kindness of the countryfolk towards the wretched soldiers who were being taken away into captivity was manifest at every step, but it was said that they treated the generals with surly rudeness. Here in Douzy only a day or two earlier the inhabitants had booed a party of generals going on parole to Pont-à-Mousson. The highways were not safe for officers – men in overalls, escaped soldiers, possibly deserters, went for them with pitchforks and tried to kill them as if they were cowards and traitors, and this legend of the betrayal was still, twenty years later, to condemn all officers who had worn epaulettes to the execration of this part of the country.

Maurice and Jean ate half their loaf, which they were lucky enough to wash down with a sip or two of the brandy with which a friendly farmer had managed to fill their bottle. But the terrible thing was to set off again. They were to sleep at Mouzon, and although it was a short lap the effort involved seemed too dreadful. Men couldn't get up without crying out because the shortest rest made their weary limbs go so stiff. Many had bleeding feet and took off their boots so as to go on walking. They were still ravaged by dysentery, and one fell out after the first kilometre and had to be left propped against a bank. Two others collapsed by a hedge a little further on, and were only picked up that evening by an old woman. Everybody was staggering and using sticks which the Prussians had let them cut at the edge of a wood – in derision, no doubt. They were now a mere rabble of tramps, covered with sores, emaciated and gasping for breath. And the brutalities went on, men who fell out, even for a call of nature, being chased back with blows. The escort platoon bringing up the rear had orders to hurry along any laggards by sticking a bayonet up their behinds. A sergeant refused to go any further, and the captain made two men seize him under the arms and drag him along until he decided to walk again. That was the worst torment of all, the face you wanted to hit, the little bald-headed officer who took advantage of his good French to insult the prisoners in their own language in biting, lashing phrases like strokes with a whip.

'Oh!' Maurice raged again. 'Oh to get hold of that man and let out all his blood, drop by drop!'

He was at the end of his tether and more sick with anger than with fatigue. Everything was getting him down, even the harsh blarings of the Prussian trumpets, which so upset him physically that he could have howled like a wild beast. He would never reach the end of this cruel journey without getting himself murdered. Already as they went through the tiniest hamlets he suffered agonies as he saw women looking at him with pity. What would it be like when they got into Germany and the people in the towns would jostle each other in their desire to greet him with jeering laughter? He conjured up visions of the cattle-trucks into which they would be herded, the disgusting conditions and tortures of the journey and the miserable existence in fortresses under a wintry, snow-laden sky. No, no, rather death straight away, better to risk leaving one's body there at the corner of some road on French soil than rot over there in some black hole in a fortress, perhaps for months!

'Look here,' he whispered to Jean who was walking at his side, 'we'll wait until we're going past some wood and then jump into the trees. The Belgian frontier isn't far away, and we are sure to find someone to take us there.'

Jean, whose mind was cooler and clearer, recoiled at the idea in spite of the feeling of revolt that was making him, too, think about escape.

'Are you crazy? They'll shoot us, and there we'll both stay.'

But Maurice pointed out that there was a chance of the bullets going wide, and after all, if they were shot, well, that would be that!

'All right,' Jean went on, 'but what would happen to us then, in our uniforms? You can see perfectly well that the whole place is full of Prussian outposts. At any rate we should have to have different clothes ... It's too dangerous, lad, and I'll never let you do anything so barmy.'

He had to hold him back, take a grip of his arm and keep it close to him as though they were holding each other up, while he went on calming him down in his rough and ready but affectionate way.

Some whispering behind their backs just then made them look round. It was Chouteau and Loubet, who had got away from Iges that morning at the same time as themselves, and whom so far they had avoided. Now these two gentry were treading on their heels. Chouteau must have overheard Maurice's words, with his plan to escape through a wood, for he took it up himself and murmured into their ears:

'Look here, we're in on this. It's a grand idea to fuck off. Some of the blokes have got away already, and we're certainly not going to let ourselves be dragged like a lot of dogs to the country of those bastards ... So what about it for the four of us – O.K. to go for a stroll and take the air?'

Maurice was getting excited again, and Jean had to turn round and say to the tempter:

'If you're in a hurry, run along ... What hopes do you think you've got?'

Chouteau was a bit put out by the straight look Jean gave him. He let out the real reason for his insistence.

'Well, if there were four of us it would be easier . . . Then one or two would be sure to get away.'

So with a firm shake of the head Jean turned it down altogether. He didn't trust that gentleman, as he always said, and was afraid of some dirty trick. He had to use all his authority over Maurice to stop him from giving in because there was an obvious chance just then as they were passing a very dense wood, with only one field full of gorse between it and the road. Did not salvation consist in running across that field and disappearing in the thicket?

So far Loubet had said nothing. His twitching nose was testing the wind, his keen, artful eyes were watching out for the right moment, in his clear determination not to go and moulder in Germany. He would have to trust to his legs and his cunning, which had always got him out of scrapes. He suddenly made up his mind.

'Fuck it, I've had enough! I'm off!'

He leaped with one bound into the field and Chouteau imitated him, running at his side. Two of the escorting Prussians at once gave chase, but neither thought of stopping them with a bullet. The scene was so brief that they hardly took it in. Loubet, zigzagging through the gorse, was certainly going to get away, but Chouteau, who was not so agile, was already on the point of being recaptured when, with a supreme effort, he dived between his companion's legs and brought him down; and while the two Prussians rushed to hold that man on the ground Chouteau darted into the wood and disappeared. A few shots went off when they remembered their rifles. There was even a half-hearted beat through the trees, though to no purpose.

But the two soldiers went for Loubet on the ground. The captain rushed over in a furious temper, talking of making an example, and with this encouragement kicks and blows with rifle-butts continued to rain down until, by the time the poor creature was picked up, he had one arm broken and his head split open. Before they reached Mouzon he died in a little cart in which some peasant had agreed to take him.

'You see what I mean,' was all Jean murmured in Maurice's ear.

The look they both cast at the impenetrable wood expressed their loathing of the criminal now running away in freedom, while in the end they felt full of pity for his victim, poor devil, who was a slippery customer and not much cop to be sure, but all the same a lively chap, resourceful and no fool. So however clever you were you got your packet sometime!

At Mouzon, in spite of this terrible object-lesson, Maurice was once again plagued by his obsession to escape. They were now in such a state of weariness that the Prussians had to help their prisoners to put up the few tents available. The camp site was in a low-lying and marshy position near the town, and the worst of it was that as another party had camped there the day before the ground was almost covered with excrement – it was a real cesspool, disgustingly filthy. They had to keep themselves out of it by putting on the ground some big flat stones which fortunately they discovered not far away. But the evening was not so bad, as the Prussians relaxed their discipline a little now that the captain had disappeared, presumably to some inn. First of all the sentries did not object when some children threw the prisoners some fruit, apples and pears, over their heads. Then they allowed people from round about to come into the camp, and soon there was a crowd of impromptu dealers, men and women, selling bread, wine and even cigars. Everyone who had any money was eating, drinking and smoking. In the fading evening light it looked like the corner of a fair, busy and noisy.

But behind their tent Maurice was getting worked up again, and saying over and over again to Jean:

'I can't stand any more, I'm off as soon as it's dark . . . Tomorrow we shall get further away from the frontier and it will be too late.'

'All right, let's go,' Jean said, for his own resistance was wearing down and he, too, was giving in to this mania for escape. 'We shall soon know if it costs us our lives.'

But he did begin to examine the people selling their wares round about. Some of the men had got hold of working smocks and trousers, and it was rumoured that kindly disposed people had set up real depots of clothing to help prisoners to escape. And then almost at once his attention was caught by a pretty girl, tall and fair, with lovely eyes, who looked about sixteen, and who was holding a basket with three loaves in it. She was not crying her wares like the others, and had an attractive but self-conscious smile and was walking nervously. He looked hard at her and their eyes met and held each other's for a moment. Then she came over with the diffident smile of a pretty girl asking if she could help.

'Do you want some bread?'

He did not answer, but made a little questioning sign. When she nodded he ventured to whisper very softly:

'Got any clothes?'

'Yes, under the bread.'

Then she made up her mind to cry her wares very loud: 'Bread! Bread! Who wants to buy bread?' But when Maurice tried to slip her twenty francs she quickly drew back her hand and ran off, leaving the basket behind. But they saw her look back and give them an affectionate and deeply concerned smile with her beautiful eyes.

Now that the basket was theirs Jean and Maurice found themselves in a terrible fix, for they had wandered a long way from their tent and simply could not find it, so flustered were they. Where could they go and how could they change clothes? They felt that everybody's eyes could peer into this basket that Jean was carrying so awkwardly, and see what was inside it. So they made up their minds and went into the first empty tent they could find, and there each frantically slipped on a pair of trousers and a smock, and hid their uniform things under the bread. They abandoned the lot. But they had only found one woollen cap, which Jean forced Maurice to put on. He thought being bareheaded far more dangerous than it really was, and gave himself up for lost. While he was hanging about looking for something to put on his head it occured to him to buy the hat of a scruffy old man selling cigars.

'Three sous each, two for five, Brussels cigars!'

Since the battle of Sedan the customs regulations had broken down, and all the Belgian riff-raff came in freely. The old man in rags had been making a very handsome profit, but that did not prevent his haggling for large sums when he understood why they wanted to buy his hat, a greasy felt one with a hole right through. He only parted with it for two five-franc pieces, moaning that he was sure he would catch a cold.

Jean, moreover, had thought up something else, which was to buy his stock from him as well, the three dozen cigars he was still hawking round. And so, with no more ado, he pulled the hat down over his eyes and called out in a sing-song voice:

'Three sous for two, three sous for two, Brussels cigars!'

This time it was deliverance. He made signs for Maurice to go on ahead. Maurice had had the good fortune to pick up an umbrella, and as it was spitting with rain he calmly put it up to go through the line of pickets.

'Three sous for two, three sous for two, Brussels cigars!'

In a few minutes Jean got rid of his wares. They hurried on, laughing: at any rate there was somebody who sold things cheap and didn't swindle poor people! Interested by the cheapness, some Prussians came up as well, and he had to have dealings with them. He had manoeuvred so as to pass through the enemy lines, and sold his last two cigars to a big bearded sergeant who couldn't speak a word of French.

'Not so fast, for God's sake!' Jean kept saying behind Maurice's back. 'You'll give us away!'

Yet despite themselves they quickened their pace. They had to make an immense effort to stop for a moment at the corner of two roads among groups of people standing about in front of a pub. Townsfolk were chatting away with German soldiers, looking quite unconcerned. They pretended to listen, and even risked throwing in a word or two about the rain which might start again and go on all night. One man, a stoutish party, kept his eye on them all the time and made them tremble. But as he smiled very kindly they risked it, and whispered:

'Sir, is the road to Belgium guarded?'

'Yes, but go through this wood first, and then turn left across the fields.'

In the wood, in the great dark stillness of the trees, when they could not hear a sound and nothing stirred and they thought they were secure, an extraordinary emotion made them fall into each other's arms. Maurice was crying like a child, and tears rolled slowly down Jean's cheeks. It was the reaction after their long torment, the joy of telling themselves that suffering might perhaps take pity on them at last. They hugged each other in a passionate embrace, made brothers by all they had gone through together, and the kiss they exchanged seemed the gentlest yet the strongest in their lives, a kiss the like of which they would never have from a woman, undying friendship and absolute certainty that their two hearts were henceforth one for ever.

'My dear boy,' Jean said in a shaky voice when they had let each other go, 'it's already a great deal to be here, but we're not through yet . . . We ought to take our bearings.'

Although he did not know this bit of the frontier, Maurice swore it was all right to go straight ahead. So they very carefully slipped along, one after the other, until they came to the edge of the woods. Then, bearing in mind the directions given by the helpful man, they wanted to turn left and cut across the fields. But as they came to a road lined with poplars they saw the fires of a Prussian post barring the way. The light gleamed on a sentry's bayonet, and the soldiers were talking while finishing their supper. So they went back on their tracks and buried themselves in the woods in terror of being pursued. They thought they could hear voices and footsteps, and beat about in the bushes for nearly an hour, losing all sense of direction, turning round in circles, sometimes tearing off at a gallop like animals fleeing through the undergrowth and sometimes standing quite still, sweating with nerves, faced by motionless oaks they took for Prussians. Finally they came out again on to the poplar-lined road ten paces from the sentry and near the soldiers who were peacefully having a warm.

'Our luck's out!' muttered Maurice. 'This wood's bewitched!'

This time they had been heard. Branches had been snapped and stones dislodged. As, challenged by the sentry, they began to run without answering, the whole post took up arms and shots were fired which whistled through the thicket.

'Oh Christ!' Jean swore under his breath, stifling a cry of pain.

He had felt a whiplash on his left calf, and it was so violent that it made him fall against a tree.

'Got you?' Maurice anxiously asked.

'Yes, in the leg. I'm done for!'

They were still listening, panting with fear of hearing the Prussians in full chase behind them. But the shooting had stopped and nothing was stirring again in the great eerie silence. Clearly the post was not anxious to get involved among the trees.

Jean tried to stand up and stifled a groan. Maurice held him up.

'Can't you walk any more?'

'Afraid not.'

Normally so placid he began to fly into a rage. He clenched his fists and could have hit himself.

'Oh Lor, oh Lor! Of all the bloody bad luck! To go and get your leg mucked up just when you've got to run! ... Really it's enough to make you go and chuck yourself in the shit! You go on alone.'

Maurice laughed gaily and just said:

'Bloody fool!'

He took his arm and helped him along, for they both were anxious to get away from there. After a few painful steps done with a heroic effort, they stopped and were again disturbed as they saw a house in front of them, a kind of little farmhouse on the edge of the wood. There was no light in the windows but the gate into the yard was wide open, showing the building black and empty. When they plucked up enough courage to venture into this farmyard they were astonished to find a horse, all saddled ready, with nothing to show the why and the wherefore of its being there. Perhaps the owner was coming back, perhaps he was lying behind some bush with a bullet through his head. They never knew.

Maurice had a sudden idea which seemed to make him quite jolly.

'Look here, the frontier is too far away, and besides, we should certainly have to have a guide. But suppose we were to make for Uncle Fouchard's at Remilly. I could really take you there with my eyes shut, for I know even the little by-roads inside out ... Isn't that an idea? I'm going to lift you up on to this horse, and Uncle Fouchard is sure to take us in.'

First he wanted to have a look at the leg. There were two holes, the bullet must have come out again after breaking the tibia. There was very little bleeding, and he simply bandaged the calf tightly with a handkerchief.

'You go on your own,' Jean said again.

'Shut up, don't be a fool!'

When Jean had been comfortably settled in the saddle Maurice took the horse's reins and they set off. It must have been about eleven, and he reckoned he could do the journey easily in three hours, even if they only went at a walking pace. But for a moment he was dashed when he thought of an unforeseen difficulty: how were they going to cross the Meuse and get over to the left bank? The bridge at Mouzon was guarded for certain. But then he remembered that there was a ferry downstream at Villers, and so he made his way to this village more or less by dead reckoning across the fields and ploughed land on the right bank, hoping luck would be on their side. Everything went pretty well at first, and they only had one patrol of cavalry to avoid, and that they did by staying quite still for nearly a quarter of an hour in the shadow of a wall. Rain was falling again and walking became very trying for him as he was obliged to tramp in sodden earth beside the horse, which fortunately was a very good fellow of a horse and very docile. At Villers luck really was on their side, for the ferry at this late hour happened to have just brought over a Bavarian officer, and so could take them at once to the other side with no trouble. The dangers and fatigues only really began at the village, and they nearly stayed there for good in the hands of sentries stationed along the Remilly road. Once again they took to the fields, going where the little paths took them, narrow paths hardly used. The slightest obstacles forced them to make enormous detours. They crossed hedges and ditches and cut through impenetrable thickets. Jean, now feverish in the drizzling rain, was slumped over the saddle, half fainting and cling-ing with both hands to the horse's mane, while Maurice, with the reins over his right arm, had to hold on to his friend's legs to prevent him from slipping off. For nearly a league and two more hours this exhausting journey dragged on, with jolts, sudden slips and loss of balance which every minute almost threw over the horse and the two men. They were the most miserable little procession imaginable, mud-stained, the horse tottering, the mán he was carrying inert and looking as if he had breathed his last, and the other man wild-eyed and haggard, only kept going by brotherly love. Day was breaking, and it must have been about five when at last they reached Remilly.

In the yard of his little farm which overlooked the village as you emerged from the Haraucourt defile, old Fouchard was loading on to his cart two sheep killed the day before. The sight of his nephew in such a sorry set-up was such a shock to him that after the first words of explanation he brutally exclaimed:

'What, me keep you and your friend here? And get myself into trouble with the Prussians? Oh no, certainly not! I'd rather die straight away!'

Yet he dared not prevent Maurice and Prosper from getting Jean down from the horse and laying him on the big kitchen table. Silvine ran off and got her own bolster, which she slipped under the wounded man's head, for he was still unconscious. But the old boy, annoyed at seeing this man on his table, grumbled away, saying that he was very uncomfortable like that and why didn't they take him straight to the field hospital, as they were lucky enough to have one at Remilly, near the church, in the old schoolhouse which had once been a convent and in which there was a very convenient large hall.

'To the hospital!' It was Maurice's turn to object. 'For the Prussians to send him off to Germany when he's better, since every wounded man belongs to them! ... What do you take me for, uncle? I haven't brought him all the way here so as to give him up to them!'

Things were turning ugly and Uncle Fouchard was talking of turning them out when the name of Henriette was mentioned.

'Henriette! What's that?' asked Maurice.

He then learned that his sister had been at Remilly since the day before yesterday, being so mortally heartbroken by her loss that to live in Sedan, where she had been so happy, had become unthinkable. A chance meeting with Dr Dalichamp of Raucourt, whom she knew, had made her decide to come and live at Uncle Fouchard's in one little room and devote her whole time to the wounded in the neighbouring field hospital. It was the only thing, she said, that would take her mind off it all. She paid for her keep and as she contributed all sorts of comforts at the farmhouse the old man looked on her with a kindly eye. When there was something to be made out of it things were always lovely.

'Oh, so my sister's here! So that's what Monsieur Delaherche meant by the big gesture I couldn't understand! Oh well, if she's here it goes without saying, we stay!'

At once he insisted on going himself, tired as he was, to find her at the hospital, where she had been on duty all night, and his uncle fumed because now he could not get away with his cart and two sheep on his butcher's round through the villages until this dratted business of the wounded man who had landed on him was settled.

When Maurice brought back Henriette they caught old Fouchard carefully looking over the horse that Prosper had taken to the stable. A very tired animal, but jolly strong, and he liked the look of it! The young man laughed as he said he would make him a present of it. Henriette meanwhile took her uncle to one side and explained that Jean would pay, and that she would look after him in her little room behind the cowshed where certainly no Prussian would ever go and look for him. Old Fouchard, sulking and still unconvinced that there would be any real profit for him in all this, did eventually jump into his cart and go off, leaving her to do as she thought fit.

Then, with the help of Silvine and Prosper, Henriette only took a few minutes to rearrange her room and have Jean carried there, where he was put into a clean bed, but still he gave no sign of life beyond a few vague mutterings. He opened his eyes and looked round but did not appear to see anybody. Maurice was just finishing a glass of wine and a bit of meat and was suddenly overcome with fatigue, when Dr Dalichamp came, as he did every morning on his way to the hospital, and Maurice did just find the strength to go with him and his sister to the wounded man's bedside, in his anxiety to find out.

The doctor was a short man with a big round head fringed by greying hair and beard. His fresh face had gone leathery like those of the peasants, with his continual open-air life of journeys to alleviate suffering, and his keen eyes, inquisitive nose and kindly mouth spoke of the whole life of a good, charitable man, a bit off the target sometimes, and no medical genius, but long experience had made him an excellent healer.

Having examined the still semi-conscious Jean he murmured:

'I'm afraid there'll have to be an amputation.'

This was grievous news to Maurice and Henriette. But he did add:

'Perhaps it will be possible to save his leg, but it will need a great deal of care and it will be a very long job ... Just now his vitality and morale are in such a low state that the only thing to do is to let him sleep ... We'll see tomorrow.'

Having dressed the wound he turned his attention to Maurice, whom he had known as a child long ago.

'And you too, my boy, would be better in a bed than on that chair.'

The young man stared straight in front of him with unseeing eyes, as though he had not heard. In his utterly exhausted state his own feverishness was coming back in the form of abnormal nervous excitement due to all the accumulated sufferings and revulsions since the beginning of the campaign. The sight of his stricken

393

friend, the sense of his own defeat, naked, disarmed, good for nothing, the thought that so many heroic efforts had ended in such distress, all threw him into a frantic need to rebel against fate. Then at length he answered:

'No, no! It's not all over, no! I've got to go . . . No, as he has got to be here for weeks and perhaps months I can't stay, I must go at once. You will help me, won't you, doctor? You will give me the means to escape and get back to Paris.'

Terrified, Henriette threw her arms round him.

'What are you talking about? Weak as you are, after going through so much! I shall keep you here, I'll never let you go! Haven't you paid your debt? Think of me as well, you are leaving me alone and now I've nobody left but you.'

They wept together. They kissed each other desperately with that adoring love of twins, closer than normal love as if it dated from before birth. But he worked himself up more and more.

'But I tell you, I must go . . . They're waiting for me and I should die of distress if I didn't go. You can't imagine what a ferment goes on inside me at the thought of staying inactive. It can't end up like this, I tell you, we must have our revenge, but on whom, on what? I've no idea, but we must have our revenge for so much suffering, so as to find once again the courage to live!'

Dr Dalichamp, who was watching the scene with keen interest, made a sign to prevent Henriette from answering. When Maurice had had some sleep he would no doubt be calmer, and indeed he did sleep all that day and the following night, for more than twenty hours without moving a finger. Nevertheless, when he woke on the following morning, his resolve to go away was still there and unshakable. There was no more feverishness, but he was gloomy, restless and anxious to escape from all the temptations to a quiet life that he felt round him. His sister wept but realized that she must not insist. And Dr Dalichamp, when he came, promised to facilitate his flight, using the papers of an ambulance man who had died at Raucourt. Maurice would put on the grey shirt and red-cross armband and go through Belgium and thence back to Paris, which was still open.

He did not leave the farmhouse that day, but remained in hiding, waiting for night. He hardly opened his mouth, but he did try to take Prosper with him.

'Look, aren't you tempted to go back and see the Prussians again?'

The ex-Chasseur d'Afrique, who was finishing some bread and cheese, lifted his knife in the air.

'Well, from what we've seen of them it's not much use . . . Since the cavalry is no good for anything except to get killed after it's all over, what do you want me to go back for? Oh no, I've got so fed up with them never giving me anything worth doing!'

After a pause he went on, possibly to stifle the misgivings in his soldier's heart:

'Besides, there's too much work to do here. The big ploughing is coming soon, and then there will be the sowing. You've got to think of the land as well, haven't you? Because of course it's all very well to fight, but what would become of us all if we didn't plough the fields? . . . You see, I can't just leave the job. It isn't that old Fouchard is much good, for I very much doubt whether I shall ever see the colour of his money, but the animals are beginning to take to me, and really this morning when I was up there in the Vieux-Clos and looked down at that bloody old Sedan in the distance I felt jolly glad to be on my own again in the bright sunshine with my animals and pushing my plough!'

As soon as it was dark Dr Dalichamp was there with his trap. He proposed to drive Maurice himself as far as the frontier. Fouchard, glad to see the back of one at least, went down to keep an eye on the road to make sure that no patrol was about, while Silvine finished mending the ambulance man's old shirt and putting the red-cross armband on the sleeve. Before they left the doctor examined Jean's leg again and could not yet promise to save it. The wounded man was still in a state of complete somnolence, recognizing nobody and not speaking. Maurice was going to leave without saying good-bye, but when he bent down to give him a kiss he saw him open his eyes very wide, his lips moved and he said in a weak voice,

'You're off?'

And as they were all surprised:

'Yes, I heard you all but I couldn't move . . . Maurice, you take all the money. Look in my trouser pocket.'

There remained about two hundred francs each out of the money from the regimental cash, which they had shared.

'Money!' Maurice expostulated. 'But you need it more than I do, for I've got my two legs. With two hundred francs I've got enough to get me back to Paris, and to be killed after that won't cost me anything ... But we'll be seeing each other again, my dear Jean, and bless you for all the sensible and good things you've done, for without you I should certainly now be in some field like a dead dog.'

Jean stopped him with a gesture.

'You don't owe me anything, we're quits. I'm the one the Prussians would have picked up out there if you hadn't carried me on your back. And only yesterday again you got me out of their clutches. You've paid twice over and it should be my turn to give my life for you ... Oh I'm going to be miserable at not still being with you!'

His voice faltered and his eyes filled with tears.

'Kiss me, boy.'

They kissed each other, and as in the woods the day before there was in this kiss a brotherly love born of dangers shared, of these few weeks of heroic life in common which had united them more intimately than years of ordinary friendship could have done. Days without food, nights without sleep, exhaustion, ever-present death, all played a part in their affection. Can two hearts ever take themselves back again when a mutual gift has thus welded them to each other? But the kiss exchanged in the darkness among the trees had been full of the new hope opened up by escape, whereas this one now was full of the anguish of parting. Would they see each other again some day? And how, in what circumstances of grief or joy?

Dr Dalichamp was already in his trap and calling Maurice, who put all his soul into a final embrace with his sister Henriette. She looked at him through silent tears, very pale in her widow's black.

'I'm putting my brother in your care ... Look after him and love him as I do.'

4

IT was a big room with a tiled floor and plainly whitewashed, which had formerly been used for storing fruit. You could still smell the good smell of apples and pears, and the only furniture consisted of an iron bedstead, a whitewood table and two chairs and an old walnut chest with cavernous depths containing a whole world of things. But in this room there was a deep peaceful calm, the only sounds to be heard were faint noises from the cowshed nearby, a distant clatter of sabots or lowing of cattle. The sunshine came in through the window which faced south. All that could be seen was part of a hill-slope, a cornfield bordered by some woodland. This private, mysterious room was so well concealed from all eyes that nobody in the world could suspect it was there.

Henriette quickly settled the routine: it was understood that to avoid suspicion only she and the doctor would go in and see Jean. Silvine was never to go in unless she was asked to. First thing in the morning the two women tidied up, and then all day long the door might have been walled up. If the patient needed something in the night he would only have to knock on the wall, for Henriette's room was adjoining. And so, after weeks of living in a turbulent mob, Jean suddenly found himself cut off from the world, seeing nobody but this young woman who was so gentle that her light step made no sound. He saw her again just as he had seen her for the first time in Sedan, like a vision, with her rather wide mouth, small, neat features and beautiful hair the colour of ripe grain, looking after him with infinite kindness.

During the first days he had such a high temperature that Henriette hardly ever left him. Every morning on his rounds Dr Dalichamp looked in, on the pretext of taking her to the hospital, and he examined Jean and dressed his wound. As the bullet had come out again after breaking the tibia, he was surprised at the ugly look of the wound and was afraid that the presence of a splinter of bone, which he could not find with the probe, might necessitate a resection of the bone. He had discussed it with Jean, who was horrified at the thought of a short leg which would make him lame – no, no, he'd rather die than be permanently disabled! And so the doctor, keeping the wound under observation, simply went on dressing it with a pad soaked in olive oil and carbolic, after inserting a drain, a rubber tube to take away the pus. But the doctor had warned him that if he did not intervene it might take a very long time indeed to heal. But by the second week the temperature did go down and things improved so long as complete immobility was maintained.

And so Jean and Henriette settled down to a regular life together.

They fell into a routine and it seemed as though they had never lived any other way and would go on living like this. All the time she was not at the hospital she spent with him, seeing that he ate and drank regularly, helping him to turn over with a strength of wrist one would not have suspected in such slender arms. Sometimes they talked, but more often said nothing, especially in the early days. But they never seemed bored; it was a very peaceful life in this most restful atmosphere – for him, still shattered by the battle, and for her, in her mourning dress, still heartbroken after her recent loss. At first he felt a little awkward because he was aware that she was above him in station, almost a grand lady, while he had never been anything more than a peasant and soldier. He could only just about read and write. But later he felt somewhat reassured when he saw that she treated him without any pride, as an equal, and that gave him the courage to show that he was intelligent in his own way, through his sweet reasonableness. Moreover he himself was amazed to feel that he had become more refined, more agile in mind, with new ideas. Was it something to do with the abominable life he had been leading for two months? He had emerged more delicate-minded from so much physical and moral suffering. But what finally reassured him was that he realized that she did not know all that much more than he did. After the death of her mother she had become at a very early age the Cinderella, the little housewife looking after her three men, as she called them – her grandfather, father and brother – and she had not had time for study. Reading, writing, a bit of spelling and arithmetic was about as far as she could go. The only reason why she still intimidated him and seemed so far above all other women was that he knew that beneath her exterior of an unremarkable little person, occupied with the trivial affairs of daily life, was a woman of the greatest goodness and the utmost courage.

They were one immediately when they talked about Maurice. She was devoting herself to him in this way because he was the friend, the brother of Maurice, his great help in time of need, and it was her turn to pay a debt of the heart. She was full of gratitude and of an affection which grew as she got to know how upright and wise he was and how reliable. And he, whom she cared for like a child, was also contracting a debt of infinite gratitude and could have kissed her hands for every cup of broth she gave him. This bond of tender understanding grew closer every day in the deep solitude in which they lived and shared the same troubles. When they finished their memories – details she untiringly asked for about their painful march from Rheims to Sedan – the same question always came up: what was Maurice doing now? Why wasn't he writing? Was Paris completely cut off, that they heard no news? So far they had had only one letter from him, postmarked Rouen three days after his departure, in which he had explained in a few lines how he had found himself in that city after a big detour on the way to Paris. And then nothing for a week, absolute silence.

In the mornings Dr Dalichamp, having dressed the wound, liked to linger there for a few minutes. He even came back sometimes in the evening and stayed longer, and thus he was the only link with the world, the great world outside, so convulsed by disasters. News only reached them through him, and his ardent patriotic heart boiled over with anger and grief at every defeat. So he hardly talked about anything except the invading march of the Prussians who since Sedan had been flooding steadily all over France, like a black host. Each day brought its own grief, and he would stay there lost in misery, slumped on one of the two chairs beside the bed, and, waving his trembling hands, tell of an ever worsening situation. Often his pockets were stuffed with Belgian newspapers which he left behind. Thus, weeks after the event, the echo of each disaster reached this hidden room and drew still closer, in a common bond of anguish, the two poor suffering souls shut in there.

So it was that Henriette read to Jean from old papers the happenings at Metz and the great and heroic battles which had started up afresh three times, after a day's interval on each occasion. These battles had already happened five weeks ago, but he still knew nothing about them, and his heart ached when he heard of the same miseries and defeats there that he had suffered himself. In the tense silence of that room, as Henriette read in the slightly sing-song voice of a careful schoolgirl dividing the sentences properly, the lamentable tale unfolded itself. After Froeschwiller and Spickeren, at the very time when the vanquished 1st corps was carrying away the 5th in its rout, the other corps, echeloned out from Metz to Bitche, wavered and then fell back in the general consternation caused by these disasters, and finally concentrated in front of the fortified area on the right bank of the Moselle. But what valuable time lost, instead of speeding up the retreat on Paris that was to become so difficult later! The Emperor had had to hand over the command to Marshal Bazaine, from whom everybody expected victory. Then, on the 14th, Borny, where the army was attacked exactly when it was at last making up its mind to cross to the left bank, with two German armies against it, that of Steinmetz, standing immovable opposite the fortified camp as a threat, and that of Friedrich Karl, who had crossed the river higher upstream and was coming along the left bank to cut Bazaine off from the rest of France, Borny, the first shots of which were not fired until three in the afternoon, Borny, the victory with no morrow, which left the French corps masters of their positions but immobilized them, straddled across the Moselle, and which the turning movement of the second German army had completed. Then on the 16th, Rezonville, all the French army corps now at last on the left bank, with only the 3rd and 4th in the rear, delayed in the appalling traffic-jam at the crossing of the Etain and Mars-la-Tour roads, the daring attack by the Prussian cavalry and artillery, already cutting these roads in the morning, the slow and confused battle which, until two o'clock, Bazaine could have won as he only had to repulse a handful of men in front of him, but which in the end he lost owing to his inexplicable fear of being cut off from Metz. The immense struggle covered leagues of hills and plains in which the French, attacked in front and on the flank, had performed miracles so as not to advance, thereby leaving the enemy time to join up and themselves working for the Prussian plan, which was to make them turn back to the other side of the river. And finally on the 18th, after the return to the original position in front of the fortified area, came Saint-Privat, the supreme struggle over a front of thirteen kilometres, two hundred thousand Germans, with seven hundred guns against a hundred and twenty thousand French with only five hundred pieces of equipment, the Germans facing Germany, and the French France, as though the invaders had become the invaded, in this strange pivoting that had come about. From two o'clock onwards there was the most terrible *mêlée* in which the Prussian Guard was repulsed and cut to pieces and Bazaine was for a long time winning, strong in his unshakable left wing, until towards evening when his weaker right wing was compelled to evacuate Saint-Privat amid horrible carnage, involving with it the whole army, defeated, thrown back on Metz and from then onwards locked in a ring of iron.

Over and over again as Henriette was reading Jean broke in and said:

'Well, and all the way from Rheims we were expecting Bazaine!'

The dispatch from the marshal dated the 19th, after Saint-Privat, in which he talked of resuming his retreat via Montmédy, and which had determined the advance of the army of Châlons, now appeared to be nothing but the report of a beaten general anxious to tone down his defeat, and only later, on the 29th, when the news of the approach of a rescuing army reached him through the Prussian lines, had he tried one last effort at Noiseville on the right bank, but so half-heartedly that on 1 September, the very day on which the army of Châlons was crushed at Sedan, that of Metz fell back, definitely paralysed and dead as far as France was concerned. By neglecting to move while routes were still open and then being genuinely halted by superior forces, the marshal, who until then might have been an indifferent commander, but nothing worse, from now on, under the influence of his political calculations, was going to become a conspirator and a traitor.

But in the papers brought by Dr Dalichamp Bazaine was still the great man, the gallant soldier by whom France still expected to be saved. Jean made her re-read certain passages in order to grasp how the third German army, with the Crown Prince of Prussia, had been able to pursue them while the first and second were blocking Metz, both of them so strong in men and guns that it had been possible to take some from them and form this fourth army which, under the command of the Crown Prince of Saxony, had made the disaster of Sedan certain. When at last he understood, on this bed of pain to which his wound pinned him down, he forced himself to go on hoping.

'So that's it, we weren't the strongest! . . . Never mind, they give the figures, Bazaine has got a hundred and fifty thousand men, three hundred thousand rifles and more than five hundred guns, and I bet you he's got something good for them up his sleeve!'

Henriette nodded and agreed with his opinion so as not to depress him still more. She was all at sea in these vast troop movements, but she had a presentiment that disaster was inevitable. Her voice stayed clear and bright and she could have gone on reading for hours just for the happiness of interesting him. But sometimes in a report about slaughter her voice would falter and her eyes suddenly fill with tears. No doubt it reminded her of her husband shot out there and kicked against the wall by the Bavarian officer.

'If it upsets you too much,' said Jean in surprise, 'don't go on reading about battles.'

She recovered her gentle kindness at once.

'No, no, I'm sorry, it really gives me pleasure too.'

One evening at the beginning of October, while a gale was blowing outside, she returned from the hospital and came into the room in great excitement.

'A letter from Maurice! The doctor has just given it to me.'

Each morning they had both been increasingly worried because he was not showing any sign of life; and especially as for a good week now it had been rumoured that Paris was completely invested, they were giving up hope of getting any news and were anxiously wondering what could have happened to him since he left Rouen. Now there was an explanation of this silence, for the letter he had sent from Paris addressed to Dr Dalichamp on 18 September, the very day when the last trains left for Havre, had gone an enormous way round and only reached its destination by a miracle, having been mislaid a score of times on the way.

'Oh, good lad!' beamed Jean. 'Read it quick.'

The wind redoubled its fury, banging the window like a battering-ram. Henriette stood the lamp on the table by the bed and began to read, so close to Jean that their hair touched. It was so peaceful and happy in that quiet room with the storm roaring outside.

It was a long letter of eight pages in which Maurice first explained how as soon as he had arrived on the 16th he had been fortunate enough to get into a regiment of the line which was being brought up to strength. Then he went on to facts and wrote with extraordinary passion about what he had learned of the happenings of that terrible month – Paris coming back to normality after the painful shock of Wissembourg and Froeschwiller and once again relapsing into self-deception and entertaining hopes of a revenge, the legend of the victorious army, Bazaine in command, a mass rising against the foe, imaginary victories, huge slaughters of Prussians which even ministers reported in the Chamber. And then he went on to say how once again a bombshell had burst in Paris on 3 September, and hopes were dashed, and the city, confident in its ignorance, had been overwhelmed by the relentless blows of fate, so that cries of 'Out! Out!' were echoing by evening on the boulevards while in the short, doom-laden night sitting Jules Favre had read out the motion for the revolution demanded by the populace. Then the next day was 4 September, the collapse of a world, the Second Empire swept away in the wreckage of its vices and follies, all the people out in the streets, a torrent of half a million men pouring into the Place de la Concorde on that brilliant Sunday, billowing over to the railings of the Legislative Assembly defended by a mere handful of troops with rifle-butts in the air. Then the mob, smashing down doors, invaded the Chamber itself, from which Jules Favre, Gambetta and other deputies of the left were about to leave to proclaim the Republic at the Hôtel de Ville, while a little door of the Louvre, giving on to the Place Saint-Germain l'Auxerrois, was opened just enough to let out the Empress-Regent, dressed in black and accompanied by one woman friend, both trembling, fugitives keeping out of sight in a cab they had picked up and which jolted them away from the Tuileries through which the mob was now running. On that same day Napoleon III had left the inn at Bouillon where he had spent his first night in exile en route for Wilhelmshöhe.

In a serious voice Jean broke in:

'So now we have a republic? ... Oh well, all to the good if it helps us beat the Prussians.'

But he shook his head, for he had always been led to fear a republic when he worked on the land. And besides, in the face of the enemy he didn't think it was a good thing not to be all of one mind. Anyway there would have to be something else because the Empire was thoroughly corrupt, and nobody wanted any more truck with it.

Henriette finished reading the letter, which ended by mentioning the approach of the Germans. On the 13th, the very day when a delegation from the Government of National Defence established itself in Tours, they had been sighted east of Paris, as far forward as Lagny. On the 14th and 15th they were on the outskirts, at Créteil and Joinville-le-Pont. Yet on the morning of the 18th, when he had written, Maurice still did not seem to believe it would be possible to invest Paris completely, and had recovered a superb confidence, considering a siege as an insolent and hazardous gamble which would collapse in less than three weeks, and counting on the relieving armies the provinces would certainly send, to say nothing of the army of Metz, already on the move via Verdun and Rheims. Thus the links in the iron belt had closed up and shut Paris in a gigantic prison for two million living souls, whence nothing came out but the silence of death.

'Oh God!' murmured Henriette, weighed down by grief. 'How long is it all going to last, and shall we ever see him again?'

A squall bowed the trees outside and the old timbers of the farmhouse groaned. If they were in for a hard winter what sufferings there would be for the poor soldiers with no fire, no food and fighting in the snow.

'Ah well,' Jean concluded, 'it's a very nice letter and it's a pleasure to get news ... We mustn't ever despair.'

And so day after day the month of October went by, with dreary grey skies and the wind only giving over so as to bring up even darker banks of clouds again soon. Jean's wound took an endless time to heal. The quality of the fluid coming from the drainage tube would not have justified the doctor's removing it, and the patient had become very weak but refused to countenance an operation for fear of being a cripple for life. So now the little isolated room seemed to be slumbering in a period of waiting and resignation, sometimes broken by sudden anxieties with no clear cause, and the news that reached there was remote and vague, like a nightmare from which one is just emerging. The unspeakable war, with its slaughters and disasters, was still going on somewhere out there, but they never knew the real truth or heard anything except the widespread muted clamour of their slaughtered country. The wind carried away the leaves under the dreary sky and there were long, deep silences in the bare countryside, where nothing was heard but the cawing of rooks foretelling a hard winter.

One of their topics of conversation was the field hospital, where Henriette spent all her time except when she kept Jean company. In the evening when she came home he would question her and he knew all her patients, wanted to know who were dying and who were recovering, and she, always wanting to talk about things near her heart, went over her days in the minutest detail.

'Oh,' was her refrain, 'poor boys, poor boys!'

It was no longer the ambulance station on the day of battle, when fresh blood flowed and amputations were carried out on healthy red flesh. It was now an ambulance station infected by the putrescence of the hospital, smelling of fever and death, clammy with slow convalescences and protracted death agonies. Dr Dalichamp had had the greatest difficulty in procuring the necessary beds, mattresses and sheets, and every day still he had to perform miracles to keep his patients in bread, meat and dried vegetables, to say nothing of bandages, compresses and apparatus. The Prussians who had taken over the military hospital in Sedan refused to give him anything, even chloroform, and so he had got everything from Belgium. And yet he had taken in German wounded in the same way as French, and in particular he was tending a dozen Bavarians picked up at Bazeilles. The enemies who had flown at each other's throats were now lying side by side in the good companionship of their common suffering. And what a home of fear and misery it was – these two long halls of the old school at Remilly, with fifty beds in each, in the bright, crude light from the lofty windows!

Even ten days after the battle wounded had still been brought in, forgotten men found in odd corners. Four had stayed in an empty house at Balan with no medical attention whatever, living God knows how but probably thanks to the charity of some neighbour; and their wounds were crawling with maggots and they had died, poisoned by their own filthy sores. This purulence, which nothing could check, raged through the place and emptied rows of beds. As soon as you reached the door a smell of necrosis caught you by the throat. Drainage tubes suppurated, dripping fetid pus drop by drop. Often flesh had to be reopened to get out still more unsuspected splinters of bone. Then abscesses appeared, that were going to discharge in some other part of the body. The wretched men, exhausted, emaciated, their faces grey, endured every kind of torture. Some, prostrate and scarcely able to breathe, spent all their days on their backs with eyelids closed and black, like corpses already half decomposed. Others, the sleepless ones, plagued with restless insomnia and soaked in copious sweat, got wildly excited as though the catastrophe had driven them out of their minds. And whether they were violent or inert, once the shivering of infectious fever seized them it was all over, the poison won, flitting from the one to the other and carrying them all off in the same tide of victorious corruption.

Worst of all, there was the condemned ward, the place for men stricken with dysentery, typhus or smallpox. Many had black pox. They were never still, but raved in a continual delirium, rising up in their beds and standing like spectres. Others, affected in the lungs, were dying of pneumonia racked with dreadful coughing. Others shouted all the time and only found relief when a jet of cold water was constantly cooling their wounds. That was the longed-for time, the hour for dressing wounds, which alone brought a bit of peace, when beds were aired and some relaxation was afforded to bodies grown stiff through staying in the same position. But this also was the dreaded hour, for not a day passed when the doctor examining wounds did not grieve to see on some poor devil's skin the bluish patches that betrayed the advancing gangrene. That meant operating the next day. Yet another bit of leg or arm cut away. Sometimes even the gangrene went higher up and the job had to be repeated until the whole limb had been eaten away. Then the whole man went, his body covered with the livid patches of typhus, and he had to be taken away, staggering, half-crazy, haggard, into the condemned ward, with his flesh dead already and smelling of putrefaction before his death agony set in.

Every evening when she came home Henriette answered Jean's questions, and her voice always shook with the same emotion.

'Oh, poor boys, poor boys!'

Then came the details, always similar, of the daily torments of this hell. They had amputated an arm at the shoulder, or a foot, performed the resection of a humerus, but would gangrene or septicaemia spare the patient? Or again, they had buried one of them, usually a Frenchman, but sometimes a German. Hardly a day passed when some furtive coffin, bodged up quickly out of four pieces of wood, did not leave the hospital at dusk, accompanied by one orderly and often Henriette herself, so that a man should not just be buried like a dog. In the little cemetery of Remilly two trenches had been dug, and they all slept side by side, the Germans on the left and the French on the right, reconciled in the earth.

Jean had become interested in some of the patients whom he had never seen, and he asked for news of them.

'What about "Poor Kid", how's he doing today?'

This was a young trooper in the fifth regiment of the line, who had enlisted as a volunteer and was not yet twenty. The nickname 'Poor Kid' had stuck to him because he constantly used these words about himself, and when one day somebody had asked him why, he had answered that his mother always called him that. Poor kid, indeed, for he was dying of pleurisy, the aftermath of a wound in his left side.

'Oh the dear boy,' said Henriette, who had developed a motherly affection for him. 'He's not doing too well and has coughed all day long . . . It breaks my heart to hear him.'

'And your bear, this Gutmann of yours?' Jean went on with a wan smile. 'Is the doctor more hopeful?'

'Yes, they may save him. But he is in terrible pain.'

In spite of really great pity, they could not refer to Gutmann without a sort of affectionate flippancy. On the very first day she had gone to work at the hospital she had been horrified to recognize in this Bavarian soldier the man with the red beard and hair, bulging blue eyes and wide, square nose, who had carried her off in his arms at Bazeilles when they shot her husband. He recognized her too, but he could not speak, for a bullet had gone through the back of his neck and taken away half his tongue. After two days of horror and revulsion and an uncontrollable shuddering every time she went near his bed, she was won over by his most desperate and appealing look as he followed her round with his eyes. Was he no longer the monster with bloodstained hair and eyes, mad with frenzy, who haunted her with a terrible memory? It needed an effort to recognize him now in this poor wretch with such a friendly, gentle expression in spite of all his atrocious suffering. His case, an uncommon one involving this sudden incapacity, touched the whole hospital. They were not even quite sure his name was Gutmann, but that is what they called him because the only sound he could manage to get out was a growl in two syllables which made roughly that name. As far as the rest was concerned, they only thought they knew that he was married and had children, because he knew a few words of French and sometimes answered with a vigorous nod. Married? Yes, yes! Children? Yes, yes! His emotion one day when he saw some flour had also made them guess he might be a miller. But that was all. Where was the mill? Were a wife and children weeping at this very moment in some remote village in

Bavaria? Was he going to die unknown, nameless, leaving his own folk over there to wait for him for ever?

'Today,' Henriette told Jean one evening, 'Gutmann blew me some kisses ... I can't give him a drink now or do the slightest thing for him but he puts his fingers to his lips in a fervent gesture of gratitude ... We mustn't smile, it's too terrible to buried alive like that before your time.'

Towards the end of October Jean was much better. The doctor agreed to take out the tube, although he was still worried; yet the wound seemed to be drying up quite quickly. Already he was convalescent and getting up, spending hours walking about the room, sitting at the window, looking sadly at the flying clouds. Then he began to get bored and talked of doing something to occupy himself and be of some help on the farm. One of his private worries was the money question, for he felt sure that in a good six weeks his two hundred francs must have been spent. So to keep old Fouchard in a good humour Henriette must have had to pay. This thought upset him and he did not dare bring it out into the open with Henriette, and so he felt a considerable relief when it was decided that he would be given out to be a new employee whose job was indoor work with Silvine, while Prosper got on with the crops outside.

In spite of the terrible times an additional hand was not super-fluous at old Fouchard's, for his business affairs were doing well. While the whole region was in agonies and bleeding in every limb he had contrived to increase his trade as itinerant butcher to such an extent that he was now slaughtering three or four times as many animals. It was said that by 31 August he had had highly profitable dealings with the Prussians. The man who on the 30th had defended his door against the soldiers of the 7th corps, with his gun cocked and refusing to sell them a single crumb, shouting that his house was empty, had set up as a general trader on the 31st at the appear-ance of the first enemy soldier, and had unearthed from his cellars huge quantities of provisions, and brought back vast flocks from remote fastnesses where they had been hidden. From that day on-wards he had been one of the biggest suppliers of meat to the German armies, and quite astonishing in his skill at finding a market for his goods and getting paid between two requisitions. Other people suffered from the often brutal commandeerings of the victors, but he had not yet supplied a single bushel of flour, cask of wine or quarter of beef without picking up good hard cash at the end of the transaction. This gave rise to much talk in Remilly, and it was considered pretty low on the part of a man who had just lost his son in the war and never went to visit his grave, which Silvine was the only one to look after. Yet all the same he was respected for making money when even the most astute came off so badly. And he just grinned, shrugged and growled in his straight-from-the-shoulder manner:

'Patriotic, I'm more patriotic than all of them put together! ... Is it being patriotic to bloody well fill the Prussians with food up to their eyes, free, gratis and for nothing? I make them pay for everything ... we shall see, we shall see how it all works out later on!'

By the second day Jean stood too long on his feet, and the doctor's private fears were realized – the wound reopened and there was considerable inflammation and swelling of the leg, so that he had to go back to bed. Dalichamp came to suspect that a splinter of bone must still be there and that the effort of the two days of exercise had finally freed it. He looked for it and was fortunate enough to be able to extract it, but only at the cost of a shock to the system with a very high temperature which exhausted Jean once again. He had never so far fallen into such a state of weakness. So Henriette took up her position again as faithful nurse in this room which was getting gloomier and colder with the approach of winter. It was now the beginning of November, the east wind had already brought a flurry of snow, and it was very cold on the bare tiled floor between these four bare walls. As there was no fireplace they decided to have a stove put in, and its roaring enlivened their solitude.

The days went monotonously by, and this first week of his relapse was certainly for Jean and Henriette the most miserable of their long enforced intimacy. Would the suffering never end? Was there always going to be fresh danger without their being able to hope for the end of so much wretchedness? At every moment their thoughts flew to Maurice, from whom they had had no more news. They did hear of other people who received messages, little notes brought by carrier pigeon. Perhaps the pigeon bringing joy and love to them had been killed by some German while in full flight through the great open sky. Everything seemed to withdraw from reach, wither away and disappear into this early winter. The sounds of war only reached them after long delays and the odd newspapers Dr Dalichamp still brought were often a week old. Their sadness came largely from their ignorance, from what they did not know but guessed, from the long death-cry they could hear in spite of everything in the silence of the countryside round the farm.

One morning the doctor arrived in a state of great distress, with his hands shaking. He drew a Belgian paper out of his pocket and threw it on the bed, exclaiming:

'Oh my dear friends, France is finished, Bazaine has betrayed us!'

Jean, dozing propped up by two pillows, woke up.

'Betrayed? What do you mean?'

'Yes, he has handed over Metz and the army. It is Sedan all over again, but this time it is the rest of our flesh and blood.'

He picked up the paper and read:

'A hundred and fifty thousand prisoners, a hundred and fifty-three eagles and colours, five hundred and forty-one field guns, seventy-six *mitrailleuses*, eight hundred siege guns, three hundred thousand rifles, two thousand military vehicles, equipment for eighty-five batteries . . .'.

He went on with details. Marshal Bazaine besieged in Metz with the army, reduced to impotence, making no effort to break the iron ring enclosing him, his prolonged discussions with Prince Friedrich Karl, his ambiguous and tentative political schemings, his ambition to play a decisive part which he didn't seem to have quite clear in his own mind; then all the complexity of the negotiations, the sending of tricky and lying envoys to Bismarck, to King William and to the Empress-Regent, who was to refuse to treat with the enemy on the basis of any cession of territory; and the unavoidable catastrophe, destiny working itself out, famine in Metz, enforced capitulation, commanders and soldiers reduced to accepting the harsh conditions of the conquerors. France no longer had an army.

'Oh Christ!' Jean swore softly to himself. He did not understand it all, but for him until then Bazaine had remained the great captain, the only possible saviour. So what were they going to do? What was happening to the people in Paris?

The doctor passed on to the Paris news, which was disastrous. He pointed out that the paper was dated 5 November. The surrender of Metz happened on 27 October, but the news of it was not known in Paris until the 30th. After the repulses already sustained at Chevilly, Bagneux and La Malmaison and the fight and defeat at Le Bourget, this news had burst like a bombshell in the midst of a desperate population already irritated by the weakness and ineptitude of the Government of National Defence. And so on the next day, 31 October, a full-scale insurrection had taken place, with an immense crowd packing the Place de l'Hôtel de Ville, bursting into the debating chambers, taking prisoner members of the government who were later rescued by the National Guard because they feared the triumph of the revolutionaries who were demanding a Commune. The Belgian paper went on to make the most insulting reflections about this wonderful Paris, tearing itself to pieces with civil war as soon as the enemy was at the gates. Was this not the final dissolution, the morass of mud and blood into which a world was about to collapse?

'It's quite true,' Jean muttered in distress, 'we shouldn't go for each other when the Prussians are there!'

Henriette had said nothing so far, preferring to keep her mouth shut about these political affairs, but she could not help exclaiming. All her thoughts were with her brother.

'Oh dear, I only hope Maurice doesn't get mixed up in all this, he's so unreasonable!'

After a pause the doctor, a fervently patriotic man, went on:

'Never mind, if there are no soldiers left some more will spring up. Metz has surrendered, Paris itself might give in, but France will not be finished. Yes, as our countryfolk say, if the body's still in good shape we'll pull through.'

But he was clearly forcing himself to hope. He spoke of the new army being formed on the Loire which, it was true, had not made a very good beginning near Arthenay, but it would find its fighting feet and march to the help of Paris. He was particularly excited by the proclamations of Gambetta, who had got away from Paris in a balloon on 7 October and two days later set himself up in Tours, calling all citizens to arms and using a style at one and the same time so virile and so moderate that the whole country was acquiescing in this dictatorship for the public safety. And wasn't there also a question of raising another army in the north and yet another in the east, conjuring soldiers up out of the ground by the sheer power of faith? In fact the awakening of the provinces, an indomitable will to create whatever was lacking, to fight on to the last sou and the last drop of blood.

'After all,' the doctor concluded as he stood up to go, 'I've often given up patients who were back on their feet a week later!'

Jean smiled.

'Doctor, cure me quickly so that I can go back to my post.'

Nevertheless Henriette and he remained very gloomy after this bad news. That same evening there was a snowstorm, and the next day Henriette came back very upset from the hospital and said that Gutmann was dead. This very cold spell was decimating the wounded and emptying rows of beds. The poor dumb creature, with his tongue cut out, had been moaning for two days in his last agony. During his last hours she had stayed by his bed, for he gazed at her with such imploring eyes. He was talking to her with his tear-dimmed eyes, perhaps telling her his real name and that of the far-off village in which a woman and her children were waiting. And he had departed unknown, trying with his groping fingers to send her a last kiss to thank her once again for all her care. She was the only one who went with him to the cemetery, where the frozen earth, heavy foreign earth, thudded on his deal coffin with lumps of snow.

Then once more, the very next day, Henriette said as she came in: 'Poor Kid is dead.'

For this one she was in tears.

'If you could have seen him in his delirium! He called me Mum, Mum! And held out his arms so affectionately that I had to take him on my lap. Oh, poor fellow, his sufferings had taken so much out of him that he weighed no more than a little boy ... And I rocked him so that he could die happy. Yes, I rocked him, he called me his mother, and I was only a few years older than him ... He cried and I couldn't help crying myself, and I still am ...'

Her voice gave out and she had to stop for a moment.

'When he died he whispered over and over again those two words he used of himself: Poor Kid, Poor Kid. Oh yes, all these brave fellows are poor kids, and some of them are so young, and your horrible war tears off their limbs and makes them suffer so much before it throws them into the ground!'

Every day now Henriette came back like this, shattered by some death-scene, and this suffering of others drew the two of them closer still during the weary hours they spent so much alone together in that big, quiet room. Yet they were very beautiful hours for, as they gradually came to know each other, there had developed between their two hearts an affection which they thought was fraternal. His serious mind had risen to new heights during their long intimacy and she, seeing him so good and sensible, forgot that he was a humble man who had followed the plough before becoming a soldier. They understood each other perfectly and made an ideal couple, as Silvine said with her grave smile. Nor had any awkwardness arisen between them, and she went on attending to his leg without ever turning away those candid eyes. Always in her black widow's weeds, she seemed to have ceased to be a woman.

All the same, during the long afternoons when he was alone, Jean could not help letting his mind wander. What he felt for her was infinite gratitude and a sort of religious devotion which would have made him thrust aside any thought of sexual love as sacrilegious. Nevertheless he told himself that with a wife like her, so tender, so gentle and yet so practical, life would have been very heaven. His own misfortune, the unpleasant years he had spent at Rognes, his disastrous marriage and the violent death of his wife – all his past life now reminded him of the tenderness he had missed, and inspired in him a vague, scarcely formulated hope of trying to find happiness once more. He would shut his eyes and let himself fall into a half-sleep, when he would see himself somehow in Remilly, remarried and owner of a small-holding that was sufficient to keep a family of honest folk with little ambition. It was such a tenuous vision that it did not really exist, and certainly never would. He didn't think he had anything left in him but friendship and he only loved Henriette like this because he felt himself to be Maurice's brother. So this uncertain dream of marriage became a kind of consolation, one of those daydreams one knows to be unrealizable but with which one whiles away hours of sadness.

But no such thoughts even touched Henriette's mind. After the dreadful drama at Bazeilles her heart remained dead, and any comfort or new affection could only enter it unrecognized, like the unperceived movement of germinating seed that nothing betrays to the human eye. She was not even conscious of the pleasure she had come to take in lingering for hours at Jean's bedside, reading the papers to him even though they gave her nothing but sorrow.

Her hand when it touched his had not even felt any warmth, never had the idea of the morrow left her thoughtful, with a wish to be loved once again. And yet only in this room could she forget or find consolation. When she was there, quietly busying herself with her tasks, she found rest to her soul and felt that her brother would soon come back, that all would work out for the best and they would eventually all be happy together and never be parted again. She talked about it quite freely, for it seemed so natural that things should be so and it never entered her mind to look more deeply into the chaste and hidden gift of her heart.

But one afternoon, as she was setting off for the hospital, the terror that froze her when she saw a Prussian captain and two other officers in the kitchen revealed to her the deep affection she had for Jean. Evidently these men had heard of the presence of the wounded man at the farm and had come to get him, it would inevitably mean departure and captivity in Germany in some fortress. She listened trembling, with her heart beating wildly.

The captain, a big man who spoke French, was giving old Fouchard a violent dressing-down.

'This can't go on any longer, what do you take us for? . . . So I've come myself to warn you that if this happens again I shall hold you responsible. Yes, I shall know what steps to take!'

Quite unruffled, the old man pretended to be thunderstruck, standing with dangling arms as though he hadn't understood.

'Beg pardon, sir, what do you mean?'

'Oh, don't make me lose my temper. You know quite well that the three cows you sold us on Sunday were rotten. Yes, quite rotten and diseased, they had died of some foul disease, and they have poisoned my men, and two of them may be dead by now.'

Thereupon Fouchard registered revolt and indignation.

'Diseased! What, my cows? It was such good meat, meat you could give a woman with a newborn baby, to build up her strength!'

He snivelled, beat his breast, declared he was an honest man, that he would as soon cut out his own flesh as sell any that was bad. For thirty years everybody had known him, and nobody in the world could say he had not had full weight and finest quality.

'Those cows were as healthy as I am, sir, and if your soldiers had the colic it may be that they ate too much – unless it was that some evil-intentioned persons put some chemicals into the saucepan.'

He confused him so with his flow of words, with such far-fetched theories that the captain furiously cut him short.

'That's enough of that! You've been warned, take care! And there's something else. We suspect all of you in this village of harbouring the guerrillas from the Dieulet woods, who killed another of our sentries the day before yesterday. So take care, you understand?'

When the Prussians had gone old Fouchard shrugged his shoulders and sneered with infinite contempt. Cattle that had died of disease, well of course that's what he sold them, that's what he made them eat, and nothing else! All the corpses the peasants brought him that had died of diseases and the ones he picked up himself in the ditches – wasn't that good enough for those filthy bastards?

He winked as he murmured with triumphant glee, and turning to Henriette, who was feeling very relieved:

'And then to think, my dear, that there are people who say I'm unpatriotic! ... Let them do as much, I say, let them give 'em old carrion and pocket their money. Unpatriotic! Well, for God's sake! I shall have killed more of them with my dead cows than many a soldier with his rifle!'

But all the same, when he heard the story Jean was worried. If the German authorities suspected that the inhabitants of Remilly harboured the guerrillas from the Dieulet woods they might at any time do house-to-house searches and discover him. He could not bear the thought of compromising his benefactors or causing the least trouble to Henriette. But she prevailed on him to stay a few more days, and he agreed, for his wound was taking a long time to scar over, and he was not strong enough on his legs to join up with one of the fighting regiments in the north or on the Loire.

The days from then until the middle of December were the most disturbing and miserable of their solitude. The cold had become so intense that the stove could not heat the big, empty room. When they looked out of the window at the deep snow on the ground they thought of Maurice buried in a frozen, dead Paris, from which there was no reliable news. They always came back to the same questions. What was he doing? Why didn't he give any sign of life?

They dared not express their awful fears, a wound, sickness, perhaps death. The few odd bits of information that still came through to them in the papers were not calculated to reassure them. After claims of successful sorties, which were always proved false, there had been a rumour of a great victory won on 2 December at Champigny by General Ducrot, but later they knew that the very next day he had abandoned the conquered positions and been forced to recross the Marne. Every hour Paris was being held in a tighter stranglehold, famine was setting in, with potatoes being requisitioned as well as cattle, private people's gas turned off and soon the streets in darkness, a darkness only streaked by the red paths of shells. Now the two of them could not warm themselves or eat anything without being haunted by a vision of Maurice and two million living souls shut up in that gigantic tomb.

Moreover the news from all directions, north as well as centre, was getting worse. In the north the 22nd army corps, made up of militia, men from supply depots and soldiers and officers who had escaped from the disasters of Sedan and Metz, had had to abandon Amiens and fall back towards Arras, while Rouen had fallen into enemy hands, for a handful of unattached, demoralized men had not seriously defended it. In the centre the victory at Coulmiers won on the 9 November by the army of the Loire had given rise to wild hopes: Orleans reoccupied, the Bavarians in flight, a march on Etampes and the early relief of Paris. But on 5 December Prince Friedrich Karl recaptured Orleans and cut in two the army of the Loire, three corps of which fell back to Vierzon and Bourges while two others under the command of General Chanzy withdrew to Le Mans in a heroic retreat during a whole week of marching and fighting. The Prussians were everywhere, Dijon and Dieppe, Le Mans and Vierzon. And every morning there was the distant crash of some fortress capitulating to shell fire. Strasbourg had fallen as early as 28 September, after forty-six days of siege and thirty-seven of bombardment, with its walls gashed and monuments riddled by nearly two hundred thousand projectiles. The citadel of Laon was already blown up, Toul had surrendered, and then came the dismal procession, Soissons with its hundred and twenty-eight guns, Verdun with its hundred and thirty-six, Neuf-Brisach a hundred, La Fère seventy, Montmédy sixty-five. Thionville was in flames. Phalsbourg only opened its gates in the twelfth week of its desperate resistance. The whole of France seemed to be ablaze and collapsing in this furious bombardment.

One morning when Jean was determined to go, Henriette took his hands and held them in a desperate grip.

'No, no! I beg of you don't leave me alone ... You are not strong enough, wait a few more days ... I promise I will let you go when the doctor says you are strong enough to go back and fight.'

5

SILVINE and Prosper were alone with Charlot in the big farmhouse kitchen on a cold evening in December, she sewing and he making himself a nice whip. It was seven o'clock, and they had had their dinner at six without waiting for old Fouchard, who must have been delayed at Raucourt, where meat was running short. Henriette, who was then on night duty at the hospital, had just left after telling Silvine not to go to bed without making up Jean's stove.

It was very dark outside against the white snow. Not a sound came from the shrouded village, and the only thing that could be heard was Prosper's knife as he busied himself adorning the dogwood handle with lozenges and rosettes. He paused occasionally and glanced at Charlot, whose big blond head was beginning to fall about with sleep. When the child did eventually go to sleep the silence seemed still deeper. His mother gently moved the candle away so that the little boy should not have the light in his eyes, and then, without stopping her sewing, she fell into a daydream.

It was then, after some hesitation, that Prosper made up his mind to speak.

'I say, Silvine, there's something I've got to tell you ... I waited until I was alone with you.'

Looking disturbed already, she raised her eyes.

'This is what it is ... Forgive me if I am upsetting you, but you had better be warned ... This morning, in Remilly, at the corner by the church, I saw Goliath as plain as I see you now, oh yes, full view and no mistake.'

She turned deathly pale, her hands shook, and the only sound she could utter was a soft moan.

'Oh God, oh God!'

Prosper went on, carefully choosing his words, and told her what he had found out during the day by questioning various people. Nobody now doubted that Goliath was a spy who had settled in the neighbourhood to find out about routes, resources and all the minute details of its way of life. They recalled his stay at old Fouchard's farm, his sudden departure and the jobs he had had since round Beaumont and Raucourt. And now here he was back again, occupying some unspecified post in the commanding officer's headquarters in Sedan and travelling round the villages, apparently employed to gather evidence against some, tax others and see that the crushing requisitions imposed on the inhabitants were being properly enforced. That morning he had been terrorizing Remilly about a delivery of flour that was incomplete and late.

'You are now warned,' Prosper said again, 'and so you will know what to do when he comes here . . .'

She cut him short with a cry of terror:

'Do you think he'll come here?'

'Well of course, it seems obvious to me . . . He would have to be very lacking in curiosity, as he has never set eyes on the kid, although he knows he exists . . . And besides, there's you, and you're not all that bad-looking, and nice to see again.'

She made a sign begging him to stop. But the noise had awakened Charlot, and he looked up. His eyes still out of focus as though he were emerging from a dream, he remembered the insult he had been taught by some Clever Dick in the village, and declared with all the solemnity of a young man of three:

'Prussian swine!'

His mother snatched him up in her arms and sat him on her lap. Poor little thing, her joy and her despair, whom she loved with all her soul but could never look at without crying, this child of her body it hurt so much to hear maliciously being called the Prussian by the kids of his age when they played with him in the street. She kissed him as though to force the words back into his mouth.

'Who taught you those wicked words? It's naughty, you mustn't say them, my pet.'

So of course with the obstinacy of children Charlot went into a fit of giggles and immediately started again:

'Prussian swine!'

Then, seeing his mother burst into tears, he began crying too and threw his arms round her neck. Oh God, what fresh misfortune was threatening? Wasn't it enough to have lost in Honoré the only hope in her life, the certainty of forgetting and being happy again? No, the other man had to come back to complete her misery.

'Now, now, come to bye-byes, my pettikins . . . I love you just the same, for you don't understand how sad you make me.'

So as not to embarrass her by looking at her, Prosper had made a point of carefully going on with carving his whip-handle. She left him alone for a minute.

But before putting Charlot to bed Silvine usually took him to say good night to Jean, with whom the child was great friends. That evening as she went in, holding the candle in her hand, she saw the invalid sitting up in bed, staring into the darkness. So he wasn't asleep? Oh no, he was turning all sorts of things over in his mind, alone in the silent winter night. While she filled up the stove he played for a minute with Charlot, who rolled on the bed like a kitten. He knew Silvine's story and he was fond of this brave, quiet girl who had been through so much, mourning the one man she had loved and having only the one consolation left of this poor child, whose birth was her lasting torment. And so, when she had shut down the stove and came over to take the child out of his arms, he noticed that her eyes were red with crying. What, had somebody given her more trouble? But she did not want to tell him – she might later on if there was any point. After all, wasn't life a continual sorrow for her?

Silvine was taking Charlot away when there was a noise of footsteps and voices in the yard. Jean listened in surprise.

'What's up, then? That's not old Fouchard coming in, I didn't hear the wheels of his cart.'

In his isolated room he had developed an awareness of the regular life of the farm, and was familiar with the slightest sounds. He listened and then said at once:

'Oh yes, it's those men, the guerrillas of the Dieulet woods, coming for provisions.'

'Quick!' said Silvine, running off and leaving him in darkness once again. 'I must run and give them their loaves.'

By now fists were banging on the kitchen door and Prosper, worried because he was on his own, was gaining time by arguing.

When the master was not at home he was not keen on opening the door for fear of damage for which he would be held responsible. But he was fortunate in that just then old Fouchard's trap came down the hill, the sound of the horse's feet muffled in the snow. So it was the old man who let them in.

'Oh good, so it's you three ... What have you got for me in that barrow?'

Sambuc, looking like an emaciated bandit buried in a blue woolly too big for him, didn't even hear, being furious with Prosper, his gentleman brother as he called him, who was only then making up his mind to open the door.

'Look here, you, do you take us for beggars, leaving us out here in weather like this?'

But while Prosper, quite unruffled, silently shrugged his shoulders and got on with stabling the trap and horse, old Fouchard broke in again, stooping over the barrow.

'So you've brought me two dead sheep. Good job it's freezing, otherwise they wouldn't smell too good!'

Cabasse and Ducat, Sambuc's two lieutenants, who always went with him on his expeditions, expostulated:

'Oh,' said the first, with his loud southern chatter, 'they're not more than three days gone ... They died at Raffins farm, where there is a bad epidemic among the animals.'

'*Procumbit humi bos*,' declaimed the other, the ex-process-server, whose excessive taste for little girls had lost him his job and who liked airing his Latin quotations.

Old Fouchard went on shaking his head and running down the goods, which he pretended to find too far gone. But he concluded as he went into the kitchen with the three men:

'Oh well, they'll have to put up with it ... It's as well that they've no meat left at Raucourt. When you're hungry you eat anything, don't you?'

Inwardly delighted, he hailed Silvine who was just coming in from putting Charlot to bed.

'Bring me some glasses and we'll all drink to Bismarck going to kingdom come.'

Fouchard kept on good terms with the guerrillas of Dieulet woods, who for nearly three months had been emerging from their impenetrable thickets at dusk and prowling on the roads, killing and robbing any Prussians they could surprise, and falling back on the farms and extorting money from the peasants when enemy game was scarce. They were the terror of the villages, particularly because after every attack on a convoy or killing of a sentry the German authorities took reprisals on places in the district, accusing them of aiding and abetting, levying fines, imprisoning mayors, burning cottages. Much as they would have liked to, the peasants did not betray Sambuc and his band simply out of fear of stopping a bullet round some corner if the deal misfired.

Fouchard had had the extraordinary idea of doing business with them. Combing the countryside in all directions as they did, ditches as well as cowsheds, they had become suppliers of dead animals. Not an ox or a sheep gave up the ghost for three leagues around but they stole it at night and brought it to him. He paid them in provisions, especially bread, batches of loaves that Silvine baked specially for them. Besides, although he had no particular liking for them, he had a sneaking admiration for the guerrillas, bright lads who made a good thing out of it by cocking a snook at everybody; and although he was making a fortune out of his dealings with the Prussians, he had a good laugh to himself, a savage laugh, whenever he heard that another of them had been found by the roadside with his throat cut.

'Your good health,' he said, clinking glasses with the three men.

Then, wiping his lips with the back of his hand:

'By the way, they've made quite a thing of those two Uhlans they picked up near Villecourt, with their heads chopped off . . . You know Villecourt's been on fire since yesterday, what they call a sentence on the village to punish them for harbouring you . . . Must be careful, you know, and don't you come back here too soon. We'll deliver your bread elsewhere.'

Sambuc shrugged and gave a fearful sneer. Never you fear, the Prussians could run after him! Then he suddenly came over angry and banged the table with his fist.

'God Almighty, the Uhlans are all very well, but between you and me it's that other bloke I should like to lay my hands on, you know, the spy, the one who worked for you . . .'

'Goliath, you mean.'

Silvine, who had taken up her sewing again, stopped dead and listened.

'That's it, Goliath! Ah, the bastard, he knows the Dieulet woods like the back of his hand, and he can get us pinched one of these mornings, especially as he boasted at the Croix de Malte today that he'd settle our account within a week ... A dirty sod who for certain must have guided the Bavarians the day before Beaumont, don't you think so, you chaps?'

'As true as that candle's lighting us,' Cabasse agreed.

'*Per amica silentia lunae*,' added Ducat, whose Latin tags sometimes went awry.

Sambuc shook the table with another thump of his fist.

'That swine is judged and condemned! If some day you get to know which way he's going, let me know, and his head will join those of the Uhlans in the Meuse. By God, yes, you can take it from me!'

In the silence that followed Silvine watched them attentively. She was very pale.

'These are all things we shouldn't be talking about,' Fouchard went on prudently. 'Your good health and good night.'

They finished the second bottle. Prosper had come back from the stable and gave a hand with loading on to the barrow, in the place of the two dead sheep, the loaves that Silvine had put in a sack. But he didn't even answer, and turned his back when his brother and the two others went off, disappearing with the barrow into the snow and saying:

'Good night, see you again soon!'

The next day, while Fouchard was alone after lunch, he saw Goliath himself come in, tall, big and pink-faced as ever, with his imperturbable smile. If this sudden appearance gave him a shock he didn't show anything but just blinked, as the man came over and vigorously shook his hand.

'Good morning, Monsieur Fouchard.'

Only then did Fouchard appear to recognize him.

'Oh, fancy, it's you, my boy! ... Oh, you've filled out a bit. You are getting fat, aren't you?'

He had a good look at him; he was wearing a sort of cape of coarse blue cloth and a cap of the same material, and looking prosperous and pleased with himself. Of course he had no German accent, but spoke the thick, slow speech of the peasants of that region.

'Oh yes, it's me, Monsieur Fouchard. I didn't want to pass this way without saying hallo to you.'

The old man stayed on his guard. What was this fellow up to, coming here? Had he heard about the guerrillas coming to the farm yesterday? He would have to watch it. All the same, as he was coming very civilly it would be best to be polite in return.

'Well, my boy, as you are so kind we must have a drink.'

He put himself out to go and find two glasses and a bottle. All this wine being drunk made his heard bleed, but you must know when to give something away in the interests of business. So the scene of the night before began all over again, and they toasted each other with the same gestures and the same words.

'Your good health, Monsieur Fouchard.'

'And yours, my boy.'

Then Goliath calmly made himself at home. He looked about him like a man enjoying seeing old scenes again, but made no reference to the past, nor, for that matter, to the present. The conversation turned to the severe cold which was going to make work hard on the land; fortunately there was a good side to snow, it killed the pests. He did show just the slightest unhappiness when he spoke of the sullen hatred or mingled contempt and fear that had been shown him in other homes in Remilly. After all, we all have our own country, don't we, and it's only natural that you should serve your country according to your lights. But in France there were some things they had funny ideas about. The old man watched him talking so glibly and being so conciliatory and told himself that this good fellow, with his big jolly face, had certainly not come with evil intentions.

'So you're all on your own today, Monsieur Fouchard?'

'Oh no, Silvine is out there feeding the cows . . . Do you want to see Silvine?'

A smile spread over Goliath's face.

'Yes of course I do . . . To tell you the truth, I came because of Silvine.'

Old Fouchard jumped up at once, very relieved, and shouted at the top of his voice:

'Silvine! Silvine! Someone to see you!'

And off he went, now quite reassured, as she was there and could protect the house. If a man can let that thing master him for so long, after all these years, he's done for.

Silvine was not surprised to see Goliath when she came in. He did not get up from his chair, but sat looking at her with his bland smile, though he was just a little ill at ease. She had been expecting him, and all she did was stop just inside the door, and her whole being stiffened. Charlot ran in after her and hid in her skirts, taken aback to see a man he didn't know.

There was an awkward silence for a few seconds, and then Goliath broke the silence in honeyed tones:

'So this is the kid?'

'Yes.' Silvine's voice was hard.

Silence fell again. He had left in the seventh month of her pregnancy and so knew he had a child, but he was seeing it for the first time. So he wanted to get things straight, being a practical, sensible fellow convinced he was in the right.

'Look here, Silvine, I can understand you bear me a grudge, but it isn't quite fair ... I went off and hurt you very much, but you should have realized at once that perhaps it was because I wasn't my own master. When you've got superiors you've got to obey them, haven't you? Even if they had sent me off somewhere on foot, a hundred leagues away, I should have gone. And of course I couldn't say anything – it nearly broke my heart to go off like that without even saying good-night ... Today, God knows, I'm not going to pretend that I was sure of coming back. But I meant to try, and as you see here I am.'

She had turned her head away and was looking through the window at the snow in the yard, as though determined not to hear. He was disconcerted by this silent contempt, and broke off his explanation to say:

'Do you know you're prettier than ever?'

At that moment she was indeed very beautiful, with her wonderful big eyes lighting up her pale face. Her heavy black hair was like eternal widow's weeds.

'Come on, be a good sort! You ought to know I don't wish you any harm ... If I didn't still love you I wouldn't have come back, and that's a fact ... But as I am back and it's all worked out all right, we're going to see more of each other, aren't we?'

She drew back quickly, looked him straight in the face and said:

'Never!'

'What do you mean, never? Aren't you my wife, and isn't that child ours?'

She kept her eyes on him and said deliberately:

'Listen, we'd better put an end to this at once ... You knew Honoré, I loved him and have never loved anyone else. And he is dead, and you people killed him ... I shall never have anything more to do with you, never!'

She raised her hand and swore this oath in a voice so full of hatred that for a moment he was quite abashed, abandoned his affectionate tone and murmured:

'Yes, I knew Honoré was dead. He was a very nice chap. Still, after all, others have been killed, there's a war on ... And then I thought that as he was dead there was no obstacle left between us. Because, as a matter of fact, Silvine, let me remind you, I didn't use force, you consented ...'

But he had to break off because she was in such a distracted state, with her hands raised to her face as though she were going to claw herself to pieces.

'Oh, yes, I know, yes, it's just that that's driving me crazy. Why did I let you when I didn't love you? ... I can't remember, I was so miserable and so ill after Honoré had gone, and it may have been perhaps because you talked about him and seemed to be fond of him. Oh God, how many nights have I spent crying my eyes out thinking about it! It's horrible to have done something you didn't mean to do and not to be able to understand afterwards why you did it ... And he had forgiven me, he had told me that if those Prussian swine didn't kill him he would marry me just the same when he came back home from the army. And you think I'm going back with you? Now look, even with a knife at my throat I shall say no, no, never!'

This time Goliath's face darkened with anger. When he had known her she was submissive, but now he sensed that she was un-shakeable and fiercely determined. Amiable creature he might be, but he wanted her, even if it meant using force now he was the master, and if he was not imposing his will with violence it was because of his innate prudence, his instinct for ruse and patience. This heavy-fisted giant disliked coming to blows. So he thought of another way of cowing her into submission.

'Right, as you don't want me, I'll take the kid.'

'The kid? What do you mean?'

Charlot had been forgotten, and was still hiding in his mother's skirt, trying not to burst out crying in the middle of the quarrel. Goliath got up from his chair and came over.

'You're my little boy, aren't you, a little Prussian ... Come along with me ... !'

Silvine snatched the boy up indignantly in her arms and clasped him to her breast.

'A Prussian, him! No! French, born in France!'

'A Frenchman! Just look at him and look at me. He's the very image of me! Is he anything like you?'

And only then did she really see this tall, fair man with his curly hair and beard, wide pink face and big blue eyes shining like porcelain. It was quite true, the child had the same yellow mop of hair, same cheeks, same light-coloured eyes, all that race was in him. She felt she was the different one, with her straight dark hair, strands of which had come out of her chignon and were hanging down her back.

'I made him, he's mine!' she went on furiously. 'He's a Frenchman who'll never know a word of your filthy language. Yes, a Frenchman who one day will go and kill the lot of you to avenge those you have killed!'

Charlot began crying and screaming, clinging to her neck.

'Mummy, Mummy, I'm frightened, take me away!'

Then Goliath, no doubt anxious to avoid a scene, drew back and contented himself with saying contemptuously and in a hard voice:

'Just bear in mind what I'm going to say, Silvine ... I know everything that's going on here. You harbour the guerrillas from the Dieulet woods, that chap Sambuc, the brother of your farmhand, a bandit you're supplying with bread. And I know that this labourer Prosper is a Chasseur d'Afrique and a deserter who belongs to us. And I know too that you are hiding a wounded man, another soldier who would be taken off to prison in Germany at a word from me ... So you see, I'm well informed.'

She was listening now, mute and terrified, while Charlot, with his face buried in her bosom, kept moaning:

'Oh Mummy, Mummy, take me away, I'm frightened!'

'Very well,' went on Goliath, 'I'm not all that ill disposed and I don't like quarrels, as you well know, but I swear that I'll have the whole lot arrested, old Fouchard and all the rest of them, unless you let me come to your room next Monday. And I'll take the child and send him back home to my mother, who will be very glad to have him, for if you insist on breaking off everything he's mine ... Do you get that? Understand that I shall only have to come and take him, because there won't be anybody else left here. I'm the master and I do what I like ... What do you decide? Come on!'

But she said nothing, and held the child closer as though afraid he might be snatched away there and then, and her great eyes filled with fear and loathing.

'All right then, I give you three days to think it over ... You will leave the window of your room open, the one facing the orchard ... If I don't find that window open on Monday evening at seven I'll have everyone here arrested the next day and come for the child ... I'll be seeing you, Silvine!'

He went off calmly and she stood there rooted to the spot, with so many ideas, far-fetched and horrible, buzzing through her head that they almost drove her silly. All through that day there was a tempest going on inside her. At first she had the instinctive thought of carrying her child away in her arms, straight ahead of her, anywhere. But what would become of them by nightfall, and how could she earn a living for him and herself? Apart from the fact that the Prussians patrolled the roads and would stop her and probably bring her back here. Then she thought of speaking to Jean, warning Prosper and even old Fouchard, but again she hesitated and recoiled from it, for was she sure enough of people's friendship to know for certain that they would not sacrifice her for everybody else's comfort and peace of mind? No, no, she wouldn't tell anyone, she would get out of the danger by her own efforts since she alone had got into it by her obstinate refusal. But, oh God, what could she think of and how could she prevent this horrible thing? For her own decency protested, she would never forgive herself all through her life if because of what she had done some disaster overtook so many people, especially Jean, who was so kind to Charlot.

The hours went by and all the next day passed, and she had thought of nothing. She went about her business as usual, swept the kitchen, saw to the cows, did the supper. In the complete and terrible silence that she clung to, what grew and poisoned her more every hour was her hatred of Goliath. He was her sin, her damnation. If he had not existed she would have waited for Honoré and Honoré would still be alive and she would be happy. What a tone of voice he had used when he told her he was the master! Of course it was true, there was now no police force, no judges to appeal to, only might was right. Oh to be the stronger and seize him when he came, this man who talked of seizing others! For her there was only the child left, for he was her own flesh. This chance father didn't count and never had. She was not a wife, and when she thought of him she only felt moved by the anger and resentment of a conquered victim. Rather than give up the child to him she would have killed the boy and herself afterwards. She had told him clearly – she wished this child he had given her, like a gift of hatred, were already grown up and capable of defending her; she saw him later with a gun, putting bullets through the lot of them over yonder! Yes, one more Frenchman, another French slayer of Prussians!

Meanwhile, she only had one day left and she had to come to some decision. From the first moment one murderous thought had been going through her poor, bewildered head, and that was to alert the guerrillas and give Sambuc the tip he was waiting for. But the idea had been a fleeting, intangible one, and she had rejected it as monstrous and out of the question – after all, wasn't the man the father of her child? She couldn't have him murdered. But then the idea had kept coming back, steadily more obsessive and urgent, and now it was forcing itself upon her with all the persuasive strength of its simplicity and finality. Once Goliath was dead, Jean, Prosper, old Fouchard would have nothing left to fear. She herself would then keep Charlot and nobody would ever again question her right to him. And there was something else much deeper, unrecognized even by her, which was rising up from the depths of her being – the need to make an end, to eliminate the paternity of the child by eliminating the father, the savage joy of telling herself that she would emerge with her sin amputated, as it were, mother and sole mistress of the child, without having to share with a male. For the whole of another day she turned the idea over, having no strength left to thrust it aside but brought back in spite of herself to

428

the details of the trap, foreseeing the smallest details and fitting them in. By now it was an obsession, an idea that has driven home its point and that one no longer argues about. When she eventually acted in obedience to this pressure of the inevitable, she moved as in a dream, motivated by some other person, somebody she had never known in herself.

On the Sunday old Fouchard, who was nervous, had told the guerrillas that their sack of loaves would be taken to the Boisville quarries, a lonely spot two kilometres away, and as Prosper was doing something else it was Silvine he sent with the barrow. Was this not Fate taking a hand? She read in this a decree of destiny, and she talked and made the arrangements with Sambuc for the following evening in a clear voice, with no emotion, as though there was nothing else she could have done. The next day there were further signs and positive proofs that people and even things were willing the murder. To begin with old Fouchard was suddenly called away to Raucourt and left orders for the meal to be had without him, foreseeing that he could hardly be back before eight; and then Henriette, whose turn of duty at the hospital did not come until Tuesday, was warned quite late that she would have to act as replacement that evening for the person on duty, who was indisposed. And as Jean never left his room whatever noise was made, that only left Prosper who, she feared, might intervene. He didn't hold with slaughtering a man like that, several to one. But when he saw his brother arrive with his two lieutenants his disgust with that vile crew only reinforced his hatred of the Prussians – certainly he was not going to save one of those filthy swine, even if he were dealt with in a foul manner, and he preferred to go to bed and bury his head in the pillow so as not to hear anything and be tempted to behave as a soldier should.

It was a quarter to seven and Charlot simply would not go to sleep. Usually as soon as he had had his supper his head fell on the table.

'Now come along, my darling, off we go to sleep,' Silvine said over and over again in Henriette's room where she had taken him. 'See how nice it is in Auntie's big beddybyes!'

But the child was delighted with this treat and jumped up and down, choking with giggles.

'No, no, stay here, Mummy . . . play with me, Mummy.'

She was very patient and very nice to him, caressing him and repeating:

'Go to bye-byes, ducky . . . bye-byes to please Mummy!'

The child at last dropped off, a laugh still on his lips. She had not bothered to undress him, but covered him up cosily and went away without locking the door because as a rule he slept so soundly.

Never had Silvine felt so calm, with her mind so clear and alert. She was prompt in decision and light in movement as though she were a disembodied spirit and acting under orders from that other self, the one she didn't know. She had already let in Sambuc, with Cabasse and Ducat, warning them to be extremely careful, and she took them to her room and posted them on either side of the window, which she opened in spite of the cold. It was very dark and the room was only very faintly lit by the reflection from the snow. The countryside was as still as death, and interminable minutes went by. At last, hearing a little sound of approaching footsteps, Silvine left and went back to the kitchen and sat there, quite still, her big eyes gazing at the candle flame.

And it still took a long time. Goliath prowled all round the farmhouse before venturing in. He thought he knew Silvine and so he had taken the risk of coming with only a revolver in his belt. But he had some misgivings, and pushed the window wide open, looked in and called softly:

'Silvine! Silvine!'

Since the window was open it must mean that she had thought it over and was willing. This was a great joy, but he would have preferred to see her there to welcome and reassure him. Perhaps Daddy Fouchard had called her away to finish some job. He raised his voice a little.

'Silvine! Silvine!'

No answer, not a breath. He stepped over the sill and went in, meaning to slip into the bed and wait for her under the sheets, for it was so cold.

Suddenly there was a furious scrimmage, with stampings and slippings, muffled oaths and snorts. Sambuc and the two others had fallen upon Goliath, and in spite of their number they could not immediately master the giant, whose strength was increased by danger. In the darkness there could be heard crackings of bones and the panting of men grappling. Fortunately the revolver had fallen

430

on to the floor. A voice, Cabasse's, gasped: 'The ropes! The ropes!' and Ducat passed to Sambuc the bundle of ropes they had taken the precaution of bringing with them. There followed a long, savage operation involving kicks and punches; the legs tied first, then the arms tied to the sides, then the whole body tied up by feel, depending on the man's jerking struggles, with such a riot of turns and knots that the man was enveloped in a sort of net, some of the meshes of which cut into his flesh. He never stopped shouting and Ducat's voice went on saying: 'Shut your jaw!' The cries stopped. Cabasse had roughly tied an old blue handkerchief over his mouth. Then they regained their breath and carried him like a bale into the kitchen, where they laid him out on the big table beside the candle.

'The Prussian shit!' swore Sambuc, mopping his brow. 'He didn't half give us some trouble! I say, Silvine, light another candle, will you, so as we can take a good look at the bleeding swine!'

Silvine was standing there with her big eyes staring in her pale face. She didn't say a word, but lit a candle and put it on the other side of Goliath, who could be seen lit up as though between two church candles. At that moment their eyes met, and his desperately implored her, for he was terrified, but she showed no sign of understanding, and stepped backwards to the dresser and stood there cold and immovable.

'The bugger's eaten half my finger,' growled Cabasse, whose hand was bleeding. 'I must break something of his.'

He was already pointing the revolver, which he had picked up, but Sambuc disarmed him.

'No, no! Don't act silly! We're not brigands, we're judges ... Do you hear, you Prussian filth, we're going to give you a trial, and don't you fear, we respect the right to a defence ... You're not going to defend yourself, though, because if we took your muzzle off you'd shout the place down. But in a minute I'll give you an advocate, and a first class one!'

He found three chairs and put them in a row, then arranged what he called the tribunal, with himself in the middle and his two henchmen on his right and left. All three took their seats and then he stood up again and began speaking with a mock dignity which, however, gradually swelled and grew into avenging anger.

'I am both presiding judge and public prosecutor. That's not quite in order, but there are not enough of us ... So: I accuse you of coming to spy on us in France and thus repaying us for the bread eaten at our tables with the most odious treachery. For you are the prime cause of the disaster, you are the traitor who, after the fight at Nouart, guided the Bavarians to Beaumont by night through the Dieulet woods. To do that it needed a man who had lived a long time in the district and got to know even the smallest paths, and we are quite convinced that you were seen guiding the artillery along some dreadful tracks like rivers of mud, in which they had to harness eight horses to each piece of equipment. When you see these roads again it is unbelievable, and you wonder how an army corps could possibly have gone that way. If it hadn't been for you and the criminal way you did well for yourself out of us and then betrayed us, the surprise at Beaumont would not have happened, we should never have gone to Sedan and perhaps we might have licked you in the end. And I'm not going into the disgusting job you are still doing, the nerve with which you come back here in triumph, denouncing and terrorizing poor people ... You are the lowest of the low, I demand the penalty of death.'

There was a hushed silence. He resumed his seat and then said:

'I nominate Ducat to defend you ... He has been in the law and he would have gone a long way if it hadn't been for his passions. So you see I'm not refusing you anything and we are being very considerate.'

Goliath, who could not move even a finger, turned his eyes towards his makeshift counsel for the defence. His eyes were the only living part of him left, and they were eyes of burning supplication beneath a livid forehead dripping great drops of anguished sweat in spite of the cold.

'Gentlemen,' said Ducat, rising to make his plea, 'my client is indeed the most stinking of rogues, and I would not undertake to defend him were it not my duty to point out in mitigation that they are all like that in his country ...

'Look at him, you can see by his eyes that he is quite amazed. He doesn't realize his crime. In France we only touch our spies with tongs, but in his country spying is a very honourable career, a meritorious way of serving one's country ... I will even go so far as to say, gentlemen, that they may not be wrong. Our noble sentiments do us honour, but unfortunately they have led us to

defeat. If I may so express it, *quos vult perdere Jupiter dementat* ...
You will appreciate the point of that, Gentlemen.'

He resumed his seat, and Sambuc went on:

'And you, Cabasse, have you anything to say for or against the accused?'

'What I have to say,' cried the southerner, 'is that we don't need all this lot of balls to settle this bugger's hash ... I've had quite a lot of troubles in my time, but I don't like joking about things to do with justice, it's unlucky ... Death! Death!'

Sambuc solemnly rose to his feet again.

'So this is the sentence you both pass – death?'

'Yes, yes, death!'

The chairs were pushed back and he went up to Goliath and said:

'Judgement has been passed. You are to die.'

The two candles were burning with tall flames, like altar-candles, on each side of Goliath's agonized face. He was making such efforts to beg for mercy, to shout words he could not get out, that the blue handkerchief over his mouth was soaked in foam. It was a terrible sight, this man reduced to silence, already as mute as a corpse, about to die with a flood of explanations and pleas stuck in his throat.

Cabasse was cocking the revolver.

'Shall I blow his face in?' he asked.

'Oh no, no!' cried Sambuc. 'He would be only too pleased.'

And turning to Goliath:

'You're not a soldier, you don't deserve the honour of departing with a bullet in your head. No, you're going to peg out like the dirty swine of a spy you are.'

He turned round and politely asked:

'Silvine, I'm not giving you orders, but I should like to have a wash-tub.'

During the trial scene Silvine had kept quite still. She was waiting, with set face, detached from herself and wholly occupied with the fixed idea that had motivated her for two days. When she was asked for a tub she just obeyed, disappeared for a moment into the cellar and returned with a big tub she used for washing Charlot's clothes.

'Put it under the table, near the edge.'

She put it there and as she straightened up her eyes once again caught Goliath's. There was in the wretched man's eyes a last supplication, and also the revolt of a man who didn't want to die. But at that moment there was nothing left of the woman in her, nothing but the desire for this death, awaited as a deliverance. She went back again to the dresser, where she stayed.

Sambuc had opened the table drawer and taken out a big kitchen knife, the one they used for slicing the bacon.

'All right, as you're a pig I'm going to bleed you like a pig.'

He took his time, and discussed with Cabasse and Ducat the way to do the butchering job properly. There was even a dispute because Cabasse said that in his part of the world, in Provence, pigs were bled head down, while Ducat protested, outraged, considering this method barbarous and inconvenient.

'Move him to the edge of the table over the tub so as not to make a mess.'

They moved him over, and Sambuc proceeded calmly and neatly. With a single cut of the big knife he slit the throat across. The blood from the severed carotid poured out at once into the tub with a little noise like falling water. He had taken care with the cut and only a few drops pumped out with the heartbeats. Although this made death slower, there were no struggles visible, for the ropes were strong and the body remained quite motionless. Not a single jerk or gasp. The only way the march of death could be followed was on the face, a mask distorted by terror, from which the blood was receding drop by drop as the skin lost its colour and went white as a sheet. The eyes also emptied themselves. They dimmed and then went out.

'I say, Silvine, we shall have to have a sponge, though.'

She did not respond, but seemed rooted to the floor, and her arms had closed instinctively over her breast like a collar of iron. She was watching. Then she suddenly realized that Charlot was there, clinging to her skirt. He must have woken up and managed to open the doors, and nobody had seen him tiptoe in, like the inquisitive child he was. How long had he been there, half hidden behind his mother? He was watching, too. With his big blue eyes, under his mop of yellow hair, he was looking at the blood running down, the little red trickle slowly filling the tub. Perhaps it amused him. Had he not understood at first? Was he suddenly touched by the wind of horror, did he have an instinctive consciousness of the abomination he was witnessing? Anyhow, he suddenly screamed in panic:

'Oh Mummy, Mummy! I'm frightened, take me away!'

It shook Silvine to the depths of her being. It was too much, and something gave way within her, horror at last got the better of the strength and excitement of the obsession that had kept her going for two days. The woman in her came back, she burst into tears and desperately picked up Charlot and hugged him to her breast. In terror she rushed madly away with him, unable to hear or see any more, with no other desire but to lose herself anywhere in the first hole she could find.

It was at that moment that Jean made up his mind to open the door of his room gently. Although he never bothered about the sounds in the house, he was surprised this time by the comings and goings and loud voices he heard. And so it was into his quiet room that Silvine tumbled sobbing and shaken in such a paroxysm of distress that at first he could not make any sense out of the disconnected words she muttered through clenched teeth. She kept repeating the same gesture, as though she were thrusting aside an atrocious vision. But at length he did understand, and he also pieced together the story of the ambush, the mother standing by, the child clinging to her skirt, the face of the father with his throat cut and life-blood ebbing away; it froze him, and the heart of this peasant and soldier was rent with anguish. Oh war, abominable war, that turned all these poor people into wild beasts, sowed dreadful hatreds, the son splashed with his father's blood, perpetuating national hatred and doomed to grow up in time to execrate his father's family, whom some day perhaps he would go and exterminate! Murderous seed sown to produce appalling harvests!

Silvine collapsed on to a chair, wildly kissing Charlot who was crying on her breast, and she repeated on and on the same sentence, the cry of her bleeding heart.

'Oh my poor child, they'll never call you a Prussian again! ... Oh my poor child, they'll never call you a Prussian again!'

Down in the kitchen old Fouchard had arrived. He had rapped on the door with the master's authority, and they had decided to let him in. And certainly he had had an unpleasant surprise, finding this dead man on his table and a tub full of blood underneath. Naturally, with his not very patient nature, he had lost his temper.

'Look here, you bloody tikes, couldn't you have done your dirty work outside? Do you take my house for a dunghill, coming and fouling up the furniture with things like this?'

As Sambuc began making apologies and explanations he grew more alarmed and more annoyed.

'What the hell do you suppose I'm going to do with this dead body of yours? Do you think it's the way to behave, to come and land a dead body on someone without thinking what he'll do with it? Suppose a patrol were to come in, I should be in a nice pickle! You lot couldn't care less, you never asked yourselves whether it would cost me my life. Well, by Christ, you'll have me to reckon with if you don't take your corpse away at once! Do you hear, take it by the head or by the feet or anyhow you like, but don't you let it hang about here, and don't let there be a hair left three minutes from now!'

In the end Sambuc got a sack from old Fouchard, much as the latter's heart bled at having to give something else away. He chose it from among the worst he could find, saying that a sack with holes in was still too good for a Prussian. But Cabasse and Ducat had a terrible job to get Goliath into the sack – his body was too big, too long, and the feet stuck out. Then they took him outside and loaded him on to the barrow they used to carry the bread.

'I'll give you my word of honour,' declared Sambuc, 'that we'll chuck him into the Meuse.'

'Above all,' insisted Fouchard, 'tie two big stones to the feet so that the bugger doesn't come up again!'

The little procession disappeared over the snow into the black night, and the only sound to be heard was the melancholy squeaking of the barrow.

Sambuc always swore by the head of his father that he really had tied two heavy stones to the feet. Yet the body came up and the Prussians discovered it three days later at Pont-Maugis, caught in the reeds, and their fury was terrible when they found in the sack this dead man who had been bled from the neck like a porker. There were terrible threats, harsh measures, searches of premises. Perhaps some people talked too much, for one evening the mayor of Remilly and old Fouchard were arrested, suspected of having been too friendly with the guerrillas who were being accused of the crime. In this extremity old Fouchard was really very fine, with the

imperturbability of an old peasant conscious of the invincible
strength of calm and silence. He marched off without any panic,
without even asking for an explanation. We should see. It was
whispered round about that he had made a large fortune out of the
Prussians, sacks of coins buried somewhere, one by one, as he
earned them.

Henriette was terribly worried when she heard about all this
business. Once again Jean wanted to go away for fear of
compromising the people who had harboured him, although the
doctor thought he was still not strong enough, and she insisted that
he should wait two more weeks, being herself oppressed with
renewed sadness at the coming necessity of a separation. When old
Fouchard was arrested Jean had been able to avoid capture by
hiding in the depths of the barn, but wasn't he in constant danger
of being discovered and taken away at any moment in the likely
event of further searches? And besides, she was worried about her
uncle's fate. So she decided to go into Sedan one morning and see
the Delaherches, who had billeted on them, it was said, a very
influential Prussian officer.

'Silvine,' she said as she was leaving, 'take good care of our
invalid, give him his broth at twelve and his medicine at four.'

The maid, busy with her usual jobs, was once again the brave
and self-effacing woman, running the farm now in the master's
absence, with Charlot laughing and capering round her.

'Never you fear, Madame, he won't go short of anything with
me here to look after him.'

6

AT the Delaherches's house in the rue Maqua in Sedan, life had
started up again after the terrible upheavals of the battle and capitulation, and for nearly four months day followed day under the
dreary yoke of the Prussian occupation.

But one corner of the great factory block remained shut up and
looked uninhabited – the room looking on to the road at one
end of the proprietor's quarters, where Colonel de Vineuil was
still living. Whereas the other windows were open and revealed

quite a lot of activity and bustle of life, the windows of this room seemed dead, with their blinds obstinately closed. The colonel had complained about his eyes and said that strong light made them hurt. Nobody knew whether it was true or not, but a lamp was kept burning in his room night and day to humour him. He had had to stay in bed for two whole months, although all Major Bouroche had diagnosed was a cracked ankle-bone, but the wound would not heal and all sorts of complications had developed. Now he did get up, but he was in such a state of dejection, afflicted by some indefinable ill which was so intractable and all-pervading that he spent his days lying on a couch in front of a big wood fire. He was losing weight and becoming a wraith, and the doctor who attended him was very puzzled because he could find nothing wrong, no reason for this slow death. He was flickering out like a flame.

Old Madame Delaherche had shut herself up with him on the day after the occupation. They had no doubt come to an understanding, in a few words and once and for all, about their definite wish to remain cloistered together in this room so long as there were Prussians billeted in the house. Many had spent only two or three nights there, but one, Captain von Gartlauben, was there permanently. However, neither the colonel nor the old lady had ever referred to these things again. For all her seventy-eight years she rose at dawn and came and took up her position in an armchair opposite her friend on the other side of the fireplace, and in the unchanging light of the lamp she began knitting stockings for poor children, while he, staring into the wood fire, never did anything, and seemed to be living and dying with but one thought, in a growing lethargy. They certainly did not exchange twenty words in a whole day, and if at any time, simply because she came and went about the house, she inadvertently let some item of outside news escape her, he always stopped her with a gesture. So now nothing whatever came in from life outside, nothing about the siege of Paris, the defeats on the Loire, the daily sufferings of the invasion. But however much, in this voluntary entombment, he refused to see the light of day and stuffed up his ears, the whole appalling disaster and mortal grief must have been reaching him through the cracks, in the air he breathed; for hour by hour he was none the less poisoned by these things and brought nearer to death.

All through this period Delaherche, very much in the light of day and anxious to go on living, was busying himself with trying to reopen his mill. So far he had only been able to get a few looms working again, in the disorganization of workers and customers. And to occupy himself during his boring free time he had had the idea of making a complete inventory of his premises and working out certain improvements he had been dreaming of for a long time. It happened that he had on the spot, to help him in this job, a young man who had found shelter in his house after the battle, son of one of his customers. Edmond Lagarde, brought up at Passy in his father's small drapery business, had been a sergeant in the 5th infantry, was barely twenty-three and looked no more than eighteen, and he had behaved under fire like a hero and with such tenacity that he had come in through the Ménil gate at about five with his left arm broken by one of the last bullets. Ever since the wounded had been moved out from his sheds Delaherche had kept him out of kindness. Thus Edmond was part of the family, eating, sleeping and living there, and now quite recovered and acting as secretary to the mill-owner while waiting to be able to return to Paris. Thanks to Delaherche's protection, and on his solemn promise not to escape, the Prussian authorities left him alone. He was fair and blue-eyed, as pretty as a woman and moreover so diffident and modest that he blushed at the least thing. His mother had brought him up and deprived herself of everything, devoting the profits of the little business to paying for his years at school. He loved Paris and pined desperately for it in front of Gilberte, a wounded Cherubino whom she looked after with friendly affection.

Finally the family was also enlarged by the new guest, von Gartlauben, a captain in the Landwehr, whose regiment had replaced the regular troops in Sedan. In spite of his modest rank he was an influential figure, for an uncle of his was Governor-General, installed at Rheims, who had absolute power over the whole area. He also was proud of loving Paris, of having lived there and of being well aware of its politeness and refinements, and indeed he affected the impeccable behaviour of the man of breeding, concealing his native uncouthness beneath this polish. He always wore a tight-fitting uniform. He was tall and heavily built, keeping his age dark, for he was very distressed at being forty-five. Given a little more intelligence he could have been terrible, but his inordinate vanity kept him in a continual state of self-satisfaction, for he could never bring himself to believe that anybody could be laughing at him.

In due course he became a real saviour to Delaherche. But in the early days after the capitulation, what dreadful times they were! Sedan was overrun with German soldiers and in terror of being looted. In time the victorious troops moved off towards the valley of the Seine and only a garrison remained, and the town fell into the deathly peace of a cemetery – houses permanently shuttered, shops closed, streets empty by dusk, with the heavy tread and harsh cries of patrols. No papers came, or letters. It was like a sealed dungeon, a sudden amputation, with ignorance and foreboding about fresh disasters everybody felt were on the way. The crowning misery was the threat of famine. One morning people woke up to no bread, no meat and general ruin, as though the land had been eaten up by a swarm of locusts, following a week in which hundreds of thousands of men had poured through like a river in flood. The town had only two or three days' provisions left, and appeals had had to be made to Belgium, and everything now came from the neighbouring country across an open frontier, the customs having been swept away in the catastrophe. And of course there were continual annoyances, a struggle that began again every morning between the Prussian administration, set up in the Sub-Prefecture, and the town council in permanent session at the Hôtel de Ville. The latter was heroic in its non-cooperation, but however much it argued and only yielded inch by inch, the inhabitants were being crushed beneath the weight of ever increasing demands and arbitrary and too frequent commandeerings.

At first Delaherche had a great deal to put up with from the soldiers and officers billeted on him. Men of all sorts of nationalities tramped through his home, with pipes in their mouths. Every night there suddenly fell upon the town, without warning, two thousand men, three thousand men – infantry, cavalry, artillery – and although these men only had a right to shelter and fire, you often had to run about and find them food. The rooms where they slept were left in a revoltingly filthy state. Often the officers came in drunk and were more unbearable than the men. Yet discipline was so strict that acts of violence or pillage were rare. In the whole of Sedan there were only two women known to have been raped. It was only later, when Paris resisted, that they made their domination brutally felt, for they were exasperated that the struggle looked like going on for ever, and were always afraid of a mass uprising and the savage warfare declared on them by the guerrillas.

Delaherche had just had to have a commanding officer in the cavalry who slept in his boots and left behind filth even on the mantelpiece, when Captain von Gartlauben arrived in his house one pouring wet night in the second half of September. The first hour was pretty rough. He talked at the top of his voice, demanded the best room, clanking his sword as he came up the stairs. But once he saw Gilberte he went very formal, shut himself up in his room, passed people stiffly and bowed politely. He lived in constant adulation because everyone knew that a word from him to the colonel in command at Sedan would be enough to get a requisition mitigated or a man released. Recently his uncle, the Governor-General at Rheims, had issued a coldly ferocious proclamation declaring a state of siege and punishing with the death penalty any person helping the enemy, whether as a spy or by causing German troops to take the wrong route when they were responsible for transporting them, or by destroying bridges and cannon or damaging telegraph wires and railways. The enemy meant the French, and the hearts of the people were outraged when they read the big white poster on the door of the headquarters which made a crime out of their anguish and hopes. It was so hard to learn about fresh victories of the Germans through hurrahs from the garrison! Every day brought its own grief, soldiers lit big bonfires, sang and caroused all through the night, while the population, now forced to be indoors by nine, listened in their darkened houses, beside themselves with uncertainty and guessing it meant yet another disaster. It was in one of these situations, towards mid October, that Captain von Gartlauben showed the first sign of some delicacy of mind. Since that morning a new hope had been born in Sedan, for there was a rumour of a great success for the army of the Loire on its way to relieve Paris. But so many times already the best news had turned into tidings of disaster! And indeed by that evening it was known that the Bavarian army had taken Orleans. In the rue Maqua, in a house opposite the mill, some soldiers were bellowing so loud that the captain, seeing Gilberte looking very upset, went and stopped them, for he himself thought that all this row was uncalled for.

The month went by and von Gartlauben found occasion to

render a few little services. The Prussian authorities had reorganized the administration, and a German sub-prefect had been appointed, which did not, however, prevent various annoyances from going on, although he was relatively reasonable. One of the most frequent difficulties always cropping up between the administration and the town council was the commandeering of vehicles, and a major fuss broke out one morning when Delaherche had been unable to send his carriage and two horses to the Sub-Prefecture. The mayor was put under arrest for a short time, and Delaherche would have gone to join him in the citadel had not Captain von Gartlauben taken simple steps to calm the storm. On another day, thanks to his intervention, the town was granted an extension of time when it was condemned to pay a fine of thirty thousand francs for alleged delays in the reconstruction of the Villette bridge, which had been demolished by the Prussians – a deplorable affair which ruined Sedan and filled it with consternation. But above all it was after the surrender of Metz that Delaherche was really indebted to his guest. The dreadful news had been like the trump of doom to the inhabitants, and the end of their last hopes, and by the following week overwhelming numbers of troops had appeared once again, the flood of men from Metz, the army of Prince Friedrich Karl heading for the Loire, that of General Manteuffel marching towards Amiens and Rouen, and other corps on their way to reinforce the armies besieging Paris. For some days the houses were crammed with soldiery, bakers and butchers were cleaned out to the last crumb and bone, and the streets reeked of sweat as though a huge migrating herd had passed through. The factory in the rue Maqua alone did not have to suffer from this flow of human cattle, for it was preserved by a friendly hand and classified only for lodging a few officers of good breeding.

So it came about that Delaherche eventually gave up his unfriendly attitude. The better class families had shut themselves up in their apartments and avoided any contact with the officers they had billeted on them. But he, with his continual urge to talk, please people and enjoy life, found this role of sulking victim very irksome. His big, cold, silent house in which each one kept to himself in the stiffness of resentment, got terribly on his nerves. So one day he began by stopping von Gartlauben on the staircase and thanking him for his kind services. Gradually the habit grew and the two men exchanged a few words when they met, and thus one evening the Prussian captain found himself sitting in the manufacturer's study, by the fire on which enormous oak logs were blazing, smoking a cigar and discussing recent events in a friendly way. For the first two weeks Gilberte did not appear and he pretended to be unaware of her existence, although at the slightest sound he glanced quickly at the door of the next room. He seemed to want everybody to forget his position as one of the conquerors, displayed a fair and broad-minded attitude, and often joked about some of the more laughable requisitions. For instance one day a coffin and a bandage had been requisitioned and that bandage and coffin struck him as very funny. For the rest, coal, oil, milk, sugar, butter, bread, meat, to say nothing of clothes, stoves, lamps, in fact anything that can be eaten or used in daily life, he just shrugged his shoulders about it. After all, what can you expect? It was annoying, no doubt, and he even admitted that they were asking for too much, but it was war, and you had to live in an enemy country. Delaherche, who was irritated by these incessant requisitionings, spoke out plainly and went over them in detail every evening as though he were going through his kitchen accounts. There was, however, just one fierce argument between them about the levy of a million francs which the Prussian prefect in Rethel had imposed upon the department of the Ardennes on the pretext that Germany needed compensation for losses caused by French warships and through the expulsion of Germans resident in France. The share to be paid by Sedan was forty-two thousand. Delaherche wore himself out trying to make his guest understand that that was iniquitous, that the situation of the town was exceptional because it had already suffered too much to be struck again in this way. As a matter of fact they both emerged from these explanations on more intimate terms, for he was delighted at having made himself drunk with his own verbosity, and the Prussian was pleased with himself for having displayed a quite Parisian urbanity.

One evening Gilberte entered in her gay, fly-away manner. She stopped dead, pretending to be surprised. Captain von Gartlauben rose to his feet and was tactful enough to retire almost at once. But the next day he found Gilberte already there, and he took his usual place on one side of the fireplace. That was the first of some delightful evenings spent in the study, and not in the drawing-room, which established a subtle distinction. Even later, when she consented to give her guest musical selections, which he loved, she went alone into the adjoining drawing-room, merely leaving the door open. Through this hard winter the ancient oaks of the Ardennes sent flames leaping high in the lofty fireplace, and at about ten they had a cup of tea and talked in the cosy warmth of the big room. Captain von Gartlauben had obviously fallen madly in love with this young woman with the merry laugh, who flirted with him as in the old days at Charleville she used to do with Captain Beaudoin's friends. He took even more care of his appearance, displayed the most exaggerated gallantry and gratefully accepted the tiniest favour, tortured by his one anxiety not to be taken for a barbarian, a brutal soldier who raped women.

Thus there were, so to speak, two parallel existences in the huge dark house in the rue Maqua. Whereas at meal times Edmond, with his pretty face like a wounded cherub, answered Delaherche's ceaseless prattle in monosyllables and blushed if Gilberte asked him to pass the salt, and in the evenings Captain von Gartlauben sat in the study listening with swimming eyes to a Mozart sonata she was playing for him in the drawing-room, the adjoining room in which Colonel de Vineuil and Madame Delaherche lived was always silent, with closed shutters, lamp eternally burning as though it were a tomb lit by a candle. December had buried the town in snow, and the dreadful news took second place in the intense cold. After the defeat of General Ducrot at Champigny and the loss of Orleans there was only one grim hope left, that the land of France itself would become the avenging land, the exterminating land devouring its own conquerors. Let the snow fall in ever thicker flakes, let the earth split open under blocks of ice and all Germany find its grave therein! Then a new anguish twisted old Madame Delaherche's heart. One night when her son was called away into Belgium on business she had heard, as she passed Gilberte's door, the sound of soft voices, stifled kisses and laughter. She went back to her own room horrified by the abomination she suspected. It could only be the Prussian in there; she had as a matter of fact thought she had noticed a certain understanding in the way they looked at each other, and she was stunned by this ultimate shame. Oh, this woman her son had brought into the home against her advice, this harlot whom she had already forgiven once, by holding her peace after Captain Beaudoin's death! And it was all beginning again, and this time it was the lowest infamy! What should she do? Such a monstrous thing could not go on under her roof. The agony of the cloistered life she lived was made worse, and she had days of fearful struggle. On the days when she came into the colonel's room sadder than ever and silent for hours, with tears in her eyes, he looked at her and imagined that France had suffered yet another defeat.

It was at this juncture that Henriette appeared one morning in the rue Maqua to try to interest the Delaherches in the fate of her uncle Fouchard. She had heard sniggering gossip about the all-powerful influence Gilberte had on Captain von Gartlauben, and so she was a little embarrassed when she met old Madame Delaherche first, on the stairs, going up to the colonel's room, for she felt she ought to explain the object of her visit to her.

'Oh Madame, it would be so kind of you if you could help ... My uncle is in a terrible position and might be sent off to Germany, it is said!'

The old lady, although she was fond of Henriette, made an angry gesture.

'But my dear child, I have no power at all ... I'm not the one to ask!'

And although she could see how upset Henriette was, she went on:

'You come at a very awkward moment, my son is off to Brussels this evening ... In any case he is powerless, just as I am ... You'd better see my daughter-in-law, who can do anything.'

She left Henriette very troubled and now quite sure she had stumbled into a family crisis. Since the previous day Madame Delaherche had made up her mind to tell her son everything before he left for Belgium, where he was going to negotiate a large purchase of coal in the hope of starting up his looms again. Never would she countenance a resumption of this abominable thing right under her nose during this new absence. So before saying anything she was waiting to be sure that he would not postpone his departure to another day, as he had been doing for a week. It meant the collapse of the household, the Prussian turned out, the woman thrown out into the street and her name ignominiously placarded on walls, as they had threatened to do for any French woman who gave herself to a German.

When Gilberte saw Henriette she uttered a cry of joy.

'Oh I'm so glad to see you! It seems such a long time, and we are getting so old in these horrid times!'

She dragged her into her own room, sat her down on the couch and hugged her.

'Look here, you're going to have lunch with us . . . But let's talk first. You must have such a lot to tell me! . . . I know you've had no news about your brother . . . Poor Maurice, how sorry I am for him in Paris with no gas, no fuel, perhaps no bread! . . . And what about this fellow you're looking after, your brother's friend? You can tell I've already heard some tales about it . . . Have you come about him?'

Henriette hesitated to answer, feeling very embarrassed. For wasn't it really for Jean's sake that she was coming, in order to make sure that once her uncle was released they wouldn't worry her beloved invalid any more? Merely hearing Gilberte mention him had filled her with confusion, and she now dared not reveal the real motive of her visit, for her conscience began to worry her and she recoiled from using the questionable influence she believed Gilberte to have.

'So,' Gilberte said again, with an arch look, 'it is to do with that chap that you want our help?'

Then as Henriette, forced into a corner, did bring herself to mention Fouchard's arrest:

'Of course, yes, how silly I am, and I was talking about it only this morning! . . . Oh my dear, you were quite right to come. We must do something about your uncle at once, because the latest news I've had was none too good. They mean to make an example.'

'Yes, I thought of you,' Henriette ventured hesitantly. 'I thought you would give me some good advice and could possibly do something . . .'

Gilberte went into a peal of laughter.

'Don't be silly, I'll get your uncle released within three days! . . . Haven't you been told that I've got a Prussian in the house who does everything I want? . . . You know, dear, he can't refuse me anything!'

She laughed louder still, with the scatterbrained triumph of a flirtatious female, holding her friend's hands and carressing her, while the latter could not find words to thank her, being very ill at

446

ease and afraid that this was an admission. And yet how untroubled and innocently gay she seemed!

'You leave it to me, and I'll send you home happy this evening!'

When they went into the dining-room Henriette was very much struck by the delicate beauty of Edmond, whom she did not know. He filled her with delight like some pretty object. Was it possible that this boy had fought in battle and that they had dared to break his arm? The legend of his great bravery enhanced his charm, and all the time the cutlets and potatoes in their jackets were being served Delaherche, who had welcomed Henriette with delight as being a new face, never stopped singing the praises of his new secretary, who was as industrious and good-mannered as he was handsome. The lunch, a foursome in the snug dining-room, was by way of becoming an intimate family party.

'So you have come to consult us about Papa Fouchard's fate?' Delaherche went on. 'I'm so sorry to have to go away tonight . . . But my wife will fix it up for you, she's irresistible and gets everything she wants.'

He laughed away as he said this with complete openness, merely flattered by this power of hers, for which he took some personal credit. Then he suddenly went on:

'By the way, my dear, didn't Edmond tell you what he has found?'

'No, what?' Gilberte gaily asked, turning her pretty, beaming eyes on the young sergeant.

The latter blushed as though overcome with rapture every time a woman looked at him like that.

'Oh, Madame, it's only some old lace that you would be sorry not to have for your mauve *négligée*. I was lucky enough yesterday to discover five metres of old Bruges point, really very lovely and quite cheap. The lady is coming to show it to you quite soon.'

She was thrilled and could have kissed him.

'Oh you are nice! I'll see you get your reward!'

Then as a pot of foie-gras, bought in Belgium, was being served, the conversation turned for a moment to the fish in the Meuse which were being poisoned and dying, and led to the danger of an epidemic threatening Sedan when the thaw came. Some cases had already occurred in November. Although immediately after the battle six thousand francs had been spent on cleaning the town and

447

burning piles of kit, ammunition pouches and all sorts of nasty rubbish, the surrounding country was still full of horrible stenches whenever the weather was at all muggy, for the ground was so full of corpses not properly buried and covered with only a few centimetres of earth. Everywhere graves made hummocks in the fields, the earth cracked from internal pressure and the putrefaction oozed out and polluted the air. And now during these last days a new source of infection had been found – the Meuse itself – although over twelve hundred bodies of horses had already been pulled out. The generally held view had been that there was not a single human corpse left in the river when a gamekeeper, looking carefully at some water over two metres deep, had noticed some white objects in it that might have been taken for stones. It was a carpet of corpses, bodies that had been slit open and so had never swollen up and floated to the surface. They had been lying there for nearly four months, in this water, among the weeds. Arms, legs and heads could be fished up with boathooks, and sometimes the mere strength of the current could detach and carry away a hand. The water went muddy and great bubbles of gas came up, burst and poisoned the air with a foul stench.

'It's a good thing it is freezing,' remarked Delaherche. 'But as soon as the snow has gone we shall have a thorough search and disinfect the whole thing, otherwise we shall all be goners.'

As his wife laughingly begged him to change to some nicer topic while they were eating, he concluded lamely:

'Ah well, the Meuse fish will be chancy for quite a time.'

By now they had finished and coffee was being served, when the maid said that Captain von Gartlauben was asking for the favour of being allowed in for a moment. There was a sensation because he had never come at this time, in the middle of the day. Delaherche at once said that he must come in, seeing a fortunate circumstance that would allow him to introduce Henriette. The captain, seeing another woman, was even more extravagantly polite. He even accepted a cup of coffee, which he took without sugar as he had seen many people do in Paris. As a matter of fact the only reason why he had insisted upon being asked in was his desire to tell Madame at once that he had obtained the release of one of her protégés, a poor workman in the mill who had been imprisoned after a set-to with a Prussian soldier.

Then Gilberte took advantage of the opportunity to mention old Fouchard.

'Captain, may I introduce one of my best friends ... She wants you to help her; she is the niece of the farmer they arrested at Remilly, you remember, after that fuss over the guerrillas.'

'Oh yes, that business about the spy, the poor devil they found in a sack ... Oh that is serious, very serious – I'm very much afraid there is nothing I can do.'

'Captain, you would make me so happy!'

She turned caressing eyes on him and he showed smug satisfaction and bowed with an air of gallant obedience. Anything she wanted!

'Sir, I would be most grateful,' Henriette managed to stammer out, overcome with irresistible revulsion as she suddenly thought of her husband, her poor Weiss, shot up there at Bazeilles.

Edmond, who had discreetly withdrawn as soon as the captain came in, now returned and whispered a word in Gilberte's ear. She leaped up, explained about the lace, which the woman had just brought, apologized and followed the young man out. Finding herself alone with the two men, Henriette was able to withdraw into herself and sit in a window recess while they went on talking at the tops of their voices.

'Captain, do have a brandy ... You see, I'm not standing on ceremony, but saying whatever I think, because I know how broad-minded you are. Well then, I assure you that your prefect is making a mistake by insisting on bleeding the town still more with this forty-two thousand francs. Just think what our sacrifices add up to since the beginning. First, just before the battle, the whole of the French army, exhausted and ravenous. Then you, and you were famished too. Just these troops going through, requisitions, repairs, expenses of all kinds, these things alone have cost us a million and a half. Add to that as much again for damage caused by the battle, destruction, fires – that makes three million. And finally I estimate the loss to industry and commerce at two million ... Well now, what do you say to that! That brings us to a figure of five million for a town of thirteen thousand inhabitants! And you are asking for another levy of forty-two thousand, I don't quite know what for! Is it fair? Is it reasonable?'

Captain von Gartlauben nodded and merely answered:

'What do you expect? It's war, it's war!'

The wait went on and Henriette's ears were buzzing and all sorts of vague and gloomy thoughts were making her dizzy as she sat there in the window seat while Delaherche was swearing on his honour that Sedan would never have been able to cope with the crisis, given the almost total lack of legal coinage, had it not been for the heaven-sent notion of creating a local token currency – paper money issued by the Caisse du Crédit Industriel, which had saved the town from financial disaster.

'Captain, do have another little glass of brandy . . .'

And he jumped to another subject.

'It wasn't France that made the war, it was the Empire . . . Oh, the Emperor took me in altogether. It's all over with him, we would rather be hacked to pieces than . . . You see, only one man saw how things really were in July, yes, Monsieur Thiers, whose present tour of European capitals is another great act of wisdom and patriotism. The wishes of all reasonable people go with him, may he be successful!'

He completed his thought with a gesture, for he would have deemed it improper to express a desire for peace in front of a Prussian, even a friendly one. But this desire was very strong in him, as it was in the hearts of all the old conservative bourgeoisie who had taken part in the referendum. They were coming to the end of their blood and their money and would have to give in, and from all the occupied provinces there was rising a sullen resentment against Paris, with its obstinate resistance. So he lowered his voice and, alluding to Gambetta's inflammatory proclamation, concluded:

'No, no, we can't go on with these lunatics. It would be massacre . . . I'm all for Monsieur Thiers, who wants elections, and as for this Republic of theirs, well, that doesn't worry me and they can keep it if they want to until we get something better.'

Very politely Captain von Gartlauben went on nodding his approval and repeating:

'Of course, of course . . .'

Henriette, who had grown more and more embarrassed, could not stay there any longer. She felt an irritation without any clear reason, a need not to be there, so she rose softly and went to look for Gilberte, who had kept her waiting so long.

But as she went into the bedroom she was appalled to see her friend lying on the couch in tears and terribly upset.

'Good gracious, what is it? What's happened?'

The young woman wept even more bitterly and would not answer, but she was in such a state of confusion that all the blood in her body seemed to have rushed to her face. But in the end she threw herself into Henriette's outstretched arms.

'Oh my dear, if only you knew ... Never can I dare tell you ... And yet you're the only one I have, and you alone may be able to give me some good advice.'

A shudder ran through her and her speech became even more confused.

'I was with Edmond ... And then, only a moment ago, Madame Delaherche caught me ...'

'What do you mean, caught you?'

'Yes, we were here, he was holding me, and kissing me ...'

Then she kissed Henriette, held her tight in her trembling arms and told her everything.

'Oh my dear, don't think too ill of me, it would hurt me so much! ... I know I had sworn it would never start again ... But you have seen Edmond, he is so brave, and so handsome! And then just think, this poor young man, wounded, ill, far from his mother! And then he's never had any money because everything at home went into his education ... I tell you, I simply couldn't refuse.'

Henriette was horrified and could not get over her amazement.

'What! It was with that young sergeant? But my dear, everybody thinks you're the Prussian's mistress!'

At once Gilberte leaped up, dried her tears and protested:

'Mistress of that Prussian ... Oh no, the very idea of such a thing! He's horrible and gives me the creeps ... What do they take me for? How could anyone think me capable of such infamy! No, no, never! I'd rather die!'

Her outrage had made her serious, with a suffering and angry beauty that transfigured her. But suddenly her coquettish gaiety and careless frivolity came back in an irrepressible laugh.

'Well, it's true I play with him. He worships me, and I only have to look at him and he obeys ... If only you knew how funny it is to tease that great lump, who always seems to think he is at last going to be rewarded!'

'But that's a very dangerous game,' said Henriette seriously.

'Do you think so? What risk do I run? When he sees that he can't expect anything he can only get annoyed and go away ... But no, he'll never see it! You don't know the man, he's one of the kind with whom women can go as far as they like without any danger. You see in that respect I have an instinct that has always warned me. He is far too conceited, and he'll never admit that I've been having him on ... All I shall allow him to do is take away memories of me, with the consolation of telling himself that he acted correctly, like a well-bred gentleman who has spent a long time in Paris.'

She thought this was very funny, and went on:

'Meanwhile we'll get your uncle Fouchard set free, and all he'll have for his trouble will be a cup of tea sugared with my own fair hand.'

But then she suddenly veered back to her fears and the fright of having been surprised, and her eyes began swimming with tears again.

'Oh God! And Madame Delaherche? ... Whatever will happen? She has no love for me and is quite capable of telling my husband everything.'

Henriette had recovered her calm. She dried her friend's eyes and forced her to put her clothes to rights.

'Listen, dear, I haven't the heart to scold you, and yet you know that I don't approve at all. But I had been given such a scare over your Prussian, and had dreaded such nasty things that this other affair is really a relief ... Cheer up, it will all work out.'

Which was wise, especially as Delaherche came in almost at once with his mother. He explained that he had sent for the carriage to take him into Belgium, as he had decided to go on by train to Brussels that evening. So he wanted to say good-bye to his wife. Then, turning to Henriette:

'Don't worry, Captain von Gartlauben promised when he left me that he would look into your uncle's affair, and when I've gone my wife will do the rest.'

Gilberte, who felt sick with anxiety, had never taken her eyes off Madame Delaherche since she had come in. Was she going to speak and say what she had just seen and prevent her son from going? The old lady said not a word, but as soon as she came through the door fixed her eyes on her daughter-in-law. With her uncompromising code she was probably feeling the same sense of relief that had made Henriette tolerant. Ah well, as it was this young man, a Frenchman who had fought so gallantly, shouldn't she overlook it as she had in the case of Captain Beaudoin? Her eyes softened and she looked away. Her son could go. Edmond would protect Gilberte against the Prussian. This woman, who had never been happy since the good news of the victory of Coulmiers, even smiled.

'Well, good-bye,' she said, kissing Delaherche. 'I hope the business goes through all right, and hurry back home.'

She went off and slowly returned to the closed room on the opposite side of the landing, where the colonel, in his dazed way, was watching the shadow beyond the pale circle of light that fell from the lamp.

That same evening Henriette went back to Remilly and one morning, three days later, she had the pleasure of seeing old Fouchard calmly coming back into the farmhouse as though he had walked back from doing some deal in the neighbourhood. He sat down and ate some bread and cheese. Then he answered all their questions unhurriedly, like a man who had never had any fear. Why should they have kept him? He'd done nothing wrong. He wasn't the one who had killed the Prussian, was he? Well, he had simply said to the authorities: 'Look where you like, I don't know anything.' And they had had to release him, and the mayor as well, for lack of proof. But his cunning and mocking peasant's eyes twinkled in quiet satisfaction at having diddled all those dirty buggers, for he was getting sick of the way they were now haggling about the quality of his meat.

December came to an end and Jean wanted to go. His leg was quite strong now and the doctor declared he could go and fight. It was a great sorrow for Henriette, but she tried to hide it. Since the disastrous battle of Champigny no news from Paris had reached them. They only knew that Maurice's regiment had been exposed to withering fire and lost many men. Then the unbroken silence, no letter and never the slightest line for them when they knew that families in Raucourt and Sedan had received notes by roundabout routes. Perhaps the pigeon bearing the news they so desperately longed for had run into some voracious hawk, or had been brought down on the edge of some forest by a Prussian bullet. What haunted them most of all was fear that Maurice was dead. The silence of that great city, gagged by the siege, had become for them, in the agony of waiting, the silence of the tomb. They had given up hope of finding out anything, and when Jean said that he was determined to go Henriette could only say in a doleful tone:

'Oh God, so it's all over, and I'm going to stay here alone!'

Jean meant to go and join up with the army of the north which General Faidherbe had reconstituted. Now that General Manteuffel's corps had reached Dieppe this army was defending three departments separated from the rest of France, the Nord, the Pas-de-Calais and the Somme, and Jean's plan, which was quite easy to carry out, was simply to get to Bouillon and then work round through Belgium. He knew that the 23rd corps was being completed with all the veterans of Sedan and Metz they could muster. He had heard that General Faidherbe was going over to the offensive, and he definitely arranged to leave on the following Sunday when he heard about the battle of Pont-Noyelle, an indecisive battle which the French had almost won.

And again it was Dr Dalichamp who offered to take him to Bouillon in his trap. His courage and kindness were inexhaustible. In Raucourt, which was ravaged by typhus brought by the Bavarians, he had patients in all the houses in addition to the two hospitals he visited, the Raucourt one itself and the one at Remilly. His burning patriotism and urge to protest against pointless violence had caused him to be arrested twice and then released by the Prussians. And so he was in a carefree laughing mood on the morning when he came for Jean with his trap, glad to be helping another Sedan victim to escape, one of these poor brave people, as he called those whom he looked after and helped out of his own pocket. Jean, who was embarrassed about money and knew how poor Henriette was, had accepted the fifty francs the doctor gave him for his journey.

Old Fouchard did things well for the send-off. He sent Silvine to get two bottles of wine and invited everybody to drink a glass to the extermination of the Germans. He was now quite the gentleman and had his money well hidden somewhere and, no longer worried about the guerrillas of the Dieulet woods, who had been hounded out like wild beasts, his one desire was to enjoy the coming peace when it was concluded. He had even, in a burst of generosity, paid Prosper some wages so as to tie him to the farm, not that the fellow had any wish to leave. He drank with Prosper, he insisted on drinking with Silvine, whom for one moment he had thought of marrying because she was so regular and good at her job. But why bother? He sensed that she would not uproot herself any more, but would still be there when Charlot grew up and went off in his turn to be a soldier. And when he had clinked glasses with the doctor, Henriette and Jean, he exclaimed:

'Here's a health to everybody, and may everybody prosper and be as well as I am!'

Henriette had insisted on going with Jean as far as Sedan. He was dressed like an ordinary civilian, in an overcoat and round felt hat lent by the doctor. On that day the sun was dazzling on the snow and it was bitterly cold. They were intending to go straight through the town without stopping, but when Jean realized that his colonel was still with the Delaherches he was filled with a great desire to go and see him and at the same time he could thank Monsieur Delaherche for his many kindnesses. This was to be his crowning distress in this town of disaster and grief. As they reached the mill in the rue Maqua they found the place turned upside down by a tragic end. Gilberte was in a flurry of dismay. Madame Delaherche said nothing but was weeping bitter tears, and her son had come up from the workshops, where work was coming back to normal, and was uttering exclamations of astonishment. The colonel had just been found on the floor of his room, where he had collapsed and died. The eternal lamp was burning alone in the closed room. A doctor summoned in haste had not understood why, for he could discover no likely cause such as an aneurism or stroke. He had been struck down as it were by a thunderbolt, but nobody knew whence it had fallen, and it was only the next day that they picked up a piece of an old newspaper that had been used to cover a book, and in it was a report on the fall of Metz.

'My dear,' Gilberte told Henriette, 'Monsieur von Gartlauben, when he went down the stairs just now, raised his hat as he passed the door of the room in which my uncle's body rests . . . Edmond saw him. He really is a very well-bred person, isn't he?'

Until then Jean had never embraced Henriette. Before climbing into the trap with the doctor he wanted to thank her for her care and kindness, for having looked after him and loved him like a brother. But the words would not come, so he opened his arms and embraced her, in tears. She was almost distraught and returned his kiss. When the horse started off he turned and they waved to one another and managed to say:

'Good-bye, good-bye.'

That night Henriette was back in Remilly and on duty at the hospital. During her long vigil she was suddenly seized with a terrible fit of crying, and she cried and cried, on and on, trying to stifle her grief between her clasped hands.

7

THE very day after Sedan the two German armies resumed the movement of their floods of men towards Paris, the army of the Meuse coming round to the north from the valley of the Marne and the army of the Crown Prince of Prussia crossing the Seine at Villeneuve-Saint-Georges and making for Versailles round the south of the city. On that warm September morning when General Ducrot, who had been put in command of the 14th corps, which had only just been formed, decided to attack the Crown Prince's army while it was executing its flanking march, Maurice, in camp in the woods to the left of Meudon with his new regiment, the 115th, only received marching orders when disaster was already certain. Just one or two shells had been enough, and a frightful panic had broken out in a battalion of Zouaves made up of recruits, and the rest of the troops had been swept along in such disarray that the stampede never stopped until they were inside the Paris fortifications, where the alarm was intense. All forward positions ahead of the forts to the south were lost, and that same evening the last thread linking the city to France, the telegraph line of the Western Railway, was cut. Paris was separated from the rest of the world.

It was an evening of terrible distress for Maurice. If the Germans had dared, they could have camped that night in the Place du Carrousel. But they were strictly prudent people, resolved to have a siege according to the rules, and they had already plotted the exact points of investment, with the cordon of the army of the Meuse to the north from Croissy to the Marne, passing through Epinay, and the other cordon of the third army to the south from Chennevières to Châtillon and Bougival, while the Prussian General Headquarters, with King William, Bismarck and von Moltke, controlled everything from Versailles. This gigantic blockade, believed to be impossible, was an accomplished fact. This city, with its bastioned wall eight and a half leagues in circumference, with its fifteen forts and six detached redoubts, was about to find itself so to speak in prison. The defending army consisted only of the 13th corps, rescued and brought back by General Vinoy, and the 14th, still being formed under General Ducrot, making between them a strength of eighty thousand soldiers, to which should be added the fourteen thousand marines, fifteen thousand volunteers, a hundred and fifteen thousand militia, apart from the three hundred thousand National Guards spread over the nine sectors of the ramparts. There might well be a whole people under arms, but there was a lack of seasoned and disciplined soldiers. Men were being equipped and drilled, and Paris was one huge armed camp. Preparations for defence grew more feverish hour by hour, roads were closed, houses in the military zone demolished, the two hundred heavy-calibre guns and the two thousand smaller ones all in use, with others being cast, a whole arsenal was rising out of the ground thanks to the great patriotic inspiration of the minister, Dorian. After the breaking off of negotiations at Ferrières when Jules Favre had made known the demands of Bismarck – cession of Alsace, internment of the garrison at Strasbourg, indemnity of three milliards – a howl of rage went up and the continuation of the war and resistance were acclaimed as indispensable conditions of the survival of France. Even with no hope of victory Paris had to defend herself so that the homeland might live.

One Sunday in late September Maurice was sent on fatigue duty right across the city, and the streets he went along and the open spaces he crossed filled him with new hope. Since the rout at Châtillon he felt that courage had risen to face the great task. Yes, the Paris he had known, so mad on pleasure and so near to giving itself up to the foulest vices, was now, he found, simple again, brave and cheerful, accepting any sacrifice. You saw nothing but uniforms, and even the least involved wore the képi of the National Guard. As a huge clock stops when the spring breaks, so social life had suddenly come to an end, and with it industry, commerce, business, leaving only one passion, to win through, and it was the only subject of conversation that inflamed all hearts and heads in public gatherings, during the watches in the guardroom and among the crowds continually blocking the pavements. Shared in common, illusions carried people's souls away and excitement flung them into the dangers of impetuous heroics. Already a crisis of unhealthy excitability was approaching a sort of epidemic fever, magnifying fear just as much as confidence and letting loose the human herd to rush off unbridled at the slightest stimulus. In the rue des Martyrs Maurice witnessed a scene which worked him up into a frenzy – a mass assault, a furious mob hurling itself upon a house where, at one of the upper windows, a brilliant lamp had been seen burning all night, obviously a signal flashed above Paris to the Prussians at Bellevue. Citizens felt compelled to live on their roofs so as to keep an eye on the surrounding country. On the previous day they had tried to drown in the round pond in the Tuileries some wretched person who was looking at a town plan he had unfolded on a seat.

Maurice, who had formerly been so fair-minded, also caught this disease of suspicion, with the uprooting of everything he had so far believed in. No longer did he despair, as he had on that evening of the Châtillon panic, wondering whether the French army would ever regain its manhood and fight; the sortie of 30 September to Hay and Chevilly, that of 13 October when the militia had taken Bagneux, and finally that of 21 October, during which his regiment had momentarily occupied the park of La Malmaison, had restored all his faith, this flame of hope which a mere spark sufficed to kindle and which consumed him. The Prussians may have stopped it at all points, but all the same the army had fought bravely and still might win. What however depressed Maurice so much was the great city of Paris, leaping from the heights of self-deception to the depths of discouragement, hag-ridden by the fear of treason in its need for victory. After the Emperor and Marshal MacMahon, were General Trochu and General Ducrot also going to be second-rate commanders and unconscious workers for defeat? The same impulse which had overthrown the Empire was now bidding fair to overthrow the Government of National Defence – the impatience of the violent militants to seize power and save France. Already Jules Favre and other members of the government were more unpopular than the ousted former ministers of Napoleon III. If they didn't want to beat the Prussians, well, they could make way for somebody else, for the revolutionaries who were sure of winning by decreeing a mass rising or by encouraging inventors who wanted to mine all the suburbs or annihilate the enemy under some novel hail of fireworks.

On the day before 31 October Maurice was attacked by this malady of mistrust and daydreaming and was now accepting sheer figments of the imagination that would formerly have made him smile. Why not? Was there any limit to stupidity and crime? Were not miracles becoming possible amid all the catastrophes upsetting the world? Inside him rancour had been slowly building up ever since the day, outside Mulhouse, when he heard about Froeschwiller. Sedan was making him bleed like a still tender wound that the smallest reverse was enough to reopen, and the shock of each of these defeats had unhinged him, for his bodily resistance had been lowered and his mind weakened by such a long succession of days without food and nights without sleep, dropped as he was into this terrifying nightmare existence, hardly even knowing if he were still alive. And the thought that so much suffering might end in a new and irremediable catastrophe drove him out of his mind and transformed this cultured man into a creature of instinct, reverting to childhood, always carried away by the emotion of the moment. Anything, destruction, even extermination, rather than yield up one sou of the wealth or one inch of the territory of France! This was the final stage of the evolution in him which ever since the first battle lost had been destroying the Napoleonic legend and the sentimental Bonapartism he derived from the epic narratives of his grandfather. He had even already left behind theoretical moderate republicanism and was tending towards revolutionary violence, believing in the necessity of terror to sweep away the incompetent and the traitors who were busy murdering the fatherland. And so by the 31st his heart was with the rioters when fresh disasters befell one after another: the loss of Le Bourget, so valiantly taken by the volunteers of *La Presse* during the night of the 27th to 28th; the arrival of M. Thiers at Versailles after his tour of the European capitals when he returned, it was said, to negotiate in the name of

Napóleon III; and finally the surrender of Metz, the absolute confirmation of which he brought back with him, after the vague rumours that had already been running round. This was the knockout blow, another Sedan and even more shameful. But next day, when he heard about the events at the Hôtel de Ville – how the insurgents were momentarily winning, with the members of the Government of National Defence held prisoner until four in the morning and then saved only by a change of mind on the part of the populace, who had begun by being exasperated with them but later become worried by the thought of a victorious insurrection – he was sorry that it had come to nothing. For this Commune might have brought salvation – a call to arms, the homeland in danger, all the classic memories of a free people refusing to die. M. Thiers did not even dare come into Paris, and after the breakdown of negotiations they were on the point of lighting up the illuminations.

The month of November went by in an atmosphere of feverish impatience. There were odd skirmishes in which Maurice was not involved. He was now bivouacked near Saint-Ouen, but got away whenever there was a chance, for he was devoured by a continual thirst for news. Like him, Paris was waiting anxiously.

The mayoral elections seemed to have relieved political tensions, but almost all the people elected belonged to extremist parties, which was a frightening outlook for the future. What Paris was waiting for during this lull was the grand sortie people had been demanding for so long – victory and deliverance. Once again there was no doubt about this, they would knock out the Prussians and walk over their bodies. Preparations had been made in the peninsula of Gennevilliers, which was the spot considered most favourable for a break-through. Then one morning came the delirious joy of the news of Coulmiers, Orleans recaptured, the army of the Loire on the march and already in camp at Etampes, it was said. All was changed, and the only thing left to do was go and join up with them on the other side of the Marne. The military forces had been reorganized and formed into three armies, one made up of battalions of the National Guard under the command of General Clément Thomas, another of the 13th and 14th corps strengthened with the best elements from more or less everywhere, which General Ducrot was to lead for the main attack, and the other, the third, the reserve army, consisting entirely of militia and entrusted to General Vinoy. Maurice was uplifted by an absolute faith on 28 November when he came to spend the night in the Bois de Vincennes with the 115th. The three corps of the second army were there, and it was being said that the link-up with the army of the Loire was fixed for the following day at Fontainebleau. And then, at once, came the mishaps, the usual blunders – a sudden rise in the river which prevented pontoon bridges from being thrown across, tiresome orders that slowed down troop movements. On the following night the 115th was one of the first to cross the river, and by ten, under a withering fire, Maurice reached the village of Champigny. He was half crazy, his rifle burned his hands in spite of the intense cold. His one desire since he had been advancing was to go straight ahead like this, without stopping, until the link-up had been made with their comrades from the country over there. But outside Champigny and Bry the army had come up against the walls of the estates of Coeuilly and Villiers, walls half a kilometre long, which the Prussians had turned into impregnable fortresses. That was the breaker on which all courage dashed itself to pieces. From that moment there was nothing left but hesitation and withdrawal; the third corps had been held up, the first and second, already immobilized, defended Champigny for two days but had to abandon it during the night of 2 December after their fruitless victory. That night the whole army came back and camped under the trees of the Bois de Vincennes, which were white with frost, and there Maurice, his feet dead with cold, and his face pressed to the frozen ground, wept.

What dreary, melancholy days after the fiasco of that immense effort! The grand sortie that had been in preparation for so long, the irresistible thrust that was to deliver Paris, had petered out, and three days later a letter from General von Moltke brought the news that the army of the Loire had been defeated and had once again abandoned Orleans. The ring was tightening still more and could not now be broken. But Paris, in a fever of despair, seemed to find new strength to resist. Threats of famine were beginning. Meat had been rationed since mid-October. By December there was not one animal left out of the huge herds of cattle and flocks of sheep that had been turned loose in the Bois de Boulogne and had galloped round in a continual cloud of dust, and they had begun slaughtering horses. Stocks of flour and corn, and subsequent requisitions, were to supply bread for four months. When flour had run out mills had had to be fitted up in the railway stations. Fuel also was running low, and was being reserved for milling grain, baking bread or making weapons. Paris, with no gas, lit by a few oil-lamps, Paris shivering under its covering of ice, Paris, with its rationed black bread and horsemeat, still went on hoping and talked of Faidherbe in the north, Chanzy on the Loire, Bourbaki in the east, as though some miracle were going to bring them victorious beneath her walls. The long queues waiting in the snow in front of bakers' and butchers' shops still sometimes cracked jokes at the news of imaginary great victories. After the consternation of each defeat illusion was born again, tenacious, burning ever brighter in this mob drugged with suffering and hunger. On the Place du Château d'Eau a soldier who had spoken of surrender had almost been lynched by passers-by. While the army, totally discouraged and seeing the end coming, was suing for peace, the civilians were demanding another mass sortie, a sortie like a flood, with the whole population, women and children, hurling themselves at the Prussians like a river in spate, carrying all before it.

Maurice cut himself off from his comrades and developed a growing hatred for his job as a soldier which kept him in the shelter of the Mont-Valérien, idle and useless. And so he found pretexts and escaped as soon as he could to get into Paris, where his heart was. He only felt at peace in the heart of the crowd, wanting to force himself to hope, like them. He often went to watch the balloons go up every other day from the Gare du Nord, taking carrier pigeons and dispatches. The balloons rose and disappeared into the dull wintry sky, and hearts ached with distress when the wind blew them towards Germany. Many must have come to grief. He himself had written twice to his sister Henriette without knowing whether she had his letters. The memory of his sister and of Jean was so remote, away in that great world from which nothing now came, that he seldom thought of them, as of affections he had left behind in some other existence. His whole being was too full of the continual storms of dejection and elation in which he was living. And then in the first days of January something else roused him to anger, the bombardment of the districts south of the Seine. He had come to ascribe the Prussian delays to reasons of humanity, whereas they were simply due to technical difficulties. Now that a shell had killed two little girls at the Val de Grâce he was full of furious contempt for these barbarians who murdered children and were threatening to burn down museums and libraries. But after the first days of shock Paris under fire went back to its life of heroic defiance.

Since the failure at Champigny there had been only one more unfortunate attempt, in the direction of Le Bourget, and on the evening when the plateau of Avron had to be evacuated under heavy artillery fire directed at the forts, Maurice shared the growing and violent irritation that possessed the whole city. The tide of unpopularity threatening to bring down Trochu and the Government of National Defence reached such a height that they were forced to make one supreme but unavailing effort. Why were they refusing to lead into the holocaust the three hundred thousand National Guards who were continually offering themselves and clamouring for their share in the danger? This was to be the torrential sortie everybody had been demanding since the first day, Paris bursting its dams and drowning the Prussians in the colossal flood of its people. The authorities were obliged to yield to this need for bravado, although a fresh defeat was inevitable, but in effect, to keep the massacre within limits, they only used the fifty-nine battalions of the National Guard already mobilized in addition to the regular army. The day before 19 January was like a public holiday: a vast crowd on the boulevards and in the Champs Elysées watched the regiments go by, led by bands and singing patriotic songs. Women and children marched along with them, men stood on seats and shouted emotional good wishes for victory. And then on the next day the whole population made for the Arc de Triomphe and was filled with wild hopes when the news of the occupation of Montretout came in during the morning. Epic stories were bandied about concerning the irresistible impetus of the National Guard, the Prussians were hurled back, Versailles would be taken before nightfall. And so what utter despair when evening came and the inevitable failure was known! While the left wing was occupying Montretout, the centre, which had got past the wall of Buzenval park, broke against a second inner wall. The thaw had set in and a persistent drizzle had turned the roads into slush and the guns, those guns cast with the help of public subscriptions, into which Paris had put its very soul, could not be moved up. On the right General Ducrot's column began moving too late and remained too far in the rear. That was the end of the effort, and General Trochu had to give the order for a general retreat. Montretout was abandoned, Saint-Cloud was abandoned and the Prussians set fire to it. By the time it was dark the horizon of Paris was a sheet of flame.

This time Maurice himself felt it was the end. For four hours he had stayed in the Buzenval park with some National Guards under the withering fire from the Prussian positions, and for days after, when he got back, he praised their valour. The National Guard had indeed behaved splendidly, which meant, didn't it, that the defeat must be due to the imbecility and treachery of their leaders? In the rue de Rivoli he ran into groups shouting 'Trochu out! Up with the Commune!' It was a re-awakening of revolutionary passion and a new upsurge of public opinion so disturbing that the Government of National Defence, as an act of self-preservation, felt it had to force General Trochu to resign and replaced him by General Vinoy. That same day Maurice went into a public meeting at Belleville and heard yet another clamour for a mass attack. The idea was crazy and he knew it, yet his heart beat faster in the face of this determination to win. When all is over can't one still attempt a miracle? All through that night he dreamed of wonders.

Eight more long days dragged on. Paris was in its death-throes, but never complained. Shops no longer opened, and the few people walking about never saw a vehicle in the deserted streets. Forty thousand horses had been eaten, and now dogs, cats and rats were becoming expensive. Since corn had vanished, the bread, made of rice and oats, was black, clammy and most indigestible, and to get the ration of three hundred grammes the interminable queues in front of bakers' shops were becoming killing. What a painful business these waits were in the siege, when poor women shivered in pouring rain, with their feet in freezing mud! It was the heroic misery of a great city that refused to give in. The death rate had tripled, and theatres had been turned into hospitals. By nightfall the formerly fashionable neighbourhoods fell into a gloomy silence and pitch darkness, like quarters of an accursed city ravaged by plague. In the silence and darkness the only thing to be heard was the ceaseless din of the bombardment, and the only thing to be seen the flashes of guns lighting up the winter sky.

On the 28th Paris suddenly heard that Jules Favre had been negotiating with Bismarck for two days with a view to an armistice, and at the same time that there was only enough bread left for ten days, scarcely time to restock the city with food. A surrender was being brutally forced on them. Paris, grief-stricken and stunned by the truth she had been told at last, just let things run their course. On that same day, at midnight, the last gun was fired. Then on the 29th, when the Germans had occupied the forts, Maurice went back into camp with the 115th near Montrouge, within the fortifications. Then there set in for him an unsettled existence, full of both idleness and feverish activity. Discipline had become very lax, soldiers ran wild and wandered about, waiting to be sent home. But he remained disturbed, nervy and touchy, full of anxiety which turned into exasperation at the slightest mishap. He greedily read the revolutionary papers, and this three-week armistice, concluded for the sole purpose of allowing France to elect an Assembly to settle peace terms, looked to him like a trap, a final act of treachery. Even if Paris was forced to capitulate, he was with Gambetta for the continuation of the war on the Loire and in the north. The disaster of the army of the east, which had been forgotten and forced to cross into Switzerland, made him indignant. The elections put the finishing touch to his fury – it was exactly what he had foreseen, the cowardly provinces, annoyed at the resistance of Paris and wanting peace on any terms with the monarchy restored while Prussian guns were still trained on them. After the first sittings of the Assembly at Bordeaux, Thiers, returned by twenty-six departments and acclaimed as head of the executive, became in his eyes the arch-monster, the man of every lie and every crime. Nothing could calm his anger, for this peace concluded by a monarchist Assembly struck him as the very depth of shame, and the very idea of the harsh conditions and the five milliard indemnity made him rave, with Metz handed over, Alsace abandoned, the gold and blood of France running away through this ever-open wound in her side.

It was then, in late February, that Maurice made up his mind to desert. A clause in the treaty stipulated that soldiers in camp in Paris should be disarmed and sent home. He did not wait, for he felt that his heart would be torn out of him if he left the streets of this glorious Paris, which hunger alone had succeeded in subjugating. So he disappeared, rented a tiny furnished room in a six-storey house in the rue des Orties, right at the top of the Butte des

Moulins. It was a sort of turret from which you could see the endless sea of roofs from the Tuileries to the Bastille. An old friend from his law-school days had lent him a hundred francs. And in any case, as soon as he was settled in he signed on in a battalion of the National Guard, and the one-franc-fifty pay would be enough for his needs. The thought of a comfortable, selfish existence in the country filled him with horror. Even the letters from his sister Henriette, to whom he had written immediately after the armistice, irritated him with their supplications and desperate longing to see him come home and rest at Remilly. He refused; he would go later when there weren't any Prussians left there.

So Maurice's life became rootless and idle, but also increasingly feverish. Hunger was no longer a problem, and he had devoured the first white bread with delight. Paris, in which wines and spirits had never been short, was in an alcoholic daze, and now living riotously in a continuous state of drunkenness. But it was still a prison, the gates were guarded by Germans and complicated formalities prevented anyone from getting out. No social life had been resumed and so far there was no work or business functioning, a whole population was waiting, doing nothing, growing more and more hysterical in the warm sunny weather of early spring. During the siege military service had at least tired out people's limbs and occupied their minds, but now the populace had slumped straight into total idleness in its continual isolation from the rest of the world. Maurice, like everybody else, just strolled about from morning till night, breathing the air that was infected with all the germs of madness that the mob had been exhaling for months. The unlimited freedom enjoyed by all finally destroyed everything. He read the papers and went to public meetings, sometimes shrugging his shoulders when the idiocies were too ridiculous, but nevertheless went home haunted by thoughts of violence and ready for desperate acts in defence of what he took to be truth and justice. And up in his little room overlooking the whole city, he still entertained dreams of victory and told himself that France and the Republic could still be saved so long as peace was not actually signed.

The Prussians were to make their entry into Paris on 1 March, and a cry of execration and rage rose from every heart. At every public meeting he went to Maurice heard the accusations against the Assembly, Thiers and the men of 4 September for this crowning shame that they had not tried to spare the great, heroic city. One evening he was so worked up that he even spoke himself, shouting that the whole of Paris should go and die on the ramparts rather than let a single Prussian get in. In this manner the insurrection sprang up quite naturally and organized itself in broad daylight among people thrown off balance by months of anguish and famine, fallen into a hag-ridden idleness and haunted by suspicions of their own making. It was one of those crises of morale observed after all great sieges, when unsurpassable patriotism has been cheated and, after inspiring people's souls to no purpose, changes into a blind lust for vengeance and destruction. The Central Committee, elected by delegates from the National Guard, had protested against any attempt at disarmament. There was a great demonstration on the Place de la Bastille, with red flags, fiery speeches, a huge crowd and the murder of one unfortunate policeman, tied to a plank, thrown into the canal and finished off with stones. Two days later, during the night of 26 February, Maurice was awakened by the call to arms and alarm bells, and watched bands of men and women going along the Boulevard des Batignolles dragging guns; and he went too, and with twenty others harnessed himself to a cannon, when he heard that the people had gone and seized these guns in the Place Wagram to prevent the Assembly from handing them over to the Prussians. There were one hundred and seventy of them, and as some of the proper gear was missing people hauled them with ropes, pushed them with their hands and got them up to the top of Montmartre with the fierce drive of a horde of barbarians rescuing their gods. On 1 March, when the Prussians had to be content with occupying the Champs-Elysées district for one day only, and even then behind fences like a herd of victors unsure of themselves, Paris did not stir from its gloom – all streets deserted and houses shut up, the whole city dead and swathed in the voluminous black crêpe of its mourning.

Two more weeks went by. Maurice had given up trying to know how his life was carrying on under the shadow of the indefinable, monstrous thing he felt was coming. Peace was officially concluded, and the Assembly was to meet in Versailles on 20 March, and still for him nothing was yet over, and some dreadful vengeance was about to begin. On the 18th, as he was getting up, he had a letter from Henriette once again begging him to join her at Remilly, affectionately threatening to set out herself if he took too long to give her that great joy. She went on to news about Jean, how after leaving her at the end of December to join the army in the north he had been taken ill with some sort of fever in a Belgian hospital, and only the previous week he had written that although he still felt very weak he was off to Paris where he was determined to re-enlist. Henriette ended by asking her brother to tell her everything about Jean as soon as he saw him. With the letter open in front of him Maurice fell into a sentimental daydream. Henriette and Jean, his beloved sister and his brother in suffering and compassion, how far removed those dear souls had been from his everyday thoughts since the tempest had dwelt within him! But as his sister told him she had not been able to give Jean the rue des Orties address, he promised himself that he would run him to earth that very day by inquiring at the army offices. But scarcely had he gone down and was crossing the rue Saint-Honoré, when two comrades from his battalion told him of the events of the night and morning in Montmartre. And all three dashed off in a frenzy.

What a day that 18 March was, and how it lifted his heart into a fateful elation! He could never remember later exactly what he had said and done. First he recalled that he had rushed off in a furious rage at the surprise action the military had attempted before daylight, to disarm Paris by getting the guns away again from Montmartre. It was obvious that Thiers, who had returned from Bordeaux, had been planning this coup so that the Assembly could safely proclaim a monarchy at Versailles. His next recollection was that he was in Montmartre himself at about nine in the morning, inflamed by the tales of victory he was told – the furtive arrival of the troops, the fortunate hold-up in the arrival of the drag-ropes which had given time for the National Guards to get their arms, and the soldiers not daring to shoot women and children, but holding their rifles upside down and fraternizing with the people. Then he saw himself hurrying through Paris, realizing by midday that Paris belonged to the Commune without there having been a fight, that Thiers and his cabinet were in flight from the Ministry of Foreign Affairs where they had been assembled, in fact that the whole government was running away to Versailles and the thirty thousand soldiers were being hastily withdrawn, leaving over five thousand of their number lying in the streets. Then again, at half past five, he saw himself at a bend in the outer boulevards in the middle of a group of hotheads, listening without any indignation to the horrible story of the murder of Generals Lecomte and Clément Thomas. Oh well, what are generals? He recalled them at Sedan, a comfort-loving, incompetent lot, one more or less didn't make much difference! The rest of that day went on in the same state of frenzied excitement that distorted everything, an insurrection that the very paving-stones seemed to have willed and which, unforeseen yet inevitable, grew and at a stroke found it had the mastery, eventually handing the Hôtel de Ville over to the members of the Central Committee, who were astonished to find themselves there.

Yet there was one memory that stayed quite clear in Maurice's mind – his sudden meeting with Jean. The latter had been in Paris for three days, having reached there penniless and still emaciated and run down by two months of fever that had kept him in a Brussels hospital, and having found a former captain of the 106th, Captain Ravaud, he had at once joined up in the new company of the 124th under his command. He had regained his corporal's stripes and that evening had been the last to leave the Prince Eugene barracks, with his squad, to go across to the left bank where the whole army was under orders to concentrate, when a dense crowd had brought them to a halt. There was a lot of shouting and talk of disarming the soldiers. He was quite coolly telling them to bugger off, and all this was nothing to do with him – he was just carrying out orders and doing no harm to anybody – when he uttered a cry of amazement, for Maurice rushed up and threw his arms round him in an affectionate embrace.

'What, it's you, Jean? ... My sister wrote to me. And to think that this morning I meant to go and inquire about you at the War Ministry!'

Jean's eyes were filling with tears of joy.

'Oh my dear boy, how wonderful to see you again! I've been looking for you, too, but where could I ever get hold of you in this bloody great city?'

The crowd was still threatening, and Maurice turned round to them.

'Citizens, let me talk to them! They are good chaps and I can answer for them!'

He took both his friend's hands and lowered his voice:

'You will stay with us, won't you?'

An expression of intense surprise came over Jean's face.

'With you, what do you mean?'

For a few minutes he listened while Maurice worked himself up against the government and against the army, recalling all that the people had gone through, explaining that at last they were going to be the masters, punish the incompetent and the cowards and save the Republic. As he strove to follow all this Jean's calm face, the face of an unlettered peasant, darkened with growing distress.

'Oh no, my dear friend, I'm not staying with you if it's for that kind of job! My captain has told me to go to Vaugirard with my men and I'm going. If the wrath of God were there I should go all the same. It's natural, surely you realize that.'

He began to laugh in his open-hearted way, and added:

'No, it's you who are going to come with us.'

Maurice let go of his hands in a gesture of furious revolt. And there the two of them stood facing each other for several seconds, one worked up by the fit of madness that was infecting the whole of Paris, a malady of long standing with its roots in the evil ferment of the previous reign, the other strong in his common sense and ignorance, still healthy from having grown up far away from all this, in the land of hard work and thrift. And yet they were brothers, linked by a strong attachment, and it was a terrible wrench when a sudden surge of the crowd separated them.

'Be seeing you, Maurice!'

'Be seeing you, Jean!'

It was a regiment, the 79th, emerging in a solid mass from a side street, which had thrown the crowd back on to the pavement. There was more shouting, but they didn't dare bar the roadway against the soldiers who were being marched along by the officers. And so the little squad of the 124th was free to follow on without any further hold-up.

'Be seeing you, Jean!'

'Be seeing you, Maurice!'

They went on waving to each other, yielding to the brutal fatality of this separation, but each with his heart full of the other.

During the days which followed it was at first crowded out of Maurice's mind because of the extraordinary events happening one after another. On the 19th Paris had woken up without a government, more surprised than frightened to hear about the sudden panic that during the night had swept away the army, public services and government ministers to Versailles, and as the weather was superb on this lovely March Sunday, Paris calmly came down into the streets to have a look at the barricades. A big white poster put up by the Central Committee summoning people for communal elections sounded very sensible, though it was a little surprising that it was signed by such utterly unknown names. In this first fine flush of the Commune Paris was hostile to Versailles because of the resentment it felt for what it had suffered and its haunting suspicions. In any case there was absolute anarchy, a struggle between the local mayors and the Central Committee, the former making fruitless efforts at conciliation while the latter, still unsure of having all the federal National Guards on its side, was still modestly campaigning only for municipal liberty. The shots fired against the peaceful demonstration in the Place Vendôme and the handful of victims whose blood stained the roadway sent the first shudder of horror through the city. While the insurrection was triumphantly and definitely taking over all the ministries and public administration, anger and fear were mounting at Versailles and the government was hastening to assemble sufficient military strength to repulse an attack it felt must be imminent. The best troops from the armies of the north and the Loire were hurriedly brought in and ten days sufficed for concentrating nearly eighty thousand men. Confidence was so rapidly restored that by 2 April two divisions opened hostilities and recaptured Puteaux and Courbevoie from the Federals.

It was not until the next day that Maurice, off with his battalion to conquer Versailles, once again saw rising out of the jumble of his memories the sad face of Jean saying good-bye. The attack by the Versailles forces had stunned and enraged the National Guard. Three columns of them, some fifty thousand men, had stormed out early in the morning via Bougival and Meudon to seize the monarchist Assembly and the murderer Thiers. This was the all-conquering sortie that had been so fiercely demanded during the siege, and Maurice wondered where he would ever see Jean again unless it were out there among the dead on the battlefield. But the rout came too quickly – his battalion had hardly reached the

Plateau des Bergères, on the road to Rueil, when suddenly shells from the Mont-Valérien fort fell into their ranks. There was a moment of stupor, for some thought that the fort was occupied by their comrades and others said that the commanding officer had solemnly sworn not to fire. A mad terror seized the men, battalions went to pieces and rushed wildly back into Paris, while the head of the column, caught by a turning movement effected by General Vinoy, went on and was massacred at Rueil.

Maurice escaped from the slaughter, and, all elated at having been in the fighting, had nothing but hatred left for this so-called government of law and order which, crushed at every encounter with the Prussians, only recovered courage to conquer the Parisians. And the German armies were still there, from Saint-Denis to Charenton, watching the edifying spectacle of the collapse of a people! So in the evil fever of destruction that took hold of him Maurice approved of the first violent measures, the throwing up of barricades across streets and squares, the taking of hostages, the archbishop, priests and former officials. On both sides atrocities were already being committed: Versailles shot prisoners, Paris decreed that for every one of its fighters killed the heads of three of its hostages would fall, and what common sense Maurice had left after so much shock and ruin was blown away by the wind of fury coming from all directions. The Commune now seemed to him to be the avenger of the shameful things they had endured, a kind of liberator bringing the knife to amputate and the fire to purify. None of this was very clear in his mind, and the educated man within him simply called up classical memories of free triumphant city-states or federations of rich provinces imposing their will on the world. If Paris won he visualized it in glory, reconstituting a France of justice and liberty, reorganizing a new society after sweeping away the rotten debris of the old. True, after the elections he had been somewhat surprised by the names of the members of the Commune, with its extraordinary jumble of moderates, militant revolutionaries and socialists of all colours, to whom the great task was entrusted. He knew some of these men personally, and thought they were a very mediocre lot. Were not the best of them going to clash and destroy each other in the confusion of ideas they represented? But on the day when the Commune was solemnly constituted in the Place de l'Hôtel de Ville, while the cannon roared and trophies of red flags flapped in the wind, he had made the effort to forget everything, and once again was borne away by boundless hopes. And so illusion began again in the crisis atmosphere of a disease at its climax, made up of the lies of some and the starry-eyed faith of others.

All through the month of April Maurice was fighting near Neuilly. An early spring brought out the lilacs, and the fighting went on amid the fresh green of the gardens, and National Guards came home at night with bunches of flowers on the ends of their rifles. By now the troops assembled at Versailles were so numerous that they had been formed into two armies, a front line one under the orders of Marshal MacMahon, and a reserve army, commanded by General Vinoy. The Commune on its side had nearly a hundred thousand active National Guards and almost as many militiamen, but only fifty thousand at the most were really fighters. And each day the Versailles tactics became clearer: after Neuilly they had occupied the château of Bécon, then Asnières, simply to close up their line of investment, for they planned to enter by the Point-du-Jour as soon as they could force the rampart by means of convergent fire from the forts of the Mont-Valérien and Issy. The Mont-Valérien was in their hands, and their whole effort was directed at capturing the fort of Issy, which they attacked by utilizing the breastworks made by the Prussians. From mid April the rifle-fire and bombardment were continuous. At Levallois and Neuilly there was non-stop fighting, with snipers firing every minute, day and night. Heavy guns on armoured trucks moved along the Ceinture railway and fired over Levallois at Asnières. But the bombardment was fiercest at Vanves and Issy, and every window in Paris shook, as they had during the worst days of the siege. On 9 May when, after an earlier alarm, the fort of Issy definitely fell into the hands of the Versailles army the defeat of the Commune was inevitable and a panic set in which prompted the wildest excesses.

Maurice approved of the setting up of a Committee of Public Safety. He recalled pages of history – had not the time come for energetic measures if their country was to be saved? Only one of the many acts of violence had really given him a secret pang of sorrow, and that was the overthrowing of the Vendôme column, and he reproached himself for that as though it were a childish weakness, for he still had ringing in his ears his grandfather's stories of Marengo, Austerlitz, Jena, Eylau, Friedland, Wagram and Borodino, and these epic tales thrilled him still. But that the murderer Thiers's house should be razed to the ground, that they should keep hostages as a safeguard and threat, wasn't that fair reprisal for the increasing fury of Versailles in its shelling of Paris, where shells were smashing in roofs and killing women? The black lust of destruction was mounting in him as the awakening from his dream drew near. If the ideal of justice and vengeance were to be crushed in bloodshed, well, let the earth open and be transformed in one of those cosmic upheavals by which life has been renewed! Let Paris collapse and burn like a huge sacrificial fire rather than be given back to its vices, miseries and the old social system corrupted with abominable injustice! And he indulged in another bleak dream, the gigantic city in ashes, nothing left on both sides of the river but smoking embers, the wound cauterized by fire, an unspeakable, unparalleled catastrophe out of which a new people would emerge. So the tales going round excited him more and more: whole neighbourhoods mined, the catacombs filled with gunpowder, all the great public buildings ready to be blown up, electric wires connecting the blast-holes so that one single spark could detonate them all together, large stocks of inflammable material, especially oil, enough to turn streets and squares into torrents and seas of flame. The Commune had sworn it would be so if the Versailles forces entered; not one would get past the barricades blocking the main crossings, for the roadways themselves would open up and buildings crumble into dust, and Paris would go up in flames and swallow a whole world.

When Maurice threw himself into this mad dream he was really doing so out of a nagging feeling of dissatisfaction with the Commune itself. He was losing all faith in mankind, and he felt that the Commune was impotent, being torn asunder by too many contradictory elements, getting more frenzied, incoherent and stupid as it was increasingly threatened. It had not been able to carry out a single one of all the social reforms it had promised, and it was already certain that it would leave no lasting achievement behind. But its great weakness came especially from the rivalries that tore it apart, and the corrosive suspicion in which every one of its members lived. Already many of them, the moderate and those who were worried, were absenting themselves from meetings. Others acted

474

under the lash of events, trembled at the prospect of a possible dictatorship and were reaching the stage at which groups in revolutionary assemblies exterminate each other to save the country. After Cluseret and Dombrowski, Rossel was going to be suspected. Delescluze, nominated civil delegate to the fighting forces, could do nothing on his own in spite of his great authority. The great social effort that had been envisaged was being frittered away and coming to nought in the isolation, increasing hour by hour, of these men, paralysed and reduced to desperate measures.

Inside Paris the terror was mounting. Paris, at first angry with Versailles and resenting the sufferings of the siege, was now turning against the Commune itself. Compulsory enrolment, the decree calling up all men under forty, had annoyed peaceloving people and provoked a mass exodus – they got away via Saint-Denis in disguise or with forged Alsatian papers, they let themselves down with ropes and ladders into the moat beyond the fortifications on dark nights. Well-to-do bourgeois had gone long ago. No factory or works had reopened its doors. No commerce, no work, and the idle existence went on in anxious expectation of the inevitable dénouement. People still had nothing to live on beyond their pay as National Guards, the one-franc-fifty now being paid out of the millions confiscated from the Bank of France, the one-franc-fifty for which alone many were now fighting, in fact one of the basic causes and the raison d'être of the insurrection. Whole neighbourhoods were empty, shops were shut, houses dead. In the beautiful sunshine of this wonderful month of May nothing could now be seen in the deserted streets but funerals of Federals killed in action, processions with no priest, coffins covered with red flags followed by crowds holding bunches of everlasting flowers. Closed churches were being turned every evening into clubrooms. Only revolutionary newspapers appeared – all the others had been banned. In fact Paris was destroyed, that great, unhappy Paris that retained the feeling of revulsion of a traditionally republican capital for the Assembly, but in which the Communist terror was now growing, a terror it was impatient to be free of amidst all the terrible stories going round of daily arrests of hostages and of barrels of explosive lowered into the sewers where, it was said, men were always ready with torches, waiting for the signal.

Then Maurice, who had never been a drinker, found himself

drawn into the general outbreak of drunkenness and lost in it. Now, when he was on duty at some advanced position or spending the night in the guard-room, he would accept a tot of brandy. If he had a second one he would get worked up in the alcoholic mists whirling round him. It was a growing epidemic, chronic befuddlement, a legacy from the first siege aggravated by the second; a population without bread but with spirits and wine in barrelfuls had steeped itself in drink and now went crazy on the smallest drop. On 21 May, a Sunday, for the first time in his life Maurice went home drunk in the evening to the rue des Orties where he still sometimes slept. He had once again spent the day at Neuilly, fighting and drinking with the comrades in the hope of overcoming his immense, overwhelming fatigue. Then, with his head in a whirl and quite exhausted, he had come back and flung himself on to the bed in his little room, having got there by instinct, for he could never remember how he reached it. It was not until the next day, when the sun was well up, that the sound of bells, drums and bugles woke him. On the previous day the Versailles forces had found a gate unguarded at the Point-du-Jour and had entered Paris unopposed.

As soon as he went down into the street after dressing at full speed and slinging his rifle over his shoulder, a group of agitated comrades he met at the local town hall told him the events of the previous evening and night, but in such a muddled way that it was hard to grasp at first. For ten days the fort at Issy and the heavy battery at Montretout, supplemented by the Mont-Valérien, had been hammering away at the fortifications, and the Saint-Cloud gate had become untenable; the assault was to take place on the following day when, at about five o'clock, a passer-by, noticing that nobody was left guarding the gate, had simply beckoned to the sentries posted at the Versailles army trenches not fifty metres away. Without any delay two companies of the 37th infantry had come in, and behind them the whole 4th corps, commanded by General Douay. All through the night the troops had flowed in like a steady stream. By seven the Vergé division was making its way down to the Pont de Grenelle and pushing on as far as the Trocadéro. By nine General Clinchant took Passy and La Muette. By three in the morning the 1st corps was encamped in the Bois de Boulogne and at about the same time the Bruat division was crossing the Seine to capture the Sèvres gate and facilitate the entry of the 2nd corps, commanded by General de Cissey, which was to occupy the whole Grenelle district an hour later. Thus by the morning of the 22nd the Versailles troops were masters of the Trocadéro and La Muette on the right bank and of Grenelle on the left bank, to the astonishment, fury and dismay of the Commune, already crying treason and desperate at the realization of inevitable defeat.

This was Maurice's first thought when he understood – the end had come and there was nothing left but to fight to the death. But alarm bells were ringing and drums beating ever louder, women and even children were working on the barricades, the streets were filling with excited battalions hastily got together and rushing to their combat positions. By noon hope was again springing up in the breasts of the fanatical soldiers of the Commune, who were resolved to go in and win when they realized that the Versailles forces had scarcely moved. This army that they had feared to see in the Tuileries within two hours was now operating with extra-ordinary prudence, having learned from its defeats and now over-doing the tactics it had learned from the Prussians at such a bitter cost. At the Hôtel de Ville the Committee of Public Safety and Delescluze, the war delegate, were organizing and directing the defence. It was said that they had turned down with scorn a final conciliatory move. This put fire into people's hearts, once again the triumph of Paris became certain, and everywhere the resistance was to be as fierce as the attack was to be implacable, owing to the hatred, fed on lies and atrocities, which burned in the hearts of both armies. That day Maurice spent in the neighbourhood of the Champ de Mars and the Invalides, slowly falling back from street to street, firing all the time. He had not been able to find his own battalion and was fighting with unknown comrades and, without even noticing, had been taken by them over to the left bank. At about four they defended a barricade shutting off the rue de l'Université where it comes out on to the Esplanade, and they only abandoned it at dusk when they knew that the Bruat division, by moving along the embankment, had taken the Legislative Assembly. They had nearly been captured themselves, and only gained the rue de Lille with difficulty by dint of taking a wide detour via the rue Saint-Dominique and rue de Bellechasse. By nightfall the Versailles army was occupying a line from the Vanves gate through the Legislative Assembly, the Elysée Palace, the church of Saint-Augustin, the Gare Saint-Lazare to the Asnières gate.

The next day, the 23rd, a springlike Tuesday with bright, warm sun, was a terrible one for Maurice. The few hundred Federals to whom he was attached, among whom were men from several battalions, were still occupying all the area between the river and the rue Saint-Dominique. But most of them had bivouacked in the rue de Lille, in the gardens of the great private mansions in that neighbourhood. He had slept soundly on a lawn at the side of the Palace of the Legion of Honour. First thing in the morning he thought that the troops would sally forth from the Legislative Assembly and push them back behind the strong barricades of the rue du Bac. But hours went by and no attack came. Only a few random shots were exchanged between one end of the street and the other. This was the Versailles plan being developed in a prudent progression: a clear determination not to run head on into the formidable fortress that the insurgents had made out of the terrace of the Tuileries, but to adopt a double thrust to left and right, following the fortifications, so as to take first Montmartre and the Observatory and then turn back and enmesh the central area in an enormous net. At about two Maurice heard that the tricolour flag was flying over Montmartre: the great battery of the Moulin de la Galette had been attacked by three army corps at once, who had flung their battalions at the hill from the north and west via the rue Lepic, rue des Saules and rue du Mont-Cenis, and then the victors had turned down into Paris, carrying by storm the Place Saint-Georges, Notre-Dame de Lorette, the town hall in the rue Drouot and the new Opera House, while on the left bank a wheeling movement from the Montparnasse cemetery reached the Place d'Enfer and the Marché aux Chevaux. The news of such a rapid advance of the army filled them with bewilderment, rage and fear. What! Montmartre taken in two hours, Montmartre, the glorious, impregnable citadel of the insurrection! Maurice noticed that the ranks were thinning, trembling comrades were quietly slipping away to wash their hands and put on their overalls, in terror of reprisals. It was being said that they would be taken in the rear via La Croix-Rouge, where an attack was being prepared. Already the barricades in the rue Martignac and the rue de Bellechasse had fallen, and red trousers were being seen at the end of the rue de Lille. Soon the only ones left were the convinced diehards, Maurice and some fifty others, who were determined to die after killing as many as possible of this Versailles lot who treated the Federals as bandits and shot prisoners behind the battle-line. Since the previous day the implacable hatred had intensified, and it was now a matter of extermination between these insurgents dying for their vision and this army in a white heat of reactionary passion and exasperated at still having to fight.

By five, as Maurice and his comrades were definitely withdrawing behind the barricades in the rue du Bac, going down the rue de Lille from doorway to doorway firing the while, he suddenly saw a lot of black smoke coming out of a window of the Palace of the Legion of Honour. It was the first case of incendiarism in Paris, and in his state of wild rage it filled him with fierce joy. The hour had struck, let the whole city go up in flames like a huge bonfire, and let fire purify the world! Then he was amazed at what he suddenly saw – five or six men had rushed out of the Palace with a great lout at their head whom he recognized as Chouteau, his old comrade in the squad in the 106th. He had already seen him once since 18 March and found him much up-graded, his képi covered all over with gold braid, and attached to the staff of some general who had kept clear of the fighting. He recalled a story somebody had told about Chouteau being installed in the Palace of the Legion of Honour and living there with a mistress on one continual binge, sprawling on great sumptuous beds with his boots on and breaking the mirrors with pistol shots just for a lark. It was even alleged that his mistress, on the pretext of going shopping in the market, went off every morning in a state coach taking bundles of stolen linen, clocks and even furniture. Now, seeing him running along with his men, still holding a can of paraffin oil, Maurice suddenly felt uneasy and a dreadful doubt came over him and made his whole faith waver. Could this terrible work of destruction be an evil thing, since it was being done by a man like that?

Still more hours went by and he was only fighting now with sickness in his heart, finding nothing left intact within him but a sullen wish for death. If he had been mistaken, then at least he could redeem the error with his blood! The barricade across the rue de Lille at the junction with the rue du Bac was very strongly built of sandbags and barrels full of earth with a deep trench in front. He was defending it with barely a dozen Federals, all lying almost flat and picking off any soldier who showed himself. Until nightfall he stayed there and used up his ammunition in obstinate, despairing silence. He watched the clouds of smoke from the Palace of the Legion of Honour getting denser as the wind blew them down into the middle of the road, but so far no flames could be seen in the failing light. Another fire had broken out in a mansion nearby. Suddenly a comrade came and told him that the soldiers, not wanting to risk a frontal attack on the barricades, were making their way through gardens and houses, battering holes through the walls with picks. This was the end, they might emerge here at any moment. And indeed a shot had been fired down on them from a window. He caught sight of Chouteau and his gang rushing madly into the corner houses on each side with their paraffin and torches. Half an hour later, when the sky was quite black, the whole cross-road was ablaze while he, still lying behind the barrels and sand-bags, could take advantage of the brilliant light and shoot down soldiers who unwisely ventured out of doorways into the open roadway.

How much longer did Maurice stay there shooting? He had no sense of time or place. It might be nine, perhaps ten. The vile job he was doing now made him feel sick, like some disgusting wine coming back when you are drunk. The houses burning round him were beginning to encircle him with intolerable heat and choking hot air. The crossing, with the piles of paving stones enclosing it, had become a fortress defended by fires with sparks raining down. Were not these their orders? Set fire to districts as the barricades were abandoned, stop the troops with an all-destroying line of furnaces, burn Paris as they surrendered it. Already he had the impression that the houses in the rue du Bac were not the only ones burning. Behind his back he could see the sky lit up by an immense red glow and hear a distant roaring as though the whole city were catching fire. To his right along the Seine other huge fires must be breaking out. Chouteau had long since disappeared, dodging the bullets. Even the most fanatical of his comrades were sloping off one by one, terrified by the thought of being taken in the rear at any moment. In the end he was left alone, lying between two sandbags with only one thought, keep on firing, when the soldiers who had made their way through courtyards and gardens came from a house in the rue du Bac to take him in the rear.

In the excitement of this decisive struggle Maurice had not thought of Jean for two whole days. Similarly Jean, since he had entered Paris with his regiment to reinforce the Bruat division, had never remembered Maurice for a single moment. On the previous day he had been fighting on the Champ de Mars and on the Esplanade des Invalides. But today he had only left the Place du Palais-Bourbon at about noon to storm the barricades in that part of Paris as far as the rue des Saints-Pères. Placid though he was by nature, he had grown more and more angry in this fratricidal war, surrounded by comrades whose one great desire was to have a rest at last after so many months of fatigue. Prisoners sent back from Germany to be put into the army were in a constant state of fury with Paris, and on top of that there were the reports of the foul crimes of the Commune which incensed him by outraging his respect for property and desire for order. He had remained typical of the very heart of the nation, the sensible peasant, longing for peace so as to get back to work, earn some money and recover health and strength. In this increasing anger, which carried away even his most tender feelings, it was the fires more than anything else which had infuriated him. Burn down houses and public buildings just because you weren't the strongest, no, that really was the end! Only criminals could be capable of such a thing. This man, whose heart had been sickened only the day before by the summary executions, was now beside himself, wild-eyed, yelling and laying about him.

Jean rushed madly out into the rue du Bac with the handful of men in his squad. At first he didn't see anybody and thought the barricade had been abandoned. Then, between two sandbags, he saw a Communard still moving, rifle to shoulder and still firing into the rue de Lille. Carried on by the inexorable fury of destiny, he ran and pinned him to the barricade with a thrust of his bayonet.

Maurice had not had time to turn round. He screamed and looked up. The fires lit them both up with blinding light.

'Oh Jean, Jean my dearest friend, is it you?'

Death was what he had wanted and sought with desperate impatience. But to die at the hand of his brother was too much – it spoiled death for him, poisoned it with unspeakable bitterness.

'So it's you, Jean, dear old Jean!'

Jean looked at him, horrified and suddenly sobered. They were alone together, the other soldiers having already gone off in pursuit of the runaways. Round them the fires flared up still more fiercely, windows belched forth great red flames and from inside came the noise of blazing ceilings coming down. Jean collapsed beside Maurice, sobbing, feeling him and trying to lift him and see if he could yet save him.

'Oh, my dearest boy, my poor dear boy!'

8

WHEN at long last, after endless delays, the train from Sedan pulled up at the station of Saint-Denis about nine, the sky to the south was lit up by a great red glow, as though all Paris was on fire. As night had come on this glow had brightened until it filled the whole horizon, flecking with blood a flight of little clouds that lost themselves to the east in the deepening night.

Henriette was the first to jump down, for she was worried by these signs of a conflagration that the passengers had seen out of the windows of the train as it sped across the dark fields. In any case Prussian soldiers had taken over the station and were making everybody get out, while two of them on the arrival platform were calling out in guttural French:

'Paris on fire ... Train stops here, everybody out ... Paris on fire, Paris on fire ...'

It was a terrible shock for Henriette. Oh God, had she got here too late? As Maurice had not answered her last two letters she had been so mortally scared by the more and more alarming news from Paris that she had suddenly made up her mind to leave Remilly. For months she had been getting more miserable at Uncle Fouchard's, the army of occupation had become more harsh and exacting as Paris prolonged its resistance; and now that the regiments were returning one by one to Germany they were draining the countryside and the towns once again as they passed through. That morning, as she was getting up at first light to catch the train at Sedan, she had seen the farmyard packed with cavalrymen who had slept there all in a heap, wrapped in their cloaks. There were so many of them that they covered the ground. Then there was a smart bugle call and they had all risen to their feet without a word, draped in their long garments and packed so close to each other that she had had the impression of witnessing a battlefield rising from the dead at the sound of the last trumpet. And now she still found Prussians at Saint-Denis, and it was they who were shouting these devastating words:

'All out, train stops here ... Paris on fire, Paris on fire ...'

Distracted, Henriette rushed along with her little case, asking for information. Fighting had been going on inside Paris for two days, the railway was cut, and the Prussians were keeping the situation under observation. But still she wanted to get through, and noticing on the platform the officer in command of the company occupying the station, she ran up to him.

'Sir, I am joining my brother and I am terribly worried about him. Do please help me to continue my journey.'

Then she stopped in amazement, recognizing the captain whose face was lit up by the gas-lamp.

'Otto, it's you! ... Oh, do be kind to me now that chance has once again brought us face to face.'

Otto Gunther, Weiss's cousin, was still smartly dressed in the tight-fitting uniform of a captain in the Prussian Guard, with the tight-lipped air of a fine, well-groomed officer. He did not recognize this thin, delicate-looking woman with her fair hair and pretty, sweet face under the widow's veil. It was only her clear serious eyes that made him remember her. He merely made a little gesture.

'You know I have a brother who is a soldier,' Henriette hurriedly went on. 'He has stayed in Paris and I'm afraid he has got caught up in all this horrible fighting ... Otto, I beg of you, help me to continue my journey.'

Only then did he speak.

'But I assure you there is nothing I can do ... The trains have not been running since yesterday and I think they've taken up the rails near the ramparts. And I haven't a carriage or a horse or a man to take you.'

She stared at him and in her bitterness at finding him so callous and determined not to come to her aid she could only find disconnected words:

'Oh God, you won't do anything ... Oh God, who can I ask?'

These Prussians, who were the absolute masters, who at a single word could have turned the place upside down, commandeered a hundred vehicles, got a thousand horses out of stables! And he was refusing with the haughty air of a conqueror whose principle was never to interfere with the affairs of the beaten natives, no doubt considering them unclean and likely to soil his nice new glory!

'Anyhow,' she went on, trying to recover her self-control, 'you must at least know what is going on, and surely you can tell me.'

He smiled a thin, almost imperceptible smile.

'Paris is burning ... come here and have a look, you can see plainly.'

He walked in front of her, out of the station and along the track for about a hundred metres, as far as an iron footbridge across the line. When they had climbed up the narrow steps and were on the top and leaning over the handrail, the vast level plain could be seen beyond an embankment.

'You can see, Paris is burning.'

It must have been about half past nine. The red glow in the sky was still spreading. In the east the flight of little bloodstained clouds had gone and the vault was simply a wall of ink on which distant flames were reflected. Now the whole line of the horizon was ablaze, but in certain places more intense fires could be seen, bright red fountains playing continuously against the dark background of the great billows of smoke. It looked as though the fires themselves were on the move like some gigantic forest with the flames leaping from tree to tree, or as though the earth itself was about to flare up, kindled by the colossal bonfire of Paris.

'Look,' Otto pointed out, 'that black hump standing out against the red background is Montmartre ... On the left there's nothing burning so far at La Villette or Belleville. The fire must have been started in the rich neighbourhoods, and it's gaining ground, gaining ground ... Just look over there to the right, that's a new fire being started! You can see the flames, a fountain of flames with fiery smoke rising ... And others, still others, everywhere!'

He was not shouting or getting excited, but the outrageousness of his quiet joy terrified Henriette. Oh, these Prussians who could watch this! She felt the insult of his calm, faint smile, as though he had foreseen this unparalleled disaster and had been waiting for it for a long time. At last Paris was burning down, Paris where

German shells had only succeeded in knocking off a few gutters. All his rancour was satisfied and he seemed avenged for the endless siege, the terrible cold and the ever renewed difficulties which still rankled with Germany. In the triumph of their pride the conquered provinces, the indemnity of five milliards, none of it was as good as this spectacle of Paris destroyed, gone raving mad and setting fire to herself and going up in smoke on this clear spring night.

'Oh, it was bound to come!' he went on almost in a whisper. 'A grand piece of work!'

As she took in the immensity of the disaster Henriette felt more and more sick at heart until the pain was unbearable. For a few minutes her own misfortunes vanished, carried away in this expiation of a whole nation. The thought of fire devouring human lives, the sight of this blazing city on the horizon, throwing up the hellish glare of cities accursed and destroyed, made her cry out in spite of herself. She clasped her hands together and asked:

'What have we done, oh God, to be punished like this?'

But Otto at once raised his arm as though delivering a reproof. He was about to speak with the vehemence of that cold, hard, militaristic Protestantism that can always quote verses of the Bible. But he caught the young woman's beautiful, clear and reasonable eyes, and one glance stopped him. In any case his gesture had been enough, it had expressed his racial hatred and his conviction that he was in France as a judge sent by the Lord of Hosts to chastise a perverse people. Paris was burning as a punishment for centuries of wickedness, for the long tale of its crimes and debauches. Once again the Germanic tribes would save the world and sweep away the last remains of Latin corruption.

He dropped his arm and merely said:

'It's all over ... Another district is catching fire, see, that fire over there, further to the left ... You can see that big streak spreading like a river of glowing embers.'

They said no more, and there was a terrified silence. And indeed sudden new bursts of flame were continually rising, filling the sky like a furnace overflowing. Every minute the sea of fire went on broadening to infinity like an incandescent tide from which there were now going up columns of smoke that gathered together above the city into an immense dark copper-coloured cloud. A light wind must be blowing it, for it was slowly moving away through the black night, filling the vault of heaven with its foul rain of ash and soot.

With a jerk Henriette seemed to come back out of a nightmare and, overcome once more with anguish at the thought of her brother, she implored him yet again.

'So you can't do anything for him, and won't help me to get into Paris?'

Once again Otto seemed to sweep the horizon with a wave of the arm.

'What's the use, because by tomorrow there won't be anything left but rubble?'

That was all, and she walked down from the footbridge without even saying good-bye, and ran off, holding her little case. But he stayed up there a long time, slender and motionless, tightly buttoned in his uniform, lost in the night and letting his eyes drink their fill of this monstrous spectacle of Babylon in flames.

As Henriette was leaving the station she was lucky enough to come upon a heavily-built lady bargaining with a cabby to take her immediately to the rue de Richelieu in Paris; and Henriette begged so hard and her tears were so touching that the lady agreed to take her as well. The cabby, a dark little man, whipped up his horse and never said a word all through the journey, but the lady never stopped talking about how, when she had left her shop two days previously and locked it up, she had been silly enough to leave some bonds there in a hiding-place in a wall. So for the past two hours, since the city had been on fire, she had been obsessed with the one idea of going back and recovering her property even though it meant going through the fire. At the barrier there was only a sleepy guard, and the cab went through with little trouble, especially as the lady made up a tale about having gone to fetch her niece so that the two of them could nurse her husband who had been wounded by the Versailles troops. The real obstacles began in the streets, where barricades blocked the roadway at every point and they had to make continual detours. Finally at the Boulevard Poissonnière the cabby refused to go any further, and the two women had to continue on foot through the rue du Sentier, rue des Jeûneurs and the Bourse area. As they were approaching the fortifications the fiery glow in the sky had lighted them up as if it were broad daylight. Now they were amazed at the emptiness of this part of the city, where the only sound to reach them was a distant pulsating roar. But by the time they reached the Bourse they heard shots and had to slip along close to the buildings. Having found her shop in the rue de Richelieu intact the large lady was delighted and insisted on showing her friend the way along the rue du Hasard and rue Sainte-Anne right to the rue des Orties. For a moment some Federals, still occupying the rue Sainte-Anne, tried to prevent their passing. It was four in the morning and already light when at last Henriette, worn out with emotion and fatigue, found the door of the old house in the rue des Orties wide open. After climbing the narrow, dark stairs she had to go through a door and up a ladder that led to the roof.

At the barricade in the rue du Bac Maurice, between the two sandbags, had managed to get himself on to his knees, and Jean was filled with hope, for he thought he had pinned him to the ground.

'Oh my dear boy, you're still alive then! Is it possible I could be so lucky, foul brute that I am? . . . Just a moment, let's have a look.'

With very great care he examined the wound by the light from the fires. The bayonet had gone through the arm near the right shoulder, and the worst thing about it was that it had then penetrated between two ribs and probably involved the lung. Yet the wounded man was breathing without too much trouble. But the arm hung down, inert.

'Poor old chap, don't be so upset! I'm glad, really. I'd rather get it over . . . You did enough for me long ago, and without you I should have pegged out at the side of some road.'

But hearing him talk like this, Jean's bitter grief came back.

'Shut up, do! Twice you got me out of the Prussians' clutches. We were quits, and it was my turn to give my life, and then I go and kill you . . . Oh, God Almighty, I must have been loaded to the eyeballs through having drunk too much blood already!'

Tears ran down from his eyes as he thought of their separation back at Remilly when they had parted wondering whether they would see each other some day, and where and in what circumstances of joy or sorrow. Was there no point, then, in their having lived days together without food, nights without sleep and with death ever present? Had their hearts been as one for those few weeks of heroic life shared together, and all to lead them to this abomination, this monstrous, stupid fratricide? No, no, he refused to think of it.

'Leave it to me, boy, I've got to save you.'

First he had to get him away from there, because the soldiers were finishing off the wounded. By great good fortune they happened to be alone, and there was not a minute to lose. Using his knife he quickly slit the sleeve and then removed the whole tunic. Blood was being lost, so he hastened to bandage the arm tight with strips torn out of the lining. Then he put a pad on the body-wound and tied the arm over it. Fortunately he had a bit of cord and he tightened this rough and ready dressing as hard as he could, which had the advantage of immobilizing all the affected side and preventing haemorrhage.

'Can you walk?'

'I think so.'

But he dared not take him away like that, in his shirtsleeves. On a sudden inspiration he ran round the corner, where he had seen a dead soldier, and he came back with a greatcoat and a képi. He threw the coat over his shoulders and helped him to put his good arm into the left sleeve. Then, having stuck the képi on his head:

'There, now you're one of us ... Where are we to go?'

That was the great problem. His anguish of mind suddenly came back amidst his renewed hope and courage. Where could they find a safe enough place to hide? Houses were being searched, and all Communards found with weapons were shot. What was more, neither of them knew anyone in that part of Paris; there was not a soul they could ask for shelter, no hiding-place where they could disappear.

'The best thing really would be my place,' said Maurice. 'The house is isolated and nobody on earth will come there ... But it's the other side of the river, in the rue des Orties.'

Jean was in hopeless despair, distraught and swearing to himself.

'Bloody hell! What can we do?'

It was unthinkable to cross the Pont Royal which owing to the fires was as brightly lit as on a sunny day. The firing on both sides of the river was continuous. And besides, they would have come up against the Tuileries in flames, the Louvre barricaded and guarded, in fact an impassable barrier.

'So it's no fucking good that way!' declared Jean, who had lived for six months in Paris after the Italian campaign.

He had a sudden inspiration. If there were any boats under the bridge, as there used to be, they might try and bring it off. It would be very long, dangerous and awkward, but there was no choice and they must make up their minds at once.

'Look, kid, let's get out of here in any case, it isn't healthy ... I can tell my lieutenant that the Communards captured me and I escaped.'

He took him by the good arm, supported him and helped him along the end bit of the rue du Bac, between houses in flames from top to bottom like huge torches. Bits of blazing wood rained down on them and the heat was so intense that it singed all the hair on their faces. When they came out on to the embankment they were momentarily blinded by the dreadful light from fires burning in huge sheaves of flame on both sides of the Seine.

'No lack of candles,' growled Jean, vexed at this strong light.

He didn't feel the slightest bit safer until he had got Maurice down the steps to the towpath to the left of the Pont Royal, downstream. They remained hidden there under the big trees by the water. For a quarter of an hour they were worried about some black figures moving about on the opposite bank. Some shots were fired, there was a shriek and something plopped into the water throwing up a big splash. Obviously the bridge was guarded.

'Suppose we stayed for the night in that hut?' Maurice suggested, pointing to a wooden office of the river transport authority.

'Not on your life! And get nabbed in the morning?'

Jean still stuck to his idea. He had found a whole flotilla of small boats. But they were chained up, and how could he free one and get the oars out? But in the end he did manage to find an old pair of oars and was able to force a padlock – not properly locked, no doubt – and having laid Maurice in the bows he at once cautiously let himself drift with the current, hugging the bank in the shadow of the bathing establishment and barges. Neither said a word, for they were appalled by the dreadful spectacle unfolding itself. As they went downstream the horror seemed to get worse and the horizon receded. When they reached the Solferino bridge they could take in at a glance both banks in flames.

On the left the Tuileries was burning. By nightfall the Communards had set fire to both ends of the palace, the Pavillon de Flore and the Pavillon de Marsan, and the fire was rapidly moving towards the Pavillon de l'Horloge in the middle, where a big explosive charge had been set – barrels of powder piled up in the Salle des Maréchaux. At that moment there were issuing from the broken windows of the connecting blocks whirling clouds of reddish smoke pierced by long blue tongues of fire. The roofs were catching, splitting open into blazing cracks, like volcanic earth from the pressure of the fire within. It was the Pavillon de Flore, the first to be set on fire, which was burning most fiercely, with a mighty roaring from the ground floor to the great roof. The paraffin, with which the floors and hangings had been soaked, gave the flames such an intense heat that the ironwork of balconies could be seen buckling and the tall monumental chimneys burst, with their great carved suns red-hot.

Then to the right there was first the Palace of the Legion of Honour which had been fired at five in the afternoon and had been burning for nearly seven hours, and now it was being consumed like a great bonfire in which all the wood is burning up at once. Next there was the Palais du Conseil d'Etat, the most immense, ghastly and terrifying blaze of all, a gigantic cube of masonry with two superimposed colonnades belching forth flames. The four blocks surrounding the inner courtyard had caught fire simultaneously, and there the paraffin, emptied in barrelfuls down the four corner staircases, had run in cataracts of hell-fire all down the steps. On the river frontage the clear outline of the attic storey stood out in black tiers against the red tongues licking its edges, while the colonnades, entablatures, friezes and sculptures took on an extraordinary relief in the blinding light of a furnace. In this building above all there was such a strong rush of flame that the colossal pile seemed to be almost lifted by it, shaking and rumbling on its foundations, keeping only its carcass of thick walls in this violent eruption that was hurling its zinc roofing up into the sky. And next door one whole side of the Orsay barracks was burning in a lofty white column like a tower of light. And finally behind all this there were still more fires, the seven houses in the rue du Bac, the twenty-two houses in the rue de Lille, lighting up the horizon, flames on flames in an endless, bloody sea.

Jean could only manage to murmur:

'Oh God, it isn't possible! The river itself will catch fire.'

And indeed the boat seemed to be floating on a river of fire. In the dancing reflections of these huge conflagrations the Seine appeared to be bearing along blazing coals. Sudden red flashes played over it in shimmering patches of flame. And they were still floating downstream on this burning water, between these palaces in flames, as if in an endless street in an accursed city, burning on each side of a roadway of molten lava.

'Oh,' exclaimed Maurice in his turn, his frenzy returning in the face of this destruction he had wanted to see, 'let the whole lot go up in flames!'

Jean stopped him with a terrified gesture, as though afraid such a blasphemy would bring a curse upon them. Could it possibly be that a man he loved so dearly, who was so well educated, so delicate in mind, had come down to such notions? He was now rowing harder, for he had passed the Solferino bridge and was in a broad, open reach. The light was as bright as a noonday sun shining straight down on the river without casting any shadow. The smallest details could be picked out with astonishing precision, the flecks of the current, heaps of stones on the towpaths, little trees on the embankments. The bridges especially stood out in blinding whiteness, so clear that you could have counted the blocks of stone, and they looked like narrow, intact passages from one fire to another over the fiery water. Occasionally, in the continuous roaring noise, sudden crashes could be heard. Flurries of soot came down and foul stenches were borne on the wind. The terrifying thing was that Paris, that is to say all the other districts further away along the trench of the Seine, had ceased to exist. On either side the very violence of the conflagration so dazzled the eyes that there was nothing but a black abyss beyond. Nothing could be seen but an enormous darkness, a void, as if the whole of Paris had been seized and devoured by the fire and disappeared into eternal night. The sky was dead too, for the flames shot so high that they put out the stars.

Maurice, now in the delirium of fever, gave vent to the cackle of a madman.

'Lovely party going on at the Conseil d'Etat and the Tuileries ... the outside all illuminated, lustres all glittering, women dancing ... Go on, dance in your smoking petticoats and flaming hair!'

With his good arm he sketched visions of the galas in Sodom and Gomorrah, with music, flowers and unnatural orgies, palaces bursting with such debaucheries, the disgusting nudities illuminated with such a riot of candles that they themselves were set on fire. Then there was a fearful crash. The fire in the Tuileries had worked its way along from both ends and reached the Salle des Maréchaux. The barrels of gunpowder had caught and the Pavillon de l'Horloge went up like an exploding magazine. An immense fountain of fire rose like a plume and filled the black sky – the final set-piece of the gruesome fête.

'Hurrah for the dance!' screamed Maurice, as though at the end of a show when everything falls back into darkness.

Jean was almost speechless and in disjointed words begged him to stop. No, no, one mustn't wish for evil! If it meant total destruction wouldn't they perish as well? He had only one urgent job, to land and get away from this awful sight. All the same he was prudent enough to go past the Concorde bridge so as not to leave the boat until the towpath below the Quai de la Conférence, beyond the bend in the Seine. Yet at that critical moment, instead of just letting the boat drift away he lost several minutes mooring it safely, with his instinctive respect for other people's property. His plan was to reach the rue des Orties by way of the Place de la Concorde and the rue Saint-Honoré. Having sat Maurice down on the towpath he went up the steps to the roadway alone, and once again he was very worried when he realized what difficulty they would have in getting past the obstacles piled up there. For this was the impregnable fortress of the Commune, the Tuileries terrace fortified with guns and the rue Royale, rue Saint-Florentin and rue de Rivoli blocked by high barricades strongly constructed. This explained the tactics of the Versailles army, whose lines that night formed a huge concave angle with its apex at the Place de la Concorde and one extremity, the one on the right bank, at the goods yard of the Northern Railway and the other, on the left bank, at a bastion of the fortifications near the Arcueil gate. But it would soon be daybreak, the Communards had evacuated the Tuileries and the barricades, and the troops had just taken over the area, amid still more fires – twelve more houses that had been burning since nine at the intersection of the rue Saint-Honoré and the rue Royale.

When Jean came down again from the embankment he found Maurice dozing as though he had relapsed into lethargy after the crisis of over-excitement.

'It's not going to be easy ... Anyway, can you walk a bit further, kid?'

'Yes, yes, don't you worry. I shall get there somehow, dead or alive.'

His worst trouble was to climb the stone steps. Once up on the embankment he moved along slowly on Jean's arm, like a sleep-walker. Although the day was not yet dawning the light from the fires near-by threw a livid dawn over the huge square. They crossed its empty spaces, their hearts aching at this dreary devastation. At the two extremities, beyond the bridge and at the further end of the rue Royale, they could just make out the phantom shapes of the Palais-Bourbon and the Madeleine, damaged by gunfire. The terrace of the Tuileries, which had been battered in forcing an entry, had partially collapsed. On the square itself bullets had made holes in the bronze of the fountains, the colossal trunk of the statue of Lille lay on the ground, broken in two by a shell, while the statue of Strasbourg hard by, still veiled, seemed to be in mourning for so much ruin. In a trench near the obelisk, which was unscathed, a gas-main, split open by someone with a pick and which by chance had ignited, was shooting up a l ong jet of flame with a hissing noise.

Jean avoided the barricade across the rue Royale, between the Ministry of Marine and the Garde-Meuble, which had escaped the fire. He could hear loud voices of soldiers behind the sandbags and barrels of earth. In front of it there was a ditch full of stagnant water with the corpse of a Federal floating in it, and through a breach could be seen buildings at the crossing with the rue Saint-Honoré still burning in spite of pumps brought in from the suburbs that could be heard throbbing. On either side the little trees and news kiosks were broken and riddled with shot. There was a lot of shouting, the firemen had discovered in a cellar the half-charred remains of seven tenants of one of the buildings.

Although the barricade cutting off the rue Saint-Florentin and the rue de Rivoli looked still more daunting, with its well-construc-ted high defences, Jean felt that it would be less dangerous to get through that way. And indeed it was quite deserted, and so far

493

the army had not ventured to enter into occupation. Abandoned cannons lay there in a heavy slumber. There was not a soul behind this invincible rampart – nothing but a stray dog that ran off. But as Jean was hurrying along the rue Saint-Florentin, supporting Maurice who was losing strength, what he had dreaded happened, and they ran into a whole company of the 88th infantry which had gone round the barricade.

'Sir,' he explained to the captain, 'this is a comrade of mine those buggers have wounded, and I'm taking him to an ambulance station.'

The greatcoat thrown over Maurice's shoulders was his salvation, and Jean's heart was beating wildly as at last they were going together down the rue Saint-Honoré. It was hardly light and shots could be heard in side streets, for there was still fighting going on all over the district. It was a miracle that they managed to reach the rue des Frondeurs without any other unfortunate encounter. Now they were only getting along very slowly, and the three or four hundred metres left to do seemed endless. In the rue des Frondeurs they came upon a post of Communards but the latter, thinking a whole company was on the way, took fright and ran off. Only a bit of the rue d'Argenteuil to do and they would be in the rue des Orties.

How impatiently Jean had been longing for four endless hours to see that rue des Orties! What a deliverance when they had turned into it! It was dark, empty and silent and might have been a hundred leagues away from the battle. The house, an old and narrow one with no concierge, was sleeping the deep sleep of death.

'The keys are in my pocket,' Maurice managed to say. 'The big one is the street door and the little one my room, right up top.'

Then he collapsed fainting in Jean's arms, which worried and embarrassed him terribly, so much so that he forgot to shut the street door behind them, and had to grope his way up this unknown staircase, trying not to bump into anything for fear of attracting attention. At the top he was quite lost and had to put the wounded man down on a step and look for the door by striking some matches which fortunately he had on him, and it was only when he had found it that he came down again and picked him up. At last he laid the boy on the little iron bed opposite the window with its view over Paris, and he opened it wide, wanting some light and air.

Day was now breaking, and he fell down beside the bed, weeping and utterly broken and exhausted, as the dreadful thought came back that he had killed his friend.

Some minutes must have gone by and he was scarcely surprised when he saw Henriette. Nothing was more natural, her brother was dying and she had come. He had not even noticed her come in, and she might have been there for hours. Now he slumped into a chair and listlessly watched her as she moved about in mortal grief at the sight of her brother unconscious and covered with blood. At last something came back into his mind and he asked:

'I say, did you shut the street door behind you?'

But she was shattered, and merely nodded an affirmative. Then, as she came over and gave him both her hands, in need of affection and help, he went on:

'You know, I'm the one who's killed him.'

She did not understand or believe him. He felt her two hands still quite calm in his.

'I've killed him . . . Yes, on a barricade somewhere . . . He was on one side and I was on the other.'

The little hands began trembling.

'We were all like drunken men, we didn't know what we were doing . . . I've killed him.'

Then Henriette withdrew her hands, shuddering, white and staring at him with horrified eyes. So this was the end of it all, and nothing would survive in her broken heart? Oh, Jean, she had been thinking about him that very evening and been so happy in the faint hope of seeing him again! And he had done this unspeakable thing, and yet he had saved Maurice once again, for he had brought him back here through so many dangers! She could not give him her hands again without a revulsion in her whole being. Yet she uttered a cry into which she put the last hope of her divided heart.

'Oh, I'll make him better – I must, now!'

Her long watches at the hospital at Remilly had made her very skilful at nursing and dressing wounds. She insisted on examining her brother's wound at once, and undressed him, but that did not revive him. Yet as she undid the emergency dressing Jean had improvised he did move, made a little noise, then opened wide, feverish eyes. He recognized her at once and smiled.

'So you are here. Oh, how glad I am to see you before I die!'
She silenced him with a gesture of confidence.

'Die! But I won't have it! I mean you to live ... Stop talking
and leave it to me.'

But when she examined the gashed arm and punctured ribs she
went very serious and her eyes looked worried. She quickly took
the room over, managed to find a little oil, tore up some old shirts
for bandages, while Jean went downstairs for a jug of water. He
never opened his mouth, but watched her washing the wounds and
skilfully bandaging them, but he was powerless to help her, for
since she had been there he had been utterly exhausted. Yet when
she had finished and he saw how worried she was he did offer to go
and look for a doctor. But she kept all her clearheadedness—
oh no, not the first doctor he could find, who might denounce her
brother! It must be somebody safe, and they could wait a few
hours. Finally when Jean talked of going back to his regiment it
was understood that as soon as he could get away he would come
back and try to bring a surgeon with him.

But still he did not go, and seemed unable to make up his mind
to leave this room, where everything spoke of the evil he had done.
The window, which had been shut for a little while, had just been
opened again. And from his bed, with his head propped up, the
wounded man was looking out. And the others, too, let their eyes
wander into the distance, in the oppressive silence that had fallen
on them.

From this high position on the Butte des Moulins quite half of
Paris stretched out below them, first the central area from the
Faubourg Saint-Honoré as far as the Bastille, then the whole course
of the Seine with the distant busy life of the left bank, a sea of roofs,
treetops, steeples, domes and towers. It was getting much lighter,
and that unspeakable night, one of the most terrible in history, was
over. But in the pure light of the rising sun, under the rose-pink sky,
the fires went on burning. Straight opposite them the Tuileries was
still burning, and the flames, and those of the Orsay barracks, the
palaces of the Conseil d'Etat and the Legion of Honour, scarcely
visible in the strong light, made the air quiver. Even beyond the
houses in the rue de Lille and the rue du Bac other buildings must
be burning, for columns of sparks were going up from the Croix-
Rouge crossroads, and still further away in the rue Vavin and rue

Notre-Dame des Champs. Quite near, to the right, the fires in the rue Saint-Honoré were burning themselves out and to the left, at the Palais-Royal and new Louvre, later fires lit in the small hours were petering out. But the thing they could not understand at first was dense black smoke that the west wind was blowing right under their window. Since three in the morning the Ministry of Finance had been burning, but without any high flames, in thick clouds of soot, because there were such enormous masses of paper in low-ceilinged rooms in a rough-cast building. It was true that the great city, awakening to a new day, no longer gave the tragic impression of the night, the horror of total destruction, with the Seine a river of blazing fire and Paris lit up from end to end, but now a hopeless, dreary misery hovered over the districts that had been spared, with this continual thick smoke in an ever-widening cloud. Soon the sun, which had come up clear and bright, was hidden by it, leaving nothing but gloom in the menacing sky.

Maurice, who looked as if his delirium was coming back, took in the endless horizon with a sweeping gesture and murmured:

'Is it all burning? Oh, what a long time it's taking!'

Henriette's eyes filled with tears, as if her sorrow had been still more deepened by these immense disasters in which her brother had had a share. Jean dared not take her hand again, nor embrace his friend, but rushed away wild-eyed.

'I'll be seeing you again soon!'

It was evening, at about eight and dark, before he could come back. Although he was so worried he felt happy because his regiment was out of the fighting and had been put on the reserve, with orders to guard this district, so that as he was camping with his company in the Place du Carrousel he hoped to be able to come up every evening for news of the sick man. And he was not alone this time, for by chance he had run into the former medical officer of the 106th, and he brought him in desperation, not having been able to find any other doctor, telling himself that this terrible man with the leonine head was a good chap really.

When Bouroche, not knowing for whom the soldier had disturbed his peace, and grumbling about how far he had to climb, realized that he was looking at a Communard he first fell into a furious rage.

'Good God, what do you take me for? ... A lot of criminals

sated with plunder, murder and arson! Your thug's case is clear, and I'll see that he's cured, that I will, with three bullets through the head!'

But seeing Henriette there, so pale in her black dress, with her beautiful fair hair falling on her shoulders, he suddenly relented.

'It's my brother, sir, one of your soldiers at Sedan.'

Without answering he took off the bandages and silently examined the wounds, took some phials out of his pocket and made a fresh dressing, showing her how to set about it. Then in his rough way he suddenly asked the patient:

'Why did you side with those hooligans, why did you do such a vile thing?'

Maurice had watched him with glittering eyes all the time he had been there but had said nothing. Now, in his feverish state, he said with blazing conviction:

'Because there's too much suffering, too much iniquity and shame!'

At that Bouroche made a grand gesture suggesting that when you went in for those kinds of ideas you went too far. He was on the point of saying something else, but decided not to. So he left, just adding:

'I'll be back.'

On the landing he told Henriette that he could not guarantee anything. The lung had been gravely affected and there might be a haemorrhage which would finish him.

Coming back Henriette forced herself to smile in spite of the blow her heart had received. Would she not save him yet, wasn't she going to prevent this awful thing, the eternal separation of the three of them who were now still united in their ardent longing for life? She had never left that room all day, and an elderly neighbour had kindly undertaken to do her errands. Now she took her place again on a chair by the bed.

Giving in to his nervous excitement Maurice kept questioning Jean and trying to find out things. Jean did not tell him everything, avoiding the blind hatred rising against the expiring Commune now that Paris was free again. It was already Wednesday. Since Sunday evening, that is for two whole days, the residents had been living in cellars sweating with terror, and on the Wednesday morning when they had been able to venture out, the sight of dug-up streets, ruins, blood and above all the terrible fires, had filled them with a terrible lust for vengeance. The reprisals were going to be tremendous. Houses were being searched and crowds of men and women suspects were being chucked in front of summary firing squads. By six in the evening of that day the Versailles army was in control of half Paris, from the Montsouris park to the Gare du Nord, including the main arteries. The last members of the Commune, a score or so of them, had had to take refuge in the town hall of the XIth arrondissement in the Boulevard Voltaire.

There was a silence, and then Maurice, gazing at the distant city through the window thrown open on that warm night, murmured:

'Well, it's still going on, Paris is burning!'

It was true; the flames had returned with the end of daylight, and once again the sky was glowing with a murderous, bloody light. That afternoon, when the powder magazine at the Luxembourg had blown up with a terrible noise, it had been rumoured that the Pantheon had collapsed into the crypt. All day long the previous day's fires in the Conseil d'Etat and the Tuileries had gone on burning, and the Finance Ministry still belched forth thick black smoke. Ten times she had had to shut the window because of the threat of a swarm of black butterflies, bits of burnt paper incessantly flying about, having been lifted high into the air by the heat of the fire, whence they came down like gentle rain. The whole of Paris was covered with them and some were picked up even in Normandy, twenty leagues away. And now it was not only the western and southern districts that were burning – the buildings in the rue Royale, the Croix-Rouge crossroads and the rue Notre-Dame des Champs. All the east of the city seemed to be in flames, and the immense furnace of the Hôtel de Ville filled the horizon with one gigantic blaze. In that direction too, like flaming torches, were the Théâtre Lyrique and the town hall of the IVth arrondissement, more than thirty houses in adjoining streets, to say nothing of the Porte-Saint-Martin theatre further north, glowing red in isolation like a haystack in the middle of black fields. Private revenges were being carried out, and perhaps also criminal elements calculated that by persisting they could destroy certain dossiers. It was no longer a matter of self-defence or holding up victorious troops by fire. Hysteria reigned supreme, and the Palais de Justice, the Hôtel-

Dieu, the cathedral of Notre-Dame had only been saved by sheer chance. It was destruction for destruction's sake so as to bury the ancient, rotten human society beneath the ashes of the world in the hope that a new society would spring up, happy and innocent, in the earthly paradise of primitive legends!

'Oh war, vile war!' whispered Henriette, looking at this city of ruin, destruction and death.

Wasn't this in fact the final, inevitable act, the blood-lust that had come into being in the disastrous fields of Sedan and Metz, the epidemic of destruction born in the siege of Paris, the final paroxysm of a nation in danger of death amidst all this slaughter and wreckage?

But Maurice, still gazing at the areas burning out there, said haltingly and with difficulty:

'No, no, don't curse war ... War is a good thing, it is doing its work ...'

Jean cut him short with a cry of hatred and remorse.

'Oh my God, when I see you there, and it is all my fault ... Don't defend war, it's a vile thing.'

The sick man vaguely waved his hand.

'Oh, what do I matter? There are plenty of others ... Perhaps the blood-letting is necessary. War is life, and it cannot exist without death.'

Maurice's eyes closed, for he was tired from the effort these few words had cost him. Henriette signalled to Jean not to argue. In her anger against human suffering she herself felt a wave of protest taking possession of her, for all her brave, feminine quietness, and in her clear eyes shone the heroic soul of their grandfather, the hero of Napoleonic legend.

Two more days went by, Thursday and Friday, with the same fires and the same massacres. The din of gunfire never stopped, and the batteries up on Montmartre, captured by the Versailles army, were mercilessly pounding the ones the Federals had set up at Belleville and in the Père-Lachaise cemetery. The latter were firing at random on Paris and shells had fallen in the rue de Richelieu and Place Vendôme. By the evening of the 25th the whole of the left bank was in the army's hands. But on the right bank the barricades at the Place du Château d'Eau and the Place de la Bastille were still holding out, in fact they were real fortresses defended by incessant, withering fire. At dusk, in the final disarray of the last members of the Commune, Delescluze had picked up his walking-stick and coolly strolled along to the barricade blocking the Boulevard Voltaire, where he had fallen, killed instantly in a hero's death. By dawn on the next day, the 26th, the Château d'Eau and the Bastille had been overcome, and the Communards occupied only La Villette, Belleville and Charonne, and in smaller and smaller numbers, now reduced to the hard core of desperadoes determined to die. For two more days they were to go on resisting and fighting furiously.

On Friday evening, as Jean was making his escape from the Place du Carrousel to go back to the rue des Orties, he witnessed at the bottom of the rue de Richelieu a summary execution which left him thoroughly shaken. For a couple of days two courts martial had been in session, one at the Luxembourg and the other at the Théâtre du Châtelet. Those condemned by the first were shot in the garden, while the victims of the second were dragged to the Lobau barracks where full-time firing squads shot them in the courtyard at almost point-blank range. It was there in particular that the butchery was frightful: men and even children condemned on just one piece of evidence, such as hands dirty with powder or feet that happened to be wearing army boots; innocent people falsely denounced, victims of personal vendettas, screaming explanations but unable to make themselves heard; droves of people herded in front of rifle-barrels, so many poor devils at once that there were not enough bullets to go round and the wounded were finished off with the butts of the rifles. Blood ran in streams and carts were taking away the bodies from morning till night. All over the conquered city other executions were going on, wherever some personal lust for revenge found a chance, in front of barricades, against walls in empty streets, on steps of public buildings. So it was that Jean saw some people who lived in that neighbourhood bring a woman and two men to the post guarding the Théâtre Français. The ordinary citizens were more ferocious than the soldiers, and the newspapers that had resumed publication were howling for extermination. The whole mob was particularly violent against the woman, who was one of the fire-raisers, fear of whom haunted people's over-wrought imagination, and whom they accused of prowling in the night in front of well-to-do houses and throwing cans of lighted oil into the cellars. This one had been caught, it was alleged, crouching in front of a grating in the rue Sainte-Anne. In spite of her protestations and tears she was flung with the two men into the trench of a barricade not yet filled in and they were shot in this black pit like wolves caught in a trap. People strolling by watched this, and a lady and her husband stopped for a look, while a baker's boy delivering a pie whistled a hunting-song.

Jean was hurrying on to the rue des Orties, feeling nauseated, when something suddenly came to his mind. Wasn't that Chouteau, the former soldier in his squad, he had just seen, clad in the respectable white overall of the working man and watching the execution with signs of approval? And he knew the part played by this criminal, traitor, thief and murderer! For a moment he was on the point of going back again and denouncing him so as to have him shot across the bodies of the other three. Oh, how heartbreaking it was, the most guilty ones escaping punishment and flaunting their impunity in broad daylight while the innocent rotted in the ground!

Hearing steps on the stairs, Henriette had come out on to the landing.

'Do be careful, today he is in a terribly worked-up state . . . The doctor has been back and he has upset me!'

Indeed Bouroche had shaken his head and been unable to make any promise as yet. It was still possible that the patient's youth would bring him through the complications he was afraid of.

'Ah, it's you!' Maurice said feverishly as soon as he saw Jean. 'I was waiting for you, what's going on, where have they got to now?'

Propped against his pillow, facing the window he had forced his sister to open, he pointed to the city, now in darkness again but lit up by a new glow from a fire:

'Look, it's starting again, Paris is burning. The whole lot of it is burning this time!'

As soon as the sun set, the fire at the Grenier d'Abondance had lit up the districts far away up the Seine. In the Tuileries and the Conseil d'Etat ceilings must have been falling in and reviving the glowing timbers, for small fires had started again and flakes of flame and sparks shot up now and again. Many of the buildings thought to be burnt out flared up again like this. For three days it no sooner got dark than the city seemed to burn up again, as though the darkness itself had blown on the red embers and revived them and scattered them to every point on the horizon. What a hellish city it was, that glowed red when dusk came and illumined with monstrous torches the nights of all that bloody week! On that particular night, when the warehouses of La Villette were burned, the light was so bright all over the great city that this time it was really possible to think it was on fire everywhere, overwhelmed and submerged by the flames ... Under a bloody sky the districts of Paris, red as far as the eye could see, were like a rolling sea of fiery roofs.

'It's all over!' Maurice said again. 'Paris is burning.'

He was intoxicating himself with these words, repeated a score of times in a feverish urge to go on talking after the heavy sleepiness that had kept him silent for three days. But a sound of stifled sobs made him look round.

'What, little sister, you, so brave! ... Crying because I'm going to die?'

She protested, cutting him short.

'But you aren't going to die!'

'Oh yes, I am, and it's better I should, I must ... You know, nothing of any value will go with me. Before the war I gave you so much trouble and cost your heart and your purse so much ... All the silly things, all the mad things I've done, who knows, they might have brought me to a bad end, prison, the gutter ...'

She stopped him again, this time angrily.

'Shut up, shut up! You've paid for it all!'

He fell silent and thoughtful for a moment.

'When I am dead, perhaps ... Oh, dear old Jean, you really did us all a damn good turn when you ran me through with that bayonet.'

But Jean, in tears too, protested.

'Don't talk like that! Do you want me to go and bash my brains out against a wall?'

But Maurice went on passionately:

'Remember what you said the day after Sedan when you maintained that it did no harm sometimes to get a good bashing. And you said, too, that if something had gone rotten somewhere, like a poisoned limb, it was better to see it hacked off and lying on the ground than to die of it like the cholera ... I've often thought about that since I've been on my own and shut up in this crazy, starving Paris ... Well, I'm the rotten limb you have lopped off ...'

He was growing more delirious and paid no heed to the supplications of Henriette and Jean, who were terrified. In a raging fever he went on pouring out symbols and vivid pictures. It was the healthy part of France, the reasonable, solid, peasant part, the part which had stayed closest to the land, that was putting an end to the silly, crazy part which had been spoilt by the Empire, unhinged by dreams and debauches. And France had had to cut into her own flesh and tear our her vitals, hardly knowing what she was doing. But the blood-bath was necessary, and it had to be French blood, the unspeakable holocaust, the living sacrifice in the purifying fire. Now she had climbed the hill of Calvary to the most horrible of agonies, the nation was being crucified, atoning for her sins and about to be born again.

'My dear old Jean, you are the pure in heart, the stout-hearted one ... Go and take up your pick and trowel, turn over the soil and rebuild the house! ... As for me, you did the best thing when you cut me out, for I was the ulcer clinging to your bones!'

He went on wandering, tried to get up and look out of the window.

'Paris is burning and there'll be nothing left ... This fire which is taking everything away and healing everything was my idea, yes, it's doing a good job ... Let me go down and finish off the work of humanity and freedom ...'

Jean had all the trouble in the world to get him back into bed, while Henriette in tears went on talking to him about their childhood together, begging him to calm down in the name of their love for each other. Over the vast space of Paris the fiery glow had spread still more, and the sea of flame seemed to be reaching the dark limits of the horizon, the sky was like the vault of a gigantic furnace, heated up to bright red. The dense smoke clouds from the Ministry of Finance, which had been steadily burning for two days without any flames, still floated across this lurid background of fires like a stately cloud of deepest mourning.

The next day, Saturday, brought a sudden improvement in Maurice's condition, and he was much calmer, his temperature had gone down, and it was a great joy to Jean when he found Henriette smiling and going back to the dream of an intimate life for the three of them, in a future happiness which still seemed possible but which she did not want to put into so many words. Was fate about to relent? She spent the nights in that room which she never left, and which her busy Cinderella sweetness, her gentle, silent care filled with a continual caress. That evening Jean lingered there with his friends and his pleasure surprised him and made him tremble. During the day the troops had taken Belleville and the Buttes-Chaumont. Only the Père-Lachaise cemetery, which had been turned into an armed camp, still held out. It seemed to him that it was all over and he even said that there were no more shootings. He simply mentioned convoys of prisoners setting off for Versailles. He had seen one that morning going along by the river, men in overalls, coats or shirtsleeves, women of all ages, some with the wrinkled faces of old harridans, others in the flower of their youth, children of barely fifteen – a stream of misery and revolt being moved on by soldiers in the bright sunshine, and whom the good people of Versailles, it was said, welcomed with catcalls and hit with sticks and sunshades.

But on Sunday Jean was horrified. It was the last day of that hateful week. As soon as the sun rose in glory on a clear and warm holiday morning he had the eerie sensation that this was to be the final agony. News had only just broken of renewed slaughter of hostages. The archbishop, the parish priest of the Madeleine and others had been shot on the Wednesday at La Roquette, and on Thursday the Dominicans of Arcueil had been picked off on the run like hares, on Friday more priests and forty-seven gendarmes had been shot point blank in the rue Haxo sector, and a fury of reprisals had flared up again, the troops executing en masse their most recent prisoners. All through that lovely Sunday the crackle of the firing-squads had never stopped in the courtyard of the Lobau barracks, which was full of death-cries, blood and smoke. At La Roquette two hundred and twenty-seven wretched creatures, rounded up more or less at random, were machine-gunned in a heap, riddled with bullets. In Père-Lachaise, which had been bombarded for four days and finally captured grave by grave, one hundred and forty-eight were thrown against a wall, and the plaster dripped great red tears. Three of them, who were only wounded and escaping, were recaptured and finished off. Of the twelve thousand poor creatures who had lost their lives through the Commune how many harmless people were there for each rogue! It was said that an order to stop the executions had come from Versailles. But the killing went on just the same. Thiers, for all his pure glory as the liberator of the country, was to go down for ever as the legendary butcher of Paris, while Marshal MacMahon, the defeated soldier of Froeschwiller, whose proclamations of victory covered the walls, was henceforward to be nothing but the conqueror of Père-Lachaise. Paris, in the sunshine, was dressed in her Sunday best and in holiday mood, an enormous crowd thronged the recaptured streets, people out for a walk went like jolly sightseers to have a look at the smoking ruins, mothers holding laughing children by the hand paused for a moment and listened with interest to the distant firing in the Lobau barracks.

As Jean went up the dark stairs of the house in the rue des Orties in the evening twilight on that Sunday he felt sick with awful foreboding. He went in and at once saw the inevitable end, Maurice dead on the little bed, choked by the haemorrhage that Bouroche had feared. The sun's red farewell stole in through the open window and two candles were already burning on the table beside the bed. Henriette, in her widow's weeds, was on her knees, quietly weeping.

Hearing a noise she looked up and seeing Jean enter shuddered visibly. He, distraught with grief, was on the point of rushing forward and taking her hands to unite his sorrow and hers in an embrace. But he felt her little trembling hands, her whole being chilled and repelled, recoiling, snatching herself away for ever. Was it not all over between them now? Maurice's grave separated them for ever, like a bottomless abyss. All he too could do was fall on his knees, quietly sobbing.

But after a pause Henriette spoke.

'My back was turned, and I had a cup of broth in my hand when he cried out ... I didn't even have time to run across the room, he died calling for me and calling for you, too, as he vomited blood ...'

Her brother, oh God, her Maurice whom she had worshipped even from their mother's womb, who was her second self, whom she had brought up and saved! Her only love since she had seen her poor Weiss's body riddled with bullets against a wall in Bazeilles!

So the war was taking her whole heart, and she would be left alone in the world, a lonely widow with no one to love her.

'Oh my God!' Jean said in tears. 'It's my fault! ... My dearest boy, for whom I would have given my life, and I have to slaughter him like some animal ... What will become of us? Will you ever forgive me?'

At that moment they looked into each other's eyes, and they were heartbroken at what at last they could clearly read in them. The past came to life, the secluded room at Remilly in which they had lived such sad, sweet days together. It brought him back to his daydream, unconscious at first and even later never clearly formulated, life down there, marriage, a little house and work on a plot of land that would suffice to keep a family of honest, humble folk. But now it had become a passionate longing, a painful certainty that with a woman like her, so tender, so active, so brave, life might have become a real paradise. She too, who formerly had not even been touched by this dream, though unconsciously giving her heart in perfect purity, now saw plainly and suddenly understood. This eventual marriage was what she herself had wanted, without realizing it. The seed had quickened and imperceptibly grown and now she loved with real love this man with whom at first she had only found consolation. Their eyes told each other all this, and now they loved each other openly only in time to say an eternal farewell. This one more dreadful sacrifice had to be made, this final tearing asunder; their happiness, still feasible yesterday, was now crumbling into dust like everything else, and being washed away in the stream of blood that had taken their brother.

With a long painful effort Jean got to his feet.

'Good-bye!'

Henriette remained motionless on the floor.

'Good-bye!'

Yet Jean went over to Maurice's body. He looked at him, and his lofty brow looked even more lofty, and from his long, thin face and expressionless eyes, formerly a bit wild, the wildness had gone. He would have liked to kiss his dear kid, as he had called him so many times, but he dared not. He saw himself covered with his blood, and recoiled before the horror of fate. What a death, beneath the ruins of a world! On the last day, amid the last bits of wreckage of the dying Commune, one more victim had been claimed! The poor man had departed still thirsting for justice in the final convulsion of the great dark dream he had dreamed, in the grandiose and monstrous conception of the destruction of the old society, Paris destroyed by fire, the field ploughed up and cleansed so that the idyll of a new golden age might spring up into life.

Full of anguish, Jean turned away and looked at Paris. At this radiant end of a lovely Sunday the slanting sun, low on the horizon, cast over the huge city a blazing red light. It might have been a sun of blood over a limitless sea. The panes of thousands of windows blazed fire as though blown upon by invisible bellows, roofs were catching fire like burning coals, golden yellow walls and tall, rust-coloured monuments seemed to be flaring up in the evening air like spurting wood fires. Was this not the final set-piece, the gigantic fountain of flame, all Paris burning like some huge sacrificial fire, an ancient, dried-up forest shooting up to heaven in a volley of sparks and tongues of flame? The fires were still burning, huge russet clouds of smoke were still billowing up, and a great clamour could be heard, maybe the last death-cries of the shot victims in the Lobau barracks, or perhaps happy women and laughing children eating out of doors after a nice walk or sitting outside cafés. From the looted houses and public buildings, from the disembowelled streets, from so much ruin and suffering, life was still stirring in the blaze of this splendid sunset in which Paris seemed to be burning itself out.

Then Jean felt an extraordinary sensation. It seemed to him, as day was slowly dying over this burning city, that a new dawn was already breaking. Yet it was the end of everything, fate pursuing its relentless course in a series of disasters greater than any nation had ever undergone: continual defeats, provinces lost, milliards to pay, the blood-bath of the most dreadful of civil wars, whole districts full of ruins and dead, no money left, no honour left, a whole world to build up again. He himself was leaving his broken heart here, Maurice, Henriette, his happy future life swept away in the storm. And yet, beyond the still roaring furnace, undying hope was reviving up in that great calm sky so supremely limpid. It was the sure renewal of eternal nature, eternal humanity, the renewal promised to all who hope and toil, the tree throwing up a strong new shoot after the dead branch, whose poisonous sap had yellowed the leaves, had been cut away.

Still weeping, Jean said again:

'Good-bye!'

Henriette did not look up, but kept her face buried in her hands.

'Good-bye!'

The ravaged field was lying fallow, the burnt house was down to the ground, and Jean, the most humble and grief-stricken of men, went away, walking into the future to set about the great, hard job of building a new France.